D1007949

# The Men and Women of the Malibu

**WILLA**—Beautiful, strong-willed, her husband's love for the Malibu would match her own, but she would find fulfillment in the arms of another.

**LENA**—Lovely, delicate, crippled from birth, she was a sharer of others' secrets, others' lives, until a sudden, explosive passion changed her own life forever.

**OWEN**—A Princeton graduate and heir to three million dollars, he would make his place in the business world of California, but he would lose what he loved the most.

**CONNOR**—A rugged Irishman, ranch hand on the Malibu, he would succumb to his hunger for Willa only to find that it would haunt him for the rest of his life.

# HERS THE KINGDOM

## SHIRLEY STRESHINSKY

BERKLEY BOOKS, NEW YORK

It's important to acknowledge the contribution of Diane Reverand, the editor
of this book, and Betty Anne Clarke, my literary agent.

This Berkley book contains the complete
text of the original hardcover edition.
It has been completely reset in a typeface
designed for easy reading, and was printed
from new film.

HERS THE KINGDOM

A Berkley Book / published by arrangement with
G. P. Putnam's Sons

PRINTING HISTORY
G. P. Putnam's edition / April 1982
Berkley edition / May 1983

ISBN: 0-425-06147-7

*For my mother,*
Edna Brinker Gaghen

*and her mother,*
Lena Douglas Brinker

*and her mother,*
Elizabeth Kerr Douglas

*and her great-great-granddaughter,*
Maria Streshinsky

# Contents

I believe that there exists deeply rooted in the nature of certain individuals some quality which inspires a natural liking for hawks.

Gilbert Blaine, *Falconry*

# Los Angeles
## December 29, 1939

You will want to know why I am writing this. I will tell you. It is not so simple.

The light this morning was searing and flat, California light. It bleaches the edges, obliterates all but the idea so that the palm I can see from my bedroom window is only the suggestion of a palm, the sort you might see in a mirage. After fifty years in California, I cannot adjust to the light.

I was beginning to dress when the postman's bell rang. My hip was hurting more than usual this morning, slowing me down. I hobbled into the hall to see Trinidad studying the envelope. It was the letter. I felt it.

A hot liquid surge slapped against my inner ear and threatened my balance. I steadied myself against the wall. Trinidad saw and put out her hand to help me. I could feel her eyes on me but I would not look at her. In her age Trinidad has become sentimental, her eyes fill too easily, and I had not the strength to comfort her. It took all I had to reach for the letter, to take it in my hand.

I slipped the envelope into the pocket of my dress and held my hand against it. Then I made my way to the library where Willa would be waiting. I do not know how early she gets

1

there. Very early, I think. She is always waiting when I arrive each morning at nine with the mail and the *Times*. It is our habit, my sister's and mine, to go through the mail together. Then I read the headlines to her, though this morning I did not take the *Times* with me, but left it on the hall table.

I slipped quickly from the glare of the hallway into the gloom of the library and for a few moments I could see nothing. I waited for my eyes to adjust, my hand pressed hard against the letter in my pocket. Slowly, the room came into focus . . . the high, dark oak, the deep red Persian carpets, Willa sitting behind the desk, her hands folded in her lap. She no longer pretends work; she has not for some weeks.

The heavy velvet drapes on the window behind my sister had not been fully closed, so that a shaft of light struck her diagonally in such a way as to illuminate her. I blinked. For the briefest moment I saw her as she had been, the girl. My heart began to race. I blinked again and saw my mistake even as I felt the stab of pain I knew to be disappointment.

"There is a letter from Kit," I said, short of breath.

"Yes," my sister answered, as if she had known.

I hobbled over to the chair beside the desk, as I did every morning out of habit, knowing that the habit was broken on this morning but seeking the comfort of it. I took out the letter and looked at Kit's small, square hand on the envelope, at the return address—the Cavendish, London. The letter was addressed to Willa. She nodded to me to read it. My hands were shaking, but I opened the letter.

"Dear Mother and Aunt Lena," Kit wrote, "wonderful news—Porter is going to be fine. The doctors assure me he will make a full recovery. He will not lose his leg."

The energy drained out of me, I could feel it going. I felt weak and sick with relief. All the fears of the past days and months rushed at me and I could hear myself sobbing. Willa waited. It was a long time, but she said nothing.

Finally I wiped my eyes and blew my nose and read on: "I have seen for myself," Kit wrote, "his wounds were serious but there will be no permanent damage, except for some scars which he can show to his grandchildren when he tells them stories of bravery, when he was fighting the Falanges in Spain." I could hear Kit, hear the tenderness in her low, husky voice.

I read on: "My stubborn twin brother is intent on saving

this sad world, as you well know. My only intent, right now, is to save Porter...to bring him home again to recuperate. He has agreed to return with me as soon as he is able to travel, another fortnight, at least, his English doctors say. I wish I could bring him back to the Malibu. I wish the only road in was the beach at lower low tide, the way it was when you first went there. I wish we could close ourselves in and be safe on the Malibu. You used to say that wishing was a kind of dreaming, Auntie. If you were here in England now, you would know that this is not a world for dreaming. You would know that there are no safe places anymore."

My eyes filled again and I could not read on. I passed the letter to Willa.

"Thank God," I whispered.

"I know," Willa answered, and I knew that she did know. *"Thank God Porter is going to be whole again. Thank God Porter will not be a cripple..."*

For a while the only sound in the library was the sound of my sniffling. Willa put on her reading glasses to finish Kit's letter. She did not read aloud.

Finally she said, in the tone of voice she might have used to discuss the dinner menu, "When they return, Kit will see to selling the Malibu."

I searched my sister's face.

She seemed to be studying the dust motes that floated in the shaft of light.

"It had to be, Willa," was all I could think to say.

"Yes," she answered, in the same flat tone.

I thought, then, what a clever girl Kit was. She would have made the decision to sell months ago, before she went to England. It was inevitable, we all knew that. But she had waited, waited until she had wonderful news—Porter would live and he would be well again. Only then could she find a way to say the words her mother had never wanted to hear—that the Malibu was lost.

I remembered then how, upon entering the library, I had been hurtled into the past, had seen Willa as a young woman, had felt the stab of disappointment even as I realized my mind was playing tricks on me. Until that moment I had not known how much I longed to hear her laugh again, to have her with me as it was, as it always has been...to have her back.

Then I saw the lilacs on the desk and I understood. It was the smell of lilacs that had sent me reeling into the past. In the springtime on the ranch at Malibu, when lilacs bloomed all about the house, Willa had always kept fresh bouquets in every room so that the scent sifted throughout the house. I wondered where Trinidad had managed to find lilacs so early.

Poor, dear Trinidad, I thought. Poor sweet simple old woman, to think of lilacs.

Willa sighed, a low, shuddering sigh.

"Take them away," she said to me, "I don't want to remember anymore."

I took the lilacs into the kitchen. Trinidad saw them and began to weep. I comforted her, holding her wrinkled old brown face in my hands, pulling her to me until her tears soaked through the fabric of my dress. I brushed the wet hair from her face and told her, as I would a child, "Porter is going to be well again, Porter is coming home."

"*Gracias,*" the old woman whispered, "*Madre de Dios, gracias.*" All her prayers, all the novenas, all the candles burned in the past weeks were witness to her longing for something she could name: that Porter, the child she had nursed and cared for and loved, be spared. But the lilacs were witness to a longing she could not name and did not comprehend.

Trinidad had been eighteen when she came to work for Willa. That was fifty years ago. She has grown old with us.

We talked quietly for awhile, Trinidad and I, in the kitchen of the townhouse where we live, three old women together, in Los Angeles. We talked about the time when Porter and Kit would return. She would make for Porter her *colache,* she would make for Porter her *sopaipillas,* her *pescado empanado.*

I did not tell her that the Malibu would be sold.

I picked up the *Times* from the table in the hall and took it to my room. I tried to read. The Russians had invaded Finland, Adolf Hitler stood on French soil on the Western Front on Christmas Eve . . . I would not read to Willa today. She does not want to remember, nor, I think, does she want to know.

Willa will be seventy-five this spring; the Malibu will be sold. Willa does not want to remember.

But I do. I knew that this morning, in the instant when the scent of lilacs had overwhelmed me. I want it terribly, I ache to remember. I need to know.

I am six years younger than my sister. Now that I know Porter will survive, I feel a new surge of energy. I need to be occupied, to have work. *Habit is the opiate of the aged.* Well, work has been my habit. I want to remember. I need to write down all that I know, and I know much.

I have been, always, a sharer of secrets, a listener. Very early in my life I came to understand that the keeping of secrets was a talent that could be developed, a valuable accomplishment for someone in my position.

*My position:* I am afflicted with congenital dislocation of the hip, a defect that is seven times more common in females than in males and twice as frequent in children born in winter as in those born in summer. The significance of these associations is obscure, the doctors say. Nonetheless, I am winter's child, the maiden aunt, the sharer of secrets. Do not misunderstand. There are advantages to my position.

I am Lena Kerr, sister to Willa Kerr Reade.

And I know most of what happened, though I do not pretend to understand why certain things happened.

Kit and Porter, perhaps, will want to know, should know. (*Perhaps . . . should . . .* I equivocate, even now. I am not sure what is best, or right. *Best* and *right;* I am not sure what they mean.)

What I know is this: I am afraid for them not to know.

Not to know *what?* That those who have loved them best have deceived them? It has always seemed to me that love is not possible without deception. (I have never much cared for the Brownings' brand of love. The Irishman Yeats is more to my liking, as "Crazy Jane Grown Old" says: *Love is like the lion's tooth.*) Still, I have been party to the deception, and it gives me no peace.

I think I was meant to tell the story. Why else would I have kept the notebooks all these years? Willa would say, I suppose, that I am a born keeper of books, that if I could not write it down I would doubt it had happened. I did keep my notebooks conscientiously, considering each Monday of my life if the past week had offered anything worth recording, only now and then interrupting the schedule for momentous events.

The notebooks will be invaluable in correcting for the vagaries of memory. It is odd, really, how perfectly I can remember a few hours in the spring of my seventeenth year, the smell of fresh-plowed earth as I walked along a lane on my parents' farm in Illinois. I remember how full I felt, how close to bursting I was with the joy of knowing that I, too, would be going to California. I remember the color of a bird sitting on a fencepost. Why, then, can I remember nothing of the days that came before, and very little of the trip West? I have also discovered that memory cannot be trusted when it comes to the great events—so often Willa's memories have differed from mine when we compare them from the distance of years. She recounts details that I have long forgotten, if ever I knew them. And I am sure that she thinks I make up my memories.

I am trying to establish a case for an orderly mind. You will want to come as close to the truth as I can take you. One more point: I have never been without pain. I tell you this only because pain has a practical purpose. It filters the foolishness, especially false romantic notions. (You have only to read Owen's diaries to know what I mean. They are full of gratuitous nonsense, which was not at all Owen's way.) It is not that people who live with pain are any more honest, it is simply that they have not the patience for romantic notions. You should know that.

Have I explained why I am writing this story? Perhaps not. I will occupy myself with the telling of the tale anyway. And then I will decide, one day soon, one day before Porter leaves again (and he will leave, I know that) if he is to know all that I know.

He will not be home long, I think. The dateline in this morning's paper read: "With the Finnish Forces near Viipuri." The story said: "Three hundred of an attacking force of nine hundred Russian soldiers were reported to be lying dead, frozen in ten below zero weather in this sector of the Finnish Mannerheim Line."

Mr. Yeats was right. *The blood-dimmed tide is loosed, and everywhere the ceremony of innocence is drowned...*

But I cannot let my mind turn to that. Not yet.

For now it is enough that Porter is coming home.

# Book I

From the Prairie
To the Ocean,
1887 - 1892

# Chapter One

From the porch I could see the buggy make the turn past the church spire at the Four Corners, a full mile away, a long plume of dust marking its passage. Gibralter, my brother, would be holding the reins high and firm, moving the team along at his own pace, steady and regular. He would be talking to the horses, but by now the visitor—the man sitting alongside him in the buggy—would have discovered that while Gibralter might talk to animals, he was not so inclined to converse with humans.

The visitor would have made a few efforts at conversation, to be sure. He might have remarked on the weather, on the freshness of the spring day, on the sudden new growth, every-where. Perhaps he admired the team, the matched bays that pulled the buggy. If he knew anything at all about the handling of horses, he would admire Gib's way with the team. And Gib would have answered, "yez," if he answered anything. It would have been a silent trip from the railroad station at Springfield. I hoped the visitor had been able to enjoy those twenty full miles of silence; I hoped he was not the sort made uncom-fortable by silence. There was, I felt, a certain peace in riding in the buggy with Gib at the reins, a steady and lovely rhythm. I squinted to try to get some notion of the man. He was big,

I could tell that, because he sat nearly as tall as my brother, who was six and one-half feet tall, like most of the Kerr men.

Mama said nothing, but she was watching. Now that the buggy was in sight, the rising tensions of the past hours were converting to anger. Her lips had begun to tremble.

"She promised," my mother said with a tremor in her voice, "your sister promised."

*Your* sister, she had said; it was an accusation. Willa was not here to meet the visitor, the man from the West who was coming to see her, coming all the way from California by way of Denver, Colorado, and it was my fault that Willa was not here because she was *my sister.*

She could not control Willa, so she would control me in her stead.

*Please, Willa,* I prayed silently, *please come now while there is time.*

I stood watching that time diminish as the buggy drew near; we were on the long porch that ran the length of the front of the house, and curved to the side. (Grandmother had called it a "verandah" or, sometimes, "the piazza," but Mama insisted on "porch," which I always thought defined the differences between the two women.) My grandfather built his house on the only rise in miles, a big white Victorian frame surrounded, now, by elm and maple and hawthorn trees, looking out over the rich black flatness of the northern Illinois prairie, The Grand Prairie, as it was called.

We watched as the two riders seemed to float above the hedge of honeysuckle that lined the dirt lane and concealed the buggy, so that it seemed as if the men were rolling along, side by side, supported by air. Soon we would be able to hear the soft, low rumble of wheels on dirt. Waiting for it, straining for the sound, seemed only to emphasize the silence. Mama heaved herself out of the big wicker chair that carried the imprint of her body in its sagging cushions.

"Burma! Malta! Servia!" she shouted to the Little Boys who had begun to tumble on the grassy patch that stretched down from the porch. Long grass stains were beginning to appear on their blouses. The train was to have arrived at noon. Mama had determined that the earliest Gibralter and the visitor could appear at the farm would be mid-afternoon. We had been waiting for two hours, all of us except Pa and the Big Boys who were plowing the north section. The three Middle Boys had been put to work in the carriage barn, near at hand. (We called them that—the three Big Boys were seventeen, nineteen and twenty. The Middle Boys were eleven, thirteen and fourteen, and the Little Boys were four, six and eight.) Every one of us, all nine of the boys and me, had been accounted for—everyone but Willa.

The sounds of the buggy made my stomach tighten. I felt, for the first time, a surge of real anger at my sister. She should have been here. I was surprised at Willa; I felt my face begin to flush.

Gibralter stopped at the lower gate, climbed out and swung it open. His passenger climbed down too, so that Gib could drive the team through and he could close the gate behind him. Standing in the shadows of the porch, I cupped my hand over my eyes to get a better look. Mama pushed my hand down roughly and I winced, feeling her mood darken.

She paced heavily across the porch, dressed in serge and bombazine, sweating in the unseasonable warmth of the spring day. The buggy began the last drive up through the avenue of poplars Grandmother had insisted Grandfather plant forty years before, to remind her of a country house in France which she had visited in her youth.

The trees were in new leaf, a bright green caught by the late afternoon light. It must be, I thought, a lovely sight, even to such a well-traveled man as our visitor, Mr. Owen Reade. In the early days an artist had drawn the farm for one of the state almanacs; the style was primitive, the viewpoint aerial, as if the artist was hanging from a cloud. And yet there was something charming about the big house, bare against the spread of the lands, the fences marching neatly all about.

It was the finest farm in that part of the state. Grandfather had settled the land, had cleared it, had built the house for his cultivated Eastern bride, had, even, added a music room on the third floor with a cherry-wood piano.

I tried to imagine how we would appear to Mr. Reade— the silent Gibralter sent to meet him at the train and then the small, bulky, restless woman marching up and down the porch, followed tentatively by a crippled girl with hands that would not be still.

*What if he thinks me to be Willa?* The idea paralyzed me.

But he would have expected Willa to be there, and I was the only young woman in sight. *No.* The word formed in my brain and bubbled there. *Please, no.* I wanted to hide, to get away. But Mama's hand was hard against my back, pushing.

"Run and greet him," she commanded.

*Run,* she had said, and I caught my breath to keep the tears from coming.

She knew I could not run. I could not even walk properly, but had to sidestep with a difficult, ugly gait, my hips moving up and over in an obscene rolling motion. My movements were grotesque; I could not stand the thought of the stranger looking at me.

At that moment I hated them all . . . Mama, the visitor, even Willa who was not here. Even Willa.

And as always, I did as I was told and went hobbling toward them, feeling a flush move down my neck and onto the rise of my chest.

The sound was, at first, unrecognizable . . . we stopped, looked. Then we heard it, a shout. Clearly, a shout. Mama, the visitor, even the Little Boys stopped to peer out to the south pasture. It was Willa, running full out, her long legs stretching, the divided skirt flaring as the wind caught it. She was running as if in a race, as she sometimes ran with the Middle Boys—to win. She waved her straw hat in the air until she saw that we had noticed her.

Pulling up short and out of breath some paces in front of the visitor, she raised one hand in front of her face to signal that she could not speak, that she needed to catch her breath. (But laughing, somehow; sensing how ridiculous she must seem, but finding it all so very funny. Willa could do that.) For a few moments she gasped, pulling air into her chest, making odd noises—all the while her eyes saying how humorous the whole thing was. In the diversion she created, I took my first good look at the visitor, at Owen Reade.

The memory is firm. In the years to come I would be reminded of it every time I saw someone meet Owen for the first time. He was a fine-looking man, beautifully formed. Yet it was not just beauty of form that made people stare at Owen; it was something more, something in his expression, in the way he looked at you, in the way he held his body. More, even: Owen was different. Always that. Owen was different in a way I could never quite grasp. There would be times when I felt I almost understood, but it would always slip away from me.

"Miss Willa Kerr?" he said with a small smile that could be banished, should the situation suddenly turn serious.

It didn't. Willa was beginning to laugh. "I have chased you, sir, for better than a mile," she told him, "I saw the buggy and raced you from the Four Corners, and Gib hadn't the courtesy to let me win."

Gibralter, busy with harnesses, looked up for the first time and a slow, sweet smile spread over his face. Seeing this, Owen looked at Willa as if to say, "And what other miracles can you perform?"

What he did say was, "I must remember never to challenge you to a footrace."

The late sun made shadow patterns from the lacy straw of her hat play over Willa's face. "Ah," she answered, "footraces are a favorite pastime on this farm. You cannot avoid them . . . and I've only been bested once."

I felt Mama's fingers in my back, pushing hard.

"Sir," I said in what was meant to be a normal tone, but in fact came out a whisper.

Owen Reade turned to us. Before I could attempt the formal introduction Mama had wanted, Willa pulled me to her, slipped her strong arm tightly around my waist and took over as gracefully as Grandmother would have, with as sure a sense of herself.

"Allow me, sir," she said, "to present my mother, Mrs. Kerr."

Turning to our mother with the slightest of curtseys, as if the most obedient of daughters, she said, "Mother, Mr. Reade."

Owen bowed and took Mama's big hand in his. He told her it was a great pleasure to meet the family of his very good friends in California. He said that Aunt Emma had sent her greetings; he said how grateful he was to Mama for allowing him to visit. He looked at Mama, and she began to quiver with pleasure.

"And this is my sister, Lena," Willa went on, pulling me close, squeezing me so I would not be afraid.

"Lena. Yes," he said, as if affirming something. He looked

at me and he did not look away. Willa squeezed me again, and I smiled at the ground.

Mama watched. She saw, she may even have felt the circle tighten, excluding her.

All this while the Little Boys had been hanging back, peering from behind bushes and trees. Now Willa called them forward and introduced them, quite formally, one by one. The Middle Boys, having heard the commotion, were walking toward us, tall and awkward in that space between childhood and manhood, each pushing the other ahead so that they came at an uneven pace.

"Come, boys, meet Mr. Reade," Willa called to them. "Mr. Reade, my brothers Persia, Berne and Turin." Looking at the tallest of the three she went on, "Bernie, I've promised Mr. Reade a footrace—a real one." Bernie smiled and said that he would be happy to oblige. It was only in the past month that he had, finally, won a race from Willa, and he was anxious to repeat his victory.

"I warn you," Owen Reade said, "I've been beaten by both the tortoise and the hare." Willa laughed as the light played over her face.

"I think you must be tired, after so long a journey," Mama said, reminding Willa to show him to the room that had been made ready for him. We watched, Mama and I, as they walked together toward the house.

"He will think her too bold," Mama told me in a husky voice, "he will think she is strange."

For once I did not conceal my annoyance: "If he has any sense at all," I said, "he will think her extraordinary, because she is."

On the pretext of checking on preparations for supper, I went into the kitchen where the hired girls were working, then up the steep back stairs to the room I shared with Willa. She was filling the basin in the corner when I entered. I knew the excitement I saw in her eyes was mirrored in mine. Too full of feeling to say anything right away, we sat close on the bed, our fingers tightly intertwined.

"Mama is furious with you," I whispered. "Where were you? Why weren't you here?"

"I was following the peregrines," Willa answered, as if it were beside the point, "I didn't want to be sitting around wait-

ing, I didn't want to think too much about it so I decided to
go hawking and I wandered too far..." It was not important,
not now. What was important was swelling inside of us, threatening to burst.

"He is..." I began, and she threw her arms around me and
we laughed, too excited to talk.

"Lena," she said, "it can't be happening..."

We hugged each other then, in the spring of the year 1887.
I was sixteen, Willa was twenty-two and we were full of wonder
at the turn of fate that had brought Owen Reade into her life
and thus, obliquely, into mine.

Fate, in this case, had a name: Aunt Emma. We called her
that, though she was not our aunt at all, but Mama's girlhood
friend. Aunt Emma, who lived with her husband, the Captain
(of what I was never quite sure), in Monterey, California, which
was south of San Francisco. She had been sixteen when she
made the long journey around the Horn to California, a new
bride. We had heard the story more times than I can remember—how the Captain had come to visit, how he had left at
the end of the month with young Emma Douglas, Mama's great
friend and companion. The Douglasses were shopkeepers in
town. There were eight children in the family and so many
hungry mouths to feed that Emma was allowed to "farm out"
to the Porters, to keep Mama company. It wasn't long after
Aunt Emma left for California that Mama married Pa, the hired
hand's gangly son who had tagged after the two girls all those
childhood years.

I suppose Grandmother looked on Aunt Emma as an acceptable little friend for her only child, in the way that Southern
girls were allowed to have slave children as playmates. Emma
Douglas was not a Negro, but her parents were poor and to
Grandmother's mind, it was much the same. As for Pa's folks,
the Kerrs, they were hired hands, that was all.

Aunt Emma's departure had been followed, in rapid succession, by a series of events which changed everything. Grandfather died, Mama married Pa, Grandmother moved to Chicago.
Mama married Pa and begat Willa, and begat Gibralter, and
begat Valparaiso, and begat Birmingham, and begat me—who
was to be the consolation of her age, as she liked to say—
before she produced six more male progeny so there would

always be a Kerr to work Porter farm.

And it was to be called that: Porter Farm.

Through all those long, childbearing years she wrote letters to Aunt Emma—great thick letters into which she poured her thoughts, her confidences. She shared everything with Emma in her letters, as they had shared everything as girls. Aunt Emma, childless, wrote back in the stolid, stilted style of a woman who was not comfortable with words, but Mama was not daunted. After a while, I think, it didn't matter who was reading the letters. All that mattered was that Mama could write them and post them. Other than several editions of the *New Popular Atlas of the World,* which she pored over and used as a source of names for her offspring, the letters to Aunt Emma were Mama's only connection to the outside world.

The letter that arrived in February began, as all of Aunt Emma's letters began, "Dear Good Friend." She wrote: "Your letter of the 14th inst. arrived with its welcome news of your family. We are well here, though the Captain complains of late of a weakness of limb."

Aunt Emma and my father must have been much alike; it was as if words pained them.

"I am putting pen to paper," Aunt Emma went on, "for a particular reason. On several occasions we have had the pleasure of having as a guest on the ranch a young gentleman, Mr. Owen Reade. On his last visit he was stricken with an illness, and at our insistence stayed with us to recuperate. Only after three months was his strength regained.

"He is an agreeable young man and during his long recuperative time I sought to distract him by reading those parts of your letters in which you talk of the children. At the end of his time with us, he asked permission to write to Willa, for the purpose of stopping at Porter Farm on his next trip to the East.

"Owen is twenty-seven years of age. His mother died when he was but a babe, his father passed from this life ten years ago, leaving his only son a sizeable bequest from his manufacturies in New England. The Captain knew his late father and vouches for his character. He fully endorses the young Mr. Reade, in whom he places much confidence.

"Owen finished his studies at Princeton College, then he traveled widely on the Continent as well as throughout the

American West. His travels have taken him many miles, as a result of which he has been able to enlarge the inheritance left to him. Neither is he content with this success, but is ambitious and has many fine plans.

"He neither drinks nor smokes, but believes both to be vices and not amenable to good health. Having suffered fevers in his childhood, Mr. Reade is careful of his health.

"He is, we believe, a man who would have won even Willa's grandmother's approval."

Aunt Emma's recommendation of Owen Reade ended on that strange note, which might have been read as caustic, given the family history.

A short time later Willa received a formal letter from Owen Reade posted in San Francisco, asking her kind permission to visit on his way to his family home in the East. His letters were brief, correct.

Mama, caught between conflicting loyalties, became querulous. She could deny her friend nothing. Still, it would have occurred to her that it could be happening again—the caller, the sudden leavetaking, the absence forever. Emma had left her, and now Willa might choose to leave. And with someone Grandmother would have approved of. It was too much for Mama to grasp, too much to try to sort out. All she knew for sure was that she could never comprehend why anyone would want to leave the farm. And yet her mother had not been happy there and Willa . . . Willa was as much an enigma to Mama as Mama had been to Grandmother.

Grandmother had longed for the old life; she had wanted nothing so much as to go back to Virginia. For Willa, it was *Ultima thule*—West, she would say to me, arms flung out, *to the farthest point* . . . West to the light, to build the kind of life where anything, everything was possible.

They were three generations of women, each caught in a web of place the others could neither see nor comprehend.

It was an amazing time, that week in the spring of 1887. The house was filled with an altogether new feeling of expectation—of what, none of us were quite sure. It was enough that the patterns of our days changed, that the long sameness was broken. We were all affected, even sweet-mannered little Servia, the smallest of the boys, who walked around with a per-

plexed look on his face. We knew the purpose of Owen Reade's
visit, though of course no one mentioned it.

The older boys accepted Owen easily. They were anxious
to ask him all about his travels in the West and he told them
what they wanted to know. He tended to be self-deprecating,
and he laughed at his own mistakes with ease. "Once," he said,
"a small band of us were riding south of the Gila River in the
Arizona territory, and we'd been told we could find shelter for
a night at the home of a Señor Lopez. Well, we found the
house all right—the hacienda, as they call it—and I saw a
dark-skinned man and called out to him, in as good Spanish
as I could muster, 'Señor Lopez, buenas días!' And this fellow
calls back, 'The name's Gilligan, friend, and I'm from Baltimore.'"

He was the kind of man who could be at ease anywhere.
He seemed to have an uncanny ability to enter into the rhythm
of a place, to become part of it, even when he was not actively
a part.

Bernie organized a footrace to be run on the course we had
cut in the near pasture. Owen volunteered to check distances
and call times, he was so much in the middle of things that we
scarcely noticed he chose not to run. When Bernie beat Willa,
decisively this time, and none of us seemed to know quite how
we felt about it, it was Owen who said exactly the right thing.
"Every champion," he announced in sonorous tones, "must
make way for new, younger talent. There is always, must
always be, the challenge."

We all cheered and clapped and the Big Boys raised Willa
to their shoulders and carried her around the running path.
Willa waved her hat and made a fine, funny speech, after which
Owen presented her with a bouquet of flowers which the Little
Boys had hastily picked—roses and honeysuckle and flags—
and we went to our beds that night feeling full and fine with
ourselves.

Something was happening and Owen was in the center of
it all, moving, making the movement. Owen set the pace, he
knew what he had to do and how long it was going to take.
Time was his only limitation. He could not tolerate diversions
and there was no place for mistakes because mistakes cost time.
(Calculated risks, perhaps; when time was the critical factor,
one would need to take calculated risks.)

Owen created his own impetus. You could not be with him and fail to feel the energy—which was not physical, though he moved more briskly than others. It was deeper, more subtle. He had an aura that seemed always to say *something important is about to happen*. When this aura was coupled with Willa's energy, which was prodigious, the air fairly crackled; her yearnings were whetted by Owen's sense of the possible.

Owen moved in a sphere that was new to us. His days were not bound by routine, his seasons not tied to the growing of crops. He ignored limitations which others embraced—in space as well as time. He had traveled to the south of France, to the Sandwich Islands, to the territories in the far West. He was, as yet, bound to no place, was without the geographical anchors so many of us find necessary. I think that Owen could not fathom the sense of peace some people get from familiar things. He had an appetite for change, for beginnings.

Willa, no less, longed for change; she wanted nothing so much as to *begin*. Each was to be, for the other, an instrument to achieve a dream, though Willa's, at that time, was not fully shaped, but only lay in the far reaches of her mind, aching to find form.

Though we could not then have known it, nor would we for a time, Owen had already developed a taste for power, and the sense of mission that was its corollary.

My memory of those days is of a flurry of activity, of high excitement and movement and tension. I had started my notebooks the year before; until then, the entries had been predictable, routine and monotonous. That one week accounted for more pages than the whole of the preceding year.

Willa and Owen spoke together for the first time, alone, on the evening of his arrival. It had not been planned. She came upon him standing in the dining room, looking at the portrait of Grandmother that hung on the south wall and was always a bit askew. We seldom used the formal dining room, so it was still Grandmother's room. Willa watched Owen for a moment and she thought: He looks as if he belongs here.

"She was twenty-six when that was painted," Willa finally said.

He turned, considered her. "I thought for a moment it was you," he said, "until I saw that it was painted by Thomas Sully." When she didn't respond, he went on, "My family knew the artist—he painted my grandaunt's portrait. She was, as I re-member, wearing that same green gown and the same dreamlike expression."

"Do I remind you of your aunt, too?" Willa asked.

"Not at all," Owen answered. "My aunt was perfectly cube-shaped, quite as wide as she was tall. But Thomas Sully made her look romantic. After he painted her portrait, the story goes, she went around with a pained look on her face, and it took a time for those around her to understand that she was trying to duplicate the dreamy, wistful smile Sully had given her."

"I know," Willa laughed, "I always felt that this portrait did Grandmother more harm than good. It became her imagined self. I assure you, she was not that romantic-looking woman you see before you."

"No?" Owen asked.

"Grandmother was a Randolph of Virginia," she went on, "always."

"What do you mean, 'always'?" he wanted to know.

"Just that she was never content here on the prairie. I doubt that she was ever content after she left Virginia. She talked about the past continually. Family, tradition, that was what she cared about."

"And you don't?" he asked, carefully.

Willa looked at him for a long moment. Then she exhaled loudly and said, "One of her ancestors was John Randolph of Roanoke. He is supposed to have said, 'I am an aristocrat; I love liberty; I hate equality.'"

Now it was Owen Reade's turn to wait, and he did.

Finally she went on, "I don't believe in aristocracy. And I don't see how you can love liberty and hate equality. And I think perhaps I should go back out and enter this room again and start this conversation afresh."

"What would you say?" he wanted to know.

"I would say, 'Well now, Mr. Reade, how was your journey from Denver?'"

"Liberty, equality and other radical notions interest me a great deal more," Owen answered, teasing her.

"What other radical notions?" Willa asked, beginning to laugh one of her trilling laughs that spilled out and over. "I have no radical notions. Please, please, let us talk about the weather . . . or Yosemite, you must have been there . . . or Yellowstone." She was laughing and Owen Reade liked it, you could see.

"At least," he said, "you do look like your grandmother, amazingly so."

"She was," Willa said quite seriously, "five feet and ten inches tall and she weighed one hundred fifteen pounds when that portrait was painted. In that way, we are exactly alike. Were, I should say. She has been dead for five years now, as perhaps you know."

He nodded. "Miss Emma told me a great deal about every member of your family—except for your grandmother. She spoke of your grandfather with great reverence, and of course she is extremely fond of your father and mother. I could tell that not so much by what she said—she says little enough— but by the way her eyes shine when she speaks of either of them. I take it your mother and your aunt were great friends, even as young children."

Willa nodded, but when she said nothing he continued, "The one person your aunt said very little about was your grandmother. I can tell you exactly what she did say—because each time I inquired, she would repeat the same thing as if it had been committed to memory—'Mrs. Porter was a great lady from a fine old Virginia family and Willa is said to be the image of her as she was in her youth.'" Willa, of course, recognized our mother's phrase immediately, and the surprise must have registered in her eyes.

"Yes," Willa said, "go on . . ."

Owen, sensing that he might be moving into hazardous territory, became wary. "You must forgive me my idle curiosity," he said, "I spend so many hours alone that I tend to amuse myself by weaving small mysteries where there are none. Perhaps I'm especially interested in families because I've never been part of one." He said this without a trace of self-pity, which Willa liked. Then he said, "Of course, the Captain explained to me how he met Miss Emma—how your grandmother's family had known his, how grateful he was to her for inviting him to come to Illinois and then for giving them their start in California . . ."

Willa was staring at him, aghast.

"You mean Grandmother brought the Captain here?" she asked.

Realizing his blunder, Owen said, "I am sorry, I seem to have . . . I'm afraid I've been clumsy, if I've breached some confidence . . ." He looked genuinely distressed.

Willa put her hand on his arm to reassure him. Her touch had another effect. They seemed suddenly to have crossed some line of demarcation, and they were no longer strangers.

At that moment two of the Little Boys burst into the room and began tumbling about Willa's skirts. She separated them with an ease born of practice, and they all went to join the rest of the family on the side porch, where the evening meal had been laid.

Mealtimes on the farm were a test of any visitor's mettle. Usually, Pa and the Big Boys would be served at the first sitting, then the rest of us would eat. In deference to our guest, it was decided that we would eat together, fourteen of us at a long trestle table on the porch.

Mama and Pa were not disciplinarians, which was rare in that day. Everyone was allowed to speak, even the smallest of the boys. The problem was that they all wanted to talk at the same time, and often did. They also had a habit of vanishing under the table. We would ignore them until something was overturned, or the noise became too great. Then either Willa or I would fish out the culprits and make them sit next to us for a time.

All the while, Mama would be giving what she called an "instructive monologue." Her voice would change perceptibly, suggesting that she was reciting, verbatim, from one of her almanacs. Once started, she seemed unable to stop. On the first night of Owen Reade's visit, she broke into the general noise to say, "Did you know . . ." Willa looked at me and lifted her eyebrows, and I shrugged silently.

Owen, unaware, looked expectantly at Mama, as if ready to be fascinated by whatever question she might have.

"Did you know," she repeated for emphasis, "that the Temple of Diana at Ephesus was built at the common charge of all the Asiatic states?"

Owen's mouth was full of potatoes, but before he could swallow and answer, Mama continued, "Two hundred twenty years were employed in completing the temple. It was four hundred twenty-five feet long, two hundred twenty-five broad, and was supported by one hundred twenty-seven columns of

Parian marble—each sixty feet high and weighing one hundred fifty tons—furnished by as many kings. It was set on fire on the night of Alexander's birth by an obscure person named Erostratus, who confessed on the rack that the sole motive which prompted him was the desire to transmit his name to future ages."

Owen's eyes widened slightly. He looked at Willa and she blinked and smiled, so that he would know this was part of the ritual.

"That's terrible," Val said, and Mama frowned.

"I mean," he went on, "to burn down a beautiful place just so people would remember who you were."

"Well," Willa answered, "it worked. How did Mama put it? 'The desire to transmit his name'—well, it's just been transmitted right here at our table. That shows you how foolish people can be . . . they should have thwarted it right away by making it an offense ever to mention the man's name again. Then people wouldn't go around burning perfectly good buildings . . . or killing presidents, for that matter."

"Killing presidents?" Owen asked, amused by the turn the talk had taken.

"Why else would Booth have assassinated President Lincoln?" she answered.

Owen came back, politely, saying, "Because he disagreed politically."

"That's the reason that is given," Willa countered, "but I think the real reason is a search for immortality . . . that is, after all, what 'keeping a name alive' means."

Mama, who had all this time been sitting looking vaguely distressed, cut in, "Willa," she said, "do you think I am foolish for repeating his name?"

Before Willa could answer, little Servia piped up to say, "What if you don't like your name?" Mama looked even more upset at this, as if it had never occurred to her that any of her boys would not like the names she had so carefully selected for them.

"Why Servia," Val said to his brother, "we don't ever have to worry about that—because our names will be sure to last forever."

The rest of us silently applauded this act of diplomacy on Val's part, and Mama flushed with pleasure, not realizing how careful the boys were to protect her.

It was to take Owen a day or two to get used to the rough and tumble of our household. He was not accustomed to small boys, especially the kind who were allowed to be heard as well as seen.

After dinner, Willa and several of the boys went to show Owen around the farm. We could hear the rise and fall of their talk, punctuated now and then by laughter.

"Seems like a nice enough young man," Mama ventured. Pa didn't answer, but to my amazement, Gib did. He said, "I can't speak for what's in his head, but he's as weak as a rained-on bee."

I thought about that for a long time, and finally I decided that Gib was right. Owen was tall and had a certain lithe bulk to him, but it was the appearance of strength, not the substance. And, I felt sure, Owen knew his limits. Why else would he so carefully avoid situations that would expose his frailty?

In bed that night, Willa told me that it was Grandmother who had brought the Captain to the farm—a fact that Mama, in all her stories, had neglected to tell us. "Grandmother must have wanted to destroy the friendship between Mama and Aunt Emma, so she found a way to get rid of Aunt Emma," Willa said.

"So Mama married Pa," I added.

"It was how she could hold on to the farm," Willa said, and we were silent for a long time then, thinking about it.

I knew what was going on in Willa's mind, and I said, "It doesn't have to be that way."

"Yes it does," Willa answered, "marriage is an economic arrangement. Always. And it is best never to forget that."

After a while, Willa asked, "What are you thinking so loudly about?" It was our private joke, one we used often when one or the other of us could not sleep.

"I was thinking," I said, "that it is hard to comprehend how such a hardy frontiersman as Grandfather could have built a house on the prairie frontier with a music room and a cherry-wood piano for a woman twenty years his junior."

Willa only sighed. Then, when I thought she must be asleep, she said in a voice so low I could hardly hear: "Maybe she married him because no one else had asked her, maybe she thought he would die and leave her a fortune."

"Maybe," I said to that, "Mama and Papa are the real lesson.

No matter why they married, they are content . . . on the farm, and with each other."

She sat next to him on the narrow and, she now realized, exceedingly hard seat of the wagon as they rolled along the road to the Four Corners, jostling over bumps, now and again being thrown together as the rough wagon lurched.

"I should have asked the boys to hitch the surrey," she remarked idly. (She had, in fact, been searching for something to say to break the silence.)

He looked at her, politely puzzled.

"I mean," she explained, "the surrey would have been more comfortable . . ."

"Do you think I'm not comfortable?" he asked, in a way that made her know he was not talking about the wagon. She could feel a swelling in her breast, the fabric of her dress felt suddenly tight across her chest. She straightened her back, and looked at her hands. She wished she had not. They were chafed and red from going without gloves, a farm girl's rough hands. She thought about Wellesley and how they had made fun of her hands, and how she had refused to capitulate. Then, her rough hands had been a sign of resistance, now she could only regret them. All the more for watching Owen's hands on the reins—long and slender, big hands, graceful and hairless. She thought: his chest will be hairless, too, and the thought made her flush.

"I am comfortable with you, Willa," he went on. "That is what is so amazing."

"Amazing?" she repeated, "why that?"

He smiled. She felt a peculiar stirring in her stomach. She had not thought he would speak so quickly.

"Expectations often fall short of reality," he pushed on, "as perhaps you have already discovered?"

She chose to ignore his question, but asked instead: "Whatever did you expect of Porter Farm?" (Not, what did you expect of *me?*)

"I'm not sure," he answered easily, moving back a pace. "Perhaps not to be so comfortable."

She felt herself flush and she knew it was with pleasure. He was not disappointed in her, then, or he would not be telling her this.

At the churchyard he climbed down and reached to help

her. For a moment they stood together, her hand in his. Finally she said, "The church will be empty; it's used so seldom these days... occasionally the pastor will come out from Springfield to hold a service..." Still he held on to her hand. She looked into his eyes, which were brown and liquid, shining, eyes deep enough, she thought, to drown in. He was smiling then, and she back, and for a moment she thought she could not breathe deeply enough to get the air she needed.

She walked ahead of him into the church her grandfather had built. Light was streaming through the high window to the north, sending shafts into the musty gloom. She shivered. The church had always made her feel solemn and cold. "Are you chilled?" he asked.

"No," she whispered, "it's not that."

"What, then?" His voice was low, intimate.

The moment was shattered by a sharp crash sounding close by. Startled, Willa lurched into Owen. He steadied her.

"A bird," he explained, "I think a bird flew into the windowpane. Against the light, it couldn't see the glass."

She strode outside, shaking. Owen was right. On the ground beneath a window was a small brown bundle of feathers. "A lark bunting," she said, bending to pick it up, "a female... probably her nest is nearby, in the grass." She could feel warmth, still, in the small broken body. When she looked up at Owen there was anger and pain in her eyes.

"One of God's own creatures," she murmured, "destroyed by the illusion of the glass." She lay the bird down, then turned and walked purposefully to the back of the church, to the well, where she began to dislodge the pail from its peg. The pail had not been used for a while, and it took her some time to disentangle the knot.

"Lark buntings are beautiful little birds," she said, speaking quickly. "The female is drab and brown but the male is in sharp contrast, in black and white. If we looked, I suspect we might find their nest in the tall grasses around the churchyard." They were silent for the few minutes it took to get the bucket free. He did not try to help her, but watched as she manipulated the old wooden pail on its rope and pulley.

As she leaned to drop it over the side, he said, "Don't fall in, you'll go all the way to China."

She pulled in her breath in a small gasp, then laughed.

"I know," she said. "When I was small I was sure that if I fell in that black hole they'd never find me."

"And did you throw in pebbles, and hold your breath until you could hear them hit the water?"

"An eternity!" she said. "One of the most delicious fears of my childhood, I do believe, was imagining what it would be like to fall down the well..."

"Delicious?" he laughed at her, "well, I'm not so..."

"Yes," she insisted, hauling on the ropes to pull the pail up. "Delicious. It was..."

He was pulling now with her, the weight of the water having become increasingly heavy as it neared the top. She could feel his shoulder against hers, the muscles pressing. She was not sure she could speak, but she knew she must.

"When the lark bunting, the male, puts on his seasonal show for the female—" *(Oh my,* she thought to herself, *what am I floundering into?)* "He climbs high, as high as you can imagine, and then with his wings quivering, he comes swooping down, singing all the way—a beautiful song. The flight is spectacular, truly." The water pail appeared, he pulled it easily to the ledge of the well as she searched for the dipper. Finding it, she began to skim off the leaves and bugs that topped the water.

"The sad thing about the lark buntings," she continued in a voice that was, to her amazement, altogether calm, "is that our farms have taken away so much of the grasslands they nest in that they've had to move south and west."

"Like the rest of us," Owen said. Then, leaning down into the well, he shouted, "Go West, lark bunting," and the words echoed deep in the well, sounding against the damp and mossy sides like some sepulchral voice from the depths of the earth.

Willa laughed her wonderful, spilling-over laugh then, and it washed over them, making Owen grin with pleasure. He dipped the water out of the bucket and let it fall in the space between them, so that she could rinse her hands.

"I like to make you laugh," he said to her.

"You shouldn't say that," she mocked him. "My teachers at Wellesley told me a lady would never laugh that way—they said it was vulgar."

"And that," he said, taking her arm, "is what is wrong with Wellesley."

She looked at him seriously, then. "For a moment I thought

I might seem falsely dramatic—about the death of the little bunting." Willa said, "and in fact, perhaps I was. I know I would have felt no such distress had a hawk taken the bunting."

She started to spread the lunch on a grassy place in the churchyard, under the old elm. A spring breeze stirred the leaves and for a time it was the only sound. Carefully, she placed a loaf of bread on the cutting board, the knife alongside it. She unwrapped the cheese and some sausages. He reached for the knife and began slicing the loaf, giving it what seemed his full concentration.

"So," he said, finally, "we share a fear of deep wells, and a concern for lark buntings. Surely that is a good start."

She did not look up at him, but continued arranging the luncheon foods. Carefully, she removed some dried apples from their bag and put them on a plate.

"Tell me more," he said, and she quickly retorted, "No, you tell me, now."

"My life story?" he asked.

"Of course," she answered lightly, "all of it."

To her surprise—she had thought it to be no more than banter—he became serious.

"I was not reared for any sort of working life," he began, and the way he spoke—a trifle pedantic—made her think that his speech was rehearsed. He went on, "My father did well in business, as perhaps you know. I was ill as a child and my parents—having lost four others—were understandably cautious about my health. I was left to my tutors and my day-dreams."

He shook his head, being careful not to frown. "One day—for a reason I can no longer remember—we were at a farm-house in New Hampshire. It was summer, and warm, and my tutor took me to read under a tree that was on the edge of a field. Men were working—harvesting, I think. I can still feel what I felt then, as I watched those men lifting and raking, the muscle ropes in their arms. I wanted to do what they were doing with all my heart. I envied those men more than I have ever envied anyone—before or since . . . the muscles, the sweat, the throat dry with dust from the fields. I even fancied I could feel the pleasure of physical exhaustion, when lying down at night. In that moment, I knew that I would not be confined to an office or a study, that if I couldn't work in the fields, I

could at least find a way to be a part of the world, the movement, the active life rather than the passive."

It was a long speech, and for most of it he had not been
looking at her. Now he turned, as if coming back. "I surprised
even myself, I think," he went on, "and I suprise myself now,
talking on so as if I were the only subject in the world."

She busied herself with the cutting of a plum cake, handing
him a large slice on a napkin.

"Tell me, now, how you happened to become so interested
in hawks," he said. "It is your turn to confide."

"First you tell me," she countered, purposefully, "what you
would have done had you been disappointed in . . . Porter Farm?"

He looked at her, chastened.

"You remember," she went on, boldly, "you said that you
felt comfortable here, and that it surprised you. What would
you have done had you not felt comfortable?"

"I don't know," he answered with surprising candor, "but
it can't matter, can it? The fact is, I do feel comfortable with
you. I am not disappointed, and I hope you are not, either."

*With you,* he had said. No pretenses, no subterfuge. He was
not disappointed in her and he felt confident enough of his own
appeal to assume she was not disappointed in him. The light-
ness, the excitement Willa had felt when his shoulder pressed
against hers was displaced by the weight of reality. Willa guessed
that she was one of Owen Reade's calculated risks; she guessed,
too, that his courting flight would be brief.

"You asked about hawks, how I came to find them so interesting," she said, in answer. "Just as you remember the
afternoon in New Hampshire, I remember the first time I sat
and watched the flight of a hawk—truly watched, I mean. Pa
had sent me out to find a cow and her calf that had become
separated from the herd, and I had to go a long ways. On the
way back I sat down to rest for a minute. I leaned against a
fencepost—it was late in the evening, after milking—and looked
up, and there against the sky was one of the biggest birds I
had ever seen. At first I thought it to be a golden eagle. It was
quartering—separating a field into sections, then moving methodically in large swooping circles until the whole of the field
is covered—and now and then it would just hover, beating its
wings in such a way as to stay in one place. I watched it for the
longest time, and when I went home I searched through all of

Grandmother's books until I found what it was—a rough-legged hawk. After that, for days, I could close my eyes and see that hawk soaring and swooping. I couldn't seem to get it out of my mind, so I read everything I could find about hawks—and I began to notice them in the fields, and they seemed, just, to say by their flight what I so often felt . . . I cannot put it into words, but sometimes I can feel what it would be like to soar . . ."

She shuddered involuntarily, but when he moved to touch her she backed away. She was deeply humiliated, chastened, by what she had revealed, all the more so because she could not know why she had accepted the acceleration of the court-ship. Was she afraid that if she made him wait, if she asked that he go at her pace, he would be lost to her?

"It is time enough for a first meeting," Mama said when Willa told her that Owen would be leaving at the end of the week. "Perhaps he will be able to visit again on his return trip," she went on, probing, trying to discover something of Owen's plans, wanting to know what Willa knew. But Willa was not in a mood to cooperate, and said nothing. Mama controlled her temper, ending weakly with, "You can correspond, you know. Letters are a fine way to become better acquainted."

Willa changed the subject abruptly, which caused me to look up from the peas I was shelling. "I think Owen would enjoy a special gala performance of the Family Puppet Show," she said. Mama's mood changed quickly. She loved the puppet shows. The year of Grandmother's death, when Willa had come home from Wellesley College to stay, she brought with her several small puppets and taught the boys how to work them. That Christmas, Pa and Gib, with Mama's help, had made a puppet that was a remarkable caricature of Willa. After that, nothing would do but that each of us have our own puppet. Willa wrote the first of the Family Puppet Shows, followed by increasingly elaborate productions devised by the boys, who seemed able to speak freely through their puppet counterparts.

We gathered in the music room after the evening meal. Val started with a comedy skit he had written. As usual, my puppet was to do a dance . . . in my brothers' productions, I was always cast as a dancer. I took my position behind the stage, and realized that I would have a good view of Owen and Willa, who sat side by side in the front row of chairs, their shoulders almost, but not quite, touching. The closeness sent a shiver down my spine.

Owen would be the only permanent member of the audience, since the rest of us would, for one skit or another, have to take part. From the first moment, Owen laughed and cheered and clapped. The Little Boys were easily infected with his good humor, and joined him. Then we all caught it and gave what must have been the most exuberant Family Puppet Show in history, making fun of the personal foibles of each of us—and making Owen Reade a party to it all.

Val, handling the puppet that was Willa, said in a high falsetto, "Oh Gib, you must not kill the nice falcon, not even if it has eaten four hundred and thirteen of our doves. Falcons are too beautiful, too wonderful, too glorious." And one of the Little Boys, trying to imitate Gib, said in a pretend growl, "Hawks are varmints, Willa. Time you learned that hawks are just plain varmints." Everybody laughed at this charade, recognizing the ongoing argument between Willa and Gib. Between Willa and anyone who believed that hawks were to be killed.

When it became too dark to see, we lit the sconces and pulled out the chandelier to throw more light on the stage. Pa and the Big Boys had been working in the fields all day, but the play seemed to revive them. Or, I think, Owen Reade's appreciation revived us all.

"Your puppet family is remarkable," he would say, clapping and laughing; I think that evening was the first time we realized it was so.

Mama, perhaps, most of all. She came to sit next to Owen while Willa and the Little Boys did their skit, and I heard her say, "Willa is the one who started the family theater. I don't know what we would do without Willa." It might have been the kind of polite, meaningless remark any mother would make. But it wasn't. It was a plea, and Owen understood.

At that moment, I understood, too, Mama's ambivalence about Willa and Owen. Willa was the spark, the organizer, the one who could move us to action. Willa had given the farm a kind of life, and Mama was worried about how we would manage without her.

That night I came into the room I shared with Willa to find her standing, altogether naked, in front of the long oval mirror, her body illuminated by the oil lamp on the washstand. She was studying herself, concentrating on the line of her hips. She was as slender as a boy; her breasts were small, compact. She was frowning.

I waited.

She put both hands on her hips and said, "I'm not sure."

"Not sure of what?" I asked.

"How I will perform in childbearing," she answered.

"Perform?" I repeated, my tone suggesting it was a strange word.

"Yes. Perform—that is part of what this is all about. Having heirs. Producing children. Like a good mare."

My chin jerked up. "Willa," I said, surprised at the anger in my voice, "that really is crude."

She looked at me and said, without the slightest rancor, "Yes it is, and we shouldn't forget it. There is something very coarse, very raw, about mating. And very practical. Men need women to give them heirs."

I looked at her a long moment, and then I said, "Or women need men. Mama used Pa to sustain her dynasty."

She arched her eyebrows. "Dynasty?" We both laughed then. With a flannel wrapper pulled about her, she perched on the foot of the bed as she often did. She was determined not to let herself be romantic about Owen Reade, determined to discuss his interest in her in economic terms, as a business transaction. Her determination, now was gaining momentum.

"Have you thought about the way Owen learned of me?" she asked.

Before I could admit I hadn't, she rushed on, "Mama's letters to Aunt Emma. Think! That was all he could know about me before he came here. Now, what would Mama have said about me?"

I thought for a while. "Well," I hesitated, "whatever she said, it was in great detail." We had seen Mama write page after page to Aunt Emma.

"Did you notice how Owen looked at you when I introduced you?" Willa went on, "as if he already knew you?"

She was right about that. I had felt that while he was a stranger to me I was no stranger to him.

"He would have been seeing us through Mama's eyes, but with his own interpretations. We knew that Mama would have told Aunt Emma about what she considers my strange fascination with hawks, how I track and study them. And she would have talked about other things she chides me for—the running, my interest in accounting and mathematics, the fact that I chose to teach mathematics at the Academy."

On the farm, Willa invariably wore a brown corduroy skirt, divided so she could ride astride, and a blue shirtwaist. It was, she always said, her "uniform"—affected so she didn't have to consider what to wear from one day to another.

"Don't you see?" Willa asked, "he came here believing me to be an eccentric. The picture he had was of a willful, independent and physically strong woman. He knew us to be related to one of the old American families in the East, so my lineage was assured. Yet lineage must not be a priority with him, because there must be countless women back East with better connections. I think he knows what he wants, and what he wants is a strong woman who can bear children, and who will fit into both of his worlds—the one in the East, and the new one out West."

I stared at her.

"Has he spoken to you of the West?" I finally said.

"Yes," she answered, "he plans to make his life there, in the southern part of California."

California. He was going to live in California. *Ultima thule. The farthest point.*

"It is what you want," I said feebly, for the first time realizing that she could go, that like Mama I could be left behind, alone. And then I felt ashamed, because it was happening for Willa, it was all coming true, and I had to be—I was determined to be—happy for her.

"Oh, yes," she said, her eyes reflecting the lamplight, "oh, yes, it is what I want. I'll give Owen Reade his babies, I'll run his ranch for him and take care of him when he is ill. I'll be strong, and I'll go West. I will."

She was too caught up in her own thoughts to notice my tears. When she felt them, finally, against my cheek she said, "Hush, hush now, Lena. Don't cry. Did you think I'd leave you behind?"

I pulled back from her as if she had lost her mind.

"She'll never let me go," I whispered, adding, "but has he asked you? Is it certain?"

Instantly I was sorry, sorry I had asked, because I was not ready to hear the answer, not yet. But Willa only said, "Almost," and left it at that.

We went on long rides, the three of us, across the prairie with its blowing grasses. Willa and Owen with me along as chaperone. I took my sketch pads as an excuse to wander away from them.

We had been born into the long, lulling sameness of the prairie. Our lives had been as much without contour as the land, with few rises and few depressions, and until that spring it had seemed that the future was as flat a vista as the land that reached to the horizon.

One afternoon the clouds began to gather, moving ominously from the south. We were caught in a sudden thunderstorm. I quickly moved into a shed Pa used to store farm equipment, but the rain began to come down in solid sheets before Willa and Owen could join me. The day was warm, but the noise of the wind and the rain made me shiver. Willa and Owen would have taken shelter someplace else. They were alone, and I was glad. The storm lasted for better than an hour. We rode home in silence that day, a warm and comfortable silence that suited the fresh, wet newness that surrounded us.

That evening, Owen and Willa took a walk down the lane with a few of the Little Boys ranging about them. I could see the children chasing fireflies, their squeals carried back up to the porch where Ma and Pa and some of the boys were sitting, watching. The katydids began their vibrant humming, the music rising and falling in the dimming light. When Willa and Owen returned, Pa rose as if on signal and asked Mama and Willa and Owen to join him in the front parlor. The katydids grew louder . . . or perhaps it was simply my perception of the noise, for it seemed to grow and grow until it reached a crescendo and I felt faint. Then all I was aware of was a silence, and the low voices of my brothers, asking if I knew what this was all about.

At that moment, Mama was learning what it was all about. "Willa has accepted my proposal of marriage," Owen was explaining, "and Mr. Kerr has very kindly heard me out, and has said that with your consent, Willa and I can be married."

Mama looked as if she had been slapped. She stared at Pa,

then at Willa. Owen said, in a low and gentle voice, "I know how difficult it must be, the idea of one's daughter leaving, and so suddenly . . ."

"Suddenly?" Mama said, "What do you mean, suddenly? You've only just met her!"

Willa took over then. In a voice that was firm and controlled, she said, "Owen and I want to be married on Saturday. We will leave the same day for Boston, and then we will go to California to settle. We would like your blessing, Mama." Willa did not say "consent," as Owen had. Willa said "blessing."

Mama looked at Pa, then at Willa, and understood at once that she had no choice. So she gave her blessing. She gave it because there was nothing else she could think to do. But she said in tones of quiet resignation, "You'll never come back, I know you'll never be back again." Willa had wanted to touch her then, to put her hand on Mama's cheek, but she had not. It had been too long since they had touched, and now it was too late.

"I will be back, Mama," Willa had promised, knowing even then that it was an empty promise.

"Why so soon?" I asked angrily. "Two more days and you are gone. Why?"

"Because Owen has a schedule," Willa answered.

"And he can't write ahead? He can't delay his business?" I demanded.

"It's not that kind of schedule," Willa said softly. "What is important now is to be married, to get on with the beginning of a family, a home. Owen is in a hurry. Once something is decided, he must do it quickly. Owen Reade is racing time."

They were married in the apple orchard on a day with a warm breeze which ruffled the ribbons on Willa's lawn dress, and scattered the scent of apple blossoms. She stood with Owen, tall and elegant, her face calm and her eyes clear. Looking at Willa through a blur of tears, I saw what Owen Reade must have seen at once: She was unique, and full of promise, and beautiful even, in a way I had not until that moment understood.

# Chapter Two

Newton Center, Mass.
June 3, 1887

Dearest Lena,

I was thunderstruck this morning. I came awake and all I could see was a mass of yellow rosebuds on the wallpaper, and I had not the slightest notion where I was or what I was doing here. It was that peculiar half-waking sensation that happens sometimes when you are in a new place, but which goes away quickly. Except that this dislodged feeling did not entirely dissipate all morning long.

Oh, I know well enough where I am. I am at Owen's aunts' home in Newton Center, which is not far from Boston. It is a big, comfortable house occupied by his two elderly aunts and the daughter of one, Minnie, who is a spinster with a wonderful, trilly laugh that can be evoked for no good reason at all.

But the fact is, I still do not quite know what has happened to me. Think of it. Six months ago I hadn't the slightest idea that a man named Owen Reade existed. (Though two of my old classmates at Wellesley tell me that they had heard of him, even when we were in school together. I was never in their social set, so I would neither have known or—for that matter— cared.)

One month ago I had never set eyes on Owen. Two weeks ago, the idea that I would be married and in Boston and soon to go west would have made me laugh. Nothing happens that fast. And yet, it has, it has ... and I am spinning. The whole of my life has changed. I find myself married to a stranger— a delightful stranger, to be sure—and suddenly trusted with his family's possessions. I am to sort through them to choose which I wish to keep. A lifetime of possessions collected by people I never knew, yet no one questions my right to do this. Owen's aunts are as dear as they can be. They call me "niece" or "sweet niece" and act as if I have always been part of the family.

It is all too much to grasp. I find myself catapulted into another world, another life, surrounded by people I have never met, who treat me with great kindness. (Of course it is not me, but Owen's wife, that they are treating with such deference. They are in awe of him! It is as if they can't believe their good fortune to be related to him. You should have seen the disappointment in their faces when he left almost immediately for New Jersey to take care of some business. He apologizes profusely for having to leave, but he has taken upon himself the job of overseeing the family businesses and philanthropies, and there is no one else to do it, it seems.)

I have to admit that I was glad to see my old Wellesley classmates, even though I had not particularly fancied them when we were in school. (They seemed to have forgotten that they once parodied me as a raw Western girl.) At least they gave me a sense of attachment to my past—which I need right now. They came, I am certain, out of curiosity. They look at me as if to see what magic I practice to have enticed Owen to marry me. I told them nothing, but only smiled when they spoke of our "courtship."

Courtship! One week at Porter Farm, Family Puppet Shows and some rain-soaked picnics. I was not going to tell them how Owen came to call on me. Let them think it is all some fairy-tale romance.

We are staying with Owen's aunts because he didn't want to open the family home and because he will be away on business almost all of our time in the East. The aunts seem genuinely delighted to have me. There has been a steady stream of visitors since I arrived. The guest list would have made

Grandmother swoon, I do believe. (It is ironic, isn't it, that I should have married into the kind of family Grandmother would have admired?)

A strange thing happened on the trip from Chicago. In some curious and unexplainable way, the conductor mistook us for brother and sister and gave us separate berths. Owen, whom I could never have imagined being embarrassed, was. He flushed and stammered when he told me of the mixup, but we agreed that we did not wish to be identified as newlyweds and be subjected to crude jokes, so we decided simply to go along with the masquerade. (I assume the other passengers thought us to be an especially affectionate brother and sister, as Owen frequently bent to whisper something in my ear and, now and again, I would forget and touch his arm in an intimate manner.) Near the end of the trip, in one of the rare interludes when we were alone, I admitted to Owen that in some ways I had been relieved to be able to get to know him a bit better before sharing his bed. He then suggested that we should look upon this traveling period as our "courtship," and should begin our "marriage" when we reach the West Coast. I am continually amazed at his thoughtfulness, his understanding of others' feelings. Everyone seems to respect and admire him. I hear nothing but praise of Owen from everyone I meet.

Still, I have discovered that there is a public Owen and a private Owen, and I have so far only had glimpses of the latter. One of these came when we went through his home. It is big and dark and gloomy, filled with heavy furniture and the musty smell of being too long closed. We were alone. In the parlors and dining room, which he never remembers ever being used, Owen pointed out certain items of special interest—portraits, a silver service crafted by Paul Revere, crystal from Bavaria. As we climbed to the second story and approached the old nursery, he fell silent. I walked ahead, and looked into the room that I knew would have been his—there was still a charming coverlet on the bed with his name embroidered on it. I asked him a question, and when he didn't answer, I turned to find tears streaming down his face, forming droplets in his beard. I started to hold out my arms to him, but he turned away as if embarrassed. He walked into another room. I could see his back heaving, so I knew he was sobbing—but soundlessly. I went behind him and slipped my arms around his waist and pressed my face into his back. He let me hold him, but he said nothing at all. When I tried to speak about it, he deflected the conversation, with false enthusiasm telling me about the architect who had designed the house and other trivial items of history.

He must have been perfectly miserable here as a child. I know from his aunts that he was desperately ill at the age of seven, and spent long months in bed. They marvel that he is now the very picture of health.

I can better see why Owen was so overwhelmed with Porter Farm—he was, did you guess? He talked on and on about the Little Boys and how they bob about, all over the place. He watched us closer than I had imagined—even remarking on how attentive all the boys are to you, the small pats and smiles you get from them as a matter of course. You remember how you worried that Owen would think us unruly—that was the very thing that attracted him. He talked about the "life and excitement and good humor" that is part of the farm.

Eula Stanton, one of the Wellesley classmates who came to call, asked how I had managed to meet the "mysterious" Owen Reade. I answered by asking what she meant by "mysterious" and Angelica Sutton, who had come with her and is much the better humored of the two, said, "What Eula means is how did you manage to get his attention when none of the Boston girls could?" My response was to laugh in as good an imitation of Grandmother as I could manage. (You remember that laugh that said, "We'll talk no more of this, my dear"?)

Yet there *is* a mystery about Owen. He needs to do things quickly; action is all-important; he speaks of time as if it were tangible. On the train he needed to meet everyone, talk to them, find out who they were and what they were about. One farmer lectured for better than two hours on pigs! Everyone else (including me) fell asleep, but Owen seemed fascinated. When I asked him in all honesty if he wasn't bored, he only laughed and told me you never could tell when you'd need to know about pigs. He has also asked me to tell him what I know about hawks . . . not, I think, because he is particularly interested in raptors, but because it is something new to learn, and he cannot resist that opportunity. He has said that reading, studying, is an old habit. It is not a bad one, I think. I watch for flaws, but I find them only in myself. Owen seems too good, too perfect. I cannot believe that we are man and wife. And yet he has said that he knew he wanted to marry me the moment he saw me gasping for breath, having raced the buggy from the Four Corners on his arrival. ("How could I not want to marry a girl who would race two fine bays?" he laughed at me.)

I rattle on; you are to be my "Emma" I think. I feel I must tell you all of it, everything. I miss you. Who else can I speak to so plainly? I worry to think of you without your friend. Do spend time with Val. He is lonely sometimes, too. Until we can be together again, letters will have to do.

Now, you will want some information. We leave for California on the fifteenth of this month, by which time I will have selected the pieces to be shipped west, and will have closed the old Reade home. Owen will then have finished his business and will join me in New York on the same day we are to leave for California.

We shall not be stopping by the farm. I am sorry, dear one. And I know Mama will be disappointed, too. I am counting on you to soothe her. Owen offered to stop if I wished, but I know that he would prefer to go directly to California and to get on with the life we will make there. Everything is ahead of us, everything. The future, all of it, and I don't want to stop until we reach the blue Pacific, for fear I will wake and find the yellow rosebuds gone, and only the empty prairie before me.

Some of my letters will have a small *o* in the lower corner of the envelope, and they are for your eyes only. Be forewarned!

All my love,
Your Willa

Near Galesburg, Illinois
June 18, 1887

My dear Lena,

We will be entering Iowa before long, and Illinois will be behind me. All of this morning we crossed the Grand Prairie. So near, so near and yet so very far away. I had not thought I would feel so sad, yet when I found myself in familiar country, knowing all of you were but a few miles away, I looked out the window over the green prairie and all I could see was a vast mist from the tears that fogged my view.

Owen, who had been talking to a railroad man about the intricacies of the Westinghouse airbrake, materialized next to me and sat very close. He reached for my hand and talked to me. It was the private Owen, again. He said that he could not truly understand what I was feeling because he had never in the whole of his life had a home to long for. And then he said, in a tone so low, and so filled with wanting that it made me shiver, "We are going to have a big house that will sit in the lee of a mountain, and a brook will flow nearby, and the house will be filled with light and with children and with pets. There will be a flower garden and an orchard where we will grow oranges as sweet as anything you have ever tasted, and I will always know you are there." His lips were close to my ear, his voice low and trembling, and I felt something warm inside of me. Little by little I am coming to know this man who is my husband.

Owen talked to me all morning long to help me get through the hurt I felt that I shall not be seeing you and Mama and Pa and the boys for a long time. (Though where you are concerned, I am determined that it will not be too long.) The frontier, he told me, is closed. The first great migration is over, the men who tamed the wilderness, pioneers like Grandfather, who had the courage and the sheer physical strength and the patience their day is gone. He spoke of them with admiration, and with sorrow. "There is a kind of man," he said, "who needs always to be separate, who does not want to be part of the civilization. And there is no place, anymore, for that kind of man. He took all the risks, he made it possible for others to come behind him, and in doing so he ruined it for himself. It's like the man who breaks horses. He risks his bones, his back, his health for the joy of breaking the beast. Then someone else takes the animal and trains it. Brawn gives way to brains. That is what is happening now, in the West. Now it is a time for the men who will shape the country to take over, and I plan to be one of them."

He sat silent for a long while, holding my hand in both of his. Then he told me about the first time he had made the westward journey by train, years ago.

"Out of Omaha," he said, "the Union Pacific line runs for

a time alongside the old Emigrant Trail, and every now and then we would pass some family going West in one of the old-time prairie schooners, their few possessions tied to its side, maybe driving a few poor head of cattle. The faces of those people were gaunt, poor and pinched and weary, and you knew that something had gone wrong for them, that they were going West because they thought it would be better for them out there. They would stare at the train as it went by, but I noticed that most of the people on the train would hardly look at them. It was as if they didn't want to see it, didn't want to be reminded."

Owen told me, too, about a banker named Sharon that he knows in Virginia City, "a well-educated fellow and a fine poker player," as Owen described him. That's what the West is now, Owen said—a high-stakes poker game. And then he added, "If you can't afford to play, you shouldn't be in the game. Because men like Sharon can smell need, and when they do it's all over. That's why that poor fellow in the Conestoga wagon and his family can't survive out West. They have too much need."

When I asked Owen if he was a gambler, he only smiled and said, "No, at least not with cards."

He has told me nothing of his financial position. I had expected him to give me some general information, at least. I suppose I should not have referred to it at all, but then I remind myself that I am his wife, his partner in this life.

I scarcely know him, yet we are that: Partners for life. I wish you were here, Lena. I miss you and I need you.

... It is some hours since I wrote the lines above. I feel better now, not quite so dreary. Before I close this letter and begin the search to find a station at which I can post it, I wanted to tell you about one more conversation with Owen. He has met several of those men who control the Central Pacific Railroad in California, and who are, he tells me, very powerful. There are four of them, though their names escape me at the moment. Owen says that they are not smart men, but rather shrewd. They were, he explains, small-town merchants in Sacramento. One had a hardware store, I believe.

"The dreamer of the big dream," said Owen, "was a man named Theodore Judah, an engineer who was certain that a railroad could be built over the Sierras that would connect the East to the West. It was Judah who convinced Congress to finance this railroad." As for the four little merchants, "They only had the sense to hang on to Judah's coattails. When he died suddenly, they took over and squeezed everyone else out."

He told me this, I believe, to distract me. But all I could think about after that was what he had called Judah—"The dreamer of the big dream." The wheels turn and the coach sways, the dirt blows in the windows and the noise wraps around and enters my head, but over and above all of it I hear in the cadence of the tracks, "The dreamer of the big dream."

I am not sure what Owen's dream is; I am not even sure of mine. All I know is that it can only happen in the West. Illinois is behind me now. We have crossed the river at Burlington and we are in Iowa.

All of my love,
Willa

Somewhere West of
Cheyenne, Wyoming
June 21, 1887

Dearest Lena,

It has been five days and four nights since we left on the Pullman palace car with its carved and gilded walnut fittings, its plate glass and tapestry carpets, its promise of the most elegant possible journey westward. That is the promise; the reality is that the motion enters your very bones; the noise and the grit thrown back from the engine seeps into you, day and night, night and day. I sit on the seat for hours on end, gently swaying in a sideways motion, and wonder if I will ever be still again, if I will ever hear real silence. Soon we will be pulling into one of the stations where we will stop to eat. Then I will be able to put my feet, for a few minutes at least, on land again. It must be the way a sailor feels after so many months at sea. In a way it is as if we are covering a land ocean. The grasses wave as we roll across the vast expanse of the plains; I feel as if I could drown in it.

But the stations! They are nothing more than clusters of buildings, clapboard or logs daubed with mud and looking as if the first high wind would take them down. They have beau-

tiful names like Papillon, Silver Creek, Plum Run—but they
are dismal cankers that have rubbed all along the railroad line.
When the train stops at one that is a dinner station, everyone
rushes off at once and descends on the one or two restaurants,
almost all of which feature a bar. (The Western men who have
joined the train invariably move up to the rail to imbibe their
dinner, and the foul smell of whiskey is added to their body
odors, which are disgusting enough.) We have fifteen minutes
in which to bolt our food—a hot beverage and tough beef,
usually—if we are to have ten minutes left over to stretch our
legs.

Owen is adept at arriving first at the lunch counters and
securing food for us. (Ladies ceased to be first almost immediately after we pulled out of Omaha.) We devour our lunch,
then we stroll up and down on the flimsy wooden platform,
concentrating so the food stays down and gives us the nour-
ishment we require. No matter, it does break the boredom.

Boredom. I am sick with myself for being bored. The whole
of the country is passing outside my window, and I want to
see it all, to remember everything...but there is a strange
sense of unreality about it. The plains are endless. Here and
there I glimpse a sod house and sometimes a few dirty children
standing outside. It seems such an empty, barren life. In front
of one of these huts I saw a perambulator—very fancy, the
kind you might see on the high streets of Springfield, or in
Boston, and I wanted to cry, it so heightened the sense of
desolation.

So far, the only Indians I have seen are those that gather in
the stations, their greasy blankets pulled around them, begging.
Their eyes are dull, their bodies filthy. The papooses, naked
and dirty, cling to their mothers. They look more like monkeys
than I thought a human could look. It is repulsive, shameful,
degrading. I try not to look at them. I would think the passengers on the train would give them wide range, but no. They
seem to find them entertaining. Even Owen crowds around
them, and when the male Indians pull out their pathetic arrows
and try to hit a target (for the promise of a coin) it becomes a
sideshow. Yesterday, at one of the stops, one of the passengers
got a bit excited when none of the Indians could manage to hit
the target, so he pulled out his Colt revolver and began banging
away. Soon four or five other guns were going off, everyone

seemed to get into the mood of it, and the tin plate that was the target was bouncing around as the train began to pull away from the station. Stupid Indians and stupid, stupid, gun-carrying men. When I vented my rage at Owen (who is one of the few men on this train who does not carry a gun, thank goodness) he would only say that they always leave a few coins behind, enough to keep the Indians in bondage to this shameful existence.

In Cheyenne I did see some real Indians—real, in my terms. Three braves were riding their beautiful ponies. They were on their way to Fort Russell, Owen guessed. They sat wonderfully erect, looking straight ahead as if the train and the town didn't exist. (As indeed they didn't too many years ago.) I could feel their pride, it was that tangible. When I told Owen I was glad to have seen them, he said only that I would do well not to romanticize Indians, that the ones I had seen in the station were a portent of what was to be for the Indians in all of the West. When I saw the braves, I thought of three hawks, soaring. It is what they were meant to do—soar.

But this letter is becoming a complaint, and I must tell you about the nicest thing that has happened to us on this journey. In Omaha, a private railroad car was added to our train. It was one of the most ornate any of us had ever seen, and in gilt along the side was the name Alhambra. Of course, all of the passengers were buzzing with curiosity trying to discover what great man was in the car. Owen was beside himself; he does love a puzzle. As usual, he was the first to find out. (Owen has an uncanny ability to draw the railroad men into his confidence.)

He came bounding down the aisle, his face alight with triumph, and I could tell that he was bursting with his news, so I decided to pretend nonchalance.

"Well?" he finally asked.

"Well?" I repeated.

"Well, I *know*," he said.

I took a few leisurely stitches of crochet, and said in as casual a manner as I could, "Really, dear—what is that?"

Unable to contain his news another minute, he blurted, "Sara Hunt."

This time my nonchalance was not pretended. I hadn't the slightest notion who Sara Hunt was or why I should know her.

"Sara Hunt is Phineas Emory's adopted daughter—his only child."

"Oh," I said, "and Phineas Emory is one of those small-town merchants who rode to power on poor Theodore Judah's dream?"

I could see at once that I had spoiled his fun—first by not knowing who Sara was, and then by reminding Owen that he had been contemptuous of Emory. So I moved to make up by suggesting that we meet her.

"Exactly what I was thinking," Owen answered, mollified.

Sara Hunt, Owen learned (how I do not know), was returning from a women's college near St. Louis, having completed her course of study. Her father, the illustrious Emory, sent his private car to collect her.

Owen has methodically set about meeting all of the passengers on our train—the drummers and the ever-present Englishmen, the women going to meet their husbands, who are surveyors or engineers or miners, and their children. I marvel at Owen's curiosity and at his tenacity. Occasionally he learns something of interest, and repeats it to me. I suppose it is a better way to pass the time than looking out the window or playing endless games of euchre, as many of the men do. But I cannot bring myself to become interested in people who seem, for the most part, to be dull and commonplace.

Sara Hunt is an exception. I am glad that Owen convinced the conductor to take her his calling card, and I am glad that he convinced me to send a note along with it.

Later that same day, at the dinner stop, one of her servants—a lovely little Chinese girl—approached us as we promenaded on the platform, and said that Miss Hunt would be pleased if we could join her in her car that same afternoon. Owen was delighted and, when I met Sara, so was I.

She was standing by one of the big leather chairs, her hands lightly touching the back of it to give her balance, the French pier glass on the far wall reflected her back. She is a small woman with a child's body and great, dark eyes. I thought for a moment that she would not be able to look at us, but I was wrong.

"Please," she said in a whispery voice, "come in, sit down." Owen set about putting her at her ease. She ordered tea, and I noticed that her hand shook not at all as she served it to us, a remarkable feat given the swaying of the train. She looked at me only occasionally, and when she did I saw what I thought to be fear, yet behind it something else. I can't quite explain it. But something else was there, behind the fear...

More important, for me, was that she reminded me so of you that I felt I already knew her, and some of that familiarity must have passed on to her, because she began to smile a bit. I cannot really say why she is like you—she does not have your small-boned prettiness, nor your clear light skin. She is, in fact, quite plain. But there is something—a certain resilience, a calmness—that is attractive.

Whatever the reason, I enjoy Sara Hunt. Owen entertains her, makes her laugh, teases her as he would a younger sister (as he teases you). And she enjoys it, that is plain to see. But when he leaves and we are alone, she seems calmer and it is as if we have known each other for a long time. I have told her about you, naturally, and once she blurted, "How I envy Lena!" (I know what you are thinking now. Don't. You *are* to be envied, twisted back and all. And we will be together again, and you will meet Sara!)

Yesterday, as we rode endlessly through the plains, she told me that her father and Phineas Emory had been business partners. Her mother died giving birth to her. Her father died when she was five. Mr. Emory became first her guardian, then her legal parent.

"How good of him," I said. And she answered, without the slightest rancor, "It was a business proposition."

Sara and Owen have sad childhoods in common. And yet they are quite opposite in character—the one bold and outgoing, the other meek and introspective.

Sara is returning to San Francisco to meet Mr. Emory's new wife, a woman only a few years older than she.

"Will that seem strange?" I was cheeky enough to ask, and she said: "Nothing ever seems strange to me." When I asked her to explain she began to stammer, and I was sorry that I had embarrassed her and I began to apologize, but she held her hand out to stop me. Then she did answer. She said: "Whatever presents itself in a certain context, I accept."

I was confounded. How can that be? How can one live by that rule? I suppose it is why she agreed to see us. We were "in a certain context."

I must admit to being glad that Sara *did* see us because she is dear to be with and because the private car is infinitely more comfortable than Mr. Pullman's magnificent palace car. Not only that, it has a bathtub. Truly. And yesterday Sara asked if I wished to take a bath.

It was like asking if I wanted to go to heaven when I die. I could have cried. The pale linen dusters that are supposed to protect our clothing are now the color of a dirty mouse. The odors of the car get stronger each day so that the windows are open most of the time, letting in more grit from the engine.

After a bath in Mr. Emory's amazing copper tub, I felt almost human again and I think I became quite hilarious. I did a small dance or two, sang a few songs for Owen and Sara, and even had the Chinese girl giggling. Today Sara is going to join me in the parlor car so that Owen can bathe. Then he promises to sing for us.

I can't tell you how sorry I am that we allowed this ridiculous brother-sister charade to happen. When I say this to Owen he only laughs and reminds me what a scandal I would cause if he should now suggest we get a double berth. Sara knows our secret; when I told her she only shook her head and smiled a little.

Owen is much the more even-tempered of us. I sometimes think he could weather any kind of storm with his charming smile and easy laugh.

Oh, but speaking of storms. Out of Omaha, at midday, we were moving alongside the Platte River when suddenly it became ominously dark. The wind rose until we began to scramble to close all of the windows. Soon it grew so close, and so dark, that the carriage lamps were lit. The storm came upon us in great, roiling clouds that moved across the plains. They were like something alive, something gargantuan. We watched the storm come; great sheets of rain overtook us, blowing so hard that the train slowed to a crawl. Owen and I went to Sara, thinking that she would be frightened.

She was. We found her huddled in a chair, shivering. "Come," I said, "let's sit together on the chaise," and she did as I suggested, like a child, trembling all the while.

The sky lightened a bit and the rain was not so driving. We were infused, then, with a curious yellow light. Far away on the plain we could see lightning crackling through the sky. We counted . . . one . . . two . . . three . . . and then felt the great rumble of thunder shake through us. We could hear the sound of the hail before we saw it—first, as a staccato drumming on the roof of the car and then, as the storm gathered fury, as balls of ice smashing at us from all sides. I pulled Sara away from the windows as Owen rushed to draw the shades as protection from flying glass. The hailstones were as big as India-rubber balls and the noise was deafening. It felt as if we were about to explode, to crack wide open. Sara had her hands over her ears and her eyes tight shut. I pulled her into the shelter of a pantry, where we huddled with the Chinese girl.

One of the plate glass windows shattered, spilling glass all about, and a shard narrowly missed Owen. Sara screamed; her face was utterly white, her eyes enormous. Owen quickly moved back to us. (He looked at me, and I could see that he was not at all afraid, but rather excited. It is hard to explain, but I knew what he was feeling. We may even have smiled at each other; I can't imagine why.)

As suddenly as it had started, it was over and there was utter quiet, the train having stopped completely. Through the broken window we could smell the wet plains grasses, the wildflowers, the earth. It was a fresh, new smell, and for the flicker of an instant I was in the real West, not enclosed in a metal container and catapulted through space.

On a path that is alongside the track came two men on horseback. They had been through the worst of the storm, in the open, and seemed not to realize that it was over. They were drawn up still as balls, tucking their heads under them for protection. In that instant I *did know* the uncompromising harshness of this land, of life outside the Pullman palace car or Phineas Emory's Alhambra. And I have been trying not to forget, but to hold on to that bit of knowledge.

Soon we will cross the great Rocky Mountains, then the Sierra Nevada. Do you know that sometimes little bands of prairie dogs sit up and bark at the train? They do! They truly do. This is the West I have dreamed of for so long. Why do I feel so insulated, so out of time in this railroad car? It is as if I am in another place, another time, as if a crucial step has been missed.

Sara has invited us to visit her in her father's home in San Francisco, I think out of gratitude for our coming to her aid during the storm. I was prepared to make our apologies, knowing how important it is to Owen to be on our way to Los Angeles. But when he heard of the invitation he was ecstatic. "We would be delighted, absolutely delighted," he told Sara, and she said, "Good." Just when I think I am beginning to understand Owen, he surprises me.

But I am delighted, too. Sara is the dearest of girls, and I am happy to spend more time with her. Too, I want to see San Francisco, the mecca of the West, before we go to what is charmingly called "the cow counties" down south. Most of all, I am happy to stop in San Francisco to put an end to our courtship, to have this marriage consummated. I touch Owen and feel a sharp electric shock, a warmth in the lower center of me. I wish the Rockies and the Sierras were behind me, I wish we were even now arriving at the City by the Golden Gate.

> My love, dear one,
> Willa

> Reno, Nevada

My dear Lena

Forgive the brief nature of this note. I have not been feeling well. I did want you to know that you might write me in care of Sara Hunt, Number 14 California Street, San Francisco. She has promised to see that your letters reach me, and I know that she will.

Out of the window this morning I watched an eagle circle and soar. I must see that this is posted in Reno, a city which is said to be "neither hawk nor vulture."

> My love,
> Willa

"I have not been well," she wrote, and it was true. It would be a year before I learned, from Sara, what had happened as the train rolled across Wyoming and into Utah and Nevada.

At first, Sara would say, Willa had simply fallen silent. The two spots of color that were always high on her cheeks disappeared, making her look strangely wan. She ceased to eat, though Owen tried to coax her and the Chinese girl rummaged through the assortment of tins of delicacies that were kept on the Emory car.

Sara was alarmed; Owen was panicked. He hovered over Willa, fretting and worrying. When Sara suggested she stay in one of the polished Satinwood folding berths in the private car, Owen readily agreed. As the fever mounted, they took turns bathing Willa with cool towels.

Willa said nothing at all, but only lay there. Her skin was hot to the touch. At times she lost consciousness altogether, or she would see things that they did not see. At Salt Lake City Owen made a frantic effort to get a doctor. None would come, and he only got back on himself by grabbing hold of the last car at the last moment, his heart pounding and his breath coming in hard gasps, so that Sara was frightened for him, too.

They took turns sitting with her; "She will be all right," Owen said—sometimes as a question, sometimes as a statement.

And then Willa had looked at them, and smiled weakly, and they knew it was going to be all right. Owen had kissed his wife's hand and held it to his cheek. Then he gently put it back under the coverlet, and turned to Sara and hugged her to him, while Willa smiled from her bed at them. For the first time in her life, Sara Hunt felt connected to another... to two others. It was to be important to all of them.

## ∿ *Chapter Three*

Letters from California, with and without the tiny *o* in the corner, arrived with astonishing regularity. I say "astonishing" because Willa was not organized and she did not believe in routine. It was, she said, dull and dulling. Rather, she functioned in bursts of energy so intense they could not be long sustained. I could only wonder at the reasons for my rich harvest of letters.

It became my habit to walk to the Four Corners to the post box. I told Mama I did this for the exercise, knowing she could not deny that need. I did not tell her that I needed the solitude as much. Often enough, the things Willa saw fit to commit to paper made me feel as if I had stolen documents on my person. I knew that Mama would not venture beyond the rose garden at the rim of the yard, so I was safe to read Willa's letters, hidden by the big elm in the abandoned churchyard, through all of that summer and into the fall.

Willa was sly enough to send, in the same post as an *o* letter, another addressed to Mama and Pa, so that no one suspected my bounty. Outwardly, my days were little changed. No one guessed that my life shifted that summer. The letters were at the center of my thoughts; they occupied me. The most

53

important moment of my day was the opening of the post box. The deepest pleasure was settling down to read page after page of Willa's large, rushed handwriting.

I do not mean to say that Willa told me everything. She did not, for instance, speak of fears or doubts—I think that she did not often allow herself to think of them. But she did confide surprisingly intimate matters. More than once my face would flush as I sat in the churchyard, leaves falling all about me.

She told me, in vivid detail, about her wedding night. "It has happened," she wrote, "I am a wife, I am truly, wholly, wonderfully a woman. I never knew, had no idea, how it would make me feel, this physical merging with a man. I know, I know, I know what I said, but I was wrong. What did I really know? Nothing. I wish I could make you understand the exquisite pain of it."

The letter, thicker than most, arrived on a warm Wednesday, a somnolent summer day that wrapped close around me. Settled in the churchyard, near a chinaberry tree, I read—ignoring the stickers from wild oats that had embedded themselves in my stockings, ignoring everything but the words on the paper.

"We came to the rooms that had been arranged for us at the Lick House (much the most *exclusive* and without a doubt the most *aristocratic* hotel in the city—Owen's words). I stood in the doorway and took a long look at the whole of the large room, as if it were a stage setting. In truth, the most important scene of our wedded life was to be played there. A new timidness came over me; I felt awkward in the presence of the man who was my husband in name, but not yet in body.

"As soon as the door closed behind us, and we were alone— wonderfully alone—I stood in the center of the room feeling wickedly free. My husband busied himself with our valises. I watched him with a cataclysmic fascination. He turned and, seeing me, stood perfectly still. I do not know how long we looked at each other, perhaps not long.

"The room itself was almost too perfect, too exquisite, the scene of an illicit encounter, except that we are licit. The appointments were exquisite, neat and in perfect place. Perfect, perfect, perfect . . . you see how often I use that word? There were elegantly embroidered towels hung on the washstand, each precisely folded. The massive bed was all carved and gleaming. I ran my hand over the shining wood and felt . . . sinful.

"I felt as if we were alone, at long last, for the first time in our married life. Private, removed, out of reach, out of time. I felt dizzy with excitement.

"Owen touched the back of my neck and I felt something hot flash through me. He kissed me then, my first true kiss. I felt as if all the time in the world had gathered in the room, and that I could stay on forever.

"Except that we were dusty and vile from the long journey, and I could not abide the thought of going to my wedding bed smelling so abominably. (If the room was in perfect order, clean and sweet-smelling, its occupants were not; occasional dabs of rosewater do not cleanliness make.) Owen called for water, and two small Chinamen, who seemed to be giggling, filled the tub with steaming water, and left us to our pleasure.

"A bath, and then bed.

"After years of hiding from Pa and the boys during our Saturday night ablutions, it felt strange to be naked in the room with a man. I liked it. I even, I believe, paraded, happy as a beetle. Owen washed my back, lathered me completely and laughed until I blew soap bubbles into his eyes and made them smart. (Unfortunately, Owen was not so willing that I should see him in his entirety, though perhaps that is understandable since there is so much more to see of the male of the species.)

"Oh, Lena, if you could but know the *wanting* . . . My hair was damp from the bath and my gown cold against my skin, but that didn't matter at all. I sat in the open air, which was chill after the heat of the bath, and shivered—but not, I think, from the cold.

"But you see, my darling husband had been thoughtful enough to order, in advance, a wedding supper and nothing would do but we wait for it to be delivered to our room. Wait! I was sure I could not eat. Oysters and champagne duly arrived, and I was ravenous. I drank my champagne too quickly, I think, liking the bubbles more than the taste, and I began to hiccough frightfully. Owen laughed at me for a while, then he gave me his special hiccough cure which I am sworn not to reveal, and shan't, since it is rather more intimate than any other hiccough cure I have ever heard of.

"I suppose we looked extremely silly, sitting there—Owen in his elegant red silk dressing gown, me in Owen's elegant cream silk dressing gown (I am, he says, to order a wardrobe while I am here; he won't have me roaming about in his clothes!).

"And then, at long last, to bed.

"It would have been romantic had he carried me, but I am too heavy. Instead, we held close together, only the fabric of the silken gowns between us, and, filled with a terrible excitement, tumbled together into the bed.

"As I thought, his chest is smooth, hairless, lovely . . . oh.

"He lay on me, and I touched that wild part of life that I had not known to exist. Beautiful, soft and hard at once. Lena—there is at the center of the wildest storm a most wonderful core of absolute design. Absolute.

"Oh, the wonder and the glory.

"The only time in all of my life that I have felt anything in the least like it was once, two years ago, in the far meadow, when I was watching two golden eagles during mating time. First one and then the other executed a magnificent dive, wings half closed, plummeting from the sky as if thrown with great force by some sky giant, reaching amazing speeds. Then, at the last possible moment, each eagle pulled out of the dive before crashing to earth—only to soar skyward again, riding a thermal up and up and up, until after a time it was no more than a dark point against the blue. I remember that the mating flight went on for a very long time and I sat, mesmerized, with everything inside of me in motion. The two eagles rolled and dived and raced the wind, until at last they were rushing at each other on a collision course—at unimaginable speeds. Just as they were about to crash into each other, the male rolled over onto his back and, from below, touched talons with his speeding mate.

"I remember crying out at the *perfection* of it.

"Lovemaking is like that. Perfect.

"Lena, destroy this letter . . . please!

"Oh, but why are we not told? Why are we made to think of mating as something dark and furtive? I remember that I said to you that there is something coarse and raw about it. I could cry at my ignorance.

"I think I know why we are not told. We must be made to wait, and if we knew we would not want to wait.

"How terribly unfair it is. Men are not made to wait. Owen did not wait. I asked him outright. It seemed not so great an intimacy, after sharing his bed. He looked at me oddly; a vein in his forehead stood out. Then, without a word, he left our room. When he returned an hour later he told me, with something akin to formality, that he did not feel he could come to me without 'experience.' He then added, as if it were an entirely distasteful subject, that he had sought only enough 'experience' to be able to understand his 'husbandly duties.'

"Duties! Such a strange word for so great a pleasure, I told him, at the same time assuring him that I did not in any way find fault with him for his 'experience.'

"Owen refuses to be shocked by me. Still, I think, this time I caused him some concern. He looked at me for quite a long time, it seemed (though in fact it may have been only a few seconds), and finally he shrugged and smiled a wry little smile and said, 'Are we then to have no secrets, you and I?'

"'Exactly,' I said, throwing myself at him with such force that we went tumbling, and Owen said the proprietors of the august hotel might very well ask us to leave for wrestling on the premises.

"I know I make Owen wonder. But he must know what I know, how exquisitely the joining of bodies defines all that we feel but cannot find words for. And how perfect a way to create new life.

"New life . . . that is a subject Owen does not tire of. I have never thought a man could be so enchanted with the idea of fatherhood. (I suppose I would be more enchanted with the idea of motherhood, had I not had so very many young brothers. Even that Owen sees as an advantage. I have had so much practical experience, he says. As indeed both you and I have.)

"I am sitting at the desk in our suite at the Lick House looking now at our wedding bed. It is immense, a great mahogany bed with a headboard that reaches, quite literally, to the ceiling. It is massively carved, with what seem to be mythical creatures—fauns and griffons and water fairies. The bed is warm, still, from our bodies. A blue ribbon loosed from my gown is entwined in the rumpled sheets. I thrill to the intimacy that bed has brought us.

"Owen is off, now, at another of his business meetings. I am to meet him at eleven at a ladies' tailor on Mission Street. He has given me such intricate directions on how to get there—involving the Polk and Central Avenue cable car and walking several blocks. Before he left this morning he announced, with what I now know to be not so much tact as a way to get what he wants, that he admires the originality of my 'uniform'— my corduroy skirts and blue blouses, and that he would like my permission to have the idea executed in a variety of different fabrics by a French seamstress. I will wear my brown taffeta to dinner at Sara's home tomorrow evening; it will have to do.

"But I didn't tell you . . . no sooner had we become settled in our hotel, than we received a formal invitation asking the pleasure of our company for dinner tomorrow evening at seven, formal attire specified. We are to dine at the celebrated Nob Hill mansion of Phineas Emory.

"Perhaps it is all a fairy tale. Certainly, I felt like a water fairy when we at last sighted the city of San Francisco. Because it sits on a peninsula, the train journey ends on a boat, thus the approach is by water.

"We arrived in a fine white fog, much welcomed after the heat of the Sacramento Valley. I envisioned us as rising out of the sea—though of course it was not the sea, but San Francisco Bay. As we crossed on the boat we could see very little and it was amazingly chill for June. The foghorns were blowing low over the water. It was an exciting sound and made me feel curiously elated. Best of all, I felt isolated with Owen. We held fast together on the deck, listening to the water slap against the hull, squinting for a glimpse of the city. It came rising out of the fog, the palest, most silvery city shimmering in a sudden glint of sunlight. It seemed as if Owen and I were the only ones alive in the universe. I had this most remarkable feeling . . . I cannot even describe it. Los Angeles is yet another four hundred and fifty miles to the south, yet I feel we are *here*. In California, at the farthest point. Illinois seems so much more than a mere few weeks in the past.

"San Francisco is only partly what I expected. There is a vitality, an urgency, here that I have seen in no other city. Yet one block will look as if it were transplanted from Boston or even Springfield, while around the corner you will feel as if you had stepped into the Orient. Celestials, as the Orientals are called, are everywhere, scurrying about, always busy, it seems, always moving.

"It makes me angry—I cannot explain why, but that is the feeling, anger—that it has been here all of this time, and I haven't known about it. It was as if San Francisco didn't exist (or, perhaps, it was as if I didn't exist, I am not sure which is right). All I can be sure of is the anger, which was . . . is . . . real. Lives have been lived in houses I am seeing for the first time, cable cars move up and down the avenues, families take picnics to the sandy stretches by the Pacific. And I didn't know about any of it until now. When I said this to Owen, he only looked at me and said, quite evenly, 'But my dear, I brought you here as soon as I knew about you.'

"We will stay at the Lick House for a few days, perhaps a week, depending on how many business meetings Owen wishes to pursue. As I may have mentioned, we came from Sacramento by riverboat. A channel has been cleared between that inland city and San Francisco along the Sacramento River. At the place where the river enters the great bay is a sprawling delta. Owen was fascinated by the expanse of marshland that could, he says, be reclaimed for agricultural purposes. He is not the first to think of these possibilities, he has learned. Already he is meeting with other men who are eager to pursue the reclamation.

"I shall write to you again after our dinner at the Emorys'. In some ways it is my 'coming out' as Mrs. Owen Reade. This is all make-believe. A fairy tale. I only wish you were here so I could tell you, see your face, hear you tell me in that quietly determined way of yours when I am flinging off in the wrong direction entirely. I count on you as on no one else. I wonder, at times, if I may simply fly off into the sky some day without you to pull me back to earth."

At supper that night I was there and not there. I suppose I did not answer when spoken to, for after a time Mama heaved a great sigh and said, "Where *are* you, Lena?" I flinched as if caught, wondering if she knew—if any of them could know— that I was, in fact, in California, that I had been there for weeks.

Willa and Owen and their new life occupied my thoughts during the day; at night, they moved into my dreams.

Willa's letters were filled with wonderful details. I could imagine myself with her and Owen on the evening they went to the Emory mansion on Nob Hill. From the heights, they looked down on the city. As they pulled up to the door in the hack which Owen had rented for the evening, Willa had smiled when he whispered, "You can smell the self-importance."

Willa was wearing a gown of the palest grey watermarked China silk, finished that day and delivered to the Lick House by the French dressmaker Owen had engaged. Willa had marveled at Owen's persuasiveness, which she assumed had been complemented by a rather large sum of money. Madame Odile would have had to work throughout the night to finish the dress. Her already dark-rimmed eyes had seemed shades darker when she came to the hotel for a last fitting. Willa had exclaimed, "Oh, but you look so very tired," with such genuine concern that the dressmaker had blinked, and waved her hand in the slightest of gestures, which seemed to say, "Ah, well, you are good to notice." When she saw the dress on Willa, she allowed herself a sharp intake of breath and a smart clap of the hands. Words, clearly, would not come.

Owen provided the words. "Madame," he said to the Frenchwoman, "the dress is beautiful, on my wife it is more than beautiful."

Willa's bones were long but not large, which caused her to move with a delicate awkwardness. Using the medium of watered Chinese silk, Madame Odile had transformed that awkwardness into elegance.

"Our old friend Thomas Sully should see you now," Owen said admiringly. For the first time in her life, Willa felt what it was to be considered handsome.

The Emory mansion was a brownstone on the very crest of the hill. There was no mistaking it. The great red pile dominated the other mansions in this most prestigious part of the city. The grounds were filled with a profusion of roses, all full-blown, and the grass was an obscene color of green, Willa thought. They walked up one small flight of stairs to an iron gate, then up another to the entrance hall. Willa felt a flutter of apprehension; Owen, sensing this, stopped on the bottom step and said in a low voice, "Well, love, shall we pay our respects to the hardware king?"

Willa giggled. "If I can't think of a thing to say, shall I engage him in conversation about nuts and bolts?"

"By all means," Owen answered, moving her up the stairs, "you must do that."

Sara was there, in the shadowy depths of the foyer, waiting.

She put both of her hands out to Willa. In the heavy context of the room she seemed even smaller than she was; her physical presence was at once so insignificant that, had it not been for her great hurt eyes, she would not have been noticed.

Willa took her hands, then hugged her.

"You're here," Sara said with what seemed to be surprise, adding, *sotto voce,* "welcome to Gloomy Caverns."

"Of course we're here," Willa laughed, "I've missed you already, and it's only three days since we left you in Sacramento."

"Think what a welcome you'll get when we've been parted the whole of a week," Owen put in, then lowered his voice too as he said, "But Gloomy Caverns?"

"That's what Charles calls it," Sara said. "He's here, someplace, you'll get to meet him too."

Charles, they knew, was Charles Emory, the nephew—and heir apparent—of Phineas Emory, and a favorite of Sara's.

Owen tucked Sara's hand under one of his arms, and with Willa on the other, moved the two women toward the drawing room where a gathering large enough to create a low drone of conversation was waiting.

Willa was surprised, and disappointed. She had not expected so large a crowd. She had supposed—presumptuously, she realized now—that they had been invited to meet Sara's family, and she had been prepared for a small, rather intimate evening. Instead, it seemed obvious that Sara had prevailed upon her adopted parents to add Willa's and Owen's names to an already long guest list.

Willa glanced at Owen. There could be no doubt at all that he was perfectly delighted with the crowded drawing room. His face was set in a smile that would make people turn to look at him, as they were indeed already doing. "If we should happen to have a large earthquake this evening, Sara," he said, "and be swallowed up on the spot, there would be nobody of importance left in California."

Sara grinned, pleased. "I thought you might like to meet some of Father Emory's friends, Owen," she said, "and in a moment you are going to meet his new bride . . ."

Helen Emory, smiling, was moving across the room toward them. There was a burnished look about her, her copper hair matched the deep tones of her dress; her skin seemed almost to glow. In the low cut of her gown a perfect, great diamond teardrop lay in the declivity between her breasts, in a nest of freckles. Willa thought that Helen Emory was as full-blown as the roses outside the gate.

She greeted them in a voice that matched her looks, all low and throaty, and it carried. Willa felt as if they were, all of them, part of some studied theatrical production. She felt, in fact, a moment of stage fright, a tightening of the throat.

In the years to come, she or Owen would meet one or another of the guests of that evening, and invariably that person would remember Helen Emory sweeping toward them, saying, "Ah, the young Mr. and Mrs. Reade, how very nice." Before Helen could say more, a young man materialized behind Sara, put both of his hands on her head so she could not turn around to look at him, and said, "I suppose you've all heard the scandalous news about Sara Hunt?"

Sara's face flushed with pleasure.

"Charles!" she laughed, reaching to pull his hands down, holding them for a moment in her own, "This is my mad cousin-of-sorts, Charles Emory."

"How very nice of you to think of us," Owen said to Helen Emory, bowing to her and smiling warmly before turning to shake hands with Charles. He accomplished this with such ease that Sara's oversight in introductions went almost unnoticed. Before Sara could recoup, Helen, smiling indulgently, said, "I will leave you cousins-of-sorts to entertain the Reades," and moved languidly away to greet another guest.

"You heard the Queen," Charles said, shrugging. Sara gave him a cautionary glance which she did not bother to hide from Willa and Owen.

"Charles spends a good deal of time polishing his sarcasm," Sara told them. "It is his one great talent."

The affection she felt for him was obvious; they seemed at ease with each other, the ersatz cousins. Willa knew they had spent parts of every summer together for as long as Sara could remember. He was as much a confidant as Sara had ever known. The sarcasm surprised Willa, in large part because Charles Emory was already running the southern branch of the Emory empire, out of Los Angeles.

Charles, it turned out, was Willa's dinner partner. The two of them were seated near their hostess, while Owen and Sara were at the host's end of the table. As they were seated, Willa caught Owen's eye. Holding her gaze, not letting it go, he bent to say something to Sara, who also turned to look at Willa with an especially affectionate smile, all the while nodding in agreement to whatever it was that Owen had said about Willa. She could feel herself flush with pleasure.

Willa had never seen such a profusion of silver and crystal and china. Candlelight made the whole of it glitter. Now and then, reflections from the diamonds worn by the women sent a glint of blue across the room. Willa felt as if she had wandered into a pleasure dome. Overwhelmed, she said on impulse, "This seems quite unreal to me."

Charles looked at her, amused.

"Do you mean unreal," he said, "or do you mean grotesque?"

Willa was startled by the question.

"Why should I mean grotesque?" she asked.

"Cultivated young Eastern ladies sometimes do," he answered, smiling disarmingly. "Sara, for instance, finds these supper parties macabre. Didn't she warn you?"

Willa looked at him, trying to understand what he was saying. She had had no disparaging thoughts at all about the gathering. She had, in fact, been enjoying herself. But now Sara's favorite relative was telling her that, perhaps, she was being naive. Or was he? She looked down the table at Sara, who, at that moment, was listening with what seemed to be total attention to a small man whose hair was plastered sideways, in strands, across his otherwise bald pate. On her side, Owen was talking with his usual animation to a portly man with muttonchop whiskers.

"You are wrong," she said to Charles Emory, "I am not a cultivated young Eastern lady. I was born on a farm in the northern part of Illinois, and I grew up there. I have been East only two times, once to go to college and once this past month, to meet my husband's relatives."

Nodding toward the man who had Sara's attention, he said, "Levi Strauss and Company, and your husband is talking to the Bank of California."

Willa turned to look at him. She did not smile back at his quizzical smile. "Surely," she said, more primly than she had intended, "surely those men have names?"

"They do, but it doesn't matter," he answered calmly, "your husband knows that."

"I'm not sure he does," Willa said, "and I'm not sure I like the notion."

"Would you call it grotesque?" Charles answered, pointedly, as if he had won a game.

Willa smiled a very small smile, a way to end a conversation she didn't particularly like. She chatted with the gentleman seated to her left, and was perplexed when he introduced himself as "a mining engineer who worked with Mr. Hearst on the Homestake" without bothering to say who Mr. Hearst was or what the Homestake happened to be.

After a time she turned back to Charles, only to find him so intent a part of conversation which centered about Helen Emory that he didn't notice Willa. In fact, she was relieved. Willa was not at all sure of herself with Charles Emory. She was prepared to like him because Sara did, but he confused her. A whole new life was washing in upon her, and she did not want to have to look at it critically, not yet.

Later that night, propped in their big bed at the Lick House with a tin of crackers and a bottle of mineral water to aid the digestion of the enormous supper they had consumed, Willa and Owen shared impressions of the evening. When she asked him about Mr. Hearst and the Homestake, Owen roared with laughter. "Welcome to the West, my love," he had said. "Lesson number one is that George Hearst—Senator Hearst—was the most successful mining engineer in the country, having discovered both the Comstock in Nevada and the Homestake in South Dakota, not to mention the Ophir and the Anaconda, all of them enormously rich mines. Legendary strikes, actually."

Each told the other which of the Emorys' guests they had met, and what had been said. They talked into the night, enjoying themselves; feeling, for the first time, the camaraderie of marriage.

"What did you think of the new Mrs. Emory?" Willa asked, with only a very slight wrinkle of the nose, enough to give Owen a clue.

"I think the new Mrs. Emory is one dance-hall girl who won the sweepstakes," Owen answered.

"But Sara said she was with the Royal Shakespeare Touring Company," Willa said, ignoring for the moment his allusion to their host of the evening.

"Yes, well," Owen replied, his voice saying she had a lot

to learn, "quite a lot of the gold towns did build what they called opera houses, and touring companies did come through regularly, but as often as not those companies would go broke somewhere along the way, and the actors and actresses would have to find whatever work they could. It was not a particularly easy life for a woman, as you can see if you look hard at Helen Emory."

Willa did not know what he meant.

"Just that she works very hard, and is adept at stage makeup," he told her, somewhat vaguely.

"Sara says her new stepmother is only a few years older than she."

"I would say that Sara is giving you the official story," Owen answered. "I would be willing to bet that she celebrated her thirtieth birthday some years back," he went on.

"But why?" Willa wanted to know. "Why would it matter? Mr. Emory is an old man . . . a fat old man, as a matter of fact."

"A fat old, shrewd old, rich old man," Owen added, "which doesn't mean he has given up on having an heir of his own. I imagine that might worry Sara's cousin Charles some."

"Ah," Willa said, as if she had found the piece to the puzzle. "I wonder if that's it."

"That's what?" Owen wanted to know.

When Willa repeated her dinner conversation with Charles, Owen munched thoughtfully on a cracker for a time. "You should understand," he started, slowly, "you should know that the people there tonight—except for Sara, who knows you now—took you to be someone else entirely. Someone more like what I suppose your grandmother to have been, from what you've told me about her: a snob, an Easterner who looks down on these grand Western excursions into 'society.'

"People are funny about social customs. You meet them on the street or in the mines or wherever they work, and they are fine—energetic and pleasant, good-natured, just plain nice to be around. Then one or the other strikes it rich, and suddenly they figure they have to *act* rich—they don't know how, it turns out, so they do the best they can, and no matter how good that is, they are sure that every Easterner is looking at them askance. It strikes me as all so foolish.

"My grandfathers—both of them—fought in the Revolutionary War, so my family is about as old as a family can be in this country. Yet that is scarcely a hundred years now. I wonder if my grandfathers worried about the English looking down on their social pretensions? I suppose they did. I do have to admit, I don't think either of my puritanical grandfathers would have seen fit to have a thirty-karat diamond dangle down into Grandmother's bosom. I kept thinking tonight that if one or two of those rich old rascals had any more wine, they were going to make a grab for that big rock of Helen Emory's."

He caught Willa off guard. She had been chewing a cracker, and the laughter rising made her choke. Owen slapped her hard between the shoulders, sending a mouthful of crumbs spewing over the coverlet. He gave her a glass of water, which she promptly spilled, since she was shaking, still, with laughter. A towel was placed over the wet place in the bed, crumbs were brushed off and, after the flurry of activity, the two of them lay back, resting in each other's arms, thinking.

*"Do* you understand? Charles said you did," Willa said.

"You mean that business about knowing men by what they do, not by what they are. That's not such a new idea, and I'm not at all sure what is wrong about assigning importance to what a man does. I suppose what he meant was that there were some very powerful, important men there tonight, and that I was aware of it. That is true. I was aware, and so was Sara— that's why she asked us, as a matter of fact. I don't think there's anything shameful about that.

"This is an exciting time to be in this particular part of the country. It is just taking shape, it is possible to play a part in shaping it. That, to me, is exciting. The men who will play major roles in California in the next few decades were there tonight. I will need to know them, that's all. I probably would have met them anyway, but meeting them at the Emorys' makes it that much simpler.

"As for social pretensions, well—I'm not distressed by them. Social forms have never interested me very much, anyway. I've never been able to understand their importance. What is important, it seems to me, is the chance we have out here. We can make our own plan, we don't have to live by someone else's."

Owen turned off the lamp, felt to make sure the towel remained over the wet place on the bed and then, touching Willa's face with the tips of his fingers, he said, "Sara is fond of Charles Emory, you can see it, so I am inclined to think there is something more to him than we saw tonight. He does seem to be a sardonic chap. Maybe that has to do with his being a nephew rather than a son, knowing you are an heir unless . . . I suppose nothing can be certain for him until the old man dies."

"Is it different for Sara, do you think?" Willa wondered.

"Sara doesn't seem to expect much," Owen answered sleepily, "I believe she really was surprised that we came."

"I know," Willa said quietly. "That made me feel sad. I thought she knew we cared for her."

Owen did not answer. She knew he was sleeping, from the sound of his breathing.

The last thing she remembered, before finally falling asleep, were Owen's words when they climbed into the hack on their way home. "We couldn't have had a better introduction to California," he had said. "Think how lucky we have been already!"

They were three weeks in San Francisco. While Owen moved about the city, "making inquiries and meeting people" as he put it to Willa, she spent most of her time with Sara. By the day they boarded the train for Los Angeles, Willa was known by the servants in the Emory mansion, and even old Phineas recognized her well enough to nod and cough and generally acknowledge her existence.

After the excitement and glitter of San Francisco, Los Angeles was not all that Willa had hoped it would be. The first letter I received from the southern city was almost petulant. "It is brown and arid," she wrote, "the sun shines all day long and the breeze, when it blows, is hot. Brown and dry, and the streets full of invalids. Ninety percent of the population, I do believe, walks or wobbles along with a cane. Everybody coughs and wheezes and the talk is interminably about health, or the lack of it. All shops sell tonics. Undertakers do a thriving business. Those who do not die, live and get better and act as testimonials to the miraculous cure this climate effects, so that the next train is even fuller than the one that came before. I am so sick of the sicklings, and the doctors who send them here for 'the cure.'"

I doubted she would talk quite so plainly to Owen. He had,

in fact, been drawn to the area for his own health. Often he would add a few lines to Willa's letters, always extolling the climate and how well it made him feel.

They did not stay long in Los Angeles, which was then in the midst of a land boom. Speculators bought and sold and even put up whole new cities out in the desert land, only to see them sifted over with sand when the great boom burst.

Real estate schemes did not interest Owen. Charles Emory, naturally enough, was caught up in the speculation. He seemed to have an uncanny ability to remove his profits only instants before the bubble would burst. In October a letter arrived with the return listed as "Shaff's Boarding House, Santa Monica, California." Willa wrote:

"Eureka! We have found it! That is what the gold miners are supposed to have exclaimed when they discovered gold— or perhaps when they discovered California, I am not sure which. I am also not sure why people shout 'Eureka!' but it expresses Owen's feelings exactly on this little seaside village, which is no more, really, than a resort town some seventeen miles to the west of Los Angeles.

"I cannot compare it to any of the villages at home—first, because it is on the very shore of the Pacific, and second because quite a number of rather wealthy people have commenced a building bonanza which is to turn the ocean front roads into elegant drives. All this, I should add, is on a bluff high above the shoreline; to reach the sandy beach one must descend ninety-nine steps—it is the fashion to count them.

"And my dear, do not doubt that the Reade house will be any the less elegant. Imagine me the mistress of an enormous house awash with cupolas and turrets and all the rest of the elaborations. Construction is under way; it is to cost twelve thousand dollars. Can you imagine? Neither could I, until I learned the extent of Owen's fortunes. I find it difficult to think of myself as the wife of such a wealthy man. I should tell you, here and now, that Owen does not want it known that he is quite so well-to-do, and I must respect that wish, even with the one I have until now told everything. I am certain that Owen would be chagrined to discover the extent of my confidences, and I am just as certain that he need never know.

"When I suggested to Owen that I admired the low, adobe Spanish-style houses of the Californios, he was taken aback.

There is within Owen a kernel of pure New England proper. Nothing would do but we have a wooden house here, which Owen says will be one of the showplaces of Santa Monica. Owen has a theory: A large, ornate house convinces the community that you are a man of substance, to be trusted. It is not the house so much as the impression it makes. I rather think he believes an adobe house would convince people we are lazy, as Owen believes the Spanish to be.

"We are staying, now, at a boarding house not far from our new home. But then, everything in Santa Monica is close by everything else. The chaparral crowds close to the streets.

"The chatelaine of this establishment, Mrs. Shaff, chatters all the day long and says nothing. She is some fussy little bird who enjoys hearing her own noise. She is also, naturally, wild for Owen, lying in wait for him in the hallways. She chatters him all the way out to the street. I do believe that Mrs. Shaff may finally cure Owen of his chronic tolerance.

"Though there are times when I am not sure if what I have chosen to call tolerance is, in fact, not instead a method of holding others at arm's length. If you listen to others well, they do not probe. There are a few people who are exceptions to this rule. I think of you, I think of Sara. And, surprisingly— a new friend I have just met whose name is Arcadia Scott. I say 'surprising' because, unlike you and Sara, Arcadia does chatter on. And yet, she listens too—and carefully. And she questions, not prying but interested, concerned. And though it is too early yet to tell, I do believe that she is not likely to gossip, that her interest is genuine.

"But I was speaking of Owen. I think, at times, that I understand him, and then he confounds me. He suffers bores so readily, and yet he often refuses to go through the simplest formalities, should they impinge on time he has allotted otherwise. No long, lazy mornings in bed for my dear husband. (Ah, I see you smile. You think I consider long, lazy mornings in bed among the simplest formalities, do you?) All I can say is, Owen reserves special time for everything, even connubial duties. I am, however, consulted, for which I am grateful."

I read those lines twice; in spite of the light tone, I found them troublesome. It was not like Willa to complain. Neither was it like her to spend long, lazy mornings in bed. The Willa I had always known was, more often than not, up before daybreak and off, absorbed in some carefully laid plan.

Even so, the letters that arrived from Santa Monica were cheerful. The ocean agreed with her, she said. She had begun to catalogue the seabirds and even to sketch them. "Sandpipers are the most wonderful, skimming up and down on the sand at the tideline, searching for food, their spindly legs skittering over the film of water left by the breaking wave. And the pelicans fishing in a long, single line, now low over a wave and then rising—like a ribbon blown in the breeze—only to plunge, one of them, headfirst into the sea to catch a fish."

Late that month, she wrote: "Owen popped into my bedroom this morning (I was lounging still, disgracefully, I know) to kiss me goodbye and he said, 'Don't I wish Lena were here to keep my girl company.' I wished so, too, but since you are not here I did the next best thing and sat down to write this letter."

Between the lines of her letters I began to sense that Willa was suffering from a peculiar type of homesickness. Owen was often away. Willa had known that was to happen, and she had been prepared for it, or thought she was. She was not a clinging woman. In fact, she had always envisioned herself as a pioneer wife, taming the wilderness. And yet she wrote: "It frightens me, how much I love being in my husband's presence. My candle flickers miserably when he is away, and burns brightly only when he is with me."

Had she been there, I would have asked if that is the dilemma love poses: When the love is total, one is diminished when the other is away. Is that it? And yet Willa had told me that Owen is happiest when he is on his way, that he is excited by the prospects of whatever business he is about.

The first snow in Illinois fell in November that year. The early winter ended my daily walks to the post box, which meant that Willa had need to be much more circumspect in her writings to me. The walking had been good for me; my face had color to it, my body felt stronger and more pliable than it ever had. There were days, when I could pretend, and almost make myself believe, that I could do my little side step gracefully.

But the snow ended my walking. Confined to the house, my body began to feel stiff and unwieldy, my movements became brittle. California began to slip away. It became more and more difficult to imagine the warm breeze off the ocean, or palm trees blowing in the bluffs overlooking the ocean, as

Willa had described them. When the moaning winter wind wrapped around the farmhouse and the boys came in at night stamping and complaining of the cold, I could not conjure up the image of purple bougainvillea climbing a whitewashed wall.

Throughout that long, cold winter the letters continued, but they seemed to be coming from farther and farther away. I read and reread them, with interest but without intimacy. Sometimes I would find myself sitting by the fire, hugging my arms about me, and I would feel as if I were getting physically smaller, as if I was being wound tighter and tighter.

Mama and I perfected our routine. We cooked and sewed and saw to the cleaning of the house, with the help of the hired girls. Women in a household of men, we were always busy. Our days were as unvarying as the prairie; flat and even, one so much like another that I could never be sure of the date, and after a time it didn't matter.

One evening we sat darning in the last of the dimming light, Mama and I, holding on as long as the deepening gray would let us, until we reached that shade where we could no longer distinguish the darning thread from the material being darned. My head was as empty as the late daylight when Mama said, "Do you remember the time when we went to Chicago, just us, when your grandmother died?"

I tried to see her face, but the shadows were too deep. I could only see that she held her hands to the window, to the last light, and that the needle moved through the shirt, though I could not be sure she could actually see what she was doing.

"Yes," I answered, and waited for her to say more, but she said nothing at all.

Did I remember? I was eleven, and I went to Chicago because Willa was away at school, at Wellesley where she hadn't wanted to go but had gone, because Grandmother had insisted, because Grandmother had said she must, and Mama and Pa had said she must *because Grandmother owns the farm, Willa.* Oh, yes, the memory is there, like old scar tissue. The night before we were to leave Pa had said there was a doctor in Chicago who might be able to help me. He told Mama that she was to be sure to take me, that the doctor would be expecting to see me. Pa had written, and our doctor in town had written, and the specialist wanted to see me. Pa said to Mama, "It's done."

It was done, he had said. Nothing Mama might say could

change his mind. I was frightened, but I also felt a wild thrill. I was young enough to dream of miracles, young enough to think that one morning I might just wake up and find my back straight, that I could run down the lane and see the poplars flash sunlight as I ran past them, my feet scarcely touching the ground. The way Willa could run, the way my brothers could run, the way I dreamed of running.

Pa took us into town and put us on the train. Mama said nothing all the way into Springfield, but just looked straight ahead, her lips pressed tight together as if concentrating. There were beads of sweat above her lip; she looked pale and sick, but when Pa asked if she wanted to turn back she hissed at him breathlessly, "No. She wants to see me. I have no choice." I could feel her panic and it terrified me. But I had no choice, either; I was going to see the doctor who might make me whole . . .

When it was time for Pa to leave he touched my arm, which was the most he was ever able to do, and I smiled and tried to swallow and whispered, "Goodbye." He patted Mama's arm, too, and she looked at him with terror in her eyes, so she closed them tight and told him, "Go."

I have often wondered how he could have left us like that, but he did. Mama clutched my hand until I thought all the little bones would snap. She sat, stiff and sweating, all the way to Chicago, breathing through her mouth, never saying a word.

Our two cousins, two stout men who had married Grand-mother's nieces, met us at the train with the news that we were too late, that Grandmother had died the night before. I remember thinking that two of them had come in case Mama should faint, so they could carry her to the buggy.

But Mama blinked at the men and said nothing. They attributed her strange behavior, I believe, to grief, and excused it. We rode in a closed carriage to the big house on Wabash Avenue. There was a wreath on the front door, with a huge black ribbon. I wanted to ask Mama about the wreath, but it didn't seem right to break the silence.

Two women of indeterminate age, the nieces I guessed, met us and led us, with tiny whimpering noises, to an upstairs bedroom where Grandmother lay propped against the pillows. One edge of her mouth sagged, and she seemed to be leaning somewhat to that side. I did not want to look at her face so I looked, instead, at the hands which lay on the counterpane, and which grasped at nothing. For months, whenever I closed my eyes I would see those hands, gnarled and grasping.

Mama pressed hard against me. I felt her shudder, heard her swallow. I wanted to comfort my mother, but I did not know how. I wanted to shield her from these strangers' staring eyes, but I could not think of a way.

She stood looking at the woman who had been her mother. She said nothing, her eyes did not leave my grandmother's face. After a time the nieces began to murmur and shift uncomfortably. Mama did not notice. Then, without saying a word, she turned and left the room, pulling me after her.

"I will see my mother's solicitor now," she announced as we descended the stairs. When one of the nephews suggested that legal matters might be left until after the funeral, she looked at him as if he were speaking a foreign tongue.

Within a few minutes a carriage was brought around and we made our way to State Street. There, in the offices of Langford, Johnston, Winthrop and Winters a tall man with silver hair assured Mama that Porter Farm was hers, free and clear.

For the first time since we left Springfield, I saw a glimmer in my mother's eyes that was neither fear nor sorrow. For the first time, I understood how monumentally important the farm was to her.

We went from the solicitor's office directly to the train station where we waited six long hours for the next train back to Springfield. The appointment with the doctor was not mentioned.

Mama did not attend the funeral services that were to be held at the First Street Episcopal Church the following day, an act of omission which was to cause all ties to the Randolphs of Virginia to be severed.

Grandmother's death released Mama from her fears of losing the farm. It also released Willa from Wellesley College, though she would wait until the end of the term to come home.

Pa did not speak to me about the doctor in Chicago after that. I tried to put it out of my mind, but at age eleven hope is not easily shattered. I had been so close, I was sure. I could not stop thinking about it. For a reason I could not then fathom, I blamed Pa more than Mama. I could not look at him without feeling my face flame, so I did not look at him at all, though I felt his eyes on me, watching...pleading, perhaps.

I had not meant to tell Willa, but by the time she came home from school, I was about to burst. It all came spilling out, the words tumbling one over the other—about Grandmother and her hands, and the nephews, and Mama's being so scared, and how we went to the lawyers and all the horses in the streets, and no one saying anything at all until the man said to Mama, "You own Porter Farm, Ma'am," and the long, long wait in the station where the windows were caked with yellow dust, and all the time my wanting to scream, to tell Mama that we had to go to see the doctor, knowing she wouldn't, knowing she couldn't.

Willa looked at me for a long time. She brushed the hair back off my face, and then she hugged me hard against her and rocked me back and forth. I think I cried, I am not sure. But I think I cried for a long time, and when the tears stopped I looked at Willa, and found her full of anger—a terrible, unrelenting, silent anger.

"I'm going to the barn," she told me in a voice that made me shiver, "I have to talk to Pa."

She left then, and I was wretched, knowing I had set in motion events I had no way of controlling. I was sick with myself, with what I'd done. I was sure something terrible was going to happen, and I was the cause of it.

But nothing did happen. I had been prepared for a storm when Willa came back, but there was no storm. She had been angry, now she seemed calm. She put her arm around my waist and hugged me to her. That night we slept together, Willa hugging my crooked spine to her.

"Mama's got what she wants, now," she told me, "but you are going to have your turn, too."

That summer after Grandmother's death I became the object of Willa's total attention. "If you can walk," she said to me, "you can ride." The idea had not occurred to me, but Willa made it seem possible.

Pa objected but he did not stop us. Mama didn't come out of the house. Only the boys argued with Willa and she argued back. "You're going to kill her," one of the boys said. Willa answered, "Nonsense. On a horse Lena will have four good legs under her, just like the rest of us." They railed and fussed at her, but when they saw that she was unmoveable, and I was determined to try, they gave in.

After a few spills, I did learn to ride. Even Mama admitted that, next to Gib, I had the best hands of anyone on the farm when it came to handling a horse. Finally, I was able to go flying down the lane of poplars, the wind in my face. It was as wonderful as I had imagined it to be. In some ways, learning to ride blunted the disappointment I would feel the following year, when Willa and I went to Chicago to see the specialist, only to learn that there was nothing to be done for a condition such as mine.

Still I knew, and I believe that Mama knew, that Willa never forgave her. She understood Mama's fears; she watched Mama's world shrink. After Grandmother's death, Mama had not been off the farm; she would hardly leave the grounds surrounding the house. Willa understood, I am sure of it, yet she was still unforgiving. I think it had to do with her belief that there is a limit to what you can allow yourself to fear, that there is a time when fear must be faced.

Willa would roam for whole days, ranging as far as the river, tracking a Cooper's hawk or a peregrine falcon or a golden eagle. The boys teased her that a proper young woman would be interested in songbirds. Willa would tell them, then, in minute and gory detail, how a peregrine could kill a sparrow in mid-flight, with its hooked bill neatly snapping the bird's spinal cord. It was, she would tell them with delight, the cleanest kill that could be imagined.

As Willa's world was expanding, Mama's was constricting. She wouldn't, or couldn't, fight it. Willa chose to believe she wouldn't, and had no sympathy. I could only feel sad. When we were little, Mama would take some of us blackberry picking in the gulleys beyond the woods. We would put on old sunhats and wear long sleeves and bring gloves to keep the prickles from scratching us. We would walk for an hour or more until we found Mama's favorite thickets. She knew all of them. I think that once she knew every bush on the farm.

When she wasn't heavy with child, she would take us to the climbing trees in the woods, and heft herself up into the branches, as high as any of us. Even when she got heavy, she could climb. She would tell us about how she and Emma were followed by small prairie wolves and had to wait in the trees until Grandfather came to rescue them. In Mama's stories, Grandfather always came to find them, he always knew where they were. Sometimes, Mama would even take us to the pool in the river where she and Emma and Pa had gone swimming. They had called it the Blue Pool and they said it had no bottom, it was so deep, and only Grandfather knew where it was.

After we returned from Chicago, Mama never went berry picking again. I remember the last time she went so far as the Four Corners, just before Owen came to visit. A peddler came through and stopped at the Four Corners to show his wares. Our neighbors came—Mrs. Fenster and Mrs. Havens and Mrs. Jameson—and Mama and Willa and I fairly flew down to the wagon to look through his supplies. We bought material and buttons and hard candies for the Little Boys. When that same peddler returned a few weeks later, Mama walked with me down to the lane, but she stopped before the end of the poplar stand. She tried, I know she tried. I could see it in her face. But she did not go on, and now the limits of her world seemed to be set: the house and the barn, the rose garden and the orchard.

"Have you ever wondered," I asked Mama, "why Willa chose to be married in the apple orchard?"

I could feel the slow churning in her head, as she struggled to understand.

"What?" she wanted to know, "Why? Willa?"

"It's nothing," I answered, dismissing it, "I was just thinking about Willa and Owen, and the wedding."

"Willa's going to have a young one," Mama said.

My sewing slid to the floor; when I leaned forward to retrieve it, I fell sideways, bumping my head.

Mama helped me, smoothed my dress and, when she saw I was not hurt, she said: "Willa wants you to come to her, she says she needs you."

I said nothing, only waited.

"Pa says it's only right that you should go. Pa says, 'It's done.'"

*Pa says: it's done.*

I had told Willa that she would never let me go, and Willa had said: You will have your turn.

\* \* \*

Willa wrote: "Dearest, you are coming to California. I did not write to you about it before, because I wanted to be certain that Pa would not change his mind. He did not.

"Our first child will be born in the spring. I want you with me. I hope that you will come to stay, to make your home with us. These are my reasons: I am sure that you will thrive in a climate which is warm and dry all year round. Owen agrees, and he is much more knowledgeable about the healing qualities of climate than I am. It is likely that you will not marry, given your physical condition. If you stay in Illinois you will spend the rest of your life with Mama and Pa, tending them in their old age. And when they are gone, what are you to do? If you join our family you will live a fuller life, one more nearly your own. As you are much more patient than I, I am sure you will make a better mother, in many respects. I propose to share my children with you. It has always seemed to me that two mothers are better than one—for children and mothers alike. If you agree, we can test my theory. Owen is as determined as I that you become part of our family, and his reasons are as selfish as mine: He travels much of the time, and knows I will be happier and less lonely if you are here. He also knows how sensible you are, and how much I have missed you.

"In spite of our admitted selfishness, I do believe a life in California will be good for you, and happier. Come and share our life. Soon, dear."

Winter broke then and I resumed my daily pilgrimages to the Four Corners to collect the mail. I wrapped myself in wool and pulled on boots on a day in March when snow threatened, but the air and the earth smelled of spring. The envelope was in the post box, the ticket in the envelope. Willa's letter said only: "Quickly, now. Come."

A cardinal flew to a fencepost across the way, and considered me, its unnatural red the only color in the whole dun-drab expanse of the prairie. Big, wet flakes of snow began to drop, melting as they touched the earth, as they touched my face and mixed with the tears that were slipping, flowing. I was laughing then, laughing out loud . . . at the silly, outrageous bird on the fencepost, at the snow that would not stick, at the girl with the twisted back who was going to California.

# Chapter Four

The pages of my journal which tell of my trip west were among those wetted when I dropped my book in the creek at the time of the big fire, so that the ink runs together, just as the details of that journey run blurred in my mind. Only here and there do a few words stand clear on the page, as a few memories stand clear in my mind. Pa and the boys on the station platform in Springfield, their eyes squinting as if against the noon glare, awkward in their leavetaking. Except for Val, who of us all was not fearful of tears. The others, my rough and sweetly shy brothers, looked away as Val hugged me, as they wished they might but could not. I remember that my heart wrenched. I remember that I was to remind Pa to stop at the dry goods store to buy three yards of muslin. I remember that I ached for the train to come and free me from the weight of their love.

In a few clear lines floating in a sea of ink, my journal tells me that for lunch on the first day of my odyssey West, I was offered crullers, pound cake, hard-boiled eggs, deviled ham, roast chicken and canned fruit, and that I was to take the hotel train that would leave Omaha on Thursday.

The train moved, all the while, westward. I rocked endlessly through the shantytowns that had sprung up along the tracks, rooted to my seat, afraid to move until the conductor directed me. I remember the grit in my teeth, coal dust from the engine;

I remember that my stomach churned as the noise and the motion entered and possessed me.

In Omaha a woman with a sickly, complaining child boarded my car and took the seat nearest me. Soon enough she had attached herself to me, sure that a young crippled girl would be grateful for her company. Strangers expect cripples to be thankful for ordinary kindnesses. I disguised my resentment and resigned myself to helping care for the sickly child. It was a task I did not want, but could not escape. Perhaps it was just as well, for it left me less time to consider the world I was about to enter, or to be awed by the world from which I was separated by the glass and wood of the Central Pacific car.

It had been arranged that I should rest in San Francisco for a few days before continuing the journey to the south of California. Sara had insisted that I be her guest at the Emory home on Nob Hill. The idea of spending two days in the home of a stranger, and a rich one, terrified me, who had never been away from home alone in my life, but Willa insisted that I must. And Sara wrote such a kind letter that I could offer no resistance.

The memory of the day I boarded the ferryboat for San Francisco remains as clear in my mind as the day itself; a sharp wind was blowing and the air seemed to define all objects. No fog, no foghorns, nothing but a peculiar clarity. In San Francisco all was noise and confusion. Everyone seemed to know where they were going, and everyone pushed and shoved until I was being buffeted by a surge of people. Then I felt a hand on mine and a voice in my ear which said, "I've come to rescue you." I knew by her big, round, and serious eyes that it had to be Sara.

"Miss Hunt?" I whispered.

"Lena, yes—I'm Sara," she said.

I thought she looked like nothing so much as a drab little freckled hen, with her rough, red skin and the gums of her teeth showing when she smiled. Yet I knew, instantly, why Willa had liked Sara Hunt. She might be drab, but she was not dull. You had but to look into her eyes to know that.

With her hand firmly on mine, she guided me to a shining black phaeton and told the servant, a big man in a thick black coat, to collect my baggage. When we were settled together in the carriage she said, "I recognized you at once. I just looked for the girl with the crippled back."

She took my breath away, demolishing what little was left of my fortitude. All of the fear that had been gathering, kept curbed before strangers, broke loose now. I burst into tears and, once started, could not stop. Sara Hunt put her arms about me, she rocked and comforted me and never once did she tell me not to cry.

Sara knew that her words had not caused my tears. She had addressed me as one cripple would another, without pity. Her understanding was complete. I could not believe that anyone else could know, but she did. I would come to know that the only difference between us was that my deformity was visible.

Settled in the red parlor of the Emory mansion that evening, next to a fire set to ward off the chill, Sara spoke in the voice I would come to know well—without reservation, as if we had made a pact, as if trust was already there.

"Your sister looks radiant," she told me. "I was in Santa Monica not long ago to see the new baby and the new house."

"Motherhood, I suspect," I said.

"More likely fatherhood," Sara answered.

I raised my eyebrows in question.

"Fatherhood has made Owen the happiest man on earth," she answered. "And since Willa had quite a lot to do with that, she is radiant." Sara's frankness amazed me.

"How old are you, Lena?" she asked suddenly.

"Seventeen," I answered.

"A baby!" she laughed.

"And you? How old are you, then, Miss Sara Hunt?" I shot back, nettled at being called a baby.

"Somewhat more than seventeen, though not much more," she laughed at me. "I am richer in experience than in years, however," she added mockingly.

"I see," I said, not seeing at all, "I am a mere girl, but you are a woman of the world, is that right?"

"I only wish it were!" she said, grinning, "I don't have any experience at all, but I do see quite a lot. Father Emory offers me a good vantage point. Shall I share it with you, Lena?"

"I would like that," I answered, politely, being confused about what she meant.

"I am serious," Sara responded, "I should very much like to have a true friend. I have never had one, you see. There has never been one in whom I could confide. We can be important to each other. Perhaps we are but girls, without experience, crippled girls. My life is as twisted as your back. I am *plain,* as they say. Ugly."

"Don't . . ." I started, but she stopped me.

"No Lena, no lies between us, not even kind lies. I need to accept my plainness, and if you are to be my friend, you must accept it too. Neither of us, I think, will marry—so there will be no husbands to complicate our friendship."

I nodded, miserably, remembering my thoughts as I first glimpsed Sara.

"I need a friend, Lena," she said. "I know you have Willa, but I hope there will be room for me in your life, too."

I touched her hand lightly. "I've never truly had any friend but Willa. I should like to spend more time with you, to know you better. But I will be living in Santa Monica. It is far, isn't it?"

"You forget," Sara said, "Father Emory is a railroad magnate. A trip to Los Angeles is nothing, not for a robber baron's daughter. Besides which, my cousin Charles lives there, and he is one of the few people I do care about."

"Robber baron?" I asked, "Is that what you said?"

"Of course," she answered, "Father Emory and his crowd, which by now includes your illustrious brother-in-law. All those men who are out to possess the great and golden West. We can have seats front row center, you and I, for that grand show."

"Owen?" I said, "a robber baron?" I was giggling now; the image of Owen roaming the countryside, holding up strangers, was too wicked.

"Well," Sara said, laughing too, "he hasn't quite reached that exalted level, perhaps . . . but he is making magnificent progress."

"I don't understand," I said, serious now. "Is Owen doing something improper?"

"Owen is doing nothing more than any of the other ambitious men of money are doing. He sees himself as a man with a mission, that mission being to guide the destiny of this new land. He needs power to do that, and money is power. It's a wonderful game they play, these men. Making money is the major effort. The goal is to be a millionaire before the age of thirty. Owen, of course, has managed to do much more than that."

"How do you know?" I asked.

"That Owen is a millionaire four times over?" she said.

I gasped, and Sara smiled at my astonishment.

"Father Emory makes it a point to know such things, and I make it a point to listen. So few people do that it is easy to learn whatever you want to know."

I studied her. "Why did you want to know about Owen?"

She did not hesitate. "Because of Willa, in the beginning. Because I care for her, and for Owen too. And then because I hoped that I could be friends with you, which would make me, in some ways, a part of the family. All very selfish, you see."

"I don't think you are," I said, "but you do seem to be, well . . ."

"Contemptuous?"

"Yes," I answered uncertainly, "I suppose."

"Perhaps I am, yes. Too much. I must watch myself."

I smiled at her willingness to criticize herself, at her habit of looking at all things with an objectivity I could never manage. I thought: You will be a fascinating friend, Sara Hunt.

"But to return to the subject of Owen," I said. "Tell me how he and Willa are being received?"

She thought for a long while; I watched her in profile, her face further reddened by the glow of the firelight. "Well," she finally said, "Owen, of course, is both handsome and charming, which is more than most men, so he was a great favorite at once. His good Yankee business sense, his old family ties to the East, the thrill he gets from making money—all those things assured his success in what is called society in San Francisco." A smile flickered, was extinguished, "Willa, on the other hand, is another story. Willa caused quite a stir. Because she is taller than most men, and she has that wonderful, glacial set to her face. In fact, I heard someone call her 'The Ice Queen,' though not to her face, of course. There is something regal about her."

"Willa?" I said in disbelief, "in her old brown corduroys?"

"Oh, but you haven't seen Willa since Owen decided to dress her. I assure you, in French silks she is stunning," Sara countered, "but I do believe the quality that bothers most people is Willa's tendency not to chatter simply to fill empty conversational spaces. It makes them suppose she is thinking, and that is fearsome. Only plain women have leave to think, and they shouldn't let anyone notice."

"But Willa *is* thoughtful," I argued.

"Indeed she is, and the only man around who seems not to mind is Owen."

"Praise be," I murmured. "Do people resent Willa, then?"

"I suppose," Sara said, "the Reades are seen as the *real* aristocracy—Boston and Virginia—it drives the shopkeepers of Nob Hill wild. It makes them feel like toads in the presence of the prince and princess. But they are invited everywhere, here and down south, and Owen accepts all of the invitations."

"Only Owen?" I asked.

"Oh, Willa goes too, but I think she would much prefer to sit alone with Owen all day and all night long. She is mad for the man, as you must surely know." She paused, and then said, "They don't want the same things, you know."

I thought about that for a time. I answered, "I *don't* know. I have seen Owen for seven days only, at the end of which he married my sister and left with her. I have only Willa's letters, but I must admit to being puzzled by some of what she tells me."

Sara stared at me until I began to feel prickly. I realized that she was not so much staring as thinking. She shook her head.

"I don't know either, I just have some thoughts. Those forbidden things. When I am about Owen I get the feeling that he is always thinking of what there is to do—and there is always something that needs to be done. He excises the superfluous parts of his life. He does not seem to believe in detours, but he wants to travel the straight line between points."

"And Willa? What does she want?" I asked.

Sara sat up as if weary. She stretched and rubbed her back.

"Only Owen, I think," she answered, and then, switching subjects, added, "did you know she was up and about only one week after the baby's birth? The neighbors saw her riding her horse, and I gather they were scandalized. Owen was away, or I'm sure he would have kept her in bed."

"From what I gather," I said, my face flushing in spite of myself, "Owen has no trouble at all accomplishing that."

Sara clapped her hand over her mouth in feigned shock.

"That makes me absolutely hungry," she said, "let's go steal something from the kitchen."

We made our way, giggling, down a back passageway that was so narrow I assumed it to be for the servants. In the kitchen we found the cold cupboard and, stifling our laughter, helped ourselves to four macaroons wrapped in gold paper. We took a different route back to our rooms, this time stealing past the library door. Peeking in, I saw a large man, his bulk overflowing the chair. We happened past at the very moment he let loose an enormous belch, an event which threatened to send us into spasms of uncontrolled laughter. Gasping, we fled up the stairway.

I was seventeen, Sara nineteen. We were young women who had never truly been girls. Now, for the first time, I felt the joy of being as foolish as any well-brought-up, pretty young woman might be. Together, Sara and I could pretend to be normal. We need not hide from each other. Never, before or since, have I trusted anyone as quickly and as completely as I did Sara Hunt; and that trust would not, in all our lives, be broken.


The journey by rail from San Francisco to Los Angeles was tame, even dull, after having crossed the Sierra. As we drew close to Los Angeles, I began to feel as if I had entered a new, exotic land. Orchards, some of them new-planted, stretched in the distances—orange and lemon groves, and what I was told were olive and guava trees. The wheat and barley fields I recognized, and was glad for because they made me feel more connected to this bright, dry land. The train slowed to an exasperating crawl as we neared the new Arcade Station. My palms grew sticky, my heart began to palpitate. I closed my eyes and willed myself not to faint, not when I had come so far.

I opened my eyes and saw Willa. She was sitting on the driver's seat of an open carriage, the better to look for me. She was squinting, her hand cupped over her eyes, searching for my face, a study in concentration. A small, excited sound escaped from me . . . *ooof*. And then she caught sight of me. Her face was transformed, she began to wave wildly. I wanted to cry, I was so happy.

We sat close together on the ride to Santa Monica, Willa's hand in mine, Owen across from us, smiling too. I was too overcome to say anything at all, and Willa kept repeating, "You're here, you're here."

When at last I was aware of where we were—in the open carriage traveling to Santa Monica—I began to look beyond the boundaries of the carriage, to the city of Los Angeles. It was like no other I had ever imagined. A peppertree threw its delicate shadow tracery onto a whitewashed adobe wall, next to a wooden structure newly built, upright and Yankee.

Owen, watching me, said, "Notice the trees—a sure sign the Yankees have come to stay. We always plant trees."

"Yet, some of the trees they plant seem out of place in this arid country," Willa put in.

"Can a tree ever be out of place, my dear?" Owen answered mildly, and Willa smiled in return.

When last I saw them together, they had been newly married strangers. Now, I realized with a certain jolt, they were intimates, having shared day-to-day concerns, having produced a child. There was a new ease between them, born of familiarity. They spoke in the abbreviated language of those who are accustomed to each other. It was as it should be, exactly. Willa and Owen were a unit, their lives enmeshed. I knew, even as I knew it could not be the same between Willa and me, loyalties had shifted.

"You got on well with Sara, then?" Willa interrupted my thoughts. Her question could not have been asked at a more propitious time.

"Oh, yes, you were right about Sara, Willa. I couldn't imagine I could become so fond of anyone in so short a time."

"Sara is not just anyone," Owen put in, "all sorts of amazing thoughts are bounding around in that little head."

"I discovered that exactly," I told him, smiling to myself and thinking that Owen would be startled to know some of Sara's thoughts.

Owen pointed out to me the points of interest in this burgeoning new southern city, once no more than pastureland for great herds, now a dusty metropolis fast burying its Spanish origins.

"Last year there was an enormous boom, everybody was buying and selling land, whole townships were being plotted out in the desert lands, it was amazing..." Owen began, and Willa took over.

"Land was being bought and sold, it was barbarous," she went on. "Now those 'towns'—which never developed beyond the beginnings of a hotel and markings for where the homes would be—are being reclaimed by the sand. I cringe to think of all the hopes smothered out there..."

"That's over now," Owen put in, "we can begin to grow in a respectable way." Lapsing into the voice of a travel director, he went on, "Fifteen years ago Los Angeles had a population of no more than eight thousand. Today it is fifty thousand. And there are six newspapers and twenty churches."

"And more saloons than churches," Willa put in. Nodding in a southerly direction, she said, "Over there is the infamous Calle de los Negros—what the Yankees call Nigger Alley— the center of gambling and all manner of vice, including opium dens and Chinese *dames de plaisir*."

"You will make Lena think the West is wicked," Owen chided.

"When do I get to see my nephew?" I asked. "I had hoped he would be at the station."

A look flickered between them. "I won't bring him into Los Angeles," Willa said quickly, "who knows what awful disease he might get—this city is filled with illness."

"Yes, of course," I muttered, feeling as if I had made a blunder.

"Trinidad—our nurse—was nettled that she couldn't come to the station, but had to stay and mind little Wen," Owen explained. "I am not sure that Trinidad will cook for us tonight, she is so angry with Willa."

"I am not troubled by Trinidad's bad temper," Willa retorted. "You should not have told her she could come with us, then she would have no reason to be disappointed."

"You're right," Owen laughed, at the same time seeing someone on the street he recognized. An instant later he called for the driver to stop, having decided to go speak to the man. He left us sitting together, glad to have a moment alone.

"I am so proud of you," Willa said. When I asked why she was proud, she answered, "That you had the courage to make that long journey alone."

I said: "I told myself that it might be the only risk I would ever be offered."

"I'm glad you're one of us, then," she said.

"Us?" I asked.

"The risk-takers of the world," she smiled back at me, and I felt myself swell inside, knowing that I had pleased her.

Before Owen returned, Willa had jumped down from her seat, bounded over to an orange tree growing in a yard, and plucked a fruit from it. "Your very first California orange," she said, as she began to peel it.

We rolled on, west on Sunset Boulevard toward the ocean, eating the sweet-smelling fruit, which combined with the warm dust, the ripe smell of the horses and the sunshine to create in me a wonderful feeling of having arrived, of having come home. I felt drowsy and happy and saturated with all of it.

"So tell me what you think of our new home place?" Owen asked. "Is it as you thought it would be?"

"No," I answered honestly, "I don't suppose I could have imagined all of this. It isn't the Wild West or the frontier, not that I expected it. There are so many things I could never in my wildest dreams have imagined... the sun, and the palms, and..."

Owen, pleased, turned his attention away.

"It is beautiful, at least where we live now," Willa said. "But I am disgusted with the falsehoods the railroads have spread, in order to entice people—poor people, many of them— to come and settle the land. 'Come to California and wear diamonds,' they say, 'the beautiful land of the Sunset Sea.' They come by the thousands, packed into what they call Zulu trains, whole families. They come expecting life to be easier here, all sunshine and oranges. And they are disappointed."

"I almost believe," Owen said, "that people who are stupid enough to believe that you can get something for nothing deserve what they get."

"Gullible," Willa corrected him, "they are not stupid, but gullible. Or naive. Or simple-minded dreamers who are tired, and want something better, and they need to believe."

"Believe what?" Owen asked. "That life is better here? It is better, for anyone who knows how to take care of himself."

Willa didn't say anything for a while, then she said, "When the big bubble burst last year, you could drive out of town— and find those lonely new developments sitting all desolate, the sand blown up over places where people thought their houses would be built. Somebody took those folks' money."

"Charles did his share of profit-taking, as a matter of fact," Owen said.

"Sara's cousin?" I asked.

"That's right," Willa answered, frowning.

There were twenty-seven rooms in the house on Seaside Avenue. It was thoroughly Victorian, with gables and cupolas and turrets abounding. The double parlors were filled with the ponderous furniture that had been in the old Reade home in Boston. Willa cared little about household decorations. In large part, Owen had directed both the building of the house and its furnishing, taking care to pay attention to the smallest details. On my first day in Santa Monica I remember Willa and I looking at it, from the front walkway. She said, "The only thing different is the palm trees."

"Different?" I asked.

"From the old Reade house," she answered.

"But you said the Reade place was gloomy, that Owen was unhappy there," I reminded her.

"True," Willa shrugged. "I suppose Owen is doing it over to get it right this time."

I looked at her for an instant, and decided against asking more. "You don't like the house?" I said instead.

"Oh, it doesn't really bother me," she replied, as if it did not. "I suppose I think it too fussy, too cluttered. I do prefer the Spanish adobe style—it is such a nice, simple way of building, and it makes sense for this warm climate. In the heat of the day, the interiors of those adobes are so cool. But I suppose a Spanish house wouldn't fit very well on this street," she said, waving at the big houses being built all along the street. "So long as it makes Owen happy, it is fine with me. Anyway," she added jauntily, "you can't say we don't fit."

"No, you certainly cannot say that," I chuckled. What Owen's house lacked in simplicity, it made up in sheer size. It was, without a doubt, the most impressive house on Seaside Avenue.

"There are exactly ninety-nine steps down the bluff to the shore," Owen said, bursting in on us. He waved his long arm toward the sea which stretched, endless blue, to the west. "Tomorrow, when you have had a good night's rest, I intend to take you down those steps so that you can take off your little shoes and wade in the great Pacific ocean. That will be your baptism!"

"We'll all wade," Willa laughed, "even little Wennie. We can dip his tiny little feet in the ocean too."

"Let us go have an audience with the heir apparent," Owen declared, one arm around each of our waists, guiding us into his home and the life he had created, so quickly, on the edge of the country.

"Tell me," I asked Willa as we waited for Owen to return with the child, "how is it to be a mother?"

"Oh," she said, casually, "I can't say that I feel any different. I saw Mama through so many of her birthings, I've been around babies for so much of my life—as you have. I don't think I have ever had any fancy notions about motherhood. I've walked too many colicky babes not to know how lucky I am with Wennie—he is a sweet child, he sleeps well, he is healthy and good-tempered, much like Servia, I think."

"May you have all such babies," I said.

"Not for a time," she answered, "not for a good long time."

At that moment a scowling, dark-skinned young woman marched into the room, carrying young Owen. The child's father bounced along behind her as if trying to take hold of the baby, but he was ignored. I wanted to laugh (Owen, behind the dark woman's back, already was), but I held it in check.

"Why didn't you dress him in the smock my sister crocheted for him, as I told you to?" Willa asked the woman.

A torrent of Spanish was loosed in the room. I understood not a word, except that the woman had terrible grievances. All the while, Owen was grinning amiably, as if this were in the normal course of events.

"Stop it, Trinidad," Willa said, exasperated, but the Spanish kept pouring out torrentially.

Turning to me, my sister had said in a very loud voice, "The poor soul can't understand a word of English, in spite of all my efforts to teach her. It is too bad that I can't introduce you."

"What? What? What you say?" came burbling out of the woman in scarcely contained anger. "I know, I know."

"Lena, I'm sorry," Willa said, mocking the woman still, pretending to ignore her, "I was wrong. It seems that Trinidad does understand some little bit of English." She turned to the woman, who was clasping the baby to her ample bosom. "This is my sister, Lena, Trinidad. Will you let her hold the baby, please?"

The "please" seemed to work. Trinidad turned to me, her face suddenly wreathed in smiles, clearly to let me know her anger was directed at Willa alone.

*"Buena, buena,"* she said, turning the baby over to me. "I am for pleased to see nice sister," she added in triumph.

"And I to meet you," I said, in what proved to be a very small voice. I wasn't sure what to think about Trinidad.

"She has memorized that speech for you," Willa chortled. The woman scowled at Willa once more, then left abruptly.

"She is wonderful," Willa told me, "you will like her. It is just that when she is disappointed, she carries on. And for some reason," here she looked at Owen in mock disgust, "Owen promised her she could take the baby and go with us today."

Owen, all this while, had been concentrating on the baby, cooing and making soft sounds, putting his finger in the baby's tiny hand. "Look at that, Willa," he said, "Wen and his auntie. That is a nice picture, isn't it?"

At that moment I swayed. Willa and Owen reached out to me at the same instant, and Owen quickly retrieved the child, who gurgled happily and spat up on his father.

"Did Trinidad tell you to do that?" Owen said to the baby. "I'll just bet she did, to punish me." He didn't mind a bit, it seemed, though Willa went for a cloth to dab off his spoiled suit.

"Come, sit next to us, Lena," Owen said. "You must be very tired after so long a trip. I know they exhaust me."

"He is a beautiful baby," I said to Owen, and he answered, as if speaking for the child, "Oh, yes I am, Auntie, my papa's pride. And my Mama is very, very happy that you have come to live with us and keep us company while Papa is away."

Putting my finger in the baby's hand, I said, "Tell your Papa that I am grateful . . ."

"Psht," Owen interrupted, "it is Papa who is grateful. Now he won't have to worry about Mama when he is away."

I would remember those words; Owen did want me to make my home with them, being convinced that I would relieve Willa's loneliness. He thought my presence would free him. I settled into the rhythm of the household more quickly than I could have imagined possible. Weeks passed, Baby Wen grew, smiled, burbled happily in his bed. Trinidad was married to the silent Ignacio, who tended our horses, and set about establishing her own family. A girl child, Aleja, would be born to them before the first year of their marriage was out.

The Pacific Ocean mesmerized me. I could not seem to look at it long enough and I could not imagine how I had lived so long without it. Porter Farm and the prairie dimmed by comparison and the weeks grew into months and the pattern of our lives took form. The ebb and flow of that life was tuned to Owen's comings and goings; he was gone for weeks at a time. I often wished that Owen could witness the transformation that would come over Willa as his carriage pulled away from the house, taking him on yet another business trip. He never saw how desolate she looked after his departure, he did not know how short-tempered and restless she could become. She rode, she studied her bird books, she tried to involve herself in all her old interests, but now they were no more than distractions, ways to pass the time until his return. I was, in turn, amazed, angry, sad and, finally, deeply troubled by it.

During my second September in California, I had my first experience of what Trinidad called a *Santana*. It was a dry, hot wind that blew from the desert, searing our eyes and our throats and fraying our tempers. It went on, hot and dry, one day and the next until it seemed everything in our existence was hot and brittle. Owen had left for Eureka.

I found Willa sitting next to the window in the front parlor, her fingers drumming on the desk.

"Wennie is fussing," I said to her, "do you think it might help if I took him down to the beach—could I let him wade?"

Willa looked up blankly at first, as if she hadn't heard me. I had started to ask again when she cut in.

"You don't have to ask me every time you want to do something with the child," she said. "Make some decisions yourself, Lena. You're old enough not to come running to me every time you have a question."

"He is your child," I said, my jaws stiff, "and I think his mother might be interested in what might make him feel better in this awful heat."

"Well, I'm not. So do what you want, and stop nattering at me."

"Nattering?" I said, suddenly furious. "Nobody *natters* at you, Willa, and that really is too bad. Your spoiled child act would not be allowed at Porter Farm."

"Act?" she hissed at me, "what do you mean, act?"

"As if you really are the Queen of the May, the mistress of the mansion, the Lonely Lady of Seaside Avenue, pining after her absent love. Look at yourself, Willa. You have everything to be happy about—your health, a good husband, a healthy good baby, and still you sit here pouting. Owen goes away and you turn into a shrew."

My skin was prickling—from the heat and the anger and, now, from fear. I had said too much.

Willa's face was cold with fury. She pounded her fist on the table and rose, too fast, turning over a glass lampshade and shattering it into a thousand pieces. She tried to grab for it, but only managed to clutch a fragment that cut into her palm. The blood splashed out.

"Oh," I cried, "Willa, you're hurt, let me . . ."

"Stay away," she said, "I don't need your help and I don't need your opinions. You have been given a place in my home, but you have no right to judge me and I will not have it. Do you hear? I will not have it. You don't know what I feel."

I watched the blood drip from her slashed hand, and felt I was drowning in it.

I said nothing at all, but turned and went to ask Trinidad to help my sister. It would be two days before she came to my door.

"Can I come in?" she asked.

"It is your house," I answered, "you can do what you please in it."

"I'm sorry, Lena, I truly am," she said. "I did not mean to say it."

"Perhaps it is best that you did," I answered, hearing the weariness in my voice. "I need to remember my place."

Willa looked as if I had slapped her. She leaned against the door, biting her lip.

"Your place is as a member of the family," she said. "You have every right to say what you said. I was angry . . . You must forgive me. I won't be able to sleep unless you do, and it is hard enough to sleep with Owen away, and the *Santana* . . ."

She sat down next to me and put her hand on my arm.

"There is nothing to forgive, Willa," I answered truthfully.

"My..." she searched for a word, "...melancholy," she finally said, "I do struggle with it, Lena."

"You told me," I replied, measuring my words, "on the farm, that week when Owen first came and you decided to marry him, you said that you understood what it was he wanted of a wife..."

She sighed. "I know. I do know, in my head. Owen has a grand plan, and nothing is going to change it. I suppose I don't want anything to change it. I also did not know how deeply I could feel about him, how I could long for him. Sometimes I wish he cared as deeply for me."

"Willa," I said, in surprise, "Owen adores you... what more..."

"What more do I want?" she cut in, "I don't know. That is what is so strange. I just have a feeling that there should be more... but I don't know what... and I know it is wrong, wrong..."

"Ah, Willa," I said, as gently as I could, "what can I do?"

She sat, shaking her head, unable to speak.

We sat listening to the rumble of a carriage as it passed on the road below. Then it was quiet again, with only the low sounds of the ocean breaking the silence.

"I must do something," she said. "I need to find the old Willa again."

"I'd like that," I told her.

"And you forgive me?" she asked.

"I will forgive the old Willa, when she returns," I answered. "I fought with her all the time."

"You never did!" she laughed, and then she hugged me to her and we both cried.

# ~ *Chapter Five*

Wen, groggy from his nap, stumbled into the sitting room that connected his room to mine. He climbed onto my lap, snuggling his head—damp with the sweet perspiration of a baby's sleep—into a comfortable position against my breast. I held him gladly. He was almost three years old, and already resisting the hugs and kisses lavished on him by a household in which he was the only child.

We heard the door push open. The high, excited voices of Willa and Arcadia Scott—pitched as if still out-of-doors, as if they were riding on the beach—sounded up the stairwell.

"Miss Lena in the *alcoba*," Trinidad answered with her usual lilting mix of Spanish and English *"con* the *nene."*

"I wonder if I'll ever be able to teach Trinidad English," I whispered to Wen, whose mouth was firmly stoppered by his thumb. I smiled down into his eyes, which were big and liquid brown like his father's.

We sat very still, as if playing hide and seek, and listened as the women mounted the steps, talking as they always did when they were together. Arcadia Scott had that effect on people: There seemed always to be so much to say when she was about.

"Wennie, sweet boy!" she cried, her hands out to the child.

"Come let me hold you, won't you please?"

Wen clung hard to me and turned his face away, so that only a muffled "no" sounded from him.

"He's just up from his nap, Arcadia," Willa said, "let him wake up." She smiled at her son and said, "Owen Two is getting to be a big boy now, and he doesn't much like us hugging and kissing him anymore."

"Oh, well, then," Arcadia said in fun, "you'll just have to get another baby for us, Willa. I simply do not think I can manage without a little Wennie to kiss."

Willa winced; I was sure of it. "Why don't you just find yourself a nice husband," I said to Arcadia in the same bantering tones, "and start having babies for us to spoil?"

"You—both of you—should understand by now," she said, as if we were a bit dense, "that I cannot get married because Willa has taken the only *perfect* man in southern California, and I certainly couldn't settle for less. I suppose I'll just have to do without a husband altogether." She heaved a theatrical sigh, pretending not to have noticed that Owen had entered the room.

"Not necessarily," he said, putting one arm around Arcadia's shoulders and the other around Willa. "We could all move to Utah and become Mormons, then I could have as many wives as I want—" his eyes on Wen, his arms out to him— "And dozens and dozens of little brothers and sisters for Wennie to play with."

The child ran into his father's arms. "Tell me," Owen said to the women, "how was the ride? What did you think of the coast to the north?"

"Are you really going to buy it?" Arcadia blurted.

"I am," Owen said, nuzzling Wen, "I have." He was looking at Willa, waiting for her to answer his question.

"Owen, it is truly beautiful," she told him. "We rode all the way to where the creek washes into the ocean. I think I've never seen such a magnificent sweep of beaches—and the mountains. It was just . . . but can you get clear title to it?"

"Oh, Willa," Arcadia interrupted, "surely you know about the Treaty of Guadalupe Hidalgo. Good, dear old Guadalupe! The Señora still prays to him, I believe!"

Owen grinned. "When California became part of the States," he explained, "a treaty—Guadalupe Hidalgo—was signed that said all Mexican property must be 'inviolably respected.' Which meant that all the great Spanish land grants, and that was something like a fourth of all the land in California, must be honored. The papers I signed this morning with Mr. Henry Kellar make me the legal owner of the Rancho Malibu y Sequit, all twenty-two miles of it."

"You bought it from a Mexican named Kellar?" I asked in mock surprise.

"Who speaks only French," Owen answered.

"Truly?" Arcadia wanted to know.

"His father was old Don Mateo Kellar, one of those flamboyant Irishmen who became Mexican citizens and who, one way or another, managed to amass quite a lot of property. He bought the Malibu from the original grantees, a family called Tapia. Or no, I believe there was another owner in between. At any rate, Don Mateo paid ten cents an acre for it. I just paid ten dollars an acre."

"That's all?" Willa said, her eyes wide.

"That's all," he answered, enjoying her surprise. "I bought it from Don Mateo's only son, a chap named Henry who was sent to France to be educated, and who hasn't the slightest intention of ever coming back to what he calls '*ce pauvre pays*' because, as he put it so elegantly, '*il n'y a rien ici.*' He was so blatantly prejudiced against Americans that I drove a much harder bargain than I had intended—with the help of his agent, a young fellow named Charlie Rich. I think Charlie figured the fatuous young fool deserved to be fleeced. Anyway, when Henry turned up his nose at my offer, Charlie Rich took him aside and told him that he could get a better price, certainly, but it would mean staying here for months, maybe a year, because there weren't all that many people with Mr. Reade's resources, that it would not be easy to sell the rancho intact . . . and that did it."

"Hooray for Charlie Rich," Arcadia said.

"Remember to buy from him, not have him sell," I put in, and Owen nodded to me in agreement.

"Except," he said, "to give Charlie his due, he did say that he hoped to do business with me again. After all, French Henry is going to disappear from these shores forever, and the Reades should be around for generations."

Owen paused to work a top for Wen. When it was spinning

across the floor, he went on. "When the papers were finally signed I told Mr. Kellar—in my flawless Bostonian French—that I had visited Italy, and that if ever a road goes through along the Malibu coast, I feel it would rival the Corniche. I also said that in my humble opinion this coast is every bit the equal of the Riviera."

"And what did he say to that?" Arcadia asked.

"He said, *'Ce n'est pas vrai.'*"

We all laughed. "How perfectly, arrogantly French," Arcadia put in, "just to say it is not true. What a boor."

"Bear?" Wen asked brightly, having found a word that interested him. The sturdy little boy looked surprised and pleased to have made everyone laugh.

"There haven't been any grizzlies in the Malibu for thirty years," Owen told his son, "but there may be a very small bear, a very nice little one just your size, Wennie, on our new ranch. Would you like to go camping there with Papa? Me and you in a nice big tent?"

"And me?" Willa asked over Wen's whoop.

"And Auntie," Wen insisted, already seeing this as his party.

"Well, not me," said Arcadia, "I'm going home now to tell La Señora that I am moving to Utah to become a Mormon."

Willa and Owen, their arms linked, went to see Arcadia to the door, the three of them chattering easily like the friends they were.

It was never possible that Owen would not have arranged to meet the Señora: Arcadia Stearns. Arcadia Bandini Stearns Baker, but Arcadia Stearns, nonetheless. The old lady was part of the very fabric of the place, part of the secret. A relic, beautiful and polished, her fingers long and slender still, the orbs of her nails pale against the olive skin, her hands as still as her face.

She was a Californio, a Bandini, one of the important Spanish families in the days before the Yankees. More important for the fable that was her life, she had been the bride of Abel Stearns. He was forty-three when he saw her, she was fourteen and a promising beauty; already she held herself in such a way as to draw the attention of Abel Stearns.

Her father, a gambler, was pleased to have Stearns as a son-in-law. The Yankee was a man who made things happen, who set things right: gambling debts, marriage banns. The good padres accepted Don Abel's generous contributions and failed to post the marriage banns which his detractors, and there were many, might use to accuse him of being a defiler of children.

A long scar ran from Abel Stearns' cheek through his upper lip, lifting it cruelly, a reminder of his own precocious childhood. Abel Stearns had run away to sea at the age of twelve. He had been many places, had done much, and carried the scars of old encounters on his face. He was called "Caro del Caballo": Horseface.

Beauty and the beast, they had lived happily together for more than thirty years. As a wedding gift he bought her the Rancho Los Alamitos. In the following years he would buy a dozen more ranches—Rancho Los Coyotes, La Habra . . . the Señora knew all about the Treaty of Guadalupe Hidalgo. Finally, his lands stretched for two hundred thousand acres and his cattle empire was the greatest in the south.

And then, in all of the year 1863 and all of 1864 there was but one rain. It would be remembered, long years after, as the time of the great drought. It was a bad time; the land was rank, the air fetid with the smell of rotting animal flesh; death rose in the heat waves over dry lands. Even the great Abel Stearns faced ruin. He lost seven thousand sheep and two hundred lambs. He sold off one thousand of his cattle, but the drought killed thirty thousand more. But he had found a way to survive, and that way had touched off the land revolution that would change the life flow of the cow counties.

Through the Los Angeles and San Bernardino Land Company, Abel Stearns sold off his land in small tracts that could be divided and divided again. The company advertised in Europe and through all of the United States. Come to the land of perpetual sunshine, they said, come to California where the warm breezes blow and happiness can be plucked off a tree.

They came from Ohio and Wisconsin and County Cork, from North Dakota and Kentucky and Paris, France. They came west as destiny and the Santa Fe Railroad told them they must. Each acre of land they bought from the Los Angeles and San Bernardino Land Company reaped a profit for Abel Stearns, so that he paid off all of his debts, he established his beautiful bride, young still, in the big house in Santa Monica and, finally, he died in honor. The great drought, the one which had defeated so many of the others, did not defeat Abel Stearns. The city of Los Angeles bears witness to it.

Arcadia Bandini Stearns married Colonel Robert Baker and lived with him for twenty years. When he died, her fortune increased. Yet through all the long years of marriage, the child bride remained childless.

She lived not far from the house on Seaside Avenue that Owen built. Two years ago, not long after the death of Colonel Baker, her grandniece and namesake, Arcadia Scott, had come to visit. She was scarcely seventeen, and blonde with a shell-pink complexion. She had a comfortable laugh and was easily pleased. She brightened the Señora's house and reminded the old woman of something. So the young Arcadia had stayed on to keep the old one company, to travel with her, to spend time tending the fable, polishing the past.

"I am so very happy to meet you," Arcadia had said somewhat breathlessly to Willa that first day, "I've so wanted to find someone to laugh with."

It had been such an earnest appeal, so forthright, that Willa had known they would be friends, and they were. After that day, the two saw each other often. Owen was delighted and so was I. He because he was away more and more, and he could think of no better companion for Willa than Arcadia Stearns' grandniece. I because Arcadia could do all those things I couldn't. She could stay in the saddle for long hours without tiring. She was fearless in the same way as Willa. They became partners in adventures that led them often enough to the edge of danger.

Had the Señora known some of the challenges they accepted, she would not have approved. "I am responsible for you," she would say to Arcadia when she did not want her to do something. "I must answer to your family, to my brother's son, your father. I cannot allow..." Arcadia had learned how to circumvent her denials. With Willa's help, and Owen's tacit compliance, the two women plotted new adventures.

They were learning to sail the small boat docked at the pier in Santa Monica. Willa would appear at the Señora's with her notebooks, and Arcadia would make a great scene of collecting her sketchpads. "We are looking for the white-tailed kite," she would say, then casually add, *"Elanus leucurus,"* to add weight to the charade. It would be true, of course. But not all of the truth. She did not tell her grandaunt that they would be tracking the bird from a small boat, tacking with the winds, working the sails. And she did not mention that her canvas day bag held, along with a lunch of bread and cheese and dried fruit, her bathing dress. Often enough, the two women managed to capsize their small boat.

After the day's ride or sail they would return to the house on Seaside Avenue full of the smell of the out-of-doors, woodsy and clean and cheeks high with color. Arcadia would stay, then, until the exuberance was spent, until she could establish the sort of peaceful demeanor required in the Señora's house. Harsh, Spanish light was not kind to old beauty. The Señora's house was a place of tranquil shadows. Arcadia Scott was learning to live in those shadows.

After a time I came to understand that the house on Seaside Avenue had two lives—with Owen and without. When he was away, which was perhaps half the time, the tempo was slow, measured. We were a household of women: Willa and I, very often joined by Arcadia and, more often of late, Sara. Willa's longtime interest in raptors—the birds of prey—had taken a scholarly turn. She spent days on end in the field making detailed observations of hawks and eagles. Her special fascination was, always, the peregrine falcon.

On horseback and afoot she followed them as they circled wide above her, quartering, their sharp eyes watching for a movement that would signal the presence of a fieldmouse or a rabbit. With her field glasses she could see a hawk rip apart its prey. Later, she would ride to where the remains—bits of fur and blood and bone—were left, and make a notation.

I, in turn, transcribed her notes on the typewriter Owen had purchased. I had become adept at typewriting, which pleased Owen and Willa, both of whom admired efficiency—and both of whom carried on a wide correspondence.

Willa began what was to become a long and detailed correspondence with falconers in Britain and in the United States. Now and then she would submit an article to a scientific journal.

"I am enclosing a treatise on the eyrie of the peregrine falcon in the coastal region of southern California," she would write, "it is the result of five months' observation of four separate eyries which produced, in all, ten nestlings. I hope you will find it of some merit, however small..." She did not explain that, to reach one bluffside nest, she had descended a thirty-foot wall of dirt and rock that dropped steeply to the sea below.

To her surprise—and delight—the research she presented was received with excitement in the society of people interested in hawks. She had signed all of her letters and articles "W. K. Reade." Invariably, the return letters were addressed either to Mr. Reade or to W. K. Reade, Esquire. Willa did nothing to correct the impression. When I asked why, she said only, "I find I enjoy being taken seriously in the company of men."

When Owen came home, life in the house quickened. It was as if a lever had been thrown, as if we breathed faster, moved faster, even words seemed to come more quickly. Everyone wanted to hear all about Owen's travels, and everyone wanted to tell him all that had happened in his absence. At first, everything was chaotic. Wen would throw himself into Owen's arms and Owen, unable to hold the child for long, would find a chair to sink into. Willa would pull a small stool up to sit at his feet, and often enough there would be a visitor to join the group. I remember once Wen took his father's face in his small hands to be sure he was looking at him. Before long, then, Willa would say, "It's time for Wen's nap, isn't it?" Or: "Isn't it time Wennie was in bed?"

Sometimes, it seemed, a signal must have gone out, because within two or three days of Owen's return, people—strangers, for the most part—would begin to arrive. Some came with letters of introduction. Even when Owen could not quite remember the writer of the letter—he met so many good people on his travels—he was never less than welcoming.

It was not unusual to find a stranger in the library, deposited there by a grim-faced Trinidad, who knew it meant another plate to set at the dinner table. Even Wen learned to deal with them.

"Are you waiting for my papa?" he would ask in his round, child's voice. "I'll fetch him for you." When Owen was at home, Wen always knew where to find him.

They came with all manner of schemes. One man had imported six thousand pineapple plants from Africa, being sure that southern California had the perfect climate for a pineapple plantation. He had the pineapples, all he needed was the plantation. Another was excited beyond all reason about the prospect of raising ostriches, convinced a fortune was to be made in ostrich feathers, a favorite ornament of ladies' clothing.

Owen listened with such genuine interest that they left with high hopes, these men, certain they had convinced him that, together, they could make a fortune.

None could know that while Owen's enthusiasm was boundless, it was in no way connected to his pursestrings. Though they had not underestimated his fortune—he had more than tripled the sizeable inheritance left him—he had not done it with small get-rich-quick schemes.

I had become a kind of office manager for Owen, handling some of his business matters in his absence, so that I knew he had, in the main, three great interests: water, oil and insurance. These three, he liked to say, would prove to be "the gold mines of the twentieth century."

"I want to go with you to Nevada City," Willa said to him. "Remember the last time we went there together? We could ask for the same suite of rooms at the National Exchange—it could be a kind of anniversary trip."

Owen's silence meant that he was not in favor of her going north with him. Finally he said, "I will be busy with meetings, Willa. I wouldn't have any time to spend with you."

"But we'd have the traveling time together . . . I want to go, Owen." This last was a plea. It was as close as she could come to begging. Owen was shaking his head.

"That was before we had Wen," he said.

"But Lena can take care of Wen," she argued. "He spends most of his time with her—I don't think he would miss me very much."

Owen looked at her steadily. "You are Wen's mother, and your place is here, with him. I think you should remember that."

Willa hugged her arms against her and looked out the window. After a time she said, in a voice empty with defeat, "Wen was conceived in Nevada City, in the National . . ."

Owen answered: "Are you saying that if I let you come with me, you will consider having another child?"

Willa's eyes flashed. "No, Owen," she said angrily. "I was saying only that before we had Wen, I was free to travel with you, to share your life away from home, too."

The air between them was taut, in danger of snapping, breaking.

Owen moved toward her. "My dear," he said, pulling her to him, "you are always part of me, even when I am away. Don't you understand that I want you with me? It is just that we have so much to do, together. This house must be full of life, open to the world. I don't want it to be shut up, waiting. When I come home I want children and friends and laughter to come spilling out the doors. I depend on you to make that happen. I need to know you are here—you and the children, in this house. But you have to remember that you are the mother. Lena is not physically strong—you know how easy it is for her to fall. You must be in charge."

She put her head on his shoulder then and told him that she was sorry.

"For what?" he said.

"Loving you too much, wanting to be with you too much," she answered into his chest.

*You and the children,* he had said. *But there was only one child.*

Owen's words proved to be prophetic. Three days after his departure for Nevada City, Wen came to me in the afternoon, his eyes bright, his face flushed.

"What is it, darling?" I asked. He whimpered and crawled into my lap, where he lay listlessly. I ran my hand under his blouse to find that his small body radiated heat. With a start I realized that he had been clinging to me all that morning. I was annoyed with myself for not having thought of it.

I glanced at the clock; it was four. Willa had gone sailing, but she was usually back by this hour. Wen became very still, his eyes were shiny with fever. Trinidad and I bathed him with cool cloths and tried to coax him to take some water, but he would not open his mouth, he seemed not to understand us.

"Send Ignacio for the doctor," I said with an urgency that caused Trinidad to clap her hand over her mouth to stifle a cry. She did not even ask if we should wait for Willa, but left to find her husband, who would be in the stables, behind the house.

I continued bathing the child, afraid at how still he was, wishing beyond all reason that he would look up at me and smile as he always did, knowing he would not, could not. My fear translated to anger, and the anger began to be concentrated on Willa.

Where was she? What right had she to be out in the water in a sailboat? Why wasn't she here to help? I made several trips to the window which looked down on the avenue, and cursed the tall trees which blocked my view. Nothing, no Willa in sight. I began to think that she was not going to come, would not return.

Such was my agitation that when the doorbell rang, I told Trinidad to stay with Wen while I went to answer it. In my haste, in my fear and excitement and need to have help, I slipped on the last step and went sprawling. The sound of my fall brought Trinidad running, crying *"Madre de Dios!"*

I convinced the doctor that he had to see Wen first. I had fallen before, and I felt certain it was no more than a bruise. The pain was almost welcome. I turned my anger in on myself. I had been so stupid, so very stupid, hurrying so, risking so much, when Wen needed all the attention, all the help

The child had influenza. He was a sturdy, healthy little boy, the doctor said. We could only hope . . . perhaps it would be a mild case. You couldn't tell. Perhaps . . .

When the doctor left, I felt afraid again. With Ignacio's help—amid Trinidad's worried scolding—I got back up the stairway and stationed myself in the child's room, looking onto the road, searching for some sign of Willa. She had never been so late. I began to worry that something might have happened to the boat. It was too much to consider, too much to bear. When the light began to fade, I decided to send Ignacio to look for her, though I regretted his leaving, because of all the servants, he was the one who inspired the most confidence.

It was dark when she came in. "Where have you been?" I snapped, furious. "Wen is very sick. What could possibly have kept you?"

My words stung, I could see. She did not answer, but went to Wen. "Let's have a look at this sweet boy," she whispered to him, but Wen turned away from her. His eyes were on me, pleading.

"I am truly sorry, Lèna," she said, and her voice was so desolate that I began to cry. She sat for a long while next to his bed. When finally he slipped into a troubled sleep, she kept watch.

My hip was aching so that I did as she said, then, and lay

on the settee in the sitting room that adjoined Wen's, close by should he wake and want me.

I woke to see her standing in the doorway, the single lamp from the child's room creating an aura behind her, so that the soft roll of her hair was lit from behind like a halo. The awkwardness between us was new. I couldn't think what to say.

She broke the silence: "I am sorry, Lena. I should have been here, you shouldn't have had to do it all alone."

"It was just," I began, "I thought that you might have had an accident..."

"I didn't mean today," she interrupted, "I mean I've let you do everything for Wen. I've tried to tell myself that you want it, need it, when really I'm the one who needs you to do it. Wen prefers you, and it doesn't matter to me. I don't know why, Lena. I love him, but I don't love being a mother. It's not that, either. It's that...it seems as if I haven't had time to be a wife. I want so to be with Owen, to share his life, all of it, and because I'm a mother, I can't. I remember that when I wrote asking you to come to live with us, I said we would share the children. But I haven't done my share, and the truth is, I don't want to. Until tonight, I've been able to avoid that truth, because you never complained. You haven't once hinted that it was hard for you."

She sat down next to me, thinking so deeply that the silence threatened to become suffocating. I forced myself to break it, to ask the question I had not wanted to ask.

"Is that why you don't want another child?"

Willa shivered, quietly at first, then uncontrollably. The tremors affected her voice and made it difficult for her to speak. Finally, with difficulty, she said, "I'm afraid for what I am not. Owen wants another child, he wants one desperately. Sometimes I think it is the only reason he sees for coming together, to make children. But I avoid that now, though I want it—more than he does, I want it. I love him, and I want to be with him, but I'm not ready for another child, not yet. And Wennie, poor little boy, so sick. If something should...if he...I am so afraid for him, and if...Owen would..."

The child's fever held for three days. All that time we sat near him, Willa and I, in turn. Sometimes he would cry out for me, and Willa would call me to come. On the third night, his small body seemed finally to find a comfortable position in the bed. We had sent a telegram to Owen in Nevada City.

By the time he arrived, the child was sleeping peacefully, his breathing normal, his body almost cool to the touch.

With Owen home, I could with a clear conscience retire to my own bed to sleep the sleep of the weary and sore. Two days later, everything seemed almost normal. On the third morning, before full light, I felt a familiar rocking of my bed, a tickling of my face. Wen had crept into my bed and was waking me by rubbing my face with one of the small fur toys Owen had brought him.

"Oh, Wennie," I said sleepily, "I am so happy to see you smiling at me."

"Papa brought this to me," he said, poking the animal at me again. At that moment Willa appeared at the door. "Wen, dear," she said to the child in an inviting tone, "come with me and we'll have something nice to eat. Let's let Auntie sleep some more." I smiled up at Willa, knowing that she would have been listening, even in deepest sleep; knowing why she had come, and being glad that at last we would be sharing the pleasures, as well as the pain, of rearing her child.

Trinidad's face was set. Her eyebrows formed a solid line across the wide forehead and one thick hand pulled at her earlobe, always a sign of distress. Since she pulled at her ear throughout our Spanish and English lessons, I could only surmise that she was in a continual state of distress whenever she attempted to speak English. The tongue that rolled so rapidly through Spanish tripped and stumbled and sometimes even got stuck trying to speak English.

"Aiii, Aiii, Aiii," she would wail then. I was determined to be optimistic, to praise her whenever possible, since criticism sent her into torrents of tears, but the most I could find to praise her for was her tenacity. "Let us please to *hablar inglés,*" she would say.

"Speak," I would correct her. "*Hablar* means 'to speak.'"

"Aiii, *sí,*" she would moan, "to speak *inglés.*"

Trinidad was only a few years older than I, but in some ways it seemed as if she had lived forever. She and Ignacio had been married for several years. I had yet to see them speak more than a few words to each other. Willa told me once that she had hired Trinidad because "she is too stubborn ever to be subservient."

"You mean you don't want subservient servants?" I had

asked. Owen had laughed out loud at that, and said how re-
freshing it was to have someone brave enough to point out
Willa's inconsistencies. Willa had glared at both of us, then,
and she did not laugh. Later I apologized to her for making
the remark in Owen's presence.

"But you don't apologize for the remark?" she had asked,
then, and I had said no, that I didn't.

I found out for myself that Trinidad was not so much stubborn as she was dogged, thorough. Perhaps proper is the better
word to describe her, though not proper in the usual sense. She
imposed an order on her life that we neither knew nor understood. She did not question, I think she could not. The old
ways were so deeply ingrained that to change them required
all of her will, all of her concentration. Learning the language
of her employers was such a change: an impossible task, but
one she would not abandon.

The lesson must be long on this day, she told me, because
of those missed during Wen's illness. Then, in the middle of
reciting vocabulary, which included the words *pen, paper,* and
*letter,* her eyes registered alarm, and she pulled from her pocket
a letter addressed to me, apologies for her forgetfulness tumbling out of Trinidad in a torrent of Spanish.

It was from Sara. She was coming to Los Angeles within
a fortnight. She would be staying with Charles in Pasadena for
a time, then she would like to visit with us, if that would be
convenient. Her asking was merely a formality. Sara Hunt was
always a welcome guest. The house on Seaside Avenue had,
in fact, a room we called "Sara's."

"How wonderful," I said out loud, "Sara is coming for a
visit."

"*Buena!*" Trinidad said, "her room I will make ready now."

"No," I explained, "she won't arrive for another week or
so, but I am truly glad that she is coming."

"*Sí,*" Trinidad answered knowingly, "is good you have *la
amiga.*"

"Friend," I corrected her.

"*Sí,*" Trinidad smiled.

It was true, Sara Hunt was my friend, my dear friend. We
visited often, usually at the house on Seaside Avenue, but now
and again in Phineas Emory's mansion on Nob Hill. Once,
when Sara and Helen Emory and I were chatting together in

the red parlor of the mansion, I started a sentence which Sara interrupted me to finish. Helen said, "Sometimes I think you two are really just one person."

"Do you mean two halves make a whole?" Sara replied. Helen did not answer, but left the room abruptly.

"Sara," I said, surprised, "she didn't mean that...she meant..."

"I know what she meant," Sara interrupted, "but I also know she has absolute disdain for weakness, any kind of weakness, if you aren't whole, Helen has no use for you. I simply wanted her to know that I know, and this seemed as good an opportunity as any to do that."

I must not have seemed convinced, because she added in a voice barely audible, "Cripples cannot afford illusions."

"So all stepmothers are wicked?" I asked.

"No," she answered, "not wicked. But in this case, shrewd. And determined. Charles has spoken to Father Emory about creating a separate inheritance for me from my father's part of the business, but nothing has been done about that as yet. So I am dependent on my adopted parents. She knows I am weak, but I want her to know I am not stupid."

Helen Emory and Sara made frequent trips to Los Angeles to visit Charles. Usually they traveled in the Alhambra. At all the little stations down the San Joaquin Valley, people would stand on the station platform and try to peer into the sleek private car, would strain to see the two women settled in the plush chairs, reflected in the high bevel-edged French pier glass, two women in a state of truce. Phineas seldom ever traveled. Business kept him in San Francisco, at the center of his financial empire. He was glad, he told his wife, that she found Sara such an agreeable traveling companion. The truth, Sara confided, was that he found any woman tiresome after the first half hour, and he was glad to have Sara act as Helen's companion.

In his charming Queen Anne style cottage—as he called it—in Pasadena, Charles Emory arranged dinner parties and teas, and all manner of pleasant diversion for the two women. There were theater parties and seats at the opera. Often, Willa and Owen and I were his guests. Just as often, Sara's visit would end with a trip to the seashore in Santa Monica.

I was glad that Sara was coming, this time more than ever.

I needed to talk with her, needed the clarity of thought that was her talent.

"Don't you find it wearing," Charles asked Willa as they stood watching Helen Emory smile up at Owen while they danced, "being married to a man women can't resist?"

The back parlor had been cleared. The music and the din of conversation masked Charles' soft, insinuating words. But Willa had heard.

"Why should Mrs. Emory be interested in my poor husband," she asked, "when she has such an utterly charming husband waiting for her in San Francisco?" From experience, Willa knew that the one person who never fell victim to Charles Emory's acerbic tongue was his uncle.

"Willa, I am quite serious," Charles insisted, though his voice said he wasn't, "women do make fools of themselves over Owen, and I have been wanting to ask you for a long time, a very long time—doesn't it trouble you in the least?"

Willa considered him then. In a teasing voice, she answered, "No. It doesn't trouble me in the least because Owen has yet to make a fool over any one of them."

"Yet to?" Charles asked.

"Wouldn't it be better for you to ask Owen these questions?" Willa came back at him, suddenly feeling very tired of Charles Emory and his baiting.

Before he could answer, she added, "Charles, you really can be tiresome, did you know that?"

"What is this, a family quarrel?" Sara asked, joining them, tucking a hand into Charles' arm.

"We've just been admiring Helen admiring Owen," Charles said, the edge of bitterness in his tone betraying him. "And I have been asking poor Willa how she puts up with all the pretty women badgering Owen."

"They simply cannot believe," Sara said in carefully measured tones, "that he is not interested. So don't say 'poor' Willa, Charles. Say 'poor' pretty women."

Willa thought, *I wish I didn't have to look into Sara's eyes*.

Large parties tired me, and Owen's parties had a way of going on into the early hours. I excused myself to Willa and slipped off to my room. Before long, Sara knocked on my door.

"I am sorry it took so long for me to get here," she began, "Helen was to leave for San Francisco a week ago, but she delayed so I couldn't leave—propriety demands, you know. Then, when Willa and Owen invited all of us to the party tonight, well, Helen wanted to come and..."

Sara often had to be coaxed to finish a sentence, but this time I had too much on my mind to probe for the rest.

"You mean, you aren't staying on with us?" I asked, clearly chagrined. "I'm terribly worried about something, about," I began to stammer. "I need to talk to you, to have you help me sift out." I couldn't seem to get going.

Sara kicked off her shoes and sat on the end of my bed. "Wait," she said. "Start over. Tell me. There's plenty of time, now."

I told her then about Willa's not wanting to have another child, about Willa's painful lack of interest in Wen.

"Since he was sick," I explained, "Willa has been scrupulous about spending time with him, giving him much more of her attention, making sure we really are sharing in his care. You know how Willa is—once she decides on a course of action, nothing will sway her. It has made Owen happy, I can see that. But Owen sees what he wants to see. I have watched her with the child, and...well...they look so forlorn together, I don't know. I think it troubles Willa terribly..."

Sara looked at me steadily. I could see that she was thinking, pulling together the threads of my rushed account, trying to find some reason. Finally she said, "I suppose...I suppose she just doesn't want to have to share Owen with anyone. Wen adores his father, and of course she has to share with him. But to bring yet another child into the world to make demands on Owen's time, well..."

"You mean, it's nothing to do with how Willa feels about her children?"

"Oh," Sara says, "it has everything, really. Some women marry men they care nothing about, knowing they will have children to love. But Willa loves Owen...it's funny, but we were just talking about that—Willa and Charles and I—about how Owen attracts women. But it's not just that, there is something about Owen that is not...how can I say it? Not forthcoming."

"Forthcoming?" I asked, not knowing what she meant.

"Not giving," she answered. "And something more," she rose and walked away from me, so I had to strain to hear, "Owen is afraid."

"Of what?" I wanted to know, worried that she had some knowledge I did not.

"Just afraid," she answered vaguely, "all the time."

"I don't understand," I said, prodding her, not willing to let this sentence trail off.

"It is, well . . . Willa loves Owen in a great, wanting way, a way I think he can't meet."

"Can't?" I asked.

"Yes, can't." Sara frowned and made an effort to be more explicit: "Except on the surface, Owen is really not all that different from all the other men of substance, the business barons. He is driven in the same way to make a substantial fortune—money for the sake of money—and to have his name on buildings and philanthropic works. He wants to wield some political power, perhaps. He wants sons, a loving family. Nothing so very different, actually. What is different, and complicating for Owen, is his health. In spite of how he looks, he *is* fragile. Willa knows it, even if she won't admit she does. Owen is scarcely into his thirties, yet he is aware of his own mortality in a way the rest of us are not. It pushes him, that knowledge. It makes him want to accomplish everything now, it makes him need to move fast. And he knows he has a limited amount of energy, that he must conserve it. Which means he must choose, must eliminate all waste motion . . . and emotion. Willa wants more than Owen can give, she wants it all. It hurts, loving like that."

I looked hard at Sara then. She turned her face away from me, but I pulled it back. I made her look at me, and when she did . . . when she turned her eyes to me, I heard a small quick intake of breath, an exclamation of sorts, and for a time I did not realize that the sound was mine.

"Oh, Sara," I said, out of breath, "who?"

I knew, of course. Charles. It had to be Charles.

"You love him?" I asked, knowing that I had to hear it.

"Yes," she answered calmly, her eyes steady on me, wide and dark, the pupils dilated, black on black.

"Does he know?" I asked.

She answered, "Yes."

I took a very deep breath, feeling tired, terribly tired, and tried to keep the pity from my eyes.

"And he?" I asked.

"He is in love with Helen Emory," she said evenly, relating a fact. "They spend as much time together as they can—my presence, of course, makes that possible."

"Sara," I said, more sharply than I had intended, "why?" I wanted to shake her, to slap her, to do anything to stop that even, accepting tone.

"Why not?" she answered, "What have I to say about it? No more than you have to say about Owen bedding Willa. No more than you have to say about Willa's feelings for her child."

Sara's eyes seemed to grow, to get larger. Her face, close to mine, expanded. Dark circles moved about the periphery of my vision and slowly, slowly began to shut down, close in, until all I could see were her eyes, huge and hurt, black on black.

Suddenly, Willa was there, fanning me.

"Too much excitement," she said, "these stupid, silly parties are too much altogether, sweet girl. Are you feeling better now, dear?"

"Sara!" I called out, suddenly frantic that she might have left.

"I'm here," Sara answered from the darkness behind Willa. "I'm here, Lena," she said again, moving forward to take my hand.

"Please," I said, too weary to speak, slurring my words, "please, Sara, don't leave."

"Sara is staying," Willa said gently, "Owen went to see Helen and Charles to their carriage."

That made me start to cry, and I could not stop. I heard Sara say, then, "I'm going to stay here tonight, Willa. I'll sleep on the settee. You go along, please."

Sara stayed the whole of the month. In all of that time, she spoke of Charles and Helen in passing, as if our conversation had never happened, as if I didn't know. Twice I worked up my courage, determined to confront her, but the words stuck in my throat. And yet . . . and yet, it didn't come between us, it did not divide us. I don't know why.

"Whatever are you doing?" Willa asked Arcadia, a note of amused surprise in her voice. They were sitting on the floor of Wen's room—Arcadia and the child—stacking bars of Poor Man's Soap like so many blocks.

"...seven, eight, nine, ten..." Wen counted.

"Where did you get all of this—" Willa tried to keep from laughing, so that the words finally popped out, "—soap?"

"This...soap...as you say," Arcadia mimicked Willa, "belongs to the Señora. And these," she pointed to a stack of books, "belong to me."

Willa picked up each book in turn: *"Mill on the Floss, Jane Eyre, Deep Down, Tom Brown at School, East Lynne, Adam Bede*...Ummm," she said.

"Ummm?" Arcadia asked.

*"Tom Brown at School?"* Willa asked.

"It was part of the...gift."

"Gift?" Willa raised her eyebrows.

"The gift I got for buying twenty bars of Poor's Soap."

"But you said the soap was the Señora's," Willa reminded her wickedly, "so how can the books be yours?"

"The Señora never reads English," Arcadia shot back, and the two women, conspirators, laughed together.

The Señora had a great deal of money but she did not like to spend it. Arcadia had no money of her own, so she had found ways to get those things she wanted. Her inventiveness became a game—and some of these games required another address. Willa, of course, had been happy to oblige. Now she sat down to help Arcadia and Wen change the wrappings on the soap—sneezing in unison as the smell of the soap took them by surprise.

"This is terrible," Willa said to her friend. "No one will ever invite you anywhere, if you smell of this soap."

"I know," Arcadia answered, laughing through the tears the soap brought to her eyes. "I'm afraid I've caused a bit of a problem this time."

"Well, you can go camping with us if you stay in another tent," Willa said.

"Camping?" Wen called out, "camping to the Malibu?"

"Yes," Willa answered, smiling at her son.

"When?" Wen and Arcadia asked in unison.

"Papa says day after tomorrow, if the weather holds..." Willa said, but Wen was already out the door, his short legs churning, running, pounding up the stairs on his way to his father's study. He sounded a long, loud "Whoooeee" that carried throughout the house.

"It is good to see him happy," Arcadia said.

"Yes," Willa answered, looking at the door through which Wen had just run, her hand poised lightly on her stomach.

Arcadia noticed. "Willa," she said quietly, "are you going to have another baby?"

Willa looked at her, surprised.

"How did you know?" she asked.

"Your hand," her friend answered, "the way you have it there, where the baby is. Women do that."

Willa sighed. "I haven't told anyone yet, not even Owen."

"He will be ecstatic," Arcadia answered.

"I know," Willa said, "it's just that, well, I want to be quiet about it still, for a while."

Arcadia nodded. She didn't understand, but it didn't matter. Arcadia did not always need answers.


"We have no say about it whatsoever," Owen was saying as he checked the cinch on his big roan. "The sea will pull back for a few hours and let us in—*mirabile dictu*—but it won't wait. We go in at lower low tide, my friends, or we don't go in at all." He lifted easily into his saddle and turned, startled to see that the rest of us were mounted and waiting for him.

*"Mirabile dictu,"* the laughter spilled out of Arcadia, and the rest of us—even usually somber Ignacio—joined in.

It was dark, still, as we made our way north along the beach. It looked as if it should be chill, but it wasn't. The air lay gentle against our skin, cool but not cold. The lower low tide was at dawn. We would have to make our way through the Natural Arch and on past Topanga Canyon by the first light.

"We look like a gypsy caravan," Willa called back to us. She and Owen led, riding side by side. They were followed by the wagon.

Wen sat between Ignacio and Trinidad on the front seat while little Aleja rode in the back. On the hard sand, where the riding was easy, Ignacio let the boy hold the reins. In a small voice made shrill, Wen called out to the team: "Watch it there, Maude. Move on, Nell." Wen's pony, Jack, was tied to the back of the wagon.

Arcadia and I formed the rear guard. We rode at a good

pace, urged on by Owen and the relentlessness of the tides. Now and then Arcadia would look over to me and smile, and I would smile back to show that I, too, felt the excitement of this trip.

Owen, wearing a pale chamois shirt tied at the neck, urged us on. "Laugh all you like, Señorita," he called to Arcadia, "when you wash out to sea, I'll wave to you."

"And I'll write you a letter from China," Arcadia called back.

Our spirits were high. Ignacio began to sing, a low and beautiful and very sad song in Spanish. When he finished there was a long pause. Then Wen began, "Oh, Susanna, oh don't you cry for me . . ." all off key, but lively. Arcadia quickly joined in. Even Trinidad, who had no notion at all what the words were, clapped and laughed and shouted, "Oh, Susanna" on every stanza.

Ahead of us I saw Willa reach out to Owen. They rode side by side, holding hands. By the time the sun had turned the sea a glowing silver and pink, we had cleared the narrow, rocky passages where the mountains came down to the water, and were safe on the long, straight stretch of beach. Safe, and sealed off from the world beyond.

"It's like a secret kingdom, isn't it?" Arcadia asked. And it was. In all of California, I thought, this must be one of the last of the untouched places. This must be the farthest point.

We stood ankle-deep in sand and looked about us: The mountains stood close to the sea, leaving only a scant ribbon of land in between—but such a ribbon, such land. We stood, saying nothing at all, listening to the quiet.

The mountains were not covered with trees, but with chaparral, so it seemed they had been smoothed, shaped by some giant hand. The sounds were those of the ocean, punctuated by a birdsong, and now by the low snorting of our animals.

The day would be clear and bright. We could mark the far line where the deep blue of the water met the lighter blue of the sky.

Willa was standing, face raised, looking all about her. I realized that this was the first time she and Owen had seen it together. Owen was watching her.

"Do you feel up to riding another half hour or so?" he asked. "There is a place I want you to see."

We stayed to establish camp on the beach. Owen and Willa picked their way up the dry creekbed, their horses moving carefully over the rocks. Soon they were climbing, and it became necessary to ride single file through the shrubbery. Then, without warning, they came into a clearing.

"Look," Owen said, lifting his arm. Below them was the sand and the sea, a long curve of it, buff and smoky blue in the distance. Above and behind them was the safe embrace of the mountains.

"Owen," she breathed out, "this is . . . exquisite."

"I know," he said, looking at her, pleased. "I discovered it on my last trip up here, and decided I would save it for you."

They dismounted and walked to where the view was open.

A peculiar sensation traveled up Willa's spine; she caught her breath with a small intake of air.

"What is it?" Owen wanted to know.

"I'm not sure," she told him, with an embarrassed laugh, "I feel so *safe* here," she said, wonder in her voice, "and that is strange, because I can't remember ever not having felt safe before . . . I'm not certain . . ."

Owen interrupted her to say, "I feel it too. I suppose we feel that way because we are safe—the mountains to our back, the sea to our front—sealing off almost all entrance. If we should ever move up here, this would be a good place for a house, don't you think?"

She looked at him. She did not know he had thought of moving to the Malibu; it was the first he had said of it. Perhaps he had only thought of it now.

"Yes," she said, "perfect."

"This land is truly virgin . . . undefiled," he went on.

"Do virgins tempt you?" she asked, so that he could not tell if she were teasing.

He was about to continue, but stopped.

"I do sometimes wonder," she went on, archly.

"Come here," he said, "sit on my knee and talk to me of virgins." He pulled her toward a fallen log which lay, like a pillow, looking out over the valley.

She began to undo the buttons on her blouse. He helped her, pulling the fabric back, releasing her breasts. He slipped his hand under one breast, bent his head and began to touch the nipple with his lips.

She looked to the sky, breathing deeply, loving the weight of his head on her breast, loving him, feeling herself warm and moist and ready.

They lay together for a long while, watching the sun poised high over them, crossed once by the unmistakable flight of a falcon. "A peregrine," she said to him, and he turned to watch with her as the bird caught a thermal and rose with it, up and up, soaring high until they could see only the place where it had been, the smallest dot on the blue.

"Do you know that in Spanish *peregrino* means 'wonderful'?" he asked.

And she answered, "Then let's call this Peregrino Hill."

She lay her head against his chest and closed her eyes, pretending to doze so that they might stay longer, knowing that they would have to leave soon, very soon.

"You are listening," he said.

"I'm listening to your heartbeats, counting them against the crash of the waves on the shore."

"Ah," he had answered, "against the beating of the ocean's heart."

Willa knew then, she told herself so she would remember, that she was as happy as it was possible to be. And she knew, too, that she had the power to make this man who lay with her, his heart beating in rhythm with the sea, happy too.

"I am going to have a child," she said, and she watched his face, saw the softness come into it, saw the tears rising.

He could not speak, but only pulled her to him and held her, and their bodies were together, she was with him as she had always wanted to be.

# Book II

## Rancho Malibu y Sequit:
### The Early Years,
### 1893 - 1895

# ～ *Chapter Six*

Trinidad moved heavily to a place behind a large rock, sheltered from the breeze that had come up off the water, out of sight but not out of sound of the rest of our party. Behind the rocks it was still and the sun felt warm on our skin.

Trinidad, grown heavy, fumbled with the front of her dress and, after much grunting and heaving, managed to free both of her great, pendulous brown breasts.

*"Uno momento,"* she said to the squirming baby perched on her hip. "Little one, do not bite your *mamacita*."

"Ah, the . . ." she searched for the word, "the tooths . . . already Pablito has the tooths."

With Pablito firmly attached to her left breast, she reached for Thad, waiting patiently, as ever. I handed him to her, holding on to him until he was tucked under her right breast, where the milk was flowing already, wetting his tiny chin. It took Thad a while to get started. Trinidad had to coax him.

"You eat, little baby boy," she scolded. "You need for to get big like my Pablito."

"Pablito's twice the size of Thad," I told her. "It's hard to believe that he's only two weeks younger."

*"Pobre* T'ad," she said. Poor Thad.

"Why are we always saying 'Poor Thad'?" I wondered out

121

loud, but Trinidad did not answer. It was not the sort of thing she thought about.

Sitting in the soft sand, we stretched our legs to the sun, secure in our privacy, and talked about the babies. It was all Trinidad wanted to talk about. Willa called her "The Monumental Mother," and she was that—both in size and in spirit. At first I had been embarrassed at the sight of Trinidad's bare breasts with their enormous nipples, at the slurping and gasping and smacking noises the babies made when the milk began to flow, at the loud flatulence as they emptied their bowels. But none of it bothered Trinidad; it was all part of being a mama. She would laugh and clean their bottoms and love her babies.

She was proud of her milk, proud that she had plenty to feed both babies, proud even of her big, bulging body. With the birth of her second child, Trinidad had left girlhood behind her forever.

When their time was near, Willa had explained that her doctor would deliver both of the babies. At first Trinidad had pretended not to hear, not to understand. When Willa confronted her, Trinidad's face became set. Her eyebrows knit to form a single line across her face. She had spoken to the *comadrona*, she said. It was all arranged, it was as it should be . . . as it had been, as it would always be for her people. The *comadrona* would deliver her baby. Willa had scolded and fussed at her, had told her that she was being superstitious and selfish and ignorant. Willa had talked and talked, but it was as if she were speaking a language that Trinidad had never heard before.

And when her hour came, the old woman—the *comadrona*—went into her room. Three hours later she emerged with Pablito, big and brown with a thatch of wild black hair, and weighing twelve pounds. In a few more days, for all of Willa's sputtering, Trinidad was back in the kitchen, expecting to take over her chores.

It had not gone so well for Willa. Her labor began in the afternoon and went all the long night and throughout the next day. It was a difficult birth. When it was over and Thad was born, the doctor had said that Willa was fortunate, very fortunate. Willa did not look fortunate, she looked as if she had known all there was to know of pain. She was weary beyond comprehension, she told me.

Thad was a small baby. When the doctor handed him to me, minutes after his birth, I thought that he looked like nothing so much as a sad little newborn rabbit, wet and wizened, too frail to utter more than a pathetic little squeak.

Now, three months later, Willa had yet to shake the lethargy that had dogged her for months. The sand and the sea and the Malibu would help her regain her strength and her spirit, Owen was sure. Even little Thad was thriving in the warm sea air. He was small, but he seemed healthy.

Life on the ranch was as different from Seaside Avenue as Seaside Avenue had been from the prairie. Our days were long and sunlit, filled with the lulling work of the ranch, the peace of being in a place apart, the sounds of the sea over it all. The long horseback ride, timed to the tides, kept all but the most determined visitors away. Here, the world could be held at bay—which is just what Willa wanted.

Owen was caught up in the excitement of becoming a rancher. He could be found in his office, surrounded by seed catalogues and government booklets explaining the latest in farming methods, full of ideas and plans.

"This is to be a working cattle ranch," Owen liked to remind us, "but we are going to grow all of our own food, too." We were going to be self-sustaining. We were going to live on the land, on this island in time, as Owen liked to call it. He was beside himself; his enthusiasm was contagious. We were all, every one of us, actors in Owen's play. We went to sleep each night eager for morning.

Owen and Willa did not build their house on Peregrino Hill, but below it—closer to the ocean and the makeshift pier, more accessible to the creekbed which would, in all but the wet season, double as a road.

It was a frame house rather than the adobe Willa wanted, for practical reasons. "The Californios who know how to make the adobe bricks best," Owen explained, "also have a habit of doing things *mañana*." He wanted the house to go up fast, and for speed Owen trusted only Yankee workmen.

The house was two stories, not nearly so ornate as the place on Seaside Avenue, but sprawling, and with a veranda that reached around three sides. Wisteria vines were being trained to give shade. In many ways, this house was a merging of their tastes; the results were compatible.

Owen and Willa spent long hours together, planning. Since Willa grew up on a farm and had more experience, Owen often asked her advice. They were, perhaps for the first time, equals in an endeavor that did not involve simply the household. It was a new experience for Willa, a new position. Her body, too thin since Thad's birth, began to fill out, to soften. She did not always walk so briskly. Now and then she would even linger over her morning tea.

A new barn was built for the farm animals, with a special section for the growing array of family pets—including a deer which had been tamed, and which wore a red and white kerchief around its neck. Owen had insisted the barn be painted a bright red because, as Willa told me, giggling, "He just has always loved red barns." It would take only a few seasons for the winter rains and the summer sun to bleach it a deep rose, a color which seemed better to fit the mood of this warm place.

Sundays were for rest. In the morning we would gather in the front parlor where Owen would read from the scriptures. In the summer and spring, Willa would go out into the fields and return with armloads of wildflowers—filling the fireplaces and vases everywhere with lilac and wild tiger-lilies or mock orange or, sometimes, simply the shining leaves of the goose-berry plant. As I played the organ, Owen would lead the singing, booming out the old songs, the hymns he loved, with Willa joining in her lovely contralto.

The ranch hands were Catholic, most of them, but they would gather outside the windows to listen on Sunday morning. Owen was certain they came out of respect for our religion. I thought they came to hear the songs, and the fervor with which Owen attacked them. *Hallelujah! Thine the glory!* he would sing, *Hallelujah! Amen! Hallelujah, Thine the glory. Revive us again.*

If the weather was at all good, as it was most of the time, we would go to the beach in the afternoon for a picnic that would last until the sun fell into the sea. The wagon would be packed with food and drink, bathing clothes and blankets, and we would all proceed—horses and animals and children in-termingled—to one of our favorite beaches.

Usually we went to a sheltered cove a scant half mile from the house. Here the waves did not pound the shore but were deflected by a reef so we could bathe in the warm, shallow water. Wen could dig holes and splash about, the dogs could fetch, endlessly, a stick thrown into the sea.

After harvest in the fall of that first year on the Malibu our brothers Val and Bernie came to visit. On their first Sunday with us, we arranged a picnic on a beach to the north of our sheltered cove, one where the waves rolled in with unimpeded strength.

Owen had returned from a trip to Hawaii with a long polished board which had been shaped something like a shark. In Hawaii, he explained, the Kanakas ride the waves on such a board.

"It takes a big man to maneuver this board," he said. "The Kanakas say there is great power in the surge of the wave." He thought that some of the ranch hands might want to ride the California waves. Willa could scarcely contain her desire to attempt it.

Like all prairie men, Val and Bernie could not get enough of the sea. Bernie had reached his full height of six feet and seven inches. His body was hard from the work of the farm and from his own need to test his physical limits in athletic contests. When Willa saw him she blurted, "I'll never ever win another race from you."

She did try, though. Willa was an exceptionally strong swimmer. She thought her experience in ocean swimming would give her an advantage. No sooner had we arrived at the beach than Willa and Bernie were in the water, swimming determinedly toward a far rock. Willa kept abreast of him almost all of the way, but you could see that she was making an effort, that she was swimming to her limit. It was only in the last ten yards that Bernie pulled ahead of her.

"Let's see what Bernie can do with this board," Owen said to Val, as the two men pulled the sleek piece of polished wood from the wagon.

"It looks dangerous," Val said.

"It is," Owen answered, "but it must also be exciting. You really should see someone ride one of these—it's as if they are flying over the water."

"Your wife is going to have to try it," Val said to Owen. Without looking up, Owen answered, "I suppose so. I haven't learned how to stop her."

"None of us ever knew how to do that," Val sympathized,

"but she's always stood up to her mistakes, I'll say that."

"Well," Owen answered, patting the board, "if she tries to ride this, I don't think she'll stand up very long. But I figure Bernie will be there to pull her out."

Later, Val would confide that he thought Owen figured things out better than we suspected.

Willa and Bernie spent most of the afternoon climbing in and out of the waves, carrying the long, gleaming board with them, trying to find a way to catch the rise of a wave and ride it all the way in. Finally, Willa gave up, exhausted. She waded ashore and flung herself on the blanket, her head in the shade of the parasol under which Thad lay. After a few moments she rolled over and kissed the baby's leg.

"You look like a big, ripe peach," she said to her son, and he beamed back a big baby smile.

"Madonna and Child," Owen said, settling himself on the blanket, careful to keep his white duck trousers away from Willa's wet swimdress.

"It's Mercury I'd really like to be," Willa answered. "If I had wings on my feet I could ride that monstrous board."

They watched as Bernie methodically stroked back out to the place beyond which the waves were breaking and prepared to try, once again. They watched as he held the board, crouching, ready to stand when he felt the water surge beneath him.

"Are you content?" Owen asked, not looking at her but squinting out to sea, to the place where Bernie waited for the wave.

"How can I be content," she joked, "when I couldn't make the waves work for me?"

"No," he answered softly, still not looking at her, "I mean . . . are you content?"

She didn't answer right away, but breathed in the soft sea air and let the breeze ruffle her hair.

"I am, yes," she said then, "I wish I could make you know just how content."

One of his hands stroked the blotched, pink skin of the baby's belly. "I was worried that you might feel too isolated on the ranch."

"But I'm a country girl," she answered.

"A country girl who could hardly wait to get out," he reminded her.

"It wasn't the farm I wanted to leave," she told him, "it wasn't even so much that I wanted to get away. I was just so ready to start, to get to . . . I was afraid that maybe . . . I needed to begin . . ."

"Begin what?" he wanted to know, now as confused as she.

She looked at him. Sometimes on these long beach afternoons the talk was idle, wandering.

She saw that he wanted an answer.

"A life, living, being part of whatever movement there was, finding some . . . well," she stumbled, "some center, the feeling of being where that would happen." As she fumbled for the words, Wen, who had been playing at the edge of the water, filled a small pail and started toward them, his face set, determined. He would be with them in a moment.

"Have you found it?" Owen asked, quickly.

"Yes!" she said, "Here, now—just this. Don't you see?"

Before he could tell her, Wen was upon them, sloshing water. At the same moment, Bernie raised himself on the board to his full height, his hands out for balance. He caught the wave and let it carry him, he seemed to skim over the water in one long, sustained, elegant motion.

"Look!" Willa shouted.

"Yes! That's it, that's it. Perfect!" Owen called.

The months that followed were like that first long, smooth ride on the wave . . . It was as if we were part of the ocean, part of the land, sun-drenched and full of the pleasure of work, the movement of life lived in the space between the mountains and the sea.

Owen was everywhere, whistling as he planned a fountain that would send water shooting into the air, welcoming anyone who came to the ranchhouse. He built a small artist's shed on a ridge that looked out over the sea, for those of us who liked to sketch. He learned all there was to learn about the best breeding methods for stock. He could tell you, to the pound, what heifers were bringing that season.

My regular Monday journal entries echoed the resonance of those years. Looking through them is like watching the morning sun rise over the mountains and reach low into one of the canyons that scored our land, illuminating the gentle wildness of the place.

I have but to leaf through the journals to see how rooted we were becoming in the Malibu.

*January 9, 1893:* Two weeks of rain have washed out sections of the wagon road so we must once again time our comings and goings to the tides. No matter. Neither Willa nor I have the least desire to go into Santa Monica. Of course, it did also delay Owen's homecoming—an aggravation to us all. In his last letter he asked Ignacio to meet him in Santa Monica with the wagon, so we are all wildly curious, knowing how Owen does love to surprise.

We got quite a start when Ignacio arrived without Owen, but with a very large smile on his face. Then we heard the whistle—Owen's special whistle which he uses to announce his arrival—and what should come wobbling up the path but Owen on a bicycle. He looked a fright! Weaving this way and that, not having mastered the skill and being altogether too large for the machine, so that his long legs angled awkwardly, almost up to his chin, with each revolution of the wheels.

Wen, who had posted himself on the veranda early in the morning, plunged headlong down the path, realizing that the bicycle was meant for him. Even so, nothing would do but that both Owen and Willa should have their turns, all the while Wen fussing at them to let him have a try.

"Give the child a turn," I chided his parents.

"Just one more minute, Wennie," Willa said, and then took a tumble into a briarbush.

"Serves you right, Willa Reade," I called to her.

"I suppose it does," she answered, trying to help Wen onto the contraption. But Wen, true to form, pushed her away. "I can do it," he insisted.

He couldn't, but that didn't matter to Wen. He spent the whole of the afternoon banging himself up quite thoroughly, but eventually he did master the two-wheeled thing. He is such a determined little boy, stolid like a locomotive. My offer to take him down to the hard sand on the beach to practice in safety went unheeded.

"Let him do it his way," Owen said, "I like the boy's spunk."

"I think you mistake stubbornness for spunk," I told him, but Owen only laughed and gave me a hearty "hello" embrace.

Owen brought with him a letter from Aunt Emma. Once more she says she is sorry, but the Captain is feeling too poorly to set out for a visit. She says that perhaps they will come to see us after the rains. I suppose we shall have to make the trip north again. No matter! They are such dears, I would travel the distance between the ranch and Monterey many times for them.

*January 23, 1893:* Happy Day! Thad, who has refused to say one solitary word—not even "Mama" or "Papa" in the eighteen months since his birth—said his first words, a full sentence! He said: "Where go Wen." As clear as day, he said it. I hugged and kissed him and shed a few tears of happiness, knowing that nothing is wrong with the child. He was happy to repeat the words to his mother and his father, both of whom praised him wildly.

*March 6, 1893:* Willa has managed to get herself in hot water again. In the current controversy over how women should ride a horse, sidesaddle or astride, she has taken the radical position that women should ride astride, and she has taken it publicly. In a letter to *Harper's Weekly* she detailed, with her usual straightforwardness, why it is neither safe, comfortable nor practical for those of us at the ranch to ride sidesaddle.

"The terrain," she wrote, "is mountainous in sections and there are deep ravines. We need sure-footed mounts and we need to be able to stay seated on them—especially when hunting or hawking." She signed herself "W.K. Reade, a rancher's wife."

The letter was published and the next issue carried six re-buttal letters, which the editor noted was only a small percentage of those received. Most agreed that cross-saddle was vulgar, showing a distinct lack of modesty. According to one English horsewoman, "Journalists short of 'copy' and women anxious for notoriety, periodically start the notion that ladies should adopt a man's saddle in preference to their own one. Anyone who takes up this idea seriously must be either mad or wholly ignorant." And Nannie O'Donoghue, who has written a whole book on the subject of the sidesaddle, wrote another scathing reply: "Modesty is, in my opinion, a woman's most exquisite attribute; once this, or the semblance of it, is lost, her fairest charm is gone. Nothing could be more ungraceful or more unwomanly than for women to ride like men . . . I maintain that a lady who knows how to sit has a far safer and surer seat on a sidesaddle than a man can ever have, and that her grip of the pommels affords her infinitely greater security than a man's 'grip of the knees.'"

Willa and I pored over the issue together, marveling at the tempest she had caused. "Such silliness," Willa said, "is hard for me to comprehend."

Owen, in New York at the time, learned about Willa's letter in a novel way.

"There I was," he told us when he returned on Tuesday, "sitting in the Olympic Club with John Bidwell—the Prohibitionist party's candidate for president, an old friend—and he hands me *Harper's Weekly* and says, wheezing, 'Now say there, Reade, you don't happen to know who this W.K. Reade woman is, do you?'"

Arcadia, who was visiting, widened her eyes and asked, "What did you say?"

"I said, 'Indeed not!'" Owen shot back. "I told him that the female members of my family were far too refined to do anything so extraordinarily vulgar." He stressed extraordinarily.

Willa looked at him fiercely. For a moment it looked as if she might fly into a rage. Then she saw the look of mock innocence in Owen's eyes, and we all had a good laugh.

*May 1, 1893:* Pa is ill. We do not know just how ill, because the letters from home are conflicting. If we are to believe Val, Papa is on his deathbed. Bernie, writing to me, paints a far more tempered picture, detailing some of Pa's problems—a shortness of breath, poor color, sweat on the brow—but he also says that Pa continues to direct the work of the farm from his bed. Mama's letters were no help at all, being, as they were, a curious mixture of recipes for the hearty soups she was making for Pa, complete with the medicinal qualities of each herb she used. She also gave us a detailed report on the weather for the past months, which she thinks has much to do with the course of the illness. Gib, whose letters are as spare as his words, said only that Pa was feeling "poorly," but the letter itself was an alarm.

*May 15, 1893:* Trinidad's baby was born at 11:25 this morning. It is a girl, ten pounds, to be called Marcella. Mother and child are fine. We do not feel that both Willa and I can be away at the same time, leaving Trinidad responsible for Wen and Thad as well as her three young ones. I will stay here while Willa returns to Springfield, traveling with Owen as he returns to Massachusetts on business.

*June 5, 1893:* Willa sends word that Pa is fully recovered and somewhat riled at what he calls "all the fuss" made over his illness. However, the doctors say that Pa has a weak heart and must not work so hard. "A man with so many sons shouldn't work at all," the doctor said, and Pa answered, "A man who does no work at all is not a man." When Willa told Owen what Pa had said, his eyes filled with tears.

"We are in Chicago now," Willa writes. "We will return before the end of the month. I can scarcely stand being away from all of you—and the ocean and the sun and the cool sea breezes. After a month in the Midwestern summer, I have come to think of the Malibu as paradise."

*September 11, 1893:* Aunt Emma and the Captain have finally come for a visit. I suppose we gave them little choice. On our last trip to Monterey we assured them that we could not come back until they came to see us on the Malibu. We are much excited, for they have not yet seen our little Thad. Being with Aunt Emma is strangely like visiting with both Mama and Pa.

Aunt Emma is a small, quiet woman with the most peaceful eyes imaginable. There is something about the way she looks at you that makes you know she will try to understand anything you might tell her. The Captain is bluff and hearty, a good-humored man who likes to play with the children. He was bouncing Thad on one knee when Pablito—a rousing big boy—marched up and firmly deposited himself on the other knee, expecting to be bounced in exactly the same manner. The poor Captain! I must say he rallied, not letting us coax Pablito away, but doing his best to give the massive child a ride.

For his part, Wen was happy to show off his prowess with the riata. He and some of the children of the ranch hands—Californios—spend much of their time practicing with the rope, swinging it over everything in sight, including each other.

Aunt Emma came to my room yesterday at four, having observed that to be the hour each day that I rest, the only time I am alone.

"I have promised your mother that I will speak with you," she said calmly. "She wants me to tell her how you are. I had not thought that I would need to ask, but I do."

I could feel my face burn. I felt ashamed, why I do not know.

"I have pain," I told her, "but less so than at home in Illinois.

The heat and the dry climate help, I believe. Is that what you want to know?"

"In part," she said thoughtfully. "I had guessed as much. I notice that when you are in Monterey, where it is damper, you seem to move with more difficulty than you have here, and I plan to tell your mama that. But the thing I wonder is—do you have full charge of the boys?"

I was startled at the question. What could she be thinking?

"No, of course not," I told her. "I do spend quite a lot of time with them. But Willa has a regular time each day with each of the boys. She makes a point of it. And Owen, well the children adore their father and he is, I think, the most loving man to his boys I've ever seen . . . when he is here."

"When he is here," she repeated.

"But that is a great deal of the time now. Owen has taken to ranching . . ."

"Owen is a good man, yes indeed," she said in her kindly way, "I've always known that to be." When she looked at me, her gray eyes were full of light. "The children are lucky to have such an auntie," she said, patting my hand.

"And I am lucky to have them," I answered, in a very small voice, knowing that she would know what I meant, this childless woman who had been banished to California before she could see any of her dear friend's children born.

"Oh, yes, yes indeed," she answered. For a moment I thought she had something more to say, and I waited.

When she said nothing, I told her, "Willa and Owen will be going East again in the spring. I plan to go with them as far as Chicago, and take the two boys to see their grandparents."

I did not say that I was taking the boys so that I would have a reason to return. I did not tell her that I had not gone back to Illinois for fear that I would not be allowed to leave.

*December 18, 1893:* Arcadia has come for a few days before Christmas, but she must return to spend Christmas Eve and Day with the Señora, much of it praying in the damp old Mission. Sara is here, too, with Charles, and they will stay through the holidays. The house is decorated with great boughs of evergreen and orange berry bushes. It has been perfectly clear, bright, bracing weather, sharp and cool in the early mornings.

Willa and Arcadia take long rides into the hills. Willa is

tracking a gyrfalcon, rare to this territory. She feels it must have been swept off course by the recent windstorms that have plagued the Southwest.

We cannot walk on the beach without having asphaltum appear on the bottoms of our shoes. It lies under the sand so we cannot see it until it appears, a sticky black mess, on our feet and shoes. An oil well spurts from beneath the ocean off the coast north of us. When the petroleum evaporates the asphaltum is left. In some places, it is mixed with sand and applied to form a very smooth roadbed.

Charles and Owen are as thick as thieves, having entered into some new oil leases in Ventura County. One day, they tell the rest of us, Western oil wells will prove as profitable as those in Pennsylvania. When I suggested they go into the business of harvesting the asphaltum from the beach, both men allowed as how there might be a "tidy" profit to be made there. I know full well that neither is interested in "tidy" profits.

The two have become known as the "terrible twins" in Los Angeles business circles, Willa told me. Indeed, they do always seem to be two steps ahead of everyone. Lately they have been talking about water rights and electricity. Los Angeles is amply supplied with water by its artesian wells, so I am not sure why they are talking water. As for electricity, well . . . Los Angeles has had electric lights for a number of years, but I can't believe that it is anything more than a spectacle—and a dear one, at that.

Charles is much involved in the municipal railway, which I must admit is proving to be a marvelous asset for Los Angeles and all the surrounding towns. You can, if you wish, play in the snow on Mt. Lowe in the morning and that same afternoon swim in the ocean—all because of the railway. Owen tells us that those big red cars have made Charles a rich man on his own, quite apart from Phineas' many millions. To which Willa answered, caustically, "That must give Charles a bit of room to breathe."

I only wish that Sara's fortune were not controlled by Phineas Emory. But Sara brought wonderful news—the best Christmas gift I could hope for. She is moving to Los Angeles. She will take up residence in the Palms, a hotel only a short distance from Charles' home in Pasadena. She has told me often enough how much she longs to live in our southland,

closer to those she cares most about in this world: Me, Willa
and Owen and, of course, Charles.

Sara seldom speaks of Helen. I do know that Helen has not
come to visit for some months, because I have asked Sara. She
is vague and says she doesn't know why, but that it is perfectly
agreeable to her that Helen stay at home and keep Phineas
Emory company. I say "amen" to that.

*April 9, 1894, Porter Farm, Springfield, Illinois:* With Willa
and Owen in Europe, the boys and I are visiting Mama and Pa
and my brothers. We came as far as Chicago with Willa and
Owen. Gib met us, and brought us to the farm. Thad and Wen
are having a wonderful time with their uncles. The puppet show
last evening had a grand finale which featured two new puppets—Wen and Thad. They were beside themselves with joy,
and their pealing children's laughter more than repaid their
uncles for the trouble.

Mama and Pa are well. Everything is changed and nothing
changes. Mama scarcely leaves the house, but I have discovered
that in time of real need, she can.

Soon after we arrived Thad chased a ball into the barnyard.
I was in the smokehouse at the time, but Mama was watching
from the kitchen window. She saw three mules break loose
from Persia and gallop full out toward the barnyard, and Thad.
I came out of the smokehouse in time to see Mama race through
the gate, snatch up Thad and wave off the mules with a towel
she was carrying. My heart was pumping madly. Even so, I
remember thinking that I could hardly believe such a heavy
woman could move as fast as Mama had moved.

Holding a bawling Thad out to me she said, "Go to your
Mama." She makes that mistake often, I suppose because she
has never seen Thad and Wen with Willa.

*April 23, 1894:* Willa writes from London: "The winter
crossing on the *Kaiser Wilhelm Der Grosse* was not the most
felicitous. Owen, for some profane reason, was not at all troubled by *malaise de mer,* as the French so euphoniously refer
to what must be the world's most wretched condition. Even
when half the crew were turning a bizarre shade of green, Owen
could still eat tins of oysters, for which I am having a great
deal of trouble forgiving him. I quite thought I would die and
at one point made preparations for just such an event. (You
will be pleased to learn that you are to have that exquisite single

strand of pearls Grandmother left me.)

"After three miserable days the seas calmed and I was able to consider the possibility of surviving. (I refuse, however, to consider the return journey and I am trying to devise some other way of returning to my native shores.)

"We are staying as guests in the home of Mr. Thomas Bayard and his wife Mary. (He is our ambassador to England.) You can rest assured that our accommodations are elegant, indeed. We have also been entertained by Mr. and Mrs. Henry White. Mr. White is with our embassy, and is a long-time friend of Owen's. Mrs. White is an *impressive*-looking lady. Recently she was painted by an American artist who has chosen to spend his life in the rare social circles of Paris and London. His name is John Singer Sargent. He has become quite in demand as a portraitist, and nothing would do but that Owen should commission Mr. Sargent to paint my picture.

"When Owen said this to Mrs. White she lowered her eyes and murmured something to the effect that she was sure that, once the artist had seen Owen, he would want to paint him. I said I thought that a thumping good idea. Can't you see a portrait of Owen over the breakfront in the dining room? It is the perfect place for a dramatic oil painting in the style of Velázquez. Wouldn't Owen have fun playing the Spanish Don?

"At any rate, it was arranged that Mr. Sargent should come to tea at the Whites', clearly to have a look at me. The talk is that Sargent is able to paint not just one's likeness, but one's *character*—hence one must have a certain amount of courage to sit for the man.

"For quite a long while the artist said nothing. He studied me quite openly, as a seamstress might have, had she been commissioned to create a gown. I decided that either I could blush and feel foolish, or I could look at him directly in order to make his assessment of my physiognomy as brief as possible. This I did.

"Finally, he announced that he would paint me in a green gown, that I would need to wear my hair pulled up and back in a Grecian mode, and that he would start in one week. I must, of course, agree to stay so long as he felt necessary. He did not mention the fee, but I know it to be enormous.

"I do honestly believe Mrs. White was shocked and mortified when I told Mr. Sargent I had no intention of agreeing to any of his conditions. 'I look bilious in green,' I said. 'It is my least favorite color, except as it appears in nature. And I choose to wear my hair in this style. I haven't the slightest plan to alter it, ever, certainly not for what might prove to be a record for future generations.' I was then quick to add that both those matters were trivial when put next to the time. I explained that I have two small boys to return to—and some soft sea sounds, and the hazy winter sun of the Malibu.

"I have been told that Mr. Sargent is difficult to converse with, that during sittings he goes for hours without murmuring a word. And yet, when I began to describe the Malibu to him, he listened with the most thoughtful attention, which I feel certain was not feigned. I tried to explain to him how bright the California light can be, how at certain hours a dark expanse of clouds can seem a perfect gray, and then a flock of sea birds will wheel in unison, flashing in a sudden burst of light. I told him how, as the birds wheel and turn, they glitter against the darkened sky, seeming to disappear only to flash silver, once more.

"To which the artist said, 'I should very much like to paint those strange lavender flecks in your eyes when you speak of California.' Truly! That is what he said. Can you imagine— lavender flecks of light? Artists do say peculiar things. Though in fact, Mrs. White tells me that Mr. Sargent has an absolutely shocking picture of a woman in his studio, and her whole upper torso is tinted lavender. I should love to see it.

"I am talking on so about Mr. Sargent, when there is so much else to tell you about London and Paris and Rome. Why do I find myself thinking so about California? Why do I find it so much more . . . what? Healthy, perhaps. The light, the sun and the sky, the air, riding horseback through a canyon, steep walls on both sides. Oh, I am so very homesick for you all.

"Owen, while at first much annoyed with me—not only for not agreeing to Mr. Sargent's outrageous terms, but for not agreeing in what Owen (and the Whites) considered an out-rageous way—changed his mind when the chill and cold of London sent him to bed with fever and cramps. Tomorrow we return to Italy, where the weather is much more agreeable. Oh but how I wish we were leaving for home . . . but it will be yet another month until my Grand Tour is complete. I hope that it is enough to earn me a reputation as being 'adequately traveled,' as Owen puts it, and that I can come home and stay there. The only advantage to travel, as I see it, is that I have my husband very much to myself between stops."

*May 21, 1894:* Owen and Willa returned on Sunday, four months almost to the day since their departure. We stood on the veranda to meet them. When Owen sounded his whistle, I gave the boys a push and told them to run and meet their mama and papa. They stayed frozen to me, Thad even hiding behind my skirts. Wen greeted his parents as if they were distant relatives to whom he should be polite. I felt so terrible for Owen, who obviously had been looking forward to the hugs and kisses and wild yelps he always gets. But he has never been gone so long before.

*June 11, 1894:* Willa lost the baby, a girl, almost before she had become accustomed to the idea of having another child. Owen has given her the most beautiful chestnut mare, which she calls Princess. With it came a special Mexican saddle, wonderfully worked by an old man in Redondo. It is a cross-saddle. "Sitting astride is safer," Owen told Willa, "I cannot have anything happen to you, not ever." He treats her with such tenderness; it is good to see.

Arcadia arrived with news to cheer us all. She came only days after the loss of the baby, when Willa was still too weak to leave her bed. Arcadia bounced in, breathless. Learning of Willa's loss, she quickly rearranged her face, but it was impossible for Arcadia to suppress her happiness.

"Tell me," Willa said, squeezing her friend's hand.

"I feel wonderful, Willa," she answered, and Willa said to that:

"You have met a young man."

"However did you guess?" Arcadia laughed, leaning over to hug Willa.

"His name is Joseph Brennan, he is a lawyer, a graduate of Fordham. He is from a family known to the Señora." (Here, Arcadia raised her eyebrows.) "He is handsome, and he has a very bright future. Not only that," Arcadia spilled out, "he has wonderful great brown eyes, quite as beautiful as Owen's, and he makes my spine tingle."

"Tingle?" Willa teased, smiling for the first time in days.

Arcadia's answer was a rippling laugh that washed over us all.

She had met Joseph Brennan in Rochester, New York, while visiting there with the Señora. They had stayed in his grand-aunt's home. He had walked into the room that first time, Arcadia told us, and bowed to his grandaunt; then he had bowed low to the Señora, then he had turned to her.

"And he never turned away?" I asked.

"Not really," Arcadia said, "I quite took him by surprise. The Señora scolded him for staring at me."

"This does sound serious," Willa told her, "can we expect a wedding?"

"Ah," Arcadia answered, "La Señora says it would be best if we become better acquainted."

"But how can you, with him in Rochester?" Willa wanted to know.

"Didn't I mention?" Arcadia answered triumphantly, "he is moving to Los Angeles!"

*July 9, 1894:* We had a great celebration on the beach for the Fourth of July. We cooked a pig and a lamb in open pits, we had flags and fireworks over the water. One of our guests, a businessman named Philpott, brought along several bottles of wine—not knowing Owen's aversion to spirits of any kind. Willa managed to purloin a bottle which she, Arcadia, Sara and I took to a cave we had discovered. It made us all feel quite naughty. Sara even suggested that we have a secret society, and on the Fourth of July each year we steal a bottle of wine and drink it all down, just as we had on this day. We all said "Hear, hear," and toasted each other. What good friends we are!

*August 6, 1894:* It has been hot and close all week; even the children lie about in the heat, it saps our energy. Sara has come for a visit. I felt that she was withholding something on her last visit. Now I know. She came alone this time, without even the usual servant to keep her company on the long ride. Owen is away, and Willa has been hawking every day for almost a week, heat or no. No one was about, but still Sara insisted we should go to the artist's shack to talk.

From her saddlebag she took a flask of wine. "Warm and travel-weary," she said, "but good enough for a toast."

"Your news requires a toast?" I asked.

She smiled wearily. "I hope so," she said.

I waited as she poured two large tumblers of wine.

"Here's to me," she said, "and to Charles."

I waited while she drank.

"We are to be married," she said.

For a moment I could think of nothing to say; words whirled around in my head; it did not make sense.

"How?" I asked, stupefied, "When . . . how did . . ."

"How did this happen?" she finished for me.

She rubbed the back of her neck as if it were sore, as if it hurt. Then she moved her head in a small circle, as if trying to make it more limber, as if trying to make it sit easier on her neck.

"Let me start from the beginning," she finally said. "I have told you, I believe, that my father was in his sixties when he married my mother. He was a widower, childless. My birth was, then, evidence that he was not impotent. Of course it killed my mother, but Father was left with his living proof. Sad to say he didn't enjoy it very long. When Father died, Phineas became my guardian so that Father's part of the business, which was substantial, should not slip from his grasp. Now I am to become Charles' wife, to insure that he will be Phineas' heir. Once again, my physical presence is important to various others in various ways."

I could feel the anger rising. I took a drink of the wine and felt like spitting it at her.

"So. Is the marriage Charles' idea? Phineas' idea? Or your idea? Or do you ever allow yourself an idea?"

She ignored my insult. "All three," she said, "the idea belongs to all of us, for three very different reasons."

"You've told me their reasons," I said, my voice harsh. "Now I should like to hear yours."

She looked at me with her wide, dark eyes and she said, "It's my only chance to live a normal life."

I caught my breath. "Normal," I all but shouted, "how can you possibly call it 'normal'?" I was amazed, aghast, horrified.

"By 'normal' I mean I would be marrying someone I care for—although I understand that he does not care about me in the same way. I would be, in the eyes of society at least, the wife of a substantial man in the community. But most of all, I would have a chance to have a child, and also a chance to be secure."

"A child?" I said, trying to understand. "Secure?"

"If I were married to Charles I would never have to worry about being left without funds. I do have to worry about that now. Father Emory controls my father's monies and he refuses, even, to speak to me about my inheritance. If he dies without specifying what I am to inherit, my fate will be in Helen's hands. I cannot allow that."

I started to weep, I couldn't help it.

"Don't," Sara said, her arms around me, "please, don't. I need you now, more than ever. I worried about telling you the truth, for fear you would have nothing more to do with me. But I need you, I don't think I can do it without you . . . please, Lena . . ."

I hugged her to me and told her that perhaps she was wrong, perhaps Charles has loved her all along and she hasn't known it. I told her that I was sure Charles had been more attentive to her of late, I reminded her of all the times I had seen him look at her with affection. She patted my hand and said, "perhaps," in a way that made me know she didn't believe what I was saying, but would allow me to believe it.

*August 27, 1894:* I have not spoken to Willa about Sara other than to tell her—at Sara's direction—that she and Charles are to be married. Neither Willa nor Owen seemed particularly surprised at the news—but then, they do not know all that I know. I long to confide in Willa, to get from her some idea of the course of action I should take. Sara did not exact a pledge of silence from me, but I know that she takes my confidence for granted, and I must not fail her. (But am I failing her by not speaking out?)

I do not think it can be a coincidence, yet it must be. The most remarkable thing has happened . . . On Wednesday last, before Owen left for Los Angeles, he perched himself on the corner of the desk where I was working and cleared his throat in the manner of someone who has something important to say.

"I want you to know about something I am doing today, at my solicitors' in Los Angeles," he began.

I looked up, waiting, only mildly curious.

"You well know that I have a substantial income . . . I have been lucky, fortunate in that. And I feel that since you are a part of this family, you should share in that good fortune."

I wondered what in the world he was talking about, my sharing in his good fortune.

"So," he said, clasping his hands on his knee, "I am putting aside trust funds for the boys and for you. I will administer the boys' trusts, but I have no control whatsoever over yours and neither will Willa nor anyone else."

"Owen, no . . ." I began, but he cut me off.

"Lena, you have earned it already, I'm not giving you anything. The children, well . . . I don't know what they would do without you. But I mean to make you financially independent. That way, you will always be secure—no matter what turn my fortunes may take."

I received the papers by mail. Owen has deposited, in my name, in the form of stocks and bonds, the sum of 70,000 dollars. When I got those papers, when I held them in my hands, I understood for the first time what Sara was talking about. Now I know what it means to be financially independent.

I should, of course, have realized that it was Willa's idea. When I confronted her she would only grin at me and say, "I think Owen is absolutely correct. Now I will know you are with us because you want to be. It frees me, don't you see?"

I could not help but think that Sara's impending marriage may have, in some subtle way, caused this new turn of events. Perhaps Willa has guessed: I cannot know without revealing what I will not reveal.

*September 10, 1894:* On Wednesday last I was at the far end of the orchard, at the small clearing near the houses where the *vaqueros* who have families live, watching Wen work the riata. The children were roping everything in sight: the dogs, Wen's pony Jack, our goat, the whole menagerie of pets Willa has assembled—even, sometimes, the family of pheasants who stay about the house, waiting for crumbs from the table.

The children were roping each other, whirling the riata over their heads, neatly swinging it so that the loop ranged wide, swinging and swinging and then, at the perfect moment, looping and pulling tight. It is wonderful to watch. And it is no wonder at all that the Californios grow up to be such fine *vaqueros*—very few Yankee cowboys can match their prowess on a horse, or with a rope. Wen, I think, may be the exception. He is not so graceful as his dark-skinned friends, but he is the most determined of the lot.

Standing there, watching, I caught sight of the covey of Chinese gardeners hurrying into the orchard, all but running with that funny little fast step. Owen says the Chinese are wizards in the orchard, and I am inclined to agree. This morning I had to blink my eyes: Towering above the rest of them by several heads was the biggest Celestial I have ever in my life seen. He must have been hired recently. Surely I would have noticed him had he been here very long.

I saw him again in the afternoon. Thad, who likes to sit with me in the arbor not far from our family garden, headed directly for the man. I soon saw the reason. The tall Chinaman was picking our second-crop strawberries, Thad's one great weakness.

"Wait, Thad," I called after him, but he is quick for such a small boy and his thin little legs were flying. By the time I pulled up, puffing, Thad's mouth was jammed with strawberry, the juice oozing out the sides, and on his face was an expression of pure delight.

"I am sorry," I said to the man, I haven't the slightest idea why. It occurred to me that he might not speak English. "Do you understand..." I began, slowly.

"Yes, I do," he answered in impeccable English.

Startled, I put my hand out for Thad, who scooted beyond my reach. I glared at the child.

"I hope you don't mind my giving the boy a berry," the Chinaman said in his remarkable Queen's English, "He asked for it so nicely, and as you can see..." and he smiled, "his enjoyment is overflowing."

I nodded at his small joke. I tried to think what to say next—what did one say to a Chinese who was six feet tall and spoke with a British accent?

"My father was in the British navy, in the port of Tsingtao. My mother was Chinese," he said.

"So many people ask?" I replied, surprised out of my confusion.

"Oh, yes, I'm an oddity among the Chinese, too—although they, as you, are much too polite to ask..."

The conversation ended there because Thad, a strawberry in each hand, was off for the arbor and there was nothing for me to do but follow. I am curious, however, and I will find out more about this strange, tall man who speaks so eloquently.

* * *

Two days later came another strange event. At midday the dogs set up a terrible barking, as they do when a stranger approaches. The St. Bernard's low bellows were punctuated by the collies' excited yelps. Before long a man appeared at the house gate. When he did not come through, but waited in the midst of the barking dogs, Willa went down to meet him, at first believing him to be one of the drifters who now and then find their way into the ranch, looking for work.

He was a thick-chested man in his middle years with a stubble of beard and stained teeth.

"I be Jacob Shurz," the man said to Willa as she quieted the dogs, "I come to see the Mister."

Jacob Shurz is the settler who lives in the mountains to the north. He homesteaded a small ranch and cut his own road through to the beach. Rather than take the longer public road to the east, on the other side of the mountains, he chooses to get his produce to the markets in Santa Monica by traveling the beach at low tide. Owen, who is continually adding to the ranch, recently bought the property through which Shurz' road was built. Willa had a good idea why the homesteader had finally come to call on us.

"Won't you come into the house?" she said, with the politeness one affords a neighbor. "My husband isn't here at the moment. He's in Philadelphia on business, but perhaps . . ."

"What I want to know," he said, making no move to come through the gate she held open for him, "is about my road."

"What about your road?" Willa asked, a trifle more formally.

"I've always passed free and clear," Shurz answered.

"I'm sure my husband will not change that," Willa said to the man, "my husband is a reasonable man."

"I dug that road and I keeps it clear," Shurz went on, as if he had been given an argument.

"I am sure you may continue to use the road," she said, a thin film of ice in her voice, adding, "even though it runs through our private property, so long as it is to bring the produce from your farm alone to Santa Monica."

She waited for a moment to see if he understood what she was saying, then went on, "You have our permission to use the new roadway we have cut along the beach, also, so long as you do not interfere with the work of our ranch."

"The beaches don't belong to you," the man countered.

Willa's back stiffened.

"The beach below the mean tide line is in the public domain," she corrected him. "That is not at issue here. I repeat: You may continue to use your road, but you would do well to remember that you pass at our pleasure."

He looked at her, turned his head and spit a long streak of tobacco juice which squarely hit one of the lizards that live near the rock by the gatepost.

"I've come to see the Mister," Shurz repeated.

Willa turned abruptly and walked toward the house; without turning she said, "Then you will have to return when he is here."

"When's that?" Shurz called after her, but she did not answer.

*In retrospect, leafing through the journals, I can almost draw a line of demarcation—a place where things started to go wrong. It was not any one action or event, but many; some were important, some not, but altogether they told, it seems to me now, that the good years were giving way, that we were about to enter a time of trouble.*

*October 8, 1894:* The heat is terrible. No sea breezes blow. Even the children lie about, lethargic. Yesterday Trinidad's little Marcella was sitting on the ground near the path to the bathhouse. Next to her, coiled, was a rattlesnake. Seeing it, Trinidad shrieked—a high, piercing cry that carried through the heavy air, slicing it, reverberating. Then there was the loud crack of a gun. The snake collapsed. Willa, seated still in her saddle, had shot the creature from twenty feet.

What is remarkable is this: I did not know that Willa possessed a gun, or that she could fire one.

*October 29, 1894:* The *Santanas* have been blowing for two days now, hot dry winds from the desert. Everything is dry, brittle. The taste of dust is in our mouths. It is too hot to eat, too hot to sleep, sleep is filled with bad dreams.

Tempers flare. Willa bit into a muffin and cracked a tooth on a bit of pecan shell which had been left in. She went into the kitchen and upbraided Trinidad without mercy. To avoid that scene I went outside and, to my surprise, startled Ignacio, who was listening, his face full of woe for his wife. It is difficult to surprise a man like Ignacio in the act of emotion.

"It's the *Santana*," I said to him. "My sister does not mean what she says." He only lowered his head and left. Strange, I thought, how these unrelenting winds flay us.

After that, Willa rode Princess into town and came back with play-pretties for each of Trinidad's children.

*January 7, 1895:* I am sick at heart, I do not know what to do. Owen is sending Wen away in the fall. He will go to a boarding school in Redlands; henceforth, he will be with us in the summers only. The child is scarcely seven years old! It is too soon! I do not understand, not at all.

Willa and I have been planning a school that was to begin this fall on the ranch. We have five children of school age, two of them older than Wen. Thad and Aleja and Pablito and the rest of Trinidad's growing tribe will need education. We were going to find a teacher, to use the beach cottage as our schoolhouse. Willa would give instruction in math and I in music. Owen knew of our plans, about which we have talked incessantly! But I think now, for the first time, that he has never joined in, never planned with us. Why did I not notice that at the time? Owen never intended for Wen to stay on the ranch for his schooling.

"Why?" I asked last evening. "Why," I said, "when Wen loves the ranch so? He is healthy and happy here, he needs to be with his family. It is not as if we aren't qualified to give him a good beginning education. Owen, you have one of the finest libraries in all of California here on the ranch..."

Owen's handsome face was set, his eyes opaque. There was to be no moving him, I could see.

"The boy needs friends his own age," he said.

It didn't make sense. Owen, to whom family meant so much. I looked at him, trying to understand.

He went on, "Wen needs to be with Anglo-Saxon children like himself."

"Anglo-Saxon?" I asked, dully, beginning to see.

"Yes," he repeated, in a tone I had seldom heard, "Californios are fine people in many ways, but they lack certain traits—energy, ambition, purpose. They are not an industrious people, and I do not want my son to be influenced by them."

"Have you ever explained this to Ignacio?" Willa suddenly

spoke. The vein on Owen's forehead stood out in sharp relief. I thought for a moment he was going to lash out, but when he spoke his voice was carefully modulated.

"We are not discussing Ignacio, but I think it would be well if you would remember . . ."

"Oh, I will remember, Owen," Willa said, her voice higher than usual. "Separate but equal as the Southern Senators like to say."

". . . if you will remember," Owen went on, "that I have amply rewarded Ignacio's exceptional service. He has a large house in which to rear his growing family."

It seemed to me—but I may be wrong—it seemed to me that Owen stressed the word "growing" ever so slightly.

"When is Wen to leave?" I asked, knowing even as I said it that I was admitting defeat.

"At the end of summer."

I went to my room then, and I have not left it since. A weight has settled on my chest. I have not been able to sleep, even though I have drunk half a bottle of Ayer's Cherry Pectoral, which almost always cures my insomnia. I wished that I had something to dull the time, to blot out everything.

Willa knocked on my door late in the afternoon. When I did not answer, she came in. I turned my face to the wall, hoping she would go away, but she did not. She sat there, her hands loose in her lap (I did not need to look at her to know that). After a while I knew she was not going to leave so I turned to her.

"Did you decide, or did Owen?" I wanted to know.

"He did," she answered, "but I agreed."

I waited awhile. There was something I had to say but I could not remember what it was, my mind was furred.

"You agreed? You?" That was it, that was what I could not pull out of my mind.

"But no one asked me," I blurted before she had time to answer. "I was supposed to share the children . . . and I have done my part, my share." I knew that, I was sure of it. "But I didn't have anything to say about it."

"Nor do I," Willa answered.

"It isn't right," I whimpered.

"No, it isn't," she agreed. "Wen is more your child than mine and so is Thad, and that is what Owen sees as the problem."

"Owen thinks I'm bad for the boys?" I cried, wounded.

"No," Willa answered in that same calm-cold tone, "he thinks they are too dependent on you, yes. But it's me he thinks bad for the boys."

I didn't know what she was saying, but she made me furious. *She had agreed.* That was all I needed to know.

"He's not seven years old and he needs to be here with us—it is too soon to send him away," I insisted.

"I know, I'm sorry," Willa said.

"Are you?" I asked, my voice shaking. "Are you really?"

I turned my face to the wall again. When I awoke, she was gone.

*March 11, 1895:* Ignacio's brother arrived from Mexico yesterday with sad news. Their mother is gravely ill, she wants to see her son before she dies. The brother rested a few hours, then returned—without Ignacio. The spring rodeo is to be held next week, we could not manage without him. Owen did not actually tell him he could not go. He shook his head in sorrow, but he did not say to Ignacio that he must leave, that somehow we would do the rodeo without him. (It has been so long since Owen took an active part in the ranch that I think he could not lead the rodeo, and Ignacio has trained no one to take his place.)

Everything happens at once. For many months, now, Owen has planned to leave on the morning after the rodeo for a business trip which will keep him away for months. He must attend the board of directors' meetings for several companies, he must deliver a speech at his alma mater, he is to attend to family business in Massachusetts, where he has funded a school for the blind and another for orphans. At one of these, he will unveil a statue of himself. Then he is to go on to England where he will advise several companies with large holdings in the American West.

This time Willa will not be crossing the Atlantic with him. This time, she did not want to go. There are good reasons why she should stay, of course. But I am not sure any of those reasons apply. I am not sure of very much, anymore.

## ~~ *Chapter Seven*

Excitement was seeping through the house. You could feel it rising out of the floorboards. Something about it—the expectation, I suppose—was sensuous and sharp, so that it was not hard to come awake. The fragrance of wood burning in the big cookstove drifted up from the kitchen. Ignacio would have started the fire even earlier than usual this morning—hoping that he and Trinidad could have a solitary morning meal together before the rest of the house was awake. But that was not going to happen this day. On rodeo day nothing was as usual. I dressed in the dark, pulling on my riding skirt and a sweater against the March chill.

Willa was in the kitchen. Even the serving girls—sluggish on the best of days—were dressed and, amazingly, had splashed the matted sleep from their eyes.

"You can see the stars," Willa said as I entered.

"I know," I answered, "it's going to be beautiful and clear, just as soon as the sun reaches over the mountains."

Willa had not yet pulled her hair back into its trim bun and it tumbled, long and softly curling, about her shoulders as she leaned over the stove to retrieve a dish from the warmer. A few wispy curls fell forward and the heat flushed her face, giving it the color I had not, until that moment, realized was missing. She looked as pretty as ever I had seen her—Willa was prettier as a woman than she had been as a girl—and yet she was preoccupied. And there was that lateral frown line on her forehead.

Ignacio was sitting at the oak table that looks onto the garden, morosely chewing as Trinidad busied herself in the kitchen. Her mind would be racing, calculating all there was to do, seeing that the breakfast was served and done with so she could get on with the serious arrangements for the big meal that would follow the rodeo.

In the midst of all the bustle only Soo Lin seemed unperturbed. He stood at the stove, cooking. As I entered he bowed to me and when I bowed back, as I did each morning, he shook with what seemed to be repressed laughter.

As I had known, there was not going to be time for Ignacio and Trinidad to be alone and Ignacio did not like it, especially now, in his time of *la tristeza*—the sadness. He grumbled and left and Trinidad sighed. Now and then I had come upon them as they sat together early in the morning. Those were the only times I had seen Trinidad in total quiet, her hands peaceful in her lap.

As the rest of the house staff began to crowd into the kitchen, anxious to eat and get on with the day, Willa nodded for me to follow her into the family dining room. A noise from the landing stopped us. We stood in place, all of us, looking up at Owen at the top of the stairs, tall and studiously somber, all in black... black broadcloth suit, expertly tailored, white ruffled shirt and on his head the wide-brimmed hat of a Spanish Don. (Nothing colorful, nothing gaudy; black and white and dramatic. Spanish. Perfect. The effect, as Owen well knew, was stunning.)

The kitchen girls murmured what sounded to be an *Ave Maria.*

"*El Patrón,*" Willa said out loud, breaking the spell. There was affection in her tone and a hint of laughter, so the servants would know they were not expected to be worshipful, and so Owen would know that she knew he was play-acting. Owen was magnificent at play-acting and he loved celebrations.

The girls clapped their hands, delighted with the appearance of this elegant, beautiful-looking man who was so perfectly the *Patrón,* the protector. In bits of English and Spanish they said how *magnífico* was his dress, how *rumboso.*

Owen lifted his hat, grinning impishly, and followed us into the dining room, padding along in his bare feet. Owen disliked boots as much as he loved hats.

He bent to kiss Willa, running his fingers lightly up her arm. She shivered and pulled away.

"Sorry about last night, sweet," Owen said in too offhand a manner, "I seem to have fallen asleep in my little aerie again, face down on a beautiful *Danaus plexippus,* small wonder I didn't chloroform myself into oblivion. You'd have had to pin me to a page in my collection."

Willa did not smile.

*Again* . . . he had said *fallen asleep again.* I wondered how many nights he had slept in the little attic room he had taken to calling his "office," going over his collections, his butterflies and antique books; I wondered how often Willa slept alone in their big bed.

She brushed her hair back in a sudden, awkward gesture and asked him, "Must you leave tomorrow? Must you go?" Her hand was clenched into a fist and for an instant I expected her to slam it down on the lace that covered the table.

Owen covered her hand with his, not letting her pull away, and finally he said, "Listen to me, Willa. I have to go. You know that. You know how long it's been planned for me to give the address at Princeton, and you know about the meeting of the board of directors, not to mention . . ."

"Not to mention . . ." Willa said, resignation in her voice, "I know." She slumped back in her chair, her hands limp in her lap.

We ate in silence.

More and more often of late our meals were eaten in silence.

A year ago Willa would not have dreamed of asking Owen to cancel one of his business trips, not even a long trip as this one would surely be. He would have to travel to the East Coast, a full week's journey in itself. Even when Willa had been heavy with child she had not asked Owen to stay with her. Why would she ask him now?

"Shall I ask Ignacio to delay . . ." Owen began.

"No!" Willa cut him short, "you cannot. His mother is dying, she may be dead already. Ignacio and Trinidad must leave tomorrow." She hesitated, then added accusingly, "You have already asked them to delay once, for the rodeo."

That was part of the puzzle, I guessed—Willa had not thought Owen would ask Ignacio to stay for so clearly commercial a reason. The spring rodeo was the most important day of the year on the ranch—all the cattle would be gathered in from the far reaches of range to be counted. New calves would be branded, ears cut in the distinctive pattern of the ranch, inferior bulls would be castrated. On a ranch as large as Malibu y Sequit, it was a grueling job. It was Ignacio who could accomplish it most efficiently—he knew the men, knew who was capable of what job, knew how to get the best work out of them. Ignacio ran the ranch. Owen was the Yankee businessman, dedicated to making a profit.

"We'll need to ship some heifers in a few weeks, do you feel confident that I can manage a crew?" Willa asked.

Owen broke a large piece of bread, buttered it painstakingly, took a mouthful and chewed thoughtfully. Finally he said, "I think you can, of course . . . but you won't have to. I've hired a temporary foreman."

She looked at him a long moment, not troubling to conceal a cold anger. I quickly excused myself and left, annoyed that whatever was between them should affect me, wanting to be free of the weight of it, free to enjoy the rodeo. Still, I could not help but wonder why Owen would not have told her sooner, would not have discussed so important a matter with her.

Before I could escape to my room a girl was sent to bring me back. "Sorry, Lena," Owen said, "but I wanted to be sure you understood that you are to continue handling the bookkeeping. I'll be straight with you, I waited too long to find this new man. I guess I thought something would come up . . ."

Willa broke in, "You thought Ignacio's mother would cooperate and die, so he wouldn't have to leave."

Owen ignored her. "I don't know what I was thinking," he said to me, "but I will feel more comfortable knowing you are in charge of the books. I haven't even met the man myself. He's been working on Judge Steven's place in the San Joaquin and he couldn't get away. He sent word he'll be here as early as he can be today. He comes well recommended for his work, but I'm sorry that I haven't met him myself, to make my own judgment. I'm told the man is restless—sound, but restless."

"Restless?" Willa asked, "Do you count that a flaw in character, Owen?"

I was surprised at the edge of bitterness in her voice. Owen, it seemed, was not. Before he could answer, she asked, "Will he—this Irishman O'Connor—will he answer to me?"

Owen's jaw was set, but his answer was even. "His name is McCord. Connor McCord. And yes, I'll tell him to see you each morning for instructions, if you like." Owen was anxious to set things right, I could sense—he would be leaving tomorrow, and he did not want to leave with anger between them.

Thad ran into the room, his two-year-old legs churning, and flung himself into his father's arms. Owen caught the child and hugged him, giving him a noisy smack on the lips which made both of them laugh.

Willa rose and bent to blow out the lamp. In the first gray light of day I saw the pain in my sister's face and a shimmer of tears held back.

"Ignacio may be back sooner than expected," Owen said, nestling the child against him, stroking his back.

"Ignacio's mother is dying," Willa answered dully, "sometimes it takes a long time to die."

For a long moment Owen was silent. Then he said, "The *vaqueros* will be here soon. I need to get my boots." As he rose, holding Thad still, he knocked over a tumbler of water. He seemed not to notice.

We stood on the verandah of the ranch house, all of us in a kind of order, a tableau. Owen, as tall and imposing a *Patrón* as Malibu y Sequit had ever seen, I had no doubt; to his left, Ignacio, the *mayordomo;* to his right, *La Patróna,* her hair loose about her shoulders still. The rest of us formed groups behind them, and all watched to the west for the first sign of the *vaqueros.* The whole of the household was there, waiting— some standing in clusters in the farmyard. Our own *vaqueros* waited in the shadows to join those who migrated from ranch to ranch for these roundups.

We knew they were coming when the dogs at the gatehouse began to bark, the St. Bernard's low tones echoing up the canyon. As the first long shafts of light slanted over the mountains we saw them, first a glitter of silver on their saddles, then the dark figures riding slowly toward us. There were more than a dozen of them, measuring the light, riding to a rhythm dictated by the sea, by the surf which you could hear pounding against the beach, all the while moving inexorably closer. It was strangely stirring.

As the dawn light reached a luminous shade of pearl gray, the *vaqueros* arrived and silently moved their horses to form a single line in front of Owen. Our own men joined them silently, not calling out *hola*, not yet. Ned and Joe Lattimore, our two raw-boned Kentucky boys, the only American cowboys on the ranch, kicked their horses into the back row. In their brown work clothes the brothers looked awkward and out of place. The *vaqueros* were dressed in black, each with a white shirt. Many of their saddles were magnificently tooled and inlaid with silver. They sat their horses like centaurs, these men, these relics of another age in California. Before the Yankees came, the rodeo was a great occasion. Families would gather from miles around to gossip and eat and dance. The men would show their skills at riding and roping. Romances would happen, marriages be arranged. Now all that was left were the black suits, which the Spanish cowboys carried in their saddlebags, and the chance to display their skills at roping and riding, branding and cutting... The Yankees had cleverly kept those parts of the ritual that added to the profit margin.

I felt a tug at my skirt; it was Thad in his night clothes and he smelled of urine. The girl assigned to care for him looked at me and shrugged. "I want to see the *vaqueros*," Thad said. He looked sleepy. The girl must have waited until the last minute, then wakened him so she could see the arrival. Willa turned, saw what had happened, but before either of us could say anything Owen said, "Let him stay."

"But..." Willa started to object.

"It doesn't matter," was all Owen would say.

"It matters," Willa replied under her breath.

The girl smiled smugly at her triumph. She would not be smiling tomorrow, Trinidad would see to that. Because *it mattered*, as Willa had said, and because somebody had to be punished for something none of us quite understood.

"*Buenos días*," Owen began. His presence pleased the men. Here was a gringo who respected their customs, a man who dressed as they dressed and spoke to them in their language. Owen's Spanish was flawless. He learned it, he told me once, in three weeks from an old Mexican who had memorized all of *Don Quixote*.

Owen told them how pleased he was that they would come to his ranch, how he looked forward to watching them work in the corral that day. He introduced Ignacio, who knew all of the men already, and each was told the section of ranch he was expected to cover. Since the ranch was twenty-two miles long and only three miles wide, some men would have a great distance to travel.

"We will hope to return, with all of the herd, to the corral in Zuma Canyon by the time the sun is overhead," Owen told the men. "Time is short, my friends, and my ranch large. *Vaya con Dios.*" He repeated this last in English, presumably for the benefit of the Lattimores, who tipped their hats and took off, happy to get on with the work of the day, happy too that they would have a small lead, since the Californios would have to take time to change into their brown work clothes.

It was not until the men left that we noticed the man sitting his horse under the big oak. "I'm Connor McCord," he said as he rode toward Owen, "I got here as early as I could."

"Yes, you certainly did that," Owen replied, obviously pleased. The man would have had to ride all night to arrive by daybreak. "I am obliged to you," Owen went on, "because we have a great deal to go over before I leave tomorrow morning, and as you can see, today is rodeo."

Owen was much the taller of the two. Most often his size, and his grace, gave him an advantage. That didn't seem to be so this time. There was a sureness about McCord, an ease in himself, that compensated for his ordinary looks.

"My wife, Willa," Owen was saying, "and her sister, Lena Kerr. Lena is our bookkeeper." McCord looked at me then. His beard was darker than his hair, which was a dusty blond. It was hard to say how old he was. I guessed he was younger than he seemed.

"I'm pleased to meet you, Miss Kerr," he said, with quiet civility. His voice was low and clear and melodious, the remnant of the Irish accent he hadn't been able completely to lose, I guessed. His smile was as beguiling as his voice. I no longer thought Connor McCord to be in the least ordinary.

"Mr. McCord," Willa said, in a voice that was coldly precise, "you are to report to me each morning at eight in the front parlor of the ranch house, which we use as an office." She added, without looking at Owen, "I will be in complete charge while my husband is away."

Owen stiffened. He had planned to say something of the sort himself, I was sure of it, but in a way that would show him to be the kind of man strong enough to turn his business over to his wife in his absence.

Suddenly (it always happened suddenly) my hip locked and I jerked, staggering and dislodging Thad from his grasp on my skirt. The sudden movement sent the child sprawling. He sat down hard, so hard that for a moment he was too surprised to cry, and then he wailed.

Owen steadied me, made sure I was all right, before scooping up his son to comfort him. Thad was wet and smelled bad, but Owen petted and kissed the boy while I made wobbly excuses to them both.

"It's all right, Lena," Owen said with perfect gentleness, "Thad knows he has to be careful not to tip his Auntie over like that."

Tears sprang to my eyes, I don't know why. Perhaps it was the pain that was even then ebbing, perhaps it was the sweetness that was as much a part of Owen as his insatiable curiosity or his love of celebrations or, even, his Yankee business sense.

"I'll be fine," I told Owen.

"So will she," he answered quietly, nodding toward Willa, "take my word, Lena—so will she."

I would have thought Owen knew what he was talking about, or at least knew more about what was between them than I did—if at that moment I hadn't seen Connor McCord's smile, and if I hadn't seen Willa's hand brush the curls from her face, the motion accenting her breasts under the cotton shirt and the curve of her hips. Willa was softer now; the lean boyishness was gone.

Suddenly I had the urge to go after Owen, to ask him to stay a while longer. But Willa had tried, and failed. There was no stopping Owen, I knew.

I was being silly, I told myself. Forebodings were Trinidad's silliness. I was thinking about men too much, I was getting loco.

"Maybe not," Sara said.

She was standing just inside the door, waiting for me. We had invited Sara to come for the rodeo.

"You've got to stop that," I laughed.

"What?" she asked.

"Reading my mind," I answered, and she laughed too.

"I can always tell when you're deep into yourself," she went on, "for a minute there I thought you might disappear altogether in a wisp of blue smoke."

Willa came in behind me, and Sara blurted, "Oh, Willa, you look so beautiful with your hair loose like that."

It was so sincere a compliment that Willa hugged Sara, which caused her to blush.

"Let's saddle up and ride out early to Zuma," Willa said suddenly, "I have to see that everything is in order and the wagons are all packed, but then we can leave."

"I want to see Thad and Wen first," Sara put in.

"They'll be at Zuma for the rodeo," Willa called over her shoulder, "if we hurry we might even get to help with the herding."

I stood looking after her; the morning's gray mood seemed to have lifted, Willa was suddenly bursting with energy. And there was something else, something it took a while for me to recognize—the old recklessness had returned. Willa wanted to take part in the herding. She wasn't going to be content to sit and watch with the rest of us.

"She's in fine spirits," Sara said.

"She was crying at breakfast," I answered.

"Willa? Crying? Has that ever happened before?" Sara wanted to know.

"Not in my memory," I told her.

"Then what is it?" she asked.

"I don't know. She doesn't want Owen to leave tomorrow, but he will. I don't know what is happening, but I have this strange feeling . . ."

Sara was watching me. "I know it sounds peculiar," I went on, "but I have this feeling that something is happening and I don't understand what it is, but it troubles me."

Sara bent her head and told me she did know the feeling. "But you'll just have to wait, you know that," she added softly. "Women like you and me, we can't change the flow of things, we can only watch . . . and wait." Her voice became impertinent then and she said, "So let's just go and watch the gallant *vaqueros* prove their manhood with the riata and the *castrata*, and in the process put more Yankee dollars in Owen's cupboard, to prove his."

I laughed at Sara's wonderful irreverence. "Maybe that's

the trouble," I said, and when I saw that she didn't understand, added, "Owen's manhood."

She leaned against the wall and frowned. "I hope not," she said, "that beautiful man . . ." but before she could finish Willa was back, breathless from hurrying. She called to us to come along. Willa had tied her hair back loosely with a ribbon, and she had changed into the delicately flowered lawn blouse that Owen had given her last Christmas, and which she had yet to wear. He would notice and consider it a peace offering. He would be able to leave tomorrow, I thought, with an easy mind.

"You'll have to ride Ranger," Willa told Sara, "all the saddle horses have been pressed into work. Ranger has been favoring his left front leg a bit, so we thought we should give him a rest—that's you, an eighty-five-pound rest."

Sara ran her hand over the big dapple gray and when he dropped his head to nuzzle her, she kissed his forelock. He was the gentlest horse on the ranch, and the largest. Willa squatted to examine his hoof, expertly thrusting her fingers into spots that could be sore, and the big horse waited patiently.

I watched the two women I cared most for in the world; the only thing alike about them, it seemed to me, was their love for animals. Sara, I felt sure, because she trusted so few people with her love. And Willa, perhaps, because she trusted so many.

Our horses waded, belly-deep, in a field of bright yellow wild mustard flowers; we were in a world of two distinct colors, yellow and the brilliant blue of the sky, and when we reached the top of the hill that looked down over Zuma Canyon, and out to sea, the whole of the ranch lay before us.

The ocean spread to the west, deep and calmly blue, only a gentle breeze blowing off the water to relieve the steady heat of the sun. Below us, against the spring-green valley, was the corral, newly built of split sycamore logs, big enough to allow six riders to work, all at once. And above us to the east were the coastal mountains that separated us from the rest of the continent.

We sat our horses, the three of us, and breathed of the mountains and the sea. "It's a kind of magic kingdom here on the edge of the land," Sara said, "closed off by the tides, it is truly an enchanted land."

I was surprised, and pleased, that Sara would speak in her poet's voice in front of Willa.

"Yes," Willa answered, "this is the center of the earth."

"The earth is round, Willa," I said. "No center."

She did not even smile. Instead she said in perfect seriousness, "I guess I mean that this is my center, my world. My safe place."

There was something haunting in her words. Sara felt it too, I could tell by the way she looked at me.

A small cloud of dust rose to the east, so we knew the first group of cattle would soon be arriving.

"Here comes the food wagons," Will said, pointing to the beach below, where hard sand served as a road. Willa spurred Princess down the hill and we followed, though she quickly outstripped both of us.

Owen and McCord stood inside the corral, Owen talking earnestly and McCord listening. Outside the corral a *vaquero* was cutting out cows and calves, putting them in one area while the rest of the herd was held in another. The cows were lowing pathetically, licking their calves all the while, as if some forgotten wisp of memory made them sad.

The pace was easy now. One or two calves were taken into the corral at a time, the *vaqueros* working together as in a dance, one whirling his lasso over the head, gracefully looping it, while the other curled his rawhide riata around the hind legs. At the exact moment each spurred his horse in a different direction and the calf was brought to the ground. While the horses kept the ropes taut, one man grabbed the hot branding iron and pressed it into the animal's hip, while the other brandished his knife, cutting the mark of the Rancho Malibu y Sequit, a notched circle, into an ear.

Some of our neighbors had come to watch. They sat on the sides of the corral, shouting their approval or groaning when one of the *vaqueros* missed. The excitement would build when the main body of the herd arrived.

Willa had seen Francisco, our oldest and most inept herder, coming from the east with a small group of cattle, and she rode off to help him. Sara and I collected Wen and Thad, who had arrived on the wagon with Trinidad, and went to the stream to hunt for crayfish.

Bordered by low growing brush, the stream was cool and

pleasant. We found one crayfish and then another. They thrilled Wen and frightened Thad, who told me, "Thad no like pinch fish, Auntie." So I took him to a grassy place and sat with him snuggled in my lap while Sara and Wen waded, absorbed in their mission.

Finally the sounds of the herd began to move in on us from all sides as hundreds upon hundreds of cattle converged on Zuma Canyon. We climbed to a grassy hillock, the four of us—Sara and Wen scrambling on ahead, Thad and I making our ponderous way behind them. We lay on our stomachs and watched the action.

The fires were blazing in the corral, the branding irons heated white hot. Some of the men had red bandanas tied round their foreheads, and every now and then you could see them wipe their knife blades flat against them, to clean off the blood, before sharpening them on pieces of oiled stone.

"Do you suppose that's why they wear red kerchiefs?" Sara asked.

I frowned. "It's cruel business, isn't it?" I asked.

"It's life," she shrugged, and added, "even in the center of the world."

The cows were licking their calves and lowing in a pitiful way, as if to comfort them, while the young bulls—the *tauritos*—milled skittishly among them, their edginess barely contained. Only a certain number of bulls could be allowed to service the herd. By law, those young bulls deemed inferior could not be allowed to roam freely. Today those would be castrated, to prevent weakening the strain.

Wen wanted to get close, so we climbed down, turned Thad over to one of the girls, and joined the others on the corral fence. Willa reached for Wen, and made way for us. The acrid smell of burning hair and burning flesh, mixed with blood and dust, fear and sweat, filled the ring—thick animal smells, edged with danger. It was the danger that produced excitement, the possibility of the spilling of blood that created the sport. And it was a sport, you could see that in the faces of some of the men.

"Look," Sara whispered to me, nodding toward a chisel-featured Spaniard. A scar ran the length of his face, ending at the side of his mouth so that his lip was lifted in a perpetual sneer. He looked evil. The knife he fondled added to the sinister quality of the man.

*"El fiero!"* a *vaquero* called, and a boy came running with the brand.

*"Viva! Viva!"* the shouts came, thick and fast, as the men pushed themselves to perform.

Ignacio sent the Lattimore brothers to replace two Californios in the corral. "Hey now," one of the Kentucky boys drawled, "we're gonna show you folks what *dos gringos* can do!"

As the two set to work, the corral rang with calls of "Hey!" and "hey-le-le!" The Spaniards cheered the two good-naturedly, willing to give them credit for the energy expended, if not for grace.

In the midst of this McCord climbed into the ring. He moved skillfully, dodging riders and cattle, making it clear that he knew what he was about. He knelt to inspect the eye of a heifer which had been trussed for branding.

"Some salt," he called, "foxtail has pierced its eye."

Owen took a few steps into the ring; he was watching McCord, he nodded his approval. Owen would like it that McCord was the kind of man to pay attention to details. He raised both hands above his head then, the signal for the men to dismount.

"Fix your saddles," he instructed them. Each man did as he was told, recinching, and at a signal from Owen they mounted their horses and began again.

"Look at the Evil One," Sara said in my ear.

The Spaniard with the knife stood ready, his stance as dramatic as a matador's, his knife glinting. Two *vaqueros* rode after a young bull, a big, dusty black creature that was wild with fear.

"Look out," someone yelled.

"The *taurito!*" another shouted.

The first rope had missed its mark and the young bull broke loose, charging for the biggest target in the ring—Owen.

Willa screamed and the sound hung there in the dusty air, piercing the dust and blood and stink.

Then a rawhide sliced the air and the bull was jerked off balance; two more riatas pulled the beast to the ground and with a single long stroke of his knife, the Spaniard slit the testicles and threw them high in the air, where a rawhide sliced out and splattered them, sending bloody remnants spraying.

Owen had been frozen to the spot, unable to move. It seemed to me his body convulsed slightly now. His shirt, so perfectly white this morning, was speckled with red, the blood of the castrated bull. He walked over to where Connor McCord was looping the riata back in place. He was thanking him, we all knew that. It was McCord's riata that had pulled the bull off balance. The *vaqueros* would not look at Owen. He had not moved to protect himself, and for that they would judge him less than a man, the victim of a failure of courage, they thought.

Owen would not mind what the *vaqueros* were thinking. He might, however, wonder about McCord. I was relieved to see the two of them squat to examine the heifer's eye.

Three hours later the last calf had been branded, the last ear cut and tossed into a box. Owen nodded to Ignacio, who began to count the bloody bits of hair and skin.

*Trescientos y dos,* he called out, three hundred and two new calves. Owen entered the date and the number in his black record book. He knew the number was correct, having counted them in his head as the work progressed.

Long tables had been set up in the sycamore grove and covered with fresh ferns for a cloth. They were heaped with food, all of it from the ranch or taken from the sea—there was mutton and fattened angora kid, rabbit and quail, pompano and fresh sardines, wild honey, a haunch of venison and bread and butter. Trinidad had made a great basketful of tortillas, and put the hot peppers on the table. It was a splendid feast, and the men ate and told stories and celebrated the day's work.

By the time we reached the ranch house the sun was casting a long shimmering reflection on the surface of the Pacific. Willa took her two dusty sons to the bath house while I saw Sara to the guest room. My back ached from the long day, so I lay down on my bed to rest a spell. When I woke some hours later, the house was in deep quiet.

*Owen's record book,* was my first thought. I would need it to make out my reports, and Owen would be leaving before daybreak, I was sure.

I lit a candle, took it over to the clock. It was two in the morning.

Perhaps Owen had left the book on my desk in the second parlor.

I heard their voices as I approached, and I stood quietly for a moment, trying to think who Owen would be talking to at this hour.

McCord, of course.

I knocked tentatively, opened the door.

Owen looked utterly exhausted. "I'm afraid I've kept Mr. McCord up half the night," he said to me, "going over all the ranch business."

At that McCord, who seemed not at all tired, rose to take his leave, and I got the distinct impression my interruption gave him a chance to escape.

I left Owen there, in the office. I do not know if, on his last night at home, he joined his wife in bed.

# Chapter Eight

The days and weeks that followed the rodeo were sunny and cool. It was that interlude between the winter rains and summer heat when the hills were a terrible, luminous green laced through with wildflowers—wild tiger lilies and columbine and sumac, and outrageous sweeps of bright orange poppies.

Wen discovered bees that spring and they were all he could talk about. We searched his father's library and when we had exhausted that source we set out to find Yang Ng, the ancient Chinese who knew where the bee caves were.

In the orange grove Wen said, "There's the big Chinaman," and ran up to Wing Soong demanding, "what are you doing?"

Wing Soong squatted on the ground next to the child and opened his hand. In his palm were three miniature green oranges.

"You've picked them too soon," Wen reproached him.

"I have picked them at precisely the right moment," Soong answered in his beautifully accented English. "Now the one orange left in the cluster will grow big and be filled with sweet juice. It will be a giant among oranges, you will see. And only because I removed these baby oranges from its nest. There is an old Chinese proverb," Soong went on, looking at me for the first time, "one big orange better than four little oranges."

When I laughed, Wen looked thoroughly perplexed, so Soong

became serious again. "You will return in a month," he said to the child, "and then, in another month, I promise you a giant orange will be here and it will be yours."

I explained our bee mission. "The old one knows more about bees than you will find in a book, I daresay," he agreed, "But he is not comfortable in your language." He was looking at Wen as he said this. Like Sara, and unlike anyone else I had ever known, Wing Soong spoke to a child as he would to an adult, out of what seemed to be some essential politeness, as if it would be rude to do otherwise.

"Perhaps you can tell me what you wish to know about bees," he said to the boy, "and I could ask the old one for you."

Wen's questions came tumbling out; some of them sensible, others childishly funny. Clearly, Wen was intrigued with the mating habits of the queen bee. Wing Soong treated each question with gravity. We were to come back the next day for the answers.

As we walked back to the ranch house Wen asked me, "Is Wing Soong an 'old one'?"

"No," I told him, "I doubt he is much older than I am." Until that moment I had not thought about it. It had, I believe, never occurred to me to think of the Chinese in comparable terms.

Each morning promptly at eight Connor McCord appeared at the door of the front parlor, which was always open, and rapped softly with his knuckles until Willa looked up. I was usually already at my desk in the adjoining room with my door closed. Still I could hear the reverberations of their voices through the wall, and I could tell by the timbre that for the first few days Willa did most of the talking. Then, as the daily sessions continued, more and more of Connor's lilting tones carried through the walls. It was almost like a song, the erratic patterns of speech becoming smoother, more rhythmic, punctuated at last by what could only be laughter.

And yet there was nothing to justify my forebodings of the morning of the rodeo. I was beginning to feel thoroughly foolish for letting my mind slip into such murky waters. The ranch was running smoothly; McCord seemed to be everywhere. The men had accepted him, perhaps because, while he worked through the afternoon siesta, he didn't expect them to change their ways. He consulted Willa on all but the most minor decisions and she seemed satisfied that she was, indeed, in control.

One morning, after her usual session with McCord, Willa came into my room, but said nothing. I was adding a long column of figures and I did not stop, but still she stayed, running a finger through the film of dust that continually covered the furniture.

I sighed and stopped.

"What is it?" I asked.

"It?" Willa answered.

"Willa," I said, smiling in an exasperated way, "you've cost me my place and now I'm going to have to add this column all over again. So what is it?"

"I've asked Connor McCord to take his dinners with us," she told me.

I looked at her.

"You've asked Connor McCord to take his dinners with us," I repeated.

"Yes."

I turned back to my adding, but she wouldn't have it.

"What's wrong with that?" she demanded.

"I didn't say anything was 'wrong,'—you did," I reminded her.

"Then what is it, exactly?"

"I don't know, *exactly*," I said. "It's just that, well, Ignacio never eats with us."

She had her answer ready. "But Connor is taking Owen's place, too, remember."

"Really, is he now?" I said in as good an Irish brogue as I could manage.

"Lena," Willa laughed, her eyes shining, "you are wicked."

"I wish I were," I sighed, "but if you have already asked McCord to eat with us, you don't need to consult me. You are the lady of the manor, but I refuse to be cast in the role of the straightlaced crippled keeper of the morals and holder of the chastity belt." I paused then, feeling a pang, and added, "But I guess we can both use a little male companionship. And McCord seems to be more interesting than most of the men who turn up around here."

Willa was looking at me with an edge of anger, and for a

moment I thought I had pushed too far. Then she said, "I think you are a little daft, Lena, and I don't particularly like your crippled-keeper-of-the-morals self-righteousness, but you are right about one thing. We do need male companionship, both of us. Maybe proper English ladies don't, but I do. And so do you."

What she said was troublesome, but it was true. I grinned at her ruefully, and she smiled to show she forgave me. Then she flicked me lightly on the cheek with her fingernails, a gesture that had always meant, "We're in this together now." I tried not to remember that as often as not it had also meant trouble in the end.

So Connor McCord joined us for dinner that night, and the nights to come, and I was proven wrong again. He came promptly at seven-thirty and left promptly at nine, after which Willa and I would sit together and sift through all that had been said, reliving the pleasure of the dinner and the talk.

Connor McCord's gift, as I was to come to think of it, was in listening with such intense interest that he seemed neither shy nor quiet. We found ourselves telling him stories of our girlhood on the farm in Illinois, we told him about Mama and her atlases, we told him things we had never told anyone else, and we were not sorry. We laughed together, the three of us, and it seemed right.

He told us anecdotes, little jokes that made us smile, but he almost never talked about himself. One evening Willa and I determined to draw him out. When he saw he couldn't slip away from our questioning, he told us about leaving Ireland when he was seventeen to come to America. His father had known the Scot who was an overseer on a great ranch in Montana, and the man had agreed to take Connor on as a hand, "to make a man out of me."

"My dad, you see, was worried that I was coddled, being the only boy in a houseful of women. I had three sisters, all of them older, and he was sure they and my mother spoiled me." He had paused a few moments, then added, "Maybe they did, if spoiling means being good to you. No matter, I found myself on a ranch in Montana that was three times the size of my home county in Ireland and I thought I had never seen such emptiness, such pure desolation in all of my life." He laughed, as if to shake off the memory of pain. "I thought I'd die of homesickness that first year. Lucky for me it isn't fatal. But I did learn that 'hard work' can mean one thing to an Irishman and another to a Scot, but if the Scot's the boss you had better accept his meaning of the word.

"I came after the ranges were fenced," he told us one night, "but the older cowpunchers would talk about the days when cattle roamed free. Whenever a big winter storm hit, they said, the whole herd would just turn south and begin to walk, and they would just keep on walking until they walked out of the storm. Then the herd would rest up for maybe a half an hour, and turn around and start back up north again. By springtime, when the big round-up would get underway, that herd would be just about back to where it had started from before the storm hit—the cowboys could find them without much trouble, they said. Even though sometimes the herd had traveled a hundred miles or more to the south.

"When the fences were built," he went on, "and a storm would hit, the cattle would turn and begin their long walk south, away from the eye of the storm, and they would walk until they came to a fence. When they couldn't get through they would begin to pace back and forth, back and forth along the fence line, and as more and more cattle came pushing in from behind they would climb on top of each other until, when the storm cleared, the rancher would find them there along the fence, in a big frozen pile."

"Is there a moral to that story?" Willa had wanted to know.

Connor grinned, his slow magic smile transforming his face, and said, "The moral is, always know how to locate the gate."

I enjoyed those evenings more than I had believed possible. I felt, for the first time ever, I thought, like someone on the inside. Connor seemed equally interested in us; the three of us took pleasure in each other. And because of that—because of Connor—the old warmth seemed to have returned between Willa and me. We were friends again, partners in the daily business of life. We had somehow managed to extricate ourselves from positions that we had seemed caught in—she as the married matron, me as the invalid dependent sister. I wondered if Willa had known all along that Connor McCord could do that for us.

Our days that spring were filled with sun and laughter. In the mornings we did the work of the ranch, the afternoons I spent with Wen and Wing Soong in the orange or the pear orchard, studying bees. Willa took off each afternoon with her sketchbooks, roaming the ranch in search of her hawks while Connor could be seen coming and going in the barns and orchards, keeping a close check on everything about the ranch.

The pattern was marred only on those days when work prevented Soong from joining us in the pear orchards, or when Connor went into Los Angeles on business. He went to the city, rather than Santa Monica, we knew, because he often spoke of the strange sights he was seeing there—the faith healers in their big tents, the new towns going up where there had been desert the last time he was there. We did not learn much about the business he conducted, perhaps because we had long since learned not to quiz Owen on business matters for fear of being bored with details. We did know that often enough Connor would have had to return in the middle of the night, on the last low tide, in order to have started the ranch day at six, as he always did. I think I have never known a man who needed less sleep than Connor McCord.

One afternoon Willa returned from her wanderings looking vaguely troubled. That night at dinner she told us about the condor she had tracked that day.

"It is the most amazing of birds," she said. "I had read about them, of course, but I had not seen one close up until today. The wingspread is twenty-five feet—can you imagine that? It was . . . awesome. Not like the hawks—condors are vultures, you know—nothing so clean and . . . precise . . . as a hawk."

Connor had, I remember, changed the subject, nudging us into a lighter mood. Before long Willa seemed to have forgotten the condor, and the shadow it had cast.

Sara was to be married on June 28. Early in April she sent word that she wanted me to travel to San Francisco with her, to help her choose a trousseau. We would make it a grand outing, she said, with trips to the theater and visits to all the grand sights. It was a new, ebullient mood for Sara and I was happy for her.

Willa said that I must go, that it would be good for me. It would be good for Sara, too—I knew that. I was only surprised at my own lack of enthusiasm. I had never been happier on the ranch, and I did not want to break the spell.

On the day before I was to leave, a fine white fog washed in from the sea. It was warmer than it had been, and I knew the interlude of bright, cool weather was over. That afternoon Wen and I found Soong waiting for us in the pear orchard. He had discovered a large section of old honeycomb and, while the house was silent around us he patiently dissected it with Wen's eager help.

When the child wandered off after a time, I told Wing Soong that I would be leaving. "I almost wish I weren't going," I heard myself say. "I mean, it has been so pleasant here these last weeks." He was looking at me with curiosity and for a moment I thought he didn't understand my English, until I remembered that his English was perfect. "I mean," I stumbled, "I've learned so much about bees..." I was beginning to feel supremely silly, but I couldn't seem to stop. "I am trying to say..."

"May I ask, please, when Mr. Reade is expected to return?" he asked, formally, shocking me into silence.

"Why do you ask?" I finally said.

He smiled then, disarmingly. "Selfishness, actually. Mr. Reade is often kind enough to lend me volumes from his library."

I was astonished.

"You know Owen?"

His answer was careful. "I do not *know* my employer, to be sure. Now and then he has stopped to talk with me, most of the time about things regarding the garden, and perhaps now and then about other things. He is a most kind gentleman, Mr. Reade."

Before I could ask what "other things" he and Owen talked about, Wen came running back with an urgent question.

Owen and Wing Soong. I couldn't think why I should be surprised. Owen had an insatiable interest in everybody and everything. Certainly he would find Soong fascinating. But it made me angry. I suppose because I thought I was the only one who knew about Soong, about his flawless English and his gentleness and... Perhaps I wanted to keep him to myself. Just once, I did not want to have to share.

The events that took place on the morning after I left I learned about more than a dozen years later. Even then the details—

the smallest, most inconsequential details—remained vivid, so that I understood what a great need she had to remember, to hold it all in her mind.

The fog had come in on that April morning, a light, white fog that settled in patches along the shore so that it was possible to move in and out of it, as you would a dream. From the verandah, you could make out the shape of the sweet bay tree in the garden, no more.

When Connor came to the office as usual that morning, they talked about an outbreak of disease among the sheep. He was afraid it could become serious. He wondered if they should take steps to isolate the sick sheep. In the middle of this conversation they heard strange, muffled sounds coming from the direction of the beach. At first they had stood quietly in the front parlor, straining to hear. Then, trying to identify the sounds, responding to an urgency they both felt, they ran onto the verandah.

The boy Sven came staggering out of the fog, sobbing and out of breath, wet to the skin and speaking in Swedish, so they couldn't understand what was so wrong.

"The horse," he finally gasped, gesturing wildly toward the beach, "the big horse in the water."

"Ranger," Connor said grimly, "I told the boy to exercise him on the beach this morning. He must have run him too hard. Sounds like he's foundered in the surf."

Connor was on his horse and riding for the beach while Willa went to the stable for Princess. She didn't bother with a saddle, but rode bareback to the beach, her heart pumping furiously with fear and anger.

By the time she got there, Connor had lassoed the big dapple gray and with his own mount had managed to drag him out of the surf.

"Dear God, is he drowned?" she screamed over the steady roar of the surf. Ranger lay there, a soaking gray mass in the sand, tangled in seaweed. He seemed lifeless, moving only when the wave washed up and rocked him, swirling eddies of foam around him.

"Clear his nostrils," Connor yelled. He was flinging himself against the horse's massive sides, pushing hard on the area around its lungs.

Willa thrust her fingers into the nostrils and pulled out a mass of slime and mucus; she clamped her teeth tight to keep from retching, so tight her jaws ached, but she did it, all the while McCord was pushing with all his weight against the horse.

Ranger's eyes fluttered, then they were wide and full of fear.

"Don't die," Willa had screamed at him, "please don't die."

"Work!" Connor yelled.

And she did work, she dug her fingers to clear the nostrils and she tried to force open its mouth. After what seemed hours but could have been only minutes, the horse's great sides began to heave.

"Watch out," Connor shouted, but it was too late.

The horse spewed bile and it splashed over, terrible in its stench. A wave washed over them, soaking them both, and she coughed and sputtered and cried.

Again and again Connor threw himself against the horse; she could see the ropes of muscle on his arms, the concentration on his face. But Ranger's sides did not heave again. Instead there was one long, involuntary shudder, then nothing. When that happened McCord stood, his hands loose at his sides, and as the waves washed around them, sucking at their feet, he pulled her up.

"It's done," he said. "He's dead."

Willa looked at him in disbelief. Then she saw the boy Sven standing there—he must have been there all along, watching—wringing his big white hands and crying.

"Get out," she screamed at him (she could hear the words, but she wasn't sure who was saying them) "get out, get away, go go go . . ." She screamed until Connor pulled her toward the water, out into the waves. ("Go back," he had called to the boy. "Wait for me.")

Their clothes were clinging wetly to their skin; she was covered with the dead horse's bile, she felt steeped in it and she couldn't stand it. She retched and he held one hand on her forehead and the other around her waist, tight, so the waves wouldn't pull her over, but nothing would come up, she could not vomit. She wanted to be washed, to be free of the awful memory of it, so they walked into the waves and let them wash over, one after another, and when he tried to pull her back she wouldn't go, but stood gasping, pulling air into her lungs until another wave crashed over them. She needed to be free, to be washed clean.

Then he did pull her back, holding her tightly with one arm, his grip stronger than she could have imagined, and with the other he had taken a handful of water to rinse her face and neck. He did it again and again, trying to rub off the bits of seaweed that clung to her.

She took off her blouse and stood there, her breasts bare, so he could wash it all away. And he did, with his hands he washed her, rubbing her breasts, cupping them in his hands. The water was cold but she did not feel it. And then his mouth was on hers; the water splashed and rocked and sucked at them and they swayed but did not fall, they held hard to each other. She felt the heat low in her groin, and a tightening, and his hard swelling against her; his mouth was on hers, his hand on her breast, and then he was walking, guiding her out of the water.

They walked together to a place sheltered by a large rock where the sand was deep and soft. The mist was all around and the air was warm and the sand was warm. They stood facing each other there, his hands lightly on her bare waist, steadying her. He was looking at her, searching for something, looking inside of her, she thought. Then she took his face in her hands. Her breasts were heaving, the nipples hard and red from rubbing against the wet suede of his vest. She held his face steady in her hands and slowly, very deliberately, with the tip of her tongue she traced his lips. When he tried to press into her mouth, she had pulled him back so he would let her continue her exploration. With her tongue she felt his eyelids, one and then the other, and the lobes of his ears, and then her hands went to his vest and she took it off.

She could hear his breathing, long and steady, as he loosened her skirt and let it drop. One of his hands went to her belly, the other was on her buttocks and he was pressing and sliding them lower, down to the throbbing, until she felt his fingers tangled in her hair, and then he was touching the place that was wet and hot and inside.

He clamped hard and held her there while she plunged her hands into his pants and found him, and freed him so that she could hold him in her hands and feel how hard he was, fully erect. She pressed him against her belly and held him there, while they explored each other's mouths, fingers and tongues plunging and squeezing and finding every tender place.

Free of all clothes, they lay in the deep sand. She opened

her legs wide to the air and the sea and the man; he ran his hands over her, fingers knowing and tongue knowing. And then she felt the power with which he entered her and she thought her heart would burst.

She met him, pushing, probing, knowing that there was a center that he must, would, touch. His tongue was in her mouth, driving, sweet and hard. He was inside of her and she was in him, and she would be a part of it, know all of it, all there was to know.

She pushed hard until he lay on his back and she climbed on top of him. She raised her hands high over her head, and he raised his, and their fingertips touched, and their toes. Then she sat up, erect, on him and arched her back as far as she could, and she moaned to the sky and the seagull wheeling overhead as he pressed both hands over her breasts and grew inside of her, farther and farther into the interior, into the very center of her.

And she had always known it could be like this, always always. He rolled over onto her again, then, and began a slow and solemn rocking, a rhythm that she joined, pushing deeper and deeper, reaching in a surging rhythm until they were together, perfectly, knowing it was there and finding it together, touching it . . . she exploded.

He waited to feel it with her, and then he exploded.

When she pressed her face into his neck and whispered, "Yes," to him, he answered in thick Irish accents, "Oh, Lord, yes."

## Chapter Nine

She was in the office earlier than usual the next morning. Now that she knew what she was going to do, she wanted to get on with it. A light breeze played through the branches of the pepper tree that stood outside the window, sending a delicate tracery of shadows over the desktop. She held her hands palms up, as if to catch them, as if to hold the moving light.

Too restless to sit, she moved to the window. The magnolia tree was in bloom. She had the urge to put one of the big blossoms in each room so the heavy, lush scent could permeate the house. She squeezed her arms together and tried to remember the fragrance of magnolias.

She had left Connor at the beach. She tried to think, now, how he had looked. She clasped her hands to keep them still.

"I thought you might not come," she said, not turning around, knowing he was neither in the room nor out, but poised in the doorway.

"Ah, why would I not?" he answered, his tone careful.

She wished she had picked the magnolia. She wanted its fragrance to wrap around her now; she wanted to breathe it into her.

"Yesterday did happen," she said. Until that moment it had not occurred to her that she could pretend it hadn't.

Connor moved into the room. He closed the door and then he looked at her carefully. She had turned and was facing him, but she had not moved from her place at the window and now she thought that she might not be able to move at all. He said, "Please, sit." When she did not move, he repeated the "please." She sat behind the desk; he stood across from her.

"Yesterday, the terrible scene with the horse," he began, "you were distraught, filled with woe. You exhausted yourself trying to save the animal, we worked very, very hard together..."

"Yesterday did happen," she repeated. Her fingers gripped the edge of the desk; she tried to keep the image of the magnolia in her mind.

"Wait," he said, his voice urgent, "I want to tell you a story. A true story. Let me do that. I've never told this story to anyone before, but I want to tell you now. Then I'll hear whatever you want to say, I promise you that."

Willa nodded, and for the first time that morning he smiled at her, a boy's sweet smile, without guile.

"You know I have not been quick to talk about my early months in this country," He began, "I was but seventeen when I arrived, and I'd no experience in the world, none at all." He cleared his throat and began to pace, moving into and out of a square of sunlight thrown into the room. "I was sent to a ranch in Montana to live with a family, to help with the work. They were a man and his wife and their three little ones, the eldest but five years. The man was big and silent and he worked himself without pity, long hours from sunup until dark, with only time to eat and sleep and be up to work again, all day and every day. His wife was young, still, though you knew she wouldn't be young for long, not in that harsh land and what with the bearing of babies and all. But this woman, she was not reared for that kind of life. She had been a schoolteacher back East, I think she hadn't a notion of how hard life on the frontier would be. She didn't complain, but you could see how lonely she felt. There was a gentleness about her, she reminded me of my sister Mag, a sweet girl for certain. So I taught this woman—her name was Susan—some of the songs my sister used to sing, and we talked together on those days I was to work with her in the family garden. She made life less lonely for a homesick boy. And it gave me great pleasure to make her smile. I came to adore her, the way a boy does when a woman is kind to him, the way I loved my sisters. I wanted to make her happy, make her laugh."

He took a long breath, moved out of the square of light so Willa could not see his face. He was, she thought, trying to raise the courage to touch a spot long sore. Finally, he went on. "One day we got word from a neighbor that a preacher was coming through—there were traveling preachers in those days, men who would go from settlement to settlement, and people would gather from miles to hear him. I was curious, having never been to another church save the Catholic, but I knew the Mister would never allow it. It would be twenty miles each direction, a long journey.

"Well, Susan decided that all of us must go. She talked and talked on it, she kept after her man, every night talking at him, but he wouldn't answer. Wouldn't say a word. Well, I don't know how she did it, but one morning she told me that she and the young ones were going, and that I would go along to drive and watch after them."

Willa sat quietly, waiting and wondering.

"Folks did come from all over, it was a real gathering," he went on. "I was glad to see Susan talking with the other women, and I kept watch over the little ones to give her some visiting time.

"The preacher got started about twilight, in a big tent that had been raised in a clearing between cabins. He was a strange, tall man with a voice that seemed to get into the head. I mean . . ." He paused, swallowed. "There was something in his voice that seemed to rouse people. It was summertime, and warm. The children were put to sleep in the wagons. For a while there was some singing, some hymns . . . then the preacher began. His voice would get loud, and then it would get very soft, very soft. Then he would be shouting again and pretty soon the people—these good, sound farm folks—they got to shouting back, and everybody was swaying and swooning. Some of the women started to cry, and one fell on the ground and began to moan. People were, I don't know how to explain it, it was as if they were . . . possessed. And suddenly Susan was leaning against me, swaying and catching at her breath and then we were outside, under the wagon."

Willa looked at his hands; the blond hairs stood out on his

fingers. When he spoke again his voice was perfectly calm. "It was the first time I had been with a woman."

Beads of sweat lay high on his forehead. "After that," he went on, "she didn't say a word to me. We drove home in silence. She never did speak to me again, except when her husband was in the room, and that was a false-hearty kind of talk so he wouldn't suspect. She couldn't look at me. She hated the very sight of me, so she erased me from her view. The shame must have burned bright inside of her, she was so full of disgust. I left as soon as I could, left with my bedroll and what was on my back."

Willa stretched her arms out straight before her, holding to the rim of the desk with her fingertips. She tried to think of magnolias; she did not want to lose the idea of them.

"Are you saying that yesterday's accident with Ranger whipped me into a frenzy that sent me reeling out of my mind and into your arms, are you saying that I didn't know what I was doing, that I'm like that farmer's wife?"

"No," he answered carefully, "no. It's not that—though I'm not sure it would have happened without the accident. The thing I am trying to tell you is that I won't let a woman do that to me again, not ever."

Willa looked at him then with astonishment. "Ah," she said, "I see."

"What? What do you see?" he asked.

"How foolish I've been," she answered, walking over to the window, looking out at the magnolia. "How foolish to have thought the decision mine alone. After I left you yesterday I went to the woods. I asked myself if it would have happened, between us, without the accident in the surf. I knew it was important. I finally understood that it would have happened, that I wanted it to happen. That I do want it . . . you."

He said, as if to make certain she understood, "It was the shame I couldn't abide. I need never have touched her again, but that she could feel such terrible shame over what had been between us."

"I am not sorry," she said, reaching across the desk, "and I will feel no shame." He took both of her hands in his. He kissed one, then the other, formally. But when she rose to move around the desk, to come to him, he stopped her. "Not here," he said, "not in this house. Now we speak of work.

That is important. If I work hard enough, and fast enough, I will be able to leave when the men take their siesta."

"Yes," Willa said, pleased that their plans had been the same. "I'll be at Escondido Canyon," she went on, and in a voice that was short of breath, gave him careful directions.

Escondido—hidden, it meant. It was just one of the places she had discovered in her trampings over the ranch. There were springs there and a small waterfall where maidenhair fern grew in thick, lush clumps and where the water ran easy over smooth stones. There was no way at all for anyone who did not know where they were going to find Escondido Canyon. There was no place in all the world, Willa thought, quite so private as the Rancho Malibu y Sequit, and no one who knew its hiding places better than she.

The springs at Escondido were only one of the secret places she would guide Connor to that summer. There were caves with Indian pictographs on the walls, and a grotto carved by the sea where they could lie in soft sand and look out at the ocean, where they could listen to the low rumble of the sea and know they were utterly alone. There were green and leafy places under the sheltering branches of a giant live oak tree, shared with the nests of birds, and there were grassy high meadows on the tops of mesas, with only the hawks soaring above them in the limitless expanse of the sky. Their trysting places were without number, their privacy inviolate, and they were without shame for the acts of love consummated in the long spring afternoons, filled with the fragrance of magnolia oil she had rubbed onto her breasts and thighs. The great ivory blossoms with their delicate yellow stamens appeared in every room of the ranch house, to remind her, to sustain her. She knew, in those weeks and days, that she was alive.

I returned in the early afternoon, riding up the beach in full sun, squinting as the light glittered on the ocean and glared under my hatbrim. It had been more than two weeks since my departure, and never had I been more excited about a home-coming. The past weeks had been the most adventurous of my life, and I could scarcely wait to spill it all out, to regale Willa and Connor with stories of Sara and her artistic friends cavorting all over wicked San Francisco with me in tow. I urged my horse to a trot, feeling the jarring to my spine but too excited to give in to the pain. I had a small packet of letters with me, including two from Owen, which I had picked up in Santa Monica, and my saddlebags were filled with presents. I had even managed to find several Chinese-language newspapers for Wing Soong, the cause of one of my adventures in Chinatown.

The dogs set up their usual barking when I reached the gatehouse. "Hush, you silly thing," I laughed at the St. Bernard, "are you blind? Can't you see it's me?" The noise was enough to alert the household, but no one came to meet me. Strange, I thought. Somehow I had expected Willa to forego hawking on the day of my return. I chided myself. After all, I had been gone but a short time, I should not expect anyone to make a fuss over my return.

One of the Mexican boys was making a desultory attempt at watering the roses. I called to him to take my horse. The house seemed empty. I paused in the parlor and noticed the remnant of a magnolia blossom in a vase. Most of the creamy white leaves had turned brown and were lying, scattered, on the tabletop.

"Hello," I called. No one answered.

As I moved through the hallway I noticed a small stool turned upside down. Putting down my satchel, I walked into the room to right the stool and tried to think what was changed.

In the kitchen—Trinidad's pride and always spotless—a stream of ants formed a double line on the floor, swarming over bits of food that had been dropped and left.

"Espiritu!'" I called, "Rosa! Luz!"

Rosa appeared in the doorway, a coarse girl in a dirty apron. The sight of her infuriated me.

"Look at this kitchen," I lashed out, "Trinidad would send you away for this. *No me gusta! no me gusta!*" I could not seem to put my fury into Spanish. The girl only stood there, the large toe of one foot making circles in the dusty floor. "Get busy," I all but screamed, "clean this place, *pronto.*"

"Ah, Señorita . . ." she began to protest and I cut her short. "Now," I said. *"Comprende?* Now."

The others were hanging back, waiting for my wrath to descend on them, too, and I obliged them. At the same time, I was beginning to understand. I had taken them by surprise, they did not know I was to return today. I wondered if Willa had forgotten.

I found Thad sitting in a pile of dusty clay, the girl who
cared for him not far away, plopped, like a large lump of paste,
in the shade of a tree. She did not move, even when she saw
me.

"Auntie," Thad screamed, his dirty little face all smiles. He
threw his arms around me and hugged me. I bent to hug him
back with mixed feelings, my delight at seeing him balanced
by my chagrin at his appearance. His hair smelled sour, his
clothes were encrusted with dried dirt as if he had wet his pants
and they had not been changed.

"Get up," I hissed at the girl, with enough malevolence to
put real alarm in her face. "Take this child to the bath house
and clean him. Then I want to speak to you." She could tell
that she was not going to like what I had to say. I bent to touch
Thad's cheek, smiling so he would know my anger was not
for him. "Sweet potato," I said to him, "I have presents for
you—and you'll get them just as soon as I see a pretty, clean
face smiling at me."

I found Wen in the garden with Wing Soong. The sight of
them, bending over the vegetables, made me feel calmer.

"How good that you are returned safely," Wing Soong said,
smiling at Wen, who was, by then, hugging me hard about the
waist, his eyes closed tight.

Stroking the boy's hair I answered, "It's good to be back,
but I fear . . ." I didn't finish the sentence, realizing that I didn't
know what it was that I did fear. Instead, I changed directions.
"Oh, but I've brought you something from San Francisco," I
said. "I found several Chinese-language papers and if the translator answered my questions correctly, there should be news
of your homeland in them. Later, not now, I will tell you how
I happened to get the papers." I knew Soong would be pleased
at my efforts but I had not expected the extent of his pleasure.

"How very, very kind of you," he said, not once but twice.
"I cannot say how grateful I am that you would make such an
effort on my account." He seemed not to be able to thank me
enough, and I began to feel awkward.

"It is little enough for the kindness you show Wen. Since
his papa forbade him to play with other boys, he has been
lonely . . . I can see I needn't have worried, about Wen at least."

He gave me a quick, searching look, then returned to his
methodical weeding, his long, smooth fingers pulling each

errant weed by the root with artistic care.

"When is Mr. Reade expected to return, if I may ask?" he said.

"I'm not sure," I answered, "I have two letters for him but I suppose my sister is out hawking, so we won't know anything until she returns."

"Mama's always hawking," Wen interrupted. "She has been out every day even on the Sabbath."

"Oh, Wennie," I told him, "you exaggerate."

But Wen did not exaggerate; Willa had been away, that was evident. Something had changed. When I saw Willa and Connor together that night, at supper, I knew what it was. The balance was gone. They tried very hard not to make it seem so, they wanted to hear all about my trip, they listened attentively to all I had to say. Yet they were watching me, too. Waiting and watching, to see what I would do. All of the excitement I had felt at coming home was gone. I had not wanted this to happen, and the dread was settling heavy in my chest. (Could I have stopped it? Had I stayed at home, would we still be three, and safe?)

"Sara surprised me completely," I heard myself chatter, "she has the most remarkable circle of friends, as it happens. They call themselves artists and it may be that they are—certainly they can afford to be. But from what I can see, much of their time and energy is spent in quite outlandish pursuits."

"Tell us!" Willa pleaded, her eyes shining. I wanted to scream "Don't, don't do this, Willa, don't. It's dangerous, don't you see that?"

Instead I said, "I'll give you one example. Sara's friend Lily—Lily Coit—would seem to be a perfectly proper young woman who has the odd habit of chasing fires. There is one fire company in the city that has, well, adopted her—they gave her a fireman's hat and a coat and she spends a lot of her time just following them to fires. Can you imagine? Anyway, when I mentioned to Lily that I wanted to collect some Chinese-language newspapers to bring back to our gardener—did you know that he is very interested in the political situation in China?—well, Lily says there is nothing to do but make a raid on Chinatown. A raid! Sara told me later that Lily dresses up like a man, hat and all, and parades around at night. It's quite a scandal, I guess. At any rate, we did get a group together, with three men along for protection, and saw what Lily assured me was 'the inner life' of Chinatown. It was amazing."

"Our Sara is a surprise," Willa laughed. "How perfectly wonderful."

"Well, perhaps not *wonderful*," Connor surprised us by saying, "but you are back, safe and sound, so all is well."

"Do I detect a bit of disapproval?" Willa chided him.

"Only a bit," Connor said, smiling at me, "only a very little bit. Chinatowns can be rough places."

"Yes," I answered quickly, "I'm sure you are right. It was a foolish thing to do. I know Owen would not have approved of my being part of the group—it was not only dangerous but..."

"Sinful?" Willa said, and the word echoed throughout the room.

"I suppose," I answered as if tired of the subject. "I'm afraid that the long trip has suddenly exhausted me. I really am quite tired, would you excuse me?" Connor began to rise and I said no, don't get up, finish your dinner, do. I had to leave.

In perhaps half an hour, Willa rapped at my door as I knew she would. I had been lying there, waiting, dreading her knock.

"Are you terribly tired, dear?" she asked, her face full of concern, soft and loving, and I thought I could not bear to see it.

"Very," I answered, making my voice as small and weak as I could.

She took my hand and held it. "I should like to talk to you," she began, her voice asking me to be with her, "it's about Connor..."

"Willa, please..." I felt myself go cold. I could not let her say what she wanted to say. "I am sorry, but I cannot, please..." I told her.

For the first time in our lives together I turned away from my sister, I refused her.

She left, closing the door without another word. A feeling of desolation seeped into me. I had never felt so alone.

Years were to pass before Willa spoke to me of that summer. We were separate during those months by choice—my choice. I saw what was happening and, powerless to stop it, tried to pretend I did not know. Instead, I took over the running of the house and the care of the children. I did Trinidad's job and much of Willa's and mine, too, and kept everyone so busy they had scant time to wonder about anything. The servants were accustomed to Willa's hawking expeditions. Perhaps they thought she was lonely for her husband. I don't know what they thought.

Word came one day that Ignacio and Trinidad would be delayed for many weeks more, they could not be sure that they would return before the end of summer. *The end of summer.* Wen would leave then, Ignacio and Trinidad would return. I dreaded the end of summer and what it would bring.

Owen wrote each week. His letters were filled with the minutia of his days, of business dealings and meetings with old friends and new. He had stopped by Washington to see Theodore Roosevelt, he wrote in one letter, "TR has become quite a politician since our student days. We shared experiences of our sickly youth, our love of the West, and our happy family lives." Owen returned from England early in May, but he had work that had to be done in Massachusetts. He would be back, he promised, in good time for Sara and Charles' wedding the end of June.

With Wing Soong's help, Wen was happily occupied that summer. The child knew he was to leave the ranch. At first he had asked me, over and over again, to explain why there would be no school on the ranch, why he must be sent away, why he could no longer play with the Californio children. I tried to be patient, I tried not to let him know my own sorrow.

"Do you want me to go?" he would ask, and while I wanted to tell him "No, no, never!" I did not. It might drive a wedge between the boy and his father, and I would not do that. Wen needed Owen.

The child seemed always to keep me in sight. Every now and again he would creep into my bed before daybreak. I knew I should not allow it—he was getting to be a big boy, and Owen would not have approved—but I did not make him leave. There were times that summer when both Wen and Thad climbed into my bed in the early hours of the morning. I made room for them both, the stolid, solemn older boy and the fragile, intense younger one.

We worked with Wing Soong in the family garden, Wen and I, and Soong shared the news from China with me. In his quiet, thorough way he told me of the concessions his country had given to England, to France and to Germany. I was astonished at the depth of his knowledge, at his grasp of history, even while I felt his point of view to be prejudiced. He was full of scorn for the Western nations, for Great Britain particularly. I could not help but wonder what part his British father played in his feelings, but I dared not ask. Whatever the reason, Soong feels that Western influence has been a disaster for his mother country. Curious, whenever Soong speaks of China, it is as if he is speaking of a person, some much-loved person.

One afternoon as he and Wen were devising a trap to catch the moles that had been ravaging our vegetables, I found myself telling Soong about my excursion into Chinatown in San Francisco with Sara's friends. "We went into the most peculiar place," I said, "an opium den, with Celestials—older men, mostly—lying about. The room was filled with this very sweet-smelling odor—why do the Chinese smoke the evil stuff?"

"Why?" he repeated. "Because it makes their lives tolerable, perhaps. Why? Because the British and the Indian traders— and the Yankees, too—introduced it, long ago, into China and the selling of opium proved too lucrative a trade to abandon. No matter the emperor banned it. Opium put the Chinese to sleep, made them pliable, kept them in thrall to the Western nations."

"I do not believe that," I said bluntly. "We would never be party to such an evil deed."

It was a peaceful afternoon. With Wen busy on the far side of the garden, Soong worked in silence for a long time. Then he said, "Allow me to point out to you that the opium trade flourishes not only in my homeland, but in yours, too. You must have known, when you visited the opium palace in San Francisco, that it is not within the law. But here, as in China, the selling of opium is a ready way for men to make a quick fortune—it is true in Los Angeles, as well." He paused, looked at me, noted that Wen was out of earshot and said, "The smuggling of opium, in fact, is done right here on the ranch. One of the common places for boats to drop caches is at a cove near Point Dume."

I looked at him in disbelief. "Do you know what you are saying?" I asked, but even as I said it I knew it was true. "But how?" I wanted to know, "And who? And however do you know this?"

Now Soong was looking at me with amusement. "I do not

know who. How is somewhat obvious: The trader makes arrangements well in advance for someone to be at the cove at a certain time. The smuggler waits, pays for the opium in gold, delivers it to those in Los Angeles' Chinatown for a large profit. As to how I know—it is common knowledge, if one listens, watches. People tell me things. I do not denounce those who take the opium pipe. It helps some of the elders to dream of the old country, the old ways. It helps them to live this life, in a land where they are generally hated and scorned. It makes their existence bearable, perhaps . . . the old men we cannot denounce, they have little else to live for." It was a long speech for Soong. I wanted to say something, to answer him, but I feared breaking the silence, lest I break the new confidence that was between us. Soong trusted me . . . he trusted *me*.

After a time I said, "Do you suppose Owen knows about the smugglers?"

"I'm sure he does," Soong answered, "just as I am sure he disapproves. I'm afraid there is little he can do to stop it. People drift in and out of the ranch and are never seen . . . just as Mrs. Reade roams wide in the hills and canyons."

His face did not change expression, his hands continued to work. It could have been a passing reference, but it wasn't. He knew. Wing Soong knew, but he—like me—would say nothing. I was certain of it. Soong was a sharer of secrets.

We resumed the pattern of our lives as if nothing had changed. Each morning I was at my desk when I heard Connor rap at the doorway of the front parlor. I heard my sister call him to come in, and I heard the soft urgency of their voices and the undercurrent of familiarity. Their intimacy was so obvious that I became nervous when anyone saw them together. And yet, no one seemed to notice. Finally I realized that Connor and Willa were, indeed, being circumspect. They took no chances. I never saw them touch. While, in my absence, Willa had allowed the household staff to become lax, Connor had done no such thing in the running of the ranch. It sometimes seemed as if he didn't sleep. He was up and about before anyone else, he seemed to know everything that was happening with the men and the animals. Everything about the barns was in good order. There could be no complaint about Connor's work. If he disappeared for a time each afternoon, during the lull when most of the men took a siesta, he left nothing undone.

*   *   *

The month of May came to an end. June arrived, bright and
clear, perfect summer weather, the ocean calm and the waves
high. Willa left early one morning packing a lunch and her
notebooks in her saddlebags. She planned to be gone all day,
she said.

Thad insisted on riding one of the Shetland ponies, so I took
him to the barn.

"Hey, Ned," I called to the Lattimore boy, "Connor promised to saddle up Bessie for Thad, here."

"Sure did," Ned drawled in his slow Kentucky way, "asked
me to take care of it for him—he had to go north up Trancos
way to check on the herd."

They would be together, then. It was easy enough to imagine
them on such a day, riding along the top of the mesa at Point
Dume, their horses in the deep grasses that blew, high above
the ocean.

It was a day that Willa would remember, and share—though
the sharing would be a long time coming.

Connor found the herd and made a careful count. "They're
all here, I'm glad for that," he told her.

"Were you worried about rustlers?" Willa wanted to know.
"Did you believe José Lopez, then?"

"I wasn't sure," Connor answered. "There has been some
bad business going on, and drifters have been seen lately heading north. But whatever they were up to, they didn't disturb
the herd."

Willa was looking at him with an amused smile.

"Is that why you wore your gun?" she asked.

He grinned. "I always wear my gun, girl, you just haven't
noticed."

"Oh, I always notice what you wear," she laughed, standing
in her stirrups and leaning far out of her saddle to put her face
to his. She could not be with him and not want to touch him.
She had never felt such a need before, ever. It was as if she
were complete when he was holding her, stroking her neck and
her back, caressing...his voice soft and lyrical, all the old
accents of his childhood ringing in her ears—the private voice,
the voice no one else heard from him.

They lay on the grass that day and they talked. All the long
afternoon they spoke of the past and of the present; they never

touched on the future. They were living a life apart, only the two of them in a world of woods and sand, with the expanse of the sky and the ocean before them, limitless, mocking their limitations. They knew it would end; knowing, Willa chose to forget.

As they lay looking up at the sky, listening to the sounds of the sea below, Willa asked, "Were you reared in a Catholic home, then?" as if she had been speaking of religion.

"To be sure," Connor had answered, "to mass every Sabbath, and confession every morning. Good Catholics, for certain."

"You believe in mortal sin, then?" she went on.

"Aye, of course, that," he answered, eyes mocking.

"If we've committed a mortal sin, do you believe your soul will be deprived of divine grace?"

Connor began to laugh; he put his arms around her and rolled over and over until her hair was tangled with bits of grass. "My darling Willa," he finally whispered, "you are divine grace, this is heaven."

He made love to her, then, slowly, with great care. Sea birds circled above them, calling. Finally he lay back, and she raised herself on one arm to look at him.

"Whenever I need to remember what happiness is, I will remember this day, now," she said.

He reached to wind a strand of her hair on his finger. "You said 'remember'—are we but making memories?"

Willa looked away. She was not ready to talk about the end, not yet.

On the return trip they stopped at Paradise Cove. Willa rode ahead, rode all the way to the secluded beach, where she tethered her horse and began, without looking back, to undress. Connor watched. She walked into the water and began to swim, not thinking of where she was going, moving with that hard, strong stroke. After a time he must have started to worry because, when finally she did look back, she saw him swimming toward her.

She went to meet him. For a sustained time they swam toward each other, one as strong as the other, two figures coming together in the ocean. They met. She held hard to him, body against body. She grasped him hard about the waist and they sank beneath the surface. If she held him with enough strength, she thought, she could feel his pain and he could feel hers. They surfaced, gasped for breath, turned and moved then, side by side, toward the shore. They pulled themselves out of the water and sank on a grassy ledge to lie motionless.

Perhaps they slept in the late afternoon sun. Then she was on top of him, her knees dug into his sides, taking him with a determined violence. It took all of his strength to hold her, to meet her. When she was through, when she was spent, he comforted her—not feeling yet the pain from the long scratches she had made in his back, the tears her teeth had made in his shoulder.

On the first weekend in June, at my continued urging, Willa agreed that we could invite Charles and Sara, Arcadia and her Joseph to the ranch. We had yet to meet Joseph, having declined several invitations to come into Santa Monica for that purpose. I knew why Willa was loath to leave or to have guests. I also knew that we must.

Wen and Thad, grateful for a break in the summer monotony, waited on the verandah to announce the arrival. We could see them in Charles' new closed brougham as they crossed the beach road, see the driver put the whip to the team as they turned toward the ranch. It was not until they drew up by the fountain—turned on for the occasion of their arrival—that I saw the fifth passenger. Charles helped Helen Emory out of the coach. She smiled, it seemed to me then, in triumph.

Without Joseph Brennan, that day would have been a disaster. A big, bluff young fellow with red cheeks and a good nature, it was impossible not to like him.

"You are right, Arcadia," Willa said, all the while looking at Joseph. "He *is* perfect for you." At which Joseph began to sputter and fluster, until Arcadia patted his arm and told him not to mind, that Willa could be counted on to be bold.

"I do think that Western women are *different* from Eastern women," Joseph rallied. "Fascinating, simply fascinating."

"Of course we are," Helen said in that insinuating voice of hers. "Western women are singular, Mr. Brennan. That is why we came West, actually, don't you think so, Willa?"

"Of course," Willa answered, flinging her arms in the old way, *"Ultima thule!* To the farthest point! That was my motto as a girl."

"And have you found what you wanted in the Golden State?" Charles asked.

Willa considered him for a moment; then she said, "Yes I have, Charles. I most certainly have."

She was being utterly honest. I thought of Owen, and I wanted to cry.

We picnicked on the beach that day for the first time since my return from San Francisco. Charles seldom strayed from Helen's side. She sat under a parasol, careful to keep the sun from her ruddy complexion. Sara and Arcadia and Joseph romped with the boys at the edge of the water, helping them build a long slide in which to send tumbling a turtle they had found. Willa moved among our guests, chatting with each in turn, but it was, I could tell, an effort.

We stayed until the sun sent long shadows on the beach. As we were gathering our umbrellas and beach chairs, a lone horseman appeared on the beach road, making his way to the ranch. I had but to glance at Willa to know it was Connor, and I could see by her face that she was not going to let him pass. I wanted to stop her, to warn her, but I could not think of a way.

My mind flashed to another time, to words that had been said: *Mama had married the hired hand.* Willa could not let him pass, could not have him dismissed. She would not do that to Connor, even when she knew that it was dangerous to do anything else.

"Mr. McCord," she shouted, waving to him. The late day's sun set a glow about him, as he walked his horse slowly toward us. I could tell he was wary. I cursed myself for not having insisted we leave earlier, as Connor must have thought we would.

Willa introduced him to each of our guests in turn. Connor did not dismount, but nodded at the men and touched his hat to each of the women, careful not to hold the eyes of any of them.

No one had the least idea why Willa was insisting they meet the temporary foreman of the ranch. Only Joseph made any attempt at all to overcome the awkwardness of the situation, and of course made it worse by doing so. Connor rode off at a fast clip.

Helen Emory, who was helping me fold a dinnercloth when

it happened, said in a low voice, "Mr. McCord is quite the man, isn't he?"

I looked at her, curious and angry. "What do you mean?" I asked.

"I mean," she answered, "that if I were a single woman like you, Lena, I'd surely be interested in that bit of man flesh."

Her words were so raw they made me shiver. I hated Helen Emory at that moment more than I have ever hated another human.

There was no letter from Owen that week, nor any the next. The third week in June a messenger arrived with a letter from Boston, written in a woman's hand, yet with Owen's name on it.

I was sure that something was wrong. I paced, waiting for Willa to return from her afternoon wanderings, sure that something was desperately wrong. I tried to read a storybook to Thad, but my thoughts worked against my tongue, and the child finally tired of poking me and skittered off. I saw Willa as she made the turn and ran to meet her, waving the letter. She did not hurry. She took the letter but did not read it at once, sensing it was the beginning of the end, I suppose. She went to the barn to put Princess away. Connor might be there, they might pass in the dim light, as if they had not been together, as if they had not touched, but knowing. When she came back to the house she handed me the letter without a word.

"My dearest wife," the letter began, "Cousin Minnie has graciously offered to practice her pensmanship and write to you for me. I know you will have been worried, and I am sorry indeed to be the cause of that worry. I have been ill. The doctors assure me that I am on my way to recovery now, that I will be up and about soon. I did not allow my aunts or my cousin to write to you until I could send good news. You must not blame them. They have been the most remarkable nurses. (I embarrass Cousin Minnie, I am afraid.)

"I long to see all of you, but you must not think of coming East. I will return as soon as I am strong enough to make the journey. I'm afraid I will not be able to attend Sara and Charles' wedding. I am sure you will tell them how very much I regret not being there on that great day.

"I am happy to know that McCord has worked out well after

all and is doing an excellent job. Please ask him to stay on and assure him I will make it worth his while.

"I will write in a few days, I promise. All of my love to my two good boys, to Lena and, as always, to you. Owen."

Cousin Minnie had added a postscript. "Dear Owen has been so frightfully sick," she said, "shaken with fevers and a weakness that we feel must harken back to his childhood. We worried so for him and for you! He does seem ever so much better now, and we feel sure he is going to be well again, but perhaps not so soon as he, or you, might wish. The doctor does not want him to travel for another four to six weeks, and we are urging Owen to heed him. My love, Minnie."

Supper that night was more silent than usual. Willa was preoccupied. She would not have had time to tell Connor what had happened. I wondered if she would say anything at supper, in my presence.

"We missed you last evening, Connor," I said, believing this to be a safe remark.

"Yes, I too . . . I was in Calabasas," he went on, "as a matter of fact, I finally met the man they call the 'Basque Grandee.'"

"You met Don Miguel Leonis?" Willa asked with some interest. "He's a dreadful man, I'm told—a smuggler."

Before I could ask how Willa knew that—smuggling having become an interest of mine through my conversations with Soong—Connor said, "I don't know much about him, but I did hear an amusing story while I was there. His men feel that he knows magic. Seems one of his *vaqueros* stole Don Leonis' watch. The old man called his men out, lined them up and stood before them with a donkey next to him.

"'One by one, as I call your name,' Don Leonis said, 'you will come forward and whisper into the donkey's ear. If you have the watch of Don Leonis, you will say "guilty." If you are innocent, you will say "not guilty." This donkey, who is my friend, will know if you lie, and he will tell me.' With great solemnity, Don Miguel led the donkey aside and spoke into its ear. Don Miguel then called each man, in turn, and each came forward and spoke into the donkey's ear. When all had stated their innocence, or guilt, Don Leonis again took the donkey aside, listened to it, nodded several times and, with a knowing look on his face, told the men, 'Now I know which of you is the thief. If the watch is returned by sunup, I say no more. It is our secret.' The watch was returned."

"Is it true?" I asked, and Connor chuckled.

"All I can say for certain is that the man who told me that story believed it. He swears Don Leonis can read men's minds."

"Or donkeys'," Willa said sarcastically.

"Or donkeys'," Connor agreed.

"But what were you doing in Calabasas, Connor?" I asked, "I've heard that is a wicked town. Didn't the outlaw Murieta hide there?"

"I was there on business," Connor answered evasively.

"What kind of business?" Willa wanted to know.

Connor concentrated on cutting his mutton chop. "I'm thinking of new lines of work, that is all."

"Not ranching?" I inquired, only half joking. "Have we worked you so hard you've been cured of ranching?"

"No, I haven't given it up, it's just that if I'm thinking to get ahead in this world, perhaps commerce..."

"Are you saying you've grown tired of country life?" Willa asked.

His answer was serious: "I could be perfectly content as the master of a ranch," he said, "it is a wonderful life...but I haven't the resources to own a ranch, so I will have to look elsewhere for an occupation."

"You mean you are interested in owning a ranch but not in working one," Willa said sharply.

"That's not what Connor said at all," I reprimanded her, "what he said was that he wasn't interested in working a farm he didn't own."

"All right," Willa said, "I didn't know you were interested in some other *occupation*." She said the word as if it were obscene, as if Connor had committed an outrage. I realized what was happening; Willa had discovered a way to talk to Connor of the future, of his plans, without committing herself to divulge her own. I was the controlling factor. In front of me, they would have to exercise the utmost care. I was greatly annoyed at this turn of events. Connor did not like it either, for he excused himself abruptly, and left. For a moment I thought Willa was going to run after him, but she didn't.

"Why didn't you tell Connor about Owen's illness?" I demanded. "He will have to know, and soon, to make his own plans."

"Damn his plans," Willa said, and left.

*   *   *

Willa did not go out the next day, but stayed in the house, working on the ranch books, catching up on small chores she had slighted in the weeks past. Dinner that night was more silent than usual. Connor spoke quietly, mostly of ranch matters. He knew, now, about Owen's illness, about his delay in returning. Connor would have guessed the conflict it would create in Willa. I was touched, that night, by the gentleness of the man. He left early, explaining that one of the animals needed tending. Willa raised her hand to him in a gesture that was at once grateful and loving.

Neither did Willa go out the next day. Connor, we knew, was on business in Los Angeles. Instead she played with the children, looking at pictures of birds in one of her many books with Thad, sketching with Wen.

We found ourselves alone at teatime for the first time in many weeks. Willa sat on the swing on the verandah, pensive, her hands quiet.

"Are you worried about Owen?" I asked.

"Yes," she answered, treading softly, honoring the silent agreement we had struck, "Yes, I am. Owen is my husband. I do not want him gone from us."

"Gone?" I asked, not understanding.

"Dead," she said bluntly, "I do not want him to die."

I looked at her, and I had to look away. There was only the sound of the swing, then, between us, rhythmical and grinding.

The wedding was held in the garden of Charles' estate in Pasadena, before a bower of roses entwined in latticework trellises. Willa stood as Sara's witness, in my place. Phineas Emory, wheezing in the heat, gave his adopted daughter in marriage. Helen Emory stood opposite me, on the edge of the gathering, waiting. The smell of roses was suffocating, funereal. Behind me a man whispered, "Charles has it all, now." His wife said, "Hush."

# ~ *Chapter Ten*

It would be August before Owen returned, more than four long months after the rodeo. A spring and a summer would have passed, days and weeks and months in which Willa and Connor, insulated in the expanse of the Malibu, would live their secret life.

That life came to an end on the day that Willa took the open carriage into Santa Monica to meet Owen, as he had asked. She was to return with Owen and with Trinidad and her children, who had been staying at the house in Santa Monica for several days, since their return from Mexico.

Willa left before daybreak. It was still, even then. It would be a hot day with no breeze blowing off the water. The light would be hard and flat, without even a shimmer on the edge of the waves. As the morning wore on, a light haze collected, as if the heat had solidified. Everything was too bright, too searing; I closed my eyes and longed for cool shadows and quiet. I longed to be away, I did not want to wait for what was to be.

Standing on the verandah, waiting nonetheless, I fanned myself with a crude fan Wen had woven from the flat leaves of the flags in the flower garden.

"Do you like the fan I made for you?" Wen asked, accusingly, daring me to say what we both knew, wanting me to say it was not a good fan, actually.

"It does the job it was made to do," I replied.

"But do you like it?" he insisted, taking a child's perverse pleasure in taunting me.

"Look!" Thad called out, "There it is." We watched the carriage approach. The boys were curiously silent. I hummed a song, trying to lighten the mood.

As the carriage pulled up to the fountain I whispered, "Go run to your Papa," and gave each a firm shove, but they would not move. I took them, then, by the hand and marched them down the walkway, determined they should greet their father warmly.

So engrossed was I in the effort that I was almost upon the carriage before I looked up at its passengers. My stomach sank.

Owen, wrapped in blankets, was gaunt. His eyes were deep-set in their sockets, his hair lank on his head. He was an apparition. I had never seen him so thin, so fragile.

Willa quickly jumped down to help him, while Trinidad and the children scrambled out the other side. There was no torrent of homecoming noise. Owen's appearance had sobered us all, even Trinidad's children were quiet.

Owen kissed each of the boys carefully. He seemed glad that they had not greeted him in the old, wild ways, but had rather shyly accepted his kiss.

I found my tongue and said, stupidly, "Owen, you *have* been ill!" Then I did something I had never done before. My eyes filled and I reached to put my arms about him. He looked so very fragile. I felt a wave of great sorrow and hurt, for all that he had been through, in the East and at home, in his absence and unknown to him.

We settled Owen in the front parlor. The morning's trip and the short walk from the carriage had spent his strength. The boys sat on the floor near him, one on either side. For a moment he rested a hand on each small head. Their silence reflected my despair. When Willa's eyes met mine, hers were full of concern and confusion, and we both looked away.

I hurt for them, for Willa and for Owen, and I was afraid, more than I could ever remember being.

"I had no idea he was so very ill . . ." I said to Willa as we passed in the hallway.

"Nor I," she muttered, shaking her head. "I would have gone to Boston," she said, "I would have. I can't imagine how he managed the train trip home."

She hurried on then, concentrating on the small tasks at hand. Returning to the parlor, she asked him, "Shall I send one of the girls to turn down your bed, or would you like for me to ready a chaise here, so you needn't walk up the stairs?"

In a voice that seemed as weary and defeated as his body, Owen said, "Let me sit here a bit, Willa. Perhaps I could have some hot tea?"

We scurried about, making him comfortable. Trinidad came with the tea tray and entered in a torrent of Spanish. It seemed to be a continuing diatribe—a curious, motherly mix of chastisement for not having taken proper care of himself, as if the sickness were all his fault, and affectionate concern. It proved to be good medicine for us all.

"Welcome home, Owen," I said. "We will suffocate you with care, whether you want it or not."

"Yes," he answered, "now that I've had a Trinidadian tongue-lashing, I do feel at home," and he gave us his first real smile, though it was a weak reflection of the glittering one we all remembered.

"Boys," he said to Wen and Thad, who had remained shyly awkward in his presence, "you must have games to be played, be on your way. Papa will talk to you later."

The boys, glad to be released, left quickly.

"They've grown," he said to me.

"Four months is a long time in a child's life," I answered.

"Four months is a long time in any life," Owen said.

I only nodded, and sipped my tea.

"More than anything, four months is too long to be away from one's family, one's own hearth," he went on, taking Willa's hand in his. "I will never leave again for that length of time, not ever." His words, it seemed to me, had a hollow ring to them, the quality of a prepared speech rather than the feeling of having come from the heart. But he had had time, long hours in bed, to think of them, to rehearse them, to wait until the moment when he could say them.

Neither Willa nor I replied. The silence that ensued threatened to become ominous, so I said, "The boys have become accomplished gardeners. The man Wing Soong has given them the most careful instructions. Wen has his own little vegetable patch and so has Thad—you will be proud of their carrots and radishes."

Owen puzzled for a moment, then he remembered. "Yes, the big Celestial—an interesting chap with a British accent. Good. Well, good." He lay back his head and closed his eyes.

"Would you like to nap now?" Willa asked. "The doctor said you should have as much rest as possible."

Without opening his eyes, Owen said, "Did McCord stay on as I asked?"

Perhaps Willa tensed; perhaps I did.

"Yes," she said hurriedly, "but he wants to leave today, and I told him that would be acceptable, now that you are home and Ignacio will be arriving tomorrow." She said it as she moved some magazines in place, as if it were a routine matter. I admired her calm.

"No, no, it is not acceptable," Owen said testily, "I want him to go over everything with Ignacio, to tell him what has been done, what needs to be done. I want a smooth transition. Surely he can stay one more day, after so long a time."

"He has another job waiting, Owen," Willa said in the same quiet tone. "He is expected in Santa Barbara."

"Call him here, Willa, I want to speak to him," Owen said, pulling the blanket about him as if to close off the discussion. But Willa was not ready to close it yet.

"Owen, you must not strain yourself, there really is no need. You forget that I know . . ."

"I must look the very devil," Owen answered with a grimace that may have been meant to seem a smile, "I suppose Charles was right."

"You saw Charles?" I blurted, "Are they back from their wedding trip? How could that be, so soon?"

"Yes, they've just returned," Owen answered me. "They got only so far as Washington when business delayed them. They didn't get to Italy after all, something came up that made it necessary for Charles to return to Los Angeles. He met me at the Arcade station with some papers that needed to be signed. I seem always to be signing papers for Charles."

I sat thinking about this new information—brooding, really. Sara had been elated by the idea of a trip to Italy, of traveling alone with Charles, of introducing him to Florence, the city she loved best in the world. I could imagine her disappointment.

"What was Charles right about?" Willa asked.

"He said I looked like death itself," Owen answered, and Willa shuddered. "I told him to bring Sara out for the weekend," he went on in the same weary voice. "I thought you would want some company. Charles says you've become hermits in my absence."

"But are you up to house guests?" Willa asked. "Don't you think we should see you well first?"

"I will be well soon enough," Owen answered, "now that I'm home." He reached for Willa's hand and held it against his chest. "I will get well, my dear. The sea and the sun and the sand will cure me, just as it did you after Thad's birth. Now be a good girl and get McCord for me."

I have often tried to imagine the meeting between Owen and Connor that hot August midday. I have tried to think what Connor would have thought, seeing the ruined health of the man whose wife he coveted. I wanted to protect Owen, though I believed Connor to be a kind man, gentle even. I could not think that he would deliberately hurt a man, especially such a sick man. Yet I could not think that Connor would go gently away, would remove himself from Willa's life without so much as a word. Unless she had convinced him that he must. Neither was I certain of Willa. Since I had removed myself from her deliberations, I was not privy to her thoughts. For that I was both sorry and glad. Had she asked my advice, I would have been hard put to separate my fate from hers, to go against my own interests.

The only thing I did know was that Connor planned to leave for Santa Barbara, that he had secured a job in a shipping firm. I sensed that he had wanted Ignacio to return first so that he could depart before Owen's homecoming.

Connor was with Owen no more than five minutes. I was in the garden, waiting, with the boys and Soong.

"You are wringing your hands, Lena," he said. (We had come to call each other by our given names when no one else was about. It pleased me to hear him speak my name.)

"I am feeling jangled," I answered distractedly.

"McCord is leaving, is that right?" he pressed.

It no longer surprised me that he should know what was on

my mind. "It is what Connor wants, but Owen is asking that
he stay until Ignacio returns."

"I see," he said.

"I wish I did," I answered.

"I believe you see too much, as it is," he countered.

"Yes," I agreed.

"Ahh," Soong said, "the curse of those who have pity for
all but themselves."

"That sounds vaguely Confucian," I replied, looking at the
house, wondering.

"You have been reading as you type," he accused me. Some
weeks before I had discovered, in a box in the library, some
rare Chinese manuscripts forwarded by Owen's agent in San
Francisco. Wing Soong agreed to translate them, so that I could
type the translations as a homecoming gift for Owen.

"Oh, yes," I said, just as Connor walked out of the house,
striding purposefully back to the barn.

"Perhaps McCord is going to leave after all," I said, addressing the issue that was on my mind. "I do want to say
goodbye to him." In fact, I hadn't a notion what I would say.

I found him in the dim light of the tack room. The smells
of oiled leather and clean straw and horses mingled. I stood
for a moment studying the way the blue shirt stretched taut
across his back.

"Connor," I said softly.

He spun around, eyes bright, his face alive.

He thought me to be Willa; our voices are alike. He was
expecting her, then.

"I'm sorry," I said awkwardly.

"Oh, Lena, it's you," he answered, struggling to cover his
disappointment.

But I had seen how he looked at her, I felt what she would
have felt, I had the briefest glimpse of what was between them.
I pushed it away from me.

"I wanted to be sure to see you before you left, to say
goodbye—things have been so confused here..." I stammered.

"I was to be off today," he answered, "but your brother-in-
law has convinced me that I should stay until Ignacio arrives."

"Tomorrow?" I asked.

"Yes," he answered.

The silence that settled between us was not uneasy, there was no discomfort in it. Connor was not a man who needed to talk into the silences. I put out my hand.

"I hope you find what you want, Connor," I said somewhat formally.

He held my hand in both of his and said to me with just a trace of a brogue, "I have always had the good fortune to meet lovely women like yourself, Lena Kerr. For that, I am thankful. But as for what I want, well—what we want we cannot always have, that's the truth of it, now, isn't it?"

I shook my head yes and left, feeling miserable. Yet even as I walked out of the barn, a wave of relief swept over me. He had, in his way, told me: He could not have her. I knew then what I should have known all along. Willa would never leave her family or the Malibu. It had never been possible, not from the very beginning, no matter what storms of passion washed over them.

Feeling free of fear now, for the first time, I hurried up to the garden and waved the boys in for their midday meal. Wing Soong, I noticed, sat back on his haunches and studied me.

"Everything is going to be fine," I called to him.

"That is good to know," he replied, repeating the words as if they were part of some private litany.

Ignacio did not return until late the following afternoon, having been delayed by a broken cartwheel. Trinidad, happy to be back in her kitchen, had been cooking all day long.

"I had almost forgotten how beautiful our vegetables are, and how huge," Owen said, caressing a large tomato. "It is good to be back in paradise."

If Willa was quieter than usual, she was at the same time ever at hand, attentive to his needs. When he touched her she did not withdraw, yet neither did she reach for him. The concern on her face was genuine. If it was mixed, as I supposed, with confusion and guilt and regret. I could only feel relief. The choice she had made had been inevitable, after all. I was only sorry that Connor could not have been away, that they could not have been spared each other's presence now that the end had come. (I could not erase from my mind the look on his face when he thought me to be Willa.) It would be easier, I was sure, when he was gone.

With Ignacio's arrival, the routine of the past months was erased, the old order returned. You could feel the change. Summer was over, in spite of the heat.

I met Willa in the hallway, alone, for the first time that day. No one was about, so I felt free to ask, "Tell me about Owen's health. What is it? What is wrong?"

"He has had pneumonia, Dr. Hadley told me. His lungs are weakened," Willa explained, "but the doctors say that he will recover, that it is a matter of time and rest now."

"Rest—will he?" I wanted to know.

"Dr. Hadley says he must, that he is to stay here for six months, perhaps more."

"No business trips, then?" I asked.

"No riding, even, for at least two months. And yes, I believe he will, Lena. He has been shaken by this illness. He is much more, well—subdued, it seems to me. Have you noticed?"

"Of course he is subdued, the man is ill," I answered, but gently. I think the question she asked was not the one she wanted to ask. "But you, Willa," I went on, searching her face, "will you be all right?"

She closed her eyes and leaned against the wall, her forehead pressed into the flowered paper. "I don't know," she whispered, her lip trembling. The house seemed heavy with silence. A circle of light played on the wall, opposite an open doorway. Willa went on in a voice that was distant. "You know how people admire eagles because they have such strong wings, because they seem to be the very essence of freedom?" she asked. "In fact, eagles aren't free, not in the least. Once full grown and mated they are tied to the nest. The same nest in the same tree somewhere in the north woods. Year after year they return to the nest, and it grows larger and larger until it fills the top of the tree, until it fills the whole of their lives. The eagle pair has no choice. It is trapped by instinct. Every year until one of them dies, the eagles must return. They are not free."

In a very quiet voice I told her, "None of us are free, Willa. Perhaps no living creature ever is."

"But the eagles soar," she said, her voice rising slightly, her eyes filling. "They seem so free as they rise on a thermal— they ride the wind and it must feel as if all that binds them to the earth is gone."

"Maybe that is enough," I said, "to soar, just to have known how it is?"

She looked at me for a long time. Finally she wiped the tears from her eyes with her fingers and, biting her lip, she said, "You wanted to know if I will be all right. The answer is yes. Yes, I will be."

I put my arms around her and I could feel how tightly she held herself, how straight and true.

We took our supper in the front parlor, Willa, Owen and I. The light grew dim, but none of us moved to turn on a lamp. It was better to sit there in the twilight, better not to see too sharply. We spoke in desultory tones. Owen, who took the lead in our conversations, lapsed into preoccupied silences. He may, in fact, have been dozing. I felt, for a long moment, that it might forever be dusk in our lives together.

It was unusually warm, yet all the doors were shut on Owen's account. For that reason we did not hear the dogs announce the approaching horsemen.

"Hallo!" a sound drifted in.

"Whoever?" Willa asked, puzzled. "Do sit still, Owen. I'll see what it is."

She returned with two men, strangers both. One was tall and had a nose with a high, wide hook to it. He seemed to be in charge. The other man was swarthy and stood uncomfortably just inside the door, his hat in his hand.

"Mr. Reade, sir, my name is Amos Proctor," the man with the hooked nose said with an official air, "I am the district agent for the Department of the Treasury." He strode across the room to shake Owen's hand. Owen did not rise, but invited the two to join us. Proctor declined for them both.

"It is a matter of some urgency—my being here," he said, looking pointedly at Willa and me as if to indicate he had come on delicate business. Owen dismissed the idea out of hand. "You can speak before my wife and her sister," he said.

Clearing his throat to give the business at hand weight, the agent said, "We have reliable information that there is to be an opium exchange off Point Dume tonight, a cache to be dropped from a sailing ship called the *Pequod*. We will need permission to cross your land, sir. We intend to catch whoever it is that is picking up the contraband on this side of the ocean."

Owen frowned. "Dirty business," he said, "I hate to think of it so close to my home."

"If you don't mind my saying so, sir, Point Dume has long been a favorite for smugglers, there's a cove . . ."

"Paradise Cove," Owen put in, "I know it."

"Yes, that's the one," the man continued, "it's perfect for the kind of landfall they need."

"Of course you have my permission," Owen told him. "No question. I want to put a stop to that degrading business as much as you do. Shocking. I won't have vermin who profiteer on other men's misery on my land."

The short man who had seemed so uncomfortable now shifted his weight, knocking against a small commode and sending bric-a-brac flying.

"We'd best be gone," Proctor said, as if to apologize for his awkward partner, who had made no move to pick up the scattered bits of glass and porcelain, but in leaving had, even, crushed a bit of crystal under his foot.

Owen seemed not to notice; Willa, not to care. I started to retrieve some of the small bits, but thought better of it and held myself to my seat.

"Call them back," Owen said, suddenly.

Proctor did not reenter, but through the door said, "Sir?"

"I want to know if you find anyone," Owen told him.

"Find?" Proctor asked, as if he did not quite understand.

"If you find anyone on my ranch, I want to know."

The Treasury agent nodded.

"Do you think there is anything to it?" Willa asked. "It seems so farfetched—desperados here, on our ranch. At Point Dume, even."

"It does sound like one of those Wild West stories the Eastern press so loves, doesn't it?" Owen admitted wryly.

I thought about Wing Soong, and what he had told me of the opium trade, but I said nothing. I did not want to draw attention to my acquaintance, or to his confidences.

I left them together, Willa reading to Owen from an old issue of *Harper's* we had saved because it was about Theodore Roosevelt and his political aspirations. Scarcely a quarter of an hour had passed before I heard Willa's step in the hallway.

I opened my door to see if she needed me.

"No," she said, hurrying on, "Owen is asleep on the chaise.

I'm getting some quilts to cover him—he sleeps so lightly, I don't want to wake him for fear he won't be able to get back to sleep."

Strange sounds moved into my sleep. I lay for a moment, trying to rise to consciousness, trying to sort them out. It was hot, close; the windows were open but no breeze stirred in the eucalyptus tree. It was the dark of early morning, a deep iron gray. Three o'clock, I guessed. Perhaps four.

They were voices, low. A murmur, then Owen's voice.

"Come down, everyone, come down!" he called in a voice that was not so much loud as urgent.

I pulled on a wrapper and made my way into the hall, colliding there with the boys who had come in search of me. They clutched at me, sleepy and frightened.

"What is it?" they said, one and then the other, "what is wrong?"

Wrong. Something was wrong, I could feel it too.

"I don't know," I said. "Come. Hold together. We'll be fine." The floor felt cold to my bare feet, in spite of the heat. In the dense dark of the hour before dawn, the house creaked with the uncommon movements.

We made our way down the stair, each of us guided by the long, smooth banister, knowing that we had reached the bottom by the quick curve in the wood as it edged against the wall.

We made our way toward a single light in the parlor. Willa was there, her hair loose and sleep-tossed. I could see that she did not know, that Owen's frenzied call had caught her, too. I could not tell if Owen was holding her to him, or if she was supporting Owen.

The servants were silently entering the room, filling the dark spaces in the corners, away from us, isolating us. You could feel their fear. Something was terribly wrong, was the sense of it. Something was happening, or about to happen. Trinidad, breathing heavily, was moving her rosary beads in steady rhythm. I thought that Ignacio was beside her, but I could see that he was not.

Owen held the lamp high; it threw its light on his face— the eyes deep-set in his skull, the skin taut. The boys held so tightly to me that I had to pry their fingers loose to lessen the pain.

"All of you, follow me," Owen commanded, and led us outside onto the verandah.

There was no moon, yet I sensed the men there, on horseback, lined to the rail, before my eyes made out their dim forms. In the quiet we could hear the quiver of a horse's breathing, a man's loose cough.

"They've caught the smugglers," Owen announced in a high, wild voice, "I want you to see, all of you . . ."

He walked away from us with his light so that it cast trembling shadows in the circle it illuminated. In the flickering light we saw, first, the forelegs of the horses and then, as the light carried, the faces of the riders in a row: Amos Proctor and the swarthy man. Between them, Connor McCord.

Connor, hatless, his hands tied behind him so that his shoulders were pulled back. A trickle of blood ran from the side of his mouth, thin and neat, as if someone had drawn a perfect line.

"No," I wailed, "you've made a terrible mistake."

Willa gripped my arm, hard. "Connor, dear God," I said, "what has happened?"

"There's been no mistake, ma'am," Proctor said in his official voice.

"We caught 'em carryin' the gold," the swarthy man put in, "ain't no doubt we got the right man."

Connor said nothing. His face had a set to it that I had never seen before, as if frozen. His eyes were locked on some middle ground, removed from us all, I would not have known him; I did not know him. I wanted him to speak, to explain, to say what had gone wrong.

Owen walked back to us, pulling Willa to him and holding the lantern high so that only the two of them fell within the circle of light.

"I wanted my family and all of the servants and workers on this ranch to see the thieves, the cowards, the filth who traffic in the opium trade. I want all of you to see how a man we trusted has violated that trust, has made fools of us."

Owen spoke to Proctor. "I employed that man and it was a mistake, a terrible mistake. He used our home to pursue his vile business. The man is scum, vermin." I had never seen Owen so agitated, his voice shook with anger.

"Who is the other thief?" Owen asked. "Does anybody

know?" For the first time I saw another of the mounted men with his hands behind his back.

"It's Rodriguez from over Calabasas," the swarthy man said, "we know that one well enough."

Proctor cut in. "Rodriguez will tell us all we need to know about McCord here," he said.

"Get them off my land," Owen told them. He was leaning against the railing, holding onto it, his face contorted with anger. For a moment I feared he might tumble over the railing, but I hadn't the courage to move to help him.

"Take them away," he said, his voice weary, his strength spent.

I lay awake in the heat, afraid to let myself think about it all. Afraid to admit the mortification of being wrong, utterly wrong, about McCord. The idea was too large to confront: I was too frightened to consider it in the dark. *Connor had been a lie . . . nothing about him had been true.* I could not bear to think of it, not yet.

I lay in my lonely bed and tried not to think of Connor, tried not to think of my sister, of what agonies she would be enduring. I heard them mount the stairs together, Willa and Owen. I heard the door close on the room they had not shared for many long months. I wondered if it ever would be morning again.

## ~ *Chapter Eleven*

Willa made her way through the days that followed as if performing a curious kind of penance. She answered Owen's every need, and the children's. She was at their command, ready to do whatever was wanted of her. She did not seek the solitude I was sure she longed for, she did not ride off on Princess into one of the canyons or quiet sea beaches which might, by their very beauty, ease her pain. She could not allow herself the luxury of solitude; she did not believe she deserved it. Had Willa been of a religious temperament, she might have sought out a church and spread herself recumbent before the altar. But for Willa there was no altar, no confessional, only this domestic atonement for her sins.

Her sin. She was guilty of the sin of believing in Connor. She was overcome with self-loathing now, was awash with disgust for that which she had committed, the sin of false belief. Connor McCord had been an article of faith for Willa. The death of that faith had thrown her into a purgatory. Outwardly, she seemed not much changed. Only a tightness in the muscles about her mouth, the set of her jaw, betrayed the gnawing within. I feared for her, I ached for her, and I could not think how to help her through this terrible time.

For Owen, the event seemed to pass quickly enough. He

spoke of it for a few days, angry and incredulous that Connor could have deceived us so. He called him a hoaxer, a serpent, a Judas, a cheat. He was full of righteous indignation, and then—for Owen, at least—it seemed to be done, forgotten.

But Willa would not forget, and neither would I. It would be months before she could bear even to think of Connor. She pushed him away from her waking thoughts, she locked that part of her away forever, sealed it off as completely as she could. She intended to erase the summer of her thirty-first year from her consciousness. If she did not sleep well, it was because Connor invaded her dreams. Dark circles beneath her eyes attested to the struggle.

I felt that I knew something of Willa's mortification for I, too, had been duped by Connor. I had not doubted him, had accepted all he said as the truth, though in retrospect I could see my mistakes—the unexplained absences, the trips to Calabasas, vague references to business opportunities. We had not thought him to be secretive at the time, which only showed how gullible we had been, Willa and I. Trusting and stupid and deluded and terribly gullible. We who had thought ourselves to be so clever and daring, not bound by ordinary convention. We had been, instead, smug and silly as girls—and unutterably dense, not to have so much as suspected. If I could feel such mortification, I could only imagine Willa's.

I did not try to talk to Willa about Connor, not then. I think I knew that she needed to excise him from her mind, that she could survive this time only if we were very careful.

She walked upright, straight. Often it seemed to me as if she were sleepwalking. Once, quite by accident, I came upon her out behind the chicken shed. She was bent over, clutching her knees and moaning. She thought she was alone, and I slipped away before she could see me. I did not doubt the terrible toll that summer was exacting. All I could do to help was to wait, wait and hope that she could maintain her composure until the wound closed. Willa needed healing time.

There were distractions enough. Owen, even ailing, saw to that. He imposed his rhythm on our lives; people began to appear. Sara and Charles were the first of our old friends to come for a weekend outing.

Sara came a day ahead of her husband, so that we might have a private visit. As soon as I saw her buggy, I moved to meet her, not even caring that she see my curious running side step, or my hips heaving up and down in my hurry.

"I had no idea you were back," I called out to her.

She accepted my worried look and welcome kiss and said, "Some things don't happen. Italy with Charles didn't happen, Lena. That's all."

"That's all!" I repeated, "But Sara, you were looking forward to it. It was your *wedding* trip."

Sara only shrugged. "Let's go for a ride on the beach as soon as we can get away," she murmured, and I nodded. There was much I wanted to say to Sara, though at that moment I had no idea if I would speak to her of Connor McCord. Sara seemed to be carrying her own burden, and I would not want to add to it, I thought.

We dismounted at the water's edge, tied our shoes onto our saddles and walked slowly down the beach, leading the horses and letting the water lap about the hems of our dresses. The weight of the wet cloth and the sand on my bare feet felt strangely comforting.

"I heard about McCord," Sara said. "Were you surprised?"

"Surprised?" I answered, my voice thick with irony, "oh, yes. Very surprised."

"I wondered . . ." she started, then stopped. I turned to look at her, still not knowing how much I would say.

"What does it all mean—Connor McCord, that business? Willa introduced us, remember? On the beach that day. It struck me as strange at the time, the way she called him over—with such elaborate respect. It seemed important to Willa, then. I've been curious."

I took a deep breath. "We felt that way about Connor—both Willa and I did," I said (realizing that I was protecting Willa, even with Sara). "We trusted him and we liked him, that's what makes it all so confusing. That we could have been so *wrong* about the man."

"Yes, it is confusing," Sara answered, deep in thought. "There is to be a trial. Charles told me. It's to be heard by one of his cronies, Judge Peal."

I knew that I was not going to be able to talk about it, not even to Sara. "Someday I'll tell you all about our friend Connor McCord, opium smuggler," I said, with a laugh that sounded bitter, I knew, "but not now, not yet. Now I want to talk about you. We haven't had a chance to speak privately since your marriage—and I want to know how you are, how everything is. How marriage is." She smiled and made a funny face.

We tied our horses to a water-worn log that had washed up on the beach, and we sat in the sun, our dresses spread to dry. A crust of sand ringed the hems and now and again a glint of mica sparkled.

"I cannot tell you how good it is to be here with you," Sara said. I leaned toward her until our shoulders touched. She added, "It is good to know that there is someone in this world I can talk to."

"Not Charles, then?" I asked gently.

"Oh, I always could talk to Charles in a certain way," she answered, squinting out to sea. Waves were breaking evenly, and every fourth or fifth wave hit with a crashing boom. "Charles is honest with me, there are no lies between us, not even kind ones. We laugh together. He trusts me, to a certain extent. I think he trusts me as much as he can anyone." She was, I could see, trying to tell me what there was between them, and in doing so only emphasized that there was not.

"Why didn't you go to Italy?" I asked. "Owen said it was business, that Charles was called back here."

"Oh, that was the reason Charles gave," Sara answered slowly, "but it was an excuse. Charles just didn't want to go. And he is good at not doing what he doesn't want to do."

"But it was all planned," I objected. "You wanted so much to go, and he had agreed."

"No, he didn't really," she said in a steady voice. "I wanted it, and I happened to mention a trip to Italy in the presence of Father Emory. Nothing would do, then, but that he give us the trip as his wedding gift. But I knew we wouldn't go, Charles didn't pretend to me."

"How did Charles explain the cancellations to Mr. Emory?" I asked.

Sara laughed. "He didn't have to. You see, when we were in Washington, Charles went to see quite a number of politicians—some of whom fall in the family retainer category—and he managed to stir them up enough to secure the right of way to some New Mexico land that Father Emory has been coveting. Of course, Charles had to come back to secure the arrangement. Italy was a small price to pay for such a grand business advantage, Father Emory agreed."

I sat quietly, trying to understand why Sara had no anger in her. As if reading my thoughts she explained, "Lena, listen to me. I was disappointed, yes, but not surprised and not angry. It would have been nice had Charles wanted to go, but he didn't. I wish there had been some way that you and I could have gone instead, but I couldn't think of how to make that happen." She laughed, thinking of what people might have said. "I would have been far happier going with you—perhaps we can arrange a tour next year, do you think? I'm taking art lessons, did I tell you? I've always sketched and you know how much I love going to museums. I may even have some talent."

I was not about to be diverted. "You haven't told me yet about . . . about your *matrimony*."

She grinned at my choice of words. "There is nothing to tell," she said in a quiet voice.

I looked at her strangely.

"Sara, I don't mean to pry . . . if you don't wish to talk . . ."

"You would never pry," she answered. "I am a wife in the carnal sense, yes. Just that. Charles drank quite a lot on our wedding night and introduced me to the married state. For me, it meant a certain amount of pain and some bleeding, which I am told by some of my friends is normal for the first time. I felt only relief when it was over. I suppose it was no better for Charles, for he hasn't repeated the gesture."

I sat up and looked at her, aghast.

"Have you spoken to him of it?" I wanted to know.

"No," she said.

"But you must . . ." I began, and stopped when I realized I had no idea what she must do, or why.

"The marriage has been consummated," she said, as if trying to explain something to me. "For legal purposes that is enough." She gave me a small, wry smile. It was all she wanted to say. I could feel myself frowning; I could not drop the subject.

"I've tried to make you understand," Sara said with a sigh. "Charles is fond of me in a certain way. But I cannot expect more, and I never intended to, you know."

"A child, you expected a child," I reminded her.

"I had *hoped* for that, yes. But it was always just that, a hope." She was biting her lower lip.

"I am prepared for that not to happen, is what I am saying," she murmured.

Because I could think of nothing better to say, I commented, "At least, Helen is out of the way."

"Helen?" Sara answered, "Helen's visiting now."

I looked at her in amazement. "Where?" I asked, "visiting who?"

"Charles," she said.

"You mean Helen and Charles are at your house in Pasadena now?" I blurted, indignant.

"At Charles' house," she corrected me. "It never was mine. That is written in the marriage contract."

"Nor, it seems, was Charles," I said bitterly. "Was that written in the marriage contract, too?" I lay back, suddenly exhausted.

"That is what I have been trying to tell you all along," Sara told me patiently. "Charles gave me a name, a legal status. That was all, and I know you think it wasn't enough—but for me it is quite a lot."

"Helen got her legal status, too," I could not help but say, "along with your husband. At least you share the same name."

Sara looked out to sea, then she turned to look me in the face. "Helen and I do have that in common, I suppose," she said without the slightest rancor.

"Oh, you have nothing in common, nothing at all," I all but shouted. Suddenly the anger and confusion and humiliation and fear that had been building within me all summer long, like some great boil, burst. I was crying, sobbing. Not for Sara and not for Willa, not for Owen or Connor or Wen, but for me. For Lena Kerr, who bore the curse of having to know.

We lay back against the rocks, Sara cradling me in her arms, and I cried for a long time. Someday, she whispered, we will talk about it all, everything. She knew, in the way she had of knowing, that my tears went beyond her own sorry situation, but she said nothing. The time would come when I would tell her all that I knew, but it was not now.

If Willa were more silent than she had been she was, at the same time, more available. She listened, seemingly engrossed, to Wen's long, convoluted explanations of how the cowboys broke the three new mustangs Ignacio had brought back with him. She brought Owen's collections into the parlor and sat with him for long hours, organizing butterfly specimens and native wildflowers, making notations at his direction, cataloging his growing library of rare books, overseeing the building of cabinets to house his Californian artifacts. She read to Thad, drew pictures for him; she took care of the collie's sore foot; she even put her cool hand on my brow when I complained of feeling warm. And they were acts of contrition, all of them. I could not but wonder how long she must serve as a penitent.

The end of summer approached. The heat did not abate. Everything seemed to move slowly, the very air was heavy. I found Willa sitting on a low stool on the verandah, facing Thad, who was perched on a chair, so that they were eye to eye. She was helping him smooth a wrinkle in his stocking which had caused him some discomfort, and the two were absorbed in the task.

"Willa," I said, determined to be heard, "Owen is feeling so much better today and it is so stifling here—why don't you take Princess for a ride along the ocean?"

Not looking up, continuing to work on the stocking, she said, "No. No, I won't do that."

"Willa," I began to argue, but she stopped me.

"I have been thinking that Princess should get out, Lena. Do you suppose you could do that for me? Take her out for at least some short rides?"

Thad, annoyed by my distraction, began tugging on his mother's arm.

"Yes, Thad," Willa said, turning to him, "how is that? Does it still hurt?"

"All right," I answered, defeated. It was, of course, part of the penance. But I did as she asked, and never had I been so happy that Willa had, almost fifteen years before when we were girls on the farm, insisted that I could ride if I but set my mind to it.

In my journal for that long, hot summer the only light, happy times I recorded were my accounts of those long rambles on horseback. They provided my only relief from the building tensions. I rode Princess regularly. She had missed the long rides with her mistress and she nuzzled me as if to say, "I'll show you just how much fun this can be." She was an excep-

tional animal, filled with good spirits yet gentle. She knew the
ranch better than I did. The few times I missed a turn and
managed to lose my bearings, Princess brought us home.

Willa came awake, not certain why, aware only that something
was changed. She was alone in the bed. She realized she had
moved to the position in the center that she had become accustomed to in the long months in which she had slept alone.
It was a comfortable feeling; she moved away from it as soon
as she understood that it was comforting.

In the early light she saw Owen's form moving about the
room. It came to her then: This was the morning Wen was to
leave for school. Owen would take him to Redlands. She forced
herself to sit up; a wave of nausea sent her reeling back onto
the pillow. She groaned.

"Ah, you're awake," Owen said, not looking round but
lighting a lamp so that he could see to dress.

"Umm," she answered, keeping her lips pressed tight.

"Stay in bed," he said, "You needn't get up—I'll send Wen
to you to say goodbye." He was not being solicitous and she
was glad. He was anxious to be on his way and did not want
the leavetaking to be protracted.

She thought: I must get up. I must. She swung her legs over
the side of the bed, but the floor would not be still, the room
seemed to lurch at her. She could not get up, she knew. With
her hand she felt for the ironstone chamberpot they kept under
the bed. It was cool to the touch; she left her hand trailing,
touching the cool pottery, and watched Owen dress. He was
humming to himself, concentrating on the detail of his dress.
When he finished he turned to her, his hands spread on the
bed's brass railing.

"You remember I am to stay over for a few days in town,"
he said in a businesslike tone, "I'll see the doctor, and take
care of some other details, but mostly I'll rest up so the trip
doesn't impede my convalescence."

"Yes of course," she said, and tried to smile. Her stomach
was churning.

"I'll send the boy up when he's had his breakfast," he said
in leaving, "don't keep him too long."

He did not bend to kiss her. He slept in her bed and he
entered her body, but he did not touch her at other times, and

she did not complain. Never again would she make demands of Owen. She would deny the body that had betrayed her.

She waited until he pulled the door closed. Then she reached for the chamberpot, leaned far over the side of the bed, and retched. When her stomach was emptied, when there was no more, she lay back on the pillows, too tired to move. She rested for a few moments, breathing deeply. Then she forced herself to sit up, and to carry the sour-smelling vessel away from her bed. Bracing herself against the wall, she splashed her face with cold water, then she rinsed her mouth, spitting the water into the basin. She could not seem to rid herself of the bitter taste; it was with her, part of her always.

She did not want Wen to smell the awful odor that was clinging to her. She raised the window and breathed the clean air. Suddenly she was swaying, she felt faint and cold. She made her way, holding to the furniture, and sank into the bed and into a brutal half-sleep in which she dreamed that Connor was riding off with Wen, was taking him away. She was trying to scream, but when she opened her mouth no sound came out and she was helpless.

We ate in silence that morning, Wen and Owen and I, until finally Owen said, "Go tell your mother goodbye, and make sure you smile."

Wen left dutifully.

"Is Willa ill?" I asked when Wen had gone.

"Ill? No, she's fine," he answered, "I think she didn't sleep well, that's all." He ate methodically, I noticed, speaking between spoons of porridge. I buttered a biscuit for a long while, knowing I could not eat it.

"Lena," Owen said in a tone which suggested duty, "I know that you are worried about Wen, but I promise you that in six months he'll come home for the holidays and be only too glad to return to his school and the friends he will make there."

I wanted to say, "How can you be so sure?" I wanted to say, "Is that what you want, Owen?" But I said nothing at all.

I watched the two of them drive off in the carriage, the tall, gaunt man and the small boy. I watched until they turned the far corner and were out of sight. When I came back into the house I knew that something was missing, and that it would always be so.

Trinidad was in the kitchen, her apron over her head, weeping copiously. *Dear Trinidad,* I thought. I had no idea Wen's departure would affect her so. Now that I thought about it, she had been upset of late. "Has Ignacio had his breakfast?" I asked, more to distract her than anything else. "No, no," she said, between wet gulps, "he is gone early."

"Gone?" I repeated.

"To Santa Monica," she replied, "To Los Angeles." I remembered then, that Owen had sent his *mayordomo* to ship the stock. Ordinarily, Ignacio would not have been sent on such an errand—but Owen had insisted he go, for reasons I did not understand.

In the weeks since his return from the East, Owen's health had made amazing gains. The open air and the sun and the sea did, as he had said they would, wonders. Each day his color improved, he moved more easily, his form seemed to fill out and his spirits to lift. By contrast, Willa grew ever paler.

She was lethargic and wan. It was as if her energy was being transmitted to him, as if she were being drained.

Owen returned from Redlands looking better, even, than when he had left. At midmorning a few days later, Trinidad and I were in the kitchen discussing the provisions we would need from town when Willa came in, still in her wrapper, her feet bare.

"Sit down," I said, "let me get you some tea." She did as I said, slumping in a chair at the table.

"Are you ill, Willa?" I asked, and when she didn't answer I repeated the question.

Willa looked at me as if I had been speaking in tongues. "No," she finally answered, "no, I'm not ill, not really."

"Then if you are well," I said with considerable sarcasm, "don't you think it time you got back to your work on the raptors? There are at least four letters that need answering. And Princess, too—you should think about taking Princess for her outings. She has been very patient with me, but . . ."

Willa sipped her tea, and I thought she had not heard me. She closed her eyes against the steamy vapor that lifted from the hot liquid.

But she had heard. "I think not, Lena," she said, in a tone that told me it was final. Before I could give her an argument she rose, saying, "You are right—I am getting lazy, staying in bed so long. I'd best get dressed."

She left me looking after her, puzzled.

Trinidad giggled.

I was annoyed. "What do you find so amusing?" I wanted to know.

*"La Señora,"* she replied, cupping her hand under her belly, *"tiene nene."*

She took my breath away. I reached to steady myself and fell against the wood stove, burning my hand.

*"Aie,"* Trinidad cried in alarm. She sat me down and began to rub lard on the nasty welt that rose on my hand. I didn't feel the pain of the burn, not then. I was too shaken by the revelation. *Willa was going to have a baby.*

Working over my hand like some mother hen, Trinidad chattered ceaselessly. "Maybe now they get baby girl," she said. "Maybe me, too," she added, patting her belly to let me know that she was, once again, with child. I knew that she was thinking how lucky it was that she would be able to suckle Willa's baby, along with her own. I had the sudden urge to hit her, to pound on her great baby-making body, on those great breasts that would pour out their bounty in streams.

Willa was dressing, still, when I knocked on the door. She was pulling on her petticoats. Her body was swelling, I could see that.

"I should have known, Willa..."

She continued hooking herself into the dress, saying nothing.

"When...?" I tried to begin, but stopped and bit my tongue.

She looked at me, her eyes wide, and she said, "I don't really know."

Owen had returned in August; *oh please*, I prayed, *not before summer, please.*

"Not knowing—" I said, trying to choose my words, "Is it...difficult?"

She walked away from me. Her dress was open in the back, I could see the tiny moles that formed a triangle at the nape of her neck. I fixed my gaze on them, I studied them as a mariner might study the stars. I saw them move, saw her shoulders heave ever so slightly.

"Oh, Willa," I moaned, my voice suddenly cracking.

She wheeled around, angry. "Don't, Lena, don't do that." She pulled herself up, so that it seemed she was talking to me from some great height. "I cannot talk now, Lena," she said. "Not now, maybe not ever. But I cannot now, please." She was firm, but I could see that the firmness bordered on collapse.

"Yes," I answered, "but . . . ask, please. I promise, I will do whatever I can . . ."

As she turned away from me again, she nodded, I could see that. She was, I was sure, holding her breath to keep from spinning apart. Owen's voice in the downstairs hallway sent me running. I did not want to be in the room when he entered. I wondered if he knew. I thought not.

"Good morning, Lena," Owen called to me, all good cheer. "I have had the most entertaining morning with our man Wing Soong. Quite a chap, actually," he assumed an English accent, mimicking Wing Soong, "his gentleman's English quite throws me off. Somehow, you don't expect a Chinese peasant to speak such beautiful English. Amazing, what?"

I tried to smile, but couldn't. "Yes, he is," I finally said. trying to hide my resentment. I had not been able to speak to Wing Soong for days. We were all so much drawn into Owen's vortex; only Owen had the leisure to choose his activities. I knew it was wrong of me, wrong and irrational and yes, even hateful—but at that moment I despised Owen Reade. He came and he went at will. He made decisions for all of us, and always so very proper, so godlike, so charming and blithe and sure of himself. And so numb to reality. It would never occur to Owen that he was as much responsible as Willa for what had happened in his absence. He deserved my sympathy, I knew that. After all, I had no idea what was going on under that brittle, bright surface. Perhaps he suspected, perhaps he was in terrible pain, too. Perhaps he was struggling to maintain the charade. Perhaps.

*Dear God,* I whispered to myself in the privacy of the arbor, *dear God, let it be Owen's.* I gripped the heavy rope that held the swing until the rough fibers cut into my burned hand. *Oh, please,* I whispered to no one at all. Even then, I knew my prayer could not be answered.

\* \* \*

I did not sleep well in the weeks following Wen's departure. October moved into November, and I lay awake each morning waiting for the first light. On one such morning I surprised myself by climbing out of bed, pulling a shawl over my night-dress and walking out to the arbor near the garden. It was the only refuge for me, the only place where I could feel some peace, perhaps because I had spent so many hours there with the boys.

I sat in the swing and picked at the flaking paint and, for the first time in a very long time, I thought about home, about Illinois and Porter Farm. I was, I realized, homesick.

I felt the tears slip down my cheeks and I tried to push them away with the back of my hand. I had left home in the spring-time, a child, full of fears and full of hope. And now it was October, seven years later. I was twenty-four years old, a woman. A spinster. I tried to remember other Octobers, but I could not. I pictured the farmhouse, letting my mind roam through it. I tried to remember my brother Servia's face, but I could not. I could only see Wen sitting, small and alone, in the victoria.

I closed my eyes and tried to think of Grandmother's dining room, with its chandelier of Bavarian crystal. I heard Willa call to me, but I did not answer. It was light and I knew I should go back, but I could not. I wanted to go home, to Porter Farm, but I could not do that either. Willa's misery over-whelmed my own, I knew. I could not leave but I could not stay, either. I could be no comfort to Willa.

"Le-na," she called, worry in her voice. "Le-na." Thad was with her. I heard him pulling at her, pulling her back. After a time she stopped calling. I sat there, breathing deeply of the quiet, trying not to think of anything beyond the sanctuary of the arbor. As the sun rose above the hills, casting an oblique light into the leafy place, the air stirred gently, surrounding me with the scent of honeysuckle.

I do not know how long Soong had been in the garden, only a few paces from the arbor. He had made no sound, he had not intruded on my silence or my sorrow, but he knew I was there. I wondered how long he had known.

He did not pretend work when I stepped out, neither did he look away from me. He was sitting, arms folded gracefully. His presence was eloquent.

"I was thinking about my grandfather's house," I told him, without preamble.

He only looked at me, and said nothing.

"There was a room in my grandfather's house which my grandmother called the Lincoln room." I had started to talk, and seemed unable to stop. "Grandmother even had a little brass plaque made to put on the door. *The Lincoln Room.* Pa liked the idea of Mr. Lincoln staying there, when he traveled the circuit. Pa even got to meet him once, and so did Mama, of course. It was Mama's home, you know. But Mama had the plaque taken off. She said that Mr. Lincoln had paid hard cash for his room and board, and that it was putting on airs to pretend he had been a guest."

Soong only nodded at this strange outburst. He was looking at me steadily, as if he was expecting something.

"I've been thinking about my home quite a bit," I added, weakly, having run out of words.

"I know that," Soong answered.

"How can you possibly know that?" I demanded.

"Because it is what I think of when events of the present become too heavy. Then I seek refuge in the past, in the memory of my grandfather's house in Tsingtao."

"Tell me about those memories, Soong," I said, close to tears, "tell me how you came to tend a garden in the Malibu ranch, tell me about the life you left in China. I want to know, I do." I could hear my voice quivering.

"Someday, Lena, I will tell you," he answered, his voice steadying me, holding me together.

"Now," I said, "tell me now."

He looking at me again, and this time there was a strong urgency in his voice. "I will, I promise you that. But not now. Now I must go to work and you must go to your sister."

*So, I thought, he knows that, too.*

Owen followed the doctor's orders with amazing fidelity. He made no move to leave the ranch after the one trip in September to take Wen to the school. He did not seem discontented. On the long burnished days before the rains came, he lay on the hammock he had two of the men hang between the two big oaks, and let the world come to him.

The world, in this case, was business acquaintances from all parts of the country. The big carriage was making almost daily trips into Santa Monica to meet the trains, carrying guests from Denver and Buffalo and Chicago. They would lumber out of the carriage and stand in front of the fountain—which Owen insisted always be spewing forth to greet them—and be amazed, as one put it, "to find this civilization in the midst of the wilds."

Owen had the servant girls serve lunch on tables on the lawn. He would instruct Trinidad to lay out the best white damask, his mother's finest china and silver. For a time he even hired a string quartet to play. For Owen, it was a form of fun. The menus would be written in the most elegant calligraphy, with special notations for those foods grown on the ranch or taken from the sea. There would be a fish course, then mutton or beef, and often pheasant. The luncheons lasted for several hours. The gentlemen would be sent on their way with packages of tangerines or sometimes a large cabbage or a zucchini. Owen was unabashedly proud of the ranch's self-sufficiency. He had his Eden, he would say, and he wanted others to share it. I was inclined to believe that it was also good business, having these men of commerce into his home. When I suggested this to Owen after one such lunch, he grinned impishly and said, "I suppose it can't hurt."

On those days when no businessmen came, Owen devoted himself to Thad's education. He was absorbed in the process of teaching Thad—now all of three years old—to read. From the depths of his hammock, Owen would write a word on a tablet, hold it high so that Thad, sitting on a stool beside him, could see it and call out the word. Whenever Thad performed correctly, Owen popped a big Muscat grape into the boy's mouth, and one into his own. The two chewed happily together, relishing the big, juicy morsels before continuing with their studies.

"Now here's a hard one, Thaddy-boy," Owen would say, elaborately drawing the words "road" or "fancy" or "seashell" on the slate, and Thad would know them most of the time, but when he didn't, Owen always said the same thing. He said: "Next time you'll get this one, I know you will." And next time Thad always did. The child wanted, I do believe, to please his father more than he had ever wanted anything. I was happy to see them together. I did not want Thad to become as attached to me as Wen had been. It was too hard.

Before Willa's condition became visible, she would join

Owen at the luncheons. It was curious to watch the visiting
businessmen with her. She made them uncomfortable, I think.
She would appear in her long, simply designed white linen
dress with only Grandmother's brooch at her neck for decoration. She would smile, and make the appropriate remarks,
but she was distant, cool. And yet, you could see that she only
added to Owen's reputation: Owen Reade was an uncommon
man, likeable but unpredictable. They didn't quite know what
to make of Owen Reade, these men in their stiff high collars
and proper shoes. And yet, they were glad to be there. Sara
told me later what Charles had told her—to be invited to one
of Owen's eccentric lunches gave one a certain distinction.
They spoke of the tall, elegant Owen in repose on his hammock,
and his wife the Ice Queen, in their enclave of civility on the
wild Malibu ranch.

Owen spent the long autumn afternoons lying in his hammock, dressed in summer white, the sunlight playing moving
shadows over his body. On those few days when nobody came,
Owen would dictate his correspondence to me and I would type
his letters. When our work was finished, and Thad's lesson
for the day done, Willa would move to his side to keep him
apprised of the news of the world. She spent an hour or so
each morning scanning all the newspapers and periodicals to
which Owen subscribed, clipping those items she felt would
be of interest to him.

Often enough Owen would announce from his perch in the
hammock, "This is Eden, it truly is. Can you think of a more
idyllic place in all the world?" Once, when he said this, I looked
at Willa and wondered if it ever would be Eden for her again,
or if the bitter taste of forbidden fruit would be with her always.

Not all of Owen's visitors were impressed with his role as
lord of the realm. Late one afternoon, as Willa was working
over Owen's historical collection, the dogs set to barking.

"Who's coming?" Owen asked, startled out of a nap.

Willa cupped her hand over her eyes to diminish the glare,
and groaned. "I'm afraid it's our neighbor Mr. Shurz again,"
she said. "Shall I tell him you aren't up to a discussion?"

Owen looked up into the oak leaves; he sighed. "Jacob Shurz
is the most confounded, dogged, stubborn creature that ever
walked this earth."

"He certainly isn't humble," Willa agreed. "Shall I send
him away?"

Owen heaved himself out of the hammock. Standing, he pulled his trousers up and tucked in his shirt. Then he pulled on a rumpled linen coat. "No," he said, "I'd best do battle now. Putting him off will mean doing it another day."

"Shall I leave?" Willa wanted to know.

"No." Owen was emphatic. "He would like that. Women make Jacob Shurz uncomfortable. He's going to have to deal with both of us. Let's not let him dictate terms."

Willa only nodded, but she would long remember what Owen said that day—how naturally he had moved her into position to oppose Jacob Shurz.

Owen, always hospitable, waved Shurz to our group, greeting him with as much enthusiasm as he would a friend. Jacob Shurz would not, however, take a seat and he did not want a lemonade, no matter how fresh and cool, no matter we had grown all the lemons in our own orchard.

"Mr. Shurz, sir," Owen said, taking the initiative so suddenly that I think even the taciturn Jacob Shurz was surprised, "I suspect you have come with some specific request. Perhaps you would like to tell us what that is?"

Shurz shifted feet and in one, sudden short movement swept his gaze over Willa and me. "I be wanting to talk to you on business," he said.

Owen smiled. "My wife and her sister know as much about the business of the ranch as I do—perhaps more," he said, leaning casually against the oak tree, his very ease punctuating the difference between the two men.

Shurz would not let go. "I want to know why my neighbors cannot use my road to take their produce into the market at Santa Monica? If they go the back way, over the mountains, it's a far longer journey, as you know. I say they should be able to have free passage over my road, to the beach—why do you say no?"

Owen was skimming a bare foot over the grass. "More and more farmers are settling in those hills beyond my property line. Soon they're going to want to use the ranch roads to get to town. Some of them do it now without my permission. They hunt on my land and they camp there, and they build fires. You know what fire can do to these hills and canyons, Shurz."

"People got a right to take their crops to market, passage is a right," Shurz said.

Owen changed tactics. "As I've told you, Mr. Shurz, you

may continue to pass over my land so long as it is my land, and you are welcome as well to use the roads I have cut in to Santa Monica. I feel it is a courtesy I must extend, since you were here before me, and the owner of the property allowed you such a courtesy before me. You see, I believe in tradition and in courtesy, Mr. Shurz. I must tell you that I find it a bit difficult to understand why you wish to turn a private road into a public thoroughfare."

"Because people have the right," Shurz repeated.

"Rights," Owen said quietly, "are often decided in the courts. I cannot believe that you would wish to take this matter that far. You speak of rights, and I would like to remind you that we—my wife and I and our children, who will one day own this land—have rights, too. I do not want an army of farmers streaming in and out of the ranch. We have trouble enough with strangers passing through. Perhaps you heard about the smugglers that were caught here last summer? I will say it again—you are welcome to use your road, to pass freely over my land. But it is my land, and you may not open it to others or I shall have to reconsider."

Shurz glared at Owen's bare feet. "The people have rights, too," he said, "maybe the people speak on this, maybe the courts have to say."

"Do your neighbors help you keep the road clear?" Owen asked him then. "Do you allow them passage in return for road maintenance?"

Shurz did not flinch. "That is my business," he said.

"No, sir, it's mine," Owen answered. "They are on my land, remember, and that is called trespassing."

With that Shurz turned his back and began to walk away. When he was no more than ten paces, however, he turned back. "This isn't the end of it," he said before walking off with that determined, stolid way he had.

Willa raised her eyebrows; Owen shrugged.

"Do you think he's one of those German socialists?" Willa asked.

"I certainly hope not," Owen answered, "the ungrateful wretch, stirring up trouble for us. What right has he to tell me what I can do? That's a dirty bunch, making demands on anybody that has more than they've got. They're making things hard on us back East, with all the union talk. And in the mines out here, it's an ugly business. Still, I'd like to avoid trouble as long as we can."

Willa looked up. "What do you mean, 'as long as we can'?"

"I mean it is going to come, sooner or later. This is one of the last of the great untouched ranches. People keep coming West, and there's little enough land for them left. It's not going to be easy, keeping them out."

"Owen, you are a pessimist," I put in, "there are still all kinds of wilderness in the West. I don't think all that many people even know about the ranch, and there's not that much land here to farm anyway."

"But it lies between Los Angeles and San Francisco, and one day Los Angeles is going to challenge the northern city. There will be calls for trains and for roads. You wait, it will happen. It has to."

To which Willa said, in a voice that was low and tense with determination: "I won't have it."

Owen was looking at the departing figure of Jacob Shurz. "Then you are going to have to fight," he said.

What had gone unsaid between Willa and me began to grow. Each day the chasm widened, until I knew that I must speak of Connor. I had to. It hovered on the edges of my mind. I waited and I watched and I grew ever more apprehensive until the bang of a door would send me jumping.

The storms that blew in from the sea that winter came one after another, with high winds that ripped branches from the eucalyptus trees and scattered them about the barnyard. Wet leaves stuck to everything; the rain saturated the verandah, a feeling of dampness crept into our clothes, into our lives.

The front hall was filled with slickers and boots. I could not step outside without confronting soft earth and clay mud. Dry creekbeds were rampant with white, frothing waters that ran to the sea.

All would be gray. For days on end we would not see the sky and then, suddenly, we would wake to a patch of blue. The clouds moved quickly, high and full. And then we could go outside in the winter sun and pretend that another storm was not brewing in the west.

The winter was the wettest in living memory. The creeks were full, the heavens wept. I watched Willa's body swell, and I knew I must speak to her, and I couldn't.

I came upon her in a lull between storms, sitting by the fountain, which was filled now with rain water, and afloat with bits of tree bark and flotsam of the winter storm. Her hands were in her lap, her eyes closed, her face turned to the sun. I did not want to invade her quiet, but I had to.

"Willa," I began grimly, "I must talk to you." I could not keep the quiver from my voice. She opened her eyes.

"About Connor," I said quickly, "about the baby."

She closed her eyes again.

"Willa, we must," I was pleading.

She reached into her pocket and handed me a small square of newspaper, folded over several times. It was creased and fragile with wear, having been read many times. The date "September 26" was penned on the top. I read: "Mr. Connor McCord entered a plea of guilty to a charge of smuggling in the courtroom presided over by Judge Efram Peal. The admitted criminal was sentenced to a term of ten years to be served in the federal penitentiary at San Quentin."

I read it twice. I said, "Guilty, he pled guilty."

Without opening her eyes, Willa replied, "I envy him his punishment." She moved her hand over her belly where the baby was growing. Her face did not change expression.

"I read something a day or so ago, a poem," I began awkwardly, "it went something like: 'I sit beside my lonely fire, and pray for wisdom yet—for calmness to remember or courage to forget.'"

Willa's eyes remained shut; I thought for a while that she had not heard me, until finally she said, "I wonder why it shouldn't be the other way—'courage to remember and calmness to forget'?"

I took a deep breath. "Can we talk about the baby, then?"

She shook her head. "Not yet," she whispered. "I can't, not yet." She turned away. I wanted so to touch her, but I dared not.

"You will find the courage," was all I could think to say, "and when you do, I will be there to help you. This time, I promise, I will not desert you."

I turned and left quickly, shaking. I had said the words out loud that needed to be said. I had exorcised the thing that was coming between us. Willa would find a way, and I would help her.

# Book III

## In the Shadow of the Hawk,
### 1896 - 1903

# ~ Chapter Twelve

Before full light on the morning of the twelfth of April, 1896, Willa came to my room. Perhaps I had been listening for her in my sleep. I am certain that I heard her hand on the doorknob, because I was at once full awake.

"The pains have started," she whispered in a voice as swollen as her body, "now I must talk to you."

"Hush, please, dear," I tried to say, but my heart was sinking. The baby should not come for another month; it was still too soon. "I'll call Trinidad, we'll send Ignacio for the doctor."

"Not yet," she said in a voice that was part command, part entreaty, "come back into bed, please..."

We pulled the covers over us and lay together as we had as girls when it was cold—tucked together like spoons, for warmth, surrounded by the heavy scent of the sleep heat of our bodies. I put my arm around her swollen belly, I could feel it grow tight, feel her pull in her breath to brace for the pain.

Between pains, she spoke in a voice that was tired yet filled with urgency. "You know how it was with Thad, how bad," she said, "it could be that way again, today. I might not..."

"Willa, let me send for the doctor," I had to interrupt.

"Wait!" she said, biting out the word. "Not yet, listen to me. The baby... Owen is not the father..."

"Willa, no," I said, but she squeezed my hand until it hurt.

"I know," she said, "believe me, I know this baby is not

233

Owen's. And it is not mine, either. I have tried to think of it as mine, but I cannot. I want you to take it, Lena. I want this baby to be yours. If it lives, it must be your baby."

"Yes, dear," I said, "whatever you want, yes, but let me go for help." Still she held hard to me.

"Promise," she said, her voice breaking, "promise me now. No matter what happens today, if there is a baby you will be its mother."

"I promise," I said. "If it is truly what you want, I suppose." Her water broke. I felt the wet warmth spread beneath us on the bed. Suddenly I was terribly afraid. "Willa, there isn't going to be time for the doctor."

"Everything will be all right now," she said in a voice of terrible calm.

In fact, everything was all right. The baby was born no more than two hours later, in my bed, a girl with a wet scatter of light hair on her head. It was an easy birth, altogether normal, with only Trinidad and myself in attendance.

Trinidad held the baby in her big, dark hands and blurted, *"Que bonita!"* It was true. The newborn was perfectly formed, without the shriveled scowling of most new babies.

"See what a good baby girl God has given you," Trinidad said, taking the baby for Willa to view.

Willa looked at the child for an instant, no more, then turned her face to the wall. "I am tired, give the baby to Lena," was all that she would say. The glance had confirmed what she already knew. The baby looked nothing at all like the boys had looked at birth. The child was Connor's.

Trinidad plumped the covers, expertly rolling Willa's body one way and then the other to change the bed linens. "What name will you call her?" she wanted to know. "A pretty name, I think."

"Ask Lena," Willa said, clearly annoyed. "Lena can name the baby. Let me sleep."

"Rose," I heard myself say.

"Rosa, yes!" Trinidad said with enthusiasm. "She is like a rose, this one."

From the bed, Willa said with a bitter laugh, "My wild Irish Rose?" She began to cough then, which sent blood coursing onto the newly changed sheets.

"Quiet," Trinidad admonished her, pushing a roll of flannel hard between her legs to absorb the flow of blood, "do not cough, be quiet!"

When Trinidad had finished, I put the baby, swathed now in soft cotton blankets, into her arms and went to my sister. I could feel the tears sliding down my face. I took her hand and leaned close to her. "Willa," I said softly, "she is a beautiful baby, it does not matter you cannot . . ."

She gripped my hand so hard that her fingernails cut into my flesh. "You promised," she said with fury, "you promised."

"Yes," I said, patting her hand, "yes I did, and I will keep my promise. Shall I call Owen now? Can you see him?"

She looked hard at me to see if I meant what I had said. What she saw on my countenance must have convinced her, because she told me yes, to call him.

The door to their bedroom was open. Owen was sitting at the edge of the bed, his back to me, head down and his shoulders in an attitude of dejection, I paused a moment before rapping, softly. *It was too soon,* I kept thinking.

Owen started, turned, his dark eyes troubled.

"It's over," I said, "it is a girl. Willa wants to see you now."

"Willa?" he asked timidly.

"Willa is fine," I smiled, trying to assure him. I was surprised to see him sink back on the bed and cover his face with his hands. I started to move toward him, but he waved me frantically away.

I closed the door to give him time to recover. It was the first time I had glimpsed the chaos that was inside him, and it frightened me. I leaned against the hall wall to catch my breath. In no more than a few minutes, Owen appeared, fully composed.

When we entered the room, Trinidad came at him with the baby. I pulled her away with me, into the adjoining room, in spite of her sputters.

Owen pulled a chair close to the bed, sat down and took her hand in his. He smiled into her eyes, and with great tenderness said, "It's all over, dear."

Willa looked at him, and her gaze was steady in spite of her great weariness. "It came sooner than you had expected," she said.

Owen's answer was ready: "The baby arrived early, yes.

She is premature. I am only glad that it was over quickly. I had worried that it might be like last time . . ."

She smiled at him then, and raised his hand to her lips.

"It is over," he said once more. It sounded like an oath.


I kept my promise. Trinidad handed me the baby in the room where Wen had once slept. It was then that a feeling came over me, slow and even and powerful . . . I looked into the unseeing eyes of the child and I knew she was mine. I *was* her mother.

I cannot remember when Owen first saw the child, or what he said about her. I know that he never questioned her taking Wen's old room, or my being in charge of her. For my part, I was happy that the baby was a girl. I think it would have been far harder for Owen, had it been a son. As it was, Rose was mine to love and protect, and I never doubted that I could give her all that she would ever need.

It was a beautiful spring, full to bursting. Owen was busy with the planting, the rodeo, the ranch. He consulted Willa about everything, so that often enough much of their day was spent together, absorbed in work. Owen regained his strength, the old elasticity. Now and again I would look at him and try to remember the gaunt Owen of scarcely a year before, and could not. Willa recovered from the birth with amazing rapidity. Often now, she and Owen would take Thad and ride off together on some errand. My spirits lifted to see the three of them together, with Willa on Princess once more. Thad was getting the attention that Wen had looked for; his attachment to his father grew stronger each day. Often I thought of the sequence of events that had brought them together, and wondered at the capriciousness of life. I let myself hope that the bad times were behind us, that the worst was over, that we were entering a season of peace and calm.

The only discordant note was Wen. Owen's prediction— that the boy would soon enough prefer school to home—had proved correct. For the first few months he took solace in food—growing soft and sullen. When he discovered the playing field, the bulk grew into muscle. His stubbornness found form in the regimentation and competition promoted by the kinds of schools where the wealthy send their children. Soon, Wen was bringing his chums to the ranch with him. To a boy they were noisy and combative, whatever manners they had were learned rather than natural. I suspected they came for the riding and fishing and swimming for which the ranch was famous. More than once I detected an attitude of superiority in their dealings with their young host. At the same time that my heart ached for Wen, I was helpless to change the course his life was taking. Some days, I felt guilty about him—as if I had deserted him for Rose, but his own lack of interest in either of us soon released me.

That I should be so much with the new baby surprised no one. Owen's lack of enthusiasm went unmarked, perhaps because he had his sons. Willa had never been a doting mother, and the household did not expect her to change for this child. Soon after Rose's birth, Willa's interest in hawks was renewed, though she had not as yet taken to wandering over the ranch as in the old days. As for me, I determined to keep Rose as much out of their paths as I could. It did not prove to be difficult.

I watched Arcadia and Willa walk across the greensward, their heads together, talking as they moved to the arbor where I was sitting beside Rose. I felt an uncommon worry. Arcadia knew us well, she was bright and quick. I could not help wondering if she would detect anything out of the ordinary.

"I've come to see the darling girl child," she called to me, "Willa's been keeping me away. I know she thinks I'm going to steal the baby right out of the crib." She pulled the netting back, leaned close, and I could hear her catching her breath.

"Oh," Arcadia said, "she *is* exquisite."

I breathed more easily. "Isn't she just?" I said, not trying to keep the pride from my voice.

Arcadia was taken with Rose. The blonde curls and blue eyes with their dark fringe of lashes had not raised any suspicions. "I've just never seen such a perfect baby," she said, "she's just almost too beautiful."

"Cadie," Willa reprimanded her fondly, "you are a caution when it comes to babies." Willa wanted to be off, I could see, but Arcadia was not to be rushed.

"What I mean is, there is something ethereal about her— she looks just like an angel, with that curly hair and those great eyes." At that moment Rose began to move her hands and feet in the air, gurgling as if in response, and gave Arcadia one of her first smiles.

Seeing that her friend was in danger of settling down to play with the baby, Willa quickly took her by the elbow and said, "Come now, you'll have your own baby soon enough...Joseph will take you to the altar this summer and..."

Arcadia's face told her that she should not continue. A shadow fell across the usually vibrant features. She turned away from us, but not before we saw that something was troubling her.

When she said nothing, Willa finally asked, "What is it, Cadie? Can you tell us?"

She turned back biting her lower lip. "You will have to know," she said in a voice so flat, so unlike her own, that I felt chilled.

Willa caught my worried glance.

"Joseph and I had planned to be married this summer, as you know," she started. "There is a very good chance that it won't happen now, I think."

"Cadie, what...?" I blurted, but Willa's hand on my shoulder stopped me.

"The Señora has asked that I not marry while she lives," Arcadia went on. "If I agree, I am to be her sole heir."

I looked from Willa to Arcadia, not knowing what to say, distressed and disbelieving.

Willa was looking at her, but Arcadia did not return the look, rather she continued to gaze down on Rose, though I think her vision was blurred by tears.

"What does Joseph say?" Willa asked quietly.

Arcadia pushed a strand of hair back from her forehead in a gesture that seemed at once languid and poignant.

"Joseph says that he will always want to marry me, this summer or next...whenever I say," she answered.

"But it could be..." I started, when once again Willa interrupted me. "It is a difficult decision," she said to Arcadia, "truly difficult."

I could not believe Willa meant what she was saying. It was not a difficult decision at all. It was unthinkable that Arcadia should consider delaying her marriage. Joseph Brennan was her perfect match; she loved him and he, her. The old woman, moreover, could live for years. Willa knew I was about to say so, and pressed her fingers hard into my shoulder to stop me.

Suddenly, Arcadia moved to leave. "I do envy you this beautiful baby," she sighed. I could feel her eyes on me, but I would not look at her. I could not.

Joseph and Arcadia did not stay the night, but left late in the afternoon to be in Santa Monica by nightfall, allowing Willa and Owen time that night to talk over the revelation.

They took supper together in their rooms, a habit recently formed. Owen opened the discussion by saying, "Joseph claims it is Arcadia's decision totally."

"Do you believe it?" Willa wanted to know.

Owen considered. "No," he said, "no, I think he wants Cadie to wait. I think he is as tempted as she."

"I can't believe that she would consider it unless Joseph agreed," Willa said.

"It is a great deal of money, no doubt. Old Abel Stearns lost a fortune, but he regained quite a lot of it before he died, and certainly the Señora hasn't wasted any of it," Owen added.

Willa winced. "Poor Arcadia has had to scrape all these years. I believe that Joseph must give her pocket money now— the Señora never has."

"Still," Owen said, not willing to be deflected from the original point, "I think it would be wrong to assume that Joseph was most responsible for the decision. We know him well enough by now to know that if Arcadia had turned the old woman down at the first mention of delaying the wedding, Joseph would have accepted that happily. Perhaps it was because she didn't . . ."

Willa nodded. "It is what I was thinking, exactly. Even to have asked Joseph his opinion was, perhaps, stating her own wishes." She was curled up on the settee sipping hot lemon tea, one hand propped against the side of her head, so that she looked unusually thoughtful. "I had to stop Lena from telling Cadie that she should have rejected the notion immediately . . ."

Owen grinned. "Dear, honorable Lena."

Willa was not thinking of dear, honorable Lena at that moment, however. "The most troublesome idea is that the Señora could live another ten years, even. She must be well into her seventies, but the Californios have a reputation for being long-lived. Cadie is twenty-seven now; in ten years it might be difficult for her to have the family she so wants."

Owen nodded, soberly. "Joseph and Arcadia could well be forfeiting a family of their own. That is a terrible price to pay for an inheritance," he said, adding, ". . . any inheritance."

Willa looked at him for a long moment. "Is it?" she finally said.

"Of course," was his answer, as if it were obvious. "A family, children of one's own, is everything. It is, quite simply, the future. Nothing is more important."

"Nothing?" she questioned again.

"Nothing at all. Can you imagine life without the boys?" He paused, then added, "And the baby, of course."

"Rose," she said.

"Rose," he repeated, as if learning the child's name.

Willa sighed.

Owen rubbed her knee. "Has Cadie disappointed you so?" he wanted to know.

"I'm not certain," she answered. "I mean, I'm not sure if it is disappointment I feel, or simply concern. I must say, I do feel that Cadie is making a mistake even to consider the Señora's preposterous suggestion. It's as if she is willing to delay living. And I think it is cruel of the Señora to suggest such an arrangement."

"Ah," Owen said, "yes, I admit I find it difficult also. Perhaps it is only because I have always had a good deal of wealth. I do see how it affects others—men tend to think it can do anything, that it will transform their lives."

Owen's voice had become removed, hard. "Some men, of course, will sell their souls for profit."

Willa could not be sure what he was thinking, who he was talking about. "And women, too, I suppose," she murmured, bringing the conversation back to the point at hand.

"You mustn't judge Arcadia too harshly," Owen said, seeming to reverse his judgment. "I think the only lesson I have truly learned in this life is to allow people to make mistakes, and forgive them."

Willa did not know if he was speaking of her or of Arcadia. "You are right," she said without enthusiasm. "Of course, Cadie is good and so is Joseph. I am only sorry they have been tempted. I think the old woman is cruel," she repeated.

"Or perhaps simply lonely and afraid in her old age?" Owen

asked. "When money is not involved, we call it duty."

Willa sighed once more. "I suppose cruelty and fear are close relatives," she said, "Arcadia is such good company, so lively and quick, she fills a house with her presence. That big place would be terribly empty without her, I am sure."

"You see," Owen put in, "it is always necessary to examine motives. It tells you so much about a situation."

"Still, it is ghoulish," Willa insisted. "Their life cannot begin until the Señora is dead. I would hate it."

"You wouldn't do it," Owen said simply.

She looked at him with surprise. "How can you be so sure?" she asked.

"Oh, I am sure of you in some ways. I do know that courage is the one thing you have in abundance, your only real fault."

She looked at him, puzzled. "Fault?" she asked.

"It can be," was all he said.

She did not know what he meant and she decided not to ask. She would, however, puzzle over his words for a very long time. She would write them down, even, so that she might study them, but her studies never seemed to enlighten her.


My days were filled with the sounds and smells and routines that are part of the care of a new baby. Days and weeks and then months went in a rush of bathings and feedings. I was content, absorbed, happy. Trinidad was full to overflowing with mother's milk, having been delivered of yet another boy child. She took great pleasure in nursing the blonde baby with her tight little ringlets and blue eyes which looked up at her, solemnly, as she nursed. Trinidad was all smiles for this *an-gelica nene,* as she called her. For the *bonita Rosa,* she was a font of plenty.

Sara was as enchanted with the child as I was. She called her a "fairy baby" and seemed not to tire of looking at her. Sometimes, when she came to visit, she would carry Rose in a sling in front of her—like a native working in the fields—and we would go for picnics in the eucalyptus grove.

More often Rose and I passed our afternoons in the arbor, shaded by the leaves of the grapevines which rustled in the breeze and made light patterns play over her. I would do some needlework while Rose napped in the wicker pram, or made quiet cooing sounds as she attempted to catch the shifting patterns made by the grape leaves. Wing Soong fashioned a plaything of shiny seashells, which hung above the pram and rocked gently in the breeze, making a pleasant tinkling sound that caused Rose to laugh.

"There is something about the child," Soong said to me one day, "that reaches into the memory."

He did not elaborate, and I knew that I should not probe for information.

I kept Soong supplied with newspaper and magazine articles about his homeland. American businessmen had begun to call for a policy which would allow all nations equal trade in China, and I thought this should please Wing Soong. I was mistaken.

"It would be good for American business, yes," he said. "I suppose it will become American policy—there has been talk of the Open Door, as they say, for some time. It makes the politicians feel self-righteous—the idea of 'preserving China's territorial integrity.' But the motives are base. They want simply to make sure they are not shut out by the European powers. China and its people have little enough to do with it."

I felt in such an odd position when Wing Soong spoke in that manner. It seemed I should defend my country, but when I did I felt naive, or that patriotism, in me, was slightly preposterous. When I spoke of this to Sara, she laughed at the seriousness I gave it. So absorbed was she with her art work that she faced Europe, rather than Asia. Her chief interest in Wing Soong was in what she called his "incredible picturesqueness."

In truth, I was not so much interested in the politics as I was in being a friend to this unusual man. I knew that strange Celestials from nearby Chinatowns were making their way into the ranch to talk with Soong, and that occasionally he went outside on some venture involving his countrymen, but I was interested only because it was of interest to him. He spoke to me of these occasions in only the cloudiest of terms when I would inquire. He neither confided nor concealed.

I suppose he knew that I had no interest in the world outside the Malibu. The house, the woods, the garden were my world. China seemed a figment of someone's imagination. I would not offend Wing Soong by saying so, but his great interest in his homeland seemed to me to be useful only in that it kept a particularly sharp and active mind occupied. If I wished, I could travel to China—having the freedom and the funds to do so. I could go wherever I wished in the world. Wing Soong could not.

Soon enough Rose was able to crawl about—not the usual baby crawl, but rather in a side motion, raising her small backside high, as if what she really wanted was to be up and running. It would not be long, I knew, before I would have to chase her. Even crawling, she could cover distances with amazing speed.

One afternoon we stayed later than usual in the garden. Soong was on the far side, hoeing. I was working on a cross-stitch sampler for the child's first birthday, which was fast approaching. My eyes lingered too long on my work, and when at last I glanced up, it was to see Rose—one small hand lifted—about to touch a great tarantula which was making its way toward her. I tried to call out, but the sound stuck in my throat.

I heard the sharp cut of the hoe before Rose's amazed cry. Soong killed the thing and scooped her into his arm in one long motion. He carried her to me before she even had time to cry out. I rose to take her and swayed. He caught me in his other arm, held me firm, and moved us both to the arbor.

I do not know what words Soong said to me in the minutes that followed, only that they soothed me, slowed my racing heart.

I held tight to Rose, who sat quiet in my lap, perplexed. Wing steadied us; my hands were shaking and my body shivered. "If you hadn't been there," I whispered, "oh, Soong . . ."

"I was there," his voice echoed from somewhere, "I will want always to be there."

His words had a strange, comforting effect. I wasn't sure why until Sara, one day, said to me jokingly, "What very strange parents little Rose has—a tiny auntie and a tall Chinaman." I laughed, but I understood that she was, in part, correct. Soong and I shared the responsibility for this child, just as we shared the garden, and the afternoons.

He planted a daisy bush for Rose. When Thad remonstrated with his little sister for pulling off the heads of the flowers and planting them in a row, Soong told the boy, very gently, that he was sure the flowers did not object.

Rose was content to stay in the garden. She found all manner of things to occupy her. One day, when she was occupied with a long game that involved two cloth animals, I reminded Wing Soong that he had, quite a long time ago, said that he would tell me about his childhood.

"My childhood?" he said, as if the idea that he should have had one was novel.

"You told me once when I was homesick that you had been too," I reminded him, "now you must tell me the rest of the story."

"You were not happy then, and now you are," he rejoined, "now there is no necessity to comfort you."

"You promised that you would," I insisted.

"I promised?" he repeated, maddeningly, and I was about to thunder at him in exasperation when Rose laughed out loud, a sound so perfectly interjected that it made both of us laugh as well.

The whole long afternoon stretched before us. Willa and Owen had taken Thad for an overnight encampment to the new ranch headquarters at Zuma. Soong was working methodically on the flower garden so that the flow of talk need not be interrupted by his task. He began to talk in that curious voice, English yet with the Chinese inflections that rendered it soft and melodic.

"My father, as I told you when we first met, was a British naval officer, assigned, however, to a German treaty port in my home province of Shantung. He was a liaison, I believe, something of the sort. He did not, however, approve of the Germans, which may be why he sought out the company of my mother. He was, I should think, quite isolated, and thus lonely.

"My mother was tall and, as I remember, quite beautiful. She had been trained to be of comfort to life's lonely men." He glanced at me to see if I understood and was offended; seeing that I was not, he continued. "I do not know all of the details, you must understand. What I was told by my grandfather could be only part of the truth, and there is much that I will never know, cannot know. My grandfather said that my father was greatly fond of my mother, that he was generous, and that when I was born he took a great interest in me. Of that I am reasonably sure, since he taught me to speak English and to read it at a very young age. I was, perhaps, an entertainment for him, a way to pass long hours."

"Do you remember him at all?" I asked.

Soong turned a leaf, plucked a large, fat green worm from the underside and put it, carefully, in a jar he kept for that purpose. He meticulously washed the tips of his fingers in a cup of water, and dried them on a linen square. I watched this ritual with a certain fascination; Wing Soong's hands were remarkably clean for a gardener's.

"I have a memory of a tall man, towering over me, smelling of leather and wool—strange, foreign smells."

"Did you like him?" I asked.

He shrugged. "I don't believe children like or dislike. I think they accept. At any rate, when I was ten years old, he left. And then my mother went away, too."

"Where?" I asked.

"She died," he said, "by her own hand."

I could not think what to say, so I said nothing.

"It was not a dishonorable act, not in China. My grandparents accepted it. My father had been recalled to England, where he had a family. He left Mother a sum of money which my grandfather then used to bring us to the gold fields of California. We were to return as rich men, you see. We said goodbye to my grandmother and my uncles. I remember it clearly, the harbor—my grandmother's face."

His voice drifted off; I think he had forgotten that I was there. I coughed, and he stirred.

"My grandfather was sure we would be welcomed," he went on. "He was certain that the barbarians would recognize our innate superiority. The Chinese feel that way, you know."

"I didn't," I said, truthfully.

"Of course," he answered, "how could you?"

We lapsed into an uncomfortable silence; something was churning in my mind, something that was not quite worked out, but Soong started talking before I could think what it was.

"My grandfather died in what the Spanish so elegantly call 'Calle de los Negros'—the Yankees call it Nigger Alley—in a massacre the summer I was twelve. They hung him with a rope from the wooden awning in front of William Slaney's shoe store."

"Dear God," I blurted, "and you, where were you when it happened?"

"There," he said calmly, "watching. There was a group of

us trying to get into Mr. Slaney's store—he was protecting others inside, to his great credit. But the mob got to us first, I tried to hold onto my grandfather's hand, but I couldn't. They just took him, and I could tell he didn't have any idea at all what was happening to him, or why. I watched them put the rope around his neck, then someone pulled me from behind and I found myself in the cellar of Judge Wilson Gray. The judge hid me and twelve others. The mob was out to kill every Chinese in Los Angeles—two hundred, about. They got nineteen in all, my grandfather among them."

He stood, reached for a pail and went for water. I watched his walk, watched the muscles in his strong arms, the loose blue garments flowing, and found myself wondering—quite absurdly—what he would look like if he were dressed like one of the ranch hands, in denims and a checkered shirt.

When he returned I asked him what started the massacre in the Calle de los Negros (delicately refraining from using the name which was more familiar).

"Superficially it was over a feud between two tongs; one had accused the other of taking one of its women. There were so few Chinese women in those days that it was seen as a great offense. A policeman was shot, a mob gathered, it didn't take long until all it wanted was blood—foreign blood. The Chinese are hated as much as—perhaps more than—the Negroes from the American South or the native Indians. Dark-skinned peoples. The darker, the more hate."

"What happened to you?" I wanted to know. "Who took care of you?"

He laughed. "I had been taking care of myself for a while by then. I was always big for my age, and Grandfather had sought refuge in the opium pipe. It took away his pain, and for that I was grateful. America was a great disappointment to my grandfather. He would never have left China, had it not been for me."

The strange, worrisome feeling prodded me again. Why "if not for me"? Before I could ask, he went on to tell me what I in fact already knew, that Judge Gray had employed him as a gardener and houseboy, that he gave him access to his library. That when the judge died, Owen asked Wing Soong to come to the ranch and work for us, and that Soong had agreed, on condition that once each year he be allowed to return to the judge's house to tend the garden and make sure the boy in charge was caring for it properly.

"Each year, on the anniversary of the massacre, Mrs. Gray finds offerings of silk and porcelain left on her doorstep, from those Celestials whose lives her husband saved," Wing Soong told me.

"Do you ever wish you were in China?" I asked.

The question gave him pause. His answer, it seemed to me, was unusually careful. "I should like one day to live in a place where I could feel that I belonged."

I did not understand, and said so.

"I mean," he went on with what I thought was purposeful obscurity, "equality is an idea that is peculiar to the West. As with many Western ideas, it sounds reasonable—when in fact, it is not. Not if *reasonable* is thought also to mean possible or practicable."

"I suppose you're right," I sighed. "Certainly the Civil War did little to free the Negroes, other than to release them from the status of being mere property."

"People of dark skin are despised in this country—whether they be Africans or American Indians or Chinese. A man's worth seems to correspond to the color of his skin, and the paler he is, the more acceptable."

It occurred to me that he was, after all, many shades paler than most of his countrymen, by virtue of his British father. It also occurred to me that I had come to feel easy in his British presence—to what might be a dangerous degree. His next remark confirmed it. "I have my father's skin," he said, "but I am my mother's son. I belong to her country, of that I am certain."

"Why did you leave, then?" I asked, a bit flustered. As soon as I said it, I had hit on what had been at the back of his mind. "If the sum your father left was considerable, would it not have been possible to have a better life in China?"

Wing Soong sat back on his haunches and studied me until I began to feel uncomfortable under his gaze.

"Ah, you have caught me out," he said. "I could have had no life at all in China. There, a half-caste is despised. My grandfather was certain that I would be accepted in American society. He reasoned that my British blood would win me admittance, and that my Chinese heritage would make me irresistible—enriching the barbarian strain, as it were." He looked at me with pained good humor, but I could not smile back.

"What a terrible dilemma," I murmured, "rejected in China for your Anglo-Saxon father, and in this country for your Chinese mother."

Rose came to rest in my lap, having tired of her solitary game. Wing Soong studied her solemnly. Suddenly, she reached for his large hand with her small one, and without so much as a murmur she kissed the long, sleek fingers.

I looked into his eyes and found there something so wild and pained that I had to look away. Rose had touched a memory, I knew that. Soong raised his fingers to the baby's cheek and brushed it, gently.

"Sweet girl," I whispered into her neck as I held her to me, "Sara was right. You are a fairy child."

Sleep would not come that night. Instead, Soong's words wound into my thoughts. I tried to understand the awful irony of it, the pity that his grandfather could not have been right. But then I would remember Soong's own sympathies—he chose to be Chinese. Yet, even while he was unacceptable in both countries, he found himself in the one he least preferred. (Still, could it be so very bad here on the Malibu? Surely he could not think so. Could he?) Restless, I walked into Rose's room to watch her asleep. I leaned close. As she exhaled, I breathed in the soft smell of her sleep breathing.

It came to me, then, that Rose, like Soong, was half-caste. They had that in common. I wondered if it had occurred to him, and knew at once that it had.

Rose called Owen "Father" and Willa "Mother." I was "Lema" and Wing Soong was "Wings," pronounced as an endearment. The arrangement seemed to make everybody happy. Willa and Owen were correct with the child, neither pushing her away nor pulling her close. Thad found Rose enchanting, especially since she did not usurp any of his parents' time. In fact, Rose's arrival corresponded to the time when Thad became an integral part of their lives. I had never seen Thad so happy; on those days when his father and mother were busy, he spent time with us in the garden, to Rose's great pleasure. Thad, thus, was so much in the center of everyone's life that he flourished.

* * *

On Wen's occasional visits to the ranch I searched his face for the boy I knew must be there—tender and hurting. I wanted so for him to come to me, to sit quietly next to me on the swing in the arbor and tell me, as he had so often, what it was that made him happy, and what made him afraid. But that Wen never came. More often now, when I watched the rambunctious boy who had taken his place, a peculiar, dull ache would settle into my chest. After a while, it came to me that what I was feeling was a kind of grief. I wrote in my daybook: "I mourn the Wen who might have been." What I did not write, what I did not admit to myself for a long time, was that I did not much like the Wen who had taken my boy's place.

The schoolmates who came with him were loud and awkward and, if not monitored, were likely to be up to some mischief. They taunted the Chinese workers unmercifully, and made rude demands of the servants. Trinidad's children learned to disappear when Wen and his friends came. I tried, once, to talk to her about Wen's behavior, but she would not let me. I suspect that she was too hurt to admit to what Wen was doing, or perhaps Ignacio and she had decided, together, how best to deal with the problem. It hurt to think that they had encountered it before, it was a part of their life that had eluded me.

Only once did Wen get his comeuppance. He and his friends made the mistake of locking little Thad—who was afraid of the dark—in one of the gloomy corn bins in the barn, where he was bitten by a rat. The child was in a state of hysteria when they turned him loose. One of the cowboys happened by, found him and carried him to the house, where he sobbed out his sorry story to Owen, Willa having gone into town for the day.

To his credit, Owen sent the boys packing. He called not for the surrey, but for one of the crude farm wagons without springs, and with hard wooden planks for seats, and sent them to their elegant homes in something less than the style they expected of the master of the Malibu. Wen spent the rest of the holiday in his room, his food—in smaller portions than he preferred—sent to him on a tray. He felt the sting of Willa's wrath later that same day. I could hear her voice, full of outrage. I wondered what I would do should he come to me for comfort.

I was, I am sorry to say, greatly relieved when he did not. After that, I made it a habit not to look too closely at Wen's face, knowing I would not like what I found there.

Late each afternoon Willa and I took tea together while the children were having an early supper in the kitchen. It was a pleasant, quiet time when we could exchange bits of information.

"Thad has been biting his fingernails again," I said one day.

"Either that or he has his hand in his pants when he thinks no one is looking," Willa answered.

I sighed. "I think I know why," I said.

She buttered a scone and raised her eyebrows in question.

"Because of Wen," I said, "he's afraid of his brother."

Willa scowled. "I know," she said. "I've tried to talk to Owen about Thad and Wen. The strange thing is, Owen rather admires Wen's bullying ways. Sometimes I think he sees Thad as the boy he was, and Wen as the boy he wanted to be."

"A bully?" I said in surprise. "You can't mean that Owen would ever have wanted to be a bully."

"No, not that," she went on, thoughtfully, "just part of the lively group, keeping pace. Owen's health has always prevented him from living what he sees as the active—and thus preferable—life."

"How can he possibly think of his life as being anything less than active?" I said in amazement.

"Yes, well," she paused, thinking hard, "it's that the matter of his health has always been preeminent, it has always been there, in control. And whenever he would think he had overcome it, well, something would happen. Like Boston, last time. He might have died, he came very close. It makes him look at things differently."

I remembered a ride Owen and I had taken a few months before Rose's birth. He had only just begun to trust himself to ride again, and asked that I accompany him on a short half-day trip to count the cattle in Soston Canyon. It had been a bright, clear day and we had ridden a good distance in silence, until he came upon a ridge which looked down into a grassy mesa where a hawk was circling.

"Willa would not approve, I am sure," I said, "but there are times when I want to shout to warn all the little animals that might fall prey to the hawk."

Owen smiled. "You needn't shout today, he's giving his own warning—don't you see it?"

I looked, but saw nothing.

"The shadow of the hawk," Owen said. "The little animals know that shadow, they know to scurry for cover—" he paused and in quite another voice said, "haven't you ever felt the shadow of the hawk, Lena?"

Those words had sent a shiver through me. At tea, I told Willa of our conversation and was at once sorry that I had, it affected her so. She sat silent the rest of the time. I wanted to say something to mend any harm I had done, but there was nothing to be said.

Rose broke the silence by running to us with her hands out—they were bright red, berry stained.

"What's this?" I laughed, "Wait! I know. You've been helping hull the blackberries."

She answered with a peal of laughter, opening her mouth wide to show a bright, berry-stained tongue. "And you've sampled a few along the way, you scamp," I teased.

"Don't touch anything until you've washed those hands," Willa admonished her.

"Mother want two nice hands on her blouse?" Rose teased, her eyes sparkling.

"Don't be naughty, Rose," I said, going for a wet cloth, but the child was away before I could wash her hands. We watched her run across the green in search of Wing Soong, doubtless to show him her red hands.

Willa had always been guarded in Rose's presence. Now she watched the child, and suddenly her face was bared of its usual careful pose.

"How can she be the product of such shame," she whispered, "and yet be so perfectly beautiful? How can that be?"

"Willa, don't," I pleaded, "don't make her what she isn't. She is just a baby, a very sweet baby. No more."

I wanted to make her understand something that I could not put into words. The set of Willa's face told me it was no use, but I had to try. The child with her blonde ringlets and blue eyes was becoming an increasingly painful reminder of the one time in Willa's life she was determined to put behind her, to bury. Somehow, some way, I had to convince her to detach Rose from that memory.

Owen and Willa seemed to be companions once more; still,

whenever Rose entered the room I could feel the air contract. They did not, I think, see what the rest of us saw: a lovely child, the light catching in her golden hair. Willa saw the betrayal of which Rose was a living proof. And though no word had been spoken between them, Owen knew. Owen knew, and for reasons of his own let the matter lie.

When Owen began to travel once more, Willa went with him. At first it was to make sure he did not overtire himself, to watch over him. Sometimes, when they were staying at especially lovely places like the big Del Monte lodge up in Monterey, or the Coronado Hotel in San Diego, they would take Thad along. These trips were good for them, I came to think, though I wondered if those journeys were taken to avoid a small, blonde girl.

That Willa achieved some peace on these travels was apparent from her letters. "We had the oddest, yet most enjoyable evening with some of Owen's acquaintances," she wrote from the Del Monte lodge, "I was hard put not to laugh, however, at the rather peculiar table manners of some of the gentlemen. The menu included double Southdown mutton chops with baked yams. We had two bottles of vintage champagne with it—the gentlemen putting on their reading spectacles to examine the labels, of course. As the Haut Brion and the Perrier Jouet bottles emptied, the cries of 'Woof! Woof!'—signs of appreciation, you understand—increased. It all struck me as marvelously funny, so much so that I finally did begin to laugh and could not stop. The gathered company, at first, seemed rather embarrassed at my hilarity. After a time, they too began to laugh (woof! woofing! all along), and we all were gasping and holding our sides with laughter and pain. Later, in our rooms, Owen remarked that he doubts his San Francisco friends will ever again refer to me as the Ice Queen. I detected a note of poignance in his voice. I think Owen was rather fond of the Ice Queen, at that.

"Last evening we strolled along the pier at Monterey, a group of us, to catch a glimpse of the Great White Fleet then anchored offshore. Over the water we could hear the sounds of the sailors singing, their voices somehow sad as they echoed over the water. I thought of our brothers—young men like them were out there, waiting to go to war, singing now of home, and you knew how lonely they must be."

The summer before, the fleet had been off our own shore on the ranch. One evening we went to the beach to watch them at target practice. We saw the flash of fire before we heard the resounding boom. Owen explained the phenomenon to Thad. The boy turned the idea—that light travels faster than sound—over in his mind for days afterwards, driving everyone but Owen to distraction. Owen was delighted by the boy's curiosity.

My preoccupation with Rose meant that I spent much less time with the bookkeeping chores. A young man named Pringle was hired for the purpose—Owen's business dealings had become too intricate for one spinster aunt. Willa undertook to instruct the new man. He was a strange, fussy creature, scrupulously neat, but he did, as Willa said, "a thorough job and he keeps to his corner." He dressed all in black and had long fingers with great knuckles, which he often cracked as he worked. He lived in a small apartment of his own, fashioned in the loft of one of the bunkhouses—separate from the cowboys as befits a clerical worker. He spent all of his time in these rooms, or in the office in the ranch house, going out of doors only to cover the distance between the two. Once each fortnight he made a trip into Santa Monica in a small dog cart, always returning before nightfall.

Charles and Sara were frequent visitors to the ranch. Owen and Charles served on many of the same boards, and their ventures were so intermingled that I had long ago lost track of them.

Willa was better aware of Owen's business transactions now than ever she had been. She had kept a sharp eye on Charles' machinations, too, ever since he expressed an interest in running a railroad between Santa Monica and San Francisco, a route that would bisect the ranch. "I told him no, never," Willa said to me, "and do you know what he said to that? He said, 'I don't believe in never.'" Willa could become angry just talking about it.

That summer, Willa and Owen sailed for Hawaii, taking Thad with them. Wen elected to stay with one of his friends from school. Thad, of course, was elated when Wen turned them down. So, too, was I—the trip would surely be a success, if only the three of them were to go.

A polite invitation had been tendered to me, and I did as I

was expected to do and turned it down. I would not leave Rose, and Rose would not be welcome. The tensions did not seem to ease as time went by, but only to gather. If the truth be told, I was rather happy that we were to have the rest of the summer before us, alone on the ranch. I worried a great deal about the tensions, and tried to think how to resolve them. Perhaps they would choose to send Thad off to school in the fall, and I would go along with Rose to keep him company. I could get lodgings nearby that would be suitable for us. After all, Owen had seen to my financial independence, for which I was increasingly glad. But would it seem strange, my leaving with the two youngest children? Would Owen and Willa allow it? I doubted they would. There was one thing of which I was certain, however. Whatever pain Rose's presence gave Willa and Owen was overshadowed by the pleasure she provided for me, and for Wing Soong and Sara.

Sara came to the ranch soon after the family's departure for Hawaii, bringing with her an inordinately large supply of sketchpads and pens. She was, she announced, going to do a portrait of Rose. She would stay until she got the necessary sketches and then she would return to her studio to finish it.

Sara's studio was a makeshift cottage on the grounds of Charles' house in Pasadena. Rose and I visited her there whenever she was at home, which had not been very often in the past few years. Sara's natural talent at sketching, once no more than an avocation, had been developed through private lessons with Cecilia Beaux, in Philadelphia—one of the foremost women painters in America, whom she had met through the good offices of Owen's family in Boston. Miss Beaux then sent Sara to study at the Académie Julian in Paris, which meant that she was much away from Pasadena, and her husband, though now and then their paths did cross in the house they shared. I say "shared" because it seemed to me, always, that she was but a guest in that house. Charles' travelings had little to do with hers. Occasionally they found themselves scheduled to spend a weekend at the Malibu, one not knowing the other was expected. They left messages for each other with the English butler, a Mr. Garvey, who managed the Pasadena household. He was a strange, stiff man of limited tolerance for Americans, an attitude that seemed to make him much sought after by wealthy families of the West. Quite clearly, he saw

Americans as an inferior race, an attitude that seemed to entertain Charles. (Though I could not but think how this same attitude, in the Chinese, was not in the least amusing.)

On one of our trips to visit Sara, upon leaving, Rose turned and with the great sweetness of a two-year-old thanked Mr. Garvey "for your nice house." The man did not so much as twitch, not even when Sara laughed and said, "Of course, of course—that's whose house it is. Garvey's!" Garvey did not approve of Sara. But then she did not approve of Garvey, either, as she liked to say, which almost made things even.

Now, contemplating her spending the weeks with us that it would take to get the necessary sketches for a portrait of Rose, I clapped my hands and said, "Wonderful!" By now I had seen enough of Sara's work to know that she would give us something extremely interesting to see, some weeks hence. Or months. I loved watching Sara at work, loved seeing the kind of concentration of which she was capable, as well as the pleasure she took from her skill. And skilled she was, indeed.

"I want to do something more than a likeness," she tried to explain, "I want to catch the light that seems to radiate . . . the child's magic quality. What the Andalusians call the *duende*."

Sara wished to portray Rose in the garden, in her favorite place, next to the daisy bush Wing Soong had planted for the child. Soong and I worked to keep Rose content in that region, so that Sara might make all the sketches she needed. I devised little games for her to play and Soong would carefully pull, scrape and wash a carrot for her to nibble on, or sometimes he would work nearby building the traps he needed to catch the pesky moles that had been ravaging our garden.

"Where go the little moles you catch?" Rose asked him one day. Soong was careful not to give her a direct answer, since the vicious scavengers were taken to the stream and drowned before being buried. "Don't you know about the mole family which lives on a hill on the other side of the mountain?" he said to the child, and proceeded to make up a long story about a mole kingdom burrowed into the mountain. In this way, Rose acquired the idea that all of the moles caught in the cages— and these numbered quite a few of late—were transported to this kingdom where they lived together in perfect harmony.

Sara returned to Pasadena with a large stack of sketches, directing me to come into town in three weeks time, when she

would have completed the portrait. I should, she said, bring
Rose with me, and we would have a tea party in celebration.
It was not like Sara to be so sure that the portrait would go
well, which I took to be a good sign.

Garvey opened the door and greeted us, stiffly. "Why, hello,"
Rose said to the towering figure, as if she was marvelously
happy to be seeing him again, "are you feeling well?" She had
only recently learned these niceties, and tended to use them
with everyone she met. Most people found it charming. Garvey
only sniffed.

Sara, the color high on her cheeks, ran to greet us.

"Is my picture finished?" Rose wanted to know.

"Yes, sweet one, it is, and I do hope you are going to like
it, because I do, immensely."

She took me by the hand, and would have ushered us at
once to the studio had I not pulled her back and insisted on
taking off my linen carriage coat first. Rose had managed to
get her hand caught in her sleeve, and was struggling with it.

My eyes took a minute to grow accustomed to the shadows
in the old shed. Then I saw the canvas, and caught my breath.
"Oh," I gasped, "oh, Sara, you *have* done it."

She had painted the child as if from eye level, so that the
viewer would see her on her own terms. The blue eyes looked
out as they often did—laughing, purely innocent. Sara had
caught the magic and had transferred it onto canvas. She had
explained everything. I could not take my eyes from the figure
on the canvas.

"It's me!" Rose cried in delight, "and my daisies. And
Wings and Lema."

I laughed. "It's you, darling, but I don't believe I see either
Wings or Lema."

"Oh, there," and she pointed to a place just off the canvas,
"there is Wings, working on the mole cage, and there," again
she pointed to a place to the right of the canvas, "you are,
sitting in your chair."

"I'm glad you put her in the yellow frock," I said. In fact,
Rose had worn several different dresses for her sittings—the
yellow had been a gift from Arcadia. It was Rose's favorite,
and mine, too.

"It's the perfect color for her, the color of sunshine," Sara said. There was something glowing about the face, with her bright blue eyes and the saucy, direct way she had of looking at you. Sara had created an opalescent color, whites shimmering with pinks and violets and yellows, that gave the whole of the canvas a radiance. It was like nothing so much as the essence of all the summer afternoons spent in the garden, and it brought tears to my eyes.

Rose laughed and slipped her little arm into mine. "My sunshine dress," she said, delighted with the idea.

"I do think it is the best thing I've ever done," Sara said.

"I wish your friend—your teacher, Miss Beaux—could see it," I said.

"I was thinking that myself," Sara answered, slowly, "But it is your portrait, I did it for you. And now that it is finished, well, it is even more yours. There is something almost private about it, isn't there?"

Knowing at once what she meant, I hugged her. "Thank you, sweet friend," I said. Rose quickly ran to hug our knees and Sara lifted her and kissed her hard on the cheek.

"I will want to leave it here, with you," I told Sara. She seemed not surprised, and said nothing, but nodded assent.

"I do have one favor to ask," I went on. "Would it be possible for Wing Soong to see it? He will be coming into the city in a few weeks to tend Mrs. Gray's garden, and I'm sure he could find his way here."

"Of course," Sara said, breaking suddenly into a wide smile.

"Whatever is so funny?" I demanded.

"I was just trying to imagine Garvey's face when confronted by a giant Chinaman—with a perfect English gentleman's accent!"

We dissolved in giggles, then, the three of us—Rose not sure why, but happy to be included in the merriment. "You will probably grow up to be the wickedest of us all," Sara told her and Rose answered, "Yes, wicked!" with such seriousness that we were sent into fresh spasms of laughter.

The family returned from Hawaii in good health and high spirits, their teeth white against the tans of their faces, the three of them exuding good health. Thad's wiry little body was deeply tanned. He had grown, I thought at first, in those few short months, but then I decided it was more how he carried himself, in imitation of his father. I saw that Owen was aware of his little shadow. He frequently touched the boy. It was good to see them so, filled with stories to tell and presents to open.

"Come with me," Willa demanded, "come see what I've discovered for us." Pulling me into her bedroom, she unwrapped a dozen long, loose dresses of various bright colors, many with flowered patterns.

"What clever wrappers," I said, not knowing what else to say of these brilliantly colored costumes.

"Not wrappers, Lena—dresses!" Willa insisted. "The missionaries fashioned them to cover the native women's nakedness—a foolish idea, to begin with. But if one must wear something in the heat, it seems to me this is the perfect answer. They are so loose and cool, no tight corsets to gird you. So I have decided that this is to be our uniform on the Malibu on very warm days. Nothing less!"

I laughed at her. "I couldn't wear such a thing, I would feel altogether . . . altogether."

It was Willa's turn to laugh. She could see that I wasn't convinced, but she was in much too good spirits to spend time trying right then. Another travel bag was filled with jewelry made from sea shells.

That first evening at home, Rose and Thad sat in the corner of the front parlor, Thad pressing a large shell to her ear so that she might hear the roar of the ocean. It was impossible not to smile at the expression on her face. Her eyes seemed to grow ever larger as she heard the echoes.

Owen sat at his desk, riffling through the papers I had put aside for his immediate attention.

"What's this?" he said, his voice puzzled. "A citizen's group has requested a hearing of the County Board of Supervisors to allow public access to our ranch roads."

Willa dropped the shell beads she had been inspecting into her lap, her face grew worried. "Neighbor Shurz?" she guessed.

"He is going to be something of a permanent thorn in our sides, I do believe," Owen answered.

"I think, then, that we should look for a way to remove that thorn," Willa answered sharply.

Owen was already studying yet another official-looking paper, and this one made him frown.

"You won't like this any better, Willa," he warned her. "It seems that there is a petition before the Interstate Commerce Commission to allow passage of a railroad line through the Rancho Malibu y Sequit."

Willa drew in her breath in a sharp gasp. "Charles?" she asked. "Would he do that?"

"He did," was all Owen answered.

"Did you know anything about this?" Willa accused him. His look told her that she should be careful.

"I can't believe he would do this without so much as warning you!" she exclaimed, clearly both angry and chagrined.

Owen's face was grim. He knew Charles well enough to know that he could be formidable. He would have to study this, have to think about what, exactly, Charles might have in mind.

"He has spoken about it in the last few years," he said, more to fend off questions than anything. "He knows I have considered the possibility of a coach road—reviving the old custom. But a railroad, no. Not a railroad."

"What will we do?" Willa asked.

"I don't know, at least right now I don't know. Except that we will have to be careful, very careful!" Seeing Willa's face, he quickly added, "I don't think we have to worry all that much. Charles likes to take surprise steps, to catch one off guard. It is part of his method. It doesn't always work, and this time it will not. That does not mean, however, that we are at war with Charles. In fact, it is extremely important that we do not seem to be at war with Charles, do you understand?"

"You may not be," Willa answered, "but I am. I can't believe he would do this, not after all the years we have known them. Even if it is only, as you say, his 'method'—I don't much like his method."

Her adamant stance made Owen angry. "Please be clear, Willa," he spoke strongly, and his glance included me, "our relations with Charles and Sara are to remain as cordial as ever. Neither of you is to speak of this matter to them. If they should approach you to say anything, deflect the conversation. We will want to be careful."

Willa started to object, when I blurted, "My relations with Sara will not change. I doubt she will say anything about the railroad. She is not Charles' agent, but if she does I shall feel obliged only to say that you have asked me not to speak of it. I cannot lie to Sara. She knows my feelings for Charles are less than affectionate."

Willa agreed. "I was about to say as much. I am sure Sara cannot like what Charles is trying to do. I think she has little influence on him."

We fell silent for a time, then Willa said, in a voice so loud it made me start, "It would be a terrible scar on the land! I won't have it. I won't. A railroad would change the Malibu forever."

"My dear," Owen said with tenderness, "if Charles had any idea how fiercely you feel about this place, he would not have the courage to challenge you."

I chuckled. "You are something of a tigress, where the Malibu is concerned."

Willa smiled, in spite of herself. "Well, Charles shall feel my sharp teeth if he presses too close."

I gathered the beads that Owen and Willa had brought me, and called to Rose that it was past her bedtime.

"I have to say that I don't understand Charles," I said to them. "You have been friends for such a long time—there are so many business connections, and Sara of course, but I must say there is something perverse about the man . . ."

A look passed between them. They knew about Helen, I was certain. "Are you ever with Charles when Helen is present?" I asked, catching them by surprise.

"A great deal more often than we like," Willa murmured, her eyes down.

Owen, annoyed perhaps by the admission that Willa had just made, snapped, "Why doesn't Sara travel with him? She has no children to keep her home—only that infernal art."

Angered, I answered more sharply than I had intended. "Maybe she doesn't like to serve as chaperone to Charles and Helen any more than you do."

Owen swore, then, something I had never imagined he would do. "Did you suppose Charles to be discreet?" I asked. Willa looked at me and I knew the sorrow in her eyes was for Sara. She had thought to spare me.

"I wonder if any of us know the dimensions of Charles' capacity for duplicity?" was all she said.

Owen had assumed that Sara's interest in art had been to blame for the failure of her marriage. In fact, it was the failure of that marriage—measured, most basically, by Sara's failure to have a child—that had caused her to turn to the serious study of art. Her travels to England and the Continent, to New York and Philadelphia, had put her into contact with some of the most famous American artists of the day—not a few of them through letters of introduction written by Owen. Soon Sara would have her own first show, and I felt certain that her talent would be recognized.

There are timetables which become clear only in retrospect; events that come together, seemingly by chance, a series of coincidences, all of which can, if the timing is precise, be fateful. We are left to ponder, long after, what would have happened if only . . .

Wing Soong went into town to work in the garden of the widow of Judge Gray (and to see Rose's portrait). He left a week after Owen's return. I marked the day in my journal, which only later struck me as strange. Still, Soong had become part of the routine of my life, and routine is often sweet in itself. Perhaps it is not so strange that I would mark his departure, since he left on a Monday and it was always on Monday that I made my entries.

"Where goes Wings?" Rose had wanted to know.

"To help a friend," I told her, and she nodded as if to say that was a perfectly good reason.

The garden did seem empty without his familiar blue-clad figure moving about on the periphery of our vision, the edges of our lives.

Owen had written the agricultural agent to ask how best to get rid of the moles that had become the scourge of our vegetable garden. As it happened, Ignacio went into town to replace a broken plow disc, traveling on the same wagon that took Wing Soong. While there, he picked up the mail, which included a reply from the agent. The most efficient way to rid the garden of moles, he assured Owen, was to mix raisins and bits of raw carrot with the poison strychnine, and place little mounds of the poison mix near the newest holes.

Owen and the diminutive Soo Lin, who cared for the garden in Soong's absence, worked together the whole of one afternoon preparing the concoction.

We went into the garden the next day. It was sunny and bright. A brisk wind made it difficult for me to do my needlework, and it blew Rose's small tin tea set about. So we moved into the solarium to keep Thad company. He was propped there on a chaise, having complained of feeling poorly. His spirits were further dampened when Willa went off to track a pair of young condors which had been sighted just north of the ranch, while Owen had shut himself in his third-floor office to concentrate on some business papers.

"What are condors?" Rose wanted to know.

Thad, feeling perverse, told her, "They are giant birds that swoop down and carry little children away in their claws."

Rose's face clouded.

"Thad, that's not true," I admonished him, "don't scare Rose like that. We've come to keep you company. Rose is going to have a tea party, do you feel like joining her?"

"I don't like tea," he answered, sullenly, wanting to be coaxed.

Rose obliged him. "Then a birthday party," she said.

"It's not my birthday," he replied.

"A pretend party," Rose said, undeterred, "with pretend cake and pretend tea."

"Pretend's no fun," Thad grumbled. "Can we have real cake?"

Rose looked at me, and when I nodded "yes" she clapped her hands with pleasure and skipped out the door, calling back to us, "And we'll have *real* flowers." I smiled, knowing she would return with a clutch of daisies.

We sat in silence, Thad and I, he looking out of the window restlessly, I concentrating on the hem I was letting out of one of Rose's pinafores. She was growing fast now.

When it dawned on me that she had been gone quite long enough, Rose appeared in the doorway. The daisies were in one hand, in the other a bulging kerchief. Her face was flushed.

"Look what I found for our party," she said, in a voice that was strangely dull.

"What is it, dear?" I asked, "Do you hurt?"

"My back, Lema," she answered, leaning against me and spilling the handkerchief, out of which scattered raisins and bits of carrots.

"Dear God, baby," I managed to whisper. "Did you eat any?"

She looked up at me, and I could see that she had.

* * *

I know every detail of the ensuing hours, every moment is burned as if by acid into my memory. No detail of that day has faded, I shall take it to the grave with me as if it happened yesterday. If I close my eyes I can see the face, the tiny ringlets of hair dark with sweat, the small facial muscles twitching uncontrollably. And then, the breath that would not come, the small, dear body hot to the touch, the eyes, blue and wide and afraid, trusting me . . . the agonies as the small body tensed and throbbed, convulsed with pain, grotesquely arching, arching, as if some demon had taken possession and was ripping from within.

I held her hard to me and prayed that I could pull the pain from her body to mine. I tried to breathe into her mouth, to give her the air she so desperately needed. Willa watched in horror, her fist in her mouth. Owen twisted his hands and held them out to help, but there was no way, nothing to be done. And then he cried out in misery, saying over and over that he had not meant for this to happen, until Willa took him away.

The doctor came, too late. She had flailed and throbbed and twisted and turned, and struggled for breath. And then she had exhaled and, with one small release, died. She died in my arms. I pressed my lips to hers and tasted the faint, bitter taste of her mouth. I sat with her until they took her out of my arms.

# Chapter Thirteen

There was medicine to help me sleep, medicine to take away the pain, medicine to see me through the day. I have no clear memory of the weeks and months that followed Rose's death; only the events of that one day are sharp. It is as if I were walking through the kind of thick sea fog that rolls onto the beach in such a way that you can walk into it and out of it, appearing and disappearing at will. I made no entries in my daybook; Mondays passed in a blur of days. What I know of that time I know from others and, out of kindness, they have never told me all.

I know I said things that should have gone unsaid. I was full of rage and fury and pain, and lashed out without mercy. I became Owen's accuser. And Willa's. The baby was buried but I was not present. And then Willa and Owen and the boys were gone, but their leavetaking did not disturb my oblivion. I did know, I was told, that they had gone to Illinois, that Pa lay ill and near death, and that he had sent for us, for Willa and me. And Willa had gone.

Sara came to comfort me and found me beyond comforting, yet she stayed on. Sara and Trinidad and Wing Soong watched over me. They nursed me, they became my caretakers. I fought them all (Sara would tell me that much). I was wild, I did not want to live and I fought them for making me. I do not remember how I learned, or when, but I knew Pa was dead, had died before Willa could get there. In my daybook, on the blank pages of that unspeakable time, I have taped a letter I received from my brother Val.

"Dear sister Lena," he wrote in a hand that was surprisingly delicate for a farm boy, "I am writing to say how sad it is to know that you are not well. Willa has told me how you grieve for the baby Rose. I have but to look at Willa's face to see how all of you have suffered. I wish I could have news that would cheer you, but I fear I have only more sorrow to add to your burden.

"Pa died peacefully, in his sleep. He has been ailing for such a long time, as you know, so that it was with great sadness that we accepted his leaving, but we were prepared as much as it is possible to be prepared.

"We were not prepared for what happened only two days later, the same day as Willa and Owen's arrival. Mama had spent much of that afternoon sitting on the porch in her favorite chair—you will remember the one. She was reading one of her almanacs. I passed by, and she looked up at me and smiled a little, the first I had seen on her face since Pa's death. I remember thinking, 'She is able to read again, and smile a little. That is a good sign.'

"An hour later, Servia came to tell me he had wanted to tell Mama that he and Bernie were going to the station to meet Willa, but that she was sleeping so peacefully he didn't want to wake her. I told him to go ahead, that I would call her in half an hour to give her time to prepare for the visitors. I did as I said I would, but Lena, I could not wake Mama. She sat there, as if asleep . . . but she was gone. Mama died only two days after Pa. The doctor says it was her heart, and maybe it was. But I cannot help but think she didn't want to go on without Pa. They were caring of each other in ways that couldn't easily be seen.

"I am ever so sorry to be the one who brings this sad news. Willa thought it would be best for us to write you, rather than send a wire, so that you might have some more details—and not be so alarmed. It is a terrible time for us all. I cannot think how it will be at Porter Farm now, without them.

"Bernie's marriage, to Martha Langley, will be delayed until after a period of mourning. We are turning the old music room into an apartment for the newlyweds, so that they can have some privacy.

"Willa and Owen will be with us for another week, then they will proceed East where they plan to put the boys into school, as you know. Willa asks that I tell you she will write to you one day soon, and that she thinks of you often. We all of us send our love. Your faithful brother, Val."

I did not weep for my parents. There were no tears in me, I was barren of all feeling, my mind and my body were numb. Sara stayed with me. She abided my crazed fits of wrath and the longer periods of silence that followed. She sketched, talked to Wing Soong, and stayed until one day she, too, received a message of death. Charles wrote that Phineas Emory lay dying and that Sara should proceed directly to San Francisco where he would meet her.

Strangely, the fog that blurred my mind lifted for Sara's departure. I stood by the carriage that was to take her away, clutching at her until Trinidad called Wing Soong from the garden.

"I can't leave her," Sara had cried with anguish in her voice.

Wing Soong had pulled me away, had pinned my arms to my sides. "I will see that she is cared for," he said. "Go." His voice was low, but there was no mistaking the command. Sara reluctantly closed the carriage door and the driver snapped his whip to send the horses away at a quick trot. Sara looked back, feeling miserable and at the same time relieved. There was something about Wing Soong that inspired confidence. She trusted him.

If Soong had been loath to make suggestions to Sara, he was not to Trinidad. The two had daily dealings. She recognized his expertise in the matter of the garden, she consulted him often and had come to look on Soong as a font of practical information. He had seldom been wrong; he knew about certain cures; he was, Trinidad had said often enough, a wise one. Which was why she agreed to refuse me all medicines, and to take away the supply of patent tonics that I kept in the cupboard in my room. Wing Soong convinced her that it must be done. No matter how I harangued her, ordering her to bring them back, to give me my medicines, her face was set, impassive. She would not.

The days that followed Sara's departure were torture. My body was filled with pain that brought me to the surface of consciousness and held me there, where I could but remember what I wanted to forget. I hated Soong. I screamed at him. I pummeled Trinidad and threatened her for listening to him. In desperation, I appealed to Ignacio to control his wife. "I will see that Owen throws you out, both of you, for doing this to me. I can do it and I will, I will," I screamed. I would see them all in hell, I said.

In the weeks past I had stored several partially filled bottles of my medicine in various places about the ranch. As soon as I could manage, I slipped out of the house to retrieve them. I went into the tack room first, to an old wooden box that had been leaning in one corner for as long as I could remember. I reached into the cobwebby recesses. It was gone.

I hurried to my next cache, worried. As casually as I could, I meandered over to the arbor and stooped by the play box where we kept old toys. I lifted the lid, looked. The bottle was there, but it was empty. Empty! I felt like howling with rage. I picked up the bottle and made to fling it, only to have Soong clamp my arm in mid-air.

"You are a monster," I shrieked at him.

"Then that is what you need, a monster."

"I am sick, I've always been sick. Can't you see that? My back, the pain . . . Soong, have you no pity?" I was pleading.

"Pity?" he said sternly. "If I pitied you I couldn't do this. I know you have pain, Lena. The pain is in your heart and you've only managed to transfer it to your body because it is more easily endured there. But it must end, and it will. Now, Lena. Now it is time to end the pain." These last words were soft, tender. I didn't feel the tenderness, not then. All I felt was resignation. He was too strong; I couldn't fight him.

Little by little, the awful pain did go away. In its place settled a lethargy, a feeling of perfect exhaustion, a dull heaviness that lay in the center of me so that it was difficult to breathe. But the pain had passed; Soong had been right about that.

I told him that he had won, that he should go away and leave me in peace. I said to him that he had saved my life, I knew it, but I did not think it was such a very great accomplishment. Trinidad's face had changed from the worried, set scowl to the soft, loving mother. She treated me like one of her children who was ailing. Trinidad fixed a chaise in the garden and Soong carried me there when I had not the strength to walk. He talked to me then—for the first time, Soong spoke freely, for hours on end, it seemed. He spoke of all that he was doing in the cause of his country. He told me things that would, at any other time, have amazed and frightened and excited me. He talked and he talked in the long afternoons, as he worked in the garden.

And one day I interrupted him to ask, "Where is her daisy bush? What have you done with it?"

He had been working sand into the soil of the vegetable garden, but my question made him sit back on his heels and look at me steadily, as if to measure the question. "I put it at the foot of her grave," he said.

I wanted to ask where that was, my baby's grave, but I could not, the words would not form.

"It is up there," he said, pointing to Peregrino Hill. "You wanted it there."

"I did?" I asked, surprised.

"Yes. You insisted."

"I see," I said, drily, though in fact I didn't see, and his saying that I had done something I had no memory of angered me. "How do you happen to know all of this?" I added, with sarcasm.

"Because Mr. Reade asked me to prepare the grave, and to tend it," he answered, carefully.

My hands were shaking. I could not seem to lift my eyes to his, I could not seem to think. Soong saw and he said, "Not yet, you are not yet ready to go. But one day you will be." The sobs started then, great and wrenching and painful, they seemed to come from some dark place so far inside of me that I could not fathom it. My body heaved and coughed and convulsed. My nose ran and I could not catch my breath. I cried and I cried. When at last I could cry no more, but lay back spent, Soong said in a voice that was more than a caress, "My dear friend, you have returned."

From Concord, New Hampshire, Willa wrote: "Lena, darling sister. I cannot tell you how very relieved I was at long last to get a letter from you. My heart pounded when I saw the familiar hand. It is so good to know—as much from the way you write as from what you say—that you are getting better. You have seldom been out of my thoughts in these past weeks. I did not write because I was not sure that you would want to hear from me. The pain, the awful pain—and so much of yours has been of my making. It is hard to bear.

"I find myself even now finding it hard to write her name— sweet Rose. It is painful to see it. But one day we must speak of her, you and I. (I echo your words of three years ago, I know that Lena, I am sorry. Oh, I am so very, very sorry for my mistakes, and it makes so little difference.)

"It is enough, for now, to say that we have suffered—you, and me, and Owen. Owen too, you must believe that. The harsh words you had for us, we know, were spoken at a time when you were filled with grief. We will not forget them, but we have already forgiven them. Just as we ask forgiveness for all that we have done, to cause you grief.

"Perhaps I should not be saying any of this in our first exchange of letters. It is just that I am so happy to know you will recover. I want so to remove any barriers that might come between us. Of all people now living, you and Owen and the boys are most precious to me.

"I cannot write, just now, of Mama and Pa. This letter is already too filled with emotion. I will only say that I found our brothers well able to carry on the work of the farm, which indeed they have been doing for some years now. And though their lives now are quite unusual—seven bachelors on a farm— I expect that will be changing soon. Bernie will marry this summer, and several of the other boys are seeing girls in town. The boys want you to return to the farm for a long visit, but I have urged them to give you some time. (Knowing that in doing so, I was asking for time with you for myself. I pray you will want to stay on the Malibu, to continue to make your home with us.)

"We have placed the boys in St. Paul's School here in Concord, where the headmaster is an old friend and classmate of Owen's. The boys will, Owen says, be well prepared for Harvard College at St. Paul's. His friend has agreed to take the boys into his own family so that they will not feel they are without ties, so far away from home. Thad is not at all happy, as you may have guessed, but his entreaties go unheard by

Owen. Wen is happy to be at the school. He seems, even to want us to be on our way even before the week is up.

"Owen seems determined to believe that his sons are the best of friends, and that Wen will act as Thad's protector. In fact, that will not happen. I feel sorry for Thad, but then perhaps that is because I know how it feels to be forced to go to school in the East when you know you belong to the West. I did get Owen to agree that we should stop by the school on our return from England, so that Thad will have our visit to look forward to. I am not sure it is wise, though. For even if we find Thad to be utterly miserable, I doubt that Owen will change his mind. And in this area, I have no influence at all.

"I am glad that you have decided to travel to Florence with Sara. It will be a new experience for you, going abroad. Florence is a beautiful city, and soothing to the spirit. We will, I suppose, pass in mid-continent, on trains going in opposite directions, as we shall be returning from Europe at about the time you propose to go to Italy. I promise to write to you regularly. Already, I look to the time when you will return, and we can begin once more on the Malibu.

"Owen sends his love, and so do I. Please write quickly, so I will know that nothing I have said offends you."

I did write to Willa, from the Malibu and then from Philadelphia, where we stopped to visit with Sara's great teacher, Cecilia Beaux, a beautifully gentle woman with a face of great kindness. She is a spinster who lives, still, in the family home, surrounded by cousins and aunts and uncles. Sara and Miss Beaux talked of the arts, of the work each was doing, and I was happy to sip my tea and listen, letting my eyes enjoy the beautifully appointed room with its lovely old rugs and Sevres vases and tapestries.

It is difficult to look at Miss Beaux's charming portraits of children without feeling a certain pain. Her influence on Sara's work is easily seen; the large, serious eyes staring out from the canvas, the light opalescent touch that makes the canvas shimmer.

On one of those sunlit afternoons, Miss Beaux rather suddenly asked, "Have you decided if you will show the Rose portrait at the Paris Salon?" Sara was caught off guard, and mumbled something inaudible as she shot a worried glance at me. Miss Beaux, sensing that she had asked the wrong question, quickly changed the subject.

Later that evening, when we were alone, Sara said, "I want to explain."

"You needn't," I told her, "don't you remember my asking if you would show the portrait to Miss Beaux? I thought you should. I wanted you to."

"I know, and I could not resist doing so. I trusted her to see it and, having met her now, you can see why I would. But I have not shown it to another soul, other than Wing Soong."

I felt a sharp, sudden shiver, thinking of Soong looking at the portrait. He had never mentioned it to me.

"He loved the child, I believe," I said, "they shared certain . . ."

"Yes," Sara agreed, but it was the portrait she wanted to talk about. I breathed deeply, and tried to prepare myself to make a convincing argument.

"It is a beautiful portrait, your best work," I told her. "I think you must show it—you must not hold back simply because . . ."

"No," she stopped me, "it's not just that, either. There is something terribly private about that portrait. I can't explain why myself, but I do not want it to be shown publicly. Perhaps when I learn why I feel that way . . . It was that she had a quality about her . . ." Sara struggled for the right words. I took her hand, squeezed it as I squeezed back my own tears.

"Someday," I said, "we will look at it together."

The tears welled in Sara's eyes. "I am so relieved to hear you say that," she said. "When you were so very ill, when you were angry . . . you told me to destroy it. I considered doing just that, but in the end I couldn't. And I felt as if I had betrayed you, in some way."

I kissed her hand, wet with tears that she had tried to brush off her face. "You were right not to listen," I said. "I do not remember asking, and you were right not to listen to me." I understood, then, why Sara had been so upset at the mention of the portrait. And I understood, too, the depth of her love for me, and wondered if I could possibly deserve it.

Sara's apartment in Florence was on a narrow street off the Via Faenza. The rooms were filled with beautiful tapestries and priceless paintings. It was as dusty and as lovely as I could imagine an old palace to be. It was let to her, Sara explained, by a distinguished Florentine family which had fallen upon hard times, and could keep the family treasures only with the aid of a rich American. There were many rich Americans in Florence, but Sara gave them wide berth. The few people we saw—artist friends, for the most part—spoke little English, and I was glad. It provided me with the kind of screen I needed. I did not want to talk very much, and there was no need. I had but to sit and smile occasionally.

By day, Sara and I did a leisurely exploration of the Renaissance city—the Duomo, the Palazzo Vecchio, the Piazzale degli Uffizi. When the weather was nice, we would climb the hills above the city in the late afternoons to watch the sun set on the burnished gold city, so foreign to anything I had ever known. Its timelessness gave me a sense of my own insignificance. If ever I were to find myself again, I would first lose myself in Florence. America was a world away. There were times when I could believe that the Malibu did not exist. The letters that arrived regularly might have come from another age, another planet.

"Dear Lena," Willa wrote, "it has been the wettest winter on record. Christmas Day we were treated to a storm that blew from the southwest, and that shook the very foundations of the house and ripped off shutters. The howling was so ferocious that I wondered, at times, if we would be blown back into the mountains.

"Arcadia and Joseph had come out shortly before the storm broke, and were stranded when fast-running streams washed out several bridges. Arcadia fretted, worrying about the Señora. At last we convinced her that there was nothing to be done about it, so she settled in to entertain us all as only Arcadia can. She was bright and happy, leading the songs and inventing new games and sparking the fun. One evening she insisted we dress in our most elegant evening clothes and, with music provided by our new Victrola, the four of us waltzed the night away. Joseph is not so good a dancer as Owen, but well able to match Arcadia's high spirits. There could have been no better companions with whom to be washed out to sea, had it come to that.

"Ah, but the big news—the great news—has also to do

with Joseph. Dear Joseph! As our representative before the county commissioners, he presented the case against Mr. Shurz and a small group of settlers (who have cited us for 'obstructing a public highway') with such marvelous good humor, and good reasoning, that he quite won over the commissioners.

"'Tell me, Mr. Shurz, sir,' Joseph would say, all ebullient good manners, 'has Mr. Reade ever denied you, personally, passage through his property?'

"The surly Shurz grumbled something that seemed to mean 'no' and said 'But—'

"Joseph quickly cut in, as if in surprise, 'You mean, sir, that Mr. Reade was actually willing to give you a key to the gate that enclosed his private ranch? He went so far as to do that?'

"When it turned out that Owen had offered keys, and the right to pass through our property, to several of the settlers who live just over the ridge, the commissioners ruled against Shurz. I think they should have thrown him out altogether, Shurz and his whining settler friends. It all seems so ridiculous to me. They demand the use of our roads, as if it were a right. That the council even gave them a hearing angers me. But we won, that is all that is important. I have said that we should build a fence across every road, and even to the high tide line on the beach. Frankly, I am frightened that more and more of the people who are settling in the mountains beyond the eastern boundary of the ranch will begin to use our roads without permission. Already they camp on our land and build fires. It would take only one careless fire to set the whole ranch to flames in the dry season.

"Owen urges patience; he seems to think we may have won only the first skirmish. I maintain that the ranch is our property, bought and paid for, and that it will remain ours.

"As for the problem with Charles . . . We feel that we may have hit upon an idea that will foil him permanently. I should say that Owen has found a way, since the idea was his. We are now the proprietors of a railroad! The La Chusa, Malibu and Southern Railroad Company. It was all so very secret for awhile. We are indebted to your friend Wing Soong for that. It was he who alerted us to watch out for the bookkeeper Pringle.

"One evening, at twilight, Owen and I were sitting on the

verandah when Wing Soong appeared at the edge of the lawn. He made no move to come closer, yet we knew he wanted to speak. Owen went to him, then, and learned that Wing Soong had seen Pringle in Los Angeles, had followed him to Charles' office, suspected that something was amiss. (I, of course, was fascinated by the idea of the huge Chinaman following the fussy little bookkeeper. I do not know why he would do such a thing, but both Owen and I are terribly grateful to him.) When Owen confronted the man Pringle, he cracked his knuckles mightily and flew about like some black bird trapped in a cage. Charles had been paying him for 'information of interest,' it seems, not only about how we expected to parry his drive for a railroad through the ranch but on the other business matters as well. Needless to say, we sent Pringle packing. He will not have an easy time securing another job, you can be sure. Charles denies the man's very existence, naturally, and we have warned others against hiring the creature.

"Wing Soong alerted us to Pringle's treachery just in time. Had he known about our plans to build the railroad, Charles might have been able to keep us from getting the equipment we needed. Our trestles are almost complete, now, and the engine house is in place. Joseph has a petition before the Interstate Commerce Commission to the effect that one railroad is sufficient to serve the needs of the Malibu—and that railroad is almost in place: the La Chusa, Malibu and Southern! Isn't Owen clever?

"The Santa Monica papers are full of news of the new railroad and the effect it will have on the people of this area. I do hope the good citizens of Santa Monica are not planning picnic excursions to our beaches. If they are, I am afraid they are going to be disappointed. Our railroad will serve the ranch— transport hides, move our workers about the ranch. I don't foresee our becoming railroad barons in the manner of the Emorys.

"Does Sara hear from Charles? He has had the good sense to stay away from the ranch, and as I seldom go into town these days, I have not seen him at all. I understand that since his uncle's death, he has been close to the bereaved widow, offering consolation. Owen insists that we must continue to be civil to him. I do not know why, other than some rather complicated business dealings.

"I have lived long enough to make grave errors in my own life. I try to remember, in order to grant others the right to make mistakes. I don't believe that one necessarily profits from mistakes. That is a rather silly notion. Just as the idea that one grows stronger through suffering seems to me not to be true. One must simply survive. But I do believe it is good to admit one's mistakes, if only to maintain honesty with oneself. That is what seems to me to be missing in Charles. He has no sense of his own fallibility. He seems to think himself above the rules. Dear Sara, poor Sara. (Do not under any circumstances let her know I said 'poor Sara.' She would despise me for it. Yet I do pity her, I cannot help it.) Owen says that Charles is truly a man of the American West—'flawed, but in a fascinating way.'"

When I repeated Owen's description of Charles to Sara, a curious smile came over her face. "I think they are more alike than Owen would like to admit," she said.

I frowned. Sara, seeing my discomfort, quickly added, "I mean only that both know very much what they want, and in certain circumstances each is capable of doing whatever is necessary to get it. Neither is afraid to wield the power he has. Owen, of course, is a great deal more circumspect than Charles."

I did not want to argue with Sara, did not want to plunge into a discussion of honor and ethics and essential good. "What, exactly, does Charles want?" I asked instead.

Sara looked at me as if to measure the extent of my interest. "Charles wants to build a railroad through the Malibu," she began, slowly. "I don't know how much he wants it, but enough to alienate Owen, which strikes me as very much, given Owen's prominence and power. Owen may well be more than a match for Charles—he has won the first round with the La Chusa, Malibu and Southern," she said, laughing without real mirth. "It's a bold stroke, and I'm sure Charles will appreciate it. But more important, now at least, and it may work in Willa and Owen's favor, is that Charles wants Helen. He wants her legally, so that he will at last be his uncle's true heir."

"How can that be?" I asked. "You are his wife."

"He'll find a way to challenge that," Sara said, with such calm that I knew she had thought it out long before.

Two weeks later, two letters arrived on the same day. Mine,

from Willa, announced with jubilation that the La Chusa, Malibu and Southern Railroad had won, that Charles' petition to run a line of the Southern Pacific through the Malibu had been rejected on the basis that one railroad was sufficient to serve the area. Joseph Brennan had been brilliant, Willa said. Charles had been dispatched; forever, she hoped.

The same post brought Sara a letter from Charles. It lay on the massive marble table in the foyer all morning long, though I knew that Sara had seen it. When it was still there in the afternoon, it began to seem ominous. I had an appointment with a physician that afternoon, a well-known man of medicine who had made a specialty of treating those suffering from my malady. When I returned, the letter was gone. I found Sara in her small sitting room. It was gloomy, but she had not yet lit a lamp nor had she called a servant to light the fire. I did both, then sat down to wait.

She shifted in her chair, as if to acknowledge my presence. Without preliminary, she said, "He wants an annulment."

"Oh, no," was all I could think to say.

Sara nodded. "He says we are cousins, and that he married me to set his uncle's mind at rest, knowing that my uncle felt I was too plain to attract anyone other than a fortune hunter. He says that he knew immediately after the ceremony that he could consider me no more than a relative, a friend. He says he hoped, of course, that it might be otherwise. All that he says is written for the lawyers, not for me."

"He is despicable," I began.

"That doesn't matter," Sara quickly put in, "what does matter is that the marriage was consummated. I am legally his wife."

I wondered why it should matter to her, but said nothing. Finally I ventured, "What will you do?"

There was something hard, or firm, in the way she answered my question. "First I will send a wire to Joseph."

"Joseph Brennan?" I asked. "Arcadia's Joseph?"

"Yes," she replied, "Joseph has been my adviser—and my friend as well, I think—for some time. I believe he is the only lawyer in southern California Charles can't control. There is real steel in Joseph. It isn't easy to see, but it is there. I've thought that this might happen, and Joseph and I made arrangements, in case Charles should act while I was in Italy."

"Plans?" I wanted to know, understanding for the first time that Sara, too, might well be a match for Charles.

"Plans for the exchange, the sale, as it were. I have something Charles wants. As a good businessman, he should know he is going to have to pay for it. If he wants to be free of me—free to marry Helen—it is going to cost him a full third of the Emory fortune."

I stared at Sara.

"A full third?" I repeated. "Sara, that would mean you would have an equal amount..."

"That is correct. It would make me the equal of Charles and Helen. There was a time, and not so very long ago, when I would have been happy to settle for the amount of my own father's investment in Phineas Emory's early business. But neither Uncle Phineas nor Husband Charles"—she repeated the titles with thick sarcasm—"could bear to part with even that small amount. It would have been enough to support myself, to give me the freedom to paint—without the humiliation of pretending to be a married woman. They used me badly, those two. I won't be used further."

"But what if he won't... what if he says 'no'?"

"He wants more than the fortune, you see," Sara explained with a stoic patience, "He wants to *be* the new Phineas Emory. By marrying Helen, he will be keeping the inheritance together. Two-thirds is better than one-half."

"For Charles, yes," I said, "but what about Helen?"

Sara nodded. "Yes, I've thought about that. What I am counting on is that Helen needs Charles to maintain her illusion of being superior. Without him, she is simply a very wealthy woman who was once a strumpet. Charles has the power to make others fear him. As his wife, she would be feared too."

"What do we do, then?" I asked, feeling exceptionally sad and weary.

"I must sail for home at once," she said, "my actions in the coming months will tell the tale. Charles must believe that I find the idea of divorce impossible. He must think that I want to continue to be known as his wife, otherwise he will never consent to so large a settlement. And I have no intention of consenting to any less."

"I'll go with you," I told her. She smiled and touched my cheek. "Thank you," she said. "I had hoped you would feel strong enough to go back with me, to help me get the Emorys out of my life forever."

We sailed for London a fortnight later, and that same week boarded the steamship for the voyage home. We had been away five months. I was not sorry to leave, nor did I look forward to docking in New York. I was most content, I believe, standing on the deck mid-point in the ocean voyage, with no land in sight, where the world was a simple choice of blues.

# ~ Chapter Fourteen

The first rays of the first sunrise of the twentieth century found them on the beach at Malibu Point, perched on a flat rock at the base of which the tide whirled, wrapped in a blanket Owen had thought to bring along. It was Owen's idea that they should see the sunrise together. He had engineered this part of the celebration as carefully as he had engineered the whole grand extravaganza—which had been going on for two days, and would last two more.

"Think of it," he said, "the dawn of a new century."

She had never seen Owen so caught up with an occasion as he was with the turning of the century. Feeling him shiver, she pulled closer and slipped her arm around his waist.

"I think this is the place I would most want to be to welcome the next one hundred years," she said, then changing subjects asked, "aren't you terribly tired?"

"No," he answered, "But I will be soon, I suppose." He had never been as strong as he liked to appear. In the past year, she had noted that his reserves seemed to be waning. He would, she knew, pay for having exerted himself so these past weeks. When the last guest left, he would need to spend several days in the hammock they had hung in the solarium.

"I hope our guests are all in bed," Willa laughed, softly, "I

doubt this place will ever see another party like this one again."
She said it to please him, as much as anything. Owen took
such pleasure in giving a good party, and this had been the
most ambitious ever, with several hundred people, including
two senators and a governor. "We'd better get some sleep
before the afternoon beach party," Willa said then, but neither
made a move to go. They sat together until the sun was high
enough to transform the vast, smooth Pacific into a mirror of
silver and pink. The edges of the waves as they broke were an
impossible shade of cerese. "I can't remember such an exquisite
sunrise," she went on, "but maybe I'm just seeing it for the
first time with my twentieth-century eyes."

She stood and shook the sand from her blanket. She was
wearing the gray silk emblazoned with crystal bugle beads,
and the morning light flashed on them. The dress was from
Worth's, a gift from Owen's recent trip to Paris. He pulled her
to him and brushed the wisps of hair the breeze had blown
over her face.

"Have I said how very handsome you looked last night?"
he asked, kissing the top of her head. She felt tired, a gray
spot was lodged behind her eyes and the champagne had caused
a low churning in her stomach. But she also felt strangely
peaceful as she rested her face against him, and relaxed into
his body.

"Do you know it has been thirteen years?" he said, and for
a moment she couldn't think what he meant. "I want you to
know," he went on, and Willa realized that it was one of Owen's
prepared speeches, "that there is never a day that I don't con-
gratulate myself on having had the wonderful good luck to have
found you." She pulled back to study his face.

"They *have* been good years," she said slowly, "most of
them, not all. But the last months have been best I think
. . . sometimes I think that our life together is really just
beginning, I think . . ."

He stopped her by kissing her lightly on the lips. "I'm
content now," he said, and it was not part of the speech, she
knew. "I'm happy with what we have had. Whatever more is
to come will be a gift from God." He pulled her close to him,
then, so she could not see his face. *A gift from God.* She
shivered, and held him. She was thirty-five, he but forty. Their
lives would span the two centuries, she thought, and so liked

the idea that she wanted to tell him; that was when she first heard someone hailing them.

"Hallo!" Joseph called out, "we've found you out, the two of you—and it was just as I deduced. Unhand that lady, sir!" He was weaving and laughing, with Arcadia on his arm. They drew unsteadily closer.

Owen waved at the pair. Had anyone else intruded on them, he would have been annoyed. But Arcadia and Joseph were part of the circle.

"Joseph said you would arrange to see the first sunrise of the new century," Arcadia laughed. "He said he knows how your mind works, Owen."

"She doesn't believe you're such a romantic dog, old boy," Joseph said, clapping Owen on the back with one hand while he waved a bottle of champagne in the other.

"We've come to toast the sunrise," he went on, "with your very best vintage, which I commandeered from the wine cellar quite without permission.

"A clear case of trespass . . . not to mention grand theft; I shall call my solicitor," Owen laughed.

"Have a drink, instead," Joseph answered, working to make the words come out straight. "Your so-li-ci-tor is second-rate anyway. Better find another."

Joseph stumbled just as Willa reached to take the bottle from him. She raised it to the morning sun, said, "To the year 1900!" and took a long swig, though it was the last thing she wanted. "Hear! Hear!" the others answered automatically, there had been so many toasts. "And I say that's the end of the toasting," Willa went on, at which Joseph and Arcadia sank onto the blanket Willa had spread on the sand.

The sun was high, it had warmed the top layer of sand. Willa and Owen made no move to leave, but neither did they join the couple on the blanket. Rather they leaned against the rock, and spoke in desultory tones.

"Quite an affair, Owen," Joseph said with a soft belch, "I doubt we'll see another like it in this century." His face was flushed with wine and lack of sleep, but still he smiled.

"What do you think the new century has in store for us?" Arcadia asked.

"In this century," Joseph answered in a parody of his sonorous courtroom voice, "I intend to make this fair lady my own."

He turned and reached for Arcadia, missed and rolled over in
the sand. Laughing, she reached to help him up, and only
succeeded in being pulled over with him. "We shall totter up
the aisle together," Joseph said, holding her loosely in his arms.
"I shall be ninety-eight, my fair bride will be ninety-six and
the flower girl, the Señora, will be one hundred and fifty-two."

Arcadia was not smiling. She extricated herself from Joseph's arms, stood and brushed the sand from her dress. "You
forget," she said in a taut voice, "the Señora will not be there.
The Señora will have to be dead."

Joseph lay back in the sand, as if spent. He put his hands,
palms up, over his eyes. Willa touched Arcadia's arm, she saw
tears waiting to well. They were all too tired, she told herself.
They had had too little sleep and too much wine. Everything
was too close to the surface.

As a social event, the Reades' New Year's party made society
columns as far away as Denver. In San Francisco, the *Chronicle*
noted that Sara Hunt Emory, identified as the adopted daughter
of the late Phineas Emory and an heiress to the Emory fortune,
had gone south for the event, and had made her private railway
car, the Golden Eagle, available to a large group of friends
from the city's first families, in which to make the trip.

Willa and Owen had loved the mention of the Golden Eagle.
It was one of the items Joseph Brennan had managed to secure
as part of the extraordinary divorce settlement he had arranged
for Sara. Joseph called it "one of the little extras." So among
Sara's closest friends the car became "The Golden Extra."

The settlement had made Sara one of the richest women in
the West. This would have surprised anyone who saw her in
the weeks before the big party. She had decided to paint a huge
mural at one end of the pink barn, above the stage erected for
the band. She put Thad, who with Wen was home for the
holidays, and several of Trinidad's children to work helping
her. All of them were happily paint-spattered for days.

"It is not what you would call a work of art," Sara said of
the big wall painting, "but you must admit, it has a great deal
of vigor."

"And it's colorful," Arcadia ventured to add, a comment
that had us all laughing, since the color choices were limited
to bright red, blue and yellow.

The bunkhouses had been sprayed to get rid of the fleas, then they were scrubbed and whitewashed and fitted with cots for the male guests. The women were staying in the big house, and various beach and guest houses close by. Tents had been set up for the servants, including a corps of new people hired for the occasion. The barn had been brushed and watered down, fresh straw was spread, banquet tables lined the length of the room and a new floor had been put down for dancing. Everyone had been pressed into service. The orchard men had a wonderful time stringing Chinese lanterns from tree to tree. The cowboys dug deep pits for the barbequed lamb and pig and steer that would be needed to feed such a large number.

Owen had managed to entice several chefs from New York, one from Delmonico's even, and all were immediately enchanted with the variety of vegetables that Soong was able to supply them. For a time it seemed as if Owen's old friend, Theodore Roosevelt—who seems certain to be the country's next president—would join us, but in the end he sent a telegram regretting that he could not come, and asking instead if he might send a young friend, a woman photographer who, he assured Owen and Willa, "is known to me, and does good work." Frances Benjamin came, with her load of heavy camera equipment, and painstakingly recorded the whole event, which she quickly proclaimed "Quite unlike anything I have ever seen, a curious and interesting mixture of the Eastern and the Wild Western cultures." Miss Benjamin was quite serious when she said this, so we tried very hard not to smile.

We prayed it would not rain for the celebration, and it did not. The thirtieth dawned bright and clear, with not a cloud to mar the horizon. The open cars of the La Chusa, Malibu and Southern Railway were draped in bunting (red, white and blue, as if the new century belonged to our country) and shuttled back and forth, delivering guests and mounds of baggage.

Hunting, hiking, fishing expeditions, balls and beach picnics had been planned, as well as sailing parties. Each would require a separate costume, and the guests came well prepared. Some brought their own servants, only a few traveled without a trunk. *"Wild* West, indeed," Joseph snorted, watching the unloading, "this might as well be Saratoga."

It was a marvel of organization, there was a place for everyone and everything. It had occupied Owen for the past several months, and as usual he had done a superb job.

"This party is to be elegant," he was fond of saying during that time, "with humorous overtones." Indoor toilet facilities would be overtaxed, so a quaint little row of old-fashioned outhouses were built, one row for men and another for women, each with its own flower box and each with an assigned servant to clean it several times each day.

The only person of any note who was absent was Charles. Owen had incurred Willa's wrath by suggesting Charles should be sent an invitation, even though we knew he was on an extended wedding trip with his new bride, formerly his aunt. Willa would not hear of it, and Owen did not press the matter.

Charles and Helen were the subject of interminable gossip, and Sara was not spared. "Imagine," an assistant editor of the *Los Angeles Times*, a young man recently arrived from New York, was heard to say, "he divorced his cousin to marry his aunt!" An older hand took the man aside to explain just why that particular joke, which was circulating, would not be considered funny on the Malibu.

It didn't matter, however. Sara knew about it, but it did not diminish her sense of triumph. Sara had done what she set out to do—she was financially independent, at last. In becoming so, she had proved herself to be every bit the equal of Helen, every bit the equal of Charles. She was just as clever, just as strong. She had shown them she was their match, and she had done it the only way that could matter to the two of them: She had secured her inheritance. Having done so, she could dismiss them from her life. Which is not to say that she did not expect to have to deal with them, in one way or another, in the years to come.

"Has it ever occurred to you," the tall young man who had claimed the third waltz said, "that you live in Paradise?"

Willa laughed—the full, thrown-back and throaty laugh that made people turn and look. "You've discovered the family secret," she said as they glided over the dance floor, "I told Owen we should never let all of you come out here—that you'd be clamoring to get in."

"Exactly, that's it," the young man rallied, "now that we've seen Paradise, you won't be able to keep us out . . . such beautiful mountains, such beautiful seas and such extraordinarily beautiful women," he said, lowering his voice.

Willa smiled engagingly; she liked bantering with this attractive young man. She wasn't the least interested in knowing anything more about him, but she liked it that he found her exciting.

"I suggest you continue to enjoy yourself," she said with mock gravity, "because once all of you leave, we are going to wave our wand and the Malibu will vanish, just like all good magic kingdoms."

He was looking at her with ill-concealed awe; she had made a conquest. She could hardly wait to tell Owen; he would enjoy knowing the young Vanderbilt was smitten with her.

At the last note of the waltz, a young lady in a white dress with blue ribbons materialized to claim the young man. His face told Willa that he would rather stay with her. "I relinquish him, with regrets, I must confess," Willa said, sighing theatrically as she disengaged his hand, "I think to console myself I shall claim a dance from that handsome gentleman," she said, nodding toward Owen.

"He is divine," the young woman gushed, "every woman here envies you, Mrs. Reade," she continued, until her partner whirled her off in an explosion of annoyance.

Sara, having heard the exchange, tucked her arm in Willa's and said, "Why is it that the empty-headed ones insist on opening their mouths to reveal pure air inside?"

Willa laughed. "If they don't," she said, "if they say nothing at all, some poor man is going to marry them before he knows the head is empty."

The two stood arm in arm for a moment, watching Owen, who was in the midst of a knot of people including the governor and his lady.

"It seems to me that Owen has changed not at all since I first saw him. Do you think? I mean when we first met you, on the train. Do you remember how he looked?"

"Oh, yes," Sara said, squeezing Willa's arm, "I thought he was beautiful then, and I think so now. I believe that was the happiest meeting of my life. Otherwise, I would never have found my family."

Willa looked at her with affection and said, "I do not think this family would have survived without you, little one. But we were talking about Owen."

"Owen," Sara said, "*has* changed. Not so much physically, but in other ways."

"What do you mean?" Willa asked. "Tell me how." And Sara was sorry, at once, that she had said it, but now there was nothing to do but extricate herself.

"I don't think he is quite so afraid as he once was . . ." she began, trying to be vague.

Willa's face said she didn't understand. "I only mean," Sara went on, "that he seems to have made peace with some of the things that once seemed to drive him . . . Don't you see it too?"

Willa thought about it. "I suppose so. He isn't in such a rush to accomplish everything today. He is more at leisure, I think. Except he can still fly about like some whirlwind—this party is proof of that."

Feeling their eyes on him, Owen looked up and waved. Excusing himself, he began to make his way around the dance floor to them, but midway a couple stopped dancing to speak to him. He was caught, Willa could see. For a moment she felt a point of anger, almost. Their life had so often been like that—dreamlike, Owen trying to reach her across a crowded room, a sea of people preventing it.

She caught herself. "How silly of me," she thought; they were no longer separate, they had never been so very much together since . . .

. . . *since the baby's death,* she admitted to herself.

The baby's death had brought them together. She would never say it out loud, not ever. But it was true.

She turned abruptly, colliding with a man and sending his champagne splashing over both of them.

She cried out. "No mind, Mrs. Reade," the man said, "none at all." He had a sharp face and a hooked nose. She looked at him to place him, and felt as if she might faint. Wen was dancing nearby. She put her hand out to him, "Son," she said, her voice tremulous. Wen quickly took his mother and guided her outside, where he sat with her for as long as he deemed necessary. Thad would have seen the confusion in her face, the pain. Wen was simply anxious to get back to the dance. "I'm fine," she told him, waving him away. "Truly, you can go." But she wasn't fine and she didn't know if she had actually seen Amos Proctor, the Treasury agent who had caught Connor McCord here, on this very ranch, almost five years ago—or

if her thought about the baby, the dead baby, had created the
illusion. She lay back against the rough side of the barn, out
of the circle of light, and closed her eyes. Did she dare go look
for him? Could he be real? No, she decided. His name certainly
had not appeared on any guest list. He was a terrible creation
of her own mind.

Owen. She had promised to be at his side at midnight. She
made her way back to the barn; the grandfather clock they had
mounted on the stage said it was twenty before the hour. The
old century was in its closing minutes; champagne was being
passed; Owen had no intention of letting this high point slide
by without ceremony.

Couples began to drift off the dance floor and to assemble
in small groups. Willa waved to the boys; Sara and I were
already at the appointed place. Arcadia and Joseph would join
us, we would see the New Year in together.

As the minute hand drew closer to the hour, the crowd
became still. Hundreds were crowded into the old pink barn,
and they were silent . . . as if waiting for an event of enormity.
You could smell the straw, the night air that wafted in . . . the
old clock began to strike.

One, two, three . . .

Owen raised his glass.

. . . ten, eleven, twelve.

"To the twentieth century," he intoned.

"To the twentieth century," we responded in unison, an
incantation.

The band struck up a march, confetti and balloons were
loosed from the ceiling, a great roar broke through the crowd.
We put arms around each other and swayed, our faces wet with
tears. It was like no other New Year that ever was, or ever
would be. We were together on the Malibu, it was 1900 and
the world looked fine, very fine indeed, said Owen in the first
of several speeches made that night.

After a time no one listened to the speeches, but danced
and laughed and were generally jolly. Somewhere in the early
hours, Sara and I found ourselves sitting at the edge of the
stage, sipping our eighth or ninth champagne, when she said
in a very loud whisper, "They've both changed. They don't
know it but they have. They've changed enough so they can,
finally, belong to each other."

I nodded gravely, as if I understood perfectly what she was saying. In fact, I wasn't even sure who she was talking about—Charles and Helen, probably. But perhaps Willa and Owen. I intended to ask her, but somehow it slipped my mind.

When Wing Soong, in his usual shadowy manner, guided me to the house where I was staying and pointed out the entrance, he had said with a certain amount of annoyance that he did not even observe this calendar, so he could see little reason for my having needed to make quite so many toasts.

Willa had long ago taught herself to forget the events of that summer, and she set about forgetting her illusion of Amos Proctor. Perhaps it was the effort that made her gasp as she was reading the morning newspapers with Sara and me, only a few days after the guests' departure.

"What is it, Willa?" I quickly asked, "what have you found?"

She passed the paper to me, her eyes cloudy with confusion.

"On Tuesday last," I read, "a man identified as Amos Proctor was found dead in the Clamber Boarding House on West Fourth Street in Long Beach. Officers suspect foul play, pointing out that the manager of the boarding establishment had recounted several suspicious circumstances. The victim is remembered in this city as an employee of the government. Identification found in his room indicates that he has been employed of late by the Armstrong Meat Packing Company of Chicago, Illinois."

"Amos Proctor was—" I began.

"Yes," Willa answered, leaving the room abruptly.

Sara read through the small notice, frowning. "The Armstrong Meat Packing Company," she finally said. "It's one of Charles'."

"Yes?" I answered, waiting.

"Nothing," Sara said, "I just thought it was an interesting coincidence."

I could tell by the way she said it that she would say no more. No amount of coaxing would get whatever she had in her mind out of her. I sighed, and gave up.

I first set eyes on Homer Lea on the morning of April 1, 1900. April Fool's Day and he was, I thought, a perfectly dandy little fool. A funny little Chinaman, he dressed like a sport, except

that his pants were an inch short of his high-top shoes. He was
a study in perpetual motion, he didn't so much talk as sputter
in a combination of Yankee slang, delivered in Chinese singsong.

Homer lived in the Lankershim Hotel, which he considered
his "headquarters." He called himself Lieutenant General Lea,
explaining to all who asked, and many who didn't, that he had
been commissioned a lieutenant general in the Chinese Imperial
Reform Army. The humor of this was evident, when it became
known that Lea had graduated from Los Angeles High School.
He was now, he explained, about to create a Western Military
Academy to train officers for the revolution.

*The revolution.* I could not understand how Wing Soong
could take the man seriously, and I didn't understand how the
two of them planned to be part of a revolution halfway around
the world. It was the first time that I had questioned Wing
Soong's judgment. In fact, he disappointed me.

When I asked Owen what he thought of Homer Lea—
knowing that Owen had a weakness for those people we call
"characters"—he said, "He's a laughable scoundrel, a poseur
certainly. But harmless, I think. A comic Asiatic Napoleon."

When I made the mistake of repeating this to Wing Soong,
he glowered at me. "Appearances deceive," he said, "and often
there is a reason for deception."

Homer brought us the first account of a rebellion in China
led by a secret society called the "Harmonious Fists." The American press promptly labeled them "Boxers." They were mur-
dering gangs who swept through the countryside, killing
foreigners. Missionaries and their families were slain, and the
Western legations at Peking were under siege. The Chinese, it
was said, were determined to throw out the blue-eyed devils
forever.

"Can you possibly condone this?" I asked angrily.

"No," Soong said, "no, I cannot, but perhaps for reasons
other than yours."

"What reasons?" I demanded.

"It is an angry outburst that has no chance of succeeding,
even in its most elementary goal: to throw out the foreigner.
The Western nations will make it harder now. It has put back
our cause." His words were bitter. I could not imagine how a
rebellion half a world away could have such an effect. I was

to be sorry for my lack of imagination.

"Listen to this," Owen said, reading from his paper. "Every town, every village, every peasant's hut in the path of the troops was looted and burned by the combined forces of the Western nations." Willa and I paused in our needlework to listen to the journalist's account of how our soldiers—along with the British and the French and the rest—had pressed inland to rescue the legations in Peking, and to put down the Boxer Rebellion.

"It's no more than they did to us," Willa said casually.

"To *us?*" I repeated, astonished. "What did those peasants do to us? More important, what did they do to anybody, including the dead missionaries?" I demanded, warming to the argument.

Willa shrugged. She did not want to argue. Clearly, it was not something she felt important enough to argue over. That was when I realized how much I was beginning to view the struggle from Soong's position. Later, when the Western powers signed a protocol which denounced China as guilty of crimes against civilization, and levied huge reparations and special privileges, I was as angry as Soong.

"China must modernize," Homer Lea would say, "the Manchu dynasty must be overthrown." Those same words were being said in China, but not nearly so publicly.

One afternoon, Soong told me, "I've become a member of a party called the Hsing Chung Hui. It translates, roughly, to "Revive China Society." The leader of the movement is a doctor, a man educated in the West. An intellectual. Homer believes he is the man who will lead China into the twentieth century."

I smiled, and knew immediately that it was a mistake.

"Listen to me," Soong said, "Homer Lea is no fool, I promise you. The work he is doing is important, and I am part of it. Homer plans, and soon, to have Dr. Sun come here, to tell us what we can do to help."

"They'll never let a revolutionist in," I said, mildly.

"They won't know," Soong replied, "he will be brought in on a boat, hidden. And when he does come, I want to spend time with him. I will need to be absent, but my absence must go unnoticed."

Ah, I thought, feeling a sudden rush of pleasure. So that is it. At last he wants something of me. At last I can do something for him.

"When it is time, tell me and I will see to it," I said.

When he returned, he said nothing at all to me about where he had been, or what he had done. I did not ask, but only waited.

One afternoon late in July, Willa returned from a hawking day with mischief in her eyes. "Come with me," she whispered, as if she had a great secret to tell me. She ducked into a side parlor, closed the door conspiratorially. Her cheeks were pink and she smelled of the woods.

"Have you ever noticed that your friend, Mr. Wing, vanishes in the afternoons?" she asked. My heart skipped.

"No," I said, worried that she might have discovered something of Soong's secret work with the Hsing Chung Hui.

But her face was too full of fun, I realized with relief.

"I know where he goes," she raced on, "I was sitting in Soston Canyon, in a little place tucked next to a waterfall. A tiercel has been hunting there, in an open space, and I've been observing him for several days, now. The falcon knows I'm there, but he seems not to mind. He abides me. Anyway, I camouflage myself in a nice little nest near a series of pools . . . lovely bathing places, actually, carved out of the rock. Oh, it's very private. I can see why Mr. Wing favors it!" She She was dissolving in giggles. "I must have fallen asleep for a time," she went on, "in my little nest of leaves and boughs, because when I opened my eyes who should be standing before me but Mr. Wing. Standing quite straight on a rock . . ." she covered her mouth to stifle the laughter, "moving his arms in strange ways as if to make shadows on a wall."

"Didn't you let him know you were there?" I asked, annoyed and a bit amazed.

"Lena!" she hissed, "I couldn't! He wasn't wearing anything, not a stitch, nothing. And, any . . ." her eyes grew wide and slightly wicked. "His maleness . . . was . . . erect!"

I felt myself flush, and I knew my neck would be glowing red as if with hives.

"Willa!" I whispered.

"Don't scold me," she answered. "Besides, he is glorious to look at, Lena. I couldn't help!"

I was angry with her, but for some peculiar reason I could not find myself ashamed for Soong.

Suddenly Willa's voice changed. Her tone became almost

businesslike, but it was with effort. "The thing is, Lena," she began, "I have been tracking this particular tiercel for several weeks now, making quite thorough observations for a paper I had planned to do for the Ornithological Society. With this trip to San Francisco with Owen tomorrow, I'm afraid my whole effort is going to be for naught. Unless you might be willing to make the observations for me?"

I looked at her, shocked at what she was proposing.

"Oh, Willa," I started, "how could you . . ." But she could, of course. She busied herself making a map, to show me exactly where the "hidden nest" was positioned. I sank back on the settee and considered my sister. I was angry with us both; and I was afraid and I was excited. I knew that I would go.

I did not take notes for Willa. Neither did I tell her that Soong had known she was there, the day before. I did not hide in her nest, I could not . . . not from myself, or from Soong, or from what he had become to me . . . someone steady, and true. A brother, a teacher and a friend. Above all, a friend.

That summer, near the falls in Soston Canyon, he became more than a friend.

I followed Soong and I waited until he was bathing in the shallow pool at the foot of the falls. Sunlight scattered through the leaves; squirrels scampered on the rocks above. One by one, I pushed away the low branches that hid me from view until I was standing by the edge of the pool, looking down at him.

For a moment I thought I had lost the power to speak. Then I said, "My back is twisted."

He said, "I should like to see it."

I unbuttoned the bodice of my summer dress; my fingers would not seem to work properly. Soong only watched, waited.

I stepped out of my underdress and stood, naked, before him.

He stood, took my hand, looking at me so steadily that I was not afraid. He led me gently into the pool. The water was cold, but I did not shiver. It rose to the place between my legs, to my belly.

Sunlight dappled our bodies and made us glow. He held me away from him, looking at me, and then carefully, ever so carefully, he turned me around so that he could see my back.

I felt his hands, firm and soft, moving along my spine,

touching, rubbing. And then I felt his lips on the small of my back. He pulled me to him, close against him, and he said, "It is beautiful, Lena. Everything about your body is as beautiful as I had imagined." And there, in the pool in Soston Canyon, Soong helped me discover the pleasures of the body that I thought would be forever denied me.

I never told anyone. I did not repeat to a living soul how Soong worked for the revolution. I did not say that Wing Soong had become a follower of the man Sun Yat-sen. We had our own society, and it was as secret as it was sweet, and there was never any need that anyone should know, not then. Not for a long time.

That September the very air crackled with the drought. Everything was dusty and dry and even the ocean seemed flaccid. Then the *Santana* started blowing hot out of the desert, playing on our tempers.

Only Trinidad's children could sleep through the night. The shrieks of a puma—wild and sharp—cut into the thick night, echoing and reverberating inside one, making sleep impossible. The young steers that had been penned in the north corral milled and bawled, made uneasy by the cat's cry. The men slept with their guns nearby.

It was only one very large cat—Ignacio and Owen found its footprints near the pump where the ground was soft. We had heard the shrieks of the puma before, but not when a *Santana* had been blowing for two days, making us raw.

We were tired, mindless and lethargic, as if the hot wind had sapped us of all energy.

"No coffee," Owen said as Trinidad approached him with a steaming cup, "lemonade is what I would like."

Trinidad only looked at him. Lemonade. She would have to go to the family orchard, pick them, and the juice would be warm, so she would have to send one of the children to the cold spring. *Aiii*, the attitude of her shoulders seemed to say, it is too hot for such nonsense. She lifted her hands in a gesture of futility, but before she could get to the door we heard the sound. We heard it because it was different. We strained to catch the sound as the winds whipped it away.

Hooves, galloping. A horse, moving fast. Too fast for such heat, no one would ride a horse so hard in such heat. So it was

important. Owen frowned. We followed him out the door,
where we stood, shading our eyes against the glare, watching
a lone rider move toward us through heat waves that rose from
the valley floor.

"It's Carlos," Ignacio said, squinting, "from Zuma."

Owen nodded, his face grim.

Then we heard what the man was shouting.

*Fuego!*

Fire.

"Where?" Owen demanded as the man pounded into the
courtyard, raising a cloud of dust, his horse lathered and heaving.

*"Norte,"* the man gasped, "over the mountains."

"By Shurz' place?" Willa shouted.

*"Sí,"* Carlos answered, "he got out, but now the wind changes
direction, it turns and it is coming . . ."

We looked to the northeast and there it was, a line of smoke.
It would not be long; soon we would see the rim of fire. It was
traveling fast, fast, Carlos told us.

Ignacio and Owen barked directions. I caught a glimpse of
Wing Soong, running with a crew to the place where the fire-
break was prepared. The animals were turned loose and
headed toward the beach. The beach was the only safety, should
it come to that. But the wind could change. It did that, it jumped
over houses and whole canyons. It might change.

Willa shouted her own orders. "The silver, Josie," she directed. "And you, Anna, get our picture books."

"I'm glad the boys left for school," I told Willa as we ran
for the house. We stopped when we saw Trinidad walking at
a languid pace away from the house.

"Where are you going?" Willa shouted at her.

"To the orchard," she answered calmly, "for the lemons."

Willa ran to overtake her, then she held her by the shoulders
and looked into Trinidad's eyes, which were glazed.

Willa held her by the shoulders and shook her.

"Wake up!" she shouted. "You wake up and do exactly
what I tell you, do you hear me?" She shook her again, so
violently that Trinidad's teeth rattled. "Get the children and
count them. Don't forget Carlotta's baby. Get them all and
bring them to me."

At that, the life returned to Trinidad's eyes. She was afraid, but she could move and talk. She began the incantation of saints' names that was to pour out of her all that day.

Willa and I made two trips into the house. There was no time for a third. The acrid smell of burning oak and eucalyptus filled our nostrils and made our eyes sting. The children cried, complaining of scratchy throats. The heat was oppressive, breathing was difficult. We loaded the children on top of the few household things we had managed to save, and started for the beach. All I had been able to save of my own were my daybooks; I cannot remember making a choice. It was what I brought.

Willa shouted the team on. "Move out, Maud," she said, "Step up there, you Nell." Behind us Pablito—a sturdy eight now—herded the family pets. We could hear the fire; there was a crackling, and an awful, angry animal sound as it moved through the low chaparral, like some monstrous, living thing. The heat flared. Sumac bushes, filled with oil, exploded. It was as if we were picking our way through a mine field.

The old team ran through the long avenue of eucalyptus. We were no sooner clear than one of the giant trees exploded. For an instant, its shadow seemed to hold against the conflagration.

"Pablito," I screamed, "hurry." He was running, keeping up, but the fire now was only sixty feet or so behind us. We were almost there. The children were wailing with the heat and the fear. Trinidad was wild, hysterical. I tried to hold her, to control her.

Then the goat Sunshine, Thad's favorite, broke loose and, terrified, ran the wrong way, into the fire. Pablito let out a screech that was as wild as the puma's.

"Let him go," I shouted, even as the fire caught the little goat and set it ablaze.

There is no way to describe the awful, acrid stench . . . of animals burning, of hair and scorched flesh. Tiny animals of the field, caught.

We reached the sea, and safety. I jumped out of the wagon, somehow, and found my way to Pablito, who was sitting in the center of the little coterie of pets, his face blackened and streaked with tears. I dropped one of my books in a pool of sea water. He picked it up.

"*Gracias,* Pablito," I said, as gently as I could.

"She was a good goat, Sunshine," he answered. "I told Thad I would care for his goat."

"Thad will understand," I tried to tell him.

But he said that Thad would not understand, not ever.

Sunshine was a good goat, the house was a good house, the barn a good barn. But all were gone, lost in the worst fire in living memory. We sat there on the beach and watched it burn. The soot fell like black snow, the heat assaulted our faces.

Most of the animals were safe; all of the men accounted for. Willa moved with determination among the stragglers on the beach, taking account, making sure.

"It's as if the earth itself is angry," she said to me in passing, "I've never seen such wrath."

I found Owen sitting on a carton, his shoulders hunched, staring at his hands. He did not look up when I said his name.

The sun, obliterated by the torrents of smoke, cast an orange-gray light over us all. It might have been, I thought, a scene from the Inferno.

~ *Chapter Fifteen*

Owen rubbed the coin between his thumb and forefinger, as if to polish it, now and then pausing to examine it, the look on his face one of strained amazement. He had been probing through the charred ruins of the main house for fully an hour and the single Spanish coin was all he had been able to recover of the collections he had spent so many years accumulating, so many long hours poring over.

Willa walked at a brisk clip through the burned stubble that had been the arbor, her step determined, so preoccupied with her own assessment of the damage that, for a moment, she was at odds to explain her husband's distress. She stopped to watch him and felt a sudden, sweeping tenderness. His face, the whole attitude of his body, told her that he was staggering still from the crushing blow the fire had delivered. He had lost more than she could fathom. For a second she understood, then it was gone, leaving her with an almost mystical understanding that he was as near defeat as she had ever seen him.

"Owen," she called softly, "perhaps we should call in a man just to sift through it all, to see what else . . ."

He shook his head, not looking up. His eyes were wet, she could see. "No," he murmured, "it's no use. Nothing could have survived the heat . . . I don't understand how this coin . . ."

His voice trailed off as he turned to look about him, disconsolate.

There was nothing to say, she knew, that could ease his sense of loss. She wondered why she, too, was not decimated, why, in fact, she felt a surge of energy, of excitement. What was she excited about? Starting over. Rebuilding, the enormous time and energy it would require. That was what she had understood, in that fleeting instant; it was what Owen could not face.

"I wonder," she started, tentatively, knowing now what she must do, "you have so many things to attend to in town—and you can't put off the trip East, we know that. Would you . . ." She hesitated, giving him time to catch up, aware that she was manipulating. "That is, if you think I could . . ." She did not want to go too far, but she knew what she would do, what he needed her to do if only she could make him agree. She cleared her throat, as if nervous. "I believe I could take charge of the rebuilding. That would leave you free to concentrate on the business . . . I feel sure I could do it . . ."

He looked at her, unsure. "Build it all back?"

"Not like it was," she answered carefully, "simpler, a smaller house. But rebuild, yes."

She had said it; now she waited. She watched him struggle with the idea. Feeling the pulse pounding in her temples, she made herself be still.

"Where would you be?" he asked, and she knew she had done it, that he was going to let her put their lives on the Malibu together again.

Most of each week she spent in Santa Monica, with Owen, setting things in motion. She was in and out of the beach house several times, nonetheless, giving orders and making plans. I was in nominal command at the little cottage which had escaped the fire. Around it, a tent city had sprung up to house the servants and cowhands. It looked for all the world like some great chautauqua meeting, tents pitched close to the beach, an air of holiday about it all. The Spanish *vaqueros* got along surprisingly well with the Chinese; many of the usual barriers seemed to ease. Wing Soong's tent was pitched only a few feet from the cottage; he was our protector, Aleja's and mine.

Trinidad had gone into Santa Monica to run the house there, leaving her eldest daughter to supervise our small beach household. Aleja was a younger version of her mother, at eleven she

was "early ripened," as Willa had observed, with rising young
breasts and rounding hips. She was a pleasant girl, devout and
hard-working like her mother, and silent like her father. The
attention some of the *vaqueros* had begun to pay had not escaped Ignacio and Trinidad. They kept a close watch on their
eldest. She was a good girl and she would marry well. The
Spanish had a hierarchy of their own.

In Santa Monica each morning Owen set off from the house
to walk the six blocks to his office in the Reade Building, the
most modern commercial structure in the growing town, oc-
cupying a full city block. From this vantage he attended to the
business interests that reached from Nova Scotia to Baja California. At age forty-one, Owen was president of the Sierra
Madre Land Company, vice president of Pioneer Oil, a director
of Southwestern Electric Company, president of the Guadalupe
Rancho Company which, in a complicated maneuver involving
buying the water rights to the whole of one large valley, opened
some thousand acres in the San Fernando Valley to settlement.
He was, at the same time, president of the Delta Land and
Improvement Company and, through a combine of syndicates,
had holdings that included two lumber mills in the redwood
forests of northern California and Oregon, as well as silver
mines in Nevada and copper mines in Arizona, along with real
estate in some of the country's fastest-growing cities.

"Money multiplies like rabbits," he was fond of saying, "all
you need is the first pair." And indeed, making money seemed
to be quite a natural act for Owen.

He also managed to be active in historical and benevolent
societies, supporting innumerable orphanages and building more
than a dozen new wings to churches. The number of boards
of directors he served on put him in league with the very men
who controlled a sizeable part of the commerce of the nation.
Though Owen went to lengths to keep his name out of the
newspapers, those with ambition managed always to find their
way to his office in the Reade Building, and when they spoke
to him it was in tones of reverence reserved for the rich and
the powerful.

Until fire destroyed almost all trace of their life on the
Malibu, Owen had carefully divided his time between the ranch
and family matters, and the businesses he saw to from his office

in the Reade Building. Now, with Willa's encouragement, he turned all of his attention to his businesses, while she took on the task of rebuilding the ranch.

We would come to speak of *before the fire* and *after the fire*. The fire became a point of reference, a line of demarcation. At first, everything was a whirl of activity. We were busy clearing, cleaning, taking inventory. My daybooks of that time are filled with lists... Willa was in the vortex, traveling back and forth on Princess, buying and then prodding shopkeepers, arguing with drayers, overseeing deliveries by land and by sea. At first, the men she had to deal with were politely condescending, and, at the same time, a bit reserved with the chatelaine of the Malibu. When she did not choose to take the many suggestions they made, they became querulous and, finally, begrudgingly admiring. For her part, Willa found the whole thing exhilarating. She enjoyed winning over the skeptical merchants and craftsmen. She felt a sense of accomplishment in realizing that she could make decisions, and that they were, as often as not, good ones.

A month after the fire, with Willa's blessing, Owen traveled to the East. He had several meetings of boards of directors to attend and he was looking forward to visiting his friend in the White House. He also had to make a trip to New Hampshire, to St. Paul's. The headmaster had twice written about problems with Wen, problems that seemed to be the sort a father could best handle.

Willa saw him off with remarkable aplomb. "It will give me a chance to get things cleaned up on the ranch. If we get the right pattern of rain, early enough, the hills will be green by spring." Her eyes were shining. I realized that she was planning to present Owen with a remarkable gift upon his return—the ranch, put together so the hurt the fire had inflicted on Owen could be repaired. It was a huge undertaking, and she relished it.

One bright afternoon late in October, as Willa and I sat waiting for yet another load of lumber to arrive at the pier, she read aloud from the letter she had received that day.

"Try as I might," Owen wrote, "I cannot seem to get the odor of charcoal from my nostrils. It haunts me, even here. I think of my collections and feel desolate. The study of hawks is altogether a better avocation than the collecting of rare oddments and precious antiquities. But you are right, my dear (I know what you will be thinking)—we did escape with no loss of life, and for that we must be thankful. Still, I try not to imagine you in the midst of that blackened land.

"You will be wondering about the boys. They are in good health, and send their love. Thad is pale, as always, but doing exceedingly well in his studies—though I do wish he knew more of the other boys, he is so often alone. Wen, on the other hand, would be better off with fewer friends so that he might spend more time on his studies. How I wish our two boys might blend their personalities . . . what one seems to lack, the other has to excess. Wen, however, has been properly chastised and he promises to reform. I will not, in all delicacy, go into the details of his transgressions, other than to say that I have, I think, impressed him with my determination that he mend his ways. I have settled his accounts for the last time. The threat of being shipped home is anathema to Wen, while Thad would leave with me tomorrow if I would allow it. Strange, those two!

"It is beautiful in New England. I had almost forgotten how lovely the autumn is here—the scattering of golden leaves on still-green lawns, the lovely musky odors of fall, the soft winds. There is, outside my window, a grove of birch that glows yellow in the afternoon light. If there is one thing I miss in California, it is the poignancy of fall, the last bright flame before winter."

I frowned. Reading my thoughts, Willa said, "I suppose he may be considering a move back East, but it will pass. I'm quite sure he could not survive the winters, and he knows it. The fire knocked the breath out of him, that's all. By the time he returns, I will have started to get the ranch back together again, so he can see it is going to be all right. You'll see, his spirits will lift when he sees all we've done."

Looking at the wild litter all about—the pier, and the great stacks of lumber and materials—I was skeptical, but in fact she was right. Owen returned to new green everywhere. The early season rains had revived the land, it no longer was scarred black like some image of hell. Owen took heart. He was amazed by the change, and I have never seen Willa so proud, so totally pleased with herself. It was, I thought, the way one must feel upon delivering a newborn child to its father.

We had our Christmas dinner on the beach that year. By then the outlines of the new ranch were taking shape. The day was bright and warm so that we took off our shawls as the sun grew high. Arcadia and Joseph were out for the day. Though everyone made a toast to the phoenix that was rising from the ashes, Owen's was by far the most touching.

"To my wife," he said, "who has worked a miracle, and put our world together again."

And she did put it together, but not quite as it had been. The new ranch house was built in the Mediterranean style, low and white with gleaming tiled floors and a red tile roof. All the rooms opened onto a verandah which wrapped around the house; in a few seasons the bougainvillea would wash in fuchsia profusion over the white walls. Owen's Victorian establishment had been supplanted by Willa's more natural, California world.

All except for the old barn, which she had replaced as it was and painted red to please Owen.

Ignacio and the ranch foremen, at Willa's request, offered suggestions on how to improve the work buildings, and she had incorporated many of their ideas into the finished plans. This earned her a good deal of respect from the men. They threw themselves into the work of rebuilding with quite amazing results. By summer, when the boys came home, we would be able to move into the house and resume our lives.

Willa's unflagging enthusiasm, her patient good humor, drew Owen into its orbit. "Darling," she would say as she whirled into the dining room early in the morning, "can you possibly spare the time to ride out to the ranch with me this morning? I'm thinking it might be nice to plant an avenue of palms leading to the house, and I want your advice."

It was the sort of question that Owen would have put to her a decade before. He looked at her admiringly, and said, "Yes, for you my dear, anything at all." They laughed easily, then, in the manner of conspirators.

Wing Soong had been given the task of planting the new orchards and gardens. Willa worked with him, and for the first time got some glimpse of his extraordinary talents. "He is a virtual wizard," she said to me more than once, and I laughingly agreed. He was that, in more ways than Willa could possibly know.

Soong had cleared and replanted Rose's grave even before

I had a chance to see it. When Sara came for the first time, she brought with her a new daisy bush to plant at the grave. I had long since found it to be comforting to visit there. After the fire, I had a new stone carved which said: *Rose, she was touched by light.*

Throughout the spring Owen and Willa continued to live in Santa Monica, but to spend increasing amounts of time at the ranch. The fire loss had been great, but Owen's resources were vast enough to absorb them with little effect. Jacob Shurz had fared less well. The fire had jumped over his house in one of its spectacular quirks, but it had not spared his barn, his herd or his crops. At Joseph Brennan's suggestion, Owen had our road crew clear the road that Shurz used to get to the beach. When Willa balked, Joseph explained, "Think how it will sound in court, Willa."

"But we've won our court battle with that dreadful man," Willa countered, exasperated, "how can you think of helping him?"

"He isn't going to quit that easily," Owen answered, "and the man is hurting, badly. I'll have the boys clear the road, and see if anyone else in those hills is going hungry."

Owen and Willa were in town on the day that Shurz appeared, hat in hand, a scowl on his face. I spoke to him through the screened door. I liked him as little as did Willa.

"Tell the mister," he said, "that Jacob Shurz didn't ask him to clear the road. Tell him it won't change my mind."

I was careful to give Owen, not Willa, the message. Owen had dealt with stubborn men before. Willa's hackles seemed to rise at even a mention of the man.

Willa was fingering the autoharp, trying to pick out the melody to a popular new song. "Oh, the moonlight's bright tonight along the Wabash," she sang, haltingly, in her lovely contralto. It was twilight, soon it would be too dark to see.

"Dashed if I can figure out where the old smokehouse was," Owen said, "or the kitchen, *or* the greenhouse. I've been trying to picture the old place and everything is all turned around in my mind. It's only two years since the fire . . ."

Willa picked away a time longer, but she was distracted. "Do you know," she said, "that really is the marvel of it."

"Marvel?" Owen asked, puzzled. "What? How so?"

"That we have so little impact on the land, that we sit so lightly upon it. Think—we lived here for eight years before the fire, and in one afternoon almost all of the traces of that time were gone—until now it is hard, even, to remember where things were, what it was like."

"And you find that marvelous?" Owen asked, annoyed.

"No, not marvelous," she came back, "but a marvel—a strange sort of marvel." She was excited, her eyes glistened as if she had come close to knowing something, but she could not convey it to us.

"A person can belong to the land," she tried again, "but the land cannot be possessed. We belong here—not so much because we have legal claim to the Malibu, that is the smallest part of it. We belong because we are right with this place. The fire was terrible, and yet... and yet I have never felt so much a part of this land as I did during the fire."

Owen sighed. What she felt did not make sense to him. He mourned the loss of the old ranch, the old time... *before the fire*.

"Mama would have understood, I think," I ventured. I could not see Willa's eyes in the gathering dusk. I wondered if she had considered how her devotion to the Malibu was like Mama's to Porter Farm.

And then, for what reason I could not guess, Owen said, "I wonder if Jacob Shurz would agree with you."

"About what?" Willa answered, her voice spitting sparks.

"About the land not being possessed, about legal claims being the smallest part of it," Owen shot back, taunting her for seeming to accept the fire's devastation.

"Perhaps," I said quietly, "Jacob Shurz' attachment is to something else."

I had meant to calm things down, but Willa turned on me. "Shurz? Attachment to what?" she demanded.

"I don't know," I lied, "he does keep talking about the public's right of passage..." My voice trailed off.

"Do you believe that?" Willa demanded.

I bit my tongue and wished I had never brought it up. Owen, however, came to my rescue.

"It *is* a delicate issue, Willa," he said. "So far, I have been able to keep it out of the litigation, but I'm not sure how long we will be able to ignore it."

"I cannot believe that any court in the land would force us to open our private roads—which we build and maintain and which cross only our own property—to the public," she repeated.

"The point," Owen came back, "is whether others have the right to pass through. Eventually, the county is going to want to build a road that connects Santa Monica to, say, Santa Barbara. They will offer to pay us for the land; if we refuse, they could try to condemn it, paying us what they consider to be a fair price."

"I don't want any pay, and I don't want a road," Willa said fiercely. "It would change the Malibu, more than a fire ever could."

"Yes," Owen sighed, tired of the argument, "but we may have no choice. The time will come when we will have to consider building a road ourselves, beating them to it—so we can decide where it is to go. I'm afraid my contention that the beach is not a public thoroughfare will not hold up much longer, if anyone takes us to court again."

Willa was obstinate. "I will fight any road. I can't believe that you truly feel we can do nothing."

"I didn't say we could do nothing," Owen rejoined, "I simply said that it may not be in our best interest to be stubborn about it."

I could feel the word "stubborn" surging through Willa. The atmosphere was charged. All was quiet for a time, then, and I was relieved that I had not had to answer her question.

I could not risk alienating my sister. I understood, perhaps better than anyone, the depth of her commitment to fight all encroachments on the ranch. It was not an issue to be argued, she could allow no opposition. Not from Owen, and certainly not from me.

As for me, my devotion was to the family. I did not plan to jeopardize my place in it—mine, and by extension, Wing Soong's. Willa was aware of his influence on me. He had become more intricately involved with the training of young Chinese militia for a revolution taking place half a world away. He did not try to hide his commitment to Dr. Sun's cause. Willa and Owen knew about it, and tolerated it because of Soong's extraordinary service to our family. Willa knew there was more between Soong and me than was evident. It had taken us so long to find each other, to reap what we had planted. Perhaps it was forbidden fruit, but it was sweet and nourishing and tender and it made my life, for the first time, whole. I believe it was so for Soong, too. We had not thought to find such joy in this life. Having found it, I intended to keep it as long as I could.

Still, the truth was, I believed Jacob Shurz to be right. I did not think that Willa, or anyone else, had the right to claim a part of the earth and to refuse others the right of passage.

Willa and Owen marked their sixteenth wedding anniversary with a quiet stroll through the young orchard. Owen broke off a small branch of orange blossoms and tucked them into the heavy coil of hair she wore twined around her head.

"You've just wasted a good part of our first orange crop," she laughed.

"Not wasted," he answered, "nothing beautiful was ever wasted on you." He held her face in his hands and kissed her, lightly, on the lips. "The fragrance makes me think of Hawaii . . . the smell of plumeria and . . ." A tender look lit his face, "Sometimes I long for Hawaii," he said, "everything so quiet and sweet-smelling. I think even death must be pleasant in those islands."

She touched his face. "How can you say that, when everything is so green and alive here?" He walked a few steps away, to examine something on one of the young trees.

"Wouldn't you like to sail off to Hawaii with me?" he asked, as if testing.

"I think the boys might want to stay home this summer," she parried, "they've been at school all year . . ."

He smiled, abandoning the idea. "You're right," he admitted, "I think I might like to do some camping with the boys this summer. Thad, especially, needs to be toughened a bit. And then," suddenly he became practical, "I have to make one trip north to a little place called Freshwater—it's a lumber town up near the Oregon border. The syndicate is set on buying the mill, and I want to see it first."

"Why don't we see if the boys want to go, and make it a family trip?" Willa put in.

"Maybe not all the way to Freshwater," Owen answered, "I'm told the accommodations there are something less than primitive. But why don't we all go to visit Aunt Emma and the Captain—that's about halfway, and I can go on from there and pick you up again on the way back."

Willa thought about it. "I would love to see them—they are getting up in years. Thad would be happy to go, but I'm not sure about Wen."

"We'll include a couple of days at the Del Monte lodge— Wen has a taste for elegance," Owen added sardonically.

Willa laughed. "Sounds wonderful," she said, tucking her arm in his. They walked along in silence, then, easy in each other's presence. Their bodies moved together, keeping pace; the familiarity of the years had replaced old uncertainties. They had been together long enough to listen for shadings of meanings. She no longer saw the handsome face so much as the flickering of expressions, and the small subtleties that told her more than words could.

If once Willa had wanted more than he could give, she had now settled for what was possible. In time, she would look at the summer with Connor McCord in the same way as she looked at the fire. It had burned bright, had been devastating in the heat it generated—but once the firestorm was over, her world had rearranged itself in quieter ways. She had passed through her seasons of discontent, of guilt and shame, and had achieved a new calm.

In the new ranch house their bedrooms were connected, but more often than not they slept apart. Still, he never failed— on those nights when he was at the ranch—to spend a few minutes alone with her at the end of each day. If it was not a marriage of passion, it had become one of real affection. There were times when Willa was convinced it was what Owen had wanted all along, and she was glad. What neither realized was that Willa's own passion, which still burned bright, had been transferred to the land. The ranch that rose from the ashes of the fire was, in every way, Willa's creation.

In June, a carriage was sent into Los Angeles to meet the boys at the Arcade station. When they returned, late in the afternoon, Wallace Sayre III was with them.

"Sorry not to give you advance notice, sir," the young man said to Owen, "Wen hadn't time, really, since I only decided to come at the last minute. My mother was sailing to France, but I've always wanted to see the American West, and Wen said you wouldn't mind."

The self-assured young man was a full year older than Wen. His legs were powerful, but shorter than his torso, which gave him a squat appearance. His eyes were a faded shade of blue, as if they had been exposed to strong light. Willa glanced at me. She, too, was trying to decide what she thought about the sudden appearance of Wen's school friend.

At dinner that night Wen told us, "Wallace is from one of New York's first families." There was an embarrassed pause.

"First in what?" Willa could not resist asking, though she softened it with a smile.

"In society, Mother," Owen answered, as if she were not quite bright.

"But I understand your family is quite distinguished, sir," Wallace said to Owen, ignoring Willa.

Owen guided the conversation in new directions, drawing out the boys on the subject of school, being as charming and entertaining as he was with adults.

As soon as the boys had been excused, Willa whispered, "Officious little snob."

And Owen answered, "Which one?"

Wen and young Sayre declined to make the trip north with the family. They preferred, they said, to stay at the ranch where they could swim and fish and do some riding. I suspected the real reason was to be free of Owen's firm hand. I was not entirely comfortable with the idea of chaperoning Wen and his insolent friend, and yet I was glad for Thad. The older boys did not hide the contempt they felt for him. I could only guess at the miseries he had to endure at school. It seemed to me Thad deserved some time with his parents; the three of them had always been happy together.

I sighed and waved them all off. Ignacio and Trinidad were to go into the house in Santa Monica to do some work while the family was away. Aleja and I would take care of the ranch house. At age fourteen, she looked fully a woman and she did a woman's work. I had grown fond of the girl in our long weeks together in the beach cottage after the fire. "Take good care of Miss Lena," Trinidad had called to her strong young daughter, and Aleja and I had laughed.

\* \* \*

Often, when Willa was happy, she would write a letter. I received the first scarcely a week after their departure. Her long, loose hand looped over the paper. She was writing quickly, as if to transfer her exuberance to the paper: "Aunt Emma is looking remarkably well and the Captain is as charming as ever, if a bit forgetful in his age. Even so, he has found the most devoted listener in Thad, whom he regales for hours with tales of his early days, sailing and soldiering. (Some of these tales, Owen wickedly suggests, are remarkably similar to stories he has read in *Harper's Monthly,* but we agree that it is eminently forgiveable, if the Captain wishes to borrow some experiences.)

"We are having, as you may have surmised, a glorious time together. I do believe that Thad grows more like his father each day, which of course endears him even more to me. The boy hopes to be able to convince his father that he should remain in the West, to finish his schooling here. He would, he tells me, even find San Francisco preferable to the East. When Sara came to see us a few days ago, the little rascal enlisted her in his campaign. She promised to look out for him, should we decide to send him to the Tucker School there. Dear, sweet Sara. But I fear their plotting will have little effect on Owen. He seems certain the Eastern 'connections' are necessary for the sons who will one day run his empire. ('Empire' is my word!)

"I have been thinking about my first night in San Francisco, at the Lick House. Perhaps the room Aunt Emma gave us is responsible for that warm memory. Owen and I have the same sort of heavily carved bedstead, and our room looks out over the hills to the sea. The other morning Aunt Emma and the Captain took Thad off on a fishing expedition before dawn, planning to be gone most of the day. Left alone in our lovely big bed, we lolled shamelessly most of the morning. Such luxury! I feel very like that girl who fell into her wedding bed in San Francisco, sixteen long years ago.

"Owen leaves tomorrow for Arcata—actually, a little town called Freshwater nearby. He will be gone only a few days, but I miss him already! (You are thinking that I sound like a silly girl, and of course you are right. But this *is* a kind of honeymoon.) I shall use the time to track a Cooper's hawk I have noticed in the pines. Thad wants to come hawking with me. He says it will make a good paper for his class in the natural sciences, which makes me think that he is prepared to return to St. Paul's.

"I hope you are getting on well with Wen and his pompous friend. Be sure to make them mind the mark. I have some doubts about that young man—and I do wish Wen weren't such a sheep. But I am too happy, just now, to worry over my eldest, and I won't. I will write again after Owen leaves. Just now, I am going to join him on the beach for a lovely, leisurely walk."

Willa's doubts were prophetic. With Owen and Willa gone, Wen assumed the attitude of lord of the manor. I had not thought him capable of such vulgar arrogance. He tolerated me, but just. What was worse, the two made demands of the servants that were, at best, capricious, and more often insulting. I found myself sending Aleja to do chores away from the house, so that she would not have to be subjected to the barrage of orders the boys could generate.

Finally I could stand it no longer, and called Wen to task. At first, I tried to explain that addressing Aleja as "girl" when he had grown up with her, had known her all her life, was a very rude thing to do. I explained that his parents treated the staff politely, that the Spanish were very sensitive to slights. In answer, he made a short, cold speech to the effect that his father had not intended for me to act as his nanny, that he was quite old enough to be responsible for himself and for his friend.

Stung, I tried not to feel the revulsion that was rising within me. He was, I reminded myself, only fifteen, and big for his age. He was really still very young; perhaps it would be well to give him some latitude.

Scarcely a day went by without some complaint being lodged against the two. I would have put it down to schoolboy pranks, had not some of their "pranks" been so cruel. Aleja came to tell me they had taken Marcella's little kitten, a fluffy bit of ginger fur, and thrown it into the pen where the cowboys were keeping two wild dogs they had found running loose in the hills. The dogs tore the little kitten to pieces in minutes.

"Oh, Aleja, they couldn't," I said.

She bit her lip and nodded, to tell me they could.

"Pablito saw it," she said, "Ned had to hold him, so he wouldn't attack Wen."

I wished that Willa and Owen would return quickly. Their presence would supply the control the boys would recognize. I considered asking Willa to cut short their trip, but they were having such a good time that I was loath to end it. I felt I could manage, a few more days.

I was sitting in the front parlor, studying the calendar. Owen was to return to Monterey today, Trinidad and Ignacio would be back tomorrow . . . Marcella appeared at the door, eyes wide and dark. She was gulping for breath.

"What is it," I asked, rising. Marcella's very presence signaled something urgent. Trinidad's children almost never ventured beyond the kitchen.

*"Por favor,"* she said, crying now, "Aleja . . ." She took my hand and pulled me, making small gasping noises. I followed her across the lawn, limping as fast as I could.

Soong was at the edge of the garden, pitchfork in hand.

He came running, then raced ahead of us to the barn, where Marcella pointed. I stumbled and paused to steady myself, but Marcella urged me on, into the barn's dim recesses.

The sounds were strange—not so much voices as growlings, rife with fear. In the dim light I saw Soong struggling with Pablito, trying to get control of the knife the boy was wielding. Wallace Sayre was thrown against the wall, his pants open revealing white, exposed flesh. On the ground at his feet, Wen's knees were pinning down a girl's arms. It was Aleja. Her dress had been pulled up and her underclothes torn away, so that she lay naked, the dark triangle of hair exposed between open legs.

"Dear God!" I screamed, and the words seemed to trigger an explosion. Wen jumped up. I ran to the girl, who lay quiet, her eyes glazed and dull.

Soong had dropped the pitchfork, and Wallace was moving for it when I found my voice. "Stop right there if you expect to get out of this alive."

Pablito struggled in Soong's firm grasp, rage fueled his young body, it radiated from him. He would, he snarled in Spanish, cut out their hearts . . . he would, he said more slowly in broken English, perform the *castrado* . . .

I covered Aleja's nakedness and held her, at the same time pulling Marcella close.

"Auntie," Wen began to whine . . .

"Stop it," I all but shouted, "be quiet and listen. If Wing Soong will help me, I'll try to get you out of here alive. Your other choice is to be horsewhipped or have your throats slit." I held young Sayre's gaze and I did not try to hide my contempt.

"They will not get away alive," Pablito said, and none of us doubted he could carry out his threat. It was all Soong could do to hold him. The epithets that came from the child's mouth amazed me; it was rage beyond anything I had ever witnessed.

"Listen to me, Wen," I said over the noise, "what you have done is bestial, unforgivable, but there is no time for that now. Soong will take you to town. Put Wallace on the first train East. Go to Joseph Brennan in Santa Monica, tell him I have directed you to withdraw whatever money is needed for the ticket. Then you stay with Joseph until your parents return. Wing Soong, tell Joseph what happened, and tell him to keep Wen safe."

Soong locked Pablito in the tack room, and they were away in a matter of minutes, leaving me with Trinidad's children— the girls sobbing quietly, Pablito cursing in rage and pounding against the door.

I felt a terrible weariness. I had saved the lives of two stupid boys. What they had done was barbaric, but I could not see them punished as the *vaqueros* would surely punish them. I put my arms around Aleja and rocked her quietly, sick with worry for her, for what their brutish attack would do to her.

If only, I thought, I had called Willa and Owen home. Poor Willa, I thought, to have her lovely summer shattered.

I could not know that Willa's world had already been shattered.

Early the next morning, Joseph and Arcadia appeared at the ranch, their faces grave and Arcadia's eyes red-rimmed. I was not entirely surprised; they would want to know, for themselves, what had happened at the ranch, Soong would not have gone into any detail. The grim look on Joseph's face was disquieting. Joseph had, always, been able to see the favorable side of things, he was always encouraging. What more, I wondered, could the boys have done?

"Lena, my dear," Joseph said, and his voice chilled me, "prepare yourself for some bad news, very bad."

"Ignacio," I whispered, "Did he . . . Wen . . . ?"

"No, no, Wen is safe," he said, handing me a telegram.

It was to Joseph, it was from Willa and it said: *My darling Owen died this morning. We are bringing him home on evening train August 4. Please tell Wen, Lena and make necessary arrangements for funeral.*

They helped me into the house and sat with me in silence. The only sounds in the still of the summer's day was Arcadia's soft weeping. I sat, holding a letter that Joseph had given me with the telegram, a letter from Willa, written only a few days ago, but in another lifetime. Distractedly, I opened it, let my eyes wander over the pages of happy, open loops that had been written in haste. My eyes caught a line, stopped. My heart fluttered, I felt faint.

"I have such wonderful news," Willa wrote, "I cannot wait to tell Owen that I am about to make him a papa again, at age forty-three. A whole new life! He will be so delighted . . ."

Owen was dead, Willa was with child.

And so, too, was I.

# Book IV

The Malibu:
Women and Children,
1908 - 1912

# Chapter Sixteen

We had been waiting on the verandah for more than an hour. Willa had never been good at waiting, her impatience was giving way to anger. She paced the length of the verandah and paused for a long moment to consider a hawk wheeling at the top of the ridge. It dipped over and under, was out of sight and then back again, circling in low, lazy arcs.

"I think my mind must be slipping," she said, "I cannot seem to remember names . . . the young woman Sara wants to bring out from Philadelphia to tutor the twins . . ."

"Sally Fairleigh," I told her.

"Yes, Sally, of course."

"Sara tells me that she is wonderfully witty, and quite accomplished for her age."

"What is her age?" Willa wanted to know.

"Almost eighteen," I said quietly, knowing that it was too young.

"She's scarcely older than Thad, then," Willa put my own thoughts into words, "but I do trust Sara's judgment, and if Sara feels the young woman would be good, then I feel we must give her a try. What do you think?"

"That's the way I feel, too," I told my sister, "I must admit I'm glad we agree. Sara says that Sally is a delight, that she is filled with enthusiasm and aching for adventure in the Wild West."

Willa smiled, absently, as she scanned the beach for some sign of a carriage. It was five years, almost, since Owen's death. She was, now, a little older than he had been that terrible summer. I considered my sister: At forty-three, it seemed to me that she had little changed. Her waist, perhaps, was a bit thicker, her hips wider, there were a few delicate webs at the corners of her eyes, lines that stood out white against the unfashionable tan of her face. Willa had stopped wearing hats altogether. My mind made a long skip to another hat, another time of waiting.

"What are you thinking about?" Willa asked, "that is so amusing?"

Caught, I confessed: "I was remembering the day Owen first came to Porter Farm . . . I was waiting on the porch with Mama, and she was furious that you weren't there—and then you came running across the field, hell bent, waving your straw hat at us . . ."

Willa's face softened. The memory of Owen pleased her, as I knew it would. She sank into the porch chair with a mock moan. "Oh, my, yes, I do remember," she said, exhaling softly.

"You were so out of breath from the run that you couldn't even speak," I went on, "and you were making these dreadful, gasping noises—very unladylike . . ."

"It's a good thing Owen wasn't looking for a lady," she answered. We smiled at each other. It had become part of our lives, little memories shared when we were alone. They nourished us like new-baked biscuits spread with honeybutter.

Willa was silent for a time. Finally she said, "It's strange, isn't it, how little his sons resemble him?"

I did not answer, I could think of no good answer. Willa and I had long since forsworn the superfluous lie.

The twins moved into our view, crossing the greensward, Porter in the lead and Kit trailing behind. The twins were four years old now, but Porter was as tall as a child twice his age while Kit was fine-boned, petite.

"Except for Porter, of course," Willa put in with a sly grin. "Everyone says Porter is the very image of his papa."

I laughed. "He certainly is that, and of course sweet little Kit takes after her auntie." Hearing her name, Kit looked up, smiled and waved at us. "Going fishing," she called, not breaking step. Porter was too intent on his thoughts to look our way.

"I know, sweet," I called back, explaining to Willa, "I thought they would have a chance to greet the boys before going off fishing with Soong. At the time it seemed rather a good idea to keep them out from underfoot, at least for a time after the boys' arrival."

"I've a mind to go someplace myself," Willa answered, "I have a dozen things I should be doing. I know their train came in yesterday, so there is no excuse for their being late—I thought Wen would want to make a point of being on time, especially since this is his first trip to the ranch since the trouble."

*The trouble.* A gray, leaden silence settled over us. Even now, almost five years after it had happened, it took a certain amount of fortitude to speak of that time—the events that burst upon us in the summer of 1903, culminating in Owen's death, and the troubled months that followed.

Remembering, I shivered.

Trinidad and Ignacio had stayed, they had not left. Their loyalty to their *patrón* was greater than the hatred they felt for his son, who had defiled their daughter. Aleja. Thinking of her, I sighed.

"Why are you making all those strange noises?" Willa asked, snapping at me because Wen and Thad were so late.

"I was thinking of Aleja," I answered, honestly.

"I finally convinced Trinidad and Ignacio to visit her at the school," Willa said, "I hope they do go."

"I think they will," I answered, "though I do believe I've never seen Trinidad so upset about anything... On the one hand, she considers Aleja to be 'ruined,' and on the other she cannot help but be impressed at her daughter's success."

"Yes, well," Willa started, and from the tone I knew she was worried about Aleja. "I hope I haven't put the girl in an untenable position. She will be one of the few Californios in the state with a higher education. No matter how bright she is—I'm wondering if she will be allowed to use her education."

"I don't understand," I said. "How can education ever do harm? Look at Soong..."

Willa flashed me a knowing look. "Exactly," she answered, turning back to a contemplation of the circling hawks.

We did not tell Willa about the attack on Aleja until after the funeral, until Wen was safely back at St. Paul's. She was sick with grief and longing, and I thought I could not bear to tell her—but there was no avoiding it. She had to know, she needed to know. It was left to me to break the news, and there was no gentle way to do it.

I will never forget her face, the shame and loathing and anger that played on it when I told her (and she insisted on the details, on everything; she would not let any of it go unsaid). Later, it would seem to me as if a boil had been lanced within her, and all the hurt and anger that had been kept inside came gushing out. She had marched out of the house, I had struggled to keep up. She marched straight to Trinidad's house, which she had entered, perhaps, two or three times only, and she walked in and confronted Trinidad. "Send one of the children for Ignacio," she had demanded.

Ignacio walked into the front parlor, with its scrubbed floor-boards, and Willa told them that she knew. She said, "I am shocked and ashamed for my son. I say to you now, if he were here I would take the whip to him. It is a terrible thing he has done, and he will not be excused. Never."

I watched them, our two old friends, and saw the tears that were close in Ignacio's solemn eyes.

"Señora," he said, turning his hat slowly in his hands, "I stay, even with the shame of my daughter. But I will never be in the sight of your son, the one who has done this. I cannot look upon him again, never in this life."

"I understand that," Willa had said, and then she added, "my son Owen will not be welcome at the ranch. When I see him, it will be somewhere else. But you say your daughter is shamed, and I cannot agree with that. The girl has done nothing wrong. It is not her fault. She must not suffer from the cowardly deeds of my son and his crude friend."

"What else is there but to suffer?" Ignacio answered. "She cannot now make a marriage. She is ruined."

Willa's face had set at hearing the words. "No," she had said, "no, that cannot be." Perhaps she had an idea, even then, to send Aleja away to school, but she said nothing. She knew it would take some planning, that she would have to work hard to find a school that would accept the dark-skinned girl.

She had done it. I don't quite know how, though I suppose

it had something to do with establishing a fund . . . but now Ignacio and Trinidad would see their daughter graduate from the university. She would graduate with honors, the first of her race and sex to do so.

I felt a moan rising within me, and stifled it. It would not do for Willa to know I was thinking of that time, those terrible months after Owen's death. I tried to force my mind from the sharpest memory, but I couldn't.

I had been sick in the night. I had pulled myself from my bed and retched into the chamberpot. My skin was damp to the touch. I felt sour and wretched and I was filled with fear. I lay there, weak and ill, and confronted the question. I could no longer delay, I would have to tell her, there was no way I could avoid adding to her burdens.

Then Willa was there, holding a night lamp that flickered unevenly, casting long shadows on her troubled face.

"Lena, what is it?" she said, setting the lamp on my night stand so that it cast its glow onto me. "My dear, you're so pale." Her voice quivered with concern. She brushed the damp hair back from my brow with a tenderness that caused tears to slide down my face. I fought to form the words. I did not want to say them, but I had to. There was no other way.

"Willa," I whispered, "I must tell you something. I don't want to, you have too much to carry . . ."

She squeezed my hand to give me courage, and waited.

"You must know . . ." I coughed, and stumbled in my speech. I was sick with fear, my hands were cold. She began to chafe them.

I was not sure that I had said the words at all. Perhaps I had only thought them, I did not know. I saw Willa look at me quizzically. She blinked her eyes, twice, rapidly.

"A baby?" she repeated.

She knew. I had said the words.

She raised her other hand to the side of my face and held it there. She looked at me for a long time, as if trying to understand something. She blinked again, caressed my face, and finally she said, "There is so much I do not know, Lena. Dear little Lena . . . Your poor back, is it possible? Is there a way for you to have your baby, and both of you be healthy?"

"Yes," I said, "there must be a way. I know there must be a way."

"You want it that much?" she asked, and I could only nod my head and cry.

She was quiet for a long while, and then she said, "If there is a way, we'll find it, sweet one. You'll have your baby and I'll have mine. It's a new start, a new life. If there is a way, I promise you, I will find it."

And she did find a way. The boys were sent East to school— Thad following shortly after Wen's departure, the unhappiest boy I had ever seen. And then Willa, in mourning, and her younger sister went into seclusion.

For seven long months we lived in darkened rooms, dressed incongruously in the bright Hawaiian overdresses Willa had brought from the islands, their loose folds hiding our growing bodies. We spoke in soft voices, and we waited. Only a few people were welcome on the ranch during that time—good Dr. Hadley, Sara, Arcadia and Joseph. It was, of course, a tragic story. Owen Reade's poor widow, who would give birth to twins before the end of official mourning, a boy named Porter and a girl, called Katharine.

Near the end, I was confined to my bed. Sara was there, of course, with a retinue of trained nurses. Sara had gone to Boston to convince the young specialist, a doctor named Eastin, that he should return with her to southern California. Dr. Eastin had performed a number of successful operations called "cae-sarean." It was the only hope, Dr. Hadley had said. Sara had been thorough. By the time she and Dr. Eastin arrived at the ranch, she knew exactly what he would need in terms of equip-ment and nursing assistance, and she set about getting it.

Willa and I, then, were prisoners of our swollen bodies, dependent on our close coterie of friends to protect and provide for us. Joseph and Arcadia handled all of the business. Willa and Sara and Trinidad and Soong fussed over me, monitored my condition, my progress, as if they were generals and my body was the battleground.

Willa and Sara deferred to Soong, who was, always, treated with respect. Whenever he appeared, they withdrew. Whenever he asked that I be given a certain herb, or a tea, they gave it. They understood my need to be with him, and they made it possible. He slipped quietly into the house, sat by my bed and with his long, graceful fingers soothed the inside of my forearm. I knew him now, knew him well enough to understand the turmoil that was there beneath the calm. He was troubled, though he never said it. He thought the risk I had taken was too great. And he was, I know, deeply distressed that I had made the decision without him.

"You would not have allowed it," I tried to explain. "It is the only time in our life together that I will ever make such a decision. Please understand, I had to. No matter what happens, it was my decision, and I had to make it."

As it had been when she gave birth to Rose, Willa's labor was short and the birth easy. The baby, though small, was pink and healthy. Two days later, my own baby was delivered by a surgical procedure in an operating arena elaborately devised in one of the parlors. The last faces I saw before drifting off into unconsciousness were those of the doctors, and the red-faced nurses in white caps.

When I regained consciousness, the first face I saw was Soong's, his beautiful dark eyes looking into me... Ah, that face, that beautiful face, filled with... how shall I explain? Rapture, I think. And gratitude mixed with love, and something wild and happy. "A boy child," he said, letting the Chinese accents be heard, "you have given us a boy child."

A gift, he knew that; a gift of our love, all that I could give so that he would know how vast, how enduring, my love was.

"Is he..." I began, and he answered, "He is perfectly formed, and big—too big for such a small mother. But beautiful, like his mother."

That moment, those words, the light in the face of my love, his lips caressing my hand—I knew it had been worth the risk, worth the pain. I knew then, and I have known always, that it was the finest moment. It was totality, completeness. I had never been so alive, I had never known such happiness.

We named him Porter, for my mother's family. He was beautiful, with dark, solemn eyes, gracefully shaped. His "twin" was as pink and delicate as he was dark and hearty. "How will anyone believe they are twins?" I asked Willa. "They don't look in the least alike."

"They are what is called 'fraternal' twins," Willa answered with remarkable calm. "Fraternal twins don't have to look alike. That is perfectly common knowledge."

I didn't believe it was, but I knew that Willa would make it seem so. She had a wonderful little speech she liked to give

when outsiders raised the question of the twins' appearance.
She explained, quite scientifically, the process that results in
"identical" twins and the process that results in "fraternal." It
was the sort of thing she was good at. No one ever questioned
her authority.

The babies were born in January. It was summer before a
new order settled into our household. The babies were together
in a new nursery with Josefa, a relative of Trinidad's who
spoke little English, but whose expertise with children was
obvious. My recovery was slow. By the time I was up and
about, Willa was working ten and twelve hours a day, having
involved herself in all aspects of the ranch and the businesses.
Joseph had seen us through the stormy business seas that followed Owen's death, when Willa had been stunned with grief
and the troubles with Wen and, not least, our two pregnancies.
Now she seemed to have recovered, and was determined to
carry on in Owen's place.

The only small stain on that contented summer was put there
by Thad. On the surface, he seemed the same. But there were
times when his mood would darken, when he would stop in
mid-phrase and walk away without a word, and not come back
for the whole of a day.

Soong told me of an incident that made me shudder. "I was
called to mediate an argument," he began. In itself, this was
not unusual; that he would tell me about it was. "A young
Chinese was mowing in the lower pasture," he went on. "One
of the family pets—a partridge—got under the blades in some
way, and was killed. Young Mr. Reade happened to be on
hand. He took a whip to the Chinese."

"Dear God," I could not help but say.

"By the time I got there, he had lashed the Chinese a dozen
times. I think he couldn't stop by himself, he seemed so totally
within the rage."

"Did no one stop him?" I whispered.

"The Mexicans were glad to see it, I think, and the Chinese
would never raise a hand against the young master."

"You did."

He looked at me, carefully. "I'm not totally Chinese, after
all. My position here is . . . unique. I think that is generally
acknowledged."

"Is that dangerous for you—for us?"

"Not unless the young masters take over. After today, I

doubt that Thad will bear me much good will."

"But you saved him from...he could have killed the Chinese..."

"He won't look at it that way."

And Soong was right. Thad did not forgive him.

And now the boys were returning, Thad having graduated from St. Paul's and Wen having finished at Harvard, an undistinguished career, at best. Joseph Brennan had been dispatched twice to extricate Wen from entanglements. Had it not been for Joseph's good nature, his willingness to help Wen, I sometimes thought that Willa would have given up on her eldest son. According to Joseph, Wen was only sowing wild oats. Sara, who spent time with the boys whenever she was in Boston, was less sanguine. She said Wen was insensitive and a snob—which is to say, like most of the other young men who fancy themselves superior to the rest of the world, for no other reason than that they have gone to Harvard. According to Sara, Thad was the loneliest boy she had ever known.

It hurt when she said it. I felt responsible. I knew it was wrong to send Thad away after Owen's death. He had, in one day, lost the father he adored and the only friend he had ever known, Pablito having been sent away to live with relatives in Mexico. Innocent victims, the two boys. It should not have happened, they should not have been hurt.

For a while I couldn't tell if the noise—the strange buzzing—was inside my head, or out. It was so steady and low that I wasn't sure if I heard it or not. I rose and walked over to where Willa was standing. She, too, was listening.

"Do you hear that?" she asked.

Before I could answer, the noise, a peculiar grinding sound, grew louder.

"That's why they're so late," Willa exploded, moving quickly down the walk, "I might have known Wen would have to buy himself a motorcar. The young fop!"

We saw it moving up the avenue of palms, a long plume of dust following in its wake; it was bright red, an open two-seater.

"I'm glad Trinidad is away," I said, "motorcars frighten her so." We could see the figures in the front seat now, at a distance.

"I'm glad she is gone, too," Willa said, grimly.

The car pulled to a stop in a whirlwind of dust, the dogs yelping crazily at the noisy monster and at the two creatures in goggles and dusters who disembarked. Thad leaped out first, all smiles, and embraced his mother. All trace of irritation had vanished from Willa's face. She was smiling, her arms were out, her pleasure at seeing her sons genuine. I felt hope stir within me; maybe, just maybe, things could be set right.

Wen, at twenty, was thickset, and new sidewhiskers gave him a stolid appearance. He kissed his mother formally, on both cheeks, holding her hand in both of his.

Words bounced out of us all. Explanations on lateness, admiration of the car, questions went unanswered, in the way of hellos.

"Wen had the fast-tourer shipped out on our train, but it didn't respond to the California climate right away. We had to hire a mechanic to get it going, and none of them had ever seen a Mercedes Sixty before. They spent all their time admiring it," Thad explained.

"Your brother buys a dandy new motorcar, and you're wearing last year's shirts," I said, jokingly running my finger around his frayed cuff.

"Oh, well," Thad went on in the same good-natured vein. "Wen's so in debt to me that one of these days I'm going to call all his notes due and take it all—motorcar, Cambridge rooms, English menswear, everything."

"My suits won't fit you," Wen sniffed, trying to match Thad's teasing tone.

"You know what Mr. Woodrow Wilson says about motorcars?" Willa put in. "He says they are a picture of the arrogance of wealth; he also says nothing has spread socialistic feelings more than the use of these machines."

"What would you expect of a Princeton man?" Thad said facetiously, and we all laughed.

"The place hasn't changed much," Wen offered when it was quiet again. "It looks greener, somehow, than I remembered."

"That's right," I put in, anxious to get it out in the open, "you haven't been here in five years. There's lots that has changed."

"Since Papa's death," Thad said.

I squeezed his hand and made him smile at me. "Come see what Wing Soong has done with the pergola you started last summer," I said, not wanting Thad's good homecoming mood to slip away.

Willa was at her desk in the front parlor early the next morning. She had sensed, from the rather formal way Wen had asked for a private meeting, that he had something on his mind. She was giving herself the advantage of being there first, taking her chair behind the desk.

For a time she sat quietly, contemplating the jacaranda outside the window. In the years since Owen's death she had learned quite a lot about dealing with men on matters of business. Most of all, she had learned to assume the initiative. She was not worried about handling Wen. He was a boy and, she knew, not exceedingly bright. Still, she wished Joseph were here. She smiled, thinking of the part Joseph so often played . . . she would greet the business caller while Joseph prowled around the room in what seemed an interminable search for a tray for his cigar, playing the bumbler, listening all the time, always listening—never missing a change in tone, a nuance, a small matter of phraseology. Joseph was a master at the power game. Owen had been, too, she surmised, but it was Joseph who had taught her how to play. She had, she knew, been an apt pupil. She saw it sometimes in Joseph's eyes, a glint that was pure admiration.

She knew now why Owen had respected Joseph, just as she knew that the motives of the two were different, quite different. In many ways, Owen had been the more traditional of the two. He had reached for financial success because it was what one did. A family and children, the ranch, all the trappings of respectability—they had been important to Owen, an end in themselves. It was what a man did . . . but Joseph, Joseph wanted something else, something more . . .

Her thoughts were interrupted by Wen's clearing of his throat. When he entered, she had legal papers spread out before her. "Good morning," she greeted him, not looking up until she had finished making a notation. Then, her hands clasped to show him he had her full attention, she said, "Have you had a chance to see all that we have done on the ranch? The cattle pens . . ."

"Yes, some . . ." he interrupted, wandering over to the window, his back to her and his hands clasped behind him. They were, she noticed, white and soft.

At that moment the twins went running across the grass, following Wing Soong into the house orchard, each carrying a small bucket.

Wen blurted, "Did you know that little Porter can speak Chinese?"

Willa tried to manage a smile. "Yes, I had noticed," she answered, trying to be light in tone, "amazing, isn't it? Kit can too, you know—but she's too shy to speak in front of anyone but Porter. I hear them in the nursery at night, chattering away in Mandarin."

Wen turned, a frown on his face. "I should think that French would be more in keeping—or even Spanish. But Chinese is, well, a heathen language . . . I can't imagine you would condone it, Mother. And I wonder if it is wise that the twins spend so much time with the Chinese gardener. They do have a governess, I believe."

Willa sighed. "Wen, let's speak plainly." She rose and stood so straight that, in her high-heeled boots, she was taller than he. "Since your return to the ranch yesterday, you have found much to complain about . . ." He started to interrupt but she raised her hand, "let me finish . . . You've graduated form Harvard and you plan to come into the family business. On that much, we agree. I am pleased, as your father would have been. I cannot say that your father would have been pleased about everything you've done since his death, but I am determined to assign that to the past, to put it behind us. What's done is done. I would like to think that we are making a beginning. Joseph and I have managed quite well together, but Joseph isn't going to want to carry such a heavy load forever. What I want to know—need to know—is just how do you see yourself fitting into the business?"

Wen leaned against a chair, but could not seem to find a comfortable place for his hands, so he sat down and put them on his knees. He had an odd habit of looking obliquely at one, concentrating on an ear or a point just above the eyes, and only now and then letting his eyes flicker into the other's.

"We are a very rich family, Mother. I wonder if you knew— if Father ever told you—just how much he was worth?"

"Your father's *worth* has no relation to the size of the estate he left," she snapped, and was sorry immediately. She was determined not to lose her temper. "Let's not be delicate, your father left an estate worth sixty million. And yes, I was surprised at the magnitude of his accomplishments."

"I thought as much," Wen said. "It is quite a lot for anyone to imagine, and I'm sure it must have been difficult for you, these past five years, having to carry the burden of the business. I am sure that Father would mean for me to relieve you of that burden just as soon as I was able. And I am able now."

Willa was stunned.

Wen cleared his throat defensively. "I have, after all, spent four years at Harvard College preparing myself. I do believe I came away with some abilities," his eyes narrowed, "as well as excellent connections."

"Excellent connections," Willa repeated, not able to keep the acid from her voice. "Yes, Joseph has told me about some of your excellent connections. And of course, we were able— your father and I, in the weeks before his death—to meet your excellent friend, Mr. Sayre."

She had not meant to say it, she had promised she wouldn't and she had, already, broken the promise. She took a deep breath to calm herself.

"I thought," Wen reprimanded her, "that my sowing of wild oats was to be in the past, I thought you were not going to bring that up again."

"Wild oats? Is that what you call what you and Wallace Sayre did to Aleja? Have you no guilt at all?" Her voice was rising, quivering.

Wen's eyes were dulled. He lay his head on the back of the chair and closed his eyes for an instant. Watching him, Willa felt chilled.

"As I am sure you know," she said, fighting to keep her voice free of anger, "I am the principal beneficiary of the estate. Your father left me in complete control of everything except the trust funds set up long ago for you and Thad."

". . . and Aunt Lena," Wen put in.

Willa paused, wondering how he had known about my trust, wondering why he would mention it. But she did not intend to be distracted, so she simply nodded. "To get to the point, I was left in control. But to underscore that it was his wish, your father left a letter in which he stated precisely that he wanted me to retain Joseph Brennan as the executive officer of his many holdings, and that if Joseph would agree, Owen suggested we form a company that would bind together his many business holdings. He suggested that Joseph be named the executive officer of this company, and that I serve as chairman of the board. As you know, this was done. We formed the Reade Land Company. Do you, then, propose to take over my position?"

For the first time, Wen flushed.

"Nothing like that, Mother. Of course I don't wish to take your place. It is just . . . well, friends of mine, people who knew and respected Father, they wonder if forming the company was the wise course of action, given the economic circumstances . . ."

She cut him off. Her patience was thinning. "Since the businesses are thriving in the consolidated company, I can't quite imagine what your friends mean, but in any case it was your father's best judgment, and since he was the one who amassed the fortune, I see no reason in refuting him."

"Yes, well," Wen said, muttering now, "Father could not have foreseen, of course . . ."

Willa was tired of the talk, tired of trying to reach some agreeable plane on which she could live with her son. "Wen," she said, "if you wish to study the business, you are welcome to join us. I know that Joseph will be happy to show you exactly what we are doing. He will explain what we plan to do and find a way for you to learn all you need to know to fit into our organization. I will have to be blunt—I have no intention of turning my position over to you, not now and not in the near future. I happen to like being at the top of a business. There will be plenty of room for you to join me, and plenty of time in which to do it. But I suggest that you aim your sights a bit lower. You will first have to prove yourself, to me and to Joseph."

These words had a peculiar effect on Wen. His face flushed deep red and he began to rub the palms of his hands on his pants.

"Prove myself," he exploded, "to Joseph Brennan? To that . . . Irishman?" He spat it out. "There are some things you don't understand, Mother. The Joseph Brennans of this world— they go to schools like Fordham and think they are educated, when really they're not first-rate. Joseph Brennan, well . . . I don't know if you have any idea ... Father certainly could not have known that Brennan would involve himself with that radical bunch that call themselves 'Lincoln Republicans.' I'm certain Father would not have approved, not at all."

Willa allowed herself a tight smile. "I do know, Wen," she said, "I make it a point to know what is going on in the world. I wonder how much you know about the Good Government League? The Lincoln Republicans are trying, with some success, to break the grip of the Southern Pacific on the state of California. If you know anything at all about the history of this family, of our long struggle to keep the Southern Pacific out of the Malibu, you should know that we are in full accord."

"On the matter of the railroad, perhaps," Wen agreed, "but Brennan and his bunch are also calling for regulation of utilities, and that will hurt us. And workmen's compensation and the conservation of forests, well—I for one don't want the government or any trade union dictating what we must pay our miners, or what trees we can cut in our forests."

She answered carefully. "Joseph and I have had more conversations than you could imagine about any conflict of interest on his part. He has offered to resign on a number of occasions, when he felt that the interests of the company were in conflict with his conscience. It has always been my opinion that good business practices can and must work in concert with the best interests of the workers, and with such things as conservation of our resources. We must not cut down all of our forests, or what will be left for your children? We must not rip all of the coal out of the earth and, in the process, kill miners as if they were dispensable because of poor safety practices."

Wen looked at her with scarcely concealed contempt. "You need me more than I thought," he said.

She had had enough. "What do you think of women's suffrage, Wen? And the initiative, referendum and recall—remember those?"

His blank look told her that he had little understanding of the political process. "Well, just tell me what you think about women's suffrage. Would you give them the right to vote?" Her tone was falsely cheerful.

"No, Mother, I would not," he answered. "The women I most admire are those who understand that their highest calling is as wife and mother, who feel that is power enough."

"Oh, Wen," she sighed, "that really is enough. I know we haven't made any decisions at all, but let's do some thinking now, and approach the whole issue again in a day or so."

Still, Wen sat. He had something more to say, and he was turning words over in his mind, trying to start. Willa waited.

"Mr. Emory came to see me when he was in Boston a few weeks back," he finally blurted. "Oh, don't worry, Mother... He started by telling me he understands that he is not well loved by our family and that he had no intention of compromising me."

"Compromising... did he use that word?" Willa asked.

"Why yes, I believe so. Something like that. At any rate, he said nothing very substantial, we had a nice chat, that was all. He can really be quite charming, Mother. After all the stories, I had expected a monster with sharp teeth."

"Was it from Charles Emory that you learned about Joseph Brennan's political activities?" she demanded.

"Why do you say that?" he came back sharply. "I know many people in Santa Monica, I have other sources of information."

"It was Charles," she said. "Stop right there, Wen. Charles Emory is a dangerous man, but you can believe what you want. If you don't wish to take my word, so be it, because I don't propose to try to convince you. I will tell you this much, however. Joseph Brennan is as good a friend as this family ever had, and you of all people have first-hand knowledge of that. He is a good and a decent man, and your father trusted him implicitly. So, too, do I. So if you expect to join the family business—which I direct, with Joseph's invaluable help—you had better understand from the start that you are going to have to earn our respect, Joseph's and mine."

"And if I don't choose to accept Brennan as my superior?" he asked, flushing.

Willa looked at him with a mixture of pity and contempt. "You will be twenty-one next year. As I remember, according to the terms of your trust you will have complete control of those funds. You should be able to live respectably—if not lavishly—on the income from your trust. Your father and I decided, when the funds were set up, that we wanted our children to be truly independent of us at age twenty-one. So it seems to me that you are free to do whatever you wish, with the exception of supplanting either Joseph or me at the company."

"When Father was my age, he had control of the whole of his father's business."

"Your father's mother was not alive," she said. She did not say that he was no match for the man his father had been at twenty-one.

"I'll be on my way, then," he said, somewhat pathetically.

"On your way? Where?" she said. "You've only just come home."

"Home?" he answered. "How can this be home, when I'm only welcome when the servants are away?"

Willa nodded. She felt a dull ache in the center of her. Something was over, done with. Wen was right. The Malibu was not home to him, and it never would be.

Watching him drive off, unable to think of any comforting words, I said only, "Thad seems to be happy to be home."

"I hope I am able to mend fences with Thad better than I did with Wen," Willa said. I put my arm around her waist, and she put hers around me. We stood there for a time, watching the red motorcar throw up its trail of dust as it roared down the avenue of palms.

Willa clapped her hands as if to clear the air. "Speaking of fences," she said, "I've decided to go ahead with the building of a fence across the beach road at Las Flores, at that point where the palisades leave only a narrow strip between them and the beach. The warning signs we've posted have done no good at all. It's time for a fence."

"Are you sure?" I asked, doubt in my voice. "It might just stir up folks—things have been quiet lately."

"Quiet, maybe, but all sorts of people are passing to and fro through the ranch. I run into some of them every time I go out, and I'm beginning to see the remnants of fires they build. Then there are the losses we've been taking in the herd— Ignacio is worried about the rustlers."

"I doubt a gate will keep rustlers out."

"You're probably right, but it will let everybody know I am losing patience with the idea that they have a right to come and go at their pleasure."

Wen had left and Willa was about to put up a fence so that whoever came, came at her bidding. I did not tell her what I was thinking—I did not say that I wondered if she were locking Wen out, along with all the others who would try to wrest control from her. I said nothing because I knew that the lines were drawn, that she and Wen would never be able to act in concert, that whatever might have been between them was no longer possible. It would not do, I knew, to look for villains. Still, I could not help noting how often Charles Emory surfaced at painful times in our family's life.

We sat on the verandah, Porter, Kit and I, in the late afternoon. The two had a large bowl of peas between them which they were to shell for our supper. I loved watching them work— Porter opening a pod, studying the groupings of the peas as if they held some secret message, counting them. And Kit, shelling three or four in the space of the time Porter took to do one, working quietly and steadily, responding to whatever he might have to say. Thad teasingly called them Grandma and Grandpa, because they were "such mature four-year olds." That made Kit spill over with laughter.

The two were a continuing puzzle to the house servants. They were almost constantly together, yet they seemed never to disagree. It was assumed that Porter was the leader since Kit almost always walked in his wake. In fact, the balance they achieved was almost perfect. He was tall, intense, always questioning while she, being smaller and quicker, tended to follow through. She never hurried him; he never failed to listen to whatever she might have to say. Others credited them with having some magical connection because they were twins.

One day, as Wing Soong and I sat watching them, I said, "He is so like you—so gentle and strong, and so filled with curiosity. I think he is going to be a magnificent man."

Soong had smiled, and—perhaps because of the homage I had paid, allowed himself to offer a rare opinion. "Sometimes I look at them—our twins—and I see you and me, without our chains. She looks so much like you, Lena—that beautifully delicate face, the same generous spirit, but without your crippled back. And Porter, though I feel his best qualities are more akin to yours, sometimes I think that he will be able to do so much more than I, because he is free of the stigma of mixed race."

Now, shelling peas, I allowed myself a secret smile. It did

not escape Kit. "Are you feeling happy, Auntie?" she asked, but before I could answer, Porter interrupted.

"My big brother Owen did not stay long. Why?"

Kit nodded. She was wondering, too. "Wen's finished college," I said, "now he must begin to work. That is what a man must do, work." I hoped it was enough.

Porter nodded wisely. "I understand," he said, "all societies are built on the labor of the working class."

I flinched. At least Willa was not there to hear. I would have to speak to Soong about sharing his socialistic sympathies with our son. Especially after Wen's diatribe, it would not do for the family to separate into opposing political camps.

"I work," Kit said. "So does Auntie. So does Mama."

"We all work, sweet," I answered, "though I do believe that you and I are doing a larger share than Porter here."

Kit laughed. "Porter gives three peas to his mouth and one to the bowl."

His dark eyes lit with mischief, and he tried not to chew the crunchy peas that he had just popped into his mouth.


Thad was out, roaming the ranch, for his first full week at home. We saw him in the evening, when he would return from a day on the range, dusty, tired and happy. His neck became sunburned, his hands raw. Everything he saw seemed to please him.

"He is transformed since his arrival," I said to Willa. "He seems so happy on the ranch, do you think he will want to start Harvard this fall?"

"Oh, I'm sure," Willa started, then stopped. "You know, Owen made the arrangements all those years ago, I guess I've always thought it was settled."

"Do you feel Thad thinks it is settled?" I prodded.

"I hadn't thought," she answered, "but you know something, don't you?"

"Not really," I answered, "nothing precise. Only that he mentioned something to me about the University of Southern California—about some of the faculty having been trained in the best Eastern schools, he said *if he had to go . . .*"

"Is that all he said?" she probed.

"Nothing was very direct. It was just a feeling I got. He kept coming back to talk of Porter Farm, and the last time he visited there—last spring. He admires his uncles, the way they live. He talked quite a lot about it."

"What does it mean?" she asked.

"I don't know," I said, "I truly don't. It's just that he made such a point that none of his uncles had gone to college, and he thought they lived quite a good life."

"I wonder what Owen would think?" she said.

"I suppose he would have been dismayed," I answered honestly, because I had thought about it. "But then, you didn't agree with Owen's insistence on the boy's being educated in the East from the beginning. I think now you must make your own decisions. You have the right to be as opinionated as Owen was."

Willa slipped her arm around my waist and gave me the briefest of hugs. It was her way of thanking me for bringing an issue to the surface, and helping her deal with it, pushing gently toward a decision.

Neither of us knew then how determined Thad was to stay on the ranch; neither of us could have guessed how relieved he would be when he met with no resistance. Thad loved the ranch in much the way that Willa loved it. There was plenty of work for a young *patrón,* though Thad's temper caused the men to be cautious of him. Still, they admired his willingness to learn, his capacity for work and his lack of pretension. Soon, the men—especially the *vaqueros*—discovered his admiration for what they called machismo, and they preened for him and basked in his envy.

The day Ignacio and Trinidad returned, Thad was there to greet them. It was the first day he had spent around the ranch house, and it took me a time to understand that he was, in fact, waiting for them.

He greeted them affectionately, which made Ignacio a trifle uncomfortable but pleased Trinidad.

"Pablito," Thad said, as soon as he could, "tell me about Pablito. What is he doing?"

Trinidad glanced at Ignacio, whose face had darkened. Thad saw and changed the subject. He would ask Trinidad when she was alone.

"Aiiie," she said, later in the kitchen as they sat across the table from each other, like friends, her hand on his. "My poor Pablito, he has brought such shame on us. First he fights with the revolution, then he fights with the dictator. He fights with whoever asks him, for money, we hear. Ignacio has forbidden me to speak of it." She shook her head, in sorrow and in perpetual sadness.

"I would like to see him," Thad said.

"Ah, and I," Pablito's mother answered, "but not here, never here I think."

Joseph spent several days each week at the ranch, bringing a clerk with him so that Willa and he could tend to business. He also brought Arcadia whenever the Señora would allow it. Once only, Arcadia convinced the Señora to accept Willa's invitation to join us on the ranch. Joseph had hired a comfortable coach for the trip. We had a guest parlor outfitted to accommodate a most important house guest. We did more than ever we had done for a guest, including Mr. Roosevelt, but it was all for naught. The Señora, it seems, had forgotten that Owen was no longer alive. "And where is young Mr. Reade?" she had demanded upon arrival. "Why isn't he here to greet me?"

"I'm not at all sure she can accept our excuse for Owen's absence," Joseph had whispered, in jest. In fact, she didn't.

"It's not at all the same without him," she told Arcadia in a loud aside, "I think I will not wish to stay."

"There were some things only Owen could do," Willa sighed. "And one of those was to make the Señora feel beautiful again." She turned away, surprised by the tears that stung her eyes. Joseph patted her gently on the shoulder.

At dinner that evening, the conversation was strained. Joseph did his best, but even he could not manage to lift the pall the Señora put on the gathering. After a bit, when the Señora dozed off, her chin sunk into her chest, we talked quietly, not to startle her. Suddenly she came awake, and announced, in a rusted voice, that Abel Stearns had come to court her dressed in knee breeches and silver buckles.

Arcadia rose quickly and moved to her side. She whispered in the old woman's ear, and soon the Señora was dozing again. The incident was important, Willa and I decided later, only because it showed something of what Arcadia must contend with, day in and day out. It made us sad.

Arcadia and Joseph doted on the twins, who returned the affection lavishly. In some ways, the twins bound us even closer to Arcadia and Joseph. They were among the few who knew the truth, our inner circle. They were among the people we trusted most in the world. We were, in turn, their family, the twins their children, as well.

The week after Wen and Thad's arrival (and Wen's precipitous departure), the twins took a bag of oranges to the bottom of the palm lane, to eat while waiting for Arcadia and Joseph's carriage to arrive. It had become their habit to ride to the house with the couple, on the way telling them all that had happened during their absence. Porter would give the running narrative, trusting Kit to fill in the details. Arcadia and Joseph loved these drives, and always asked their coachman to go slowly to prolong the time with the twins.

"Sara's in town," Arcadia called to me as soon as the carriage halted, and the twins came tumbling out. "She's finishing up some business in Santa Monica today, and she'll be along shortly."

"Wonderful," I exclaimed. Sara had been in Paris for most of the spring. We had not expected her for several weeks.

"Not so wonderful, I think," Joseph put in, "Charles is champing at the bit."

"Charles?" I said, wary.

"We've been giving the Southern Pacific a good deal of trouble," he answered, speaking of the Good Government League. "Charles is angry that we were able to get the documentation on rebates that will enable us to take our case to Washington. He's out for bear."

"Joseph," Willa said, "behind that cigar and gathering girth, you really are fearless."

Joseph erupted in one of his great laughs, throwing Kit into the air and catching her, then giving her a big kiss before gently setting her down. "Porter," he said then, "I think we men had better retire before the women pick us to death. Let's find Wing Soong."

That, too, had become part of the ritual. Shortly after arriving, Joseph and Porter would make their way to Wing Soong's little cabin. There, Joseph would light his cigar and the two men would talk, while Porter listened. They spoke of politics, they talked of revolution, they covered a whole range of subjects. In Soong, Joseph had found an inquiring mind to rival his own. Owen had been fascinated with Soong, but not intellectually. Joseph, on the other hand, plumbed the depths of Soong's Oriental mind. While Owen had been a captain of industry, Soong and Joseph were men of conscience with goals that far outstripped anything Owen Reade had ever imagined.

Porter listened, now and then asking a question. Most of the questions were a child's but all were answered. I wondered, at times, how much of what he heard would stay in his memory. I wondered, more often, what effect it would have on our son, these long, convoluted discussions about morality and ethics, about duty and the dignity of work.

Porter had been told that Owen Reade was his father. Joseph was Porter's godfather, Soong his good friend. Even before Porter had much of a notion of what a father should be, he selected his own. I will never forget the words. He said to me, "I have chosen my father." He paused, continued, "Soong for half, Joseph for half." When I told Soong, his pleasure was real. "A wise man, our Porter," he said. "His judgment is sound. How agreeable to be able to choose one's own father, and to be fortunate enough to know such a man as Joseph Brennan."

Sara arrived on Saturday and we celebrated with a beach party, the first of the season. We set our umbrellas and chairs in the sand, and watched as the twins romped off to the surf, squealing with pleasure as the waves washed over them, letting the water lift and carry them, belly first, onto the hard, wet sand. After a time they tired of riding the waves and came to fetch Sara. The three wandered off to comb the beach.

Sara and Porter were squatting by the tide pools along the rocky ledge, jumping when the surf washed too close, returning then to stare into the pools. Kit approached with a starfish in her hand.

"How beautiful, love," Sara enthused. Porter moved to Kit's side, examined the starfish and announced, "It was a shooting star, you know, when they fall into the ocean, this is what happens to them."

Kit looked at him, saw that he was serious, accepted his explanation. It never occurred to her to doubt Porter.

"That's a lovely idea," Sara said, considering her godson carefully. Later she would tell me, "He has the most remarkable presence. Sometimes I think Kit is the only one who truly understands him."

"And Soong," I added. Sara smiled, "Kit and his mother and father, I should have said."

"Oh, not me," I assured her, "I don't have the same sort of thought processes they have—Porter, Kit, Soong—or you or Joseph, for that matter. You're all much too quick for me."

Sara took my arm, then, and we walked down the beach together feeling fine with each other. I tried to explain, to put into words, what the twins had done to change all our lives, but I could never quite manage. It was fascinating, and somewhat strange, but we were a family again. After Owen left, the pattern had been shattered. We all missed the excitement, the cohesion, he had brought to our lives. There were times, in those months following his death, when I despaired of our ever being together, a whole, again.

And then the twins came. Our days formed around them. We came together, our circle of friends who were more than friends, more even than family. Willa was able to enjoy her daughter as she never had her sons. Perhaps it was just that Kit was a girl, perhaps it was something else. I didn't know, it didn't matter. Kit and Willa had lovely, laughing times together. Whenever Kit awakened in the night, it was Willa's bed she went into.

On the Sunday after the beach party, Willa and Arcadia rose early to go to the boat dock to do some sailing, a sport they had revived for themselves. As they walked toward the barn to get the dog cart, Thad, shirtless, leaned from an upstairs window and called to them, "Can you use a crew?"

Arcadia shielded her eyes and looked up at him. "Come along, sailor," she called.

"We'll go ahead and get the boat ready," Willa added, "come along when you've had some breakfast. We'll be away all morning."

"Right behind you," Thad shouted, slamming down the window. In a few minutes he was racing across the yard, eating biscuits on the run. Sara and I watched from the kitchen window. "How nice to see that boy so happy," Sara said, "he doesn't seem at all the same Thad I saw in Boston. Not the same boy."

"I know," I answered, "Sometimes I think there are several Thads—but this is the one I like best."

Joseph joined us, and Trinidad was right behind, shooing us out of her kitchen and onto the verandah where we were to allow her to serve us a leisurely breakfast. Joseph was her clear favorite, eating everything she put before him, as she clucked and cajoled all the while.

"Trinidad, you are a wonderful woman, but you are ruining my figure. I'll never be a slim man again, I fear, and it is your fault, all of it."

"No, no," Trinidad murmured, as she might to a lover.

Sara shot Joseph a wry, affectionate smile. "When I try to explain to my friends in Europe, or even San Francisco, what it is I love about the Malibu, I never can. How does one explain the noises Trinidad makes as she serves sausages in the morning?"

"One doesn't," Joseph answered. "Never try to describe a state of mind, of being . . ."

"I suppose it is the way a few lucky people feel about home."

"Strange you should speak of home," I put in. "We had rather a large disappointment earlier this week. Wen came out with Thad, you know. It was his first time on the ranch since the trouble, and Willa had gone to great lengths to get Trinidad and Ignacio to visit Aleja . . ."

"Oh, yes, and did they actually see her?" Sara put in, breaking my thought.

"Yes, they finally did—and it seems to have been a remarkable visit, their seeing Aleja on the campus of a university, where she is actually taking the course prescribed for men. But I'll tell you about that later, what I started to say was that Wen only stayed long enough to tell Willa he expected to take over the reins of the family business. When Willa objected, he left. That in itself hurt her, but I think she was just as hurt when Wen said the Malibu wasn't his home."

Joseph stopped eating. He was looking at me intently, but I knew he was not really looking at me, he was thinking. It was his way, it was how he put things together.

"I wondered what had happened," he finally said. "As soon as he came back to town, he stopped in the office and asked some very specific questions about the legal organization of the company, specific and rather sophisticated questions."

"He's not smart enough for that," Sara said bluntly, "so they were someone else's questions."

Before Joseph could answer the dogs set to barking. We heard, then, the unmistakable rumble of a carriage.

"Willa didn't get the gate up in time," I muttered. A few

moments and the carriage came into view. None of us moved
to meet it, nobody went to greet Charles Emory when he
emerged. For a long moment no one said anything. We watched
Charles blink, look about as if he had arrived on a social outing.
Finally, he walked over to where we sat together, the three of
us. Joseph was the first to speak.

"Out for a Sunday ride, are you, Charles?" he asked, his
tone innocent humor.

"Owen always did say that the coast road rivaled the Grand
Corniche," Charles shot back, reminding us that he had once
been part of our lives. I felt a sudden surge of fear.

Charles was looking directly at Sara. He did not take his
eyes from her for several long minutes, but let the silence grow.
Sara met his gaze, she did not waver. Finally he said, "I would
like a private word with you, Sara."

"Hello, Charles," I cut in, reminding him that he had ignored
the civilities. I rose, moving between him and Sara, but she
was quicker than I and managed to be up, her arm around my
waist. With the gentlest of motions, like some sweet waltz
step, she handed me over to Joseph, who tucked my arm in
his and led me into the house.

Charles and Sara went into the front parlor and shut the
door. Joseph and I waited in the next room. I sat with my
hands in my lap while Joseph paced. It was not a nervous
pacing, but rather thoughtful, as if he were trying to piece
things together.

We could hear the low undertone of the voices from the
next room: Charles' high and staccato, Sara's low and soft.
Had we heard what they were saying, I would not have understood, not then. Not until much later.

"I suppose," Charles opened the conversation, "this should
make you feel good, forcing me to come searching you out
like this."

Sara looked at him. "You never did have even the vaguest
notion of what makes me feel good, Charles. But I will give
you a hint: Your coming here does not make me feel good. So
state your business and be on your way before Willa returns
and cites you for trespassing."

"Yes," Charles said, with his old grin, "Willa would do
that."

"What is it?" Sara said, her voice sharp.

"I want you to stop cooperating with Brennan and that bunch

of bastards that call themselves the Lincoln Republicans. They're out to do the Southern Pacific in, and you are feeding them the information they need. We know it. We even know how you do it. Your sources are being closed. But you should consider something else—your spite is going to hurt you, as well as us, since you are a major shareholder in the company."

Sara walked to the window, turning her back on him, letting her hand trail casually over the back of a chair. She considered telling him that her motive was not spite, but decided against it. Better he think her spiteful than resourceful. Better he think she was doing it out of misplaced vengeance than from preservation. She was, she knew, the only one who could protect the Malibu from Charles this time.

"You've accused me of cooperating and you want me to stop," Sara said, "but you wouldn't come all the way out here unless you had something more to tell me. You want me to stop or . . . or what, Charles?"

"I've told Helen you're a good deal smarter than she gives you credit for," he said, his voice insinuating, mean. Sara was careful not to move, not even her hands. She would not give him that. He sat down, crossed his legs as if he planned to stay, began unwrapping a cigar. "It's quite nice out here on the ranch—different, though, from what I remember. But nice, still. I can't imagine why Wen doesn't feel welcome here . . ."

Sara's back straightened; Charles noticed, smiled.

"He's come to work for us, you know."

"I didn't know," Sara said, looking at him with ill-concealed contempt, "but I'm not surprised. He's a stupid boy, perhaps you'll find him usable sometimes, but that's not all you have. I don't want to waste the whole of my day waiting for you to divulge your little mysteries. I'm not a wife, Charles, I have no duty to listen to you . . ."

He ground out his cigar in sharp, hard swirls. "All right, Sara, here it is. Stop feeding information to the politicians. Stay out of it or you will find how hard I can hit. I know what this place means to you and your precious friends, the . . . Lena and Willa. I can bring this place down, Sara. I can destroy everything . . . Lena and Willa and the little . . ." he paused, dramatically, ". . . twins, the remarkable little twins . . . with it. Do you understand what I am saying, Sara? Don't underestimate me."

Sara's mind was racing—the twins. He knew, of course he

would make it his business to know. Too many people were involved. She would have to be careful now, too much was at stake.

"I have never underestimated you, Charles," she answered, "that is why I am here today. But you have consistently under-estimated me. Let me ask you a question now. Do you happen to remember a man named Proctor, Amos Proctor?"

Charles' eyes narrowed, the pupils seemed to diminish to pinpoints as if flooded by light. "He was a Treasury agent," she continued in a soft voice, barely more than a whisper, "and he met with an unfortunate..." Sara paused, then continued, "accident. It was on the second day of the new century, in a boarding house in..."

Charles bolted out of the chair, for a moment she thought he might strike her. She felt a rush of elation, and turned away to hide it.

"Strange that our marriage wasn't more of a success, Charles," she continued, calmly, "you can't say I wasn't an apt student. You taught me how to...negotiate, shall we say?"

"I'll see you in hell, woman," he spat, his voice out of control, as he strode out of the door and stormed into his carriage, barking at the driver to be off.

"Give my stepmother my regards," Sara said, too softly for anyone to hear.

Her face reflected victory. Sara linked her arms in ours, Joseph's and mine, and guided us across the lawn toward the pergola where the twins were playing.

"He's not a man to underestimate," Joseph warned.

Sara smiled up at him. "How odd you should say that," she laughed, "that's just what Charles told me. And I answered him as I will you—truthfully. I never have."

Joseph stopped, looked hard at Sara, then broke into a fine laughter. Soon we were all laughing, our arms about each other.

"Sara," Joseph finally said, gasping for breath, "you are a wonder. A perfect wonder."

"Are you just finding that out?" I asked him. "I've known all along. If Sara were a man, she'd have all of you by the throat."

"Then I'm glad I'm not a man," Sara said, holding out her arms to Kit, "because I have everything I want right now..."

Kit threw herself into Sara's arms and hugged her. "Look here, Joseph, at our godchildren. What more could one ask?"

Joseph was smiling on the children, and it moved me to say something that, perhaps, should have gone unsaid. "I suppose it's terrible to say, Joseph, but we have benefited so from your being free to serve as father to the children. No one could be a better father than you have been."

"I'm afraid I've failed with Wen," Joseph sighed.

"You've guessed, then?" Sara said, and Joseph nodded. "It makes sense," he went on. "Wen's ambition far outstrips his abilities. He thinks the old school tie business will see him through, but I don't. Not here in the West, at any rate. Here, even Harvard men are supposed to have some abilities. Since I'm the one who has witnessed Wen's failures first-hand, it is understandable that he would dislike me. By throwing in with Charles, he hits at his mother and me in one stroke. It stands to reason that Charles would try to make use of such a situation."

"But what could..." I began, then a hard knot of fear formed in my stomach. "Wen doesn't know?" I whispered, looking at the twins.

"No," Sara said firmly, "and I think Charles will find out soon enough that Wen isn't going to do him any good, and he'll let him go then."

I felt immediate relief. I knew that Wen could cause quite a lot of trouble for all of us, if he could prove that Porter was not a legitimate heir to his father's fortune. He could discredit his mother, could cause all manner of grief to all of us.

The matter of Porter's being an heir bothered me more than I cared to admit. I had, in fact, asked Willa to disinherit Porter. Money was no real object. I would have a tidy income to leave him, and I knew the twins were to be Sara's principal heirs. But Willa, and Joseph was in agreement, felt that it was too soon to make such a legal move, that it would raise questions we did not want to answer.

"Wen isn't your failure, Joseph," I said. Sara, suddenly angry, agreed. "Wen is Wen's failure," she said, "I wish you two would stop acting as if either of you—or Willa or Owen, for that matter—had anything to do with making Wen what he is. He has committed the most despicable acts—holding Aleja down so his schoolmate could rape her, then all those disgusting escapades at school...fornication and blackmail and God knows what all else..."

"Gambling," Joseph said, drily, but Sara was too riled to catch the note of sarcasm.

"I don't know what happened to Wen," Sara went on, "I do know that others—Owen, for example—had a more difficult time as a child, and were able to overcome it. If Wen is going to throw in with Charles, so be it. He will find out how hard the world can be. Maybe it is what he needs—with no Owen, no Joseph to rescue him."

"Sara, my girl," Joseph said, gently mocking, "such a sentimentalist you are."

~ *Chapter Seventeen*

Sally Fairleigh sprawled under the big oak, one arm looped around Kit's shoulder, the other hand holding the book. Porter lay close by on his stomach, feet in the air. All three were barefoot, and the bottoms of their feet were blotched with black asphaltum from the beach. Each afternoon, if Sally deemed their schoolwork properly done, she read to them aloud. At first she had chosen books she thought they would enjoy—rhymes and fairy tales. Now, at Porter's insistence, she was reading from *Huckleberry Finn*. She read with gusto, throwing herself into all the parts without the slightest hesitation—even Jim: *"We's safe, Huck, we's safe! Jump up and crack yo' heels! Dat's de good ole Cairo at las', I jis know it."*

The twins were transfixed. They had been munching on apples, but now they were too engrossed to remember to take a bite, or even to notice that one of the pet chickens was about to rush at Porter's apple, outstretched in his hand.

Soong and I watched, unseen, from the arbor.

"Trust Sara to understand what is lacking, and supply it, before anyone else has so much of a glimmer that there is a need."

"That's rather enigmatic," I replied.

"I mean, what the twins need—what everyone needs—is a

349

schoolteacher who goes barefoot, eats apples and reads Mark
Twain to five-year-olds."

I laughed, delighted. "Sally does stir things up, doesn't she?
And you're right, we did need stirring. We were getting quite
stale, I think."

"It's the wild red hair I find fascinating," Soong went on,
"the color of it, and the way it crinkles and sticks out . . . and
all those strange marks on her face."

"Freckles!" I giggled. "I forget that you haven't seen many
redheads—or any, I guess, if you haven't seen freckles. Most
redheads have them. What a sheltered life you've led, Soong."
I gave him a mischievous grin. "Redheads usually hate their
freckles, but Sally claims she quite likes them. Her father told
her, and she told me, that freckles are vastly underestimated
as marks of distinction, except in some tribes in deepest Africa.
She had therefore, she said, decided to be content with her
looks."

Soong shook his head, smiling. "One never quite knows
what the young lady is going to say, does one?"

"No," I agreed, grinning at him again, and mimicking his
suddenly stuffy English accents, "one doesn't. Has she convinced you to teach that field course in botany? I am to do my
stint in music. She has already scheduled me for three hours
each week, Mondays, Wednesdays and Fridays at eleven in
the morning."

"I think I must speak to your sister first, to see if she would
find it agreeable."

"Whyever?" I asked, surprised. "You know Willa won't
object."

"I think not," he answered, slowly, "but I also think that
young Thad feels I already 'take advantage' of a special position
in the household."

"Has he said anything to you?" I demanded.

"No, no. And I doubt he has said anything to his mother
yet, either. But I feel sure it is coming, and I think it wise to
take precautions now."

"Thad is no threat," I assured him. "I am a bit peeved with
him now for his treatment of Sally. He doesn't seem to have
cottoned to her at all, and I can't imagine why. She has delighted the rest of us no end."

"Perhaps that's why," Soong answered.

There were times when I wondered where he got his ideas. "I think you should teach the botany 'field class,' as Sally calls it. In fact, I suggested that she ask you—I know you read every botany book in Owen's library last year, and you know more about plants than anyone in all of southern California, I think. So why shouldn't you share with the twins?"

"There are times when you should listen better, Lena," he said.

"Do you want me . . ." I started.

"I always want you," he interrupted, looking at me in a way to make me blush.

Flustered, blushing in spite of myself, I continued, "I started to say do you want me to collect the books again?"

"OK, Missy," he teased, using the singsong cadence of the Chinese, "This Oriental man knows many mysteries, many secrets . . . he knows of places, high in the mountains, places of great beauty, where a man and a woman . . ."

"Soong," I whispered, raising my hand to his lips, "you embarrass me." He only smiled, and looked at me in a way to make me flush and feel warm.

"In the Soston Canyon, at three?" I asked, and he nodded yes.

A few minutes later, Sally intercepted me in the courtyard. "Miss Lena," she said, smiling, "you're all pink—you look pretty enough to put in a vase."

To her surprise, I gave her a quick hug. "There," I said, "I've been wanting to do that ever since you arrived . . . what? Three months ago, now? I am so very pleased that you've come to us."

Her brown eyes grew wide with pleasure. "I can hardly believe my good fortune," she answered, "six months ago I was more alone than I had ever imagined a person could be, and my prospects were dreadful. Now, here I am in Paradise— with you and Miss Willa and the twins."

"It must be those freckles!" I laughed; she looked at me for a moment, raised her eyebrows in an elfin expression, and said, "Of course, that's it! I knew they must be magic."

What brought Sally to us, in fact, was a combination of events, not all of them happy. Sara had happened to be in Philadelphia not long after the death of Sally's father, Justin Fairleigh. He was a learned, doubtlessly eccentric man who earned a modest living by translating scholary papers. His wife had died in childbirth when Sally was three, and he had insisted on rearing his daughter by himself, without so much as a maiden aunt nearby. He even provided her education, which was, as Sara explained, "classical, elegant and exuberant."

When Justin Fairleigh died, leaving his only child an exceptionally modest inheritance, she decided to go West. Since the only respectable way a single woman could go to the territories was as a schoolteacher, Sally made contact with an Ohio group which found positions for teachers. She was packed and ready to go when Sara learned of her situation, and persuaded her to postpone her departure until she could write to her friends on the Malibu. The rest, of course, is history. Happy history.


The beach cottage had been turned into a schoolhouse. Sally, the twins and several of Trinidad's children studied there each morning. We took our midday meal together—Willa, Thad, the twins, Sally and me. As the weeks wore on, we discovered Sally's first failing. She was not punctual. More often than not, she and the twins came running in late, out of breath and with hands dripping water from a hasty washing. We would hear them race up to the porch, Sally entreating the children to rush. "Hurry, love, hurry," she would say, and the twins would be giggling and rushing at the same time, and enter breathless.

Willa seemed unperturbed, but Thad did not. After three days of this, Willa did allow a mild reproach. "Trinidad doesn't like it if the bread is cold," she said.

"I know, I'm really very sorry. I shall try not to have it happen again," Sally had said.

But it did happen again, and this time Thad exploded.

"Kit," he said sharply, "your face is filthy. Go give it a proper scrub. And you, Porter, look at your hands."

Silence. We watched Kit's eyes, big and blue, fill.

"Mr. Reade," Sally said, "I'm afraid it's my fault. I rushed them so . . ."

Porter sat tall, staring at Thad, angry.

"Go!" Thad shouted at him.

For a moment I was afraid, for my son did not move, but continued to stare at Thad.

Willa took over then, standing and taking each of the children by the hand. "Enough, Thad," she said, "I'll wash them up, don't make such a fuss. Perhaps what we do need, Sally," she said over her shoulder as they left, "is a clock in the schoolhouse. Take the one in the second parlor. Thad, you can do that for Sally."

Thad sat, glowering at his plate.

Sally, trying to heal the breach, turned to Thad and said, lightly, "I deserve your wrath, Mr. Reade. I admit it. And I plan to reform. I'm sure I won't be late again, even without the clock in the parlor. In fact, I have my father's pocket watch packed away. It has a lovely chime, and I will keep it on my desk. So you really needn't go to the trouble of bringing in the clock."

Thad did not so much as look up. His rudeness—and his anger at the twins—made something boil up in me. "Your father's watch should be kept in a safe place, Sally. Especially so near the ocean, where sand or salt air can ruin it. The clock in the parlor is sturdy, and it chimes on the quarter hour. You will be adequately reminded. Isn't that right, Thad?"

I had used that tone with Thad no more than three or four times in the whole of his life. It brought him up, stiffly.

"Yes, Aunt Lena. I'll be happy to bring the clock this afternoon."

From the window of the cottage, Sally watched him approach, on horseback, across the stretch of dunes, picking his way carefully around clumps of dune grass. The clock was tied to the rear of his saddle, which caused him to dismount by swinging his leg forward and over. She noticed how gracefully he executed the awkward motion. It was not the first time she had watched Thad, unseen, not the first time she had noticed how easily he sat his horse. He was not so much taller than she, but he was tanned and lean, and he moved easily in this magnificent country. There was something in his face that she did not understand, but that touched her. She frowned. She had had so little experience with young men, men her own age. She hadn't a notion what it was about her that he objected to. Yet she knew there was something, and she knew she would have to find out what it was. Because Thad Reade could send her packing. He could cause her to lose her position, and she couldn't bear it. The place, the women, the children. No, she could not bear to lose them now.

She opened the door before he could knock, so that he needn't break stride while carrying the heavy timepiece. She directed him to the place she had cleared, in plain view of the table that served as her desk. "Wonderful," she said, clapping her hand. "Now we shall never be late again, I promise!"

To her surprise, Thad smiled. It was a shy smile, flickering as if to go out. "I am sorry to have made such a fuss. It wasn't worth having little Kit cry. She really is a nice little girl."

Sally looked at him then, weighing the risk, even while she knew she would take it.

"Why don't you like me?" she asked.

It brought him up short. Thad turned, walked to the window that looked out onto the beach. Without saying anything, he turned back to the clock and began to check its mechanism, busying himself with the setting and winding. And all of the time he was silent, he neither looked at her nor seemed inclined to answer.

Sally knew to wait.

He turned, sat on the table almost nonchalantly and smiled, widely this time. It was an engaging smile, very like his father's, though Sally could not know that. She only knew that it was the most charming smile she had ever seen.

"I've been wondering about that myself," he began, slowly. "At first I thought it was simply that you reminded me of the East—all the girls I met when I was in school in New Hampshire. There wasn't much that I liked about the East, and the girls seemed particularly silly."

"But..." she started, and he stopped her.

"You asked a question. Let me answer. It was obvious, rather quickly, that you weren't at all like the Eastern girls I had known, so I have been trying to think of what else it could be. The answer is hardly admirable."

Now he seemed to grow uncomfortable, his smile faded. "I didn't want to go away to school, not ever. All I wanted was to stay here, on the ranch. But my father and mother would not allow it. They insisted I be sent East to get an education. They said it would be impossible for me to be properly educated here. So I spent all those years—the better part of my life—in the East, and I cannot remember even one day when I felt happy there. Not one day."

Again, Sally waited, sensing his need to finish.

"Now, of course, the twins are to be educated here, on the ranch. Suddenly, it is not only possible to get an education here—it is possible to get an *extraordinary* education. You should hear what they have to say about your abilities as a teacher! You are an absolute wonder, they say. By the time the twins are ready for high school, they will be so far advanced that they might as well sail right into the university, they say."

Sally smiled, a very small smile.

And Thad smiled, too.

"They're right, of course," he went on. "You are a fine teacher—that's easy to see. But then, I've known all along that it was possible to stay right here, and learn all one need to learn. I've known that you don't have to go to Massachusetts or New Hampshire to get a proper education."

"I agree, of course," Sally answered, cautiously.

"So you see, I've resented you—unfairly, I know that now. It's not your fault that I wasn't allowed to have a Miss Sally Fairleigh. And it's not the twins' fault, either."

"Whose, then?" Sally asked, and the question surprised him.

"My parents," he said, "my mother."

"Could it have been that your father simply wanted his son to follow in his footsteps? Sometimes Eastern men, especially those who have gone to schools like Harvard and Princeton, have a special sort of attachment to the place. Could that have been?"

"No, I don't think so," Thad answered. "My father always said he wanted me to go East, but I think my mother could have changed his mind, had she wanted to. And remember, I was only nine when he died. After that, she sent me away."

"I don't know," Sally said, looking at him thoughtfully. "I suppose I'm only glad that she decided differently for now, for the twins. Perhaps it is selfish of me, but I'm terribly happy to be here. And perhaps it's arrogant of me, too, but I do believe I am as good a teacher as can be found in the East."

Thad smiled again, the clear, beautiful smile. "Now I have apologized, and I promise never to be rude to you again."

"And I promise never to be late again," she answered.

"I wonder which of us will break our promise first?" he asked.

"Me! I will, at least I hope it is me—because I think I couldn't bear having you feel annoyed with me again."

"But if you are late, I will be annoyed, won't I?"

She laughed, easily. "I know I shouldn't . . . but I have this terrible habit . . ." He was grinning, so she went on. "Your aunt has said you have a magnificent collection of shells, one started by you and your father, and she says you know a great deal about sea life. I'm wondering if I can tempt you to . . ."

"You do tempt me," he said. "No, I know what you mean, don't blush—your color is high enough—I can't take on any teaching duties for the time being. Ignacio is teaching me, I want to learn as much as I can about the ranch, and he is allowing me to do much of the work of the next rodeo. When that is done, I may have some extra time."

"I don't give up easily, I'll remind you," Sally said, following him to his horse.

"You won't have to," Thad told her.

She watched him ride away with a mixture of feelings. She was relieved that the tension between them had been banished, yet puzzled and troubled by his explanation, which signaled trouble between Thad and his mother. She admired Willa; she had felt a kinship to her—and now there was doubt. Why, she wondered, hadn't Willa allowed Thad to stay on the ranch, when clearly he loved it so? *Take care,* she told herself, *perhaps there is something you do not know. Be satisfied to have solved your own problem.*

Still, she couldn't dispel the small knot of regret that had gathered inside of her; she *was* pleased that Thad did not dislike her, so why should she have this small, nagging worry?

"You certainly look handsome these days, Thad," Willa remarked one morning as Thad happened on to us in the kitchen. "Don't you think so, Lena?" she asked me.

"Thad always looks handsome when he's happy," I said, looking into his eyes. "Of course, it is also true that Thad is always happy when he's on the ranch, and from what Ignacio tells Trinidad—and she tells me—Thad is fast becoming the new *patrón* of the Malibu."

He smiled with pleasure, and gave both of us a quick kiss on the cheek as he made his way out the door.

Willa looked at me in amazement. "A kiss!" she said.

"Don't be such a goose," I told her, "you know what makes a young man act like that."

My sister's eyes rounded in wonder. "Sally? Could it be?"

"It could and it is," I laughed.

Willa grew serious. "Oh, my," was all she said.

"Sally is probably the very best thing that could happen to Thad," I scolded her.

"It's not that, of course I approve of Sally. It's just that, well . . . I don't want Thad to be disappointed again. There have been too many disappointments for him, and they are both very young. . . . Sally is not the usual sort of girl, she has ideas—plans. I am not at all sure that her plans won't be in conflict with his."

I nodded. Sally had confided in me, too. I knew that marriage was not in her future plans, at least for some time. "I suppose I was only thinking in terms of now," I explained, "of the friendship that Thad needs. They are such children, really. . . ."

"She is eighteen," Willa answered. "At eighteen I felt I was quite grown up."

I nodded. "Perhaps you are right, should we speak to Sally?"

"I think not," Willa quickly said, "I think there is nothing for us to do but take care not to interfere. I trust Sally's good judgment . . . I only hope she sees, in time, how very vulnerable Thad is."

"What I said about Ignacio was true," I put in, "he is very pleased with Thad's progress this past year. I hardly see what can go wrong for Thad now—all he ever wanted to do was run this ranch, and that is what is before him, now. You've made that clear to him."

Willa smiled. "I can't help thinking how Owen loved to play at being the gentleman farmer—and how Thad really is one. He knows so much more about the ranch than Owen ever did. And the men are becoming more accepting of him. He seems to have his temper under control. As soon as they become convinced, he will be able to earn their respect."

Without thinking, I said, "Isn't it strange, Owen got their respect and he knew so little about the work. Thad can do so many things so much better than Owen. Some men just seem to command respect . . . Owen, and . . ." I stopped myself, surprised at the name I was about to utter.

Willa said it for me: "Connor. Connor McCord, you were about to say."

"Willa . . ." I stumbled, "I can't imagine why his name popped into my mind."

"Because he did have that about him . . . one just believed in him, I don't know why." She shook her head. "I haven't thought about Connor in a very long time."

"No?" I said naively.

"No!" she answered, sharply, surprising us both.

"Are you still that angry?" I asked.

She shrugged. "At myself, I suppose. It's hard to believe I could have been so stupid, could have allowed my . . ." she paused, searching for a delicate phrase ". . . my physical nature to so overwhelm my reason."

We sat, locked in separate silences. Finally I asked, "Do you think 'physical nature' was all of it? Could it be . . .?"

"No, it was all," she said, "awful, physical attraction. But that is buried now. Dead. Owen is dead, and so is Connor for me."

I thought it best not to tell my sister, at that moment, that Connor McCord was very much alive. Sara had told me on her last visit. We had gone up to the artist's shack on the hill with a bottle of vintage wine, we had talked and sipped and she told me she had seen Connor in San Francisco. "He's doing well enough for himself," she said. "He used the years he spent in prison studying hard-rock-mining techniques that were developed in England. Then, when he got out he made a survey of gold mines in the northern diggings, concentrating on those that had played out. He bought the old Empire Mine in Grass Valley, got it for a good price. The owners went around congratulating themselves for having unloaded it on this 'green Irishman.' They thought that a grand joke—*green* Irishman. Connor, however, got the last laugh. He's taken several millions out already, and says there are untouched veins that should produce for a decade or more."

"You seem to know quite a bit about it," I offered, delicately.

"Oh, I know a good deal about business dealings in San Francisco. It's how I spend my time—on gossip." She did not look at me as she spoke.

"I wonder where he came upon the money to buy the mine," I pushed on. "Certainly he didn't have a cent when he left here."

"I'm told he paid his investors off handsomely," Sara an-

swered. Then she insisted on changing the subject, so I knew
she would tell me no more.

I can't say why, but I decided against saying anything to
Willa about it. There was little chance that she would find
out on her own, I knew. Since Owen's death, Willa seldom
ventured beyond Santa Monica. Joseph was, in fact, running
the Land Company, but since we had no holdings in gold
mines, I doubted that he would come into contact with Connor, either.

I felt certain that Sara had decided to back McCord's venture, I had no idea why, and I knew I would not find out until
Sara was ready to tell me.


The twins dictated the rhythms of my life; they were gentle
rhythms, gentle years. I moved between the nursery and the
kitchen and the garden and the school. There were fishing trips
with Soong, music lessons, field trips, puppet shows, and galas
on the lawn. On Sundays, we picnicked on the beach and Thad
was always talked into giving impromptu lessons on whatever
sea life the twins were able to discover. He and Kit became
so involved in tide pools, and their secret life, that even Sally
began to clamor for more romping, less studying. And of course,
as Thad was drawn into the vortex of the family, he was thrown
ever closer to Sally. At times I would have to look away, not
to blush at the look on his face as he watched her. He was in
love, totally, as Thad always loved. I could only wonder how
Sally intended to deal with it.

I looked at the two of them together: The slim, handsome
young man, the rather plump, freckled girl (who would have
been described as plain, had it not been for her remarkable
expressions), and I could only shake my head in wonder.

"You're thinking that any girl in her right mind would be
panting after him, aren't you?" Willa asked.

"Actually, I wasn't," I answered. "Women on this ranch
have a habit of not being in their right mind, you know."

"She's braver than we were—braver than me, than Arcadia," Willa said. "I admire her, and yet I fear for her . . . for
Thad, too."


"They've torn it down again, Mother," Thad called, scraping
caked dirt off his boots before entering the kitchen, "it looks
as if they hitched a team to the fence and pulled the whole

thing down. Must have done it last night."

"Damnation!" Willa cursed, "that's the sixth time in as many months. I've got to think of something to stop it . . . those settlers have gone too far."

She was in a dark mood all morning, pacing through the house, as if trying to solve the problem of the bench gate in one fell stroke. On the days when she was at the ranch, Willa had taken to wearing a buckskin vest with her corduroy riding skirt. Now, when she went riding off alone, she strapped on a gun belt. It was, she told Sally and Kit, simply a precaution against rattlesnakes. They could not know that for a long time she had not worried about rattlers.

By mid-morning, Willa seemed to have worked something out. "I'm riding out to the north forty to find Ignacio," she called back to me, striding with determination toward the barn. I stood, watching, so that I saw Ignacio walk to meet her. They stopped under the pepper tree, she listened as Ignacio stood, turning his old straw hat in his gnarled hands, talking at unusual length.

"Twenty more pigs are gone today, that makes fifty this month, a hundred fifty this year. It's rustlers, we see the tracks," Ignacio said.

"Did you follow them?"

"*Sí,*" he nodded. "Into the mountains, through the pass by the Silver Lake."

"Who's the settler up there? Harding, is it?"

"*Sí,*" Ignacio said again, "there are three of them close by. All Yankees." His voice was flat; he was offering no comment.

"That's how they're doing it, then—the rustlers. The settlers are working with them, giving them a holding pen until they can get our livestock out."

Ignacio was impassive. Willa seemed not to notice.

"First things first," she said then. "I want a gatehouse built by the gate on the beach, and someone to be there all the time. Put some carpenters on it today. Next time someone decides to tear down the gate, we'll have a witness. The settlers have to know I mean business."

Ignacio turned to put her plan into action.

"Think of someone to put in the gatehouse—someone who won't be missed much."

Ignacio stopped, scratched his head.

"What about old Francisco?" she asked. "He sleeps most of the day as it is."

"Francisco, he is a very old man," Ignacio said.

"Then he will probably be happy with such an easy task," she answered, a little surprised that Ignacio should seem doubtful about her choice, since she knew he favored the old man.

I told her what Ignacio would not, that old Francisco might not be able to deal with whoever was tearing down the gates, that he might get hurt.

"If I thought that for a moment," Willa said to me coldly, "I would never put him there. No, the rustlers aren't coming through the front door. They travel over the mountains. It's the settlers who are tearing down the gate, and they know better than to attack one of our people."

"I hope you're right," I answered.

"I know I'm right," she told me.

When I didn't seem convinced, she went on, "Listen, Lena, I have no choice. It's no good complaining to the authorities in town. They only say they haven't the men to patrol my ranch, and they point out that since the whole matter is right now before the courts—the right of way—they are not sure they should be keeping the settlers off my roadways. Joseph is half-hearted about pursuing the matter. I've had to hire outside lawyers to take the case. I'm afraid my patience is fraying. I must do something, and I don't want to put a young firebrand cowboy down there who might provoke a fight. Francisco is perfect. He's not going to do much of anything but tell the settlers they can't pass. Then, if they go without permission, we'll at least know who they are."

Within two weeks, Francisco was installed in his new home and he was, as Thad put it, "happy as a clam." The ranch hands made an occasion of it, taking gifts of red peppers and tequila, giving him a proper housewarming. The toothless old herder welcomed everyone into what he proudly called his *castillo*, though it was hardly that. Sally and the twins made him a large picture of a herd of sheep, the mountains behind, "so that he wouldn't feel lonely."

Two days later, Willa popped her head into my office to say, "Ride with me to pay Francisco a visit?"

"My joints do feel stiff," I answered, only a bit reluctant to leave the books I was working on.

"It'll do you good, then. Come along," she said.

I quickly gathered up some oranges from the family orchard, packed them in a basket and we were off. It was a dazzling, fresh morning, so bright I had to shield my eyes as we rode down the beach, avoiding the glare of the sun on the water.

The old man stood in the doorway, waving a dirty towel at us.

"Have you had any other visitors?" Willa asked, after all the greetings were taken care of, and he had thanked us profusely for the oranges.

"*Sí*," the old man said, pleased with himself. "Yesterday, Señora Shurz and his neighbor, they come. They say, 'Let us pass, old man, it is our right.' And I say, 'No, señores, you cannot pass, I am very sorry,' I say."

"And what happened then?" Willa asked.

"He say he will have me arrested, and I say if that is so, that is so, but he cannot pass."

We smiled. "He can't have you arrested, Francisco," Willa told him. "Don't worry, I wouldn't let that happen to you."

The old man beamed at her.

"Señor Shurz, he made the ugly *gringo* face, but he left."

At this, both Willa and I burst out laughing, much to poor Francisco's dismay. *Gringo*, he realized now, was an insulting word.

"It's all right," I told the poor man, "Jacob Shurz is exactly that—an ugly *gringo*."

Riding back, we saw a hawk circling above the palisades, and Willa stopped to watch. "It's a peregrine," she said, "a female. She probably has a nest in those cliffs." She sighed. "I suppose I'll never again have the time I'd like for the falcons."

"Why don't you let Thad take over the ranch work you do, at least. He's certainly capable."

"Capable, yes," she answered. "It's just that he doesn't agree with me, either, on the matter of the right of way for the settlers."

"Oh?" I asked.

"He thinks I'm being too *inflexible*—that's Joseph's word. I'm sure the two have discussed it," she answered, irritated.

"I think it's a good sign," I came back, "Joseph and Thad talking together, I mean."

"What is a good sign," she said, calling back over her

shoulder, "is that Shurz turned back, as I was sure he would. I was right about that." She galloped off, then, her hair tumbling out and streaming behind. She raced down the beach, and I watched her, glad for her happiness, her triumph. Glad she had ridden off so abruptly, so I would not have to say what had been on my mind: That Shurz might be an ugly *gringo*, but he wasn't the sort to pull down gates. He was the sort to wait her out in the courts.

At sundown the beach was bathed in golden light, so that even our skins seemed to glow and our shadows flung out long behind us on the sand. Sally and the twins were far ahead, peering at the edge of the waves to see what might have washed in on the tide. Thad and I trailed behind.

"Let's sit on that log a bit, Auntie," he said, helping me lower myself.

We gazed out on the open sea, following the progress of a Panama steamer. "Your father always called this the 'sundown sea,'" I told him.

"Umm," he smiled, "I think of him still." We listened to the call of the pelicans, fishing long and low in a single row parallel to the shore, one and then another and another diving, headfirst, into the water and disappearing below the surface.

"I've often thought about Rose, too," Thad said.

"Rose?" I was surprised.

"For the longest time I had nightmares about that night," he said. I had to strain to hear over the sound of the sea. "It was always the same, the dream. She was in the solarium, in the bed by the window . . . the one where I had been that day. And I would hear the sounds—those terrible sounds she made when she was trying to get her breath."

"Oh, no, Thad—you didn't hear that, you weren't there?" He only nodded his head. I shuddered for him. I hadn't known that he was a witness. Dear God, I thought.

He went on, "I've never been able to forget those sounds. And then, in my dream, everything gets very quiet, and everyone knows she is dead and that I did it. I gave her the poison. No one blames me. They just won't look at me or say anything to me and I know, in my dream, that they all know I did it."

"My dear boy," I blurted, distressed. I reached for his hand, and he gave it to me.

"It's all right, now," he said in the same soft voice. "If it weren't, I don't think I could be telling you about the dream. I know I didn't kill Rose, I've always *known* that. But for a long time I thought that maybe if I had done something differently—if I had been nicer to her that day—maybe it wouldn't have happened. I remember thinking, in the early days when I was really young, that if I had just been nicer to her I wouldn't have been sent away, I could have stayed on the ranch."

I squeezed his hand. I could hardly bear it, thinking of the pain the boy must have endured. Thinking of how little use I had been to anyone during those same months of that terrible year. "You had nothing at all to do with Rose's death, Thad," I said, weakly, "as a matter of fact, you were especially sweet with her and she cared for you quite a lot. No one was to blame for her death—though I believe your father blamed himself, because he was the one who had bought the poison and had put it out. He wanted to kill some moles that had been troublesome in the garden. Did you know that?"

Thad shook his head. "No one ever told me, no one ever talked to me at all about Rose's death, so I didn't really know what had happened, except that in the morning she had been having a tea party or something like that with me in the solarium, all laughing and happy, and then she was dead. I knew that she had been poisoned, but I never knew any of the details. I don't have much of a memory about the trip East, except that it ended with me being left with Wen at St. Paul's. And Grandmother died," he looked at me, as if to apologize. "Even Papa was quiet and wouldn't talk to me. So I thought I must have done something to cause it."

"We were, all of us, in a dreadful state at that time," I tried to explain. "You were sent off to school only because of our unhappiness at the deaths—Rose, then our parents in quick succession. It was almost more than we could bear, Willa and I. You hadn't done anything in the least wrong, darling—you were perfectly innocent."

"I know that now," Thad told me, pressing my hand in reassurance. "Truly, Auntie, I do." He looked up to see Sally approaching. His face softened, he could not help smiling.

*Dear Sally,* I thought, *how lucky for us all that you have come to heal old wounds.*

\* \* \*

And it was a time of healing, of healing and laughter, and learning and . . . fun. Not just gentle, everyday fun where people smile at each other and make little jokes, but often outrageous, uproarious fun. I can remember laughing as I wrote in my journal: "It has taken many months, but finally Sally knows us well enough to reveal her second great flaw. She is a prankster of high order, or, as she dubs herself, 'the Grand High Wreaktress of Havoc.'

"It started innocently enough when I discovered a tarantula in my sewing box. I had flung it across the room, its contents scattering hither and thither, before I realized that the twins were squealing with laughter and the spider was in fact made of wire-covered yarn.

"Thad laughed with the rest, but soon the laugh was on him, too. I didn't know he could curse quite so well, until I heard him trying to pull on trousers whose legs had been sewn shut, and this before dawn on a morning when he needed to be off quickly. I must admit that Thad was a good enough sport about it when he discovered that Porter had done the stitchery, knowing that Porter's tutor had been the instigator.

"One prank fell upon another. The twins quickly became Sally's lieutenants, and they found more silent partners than I could have imagined. (Soong, I am sure, aided and abetted them on a number of occasions.) Willa met herself the other afternoon—*herself* being our pet donkey, all dressed up in some of Willa's cast-off finery, including the gray silk dress bought long ago at Worth's in Paris. With the gray, they had fashioned an extraordinary pink hat filled with flowers—the donkey's ears sticking through the flowers.

"How many more pranks? I can hardly remember them all. It is nothing to be playing the piano, have the F sharp suddenly make a rude noise. When we celebrated Thad's birthday two weeks ago, Sally insisted on making the cake. It was beautiful, and caused much tittering among the twins. Luckily, we had dinner that night—a warm evening—in the arbor, for the cake was a cardboard confection filled with *frogs* . . . real, live frogs that began hopping all over the place when Sally cut into the box. We had invited a group of young people for a party— most of whom Thad had known slightly, or who were known to Arcadia—and at first they seemed shocked. Then the laughter started—and even the proper young ladies got into the spirit, and helped chase the frogs about the lawn . . . squealing with feigned abhorrence all the while.

"The other young ladies seemed not to know what to make of Miss Sally Fairleigh. They waited and, when the young men seemed inclined to accept her, decided it might be a nice idea. I was pleased with them. It is nice to see Thad and Sally among a group of young people. They played songs on the Victrola, they danced and they strolled the beach, and at sunset—before the carriages left for Santa Monica—they had a sing. Kit and Porter hid in the arbor, and watched. Kit seemed to like what she saw, but Porter was vaguely disapproving. I wonder if he is a bit jealous that Sally seemed to prefer her visitors to him?

"Sally's birthday was yesterday. I must say, Thad managed to return the favor. He outdid himself, and I do believe he has had the last word in pranks. Joseph and Arcadia came for the weekend. Nothing much had been said of Sally's birthday. In fact, we had planned a quiet little celebration, with a cake and a few gifts. Before daybreak, I heard a knock on my door. It was Porter urging me to get up, and dress quickly. I heard Kit go to her mother's room, and Thad downstairs, waking Joseph. Arcadia was already up, to my surprise. (I should not have been surprised; Arcadia would, of course, be Thad's accomplice.) We went by horseback to the cottage by the beach where Sally lived.

"'Shhh,' Porter warned us, 'be very quiet.' We dismounted some distance from the cottage, and waited. 'Whatever is this all about,' Willa scolded, pulling Kit close to keep her warm in the morning chill.

"At first light, I caught a glimmer of something off the coast—a boat, two boats . . . three. As the sun broke over the mountains, they moved closer into sight: Three long skiffs, filled with men in brightly colored uniforms. As the sun caught them, and sparkled off the brilliance of uniforms and brass instruments, they broke into sound: music. They were playing a rousing march, a Sousa march . . . louder and louder until you could hear the sound over the water, loud and clear. The boats beached, a runner jumping out to pull them ashore, and out marched a full-scale, brightly uniformed marching band. Without a moment's hesitation, they marched right up to the cottage—in perfect step now, even in the soft sand, and played 'Happy Birthday.'

"Under cover of the noise we had moved around, in front

of the cottage, so we could see the moment of truth.

"Sally came onto the front porch in her nightdress, her hair flying in all directions . . . and she didn't seem to know where she was. She must have been sleeping soundly, so soundly that she walked onto the balcony as if in a dream, having no notion where she was, and she walked ahead, and fell off.

"It was a short drop to the sand; she landed on her knees, and the shock was all she needed to come full awake. She sat back on her haunches, looking at the band in wide-eyed amazement as they blasted out their music. Then she began to smile, to laugh. She saw us, let her eyes wander over each of us, let them come to a full halt with Thad.

"'You!' she shouted, and was up and running in an instant, chasing him. He raced ahead of her down the beach, turning to see if she was gaining, she still in her nightdress, her red hair blazing now in the first light, laughing. He ran into the water, splashing with his boots, and she was after him there, trying to dunk him under the wave.

"It was the beginning of a full day of games and fun for the young people—a boatload of whom had come out with the band, having set out in full darkness in order to be there for the surprise.

"Thad had planned separate picnics for the band members— which included the Loyal Order of the Oaks, as well as the high school musicians. It was, everyone agreed, exactly the sort of birthday surprise one should plan for Sally Fairleigh. And nobody enjoyed it more than Sally herself, unless it was Porter and Kit. This time, Sally made sure they were included in everything.

"Thad walked Sally back to her cottage that night. The sun had set, but it was not altogether dark yet. She felt at peace, and happy. 'Thank you,' she said to him.

"'Thank you,' he answered, and touched his lips to hers.

"She looked at him, ran her tongue across her top lip carefully, and said, 'That was very nice.'

"Thad smiled his beautiful smile, and kissed her again."

"I would like for you to see your brother," Willa said.

"Why?" Thad wanted to know.

"Because. Because I don't want to sever all contacts with him," she went on, "because he's my son and your brother and

I hope that someday, in spite of all he's done, we might be friendly again."

"He doesn't feel very friendly toward you," Thad said, watching to see how she would respond.

"Then you have already seen him?"

Thad nodded. He had been leaning far back in the swivel chair in the office, but now he came forward, his face softer.

"He sent me a message asking to see me. That was about three weeks ago. So the last time I was in town I went to his office."

"Why didn't you tell me?" she asked.

Thad shrugged, "I'm not sure. I suppose I felt as if I would be spying or something. I don't know. Maybe it was because I'm out here with the family, and everything is good with me, and Wen isn't having such a good time of it."

"What do you mean? What about his job with Charles?"

"He quit. At least that's what he says. I think Charles gave him the boot. So Wen has opened his own law office, but I got the idea that business isn't too good."

Willa's face became a study in confusion. Thad knew what she was thinking.

"No, don't try to help him, Mother. You've always done that, you and Papa and Joseph. This time let Wen work it out himself."

"That sounds like Joseph talking. Is it?" Willa asked, but in a friendly way, so he wouldn't mind admitting it.

"Yes, I have talked it over with Joseph. I had to."

"You *had* to?" She didn't understand.

Thad became uncomfortable. He stood, walked around the room. Willa decided to change the subject. "How is your brother doing otherwise?" she asked.

"He's gained some weight. He has a couple of rooms in a hotel on Broad Street, not very fancy."

"Poor Wen," she said with a small smile, "he does so love elegant surroundings. Perhaps it will teach him some humility."

"I doubt it," Thad answered, "he's going to be married, to Abby Fleet."

Willa was shocked.

"Married? Why?" she blurted.

"Why?" Thad laughed. "I can think of all kinds of reasons, but in this case it is because she has a big inheritance, and because she has what Wen considers to be, as he put it, 'excellent family connections.' Abby Fleet is going to see that Wen is welcome in all those monstrosities on the beach at Newport."

"Thad, be serious now. What's she like, this girl?"

Thad was serious when he said, "I'll be kind and say only that she is plain, so plain in fact that her family couldn't even buy her a lesser title in England or on the Continent."

"I'm not concerned with her appearance, Thad," Willa insisted, "tell me what sort of person she is."

"I don't know, Mother," Thad answered, "I've only just seen her a few times. Someone told Joseph that she is exactly as interesting as she looks."

Thad could see that Willa's hands were shaking as she rose.

"Mother, I'm sorry," he started, but she silenced him with a small wave of her hand. He waited.

"When?" she asked in an even voice. "When is the marriage to take place?"

"Next month, I believe. It is to be a small, private affair—five hundred of the best people, Wen says."

After another long pause, she asked, "What has he said about us, about his family? Surely the Fleets want to know something about us?"

Thad cleared his throat. She could see he was reluctant to go on, that he was trying to decide how much to tell her. "Don't try to spare me, son," she said, "I need to know it all. If you've had to go to Joseph, there must be something more I need to know."

"Wen asked me to go East with him, to stand with him at the wedding as a family representative. He has painted you as a recluse. Our 'family' is to be represented by Charles and Helen Emory."

Willa flinched, but motioned him to continue.

"I told him that I could not go with him, not under the circumstances."

"Is that all, then?" she pushed, knowing there was more to it.

"He asked me to find out if he had been disinherited," Thad said.

She reeled back as if she had been slapped.

"I'm sorry, Mother. Joseph said we shouldn't bother you

with this, that it would only hurt. Wen is convinced that you are going to leave everything to the twins, that you plan to cut us out."

"What?" she said, amazed. "Why does he think that?"

Thad shrugged again, anxious to be done with it. "I told him that, so far as I knew, there had been no change in Papa's will, and that you didn't plan any. I wasn't being entirely truthful, because I didn't tell him what you said about the ranch—about leaving it to me."

"Thad," she told him in a voice of great patience, "the ranch is only part of our family holdings, and it is not even an eighth of the whole. I plan to leave an equal share of whatever the inheritance is to each of the four of you. Joseph knows that, he could have told him."

"He did," Thad answered.

Willa bit her lip. Of course Joseph would have told him. Dear Joseph, he would have tried to spare her this.

Thad slipped his arm around his mother's shoulders. "Try not to be too disappointed in Wen," he said, "he is getting what he wants. That should make him happy."

"He will live in the East, then?" she asked.

"No, I thought he would, too. But Abby seems to want to come West. Or maybe her parents want her to come West. I understand that they will be able to live quite nicely on the combined earnings from their trust funds. Not lavishly, but nicely, Wen says. But he seemed happy enough at the prospect of coming into his share of the Reade properties, which Joseph assured him would compare nicely with Abby's inheritance."

"So he will be practicing law in Santa Monica?"

"In Los Angeles, actually. He says Papa's name is an advantage, out here especially. He'll need all the advantages he can get, I suspect, because I don't think he is a very good lawyer."

She squeezed her son's hand, but her mind was elsewhere. She was thinking about another marriage, about an apple orchard and her brothers all in a row, about Wen's birth and Owen's unbounded delight.

She tried to remember the last time she had felt delighted with Wen.

It was no accident that on the day in June 1911 when Wen was to have been married at the Berwinds' "The Elms" in Newport, in a garden wedding that would receive mention in society columns in Boston and New York, Willa chose to give a tea dance at the Malibu. It was the first time she had entertained formally since Owen's death, eight years before.

It was a soft, summery day, the ocean breezes riffled the palms and stirred the egret plumes on the ladies' afternoon hats. Chinese lanterns were hung in the trees, and Japanese parasols shaded the rattan garden chairs that ringed the greensward. A new dance floor had been built and covered with filigreed lattice work. The dance orchestra warmed up by playing popular tunes—"In the Good Old Summertime," a great favorite, and "Come, Josephine, in My Flying Machine." A yellow and white striped marquee had been raised as a place to dispense refreshments and, later in the day, a cold supper. We marveled at the carnival air and how pretty it all looked.

A list of more than one hundred names had been given to Francisco at the gate, a source of amusement to those of us who knew the old man could not read. Joseph described how Francisco had met them, asking for the names of the guests they had brought with them, and making a great show of crossing them off and waving them through the gate with welcoming flourishes.

Sara, Joseph and Arcadia stood with Willa in an informal receiving line, while I sat close by with the twins. Willa, in ice-blue lace and an afternoon toque that framed her face, looked the picture of elegance.

A group of Thad's friends—and Sally's, now—roared up in a Haynes Touring Car, following by others in an Oldsmobile. They gathered around the machines, admiring the shining brass fittings and, out of the corners of their eyes, each other. The girls were wearing lingerie dresses, all in white, sheer linens and lace insets, while the young men were natty in summer white suits and straw boaters. They were glorious to see, and they knew it.

Only Porter fussed at the finery. At the age of seven, he considered his short pants and blouse altogether silly. Getting him dressed for any formal occasion was a trial. "I should rather spend the afternoon off with Wing Soong," he argued, "or even in the schoolhouse, I should sooner be working on my history theme."

"Porter," I tried to sound stern, "it is equally important that you learn how to conduct yourself in company."

"Why *equally*," he wanted to know, "I can't believe it is *equally* important."

Kit came to my rescue. "Hush, Porter," she said in the voice of quiet reasonableness, "you cannot always do what you like. One way to learn discipline is to do things you don't like."

Porter looked at his sister and I could tell that he accepted, if not her logic, his fate. He took a seat, gazed ahead stoically, folded his hands. By mid-afternoon, I knew, Kit would have devised a game that would keep them happy and busy.

"Look at Miss Sally," Kit cried. Our eyes turned to see Sally, in a lovely white dress of the softest batiste with a pink ribbon in her hair. "Only Sally would think to wear pink and red." I smiled, watching as a young man led her to the dance floor.

The music began, a waltz. Couples drifted to the dance floor, moved effortlessly about in widening circles, smiling and swaying gracefully. "I suppose we should think about the two of you taking dance lessons," I teased, looking at my son. Kit and I burst into laughter at the face he made.

Music and dancing, filtered sunlight and champagne, leaves stirring gently in the breeze, the echoes of the ocean rising and falling; it was lovely enough, almost, to blur the image of another celebration on another seacoast.

"Wen will have been married by now," Willa said wistfully to Thad, as he waltzed her around the dance floor.

"I promise that you shall be the first to be invited to my wedding, Mother," Thad replied, "we'll have it right here in the garden, you can wear that Alice-Blue-Gown, and all the men will be looking at you, just the way they are today." The dress was of the softest voile. A high neck edged with delicate Valenciennes lace framed her face, and inserts of lace trimmed the bodice and tumbled down the skirt. It made her look soft and fresh, and ten years younger than her forty-seven years.

Willa smiled at her son's effort, and she thought, "At least I have you, Thad. At least we are friends now."

"We'll have a wonderful wedding for you, dear. I trust you will give me good notice."

"That I will do," he laughed, whirling her around in a wide circle, causing the other couples to look at them, and smile.

\* \* \*

What Thad had said was true. Willa did look stunning, and she was seldom off the dance floor. When she could, she begged forgiveness to do an errand. Wanting a few moments alone, she made her way to the library to search for a book she had promised one of her guests.

The house was quiet and dark. All of the servants were occupied out-of-doors. She moved easily through the hallways, into the library. If she remembered correctly, the volume she wanted was on one of the top shelves. She pushed the ladder along the wall, then climbed two steps and was reaching when a voice spoke out:

"Please don't be startled, Mrs. Reade."

She *was* startled; for a long moment she stood, with her arm raised in mid-air, swaying.

"That was what I was trying to prevent," he said, reaching to steady her, "I'm Philip Bourke, and I'm afraid I've frightened you. Forgive me, I'm clumsy on the dance floor as well and I sought out this place as a retreat."

Willa opened the draperies and let the afternoon light into the room. He was tall and wearing a rumpled linen suit. "Mr. Bourke," she said, "I don't think that we've met before."

"As a matter of fact we have," he told her, "eleven years ago I managed to get myself invited to the party you gave to welcome in the new century. You were wearing a gray silk dress and you danced with me, once. I'm not surprised that you don't remember, however, because you danced with the whole lot of us smitten young fellows that night."

"And you've been here, in California, ever since?" she asked, choosing to ignore the flattery. In fact, she had heard about Philip Bourke. He was one of the "progressives" who were working with Joseph to break the Southern Pacific's stranglehold on California. Joseph thought well of him, she knew, though she was not at all sure how she felt about the radicals.

"No, I haven't been in California all of that time," he answered. "As a matter of fact, I was only visiting then."

"Do you spend a good deal of time, then, at tea dances and New Years' celebrations?" she asked, pointedly.

"Not much at all," he countered, sipping on a glass of champagne he had with him, "the Reades are not that approachable, you see. I only go to tea dances as a subterfuge."

"Perhaps we should return to the dance," Willa murmured,

suddenly wary. Her business training had taught her to deflect requests for help—what she called "give me" sessions.

"Please, Mrs. Reade," he stopped her, "I promise not to keep you long. I only want answers to a few middling questions."

"Middling?" she asked, with a small smile.

"That night, eleven years ago—I was twenty-four years old and working on what was my first big job . . . I was a special investigator for the government, looking into charges of graft, corruption, internal problems. Just the sort of thing to get a young man excited." He grinned, "As a matter of fact, your husband's old friend, Mr. Roosevelt, managed to get my name on your guest list."

"You know Mr. Roosevelt?" Willa asked, her eyebrows raised.

"Not really," he answered, "I was just one of the young boys he was turning loose in his crusades to clean up the country. I arrived at your ranch successfully, I had more than a successful dance, from my point of view, with my hostess. But I was never able to speak to her husband. He was surrounded, even past daybreak."

Remembering, she felt a sudden surge of anger. They had been watched, that night on the beach.

"I am sorry," he said, contrite, "it was inexcusable to observe you. I can't tell you how I envied your husband . . . he seemed to me to have everything."

"Go on," she demanded in clipped tones.

"There was a man here that night who wasn't on the guest list. His name was Amos Proctor, and at one time he had been a Treasury agent. Two days later he was found dead in a rooming house in Long Beach."

Willa stared at him.

"Mrs. Reade," he pressed on, "I had been investigating Amos Proctor. His death ended that investigation, but I've always been curious about his appearance here that night. It's like an old puzzle with a piece missing. I'd like to complete it, to set my mind at ease."

"Is that why you came today?"

"In part."

"I see," she said. "And you don't wish to dance?"

"I do, I do very much. But first I wanted to explain to you, and I wanted to ask what Amos Proctor had to do with your family—how did you know him? And what did he say to your husband that last night of the century?"

"He spoke to my husband?" Willa asked.

"You didn't know?" he countered.

"How could I possibly know everyone my husband spoke to that night? You were there, you saw the crowd. As you say yourself, Mr. Proctor was not invited, and until this moment I didn't know for certain that he was on the ranch that night."

"You said 'for certain,'" he noted.

A voice called out for her. "Willa." It was Sara. "Where are you?"

Willa stared at Philip Bourke. "Here, Sara," she answered "in the library." She was grateful for the interruption, a fact which did not escape Sara.

"Mr. Bourke," Sara said, "I wondered where you had disappeared to." Then, ignoring him, she said to Willa, "Senator Bard and his wife have arrived and Joseph said you would want to know."

Willa left quickly. Philip Bourke would have followed had not Sara blocked his way. "When we spoke in San Francisco last month, I thought we had agreed that Mrs. Reade was not to be troubled by these questions. It was my understanding that if I helped you, none of my friends on the Malibu would be approached."

"Miss Hunt," he said to her, "I made no such agreement, I would not have. I am sorry if you misunderstood. I am trying to solve an old mystery, that is all. I'm wondering why you are so nervous about it. Unless, of course, you are trying to protect your former husband, and I've been told that isn't likely."

Sara recognized the bait, but refused it. "You want to solve an old mystery, you say," she went on quietly. "Mr. Bourke, I can only tell you that the memories you are stirring are painful. No good can come of your questioning Willa . . ."

"If I were certain of that, I would cheerfully stop, Miss Hunt. I admire Mrs. Reade, I have for quite a long time." He smiled. "But there are troubling coincidences. Amos Proctor was murdered a night after speaking to Owen Reade. Three years before, something brought Proctor out to the Malibu— something other than the opium smuggling ring he broke here. The name Connor McCord rises to the top of the broth—the

same Mr. McCord who is a rising light in San Francisco business circles. And at about the same time, Mr. Reade broke
with your former husband, who happens still to own a voting
majority of the California state legislature. There is a puzzle
there, Miss Hunt, and I would like to solve it."

Sara sighed. "Let's be frank, then, Mr. Bourke," she said.
"It is not some puzzle you want to solve, not just that. What
you want is to wrest the state of California from the control of
the Southern Pacific."

"From Charles Emory."

"Yes," she agreed, grim. She tucked her hand into his arm
and guided him to the hallway, where she could scan the house
for any unseen guests. Then she drew him back into the library
and closed the door.

"Joseph says he trusts you," she said, "and so now must
I."


Before the day was over, Philip Bourke would claim his dance
from Willa. "You were not truthful with me," she said, as they
moved about the floor, "you aren't the clumsy dancer you
claimed to be."

He smiled, looking at her directly, saying nothing. She
wondered if he would return to the subject of Amos Proctor.
If he did, she had decided, she would refuse to say more. If
Owen had spoken to the man that night, there was no way
anyone could know what was said. Owen had not told her; and
both men were dead now.

But Philip Bourke said no more about it. He was among
the last to leave that evening. He stood with Joseph at the edge
of the greensward, talking easily, not anxious to be off. It was
difficult not to notice Philip Bourke. He was tall, good-looking,
even his rumpled suit seemed to fit with a casual elegance. He
was the sort of man who was attractive precisely because he
didn't try.

When the stableboy brought his horse Bourke turned to
Willa, kissed her hand. "I suppose if I come to another of your
parties nine years from now, you'll look that much younger,
and lovelier still." He said it as a matter of fact.

"I hope you'll come back sooner than that," Willa heard
herself saying.

"May I?" he asked.

"Of course," she answered, "though I hope there will not be any more puzzles to solve."

"I promise," he smiled down at her from the horse.

"Then come whenever you like," she told him.

Behind her, Joseph looked at Arcadia with the slightest arch of his eyebrows, and she shot back a knowing look, registering both surprise and pleasure.

Philip Bourke would be back. He would also keep the promises he made that day—one to Willa, another to Sara.

Everyone agreed that the tea dance had been perfect . . . the weather, the music, the laughter. It had been a *charming day,* an absolute *delight.* Couples walking about, ladies rocking in the swing in the pergola, the smell of orange blossoms in the air.

"A dream," Arcadia had said as Joseph gently guided her around the dance floor, "a perfect dream."

The sun had set by the time Thad walked Sally back to the beach cottage. Halfway there, she insisted on removing her slippers and stockings, and Thad gallantly turned his back as she stripped them off, giggling.

"I think you've had too much champagne," he told her.

She hiccoughed as if in answer, which sent them both into a spasm of laughter.

"How can I be serious with a girl who hiccoughs?"

"Why should you be?" she wanted to know.

"Because my mother wasn't invited to her son's wedding today," he answered, cryptically.

It had the effect he had wanted.

"Whatever can you mean?" Sally pleaded. "Tell me, you must tell me."

He told her about Wen, about his mother's disappointment. "I think that in some strange way, the party today was for Wen. Except that Wen wasn't here." He paused, then added, "Which is probably a good thing, because he would have managed to ruin it somehow."

She looked at him, trying to fathom what had happened. "I'm sorry, that wasn't kind of me," Thad said, reproaching himself. "But I do feel Wen has acted badly, and has hurt Mother without good reason. I've told her that she will be the first to be invited to our wedding."

She looked at him, not sure she had heard him correctly. He smiled and pulled her to him. "I want to marry you, I'm asking you," he said.

Still she could not answer. Her mind was racing. He was dear to her, she knew that. Dear, terribly dear. She supposed she loved him. Yes, she did love him, she knew that. But she had not wanted to hear this, had not expected it and did not want it.

She raised her face and he bent to kiss her. Before she understood what was happening, she had wrapped her arms tight around his neck, their bodies were close. His hands caressed her back, stroked her sides so that he could feel the swell of her breasts. For the first time, they touched with passion. His mouth was on hers, moving, and she met him.

She pushed him away, hard. "Thad don't. Please, listen to me."

"Sally, I'm sorry," he said, not understanding, "please, I didn't mean to do that. I want you to marry me, that's all. I will wait for the rest, I promise I'll wait."

"No, it's not what you think . . ." she started, then stopped.

He was confused, she could see it flicker over his face.

"Listen to me, please," she said in a voice that ached with hurt. "I love you Thad," she said, "I do, I know I do. And I loved kissing you now, it wasn't that I wanted to stop. It's something else. I can't marry you now, not now. Maybe not ever. I don't know for certain, but I know it can't be soon."

"Why?" he cried out. "Why, when you say you love me? I want you to be my wife, to have my children. You know what our life will be—here, on the ranch. You said you were happy here."

"And I am," she sighed. "Today, today was a perfect day, an idyllic day. And this is the most beautiful place I've ever seen, and I love all of the people. And that is part of what is wrong, Thad. It's all too perfect, too easy. The future is all laid out, and I'm only just twenty-one years old. There is so much I don't know, so much I haven't done . . ."

His face darkened. "If you don't want to stay here, then . . . well, then we can live someplace else."

"Thad, don't," she said, "you belong here, it's all you've ever wanted. You've been other places, and you know. How could anyone who loves you even think of asking you to leave?"

He turned and walked away. She ran after him, tearing the lace of her dress in the ragged dune grass.

"Thad, please wait." She grabbed onto him and held him in a tug-of-war that ended only when he stopped. She stood in front of him, her chin out. "I do love you. Any woman in her right mind would say yes, and throw herself into your arms now. I'm not in my right mind, I'm sure. You of all people should know that. Please, Thad, give me time. I need more time."

He looked at her. "How much time?"

"A year, at least a year. There is so much to consider."

"What, exactly?" he wanted to know.

"Well," she stuttered, "children. I'm not sure if I want to have a whole passel of children."

"You're wonderful with children," he said, surprised.

"Maybe, but I'm not sure if I want to spend my life rearing them."

He looked at her now with affectionate exasperation. She had not said *no,* she had said she loved him and that he must wait.

"I have to decide what I want to do with my life," Sally said.

"What you want to do with your life," Thad repeated. His mocking tone made her wheel and walk quickly away, but now he was behind her. He caught her and held her, and when she stumbled he swept her up and carried her into the cottage.

She could easily have laughed or cried. She chose to laugh. He made her heart quicken, this young man. He made her feel warm and he made her breath come in short, sweet gasps.

He sat on her narrow bed, holding her in his lap, the swell of her breasts under the lacy bodice pressing into him. She found his mouth with hers, and let herself breathe into him.

When he had kissed her, he held her tight, rocking back and forth. And then he said into her hair, "I'll wait. I'll wait for a year."

She reached for his mouth again and kissed him with such violence that they fell back onto the bed. She moved into the curve of his body, and for an instant they arched together. Then he stood, pulling her up with him, holding her arms to her sides.

"I'll wait," he whispered harshly, "we'll wait together.

There's been no one before you and there won't be, not until
our wedding night."

She thought she couldn't bear it. She opened her mouth and
kissed his neck, thrusting her tongue into his flesh, feeling as
if she would burst. He moved his lips to her ear, and through
the tangled mass of her hair he whispered, "Do you think I
don't want you?" With his hand he guided hers to his trousers,
so that she could feel how hard he was through the cloth of
his suit.

"That's how much I want you," he said, "but I will wait."

We went to our beds that night in varying states of grace. I
felt as if I had watched a fairytale unfold. Willa was wistful
about Wen, but went to bed thinking about Philip Bourke.
Joseph and Arcadia kissed lightly on the lips, and went to their
separate rooms, wishing as they always wished that they could
sleep in each other's arms.

I woke before dawn to unfamiliar sounds; then it was quiet,
ominously quiet. I could not say what it was, until I heard the
sounds of boots on the stairs.

"Thad, what is it?" I called to his back as he descended,
strapping on a gun belt.

"Francisco," he called back.

In the kitchen, Willa was strapping on a gun belt as Trinidad
made the motions of starting a fire in the wood stove.

"Don't," Willa told her, "there will be no time."

My sister looked at me, her face grim. "I was wrong," she
said. "Francisco was killed, bludgeoned to death."

*Dear Lord.*

"Who? Where are you going?" I could not think to ask the
right questions.

"Ignacio thinks it's rustlers, and that means they're going
after the herd. They have an hour's lead, no more. We're going
after them." Her voice was taut, angry.

Joseph came into the kitchen, pulling on his suspenders.

"Wait, Willa," he said. "Send someone into town to talk to
the sheriff first. You don't know what you're up against."

"You go into town and tell the sheriff, Joseph," she came
back, her voice filled with fury. "This time, I'm going to stop
them. This time they won't get away with it."

The ranch hands were mounted and waiting in the back

courtyard, some of them with rifles across their saddles and others with guns strapped to their hips.

Trinidad ran to where Ignacio was tightening his cinch, and handed him a napkin filled with food. He put it in his saddlebag without saying anything. She stood, her hands limp, her body an expression of concern.

"I hate this," I said to Trinidad when they had left, "the guns, the fear, the violence. I hate it."

The morning was interminable. The twins occupied themselves with picking up bits of ribbons and colored papers from the lawn, the remnants of yesterday's tea dance. Suddenly yesterday seemed not real, a frivolity that could not have been. Today was real.

Joseph hitched a team to his brougham and left early, eager to get Arcadia into town and report to the sheriff before returning. He was intent on returning, he said, and I did not try to dissuade him, though I knew it would be difficult.

Soong worked in the family garden, staying close by, I felt sure, to watch after us. Only the Chinese, and a few old men— old hands like Francisco—were left about the home place. It could happen that the rustlers would swing back, though we knew it not likely. "Joseph agrees with Ignacio, and so do I," Soong told me. "It makes sense that they would think we would not expect a raid on the morning after a celebration, a Sunday. Probably they thought the old man would be asleep, or drunk. It's possible that he surprised them, challenged them."

"He would have," I answered, "I think the poor soul took his position so seriously, he would have tried to stop them."

Sally waited with us. Thad had raced down to the beach as soon as he heard, to make sure she was safe. "I was still awake," she told me, shyly. "I hadn't been able to get to sleep. That's how I know they passed less than an hour before Thad came for me. I heard the horses on the beach road."

Only Soong was able to work as the morning moved, ponderously, into the afternoon. The rest of us, our minds dulled by dread, could only wish the minutes away. We thought we heard the reports of rifles, but we couldn't be sure. Sounds played tricks in the mountains; it might have been a tree falling, a rockslide.

At four o'clock, they came riding in by ones and twos, silent. We ran out to watch them; we stood as they moved toward us. Sally saw it first: a horse without a rider, behind Willa. On it, a figure covered by a blanket.

Trinidad screamed. Sally caught her, and the two slumped to the ground.

It was Ignacio's horse. The body it carried was Ignacio.

# Chapter Eighteen

"Mama wants you to come to our house, Miss Willa...and Miss Lena, too," Aleja paused, and with a tiny intake of breath added, "...if you would be so kind."

*If you would be so kind*...It was a formal invitation, delivered by the solemn, dark-skinned girl in her black dress with its neat white collar. A Yankee dress, and Yankee words...*if you would be so kind*...Aleja had become a hybrid, too cultivated, too Yankee for her Mexican household, too dark-skinned, too flat-faced for the Anglo world.

Aleja had stayed close by her mother since the funeral. For most of that time, Trinidad had sat in the straight chair in the parlor of the house that she had shared with Ignacio, her hands in her lap, talking about the silent man who had been her husband. She told of small kindnesses, bringing out each memory as if to hold it in her hand like some polished, precious stone to be admired. His death had released her from the secrets, his goodness could now be told.

We listened, and nodded, and told our own stories; we spoke of the good times, the good things. It was, I thought, a stately way to mourn. In time, Trinidad would return to the present, to the future.

Willa strode ahead of me while Aleja waited, too thoughtful

to leave me behind. By the time we climbed the stairs and crossed the threshold, we could hear Trinidad's strangely stern tones: "Be silent, my son," she commanded, and the big, bearded man who stood beside her, dressed in the rough clothes of a peasant, was silent.

"Pablo!" Willa exclaimed, having finally recognized the boy in the man.

"Someone has sent to Pablo the message that his father is killed dead. Ignacio has said to Pablo, do not come here no more. But he comes, as you see, and he says to me, 'I must speak to Miss Willa.' I say no, but Pablo says 'let her say.'" Trinidad's voice was losing its firmness; a quiver had come into it. Her eyes would fill in another moment.

"I will speak to Pablo, Trinidad. It is good that you called me." Then, turning to the man, she nodded for him to follow her outside. "I don't want to disturb your mother," she said so that Trinidad could hear, "we can talk in the garden."

Trinidad was weeping quietly. Aleja went to her, and so did I.

In a while, I asked, "Who sent the message to Pablo?"

Trinidad would not look at me, but bit into her knotted handkerchief.

"Thad," Aleja answered. "Mama told him how to reach Pablo many months ago. They have been meeting, in San Diego I think."

Willa and Pablo walked toward the orchard. He was taller by a head than she, and thick. He wasted no words: "Do you know who killed my father?"

"No," she answered, "we surprised a gang of rustlers—about six in all. They had killed the old man, Francisco, and we went after them. We found them in a small box canyon near the Harding place. They fired first, your father fell at once. He was dead by the time we reached him. We stopped for him, and they got away."

Pablo nodded to the ground.

"Did you see any of them?" he asked.

Willa looked at him squarely, then she nodded.

"Did you know any of them?"

Willa continued to look at him, not wavering. Pablo frowned, repeated the question.

"I may have known one, but I don't know if he was the one who fired the shot that killed your father."

"What is his name?" Pablo asked.

"I'll tell you his name," Willa answered, "but I want something in return."

Her anger spilled over then. There was nothing in his eyes that could match the cold fury in hers.

"I want them caught, every one of the men who came onto my land and killed Francisco and your father. I can tell you a name and a place, and I can give you a description of each man and his horse. You will have to find out the rest. But first, I want you to do something for me."

He was wary now, but he waited to hear what she had to say.

"I want an army, Pablo. I want men who can fight, who will be a match for any who come onto my land to kill and steal."

Pablo walked over to the old split-rail fence, leaned back on it, the heel of one boot caught in the lower rail so that he looked the part of a man who had all the time in the world.

"How many?" he asked.

"How many will it take?" she answered.

"You are prepared to pay?"

"It's to be a business proposition, then?" she asked, just a hint of sarcasm in her voice.

Pablo shrugged.

"I can pay, you know that."

He nodded. "I will return in two weeks with fifteen, no more than twenty *vaqueros.*"

Willa walked a few steps from him, turned her back and clasped her arms together. Pablo waited. Finally she turned, exhaled deeply and said, "Manuel Rodriguez. Calabasas."

"How do you know this?" Pablo asked.

"Once, twelve years ago, two men were arrested on the ranch for smuggling. Rodriguez was one of them. I saw his face that night. It was the same man."

"And the others?" Pablo pressed.

She gave him some details, descriptions she had written on a notepad that same day. She did not need to refer to the notes because she remembered everything. She saw the faces of the men, their horses, in her dreams, night after night, riding around and around the canyon, shooting and then riding again in the same long, leisurely loops.

Pablo left without a word, but Willa seemed not to notice. She found herself gripping the fence rail so hard that a splinter lodged in the palm of her hand. She did not take it out, but stood looking at it, pleased at the pain it inflicted.

She had made up her mind. She would fight.

She found Thad in the barn and announced Pablo's arrival.

"I know," Thad said, "I sent for him."

This puzzled Willa, and for a moment deflected her from the subject she had meant to talk about.

"Why?" she asked. "How did you know where to find him?"

Thad did not look at her, but busied himself with a steam gauge he had been trying to fix.

"I got Trinidad to tell me," he said, adding, "she didn't want to. I convinced her."

"But why?" Willa insisted, "I want to understand."

Still he wouldn't look at her. "I thought he had a right to know that his father was dead."

Willa sat down on a decrepit chair, steadying herself when it wobbled. "Of course," she said, "I thought of it, too, Thad. But Ignacio had made such a point . . ."

"You were looking at it from Ignacio's view. I was looking at it from Pablo's."

She nodded slowly, agreeing. Or seeming to agree; she wasn't sure what, exactly, she felt.

"I've asked him to stay," she said, "I've asked him to hire some *vaqueros* to help us protect our herds, and our people."

Now it was Thad's turn to look to his mother with surprise.

He would say to Sally, later on that day, that he wished, just once, his mother would do the expected; he wished, just once, he could understand what makes her do the things she does.

And Sally had said, "You can see things from Pablo's view, but not from your mother's. Why is that?"

Thad had not expected Joseph to be so adamant. "I think it is a dangerous idea, hiring *vaqueros* to patrol the ranch."

"I don't see why," Thad countered. "The law won't do anything about it, and we've complained. The sheriff himself told me it would take every one of his deputies to go after the thieves who've been ransacking our herds—and he said he didn't think the taxpayers would think much of the idea, especially since Mother doesn't want any of those taxpayers setting a foot on the Malibu."

Joseph grimaced. "Even so," he said, "I wonder if it wouldn't be just as well to take the losses, considering . . ."

"That's what we have been doing, Joseph," Thad said, "until they killed two good men. The other thing we can do is arm every one of us—all the ranch hands, the servants, the orchard men. Or we can bring in men who already know how to use guns. Pablo has been a soldier for the past four years. He has the training . . . why not put it to good use to protect the ranch?"

"We're talking about hired guns, Thad," Joseph said with a sigh, knowing he had lost. "Do you think you and Willa can control them?"

Thad smiled somewhat condescendingly to Joseph, as if the older man were timid. "I think so," he said. "When you meet Pablo again, I think you will feel altogether better about it."

"You know him that well? He's been gone for quite a long time, Thad . . . men change . . ." He was careful to say "men," careful not to offend Thad.

"He hasn't changed," Thad said with certainty. "I've kept in touch."

Joseph started rummaging in the drawer of his desk. While fumbling, he managed to ask "How did that happen? I mean, how did you two fellows get together?" He might have been inquiring about a sporting event.

"We met a couple of times in San Diego."

"He crossed the border so easily?" Joseph asked over the jumbling noises he made in his awkward efforts to find an ashtray.

"He was working for the president . . . Diaz . . . he had something to do with the police, so he could come and go as he pleased."

"That was before Diaz left, I suppose?" Joseph asked idly.

"That's right. Before."

"So Pablo had to clear out, too? Is that right?"

Joseph's casual questions had thrown him off guard; now his face became set. "I suppose," he answered. "I don't think politics makes much difference to Pablo. I think he only wants to be a good soldier—and he is that."

Joseph smiled, to take the edge off what he was about to say. "I wonder—can a man be a good soldier if he doesn't believe in his cause? Old Ignacio told me, once, that he did not like Diaz, that Diaz was not good for the peasants—Ignacio's people. That was why he did not want to see Pablo. Did you know that?"

He could see the anger rising in Thad, and for a moment he feared he had gone too far.

"If you had seen Ignacio's face blown away," Thad said, "if you had seen Mother's dress splattered with his blood . . ."

Joseph put his arm around Thad's shoulders, then, and pulled him to him in a hug. "I know, son. I can imagine," he said. "I only hope that Pablo and his *vaqueros* can prevent another scene like that. You will tell him, won't you—prevention is what is necessary, protection."

Since Ignacio's death, Willa had been out of my reach. It was as if she were tightly coiled. I feared that the slightest disturbance could make her snap, could send her flying apart. She spoke in short volleys to give commands or ask questions. She had the same, frozen look on her face all day long, and there were times when I wondered if she had turned herself into something mechanical. None of us, not even Kit, seemed to know how to talk to her. We skirted any issue we thought might make her even tighter. We did not speak of Francisco or of Ignacio.

Willa had not cried and, so far as I could tell, anger was all she felt. The tension was building in us all, it was becoming oppressive.

In the midst of this, Philip Bourke appeared—without notice or invitation.

"You said *any time,*" he said pleasantly to Willa, with that half-smile that might have been mocking. I wondered if he knew all that had happened since the day of the tea dance.

"I heard about the trouble," he said, answering my question. "Bad stuff, very bad." Then he asked. "What are you going to do about it?"

Her eyes were flashing, and for a moment I thought she might strike him.

I tried to intervene. "Mr. Bourke," I began . . .

"Be quiet, Lena," Willa snapped, so rudely that I would

have been hurt, had I not been so frightened.

All the while, Philip Bourke was standing in the entrance to the parlor, his hat in his hand. Now he tossed it carelessly onto a settee, and walked inside. "Miss Lena," he said, "I wonder if I might trouble you for a glass of water? It's been a long, dry ride."

I understood that he was asking me to leave, but I stayed outside in the hall to listen.

"Do you think you are responsible for their deaths—the two men who worked for you?" he asked bluntly.

"Yes," Willa blurted, all impatience and anger mixed, "of course I'm responsible, who else? I gave the orders . . . I *am* responsible."

"All right, good," he said, as calm as she was riled, "I'm glad you've got that straight, at least."

I could not see Willa but I heard the sounds she made— words, jumbled, as if trying to form thoughts. Philip Bourke's calm seemed to confuse her, but to release something, at the same time. He didn't push her, though, but just waited for the words to get in order. At last she said, "I presume you didn't come for a social outing because as you may have noticed, I'm in no mood to be pleasant."

I went quickly for the water, and when I returned I paused again before entering, hearing Philip say, "A man named Rodriguez was found over by Calabasas—his throat slit. And two others, the same night—same style of knife work. Very fancy. The rumor is they were part of a gang that stole just about anything they could get their hands on. I wondered if they might be your rustlers."

I entered the room in time to see Willa's face go cold.

"*My* rustlers?" she said in a way that could make water freeze. "What do you mean, *my* rustlers?"

"I mean the men who have been cleaning out your livestock."

"How would I know? What are you trying to say?" She kept asking questions in a belligerent way. Though it was making me uncomfortable, it didn't seem to faze Philip.

"I thought you might have gotten a look at the men—you were pretty close, after all. I thought you might have recognized one of them . . ."

"I don't quite know where you get your information, and

it is beyond me that you should think I socialize with cattle thieves."

He smiled. "You socialize with me, so I figured you weren't too particular."

To my absolute amazement, she laughed. Willa actually laughed. I had expected her to explode, I thought the anger she was holding in would spill out, but instead, she laughed.

Just as suddenly she was serious again, but it was a more peaceful kind of seriousness. "I was riding next to Ignacio when he was shot," she began, "it was . . . it was the worst . . . I couldn't . . ."

"Yes, of course you couldn't," Philip said in the kindest possible way.

"I am sorry that I was so rude to you," Willa said, "and of course I remember telling you to come any time. I'm pleased that you did."

I made an excuse to leave then, but later on Willa would confide in me what happened.

She said to him, "You asked what I intended to do about the trouble here. I'll tell you. There is a young man, Ignacio's son Pablo, who is the same age as my son Thad. Well, Pablo has been a soldier in Mexico for the past several years—but he was born on this ranch and raised here, he knows it well and feels some affection for it, I believe. He is going to recruit a group of men—*vaqueros*—to serve as protectors."

"Whoa!" Philip interjected, squinting at her in a curious way, *"Banditos*—hired guns. That could be rough, you know."

"Have you been talking to Joseph?" she said, accusingly.

"No, I promise I haven't. But I know Joseph wouldn't like it."

"I said *vaqueros,* not *banditos,"* she replied.

"Men handy with guns and knives," was all he answered.

"They aren't here yet," she came back. "Pablo won't be back with them for two weeks or so."

"So you are declaring war, then?"

"Not war," she answered, "why do you put words in my mouth? All I want to do is protect my people and keep my land free. I want to be left alone, that is all."

"By alone, do you mean you want to keep the settlers from passing through, as well?"

"Yes," she was definite. "We offered them a reasonable right of passage and they refused, saying they should be able to come and go as they please, using any route they wish. That is unacceptable, and now I am tired of arguing with them. Especially since I feel sure they are aiding the rustlers."

He looked at her and said, "I'm afraid you're asking for trouble, my friend."

"Are we to be friends, then?" she answered, in the same offhand way.

"I hope so," he said.

"Then I will try once more to make you understand—I'm not asking for trouble, I'm simply answering it."

"I wonder what your friend Mr. Roosevelt would have to say about your big stick."

She touched her hand to her hair in a gesture that was, somehow, delicate. "I know Mr. Roosevelt thinks this coast to be one of the most beautiful he's ever known. I know he hopes it might survive man's intrusion. He told me as much."

"Is that why you want to keep everybody out?" Philip asked.

"It's at least part of the reason . . ." she said, thinking. "Perhaps you know that I have a particular fascination with raptors—for peregrine falcons especially. Like so many other birds, they are being forced out of their nesting grounds . . . It seems to me that we must leave some places on this earth where the hawks can fly."

"Are hawks more important than people, then?" he asked.

She answered truthfully. "I don't know. Perhaps you expected me to say 'of course not,' but I'm not sure that man is inherently so much more important than other living things. No, it's not even that—it's that I believe man has to take some notice. I am so often appalled at the havoc men wreak when they move into a beautiful place. I don't want that to happen here."

Philip Bourke turned the conversation back to hawks. As it happened, he knew a good deal about peregrines. His uncle had been a falconer and he had been fond of that particular uncle.

After that, the talk ranged over a wide number of subjects— people they both knew, places they had been, amiable talk that happens when two people are becoming acquainted. In the course of the conversation, which went on for better than an hour, Willa happened to ask, as if it were of no consequence whatever, "How did you happen to know about the killing of the rustlers?"

And Philip had answered, with as little concern, "I read about it in the papers."

"The *Times*?" she asked.

"Not at all," he laughed. "I try never to read Mr. Otis' sheet—his hatred for the Southern Pacific is genuine enough, but so too, I'm afraid, is his contempt for reformers, in which class he happens to put me. No, I think it was one of the local papers—perhaps the *North County News*. I can't remember, for certain."

"So you are another of the wild progressives, are you? I'm not sure my reputation can withstand association with any more radicals."

"I promise not to try to convert you," Philip had said.

And Willa answered, "I am not a political person, Mr. Bourke. You should know that."

"Philip," was all he said.

"Philip," she agreed.

Philip Bourke came often after that. Sometimes he rode out with Arcadia and Joseph in Joseph's new Oldsmobile, other times he turned up on horseback. He was one of the most unassuming men I think I've ever met. From Joseph, we knew that Philip had made a small fortune in real estate, enough to allow him a certain freedom. He was far from wealthy, but then wealth had never been his goal, he told Willa.

"Do you think that odd?" I asked her.

"Why, yes, I suppose I do," she answered. "Don't you?"

I could only shake my head at her. "Sometimes I wonder, sister, how you can know so much about the behavior of hawks, and so little about the behavior of men."

This conversation took place during our mid-morning session as she sat at the edge of my desk. As usual, when she tired of a subject, she simply changed it.

"Aleja plans to stay on here with her mother, she says—if there is some work she might do."

"What kind of work?" I asked, worried. We had been trying—Willa and Joseph, and Sara, even—to find Aleja a business position, but without success. What had become eminently clear was that if we forced the issue with the companies in which we could wield power, Aleja would be employed, but only under duress. It would not be pleasant for her, we knew. Aleja was too shy to endure the kind of unpleasantness she would most certainly have to confront. Even Joseph was amazed at the resistance to hiring a woman. "A college-trained woman is bad enough," Philip had said one recent evening, "but a college-trained Mexican woman, well . . . you might as well ask them to hire an Eskimo."

"She says she is willing to do anything—cleaning, cooking . . ."

"Oh, Willa, she can't," I groaned, "not after all that training. We must find something better than that."

"What do you have in mind?" Willa asked, quietly.

I understood at once. "We've run this ranch office in the most slipshod manner possible," I came back. "I'm always so rushed with everything, and you have more than you can manage with the other businesses. Why not make her office manager here? I can train her, then she can take it all over and it will be handled ever so much better."

Willa hugged me. "I just didn't want you to feel pushed out," she said.

"I'll gladly dance out of here," I answered, feeling especially fond of Willa for the way she had told me.

"Thad seems to be doing well as the head boss man now," Willa went on. "He doesn't command the respect they gave Ignacio, but I'm not sure that anyone can. And Ned Lattimore has been surprisingly helpful. Thank goodness for Ned."

"He's worth two men," I chuckled, "and it's a good thing too, because his brother has been drunk for three days now— or had you noticed?"

"I noticed," Willa sighed, "but he's harmless enough when he's drunk, and as you say—Ned does the work of two, so I guess we needn't complain."

"I think you'd better tell Thad, then," I said, "because I heard him complaining to Ned the other day—and I don't think Ned liked it one bit."

"Oh, dear," Willa answered, "I do wish Thad would grow up and discover the meaning of compromise."

"Maybe," I said wickedly, "the two of you can learn together."

She was still too pleased with me on the matter of Aleja to be angry.


Pablo returned as he said he would, within a fortnight, bringing with him sixteen men, who, in turn, were followed by a dozen women—some walking, some on wagons—as well as half a dozen dirty children. The men wore sombreros and had cartridge belts crossed on their chests. Willa's army had arrived. She went on to review the troops, feeling a mixture of excitement and fear.

To Pablo she said, "Who are these women? Why are they here?"

"*Soldaderas,*" Pablo answered. "In Mexico they go to war with their men. They cook, they provide all their needs, it is easier that way."

"These men are soldiers, then?"

"Most were *rurales*—what you call federal police. They worked for President Diaz."

"Diaz is in exile," she reminded him.

Pablo nodded.

"So these men are deserters?" she asked.

Pablo did not answer.

All the while the men sat their horses, staring at Willa. I knew, by the way she held herself, that she was struggling to maintain a presence. She was playing *La Patróna*.

"Put them in the far bunkhouse," she ordered, "I've had it cleared. There should be enough room."

"They want to make camp on the beach—at Indian Point."

The *rurales* watched her, their dark eyes waiting.

"The bunkhouse," Willa said firmly. "If they want to camp there's a clearing behind it, but tell them to mind their fires. Be firm about that, you know the fire danger here."

Pablo did not like it, she could see. For a moment she was afraid he would argue with her, and she would have to explain to him that she did not want those men close to the schoolhouse, which Sally now shared with Aleja, and where the children were each day.

But Pablo seemed to think better of it, and simply repeated what she had said. The men talked among themselves. They were not pleased, it was easy to tell. The women and the children moved closer, staring at us with bold eyes.

"They are called *Adelinas*, sometimes—the women," Aleja told us under her breath. "Those with the very dark eyes and blue-black hair are Indians, those with paler skins, Spanish. They actually go into battle with their men, sometimes the children act as gunbearers. They say that when a man falls, his *soldadera* will pick up his gun and fight on."

"What a barbaric life," Sally said, staring back at the women without blinking.

"Pablo told me the government allows it to save money. The women feed the men—they steal or barter or, when they can, buy food, they nurse them when they are hurt or sick, they keep them happy."

At this, to Aleja's great embarrassment, Sally guffawed.

"In other words," she said, "the government uses the women to do their dirtiest work."

"It is a hard life for the women, and for the children," was all Aleja would allow herself to say.

"It is barbaric," Sally said again, unwilling to give in, "and it produces barbarians." As she said this, one of the children— a boy, perhaps nine, with two long streams of mucus running into his lips—walked purposefully over to a lemon bush at the edge of the courtyard and proceeded to pick three of the largest fruit. What was amazing about the act was that he looked at us the whole time; clearly, it was an act of aggression. The men were still occupied among themselves, trying to decide if they would accept the order to repair to the bunkhouse, but the women saw, and they waited to see what we would do.

Porter came slamming out of the house at this critical juncture. He saw what had happened and, without breaking stride, headed for the boy saying, "Put those down!"

Sally put her hand on my arm, a silent message.

Porter was at least two years younger than the boy—and a full head taller. Still, I knew he loathed the idea of physical conflict. I had never seen him confront another child in this manner.

"I said put it down," he repeated. The message was clear, it did not have to be translated. (Later, I wondered why Porter didn't speak in Spanish—he knew well enough how to.)

The boy threw the lemons at his feet, trying to mask defeat in contempt. Porter calmly picked them up and, surprising me once again, handed them to Willa.

It was a small incident, but it had its effect. The *soldaderas* now looked away, allowing their eyes to roam over the house and the hills beyond, not looking at the knot of women who stood together on the arcade.

"They say the bunkhouse will do," Pablo said to Willa.

"Tell them to be careful about fires," Willa repeated once again, as much to exercise control as anything.

With the arrival of the *rurales* and their *soldaderas,* the whole tenor of ranch life changed. Their very presence—the sounds and smells that emanated from their camp, the raucous laughter and, sometimes, the arguments—made it seem as if we had been transported to another country. Knife fights, we knew, were not unusual. Occasionally a gun would be fired.

"Sometimes I think they will declare war on each other and we will wake up one morning to find everyone in that encampment dead," I told Soong.

He was wary of the *rurales,* and with good reason. They had quickly established an attitude of disdain for the Chinese orchard men and gardeners. In the first week there had been several incidents that could have been ugly. The *Adelinas* and their children were like some pestilence in the orchards, stripping a tree of its fruit in a single hour. When the Chinese objected—in their smiling, deprecatory way—the Mexicans only spat on them. Only Soong—because of his size, I believe, and his Spanish—could dislodge them from a tree. This, of course, did not endear Soong to the Mexicans, and he became a target.

"I've already spoken to Willa about the way they treat the Chinese," I told Soong, "and I'm going to say something to Thad and Pablo. If anyone can control these strange creatures, it should be Pablo."

"Remember," was all he said, "I was the one who helped Wen escape after the attack on Pablo's sister. Don't think he has forgotten. And Thad, too—I interceded when he whipped the young Chinese that time. Those two, Thad and Pablo, have long but selective memories. Don't count on their help."

Still, we lost no more pigs that year, and our herds went unscathed. Trespassers—including surveyors who came with court orders to lay out a county road—were turned back. When they returned with lawmen to oversee their intricate measurements, they were carefully watched. (These same careful measurements were undone by pigs turned loose to root up the place.)

Rumors began to circulate in Santa Monica. It was said that men had disappeared into the Malibu, that they had gone in and nobody had heard from them again. It was said that Willa Reade herself patrolled the borders, a six-shooter on each hip.

That much, I knew for sure, was wrong. Willa occasionally did visit what she called "border points" but now she was driving her Pierce-Arrow, and she kept the gun in the pocket compartment.

Sara had spent the fall and the early part of the winter in Paris. The Atlantic crossing had been a trial, she said, and she had looked forward to nothing so much as relaxing at the ranch, where she expected the usual pastoral peacefulness.

"What has happened here?" she moaned, "the Malibu feels like an armed camp."

In fact, we had grown somewhat used to it by now, had even learned to coexist with the separate camps—the *rurales* and their women, the ranch hands and the Chinese. Until Sara arrived to point it out, I had become inured to the tension that existed.

Minor incidents continued to occur. Early one morning I went to the family orchard to pick some tangerines for breakfast, and surprised one of the *Adelinas* stripping a tree.

A Chinese gardener—little Loo Sin—was watching her, but had said nothing. My appearance reminded him that he must make an effort to protect the trees, and he came running at the woman, urging her in rapid Chinese to stop.

Fear flickered momentarily over her face at the sight of the two of us, then it was replaced by bravado. She flew at the poor little Chinese and pummeled him to the ground, screeching all the while. I ran to his aid, trying to pull the woman away, and before I knew what had happened, her fingernails tore a long slash down my cheek.

Then I had a sense of her flying through the air. It took a long moment to realize that Soong had arrived and had flung her from me with such force that she hit the ground with a hard thump. She sat there, stunned—looking at Soong with purest hate in her black eyes, muttering imprecations under her breath.

"Get out of this garden," Soong said to her in his perfect English, then he repeated it in Spanish, adding some words I was not familiar with, and which produced an animal, hissing sound low in the woman's throat.

I went to find Thad and Pablo, ignoring for the moment

Soong's wish to wash and clean the scratch on my face. I wanted them to see it, to see what the Mexicans were capable of doing.

"You must do something about those women, they are stealing everything they can get their hands on . . ." I began.

"It is their job to get food for their men," Pablo said.

"They are given enough food and you know it," I told him. "They have no right to scavenge—to act like animals."

Thad looked at Pablo, who looked away.

"We'll straighten it out, Auntie," Thad said, "you'd better get that scratch cleaned out."

"That woman, she threatened Wing Soong," I insisted. I would not let them ignore it. "I want it stopped—this terrible disdain for our Chinese."

"They may be your Chinamen, Miss Lena, they're not mine," Pablo said, with an insolence that was new to me.

I was struck dumb. "I helped rear you, Pablo," I said to him, "and so did Wing Soong and the other Chinese. They were kind to both of you when you were children, and both of your fathers admired and respected Wing Soong. You would do well to remember that."

"I remember times when the big Chinaman worked against us," Pablo said, his face set.

Soong's words came back to me, and I shivered. "I'm sorry you have such a selective and faulty memory," I said, as cold as he, "but I have to insist that you keep those people out of our gardens, and away from the Chinese."

"Mother's already given us a lecture on the subject," Thad said, drily. They turned and started to walk away from me. "Stop, both of you," I said. "I want an answer. Are you going to do anything about what is going on here?"

Pablo answered, "I cannot control human nature—it is in the nature of the Mexicans to hate the Chinese heathens."

There was little time for us to be alone. Soong was preoccupied with the gardens as well as with the work with Homer Lea, training young Chinese at his Western Military Academy. I was beginning to believe that the long, private afternoons in the hills were a thing of the past. The few times we managed to go off together, Soong was wary the whole while. I knew he worried that one of the Mexicans would follow us and discover our secret. It would be a powerful weapon to use against us.

For this reason, I was surprised when Soong said we must meet. We chose an isolated spot near the beach, a place overgrown with maidenhair fern, warm and sheltered from the winds. It was, in fact, our favorite place. We had spent long, pleasant hours there, but this was not to be a time of pleasure.

"You are troubled. Tell me why," I began.

He smoothed my hair from my face with his hands, holding to me at the nape of my neck, looking as if to see within me.

"Troubled . . . yes. Things are not as good at the ranch, you know that. I worry that you or the children may be caught . . . hurt." With a finger he gently traced the scratch left on my face by the *soldadera*. "She-devil," he said under his breath. "The *rurales*, they deserve their reputation."

"Reputation?" I asked.

"For being vicious, cruel. The peasants of Mexico hated—dreaded—them. That is why Ignacio was so ashamed of Pablo, for being one of them."

"I should tell Willa; if she knew . . ."

"She knows," Soong said cryptically, but before I could question him, he went on.

"I think you should go into the city with the children. Say you feel they should be in a school for a time. Say anything you need to say, but go."

I was shocked. "Go into the city . . ." I echoed him. "Soong, why would we do that? Sally is teaching them here, she is remarkable, you said so yourself. And the ranch hands' youngsters, they get the benefit of the schooling too. How could I possibly close the school? What would Sally do?"

"I know," he said, walking away from me, folding his arms and looking out to sea. "But when Sally leaves . . ."

"Leaves?" I said, further surprised. "Why would she leave? She hasn't given even a hint that she is dissatisfied—except, of course, with the *rurales* and their women, like the rest of us."

"Pablo has had an effect on Thad," was all Soong would say. "And that has to have an effect on Thad and Sally."

"Even if Sally should leave," I went on, "why should I take the children away from here—from you? They belong with us both, I belong with you."

He took my hand and pulled me close.

"Yes, you do, my love. And we will always be together, even when we are apart." It was a solemn pronouncement; I did not want to understand.

I looked at him, and knew my eyes told him not to say it, not to go on.

"We must be apart."

He had said the words. They came crashing on me with such force I thought I would suffocate, thought I could not breathe. I let the silence grow between us until it became too heavy to bear. Pushing it back, pulling away from the darkness, I said, "When?"

"Soon," he answered. "Sun has sent for me. The revolution has started, at long last. The last contingent of officers are trained. Homer is with Sun in France now, raising needed funds. I am to go directly to Nanking."

Dark edges moved about the periphery of my vision. Concentric circles of darkness closed in, until I could see only Soong's face. I pressed into his chest, trying to hold the darkness back. I would not allow it to engulf me.

I opened my eyes wide, took a deep breath.

"It is decided, then? Everything is decided?" I asked.

I knew the answer. It had happened. I had tried with all my might to think that it would not, I had pushed it away from my consciousness . . . even while I knew, I must have known, that it was to be. I could not let him go, I could not survive without him. And I knew that I could, that I would. That I must.

"Why?" I whispered. "Why must you go?"

He traced his long fingers up and down my arm, and in a voice meant to comfort, said, "Why, when I have a family here? Why, when I have happiness that I thought would be denied me in this life? Why, when I feel for a woman more than I imagined possible to feel for any being? Why, when she has given me a son who is beautiful in every way? Because of that, just. Because there is a greater need, greater than personal happiness, greater even than duty to family.

"I believe," he continued, "in Sun Yat-sen's mission. It is my own. I need to take part in the struggle, the greater struggle."

I tried not to cry, but I could not stop the tears. They fell softly, steadily. Soong spoke in lulling tones.

"If I should stay, Lena...and you know this...one day my son would see me as Thad and Pablo do—as a servant, an inferior...as a Chinaman."

"No," I cried out, "he would not. Not Porter."

"Perhaps not," he said to placate me, "but he would hear the others, and there would be a day when he would grow embarrassed to find his old friend Soong's life had been spent growing vegetables...There can be nothing else for me here. Look at me, Lena. Listen. You know it is true...you see what is happening to Aleja. Willa and you are trying to make a place for her at your table, while her mother still serves that table."

"Trinidad does not have to do that," I objected. "We don't think of her as a servant..."

"Don't you?" Soong asked. And then he added, to ease the sting, "Even if you didn't, Trinidad herself feels more comfortable in that position...she has served for so long, it is how she thinks of herself."

"What has she to do with you?"

"Nothing," Soong answered, "and everything. If I remain here it can only be as a servant, and there is nothing you can do to change that, not ever. Our life together has been magic, but it is also secret. Willa believes that she will be able to stay here forever, sealed off from the rest of the world, but that cannot be. The Malibu will not always be a sanctuary. A day will come when all of us will have to leave...that day has arrived for me, Lena. I go on Sunday."

"Sunday!" I gasped, "So soon...and you won't be able to return, once you've left...the Exclusion Acts."

He pulled me to him, held me close. I closed my eyes tight and tried to imagine staying there forever like that...I wanted to remember everything...the smell, the touch, the sounds of his heartbeat.

"I should like to think that my son will remember Wing Soong not as a servant, but as a man," he said. "One day, I believe, he will understand why I left...that there was a purpose to my life that was larger than the gardens of the Malibu, that I had a larger garden to tend than those on the Malibu. If ever he should discover who fathered him, he will not need to feel shame."

I could not speak. Words would not rise from the ache at my center. I could only cling to him and try to hold the moment.

"You know," he went on in the same lulling voice, "it is why you could love me, why you could risk your life to bear our child...I have been, for you, a man. You cannot know, I think, the power that gives me. I have delayed as long as I can, Lena. The thought of leaving you, our son, pains me...I should like to see him grow to manhood. He will be extraordinary, our son. I feel it, I know it. But I must go, and you must help me. Joseph knows...I didn't tell him, he guessed. I did tell Sara, and I hope you can forgive me for telling her first, but she loves you almost as much as I do, and she has the capacity to protect you and Porter. Far more than I can, in reality. You have strong allies in Joseph and Sara. They will not desert you."

I bit my lip and nodded into his chest, and I wondered if I would ever be able to breathe easily again.

On Saturday, Soong took Porter into the mountains. They were gone the whole of the day, returning only at sundown. I watched them part at the gate. They turned to each other, bowing slightly, it seemed, though in fact they may only have been talking...and then Soong did something that was rare...he raised his hand, once, and stroked his son's face.

On Sunday, before sunup, I rode with Soong down the beach road. We stopped short of the gatehouse, where he dismounted and handed me the reins to the horse he rode.

Everything had been said. He looked at me, he bowed formally, he turned and walked away, down the beach.

I watched until he was but a dark point on the beach, a tiny mote against the sweep of the sand and the sea...and then I closed my eyes to hold that mote in my mind.

The barley fields, that morning, rippled in the wind. Heavy, nearing harvest, they bent in undulating waves, showing the deep blue undersides. I rode slowly back to the ranch house knowing that a part of me—perhaps the best—was walking even now toward Santa Monica and the port, that now and forevermore my very existence would be separated. There would never be a day when I would not think of him, and miss him, and know that he, too, felt the connecting thread of our lives.

There are times in a life when we live on the surface because the interior is too painful. The days and weeks following Soong's departure were like that for me. The surface of my days seemed smooth, without event, even dull in their sameness. We spoke of daily concerns. Women knitted and children played and grew. We tended to the small urgencies of living and we did not complain. And all the while, below that placid surface a cataclysm was taking shape, was forming, and we did not notice because of the very ordinariness of the days.

The winter rains sent us indoors for long periods that year. Dry washes were turned into torrents. Hills drifted toward the ocean, so filled were they with water. Each day brought mud-slides which closed off the beach road, sometimes for days on end. Willa, disgusted when the Pierce-Arrow got mired for a third time in almost as many days, had it put up on blocks in the barn to wait for the dry season.

The *vaqueros* and their women were quiet, the rain damping their contentiousness. Willa was preoccupied with her court cases. When she was not plotting with the batteries of lawyers that came and went, she was roaming the hills, tracking a pair of peregrine falcons, with Philip.

The hawking was, I suspected, their excuse for spending time together. Willa was surprisingly touchy about Philip's attentions. It took me a while to discover why.

One afternoon late, the two came back from a long ramble along the cliff, their faces high with color from the ocean wind. "We saw a wonderful chase," Willa said, removing her mud-spattered boots. "A young hawk made the most amazing stoop, careening down through the sky at speeds of, oh . . . what would you say, Philip?"

"Close to a hundred miles an hour, I would think . . . terrific speeds. He hit the quarry, snapped its neck so fast it couldn't have known what had happened. All we saw was a flurry of feathers."

When Philip left and we were alone, Willa and I, I teased her by intimating that Philip was more interested in her than in peregrines.

"Don't be silly," she snapped, "Philip is a good twelve years younger than I. You know that."

"I hadn't thought about it, really," I answered truthfully.

"Well think about it," she said as she flounced out of the room. I did as she said, but all I could think was how strange that Willa should care about age. It wasn't like her. That, in turn, made me ask myself: What *is* Willa like? More often of late, she surprised me. She was preoccupied with the ranch. Or was it the ranch? I wasn't sure. What I did know was that the forces without were gathering. Los Angeles was growing. Santa Monica was growing. All the little towns that had once been no more than villages surrounded by orange groves were growing. The county was building a fine new road that would end at the entrance of the Malibu. Already Willa's name was appearing in the newspapers of the coastal towns, and they were not saying nice things about the woman they called "the Duchess of the Malibu."

Months later, I would search my journals for some hint, some small clue, that might have been a warning. I found nothing. The entries for that time were as routine as our lives, enlivened only by the messages I had begun to receive, with what would prove to be a lovely regularity, from Wing Soong.

And yet there were indications, had I but been sensitive enough to notice. For example, early in December I wrote:

"Sally complained that the twins had been allowed to witness a cruel game played by the *vaqueros*. The men bury a live chicken in the earth, then they ride on horseback—galloping at full speed—and the rider swoops down and plucks the chicken out of the ground. To win, he must not kill it. Thad did not understand Sally's objection, saying that the *vaqueros*' horsemanship is a rare thing, to be admired. His own feeling, he said, was that it should be a privilege to watch.

"Sally would not give in. 'It is cruel to use a live animal,' she said, her chin up in its stubborn position. Unfortunately, Thad did not seem to notice. 'How silly,' he teased, trying to josh her, 'do you know how many chickens' necks get wrung around here in a single week?'

"'I suppose you approve of cockfights, too?' Sally shot back at him.

"It was Thad's turn to frown. He glanced at Willa, knowing that the cockfights were a sore topic. Surprising us all, Willa came to his defense.

"'I've tried my best to discourage the cockfights,' she told Sally, 'but the Mexicans persist. They slip off into the hills and hold them. Sally is right, however, Thad. The children should not be witnesses to the cruel games the Mexicans will play.'

"Nothing more was said, but the exchange had left us all in a bad frame of mind."

Another journal entry, made during a sunny spell between winter storms, told of a "Play Day" Sally was planning for the friends she and Thad had made in Santa Monica. Strangely, this entry, too, had to do with games.

"Sally today coaxed Aleja—dear, sedate Aleja—into trying out some of the games she is planning. The two have become such solid friends since Aleja joined Sally in the cottage. It would be difficult to imagine two more different girls, but they are friends nonetheless.

"Sally explained how the 'sack race' is run, with two people standing side by side, their inner legs in a single sack. For this, she had procured an old flour sack still dusty white. Kit and Porter drew the starting and finishing lines in the sandy stretch in front of the cottage. Sally and, with some difficulty, Aleja, managed to get one leg each into the sack—modesty causing Aleja to flush, while Sally kept up a steady stream of instructions.

"Porter shouted 'Go!' Sally took off full tilt while Aleja only looked startled. As a result, the two went tumbling head over foot, black stockings and petticoats all in a tumble, red and black hair tangled together—and through it all laughter spilling out and over, not the least from Kit and Porter and me.

"It was a funny thing to see, Sally pulling Aleja up and, grasping her tightly about the waist this time, setting off once again—only to go a few steps and fly into the sand.

"Thad and Pablo rode up in the midst of this, to find all of us so in the grip of laughter that we had no breath left to call hello. Sally and Aleja sank back, a tumble of arms and legs, in the sand. Weak from laughter, Sally could only hiccough.

Thad grinned, then he glanced at Pablo and became serious.

"Pablo, in angry Spanish, ordered his sister—and these were his words—to 'get up off your back.' Thad said nothing at all, but when Pablo wheeled to leave, he followed."

The last incident I recorded was a snippet of talk from a dinner party held during the holidays. Arcadia had not been able to come for Christmas, the old Señora having taken a turn for the worse, but Sara was down from San Francisco, and Joseph and Philip joined us. It was what Willa and I called our "family" group. (Wen and his bride had been invited. Willa had written the invitation by hand, and had it delivered to the couple's home with instructions to wait for a reply. The delivery boy was sent back with neither reply nor message.)

We sat at table, talking in the usual easy way. Sally interjected—rather awkwardly, it seemed to me at the time—a conversation about the position of women in our society. Thad made a little joke about it, but Sally said that to her it was not a matter to laugh about.

"Did you know," she said in her teacher's manner, "that one-fourth of the states deny women the right to own property? And that four-fifths of the states deny women the right of equal guardianship of their own children?"

"The Malibu is hardly a male bastion," Joseph noted amiably.

"The Malibu is hardly the real world," Sara countered, "besides which, Willa's property—hence her power—and mine as well, are derived from men. We didn't come by it on our own."

"But you could have," Sally put in, "you and Miss Willa, you are extraordinary women."

Willa was embarrassed, and started to say something, but before she could, Thad interjected, addressing Joseph and Philip. "I believe they are trying to tell us we men aren't needed around here."

Which, of course, elicited a female chorus of assurances that we could not do without them.

It would make an interesting course of scientific study, I should think, to plot how life's important decisions are made. Sally was struggling, I knew that. But it would be some time before I learned—from Aleja—of the night that Sally finally understood what she must do.

Sally and Thad walked on the beach but they did not touch. She was searching for words that would break through the wall that seemed, more often of late, to fall between them. She turned one subject in her mind, dismissed it for being abrasive, then thought of another, her eyes on her feet rather than the hills and sky and the sea. She was so deeply into the task that for a moment his words did not penetrate.

"What is it you have against Pablo?"

She stopped, searched his face. "I don't know if I have anything against him. I've scarcely spoken to him . . . but . . ."

"But?" he prodded.

"But . . . well, I'm not sure I like the effect he has on people."

"People?" he persisted, not able to keep the sarcasm from his voice.

"You . . . and Aleja."

"What do you know about Aleja?" he said, in a way that meant she knew nothing at all.

"I know that she was attacked by your brother and another young man, a schoolmate of his. I know that they attempted to ravage her . . . and that she seems to believe that she should be ashamed—as if the shame is hers."

Thad was surprised that she knew, that Aleja would have spoken to her about the attack, but all he said was, "That's the way they think."

"They?" Sally said, hearing her voice rising even though she had vowed not to get angry. "Who is this *they* you speak of—one of the *Adelinas* told me she had been taken by three men during the wars in Mexico, and she didn't seem in the least ashamed. She seemed almost . . ."

"It isn't the same," Thad interrupted.

"No?" Sally's eyebrows lifted.

"Sally, for heaven's sake, you know what those women . . . they're not the same . . . Aleja was a good girl, from . . ."

"A *good* girl . . . *was?*" Her eyes snapped with anger now, there was no holding it back.

"Is," Thad said, grim. "Sally, listen to me. I don't know what's happening—you seem angry with me so much lately. Is it because I spend time with Pablo?"

His sudden change caught her by surprise. She shook her head and looked at him, trying to understand. Thad went on, "I've told you about Pablo, about how we grew up together. He taught me how to ride and how to fish . . . some of my happiest memories are of the times when we were kids. I wish you could have known . . ."

She raised her hand to touch his face, he pulled her to him then, and rocked back and forth, relieved to be holding her again.

She wrapped her arms around him, and for a while said nothing at all.

"Pablo . . ." she started, softly, "does he think that Aleja is shamed?"

"I'm not sure," Thad muttered, pulling her closer still.

They stood like that for a long while, Sally with her face burrowed under his chin, her lips all but touching the hollow of his neck. She held to him because she loved him, and because she did not want him to see her face.

When Aleja came into the cottage that evening, Sally was sitting with her back to the door, her eyes unfocused, her face so wet that strands of hair were sticking to her cheeks.

"Sally?" Aleja said, softly.

Sally shuddered. She looked at the older girl. When she spoke, her voice was weary: "How can it be, Aleja, that you can love someone and know it is wrong?"

Aleja sat beside her, took her hand. They did not talk, but watched the gathering dark.

Finally a long sigh shuddered through Sally. She said, "I cannot marry him. It would be a terrible mistake."

Aleja only nodded. Sally leaned against the wall, her eyes closed. A last glimmer of light lit her face, and Aleja could have cried for the pain she saw there.

"What will you do?" she asked, absently.

"Do?" Sally repeated. "I'll have to leave."

"Must you?"

Sally nodded, miserable. "But please, say nothing yet . . . Thad doesn't know, and I must tell him first . . . And, I need time to think, I want to do this as . . . easily, I suppose, as I can. The children . . ." Her eyes filled at the thought of them. She cried, then, long wrenching sobs came out of her, and all Aleja could do was hold her hand. She did not try to tell Sally she should reconsider. Aleja had known for some weeks the struggle that Sally was waging. She knew, too, the decision she would have to reach.

At last Sally sat up, blew her nose, and attempted to smile. It was a warm evening, the moon had lifted above the mountains and transformed the ocean into a silver shimmer.

"Do you feel like a walk?" Sally asked. They pulled on shawls against the evening cool, and started down the beach.

"I think I'll never know such a place again," Sally said. "I can hardly bear to think of leaving."

"What will you do?" Aleja asked.

"Go East, I suppose. Perhaps to Washington. If I can, I would like to work with those women who are trying to get the laws changed . . . perhaps I'll become a suffragette."

Aleja linked her arm in Sally's. The two walked in the soft sand, sharing the sadness . . . now that it was said, and in the open.

"Don't leave before you know where you are to go," Aleja said. "Promise me that."

/ Sally hugged her friend. "I cannot promise, but I will try."

Sally knew her secret was safe with Aleja. I could only wish, from hindsight, that she had trusted me with it as well, for I might have helped her move quickly. I would not have relished seeing her go—but I would have helped her, had she confided in me. Soong's words, his premonition, as it were, would have cushioned my disappointment. If only . . .

If . . . if . . . if . . . the sequence of events was unfolding. Soong was gone to China, though I had not yet become accustomed to going to the garden and finding him gone. Joseph was in the East on business, Sara was in London preparing for a new show, Ignacio was dead . . .

I heard the voices rising in anger, and I knew the argument was a continuation of the discussion they had started several days earlier. As the winter gave way to spring, we seemed to shake ourselves out of the lethargy that had prevailed.

"No, Thad. No. I do not approve. Your father never allowed it, nor will I—and I can't imagine why you would bring it up again. We've gone over it a thousand times. Bullfighting is calculated cruelty. I won't have it."

Silence. Then Thad's voice, low and surly. "The Mexicans don't see it that way. To them, it is a test of a man's courage."

"Courage," Willa spat, "what can possibly seem courageous about slitting a poor beast's tongue and placing hot peppers in it to enrage him, so that he attacks—and the brave *vaquero* then kills the bull with a sword, not without help, of course."

I could not hear Thad's reply, only the low, urgent tone of his voice.

"I will not have it, Thad. That's all."

"Do I have no say?" Thad shouted. "I thought I was to be *El Patrón*, but obviously I rule only at the queen's pleasure."

There was a breath's pause, a slap and a sharp cry from Willa. "Oh, no," she said, "Thad, I didn't mean . . ."

He left without a word. A moment later she stood at the

doorway to the parlor where I worked, her eyes wide with dismay.

"Lena," she said, "I've done the most awful thing..."

"So there is to be a bullfight after all?" Sally said to Aleja.

"Pablo says yes. He says Mrs. Reade has agreed."

Sally's distress was evident, though more sadness than anger now. She wondered how Willa had been won over. Thad had had something to do with it, she guessed. She had been so sure Willa would not give in, so sure that she had not allowed herself to reply when Thad told her about the bullfight, about how the *vaqueros* were insisting they be allowed to hold one after the spring rodeo.

Sally had not yet told Thad that she was leaving. She hoped that he would see, himself, that their union would not be wise. The bullfight was a culmination of all that was wrong between them. They did not share the same ideals. Thad was unable to see how contrived, how sadistic the bullring could be. Though he was careful not to say it, she knew he shared the *vaqueros'* notion that there was something manly in facing an enraged animal.

"Would you want me to turn tail and run?" he had asked her once, and she had answered, "There are times, yes, when the wisest thing a man can do is run."

Owen Reade would have understood—Owen, who knew about limits and limitations. I remembered the day, twenty-five years before, when with consummate grace Owen had managed to avoid a footrace at Porter Farm. I could not help but think that, had he lived, Owen might have been able to make his son see how little brute force had to do with bravery, how facing a mad bull had nothing at all to do with being a man.

Sally decided to wait until after the rodeo to tell Thad she was leaving. She did not, she reasoned, want him to think that the bullfight—or rather, his support of it—had anything to do with her decision. It had become so important to him, and such an unspoken point of contention between them, that she wanted it done with first. Then she could try to explain, could at least attempt to tell him why they could not marry, why she must leave. Perhaps she thought that he might have a change of heart, perhaps she hoped for a miracle. She did love him, of

that she was sure. She was just as certain that love was not
enough.

It was the first rodeo since the advent of the *rurales* and their
women, and they intended to make it a day of celebration. We
gathered—Sally, Aleja, the twins and I riding together—at
midday at the corral at Zuma. The Mexicans trailed behind us
on the beach, raucous, as if off to a carnival. The men had
refused from the beginning to do any herding, so Thad had had
to bring in the *vaqueros* who worked the ranches. Willa had
not liked it, had been so annoyed, in fact, that she declined
even to make an appearance today. I suspected that Thad did
not regret her absence. He found it easier to exert his authority
when his mother was not about.

I leaned against the rough wood of the corral, felt the sun
hot on my face and remembered another rodeo when Thad had
been a very small boy, frightened by crayfish in the stream.

On that long-ago day, Owen had been dressed all in black,
the very model of *El Patrón*. Owen and Ignacio, what a pair
they had been, the *Patrón* and his *mayordomo*.

Thad did not have his father's *presence*. It was hard even
to imagine Thad in the black suit. All the pageantry was gone
from the rodeo now. Ned Lattimore, who had been a solid
young cowboy from Kentucky then, was wiry now, his hair
was thinning.

"Hahle!" someone called out, "the *taurito*," and the words
spun me back to that other rodeo, when the young bull had
rushed Owen. I could almost hear Willa's scream, the rawhide
slicing through the air, jerking the bull to its knees. . . . Connor
McCord's rawhide. The glint of the Spaniard's knife, then,
and the *taurito*'s bloody testicles had been tossed into the air.
I shivered involuntarily and tried to push the image from my
mind, but it would not go. Through the dust and the heat and
the animal stench of the ring, I could almost see Owen walk
over to Connor. The *vaqueros* had looked away, assuming a
failure of courage on Owen's part, judging him by standards
Owen did not accept. If only Thad could be made to understand . . .

Trinidad insisted on overseeing the rodeo dinner, which she
considered the most ceremonial work of the year. Aleja helped
her mother with the food. I watched Trinidad shoo away one

of the *rurales'* children. She had made it obvious that she expected to feed only those who worked. The *rurales*, for their part, made a great show of ignoring the rest of us.

They lined the section of the corral that we usually took, climbing onto the fence in a noisy mass, lifting their dirty-faced children for a better view. Once the work in the ring was underway, the ranch hands roping and branding, the Mexicans began to shout and call out, abusing those who made a bad show. They kept up a steady stream of peppered Spanish, some of it obscene. I noticed that Aleja winced often. One woman, whose dirty, dark hair reached to her waist, was particularly fierce. Her shriek could be heard above the noise of the ring.

The cattle began to pour in. Dust was rising. The sounds of the animals' bleating created the usual controlled chaos. When three cowboys were working at a time and the ring was filled with the cries of *"Hola!"* Thad decided to try his hand at the rope. He was, I knew, as good as the next ranch hand—which is to say, competent. Still, as *Patrón*, it was not his place to work the ring. I wondered if Sally's presence had anything to do with it. When I saw him glance at her, I had my answer.

He sent the loop flying, long and open, over a calf, and missed. At that precise moment, there was a lull in the noise—as happens, at times, in the midst of so much action—and the black-haired *soldadera's* obscene laugh rang out. She made, with her hand, a motion so insinuating that I felt sick. Her meaning was not lost, not on any of us. Even Kit hid her face in my skirts, and Porter stared ahead without seeing, so I knew he was girding himself.

Sally tried not to look at Thad. I could feel as much—just as I wanted not to see either of them, but did. I could feel Thad's humiliation, and Sally's anger—at the woman, at Thad for letting himself be humiliated.

"It shouldn't matter," Sally said under her breath. "How can I make him understand that it shouldn't matter?"

Only Aleja and I heard her, and neither of us could answer.

Thad did not attempt another throw. Instead Pablo, who had been working the inner ring, easily slipped his rope over the calf, preventing it from interrupting the other work.

"Pablo to the rescue," Sally said, irritated.

Aleja's soft voice answered, "Pablo waited. He gave Thad

first try, and he waited to see if he would recover."

Once again, the woman's derisive laugh rang out, and when we looked at her she thrust her tongue at us. Sally and I left with the twins soon after, having decided against staying for the rodeo feast, spread as always under the grove of oak trees near the corral.

We left early for a number of reasons, not the least of which was a great, black bull tied to a single tree on a hillock nearby, outlined by the sky, looking fierce. Once the work of the day was finished, the corral would be converted into a bullring. The *rurales* and their women were girding for it. We had seen the flasks passed among them, had noticed the laughter getting wilder, more raucous. The bull would be brought down from the hillock, his tongue would be slit and hot peppers placed in it . . . and the men would perform, one at a time, in the ring alone with the beast.

It was Aleja who came for us, riding hard, out of breath so that she could hardly speak, but finally gasping out the awful news.

"Send for the doctor," she panted.

Willa grasped her shoulders, shook her slightly, "What is it? Who is hurt?"

Nearly fainting, Aleja slumped in Willa's grasp. "Thad," she whispered, "it is Thad . . . gored . . . gored by the bull."

Sally was already running for the barn and her horse, her red hair flying, her face set.

"Where has he been gored, girl? Tell me!" Willa demanded.

"Here," Aleja whispered, doubling over, her hand in her groin, "here."

Sally saw the dark-haired woman first, the she-creature who had taunted Thad. Of all the people gathered around him, it was that woman Sally saw first, her eyes flashing, as if hot from the pleasure of blood . . . the woman who had goaded him, had stung him. . . . And Sally wanted to go at her, to rip her eyes out of her head. She wanted to pound the creature's terrible face into the earth, she wanted to choke off the air from her throat . . . Sally stood looking at her and she hated her more than ever she had hated another human, the sour body smells came rushing at her and Sally wanted to destroy her.

And then she saw Thad, on the ground, his knees drawn up to his chest. She saw they had thrust a white shirt between his legs, and she watched the wide blotch of red grow, spread on the shirt. She stood looking down upon him, she felt herself swaying, she heard the woman's voice, soft now and thick with pity. *"Que lástima,"* the creature sighed, "the *gringo's* manhood, gone."

# Book V

Porter and Kit,
1913 - 1922

# Chapter Nineteen

Sara struggled with the cork, finally dislodging it from the champagne bottle with a loud whoosh which sent it ricocheting against the ceiling, only to come to rest in my lacy fern.

"Aha!" she laughed as we thrust our glasses out to catch the bubbles. "Here's to us, together again." Then she settled herself comfortably on the rug in front of my fireplace and demanded that I catch her up, every detail.

"It's been almost a year since the rodeo, and I've written you everything, you know..." I began.

"Oh, the trouble with letters is always that the receiver can't ask questions. I much prefer the telephone.... I'll be glad when I can pick up the telephone in Paris and call you here in Los Angeles, then we can talk every..."

"Talk! Are you mad, Sara? I can scarcely get used to the idea of speaking to someone across town..."

She only laughed at me, and I had to smile myself, to think how caught up in all the new contraptions Sara was. She could drive a machine, and even knew some women who were flying airplanes.

"I need to know what Sally is doing in Washington. And Thad, has there been no word at all? I know Willa has detectives looking for him, because they contacted me. And this house, what made you decide to buy it and move into Los Angeles . . . apart from the twins and school, that is. I know there has to be more to it than that."

I held out my glass to be filled. "I might as well drink until you get through asking questions," I said, drily.

"This is Soong's Promise, right?" she said, pouring, and I lifted my glass in answer and said, "To Soong, and the limit he put on my drinking."

"I'll be sure to tell him how religiously you keep that promise," she answered. "He writes me, you know—the most remarkable letters. I'm saving them all . . . for Porter. But I think that someday I would like to have them published . . . with Soong's permission, of course."

Her words warmed me.

"The thought of him still lights your face," she said. "I must remember to tell him that."

I stretched, as comfortable as always with my old friend. "I think you have just confirmed something that Soong was trying to explain to me," I told her. "The idea of his thoughts being published, that he is taking part in . . . well, in *history* . . ."

"In the making of history," she gently corrected me.

"Yes," I went on, "the idea of others coming to respect Soong, that pleases me."

We were silent for a time, in front of the fire, each of us thinking our own thoughts. I shook myself finally, and started to tell her what I knew she would want to know. "It was Soong's wish that I move into town with the twins. I never told Willa that, and I suppose I would rather she not know."

"Why not?" Sara asked.

"Because, well, because Soong was somehow able to see what was coming. He worried about the influence Pablo had over Thad. He even told me he thought Sally would leave. He was afraid for us . . . still, I wouldn't have left Willa there, alone, except . . ."

"Except?" Sara prodded.

"Oh, Willa sent Pablo and that crazy bunch of *rurales* and their women packing—and turned right around and replaced them with a small army of more manageable *vaqueros*. Then she became so preoccupied with Thad . . . you wanted to know about Thad." I sighed, and felt the small knot of sorrow that seemed permanently lodged in my breast for Thad. "It wasn't all that dramatic, the way it happened. After the accident he just got quiet. He ate, and seemed to go on about the business of the ranch. He would answer when you asked a question, but he seemed to keep moving farther and farther away. Then one day, perhaps two months after the accident, he moved into the artist's house on the ridge, and a week later he was gone."

"Without a word?"

"Without a word. It has been eight months now."

Sara thought for a while, then she said, "What about Sally? What did she do all this while?"

"Oh, she did what she could, but Thad acted as if there was nothing between them. She tried, again and again, to talk to him—but all she got was that terrible, removed silence. It was as if he had . . . well, as if he had left already."

"How did Willa take all of this?"

"She was frantic, absolutely frantic. She even seemed to blame Sally for a time, as if Sally's rejection of Thad had something to do with his climbing into the bullring. We all know Willa was out of her mind with grief. We didn't dare tell her about the *rurales'* woman who taunted Thad because we figured she would take a whip to her, or a gun. After a time she calmed down. I think she blames herself most of all, for giving in to the bullfight."

"Poor Willa," Sara said, "she's had so much sorrow in her life, and now this. It is almost too much for any woman to bear." She paused, deep in thought. Then she said, "Isn't it strange how often we look to women for reasons?"

"How do you mean?" I wanted to know.

"Just that we seem to need to accept guilt—I don't think either Willa or Sally or, for that matter, the Mexican woman had anything to do with Thad's climbing into that bullring. It had to do with Thad, and his dissatisfactions, and with chance—fate, call it what you will. Maybe that's why we seem so ready to take responsibility . . . it's a way to deny chance, a way to maintain the idea of control."

A heavy silence settled over us and we sat there for a time, thinking. Finally Sara shook herself. "How bad were Thad's injuries?" she asked.

"Bad," I answered. "The doctor told Willa that he would never be able to function normally, as a man."

"Lord," Sara whispered, "those two boys—Wen and Thad . . ."

"Wen has turned up, too," I put in. "Now that Thad has

disappeared, he wants control of both trust funds. I thought Willa would faint when he asked her to turn over Thad's trust to him. In the end, she only said that it would remain intact for now, that when Thad returned it would be there for him."

"I can't imagine even Wen being so crass," Sara replied.

"According to Arcadia, Wen and his wife live well beyond their combined incomes. Wen feels cheated, I'm sure."

"He must be the only attorney in Los Angeles who isn't making a fortune," Sara put in caustically.

I grimaced. "The irony is that Willa is creating fortunes for a whole covey of lawyers. Joseph has been trying to talk to her about it, but she won't listen. She is getting a reputation for litigation."

"Joseph talked to *me* about it," Sara admitted. "He's worried, and with reason. The companies are doing well, but most of the profits are going right out to Willa's lawyers. In the end, they are the only ones who are likely to benefit."

"You don't think she can keep the Malibu free?" I asked.

"Not forever. At best, she can fight for delay. Why do you suppose she is so absolutely intent on keeping everyone out?" Sara wanted to know. "Philip thinks it is a matter of conservation—that she wants to keep it wild and free for, as the conservationists like to put it, *future generations*. He considers her something of a heroine for her stand."

I smiled, thinking of Philip. "That's part of it, I think. I'm not sure . . . I've been trying to puzzle it out for myself, but I know there's more to it than that. She's lost so much—Owen, then Wen and Thad. The Malibu was supposed to be the promised land . . . *ultima thule* . . ."

"What?" Sara asked.

"*Ultima thule* . . . the farthest point . . . it is what Willa used to say, when we were girls in Illinois. She wanted always to go West, as far as she could go. I'm not sure, I've often tried to understand what it is about the ranch that so absorbs Willa. You remember my telling you how our mother wouldn't leave our farm—Porter Farm—how near the end of her life she hardly left the house? I mean, it wasn't a matter of choice. She couldn't—it would make her physically sick to try to leave . . ."

"And you think that is what has happened to Willa?"

"No, not exactly. It's not the same, and yet something about it is . . . I think that for Willa, the Malibu is where she feels safe . . . where she feels she is in control, that if she seals herself in and keeps everybody else out the world . . ."

Sara was shaking her head. "It doesn't make sense," she said.

"I know," was all I could answer. "It doesn't make sense, and yet I don't think she can help herself now. I think she has to fight all those forces that are gathering, the people who feel she has no right to close off the ranch. Sometimes I think if she would only listen to them, would only be willing to make some concessions. But she can't, she just can't."

"And that's why you left?" Sara asked.

She caught me off guard. I hadn't thought of it, but there it was. "I didn't think so," I said truthfully, "but maybe. Maybe." Quickly I added, "You've helped Willa some, I know."

"A little," Sara answered. "I managed to keep Charles out of her hair that time when he was so intent on ramming a railroad line through the ranch. It wasn't difficult."

"Part of the divorce settlement, I believe? The price of freedom—if you can call his life free."

Sara shook her head, and ran her hands through her hair. "Poor Charles, he's been done in by so many people lately— and he deserves it. I haven't a whit of sympathy for him. When he lost his sense of humor and became so almighty greedy . . . Still, he did provide a nice target for Philip. Did you know how he managed to remove Charles' influence in the legislature almost totally? It must rankle Charles to know that his nemesis, Philip Bourke, is what the newspapers call 'Mrs. Owen Reade's *frequent escort.*'" She laughed, but without mirth.

"I remember your saying you had bumped into Charles and Helen in London."

"Humm," Sara laughed, genuinely this time. "Helen was wearing the most expensively grotesque pearls I have ever set eyes upon. At her elbow was this anemic little Duveen man, an art dealer who has 'taken over' the rich American lady, as the English put it."

"What was Charles doing?" I wanted to know.

"Looking so hangdog that I had a notion to give him a hearty clap on the back and tell him to buck up, the way he used to clap me on the back when we were children."

"So you've forgiven him, is that it?"

Sara crossed her legs so she was sitting Indian style. She poured herself another glass of champagne and looked at me, an impish grin on her face. "There was never anything, really, to forgive. I've never wanted revenge, nothing like that. Those kinds of feelings—hate, revenge, pity—are corrosive, they eat at you. I couldn't afford them, ever. No, I've been struggling not so much against Charles as against myself. In the meantime, I had to learn how to deal with Charles, and I'm glad I could help others who needed to deal with him. He is, after all, a terribly bright man. Able. And he used to be funny. That was the best thing about him, his sense of humor. Pity he lost it."

"Helen's fault?" I asked, feeling mischievous.

"Bosh!" Sara all but shouted, "Charles' fault . . . and fate's, for giving him Phineas Emory as an uncle.

"Lord, this is grim talk," Sara said, rising to fix the fire. "Tell me about Sally. That should cheer us up."

The thought of Sally made me feel better. "She is absolutely proselytizing about the women's suffrage movement. She has joined a group which is supposed to convince legislators to pass laws that will limit the hours children can work in factories—child-labor laws. And she is also involved in the movement to set a minimum wage . . . and then there are the blind babies . . . Oh, she has so many good works going, and her letters are filled with her convictions. Can't you just see Sally up on a soap box, red hair flying, exhorting the women of the world to rise and fight for the vote?"

I rummaged through my desk until I found the Brownie snapshot Sally had sent in her last letter. There she was, one of four young women, each wearing a derby hat and each with a big, black cigar in her mouth.

"That's our Sally," Sara laughed, pleased. "I do believe she has found her proper niche."

"I know you are helping her," I said.

Sara only shrugged. "Never could smoke cigars myself," was all she would say, "better to have someone smoke them for me."

"It makes me sad to think we won't see T. R. in the White House again," I put in, "It's a pity that he lost this time."

"Too bad he didn't get the Republican nomination—splitting the vote was surely what threw the election to Mr. Wilson."

Our discussions, Sara's and mine, tended to roam over all kinds of subjects, touching this and that, the serious mixed in with the frivolous, so it didn't surprise me when Sara abruptly changed the subject. "We are women without men, aren't we? You and me, Willa and Sally and Trinidad and Aleja. Everyone except Arcadia . . . and in a way, she fits the description too."

"Oh, no, not Arcadia. Joseph is the most devoted of husbands . . . it's just that he's not totally a husband, or . . ."

"I know," Sara put in, "I know exactly what you mean. Too, I don't suppose we can put Willa on the list. She does have Philip."

I rose to my knees. Sitting so long had made one of my legs feel stiff. As I rubbed it, I said, "Philip is smitten with Willa, I know that. I even think he would like to marry her. She hasn't told me . . . we don't get a chance to talk privately all that much anymore . . . not since the trouble with Thad, and my moving into Los Angeles."

"He does want to marry her, he told me," Sara said. "Willa won't have it, because of the difference in their ages. Philip says he can't understand why the age difference bothers her so, when Owen was that much older than she . . ."

I chuckled. "Good for Philip," I said. "I do like that man."

Sara glanced at me in a way that meant she was trying to decide if she should reveal something. "Do you think Willa knew that Connor was younger than she?"

"Was he?" I asked, surprised, "How do you know?"

"I see him now and then," she answered, offhand.

"After what he did, Sara—to Willa, the smuggling—how can you see him?"

Sara moved her finger around the rim of her glass, then she poured herself another small sip of champagne and seemed to study the tiny rise of bubbles. "I'm glad Soong didn't ask me to limit my drinking," she said.

"You never needed to," I answered, "but you do need to answer my question. Why do you see Connor?" I paused, then plunged ahead. "And why did you finance his mining venture?"

"Maybe," she said slowly, still running her finger around the rim of the glass, "maybe it was because of Rose. Not just that he never got to see her, but because he never even knew about her—that she was his. And I did know, do know. Maybe . . ."

"But he did a terrible thing, Sara . . . and we had believed in him, trusted him . . ."

Sara lay her head back on the chair behind her and closed her eyes.

"Have you ever wondered why he did what he did?" she asked.

"Why? What do you mean?"

"I mean, I've always wondered what Connor could have wanted so much that . . ."

"Money," I interrupted, "he wanted money and power, both of which he seems to have now, thanks to you."

"No thanks to me, Lena, I assure you. The man has earned what he has and in doing so he has earned quite a tidy little sum for me, too. Someday that sum will be Porter's. I'm still trying to figure a way for Porter to be left out of the Reade will without causing suspicion. Joseph and I have pondered the question, and frankly we still haven't come up with a good answer."

"I know," I sighed, "but we've got to do it. Wen is beginning to stir things up again. He is furious with Willa, says she is squandering the estate."

She had deliberately changed the subject, and I allowed it. There were times when it was best not to push Sara. She had, I felt, said as much as she would say about Connor. I also knew we would come back to him, that he would figure in our lives once more, in some way.

"Sometimes I think Porter himself will give us a proper reason for being disinherited," I said, "every time we go to the ranch, he manages to get into a conversation with Willa about land reform. Henry George is his latest hero. Sometimes I wish the boy would read dime novels instead of economic theorists."

Sara laughed. "How does Willa take it?"

"It's a good thing he isn't her son, in fact," I grimaced. "She can afford to be tolerant, but of course she doesn't much like it. And I can't think of a way to quiet him . . . I mean, what can I say? 'She isn't your mother, she's your aunt so be nice to her'? He's supposed to be able to tell his mother what he thinks. And already he has said he doesn't much like being part of the capitalistic class."

"That's wonderful, absolutely wonderful." Sara could barely contain herself, and I thought for a minute that she would choke

laughing. "Of course, that is it. We'll simply wait for a bit and
have Willa politely give him his way, and remove the burden
of capital."

"Do you think we can, without raising an alarm?"

"I don't see why not. Willa would be seen as the hero,
giving her socialistic son what he deserves."

"But he's such a child..." I began.

"We'll wait until he's thirteen. Four more years."

"Are you going to tell him about your legacy?" I asked.

"Not until he reaches what I consider to be an age of reason."

"Which is?" I wanted to know.

"Oh, twenty or twenty-one. Then he can do as he likes with
his inheritance."

"At this point I believe he would turn it over to the Wobblies."

"So be it," Sara said, and she was serious. "But tell me
about the two of them—Kit and Porter. That always cheers
me."

There followed a lively conversation that went far into the
night. I was terribly proud of the children, I must admit. The
details of their lives filled mine. As we had guessed, Sally had
prepared them well for their entry into formal education. Their
teachers would have advanced them two full grades had I not
objected. As it was, they were with children a full year older
than they.

Neither Kit nor Porter objected to the move to Los Angeles.
Kit did not want to leave Willa, but she was content to come
when Willa agreed to spend a few days of each month with
us. And of course, we went out for weekends quite often.

I visited with Arcadia every day, since the Señora made it
difficult for her to leave the house. *Difficult* is too mild, *impossible* is closer to the truth. Joseph worried so about Arcadia's
isolation. I do believe my visits helped him as much as Arcadia.
At any rate, I thoroughly enjoyed our hours together. Cadie
has never lost her gift, which is, simply, to make others feel
good. The Señora complains about my visits, I know. Almost
as soon as I arrive, she begins to ring the bell she keeps by
her bed to summon Arcadia. She continues ringing it throughout
my visit, but I am obstinate. I will not bend to the old woman
who uses her age as a weapon.

"Her age and her station and, not least, her *fortune*," Sara reminded me, yawning. "God save the wicked queen. Let's go to bed now so I can go with you tomorrow to visit Arcadia."

Sara insisted on driving her motorcar, a dazzling cream-colored monster which had arrived on the train with her. I was thoroughly shaken when we arrived at the Señora's big house, so much so that I didn't see the doctor's carriage right away.

Joseph met us at the door, and his face told us everything.

"Shall we leave?" Sara asked.

"No, no, don't do that. Come in, if you will . . . if you don't mind . . ." He was stumbling in the way he did when he was particularly upset, which is to say, not purposefully. Clearly, the Señora's time was close.

Arcadia joined us in the dark, old drawing room. She kissed each of us in turn, holding us to her for a long moment. Her face was lined. For the first time I looked closely at her, to see that the girl had become the matron. Cadie was no longer young. The thought came to me, as well as the knowledge that it was quite out of place, that I could never think of Arcadia as anything but a girl. I wondered why that was. Perhaps because she had never married, never had children when it seemed so right that she should.

At that moment the doctor appeared, motioned to Arcadia, and she left.

For the next half hour no more than a dozen words passed between us. There was nothing to say, we could only wait.

When Arcadia appeared in the doorway she had a strange, dazed look on her face. She started to walk toward us, but it was as if she had trouble finding the floor. Joseph was at her side in an instant, his arm around her as he directed her to a chair.

"Is it over, Cadie?" Sara asked.

Arcadia blinked and looked up at Joseph. In a voice amazingly free of emotion she told him, "Her words to me—her last words—were 'Never have children. They steal your beauty.'"

We sat in stunned silence, Sara and I. I heard myself saying, "Come home with us, Cadie, now. Right now. Get out of this house."

Joseph and Sara, in unison, said, "That's right." And we had her in the motorcar before she knew what was happening.

* * *

Arcadia Bandini Stearns was given the kind of burial usually reserved for heads of state, for royalty. She was that, in a way—the last of the great Californios, a symbol of an era gone long enough to be romanticized. For some, her passing signaled the end of Los Angeles' beginning. They mourned her for her beauty that was lost, for the legend she symbolized. Those of us who knew the price she had exacted from her niece, the pretty blonde namesake who had come to visit twenty-five years before, did not mourn. We felt, instead, relief.

And yet, Cadie's grief was genuine. She had spent so much of her time tending to the old woman, her schedule had been so tied in to the invalid's, that at first she could not adjust to the freedom, the time to herself. Sara stayed on to help. Together, we talked Cadie into her new life.

It was on a Thursday that old Mr. Kimble came to call on Cadie. I remember precisely the day, for no good reason other than it was late in the week following the Señora's death. He had been the old woman's solicitor for half a century. She was, I suspect, the last of his clients. He climbed our porch with difficulty, crippled as he was by arthritis. Joseph knew he was coming and was waiting for him. He helped him into the house and led him to the library, where Arcadia, looking pale in her mourning dress, waited.

After no more than ten minutes, the old man came limping out again, making small groaning sounds under his breath, as if to help the aches and pains of age escape.

Sara and I watched silently as Joseph helped the old man out of the house and into his carriage. When Arcadia did not emerge, we went to see what was wrong.

We found her sitting, bolt upright in a chair, an amazed look on her face.

"What is it?" I blurted. "Tell us!"

She began to laugh then, a terrible, hysterical laugh.

Sara strode past me and grasped her by the shoulders. She shook her, but Arcadia would not stop. Sara slapped her then. Once. Hard.

Cadie blinked; her eyes focused and filled with tears.

"Do you know . . ." she whispered gulping to keep the sobs back, "do you know what it means to die *intestate*?"

Not believing, not wanting to let myself believe, I said, "It can't be. No."

"Oh, yes, oh, yes," Cadie said, her voice quivering. "She didn't leave a will . . . and she meant not to leave a will."

"That means . . ." I began, but I hadn't the heart to finish. We all knew, at any rate. We all knew it meant that Cadie would get nothing at all from the Señora's estate. There were too many relatives with closer ties.

Sara held Cadie to her, hard. I listened to the sobs wrenching out of Cadie and tried not to think. Joseph was with us by then, and I could see that he knew. The old man would have told him. He looked at Cadie, and I wish I had not seen the look on his face.

We left them together, then. But not before Cadie had managed to tell us why she was crying. It was not the inheritance, she said. "It was that she could have despised me so . . . to want me both childless and penniless . . ."

I avoided looking at Sara for a time. I knew her well enough to know that she would not see Arcadia as the victim of the Señora so much as she would see her as the victim of her own conflicting loyalties—her distorted sense of duty, confused by what once might have been greed but had been transformed, over the years, into guilt.

I was not so sure. I did not think it quite so easy as that, quite so simple. All I knew was that something had been lost. At the very least, time. Youth. A chance for . . . what? I wasn't sure.

"Cadie simply couldn't believe the old woman could be so perverse," Sara interrupted my thoughts, "that's all." It wasn't all, but I could only sigh and say that I wished there was not so much venom in the world.

Later we would talk about it together—Joseph and Arcadia, Willa and Sara and I. Joseph would say that they were better off free of the old woman's money, that it never need taint them. And we would nod in agreement because it was the kind thing to do.

Arcadia and Joseph were married in a private ceremony in the garden at the Malibu. The wisteria was at its height, the heavy lavender blossoms formed a fragrant arch under which they said their vows. Willa and Philip stood as witness for this long-awaited day. None of us could believe it was, at last, to happen.

I watched through a shimmer of tears. Kit held my hand, squeezing it to give me courage. Then she and Porter sent the newlyweds off in a shower of rice and rose petals. Sara had arranged a tour of Europe for the two as her wedding gift. As we waved them off, I tried not to notice how portly Joseph had become, or how faded Arcadia's prettiness.

Late that afternoon I did what I have always done when I need solitude—I settled into a quiet little nest behind a bank of flowers in the pergola. I had been there no more than ten minutes when I found myself in the embarrassing position of overhearing Willa and Philip in the grove, close by. They were laughing—the soft, urgent laugh of lovers. I was about to clear my throat to signal my presence when I heard—or perhaps felt—the sounds of passion. It silenced me. Willa, breathless, said, "You can't have marriage fever, Philip—I won't allow it. Tell me you're not a sentimentalist after all."

"But think of all we could do if we were married," he answered.

"What that we can't do now?" she wanted to know.

"Travel. We could travel together if we were married."

"We can travel together now, Philip," she told him. "You can tell everyone I'm your old Auntie."

"Damn you," he said as clear as day. "Damn you, Willa, for being a silly woman after all."

"Not silly," Willa told him. "Never silly. Impulsive, perhaps. Mistaken, often. Practical, sometimes. But not silly. My life is set, Philip. I belong here, right here on this ranch. So long as you want to be here with me, so long as you want to share my bed, you will. And when you want to go, you will go."

"Not 'whither thou goest' then?" Philip said.

"No," she answered.

And he said, "I see."

## Chapter Twenty

The years between 1912 and 1919 saw us in the townhouse I had purchased in West Los Angeles. I selected this location because it was close to a very good private school. Fortunately, as it turned out, it was also close to the public high school, which Porter was to insist upon attending.

My journals for those years are filled to overflowing with the mementos of growing children—piano recitals and school plays, letters written from a trip East with Willa one summer, notes included in birthday and Christmas gifts . . . and photographs, many of them out-of-focus, of the twins in front of the Ferry Building in San Francisco, the twins on horseback in Yosemite Valley, the twins at the beach . . . all the happy litter left over from their growing years. Good years they were, too. The children were at the center of my world and I reveled in being their guide on the journey through childhood.

Ours was a lively house. Visitors came and went so that the guest rooms seemed always to be occupied. Kit collected friends as easily as Porter collected stamps and marbles and bits of string, not to mention subscriptions to magazines I scarcely knew existed. Porter got on well with his classmates. He might even have been popular had it interested him. Since it didn't, Kit remained his only close friend. There were times when I worried that his course of action limited hers. It was not a major worry, however, since Kit seemed perfectly happy in the company of the boy she believed to be her twin. They gave me little enough to worry about, the two of them—and unbounded pleasure. Riffling through the pages of my journal, I remember all the good times. It was a happy time for them as well.

*February 6, 1913:* Kit came from school today glowing with pride. Her marine zoology exhibit has taken first honors in the All City Science Exposition. The notation on the prize said: "Seldom do we see such sophisticated scholarship in the fourth form."

"My teacher asked if I had help from my family," Kit told me, "I said my brother Thad used to teach me about sea life, but that he left."

Porter, who had been listening, quickly put in, "Did you say he ran away?"

Kit shook her head. Her eyes were so wide, so questioning that suddenly it became clear to me how sadly confusing Thad's disappearance has been to them. With a wrench, I remembered Thad's confession about Rose, how he had thought that he might be responsible for her death. Could either Kit or Porter be thinking such thoughts about Thad's leaving? I sat them both down and tried to explain. I know they are too young to understand, but I had to try. There is so much we cannot know about the minds of children.

*March 23, 1918: The United States* vs. *Willa Kerr Reade* was decided today. Willa claimed a victory over the federal government. The court dismissed the complaint—which was that by putting up gates and fences on the Malibu she was in violation of acts of Congress for "enclosing public lands." It was that old notion of "implied right of way" rearing its head again. The court found, and I quote, that the gates and fences were a "reasonable and proper and appropriate" way of protecting her land from encroachment.

Willa, of course, is ecstatic. Privately, Joseph is not. I am sure that he felt a defeat this time would force Willa to come to terms with the settlers. And it's not only the settlers that want free passage into the Malibu. The county is proceeding to improve the road between Santa Monica and the eastern boundary of the ranch. Once that road is finished the townsfolk are going to clamor to get inside. They seem to feel that the Malibu beaches are more beautiful than anything to the south. By making it a mystery, Willa has succeeded in whetting the public appetite for access to the Malibu's natural beauty.

I went to the courthouse with Arcadia and Willa. We saw Jacob Shurz there. I must wonder at the tenacity of the man. From the looks of him, he could have chewed us all up and spit us out. He is, I think, every bit as stubborn as Willa.

The twins joined us at the Plaza for a victory luncheon. I made sure Porter sat at the far end of the table, away from Willa. His questions only irritate her. I wish he didn't insist on so many details. Joseph, bless him, knows just how to deal with Porter. Willa does not.

*April 14, 1913:* Sleepless nights, with no good reason. The back pains, yes . . . but they have always been there. I waken at three each night, the loneliest hour of all. I waken and lie there and miss Soong. Last night he was so close I wanted to reach for him. That is when the idea that I could never see him again assaults me. I don't want to think it.

To ease the fear I attempted to write Soong. "We mark the twins' growth on the doorframe of the passageway by the pantry. Porter has added two full inches since you left. You asked that I write you about their schoolwork. Kit's marks are evenly excellent. Porter's, as you might expect, tend to the extremes. Whatever he feels is of interest he does well in. If he feels a subject has no value, he ignores it. I had thought he would not be in the least interested in the physical culture program at school, but once again our son surprised me. He is running on the relay team and plays field hockey. And of course, he does these things well . . ."

I stopped writing. For some reason I could not fathom, it seemed certain to me that Soong would not read the words I had set to paper and I could not go on.

*June 23, 1913:* This letter arrived yesterday; from Soong, it was dated April 14. "My Lena," he began, "I must write to you today because I am having a difficult time imagining myself with you on the Malibu. This world—the sights, the smells, even the way people speak to each other, is so different from what we knew together that at times I must shake myself to know that you exist. You and Porter and Kit, my loved ones, in a house in Los Angeles. I must tell myself over and over again that it is a real place, that you breathe and talk and sing and laugh.

"It is warm now, and I am glad. The winter was long and cold and I thought it would never end. I long for you . . . you must feel it. At times I am overcome with such a need that I reach out for you. You must know. The work I do here tries my patience. There are times when I despair, and it is always at that lowest moment that I meet someone who renews my hope.

"Such is the case with my young friend Sung Chiao-jen. He is wonderfully bright and witty and totally dedicated. He is able as well, which makes him unique among Sun Yat-sen's followers, who tend to be either adventurers or idealists. Sung is able as so many others are not to rise above the old ways, the personal ambitions. He makes me believe that it is possible, after all. *It* being the transformation of a country, and the introduction of the Anglo-Saxon notion of personal freedom, of individualism. "In China, loyalty has always been given a monarch, a person. People are poor and ignorant and the task of educating them is enormous. Yet it must be done, if we are to create a republic. My friend Sung says it is possible. Watching him in action one can almost believe. He has molded a new party which promises to be the vehicle we need. It is called the Kuomintang.

"Those of us who follow Sun have been educated outside of China, the majority in Japan. (Sun and I are among the few who have experience in the Western world—he in Hawaii and Europe.) Sun toys with a few socialistic ideas, most notably Henry George's land reform—but he is by no means a Marxist.

"Sometimes I go with him when he speaks, and I must work not to smile when he shouts out to a gathering of peasants, 'I am a coolie and the son of a coolie. I was born with the poor and I am still poor. My sympathies have always been with the struggling mass.' It is very good rhetoric, even if it is not accurate. Sun comes from the peasant class, that is true enough, but his father became a village elder and Sun himself has been educated as a surgeon. I only wish he had been trained as an administrator or even a soldier. The revolution was, in retrospect, comparatively easy. The hard part is upon us now. The coalition that gave us victory was united, I fear, only in its opposition to the Manchus. Now we must try to create a government. The difficult times begin. I will write as often as I can."

His letters ended, always, with endearments that I would read over and over again, basking in the warmth they created in me.

*August 18, 1913:* Yesterday I received, from Homer Lea himself, this hurried note from Soong. "Darling Lena," he began, "forgive the haste, but I must go into hiding and I am not at all sure when I will be able to get another message to you. My channels to the outside world are closing.

"Events demand that I write, and I cannot go into a long explanation, not now. Suffice it to say that for the past weeks I have worked closely with my friend Sung Chiao-jen to create a viable National People's Party, which we call the Kuomintang. Sung did his work well; too well. He has been assassinated on order of the new provisional president, the head of the New Army, who has taken Sun's place. We run for our lives now. Intrigues abound. Know that I love you. It is the only certain thing in my life."

*August 25, 1913:* Invariably, I wake each morning at three and lie thinking of Soong. Where is he? What is he doing? Above all, is he safe? Willa has sent Trinidad to stay with us while she goes East in yet another attempt to find Thad. Lost sons, lost lovers. No. If Soong is alive he is not lost to me, not in the way I fear Thad is lost. It is so awful, the not knowing.

*September 22, 1913:* I rented a car and a driver and took the children to the Arcade station to meet Willa. Her journey has ended in disappointment once more. The news she did bring was cruel. One of the investigators put on Thad's trail had discovered that Pablo was killed in a knife fight in Oaxaca four months ago. Willa must tell Trinidad. She looked so worn and despondent that I pleaded with her to stay with us for a day at least. She cannot. Trinidad must know. We did not speak of Thad, or of Soong. Talking does not ease the empty ache.

On the ride, Kit sat close to her mother and held her hand. She is a thoughtful child, seeming always to sense how others feel. My thoughts were with another child. In my mind's eye I could see Pablo on the day of the great fire, weeping because he could not save his friend's pet.

*December 22, 1913, the Malibu:* We have come to the ranch

to spend the holidays. Sara, Joseph and Arcadia will arrive on Wednesday for Christmas Eve. Aleja, we have discovered, has a talent for decorating and she has transformed the house into a wonderland, with pine boughs and red berries and baskets of oranges and nuts everywhere. We are to have a tree-trimming party tonight for the children, which includes two of Trinidad's grandchildren. Her tribe increases, and gives her comfort.

Philip is here. He seems so much a part of the household now. Willa tells me that Governor Johnson has asked Philip to accept an appointment to the bench. Philip a judge! He is considering it, Willa says. She is determined that he should take it. Philip teases her that it is only so he may then use his influence to seal off the Malibu. Trinidad told me that she heard Philip say to Willa that he would take the judgeship if she would marry him.

Willa has been tracking two peregrine falcons. She has stalked for thirty days running, going off on horseback each morning. Often she tethers her horse and follows the falcons on foot.

I have never seen her so intensely involved with raptors as she is now. On the day of our arrival she came in, trailing cold air and with bits of leaves tangled in her hair, in a state of high excitement. The tiercel had allowed her to watch him—in the open—from a distance of no more than thirty yards.

Breathless, she recounted the adventure: "He had just taken a gull and was perched in a tree on the edge of a pasture, ripping the bird apart and glaring at me. I just stood still, absolutely still, and stared back. Those eyes! They are great, monstrous things. Then it happened—he flew at me and hovered over me as if to attack . . . I thought the sound of my heart beating would frighten him off. But I didn't move, I didn't even raise my arm to protect myself. I just stood there staring into those great, globular, fiendish eyes—Lord, I know now why the prey turns its head to the hawk before it snaps the necks . . . you can't resist those eyes . . ."

Porter, mesmerized by the account, said, "And did he attack?"

Willa laughed, and the color in her cheeks seemed to glow. "No. But he flew to me twice more after that, and he gave me a very good looking over. He is curious about me. He wonders what I am."

"Maybe he thinks you are a hawk," Porter suggested.

"Maybe he does," Willa agreed. "At least, part hawk."

Kit put in, "Would you rather be the hawk or the prey?"

Willa did not hesitate. "The hawk, of course. Even though it is harder to be a hawk. They must kill to live...if they don't, they soon become too weak to hunt. And they can never really rest—even when they sleep, they must be aware of the movement about them, the shifting patterns of the light. Everything."

"I think I'd rather be a bunny, or a field mouse," Kit answered, "they can live on greens, and never grow hungry."

"But bunnies can't soar, darling," Willa answered. "Think how it must feel to glide high in the sky..."

"Before you turn into a hawk woman," Philip interrupted in his lazy, joking way, "I think I might point out the possibility that your falcon is using you quite efficiently. Isn't it likely that, earthbound as you are, you are flushing prey for him?"

Willa gave Philip a haughty smile, at the same time rumpling Kit's hair affectionately. "Come on, little field mousie," she said to her daughter, "come keep me company while I take a hot bath."

*February 2, 1914:* Last evening at a quarter past seven Homer Lea appeared at the kitchen door of the townhouse, frightening our cook, Manuela, out of her wits. She sent several pans clattering to the floor, which brought me to investigate.

"Homer," I said, genuinely delighted, "I thought you were in China." Before he could speak, I saw the letter he was carrying and I knew it was from Soong.

"I am safe," my dearest wrote, "in Saigon, where the French government suffers our presence, for now. In mid-April I must be in Hawaii. If it is possible, I would be happy beyond words if you could meet me there, and happier still if the children were able to come, too. Trust Homer or his agent with your reply. I pray, my love, that you are well, that the children grow and are strong, and that you will find a way to come to me."

I suppose I was laughing and crying at the same time, for Homer and Manuela were beaming at me and clapping their hands together silently. All I could think to do was to clap my hands together, too. *God in Heaven,* I said, *Thank You.*

*April 13, 1914:* Aboard the ocean liner *Northstar* en route

to Honolulu. Tomorrow we dock. The skies are blue overhead,
the ocean vast and calm, quite unlike what I feel inside. I try
to imagine how it will be when I see him again.

Porter and Kit are wildly excited. They look beautiful in
their tropical whites, tall and slim ten-year-olds on their first
trip to the South Seas. Porter is an avid reader of Mr. Jack
London, he often reads aloud to us from his writings.

Sara is with us. Willa had planned to come, but at the last
moment had to stay behind when the county board of supervisors granted her a chance to appear before them to plead her
case against condemning land through which to run a road all
the way up the coast. If she is not successful, she will have to
start yet another round of costly legal appeals. Joseph has a
perpetual frown when the subject arises.

Sara has just gone to join the twins on the promenade deck.
She says I am impossible to be with, and she is right. I can't
seem to keep still. Every particle within me is in motion, some
going in tiny circles and others bumping into each other. I want
it to be tomorrow. I want this sea to end, and the islands to
come into sight, and I want to see Soong.

Sara has given me the most beautiful traveling suit of Italian
linen, white with elaborate cut work and hand embroidery. It
is fashioned so as to minimize my deformity. With it I shall
wear my straw hat with the Chinese silk band. I shall be beautiful.

What nonsense! I'm acting like a moonstruck girl, instead
of a woman of forty-three years. I am not beautiful, but it
makes no difference. None at all. I only hope Soong finds me
not too changed.

*April 15, 1914, Waikiki Beach, Oahu:* I know about Paradise
now. I will write it as it happened.

As we docked we were greeted by a procession of dark-
skinned natives of these islands who lifted flower boughs over
our heads. It was the most gracious welcome any of us have
ever had, and it made all of us wonder what was to come. We
have not been disappointed. We are to stay in a cottage on the
beach, a cozy place open to the sounds of the sea. It is a different
ocean here—green in color at times, at times an iridescent
blue. The beaches are sparking white; the sounds and the movement are languid. It is as if we have entered a new and beautiful
world which moves at a gentler tempo. It is sweet, just to listen

to the wind in the palm fronds.

No more than an hour had passed when a Chinese appeared at our doorway and said something in French. Sara translated. If it was convenient, he said, he would return in one hour to take us to a house where "the tall one who is your friend" awaits.

He did as he promised, returning with an open, horse-drawn carriage in which we made our way through the narrow streets of Honolulu, into the Chinese quarter. We turned down a street so narrow there was room only for our carriage. I was wondering whatever we would do if we met another vehicle coming the other way, when suddenly we stopped. I saw nothing but high walls on one side, and what appeared to be a vacant warehouse on the other. Nonetheless, the man motioned us out of the carriage and we did as we were told. I had not noticed a small gate in the high wall. This he opened, and we followed him through it.

Magically, it seemed, we were in a beautiful garden, alive with the exotic blooms of the islands—red and white hibiscus and orchids, and the sweet-smelling plumeria.

He was standing at the far end of this garden: Soong.

Porter was striding toward him, Kit trailing behind.

"Wing Soong," Porter said excitedly, "it really is you!"

I saw the father look at his son. I saw his eyes shining with love and pride. And then Soong's eyes found mine, and the world was whole again.

Sara, beside me, was weeping. I turned to her, embraced her and kissed her on one cheek, then the other. "It is all right now," I told her, feeling the calm permeate, "everything is right now."

Soong said to Kit, "What is it, little one? Why are you shy with your old friend?"

And Kit answered, timidly, "Excuse me. It's just that you seem . . . different."

A great pride welled in me then, because it was true. Soong, tall and stately in his simple gray cotton uniform, was clearly a man of substance, an important person. Wing Soong had not changed, only the way the world considered him had.

And then we were alone in the garden, Soong and I, and I was where in my dreams I had longed to be—in his arms, touching his face, feeling the weight of his mouth on mine.

We are to have one week together. It is arranged. My body hungers for him. I understand something now that I did not know before. When our bodies join, in that instant when we are most totally one, his body answers mine and we are reaffirmed. It is, I know now, different from the kind of understanding known by a man and a woman who spend the whole of their lives together, sharing a bed each night. When our bodies join, we understand that which is beyond words. Our bodies say what is true. That life is, at best, an exquisite blending. That good is possible. When our bodies are together, I know this without reservation. I understand that truth that cannot be explained.

We will lie together today, and tomorrow, and then again for all of one holy week, one week when we are whole. And it will be enough.

*July 5, 1915, San Francisco:* The twins and I are spending part of our summer vacation with Sara in her new *petit palais* on California Street, almost directly across from Phineas Emory's old mansion, the one that was destroyed in the great 1906 earthquake and fire. Sara brought an architect from New York to design her little mansion, now the talk of the town, with its wonderful french doors, etched glass and graceful ironwork. It looks out onto a marvelous little park. Not only will we go to the theater while we are here, but we will also see Sara's new showing of paintings at the gallery in the City of Paris.

Porter has embarked on a series of mail-order self-improvement courses. He rises at five each morning and does such a thumping set of exercises that he literally rocks the house. Later, we must all serve as his audience as he orates in the manner of a chautauqua Bible-circuit lecturer.

"One thing about Porter," Sara said with remarkably good humor, "when he has a passion, it is a first-rate passion."

Our visit has been marred for me by something that Sara has told me. Confessed is a better word to use, in truth. It has caused me concern.

"Some weeks ago," she began awkwardly, "Connor McCord paid me a visit. He is building an estate south of the city—a great manor house and gardens—which he calls Wildwood. He asked me to select the paintings and tapestries that are to hang there. He asked, too, that I include a number of my own works.

"We went together to the gallery where I store my larger oil paintings, and began in a relaxed way to look through them. To be truthful, I didn't pay much attention when Connor strayed to another set of paintings. He began looking through them, and all of a sudden he called out to me. He had come upon . . ."

" . . . the portrait of Rose," I finished for her.

Sara nodded, solemnly.

"I tried to turn him away from it, but he wouldn't be turned. He just couldn't stop staring at the portrait."

"Who is she?" Connor asked. "Is her name Rose?"

Sara said yes. Only that, but something about the way she said it made Connor look up and study her face.

"Why do you keep it here, packed away?" he wanted to know.

"Because it is a flagrant copy of my teacher's style," Sara said forcefully, "it is embarrassing, and I won't have it seen, for that reason."

Connor carefully put the portrait back, walked a few steps to the window and painstakingly began to take the wrappers from a cigar. He concentrated on this task for several minutes, never once looking at Sara. She waited, feeling a rising sense of panic.

"I want it," Connor finally said.

"It's not for sale," Sara told him.

"Why not?"

"I told you, my professional reputation is at stake."

She had to make him believe her.

"If you let me have it, I won't show it. I'll hang it in my bedchambers. This bonny lassie will be all mine, then, and I needn't worry about sharing her with the world."

"Those words impaled me," Sara explained, her eyes huge and dark. "He said, 'this bonny lassie,' . . . Lena, she *was* his . . . I didn't know what to do. I told him I could not sell it, but that he might keep it for a time, if he promised me it would never be shown."

"And what did he say?" I asked.

"He said that it would be in his bedroom. And when I said I didn't know who might occupy his bed besides himself, he said no one, at least not that particular chamber. He said I had his word."

"And you take his word?" I asked.

"Yes I do," she answered. "I'm sorry, but you have to know

this—I have reason to trust Connor."

I bit my lip and nodded. I did not ask her reason. It was not that I objected to his seeing the portrait. It was more that it seemed, somehow, dangerous to raise those old, painful memories. I wanted to forget them. Rose was dead, Owen was dead. It was done with, that time. There was something disturbing about the idea of Connor sleeping with the image of Rose there . . . that portrait that so caught her charm, her magic.

The portrait I still could not bring myself to look at.

*January 10, 1916:* We had intended to spend yesterday at the ranch, but returned home early when Porter managed to anger Willa thoroughly by suggesting that she has no right at all to refuse the settlers the right to cross the ranch. I must admit that Porter can be exasperating, but Willa entirely lost her temper.

"He is only twelve years old," I tried to remind her.

"He talks as self-righteously as a twenty-year-old," she shot back.

"He's only a boy, Willa," I tried again, then—my ire aroused—added, "and I am wondering why it is that you can't allow any of us to disagree with you? Must we all think you are right all of the time?"

She blinked and for a moment it seemed as if the starch had gone out of her. Then she straightened and said, "Sometimes I get the feeling you are all against me. I have to fight every day to keep this ranch . . . every day of my life."

"You're not a hawk, Willa," I snapped. I haven't the vaguest notion why I said that.

*July 24, 1916, San Francisco:* I must record this while it is fresh in my mind, though I am shaking still with fear, thinking how close we came to disaster.

We are visiting with Sara, and of course nothing would do but that we attend the Preparedness Day parade on Saturday. Porter has announced his opposition to our entering the war in Europe, as have the labor leaders. They don't believe that Americans should fight in Europe for a war created, according to Porter, by the merchant and capitalist classes. I find myself in the peculiar position of trying to keep abreast of the news in order to be able to argue reasonably with my twelve-year-old son. The irony of this does not escape me.

Sara agreed that we should go to the parade. She thought

it might also be enjoyable to go to the reception in the city offices afterward, and meet Mayor Rolph and Governor Johnson, who will ride in the parade. Philip has arranged invitations, having worked closely with the governor for many years. We decided to find ourselves a suitable place from which to view the parade, and settled on Market Street near the Embarcadero.

I've always loved a parade, though I must admit to feeling a bit ashamed at enjoying one that was in support of our entering the war. We placed ourselves close to the curb. The crowd was jolly enough as we waited for the parade to pass our way. Then I noticed a group of men carrying placards, and a rough cry came up from them.

It all happened so quickly.

One moment we were standing about, waiting. Then there was an awful noise—then smoke and the smell of cordite . . . and such awful screams and cries . . . terrible cries.

I stood there, stunned, pulling Kit close. Her face was white, her eyes filled with fear. Everybody started running this way and that, shouting and crying. The crowd surged, pressed in on us . . . Then someone near to lifted me off the ground. I looked. I could not believe . . .

The children, Sara and I were pulled into an alleyway where we were quickly pushed into a touring car. The driver was instructed to get us out quickly.

"Who was that?" Kit whispered.

"A friend," Sara said.

"Connor McCord," I heard myself say. "His name is Connor McCord."

"Connor McCord," Kit repeated, as if to remember.

Then I looked at my son, who sat staring out of the window—his hands splayed against the glass, as if to understand what it was that had happened to us in those few chaotic, awful moments.

The morning papers tell a terrible tale. Ten died and forty were injured by a bomb blast. A suitcase filled with explosives was leaned against a building at Steuart Street, only a short half block from where we stood. It was, according to the police, the work of extreme radical revolutionists. Arrests would be made shortly, they said. Several revolutionists with experience in explosives are known to be in the city at the present time.

Porter reads the papers from cover to cover, trying still to understand. He says little, and that troubles me. Until now, Porter has been happy to talk at length about his newly discovered political theories.

When I asked Sara what Connor had been doing, she admitted that he cautioned against our going to the parade, saying that there was a good chance there would be violence. She had not believed him, she said. She was wrong and Connor was right. She supposed he had appointed himself as our protector. Perhaps he feels obligated to Sara, for all the help she has given him. Whatever the reason, I must admit that I am grateful to Connor for his help. I shiver to think what would have happened to us, had he not been there.

At the same time, I have suggested to the twins that we not disturb Willa by telling her about our adventure.

*October 7, 1918:* I passed by the library today and glanced in, to see Kit sitting on the Persian carpet in a pool of October sunlight. I thought: How lovely she is becoming. Her child's body is budding. She is fourteen now, slim and delicate. Her eyes are a smoky hazel, and wonderfully direct. She is not nearly so tall as her mother, but she has the same slim body, the narrow hips, the way of moving that is a study in grace. The boys have already begun to take notice. Wen, who always had an eye for attractive women, told her she was going to be the belle of the ball. Kit looked at him with her wide, direct eyes and replied, "Why should I want to be?" As usual, poor Wen didn't know what to make of her response.

*January 13, 1919:* The Los Angeles *Times* tells us that a forty-million-dollar state road bond issue has been passed and, it says, this ushers in a grand new era in road building unseen in two thousand years. (A bit of hyperbole, perhaps. Just a bit.) The *Times* is ecstatic—as, I suppose, is Mr. Henry Ford. The *Times* also tells us that the southern counties have coordinated their own road-building programs, and that Route 60 is to follow the shoreline through three counties. It is to be concrete, twenty feet wide and six inches thick.

Imagine a concrete roadway all the way up the coast! Imagine it, however, without Willa's twenty-two miles of shoreline. She will have nothing to do with it, nothing at all. Says she won't have a concrete slab slice through her land. James Irvine of the Irvine Ranch—one of the last of the great land grant ranches still intact, along with the Malibu—has up and donated the right of way through his property. Of course, this has made him something of a hero to the local folks, not to mention the highway commission. Willa says he's a fool. Joseph says he's shrewd, since he has managed to route the road where he wants it. I agree with Joseph, but it doesn't do to let Willa know. She glares you down as if you've put in with the Devil.

Ah, Willa. We have taken to calling her What Next Willa. What is next has thrown us all for the proverbial loop. She has engaged an architect to create what she calls "The Big House." She is going to build a mansion on Peregrino Hill; it is, she says, her first order of business. The word "mansion" is right. The plan is to have some fifty rooms, not to mention a ballroom large enough to accommodate the Philharmonic.

Last weekend, with Porter at the wheel of his new roadster, we drove out to the ranch, and I was amazed to find Charlie Rich there. Charlie was the agent who procured the Malibu for Owen almost thirty years ago. He has not aged well, but is fat and bald and laughs too much. His fortunes have fluctuated, though never his grandiose plans. He is trying to interest Willa in a money-making scheme to lease some beach property to rich people. Owen used to say his ambitions outstripped his talents, but when I mentioned that to Willa she said she was quite sure Owen had said no such thing, that my memory was faulty. That sent me on an hours-long search through my journals—and there it was, big as day: "Charlie Rich is a funny little man. Owen says he is one of those men who want a great deal more than their capabilities will provide, and that someday it will get him in trouble."

I said nothing of this to Willa. She does not like to be proved wrong.

Business has been good. The Reade companies are making money faster than Willa can spend it—*only just,* Joseph says. Wen sputters and fumes, and keeps after us all to "do something" before she sends everyone to the poorhouse.

Wen has taken to dropping by the townhouse with some regularity. His wife came once. As Porter said afterwards, "The lady does not approve of our laissez-faire household." I suppose she didn't, for she has never come back nor have we been invited to her home. I am glad for that small favor, for I'm sure I couldn't talk the twins into going.

Porter, that cheeky lad, takes uncommonly perverse pleasure

SHIRLEY STRESHINSKY

in Wen's visits. Happily, Wen seems not to notice Porter's tongue-in-cheek sallies. For example, after a few pleasantries Wen will settle down in the big chair and say, "Mother has taken leave of her senses, I do believe."

Porter then puts in, sotto voce, "Spending money faster than we can make it."

To which Wen, solemnly nodding, says out loud, "Spending money faster than we can make it."

Then Kit, primed by her brother, chirps up, all perky innocence: "Then we can make it, the nerve."

And Wen hasn't the good sense to know he's being joshed, poor thing. Still, I encourage his visits . . . I suppose I cling to the hope that, deep down, something remains of the boy I used to know.

I have asked Wen several times if he won't bring his two little girls to the townhouse for a visit: Caroline is five already and Lucy, just three. I suppose their mother won't have it—more's the pity!

*April 28, 1919:* I am so angry I could scream. I am livid. I am beside myself. At Abby, Wen's thoroughly despicable, simpering depressing wife. And at myself, oh, yes. At myself for not having had the presence of mind to excoriate her for having had the unmitigated gall to say what she said about Kit.

Oh, I am so mad! Why couldn't I think how to answer her? If she had called Willa instead of me—oh, my, then the fur would have flown. Willa would not have been such a simple fool as I was. "Thank you for calling," I said. Like some silly old fool. Even "thank you"!

I hate to talk on that infernal telephone. It makes me nervous. And Abby had never called before so it came as a shock to hear that whining little voice. How did she put it? She said she had something of "a delicate nature" to tell me, that she was sure I would want to know what people were saying about Kit.

"What people?" I had asked.

And the mealy-mouthed gossip answered, "People who know that Katharine Reade is my husband's sister, and who know we would be concerned about the family name."

The family name! I should have told her to ask Wen about honor and the family name. Why didn't I? Why did I even listen to her when she told me that Kit had been seen in places where "nice girls don't go," when she said it was "common knowledge that Kit smokes and drinks." And that she drives about town in a roadster, going "quite fast actually." Then she had lowered her voice, and said something about Kit's being seen in a parked car with an "older man."

I put the telephone receiver down and sat there in the front hall, shaking with fury. Porter walked in and, concerned, all but lifted me across the hall and made me lie down on the sofa. My anger spilled over then, and I blurted it all out. I could hardly keep my voice steady.

The worried look on Porter's face dissolved into relieved laughter. He took both of my hands in his and squeezed them, as if to make me pay attention. "She's right," he said, "Kit's a regular desperado. She does pretty much what she wants to do, you know that. She doesn't do it to shock anybody. Why shouldn't she go into beer halls now and then? I think she even has a beer sometimes. You know she smokes, and you know she's been seeing Joe Ainsworth, who goes to USC. He's maybe twenty. I guess that makes him an 'older man.' It's just that Kit is straight, and honest. And that bothers people. But you know all of that, so why are you so angry?"

I bit my lip and wondered myself. "I don't want people to talk about her that way. It hurts," I answered, childishly.

Porter *would* tell Kit, of course. And Kit was more concerned about my distress than anything Abby had said.

"I've heard it before," she told me, tucking her hand in mine the way she did. "The war is over, Auntie. Things are different now. A lot of the old ways don't work anymore. It's time for a change."

"Do you mind the gossip?" I asked.

She lit a cigarette and sat, holding it, thinking.

"When Betty Woodson told me that her parents had asked her not to see me anymore, I minded. We had been friends, I thought. She said she didn't want to obey, but she did. That's what I minded—that she gave in so easily."

"You wouldn't have," I said. "It must have hurt."

She smiled and gave me a quick kiss on the cheek. I couldn't think of anything else to say. The only thing I was sure of was that the next time Wen dropped by and deposited himself in my drawing room, he was going to be treated to a well-rehearsed diatribe. I would say everything to him that I should have told his wretched wife. His ears would burn.

*June 9, 1919:* The Senior Class Prophecy was published today, along with the Class of 1919's yearbook. According to the prophecy, in the year 1939 "Porter Reade was elected the youngest president in the history of the country at the age of thirty-five, while his twin sister, Katharine Reade, the First Lady of the American stage, gave a command performance before the bachelor king of England, which set tongues wagging on two continents."

After shrugging the prophecies off as "not terribly original" Porter could not resist adding that his first action as chief executive would be to issue a full pardon to Tom Mooney and Warren Billings, who continue to languish in San Quentin prison for the Preparedness Day Bombing in 1916, in spite of massive evidence to prove their innocence. I do believe that whole episode has done more than anything else to form Porter's political persuasion. He can scarcely speak to Willa anymore. Porter refuses to go to the Malibu, and Kit goes only occasionally, and only to see her mother.

*June 16, 1919:* The twins graduated last week, some months short of their sixteenth birthdays. It has been a busy time, what with examinations and then a full week of graduation celebrations.

About the only decision we have made is that we will spend the summer on the ranch. I am determined that Porter should mend fences with Willa. He does not know it, but I have spoken to Willa and she has agreed. The twins—even I think of them as that!—want time to ride and swim and explore after their long siege with studies.

It seems strange to speak of "siege" in terms of studies, when these were also the war years. Strange, and yet the war was far removed from our coast. Porter kept a large map of Europe in his room, on which he plotted the major battles with colored pins. Still, except for items in the newspapers listing casualties, and an occasional parade, the war has seemed distant. I am almost ashamed to admit that, for the family, the major effect has been economic. Owen's investments—oil and gas and the mines—were stimulated by the war, and have flourished. The last time we were at the ranch, Willa was decrying some new taxes, and Porter managed to raise her ire by pointing out what he chose to call the "war profits" the

Reade Land Company had reaped.

After the summer, I am not sure what will happen. Willa and I have encouraged the twins to wait a year before entering college. Porter plans to go to the University of California at Berkeley rather than Stanford. Kit isn't sure if she wants to go on to school.

Now that the war is, at long last, over, we'll be able to go to Europe again, though not for a time. Porter would like to visit Washington to observe the government. It would be good to see Sally again. But for now, only the Malibu . . . sand and sun and relaxation. I feel as if I am coming home again. Perhaps I will move back. Willa would like it, and there is no reason not to if Kit and Porter are away.

*June 23, 1919:* I feel I should begin this with a prayer. Lord Have Mercy, is all I can think to say. I am not a religious woman, but at times the old phrases are comforting. Here is what happened: Several days after our return to the ranch, one of Willa's *vaqueros* rode up to tell her that soldiers had made camp on the beach, that they said they planned to stay. Willa threw up her hands.

"I knew it," she said, "squatters! All those stories circulating again about the illegality of old land grants . . . how many times do we have to prove we own this land? Now I've got war veterans gathering like locusts . . ."

"It's terribly sad . . ." Kit began, but Willa cut her off.

"Of course it's sad, Kit. There are all sorts of sad people all over the country. Should I gather them all in? Should I empty the mental hospitals and the old people's homes and give each of them a slice of the ranch?"

Porter entered at the moment and I knew if he said anything at all we were in for it, so I quickly marshaled the two of them to go with me to, as I put it, reconnoiter the situation. I felt sure it was the only thing that would deflect Porter.

From a distance, we could see the men in the familiar drab uniforms clustered on the beach. The fires they had lit seemed out of a dream, but we could smell the food they were cooking.

"I suppose they have nowhere else to go, no homes or families," I said. "Coming here must be a last resort."

"Resort is what I believe Mother has in mind for the Malibu," Porter said caustically.

"Porter!" I warned him. I pulled my horse up short of the

encampment and Kit stopped with me, but Porter pushed on. We watched him, tall and lean and sure of himself, dismount and walk into the group of men. He seemed to be talking easily and then, suddenly, he wheeled, jumped onto his horse and returned to us in a state of agitation.

"Auntie, come quickly," he ordered, and I did as he said.

Porter lifted me from my saddle and all but carried me to a small cluster of men. Two were standing by another, who was sitting on a log, staring at the ground. He raised his eyes as the three of us approached. I fell against Porter.

"Dear God in heaven," I heard myself saying.

It was Thad.

## ~ *Chapter Twenty-One*

Thad had made his way home again, home to the Malibu. He did not seem to know who he was, or even where he was, but he had come back to the beaches and mountains he loved. He did not recognize us, not even Willa. After one short, heart-breaking sob she pulled herself erect and said, "He's home, that is all that matters now." It was a refrain she would repeat in the days and weeks to come, days of turmoil and weeks of despair.

Slowly, very slowly, the facts of Thad's long odyssey began to emerge. He had volunteered for service in the AEF, American Expeditionary Force, and he had been through the dark and brutal battles of Château-Thierry and Belleau Wood, and the Meuse-Argonne offensive. He had been gassed; his mind was a haze, his lungs weakened. In the end, when it was over at last, he had drifted with the others, the men who had fought and come home to nothing. Some of the men—those who had known him before the gas weakened his lungs and the horror, his mind—knew that he had once lived in California, by the sea. Even then, they said, he seldom spoke of his past. Now he scarcely spoke at all.

The summer of fun and relaxation the twins had planned was no longer possible. Willa was preoccupied with Thad. We could see how tightly she was coiled and the tension affected us all. And yet, her concern had some unexpected effects. Porter, for the first time, was able to feel sympathy for Willa and he became more tolerant. And Kit—Kit in those terrible months amazed me. She moved to her mother's side, she saw what she could do and did it. She offered encouragement when it was needed, and was quiet when that was best. She never backed away, never shirked an unpleasant task. Kit grew up in those months, and I was proud of her.

In the fall Porter went off to Washington. He asked Kit to go with him, but she wouldn't. By then she had taken over some business tasks in order to relieve Willa, who had thrown all of her energies into seeking medical help for Thad. Kit was patient and tender with her older brother. Willa thought Thad favored Kit, though I couldn't see that he favored anyone or anything. He seemed in a trance, willing to do whatever anyone told him to do. He accepted us as he had accepted his soldier friends. When they left, he registered no surprise, no emotion at all.

For the first time in years, Willa had reason to leave the Malibu. She went off to New York and Europe to consult with psychiatrists. I urged Kit to go with her, feeling it would do her good to get away, but Willa wanted her to stay behind with Thad.

Occasionally Kit had friends out from town, or she would go in for the weekend, to a party or a dance. But as the months passed she accepted fewer invitations. She became more and more involved with the Land Company, she seemed to be drawn into the ranch. I began to fear that she was becoming isolated.

A year passed, then another. Willa's energies remained focused on Thad's well-being. She was convinced his mind could be cured, even if his body could not be. And Kit was becoming indispensable to her. Except in looks, they were more alike than I had thought. It was good to see them together, to see how close they had become. But it was worrisome, too, because Kit's life was just beginning while Willa, at fifty-seven, had seen as much of the world as she cared to see. I tried to talk to Willa about Kit, but she could not see why I was worried. Kit was in good spirits, she pointed out, she seemed happy and busy. Could it be, Willa implied ever so carefully, that I was a bit jealous that Kit *was* content on the ranch?

I had asked myself the same question. I had also asked Sara and Porter, now in his second year at Berkeley. They felt my alarm was justified, and convinced me that we should act to get Kit away from the ranch for a time.

Late in the spring of 1922 I talked Kit into going north with me, to San Francisco, for several weeks, Sara had arranged for Kit to meet several young women who were involved in various enterprises. We thought that if we could just show Kit what else was available, she would at least take a close look at the path her life was taking.

The best of plans can go awry, and ours did. Two days before we were to leave for San Francisco I received a letter from Wing Soong. He was to be in Canton, in the south of China, for the summer months. Canton was close to the Portuguese treaty port of Macao. If I could travel there, it would be an excellent opportunity for us to be together. He would not wish me to make the trip alone, he said. Sara had often expressed a desire to see the Orient, to study its art. If this was an appropriate time, he would be overjoyed to see both of us. I said nothing to Kit, but waited until we arrived in San Francisco so that I could speak to Sara first.

Sara took no time at all to make up her mind. "I can book passage and we can be away in four days' time," she said, her eyes sparkling.

"But what about Kit?" I moaned.

"Kit will keep," Sara answered tartly, "in fact, leaving her here on her own may be the best idea of all. She has too many of us hovering over her. Let's let her breathe. And Porter's here, after all."

So we left. It would be many months before I learned all that happened that fateful summer of 1922.

"What does Aunt Lena say?" Porter asked, in an attempt to draw her out.

Kit walked to the window and pulled open the drape so she could look out onto the greenery of the Flood mansion across the way. A fine, white fog made the bushes glow a garish shade of green. She pulled Sara's dressing gown close around her.

"Oh, Auntie . . . well, she is careful. You know how easily she treads where Mother is concerned. But I think she'll be glad if I decide to get out."

"You've got to get out," Porter cut in, "the ranch is no place for you now. Mother's obsessed with Thad, and he's one of the walking dead . . ."

"Porter!" Kit reprimanded him by the urgency of her tone.

Porter only shrugged. "They're all over, you know. I was at one of the Old Soldiers' Homes a few weeks ago, and the men—they've lost parts of their bodies or they've been gassed, like Thad, and something is missing in their minds."

"The awful part," Kit said softly, "is that sometimes he looks just like the Thad I remember. I'll come upon him, he'll be working in the barn or fishing and I forget until I look into his eyes, and . . . nothing is there." She was silent for a time, then she continued. "Mother talks to him as if nothing has happened. She uses this very reasonable tone, and when he doesn't answer she just keeps on talking as if he had. I can hardly stand to be around her when Thad is in the room. I know what she is trying to do but . . ."

"What *is* she trying to do?" Porter wanted to know.

"One of the doctors she searched out in Austria—the psychiatrists—told her to continue to treat him as if he were normal, to try constantly to draw him out."

Porter grimaced derisively. "Thad is burned out."

"I feel that, too," Kit told him, still looking across the street, "and in spite of the fact that it annoys me—the way she talks to him—I almost admire her for her hope. And yet, I can't but wonder if it wouldn't be more realistic to accept what he is . . ."

"Thad's an empty shell," Porter put in. "Maybe she thinks that someone else will come live in it, like a hermit crab . . ."

Kit turned back to him, put her hand on his arm for an instant before she curled up on the chair opposite.

"I heard from Philip a few days ago, just after Sara and Auntie decided to go to Macao," Porter said, "I wrote him that you would be here for a short while, and I expect he'll come to see you."

"He's in Sacramento now?"

Porter nodded. "But he will have an office here in San Francisco, too, now that he's moved up to the Supreme Court. I'm glad for that—he needs something after Mother kicked him out."

"She did not kick him out," Kit sighed.

"He thinks she did."

"Well, I was there and it wasn't like that. I don't even know if anything was said . . . it just became clear that there wasn't going to be room in her life for Philip." She hesitated, as she always did when she felt pulled between Porter and her mother "She felt that she would have to break with Philip soon anyway, that the age difference between them was becoming more . . . difficult, for her."

"That was her excuse," he said.

"You think so?" Kit asked.

"I think she has her hawks and the Malibu and Thad. And Philip has the habit of cutting through to the truth of things . . . and Mother, more and more, doesn't want to see what is, only what she wants . . ."

"Maybe," Kit said quickly, determined to stay away from this particular conversation. "I'll be happy to see Philip. It will give me something to look forward to, now that Sara and Auntie are off for who knows how long . . ."

"From my last letter from Soong, I'd be willing to bet he will be in Canton for weeks, months maybe. You may be here alone for quite a while. I could move over, if it bothers you— being alone in this house."

Kit shook her head. "That's silly. You've got your place in Berkeley, and you have trouble making it to class in time as it is. I'm not in the least worried about being here alone. And the Weatherlees are here, after all."

"The faithful servants, yes," Porter murmured, but he was grinning too. "The saving grace is they don't seem to think they're servants. At times I think they run Sara."

"When she left, Mrs. Weatherlee promised she'd look after me, 'like her own mum.'" Kit grimaced.

Porter looked at the clock and stood, rubbing his eye with a fist that was ink-stained.

She touched his hand. "You're grimy," she said.

"Too little sleep and too much writing," he answered. "I can't afford to loll around until noon, as you've just done. If I hurry I'll only be an hour late for my meeting."

Kit laughed at him fondly; he seemed incapable of being on time, anywhere.

"Perhaps I should go to college, if for no other reason, to see that you manage to get to your classes."

Porter frowned. "You don't want to go to college, Kit . . . you're only considering it as an acceptable way to leave the Malibu. Why do you feel you need an excuse?"

She tucked her arm in his, and walked him to the door. "I don't, really. In some ways I'm happy there. It's just that Mother, well . . . She seems so locked in . . . Sometimes I feel I'm one of the last links for her . . ." She paused, then said, cautiously, "Mother wants me to learn about the business."

He had opened the door, but now he closed it again. He looked at her carefully, as if to read her mind.

"Does that interest you?" he asked.

"I think it does, Porter . . . I mean, it seems logical that I should prepare myself. You won't, and Thad can't, and Wen . . ."

"Wen is a jackass," Porter said.

"Yes, so maybe I should be the capitalist of this generation."

Porter looped his arm around her and gave her a hug. "Lord," he said, "my twin."

She looked up at him, anxiously at first, then she relaxed. "You don't mind? I wasn't sure . . ."

"Be sure," he said, "I'm sure of you. Just don't go back to the Malibu until we can figure out something to occupy you."

"Go to your meeting," she laughed, pretending to push him out the door.

As he ran down the steps and onto the street he called back, "Tell Mother you have to stay to help me get organized . . . that'll satisfy her."

A cable car came rumbling past and he loped after it, jumping on just as it began the descent down California Street hill. He waved his cap at her, and she stood smiling, still wrapped in Sara's old dressing gown.

She was about to step back inside when she noticed a large green Pierce-Arrow stop in front of the mansion. A man emerged from the back seat, said something to the driver and was at the door before he noticed Kit.

"I'm sorry," he said, taken aback. "Is Miss Hunt in?"

The fog was blowing in gusts. "Come in, please," she smiled politely. She did not want to stand on the street to explain.

He stood only inside the vestibule, his hand still on the door handle. "I have a luncheon appointment with Miss Hunt . . ." he began, formally.

"I'm afraid there has been some mix-up," she told him,

"Sara left yesterday for what promises to be a long trip—she must have neglected to notify you..."

"I see," he said tersely, "I'm sure she left word with my secretary. I'm just returned from a trip myself and I haven't yet checked with my office. Thank you." He turned to leave.

"I *am* sorry," Kit said, putting her hand out to him, "I'm Katharine Reade. Sara is my godmother. She left yesterday with my aunt to meet an old friend of theirs in Macao. It happened quite suddenly—they were off as soon as they could book passage."

"I see," he said again, stiffly in spite of her attempt to be friendly. "In that case..." He turned to go, but now Kit's curiosity was whetted.

"May I tell Sara who called?" she asked.

For a moment she had the curious sensation that he was not going to answer, that he did not want to tell her his name.

"McCord," he said, "Connor McCord."

"Oh my!" Her face changed; a smile of recognition broke through. "Connor McCord, at last. You can't know how long we've wanted to meet you—my brother and I—he's only just left, and he will be disappointed. But you can't go now. Please. You got us out of trouble that day—the Preparedness Parade. Please don't run off."

"You're getting chilled standing here," he said, smiling slightly.

She looked down at the dressing gown, pulled it close about her neck and, to cover her embarrassment, wrinkled her nose and said, "It reeks of oil paints—Sara must work in it. But, please...I am so glad finally to meet you. I should like to talk a bit." She grinned at her own awkwardness. "Can't you wait just a minute while I dress? I can be back in no time."

He hesitated. He was, she could tell, trying to find a polite way to leave. But he did hesitate, and Kit took advantage of it.

"To be truthful," she told him, "I'm afraid I'm at loose ends today. My aunt and Sara rushed off, Porter is busy and I have been trying to think what to do. I don't suppose I could invite myself to lunch? I know that's terribly forward, and I'm not Sara, but..." She laughed then, so disarmingly that he smiled in return, a boyish smile that made her feel she had said the right thing. Before he could answer she started up the stairway.

"It won't take me a minute, I promise, to wash my face and throw on some clothes. Promise me you'll wait?"

Halfway up she turned back so that she could see him. "Promise?" she said.

And he nodded yes.

Passing a mirror in the hallway, she was surprised to see the excitement in her eyes. He was, she thought, terribly attractive, this man.

It was not until they were seated across from each other at a table overlooking the ocean, the surf crashing on the rocks below them, that she could study his face, strong, lined, but still young. He had a thick shock of hair, scattered with gray. He moved as if he were sure of himself. There was, she noted with pleasure, nothing awkward about him, nothing at all.

They talked easily. He drew her out so that she talked a good deal more than was usual for her, hearing herself say aloud the thoughts that had been going through her mind. He was studying her, she knew that. She was pretty enough, and wealthy enough, to understand something of the effect she had on men.

She knew he would find her informed as few women her age were. When he remarked on this, she said, "When you meet Porter, you'll understand why. It's not just Porter, of course. You know Sara... The people I seem to care about, most of them, are..."

"Fascinating?" he put in for her. "Unorthodox?"

"At the very least!" she laughed.

At one point she looked at her hands, which were raised, palms open, as if they were struggling to help her find the precise words that would explain a concept she was trying to grasp. She let her hands fall and looked at him in distress.

"This is terrible," she said, "I'm babbling away, you must think..."

"No," he said, looking at her through the smoke of his cigar. And then he smiled, and she felt pleased. Enormously pleased.

She took a breath.

"Tell me then how you happened to be there that day, why did you rescue us?"

"Nothing mysterious," he answered so carelessly that she knew he had prepared his reasons. "I happened to be watching the parade at about the same time from the same vantage point.

I'd been told that there could be trouble, that wasn't much of a secret. I had my car parked close by, in a place I knew would offer an easy egress... I've known Sara for a long time. She has been a good friend... a very good friend. I noticed her standing there, it was clear that you and your brother and your aunt were in her party. So when the bomb exploded, it seemed the proper thing to get you out of there."

She was looking at him steadily. "Coincidence, then?"

"More or less," he answered.

"My Aunt Lena says she will be forever in your debt for that day. Did she write you that?"

"I believe she did," Connor answered, for the first time uncomfortably, "it was a long time ago. I seem to remember a very small girl with great, frightened eyes."

"I was frightened, terribly so... I remember it so clearly. And Porter, well it had the most profound effect on Porter. He still works for the release of the two men—Mooney and Billings."

"Yes," he said, "it's exactly the kind of case that points up the flaws in the judicial system."

"But letting innocent men stay there—locked up, when their innocence has been proved. It is beyond my ability to understand... I don't know what life in San Quentin is like, but from what Porter tells me it is dreadful..."

He shifted uncomfortably in his chair and looked out the window as if searching for something on the horizon. "Did I say something?" she asked, not understanding the sudden silence, the shift in mood.

"No," he answered, turning back to smile again, "nothing at all."

He asked questions, she answered with her own questions. They laughed, and the afternoon passed until, when finally she did look around her, she was amazed to find the restaurant empty.

"I'm surprised they haven't asked us to leave," she said.

As if on signal, the head waiter appeared with a chit which Connor signed.

"Can we walk for a bit?" she asked. "We've been sitting for such a long time, my legs feel numb."

She tucked her arm into his as they moved down the steep walkway to the beach below.

"Do you come here often?" she asked.

"Every morning, as a matter of fact," he answered, bending to her so the wind wouldn't pull away his words. "I swim every morning at about six. Keeps my legs from getting numb in the afternoon."

"You swim in the ocean—this ocean?" she said into his ear.

"You mean this cold ocean . . . not the warm Malibu beach."

She looked at him, blinking the wind from her eyes.

"Do you know the Malibu beaches?" she asked, surprised.

"I was there once, a very long time ago—long before you were born. In my cowboy days, you could say."

"You mean you worked on our ranch?"

"That's right," he said, turning her into the wind so that any more talk between them was impossible. Foghorns were wailing. The sound carried over the waters and made her feel as if they were, somehow, isolated on this bleak seashore, and she felt suddenly sad.

In the car the formality returned to his voice. He said that he had enjoyed meeting her, that having taken lunch with her was an unexpected pleasure, that he would be sure to tell Sara how kind she, Kit, had been to substitute for her.

Kit cut in. "It *was* a pleasure. Do you suppose we might lunch together again?"

McCord did not answer for a long moment, but looked out of the window of the car as it circled along the ocean drive. When he spoke, the false formality was gone, and in its place a somber tone. "Katharine," he said, "I mean it when I say that today was a great pleasure. But my life is complicated, extremely so . . ." He was, she thought, being purposefully vague, he wanted her to think that there was something he could not tell her. "There are other demands . . . business, personal . . . I wish there were more time."

"I don't understand. Surely we could have lunch?"

He spoke carefully. "I've never married, you know, but if I had a daughter . . ."

"Don't do that," Kit snapped. "Please, just don't. I'm not your daughter, and I don't think that's a very good way to dismiss me."

Connor thrust his hands in his pockets and turned away. When he turned back again he was smiling, a curious smile she could not understand.

"Perhaps when Sara returns, we can all . . ."

The car had stopped at an intersection and Kit quickly opened the door and darted out, taking him—and herself—by surprise.

She walked briskly, the wind blowing the folds of her dress against her body, and stinging her face so that tears filled her eyes. Connor caught up with her and took her arm.

"You are angry and I'm sorry," he said, an edge of humor in his voice, "I suppose it runs in the family."

She didn't know what he could mean, but she felt too peculiar and confused to ask. Not knowing what to say, she said nothing.

"I cannot give you all the reasons I shouldn't see you again," he said, bending down to speak close to her face, "you will have to take my word that they exist. There are too many complications." He was firm, he was not pleading.

She found her voice. "Do you want to see me again?" she asked breathlessly.

"Yes," he answered. "Let's go now." He guided her back to the car, and she said nothing, nothing at all. But she felt a remarkable surge of energy, a feeling of triumph. *He wanted to see her.*

"I'm terribly sorry," the secretary told her, "Mr. McCord is not available. Yes, he is in the city, but he cannot be disturbed."

Kit found two other numbers for Connor in Sara's book. She called the first.

"Yes," he answered, peremptorily.

"This is Katharine Reade," she said, working to keep her voice even, "will you meet me for lunch?"

Silence. She waited.

"I'm sorry," he said, "I can't." He was abrupt, not rude. She thought that perhaps someone was with him.

"Here then, tomorrow. At Sara's. I'll cook."

"I'm afraid I can't do that, either."

"All right," she said, keeping her voice quiet, "but I think it only fair—either you tell me why you can't see me, or you see me. I can't think I'm asking all that much."

"I . . . Can you . . ." He was stumbling.

"Tomorrow then," she said, quickly, "at noon, here. Please!"

She hung up before he could answer, then sat looking at the telephone for a full ten minutes, expecting it to ring. She had never pursued a man before, not like this. She repeated, over and over again, his answer when she had asked if he wanted to see her again. *He did.* She was sure of it. He had been drawn to her. Why was he resisting her? She shook her head and said out loud to herself: "Kit, you're acting like a spoiled child." She paced back and forth, glancing at the telephone, waiting for its ring.

Finally she decided to get out of the house. She dressed and left for Berkeley, where she spent the day with Porter. After his last class they went to a movie, had dinner, and she caught the ferry back. When she came into the house Mrs. Weatherlee fussed with her for not having called for the car to meet her. Only as an afterthought did the woman say, "Oh, yes, there are flowers for you in the drawing room—and a card."

She looked at the card for a full minute before, sighing, she opened it, knowing already what it was going to say: *Katharine, I can't. Understand. Connor.*

Sinking into a chair, she said out loud, "No. I will not understand."

She sat for a long time, still in her coat. She did not turn on the light; she was thinking. When finally she stood, she knew what she was going to do.

For three days she distracted herself with trips to Berkeley, where she and Porter went to coffeehouses where they listened to political speakers, or to the moving pictures, or sometimes took long walks in the eucalyptus groves, which made her think of the ranch. Porter tried to get her to talk about her future, and when she wouldn't he accused her of being evasive.

"True," she told him, "but I'm not going anywhere, not for a while. I'll tell you when I'm ready."

She shopped at the City of Paris. She even agreed to lunch with an acquaintance from school, regretting it immediately. The girl chattered incessantly.

On the morning of the fourth day she rose at five, dressed carefully and warmly, pulled on sensible shoes and a woolen scarf and drove Sara's yellow Stutz out to the beach.

She arrived just after six; the green Pierce-Arrow was there. She caught her breath. She could feel the blood throbbing in her temples. She slowed, doubt assailed her. She all but turned the car around, but, instead, stepped hard on the gas pedal, and pulled up next to the big car.

"Hello," she called to the driver with false cheerfulness,

"I'm late, I'm afraid. I take it he's already gone in for his swim?"

The driver looked at her, confused. Then he recognized her and smiled politely. "Yes, miss," he said, "no more than five minutes ago. He'll be twenty more, at least."

"You can put his things in my car," she said, "I'll take the towel and wait for him."

"Ma'am?" the driver said, confusion flickering over his face.

"Didn't Mr. McCord tell you that I would be meeting him here, to drive him back?"

"No, ma'am, he didn't."

"Perhaps he didn't think I would make it on time," she laughed, a warm, girlish laugh. "That scoundrel!" He laughed too, then, sharing the joke. While she had the advantage, she quickly reached for the towel. "You are to have the morning off, I believe. If you'll just put his things in my car there." She nodded toward the flashy little Stutz. "Well, in truth it's Sara Hunt's car, but I pretend it's mine."

"Miss Hunt, oh, yes," the driver said jovially, gathering up his employer's clothing.

She did not wait, but walked off toward the water's edge as if to wait, searching the foggy waters for some sign of the swimmer.

When she looked back, the Pierce-Arrow was driving along the highway. She pulled the towel close around her and laughed; the first part of the plan had worked. He could not avoid her now.

She caught sight of him, stroking steadily, riding a wave as it surged forward out of the fog. Then he was standing, walking toward her. His body was tightly muscled, she noted, his chest covered with wet, gray hair, his legs slim. A good body, she thought, and felt her own stomach tighten.

He did not break pace, but took the towel from her without a word and began to dry himself as he must every day, not looking at her now but attending to the business at hand.

She waited. She had thought she would say something witty, something glib, but words seemed locked inside her. Her smile felt fixed; she could not speak.

They walked together toward her car on the deserted beach. From the roadway above, they would have looked as if they knew each other well enough to walk without speaking, they would have looked as if they knew where they were going.

He reached into the car, pulled on his clothes, tucked in his shirt without the semblance of embarrassment at buttoning his pants in front of her. She could scarcely bring herself to look at his face, such was her discomfort. When she finally did, she could not tell what he was thinking or feeling. His face was not readable.

Suddenly she felt angry, it welled within her and spilled over. "Damn you," she said, "just damn you."

She started the car, every motion a jabbing anger. She pulled out of the dirt in a spray of sand and gravel. Connor slammed his door shut, but a quick turn sent it flying out from him so that he struggled a few moments.

She slammed on the brake. "I have been stupid... stupid and childish and..." She had turned toward him, and now she looked at him. "I don't have the slightest idea why I would do this, and I am terribly sorry and embarrassed. Tell me where I should take you."

He smiled then, a small and careful smile.

"I'll take you home," she said, disgusted with herself. "And I won't bother you again, I promise."

He spoke, then, for the first time: "Surely you had some plan, something more than taking my pants, that is."

"It wasn't your pants I was after," she said, the anger returning. "Though please... don't tell me I'm too young for that, too. I'm not."

"Whoa... wait one minute, slow down," he said to her, laughing now at her anger, "you've successfully kidnaped me, the very least you can do is buy me a cup of coffee."

She closed her eyes, took a deep breath and whispered, "Where?"

"There's a diner down the way."

"Your pants are wet," she answered.

"Maybe no one will notice," he said.

Sitting on stools in the brightly lit diner, sipping bad coffee from heavy mugs, she told him, "It really was a childish thing to do, especially when I'm trying to convince you I am not a child, but I wanted to see you and you wouldn't..."

McCord said nothing, but sipped the steaming coffee. He was wearing his wet swimsuit under his clothes, but if it was uncomfortable, he didn't show it

* * *

Porter sat in his usual sprawl on the lounge in Sara's morning room, turning a chambered nautilus from Sara's collection of shells over and over in his hands, studying it while listening intently.

"I have been trying to understand why I've been acting so strangely," Kit said. "He is an interesting man, that's part of it. And I wonder if it's because I've never had anyone push me away before, I mean any man I was interested in..."

"Have you ever been interested before? I mean, that much?"

Kit shook her head. "I suppose not, but it's not just silly romantic notions, Porter. I enjoy him, yes. There is something exciting about the man. But..." She shook her head, dropped her hands. "Maybe it is just because he won't see me, maybe that is it... maybe that's all there is to it."

"Maybe," Porter said. "It looks as if it is keeping you from doing anything else, so you had better find out."

"Thanks for the sympathy," she said.

"What the hell do you need sympathy for?" he answered, and she patted him on the sleeve to let him know she didn't.

"Push him," Porter said. "Just keep after him until he explains why he can't see you. Maybe he's got a wife and kids stashed away—hidden in that big house he owns out by Crystal Springs."

Then Porter smiled. "I still can't quite feature the beautiful Kit, Queen of the May, hiding a man's clothes from him."

She threw a pillow at him and he, catching it, caught her too and held her easily at bay with one hand. She flailed at him helplessly, until she began to laugh and he joined her.

"I'd like to meet him too," Porter said. "I've always wanted to know what he thinks about the Mooney case... he was there, that day. We know that."

"Well you can't see him, Porter. Not until he agrees to see me, at least."

"Too bad Sara isn't here," he said, "maybe she could help."

"I rather doubt it," Kit answered, biting her lower lip. "I have a feeling that Sara wouldn't approve. Otherwise, why wouldn't we have met Connor before? He and Sara are friends, good friends. And we have wanted to meet him, we asked ... remember?"

Porter did remember. "It is a mystery, isn't it?" he said. "Maybe Philip knows something. He's coming next week, we can find out."

Philip took a long time to study the menu, then he asked for a wine list and took an equally long time to decide on his choice.

Porter looked at Kit and raised his eyebrows. She knew what he meant. Philip knew something and he was trying to decide how much to tell them.

Kit's stomach tightened.

"He is, I think, quite an interesting man," she said, trying to sound casual, "McCord, I mean. But he doesn't seem to want to see me. Naturally," she mocked, "I find that terribly difficult to understand." She frowned. "Even more difficult to understand is *why* it angers me so—I don't know any man, other than Porter, who can make me angry."

Philip smiled at her, patted her hand. "Kit," he said, "could it be, well—could he perhaps think you too young? He is a man of experience, and . . ."

"For Christ's sake, Philip," Porter started, but Kit stopped him.

Philip shifted uncomfortably. He knew what Porter had been about to say. "I'm sorry, Kit, really I am," he said, "you're more mature than most of the women I know, and damned attractive as well. I suspect it's something else. Have you thought, well . . . have you thought that there might be another woman?" He said this with a certain delicacy.

Kit leaned across the table as if to share a confidence. "I am not necessarily applying for the position of mistress of his household," she whispered, "I simply want to get to know the man."

Philip and Porter exchanged glances.

Porter leaned back in his chair and began tapping a spoon against the crystal. In his shabby corduroys, he should have seemed out of place in the elegant little restaurant; instead, he seemed so perfectly at ease that the waiter, annoyed by the clinking of the crystal and the fact that Porter's long legs rested in the walkway, still could not bring himself to say anything to the young gentleman.

"Could we settle this romantic problem so we can get on

to other, perhaps equally important, subjects?" Porter said.

Kit smiled sweetly and put her hand over the spoon. "Stop making noises, dear heart," she said, "and stop referring to my interest in McCord as 'romantic.' It's condescending."

"Kit's right," Philip said. "I do know a bit about McCord, nothing that isn't common knowledge, I suppose. I know, for example, that he spent a few years in San Quentin some time back."

"Really?" Kit and Porter said in unison.

"A long time back, actually. After that, he seems to have made quite a spectacular fortune with a gold mine in Grass Valley, I believe. He developed a way to reach the deeper veins in the old mine. Sara's done business with him."

"Of course Sara's done business with him," Porter laughed. "Count on Sara."

Kit was thinking about their conversation at the restaurant at the beach. She had mentioned San Quentin and he had looked away, had seemed uncomfortable. Was that it? Was that why he wouldn't see her?

She turned the talk to Philip's work on the court, and they went from that to their own futures, hers and Porter's. They spoke of Wing Soong in Macao with Sara and their auntie. They talked of politics and power and Philip, feeling the warmth of the wine and the good feelings of old friends, told them once more what a remarkable pair they were, how extraordinarily intelligent he believed them to be.

Philip sat up late that night in his room at the Palace Hotel, trying to decide. He went through it all in his mind, covering every point as he might a case. He was concentrating as hard as ever he had, trying to determine what was just . . . understanding that justice often had little enough to do with fairness, or right. It was a case that he had considered for a very long time and he knew, he was certain, that in some way he was a participant, that he was inextricably involved in its resolution. He wished he were not. He wished he were merely an observer, not feeling the need to act.

"Are you playing God?" he asked himself. Willa would say so. Willa would accuse him of taking revenge.

"Is that right?" he asked himself. "Is it because she couldn't love you enough, is that it?"

He puffed on his cigar, and looked out over the buildings

on Market Street. He blew one circle of smoke and then another, letting them float out of the window to disperse. No, he
said to himself, that's not it either. He had come to terms with
Willa Reade. He accepted, finally, what Willa must have known.
That there was not enough between them. That he—or she—
was lacking some final wellspring of... of what? Need, perhaps. It wasn't there, or, if it was, it wasn't powerful enough.
He lay back, closed his eyes and dozed fitfully.

Connor opened the door himself, and led Philip into a darkly
paneled room in which a fire had been lit. He motioned his
guest to have a seat in one of two leather chairs pulled to the
fireplace.

They covered the amenities quickly. Each knew the other
by name, by reputation. Connor was cautious, waiting to find
out what Philip Bourke wanted of him.

"We have a good many mutual friends, I suspect," Philip
said. "Sara Hunt, for instance."

Connor nodded, but waited still.

"And Kit Reade. I've known Kit most of her life. We had
dinner together last evening.

Connor leaned forward and poured two brandies. He took
his time, swirling the amber liquid in the snifter as if to study
it before handing one to Philip.

"Thank you," Philip said absently, leaning back and sighing.
"Look," he said, "the advantage is mine. I know a good deal
more about you than I think you know about me... though I
am told you make it a policy to know a good deal about many
things. However, since I feel I do have an advantage, why
don't I attempt to rid myself of it, so that we can talk straight-
forwardly?"

Philip started at the beginning, with his first trip West as
one of T.R.'s boys. He told Connor all that he knew, traced
all of the connections, talking for three quarters of an hour
without interruption. Connor listened, occasionally taking a
long swallow of brandy, sometimes looking into the fire with
a pained look which might only have been a reaction to a deep
swallow of the drink in his hand, or something else entirely.
Philip couldn't be sure.

When Philip finally fell silent, Connor asked, "Why are you
telling me this?" His voice was calm but his eyes were wary.

"Ah yes, my motive," Philip said. "I sat up half of last night asking myself that same question." He went then, step by step, through his reasoning. He spoke of Calabasas and Rodriguez, he spoke of Charles Emory and of Amos Proctor. He spoke, even, of Willa and himself. Very carefully, methodically, he marched through each of the possible motives, speaking at times as if he were alone in the room, yet knowing full well the risk he was taking.

He was not sure how much of what he said Connor already knew. He was not sure what Connor knew that he did not. And he had no way of knowing what Connor would do with the information he gave him.

"I came because of Kit," he finally said.

Connor began, "It was an accident, my meeting her. I assure you I . . ."

"I know that you've discouraged her, and I tried to also. It didn't work, and it won't . . . I know Kit well enough to know it won't. She is determined to know you. I suggested to her that you might very well have someone . . . that there might be a woman . . ."

"No," Connor said firmly, "no one."

Philip looked at him directly, then. "Is it because of her mother?"

Connor only shook his head. "Do you mean, is Willa Reade the reason there is no woman in my life, or do you mean, is Willa Reade the reason I won't allow myself even a casual acquaintance with her daughter?"

"Both, I suppose," Philip answered, not sure that he wanted the answer but certain he would have to accept it.

"Willa taught me a major lesson, she taught me that women were a peculiar weakness for me . . . that I could become too . . ." he paused " . . . dependent. When I discovered that to be the case, I decided not to let it happen again. I haven't. That's all. I have no feelings for the woman now, haven't had for a very long time. You know enough of the details to know why. As for Katharine, I simply feel that it would be a mistake to bring it all up again. It could only cause trouble—and I understand that she and her mother are . . . that they care a good deal about each other. Sara has been careful to keep us separate."

"Except for the parade, when you rescued the twins."

Connor grimaced. "I'm afraid that was purposeful. I knew

there would be trouble, I tried to warn Sara but she wouldn't listen. And I knew that Lena and the children would be along—I've always had a fond feeling for Lena. I could say it was duty—I owe Sara everything—but it wasn't just that."

"What then?" Philip wanted to know.

"Curiosity, perhaps. I seem unable to avoid the Reades."

"Do you want to?" Philip asked.

Connor frowned, his face flushed. "Damn!" he said under his breath. "Yes. I do. I have to stay clear of them."

"Kit is extraordinary, as you've already discovered. My advice would be to see her. Not seeing her might be the real mistake. Remember, too," he said, "she was born after it was over, all of it."

"She's a child," Connor said.

"Don't make that mistake," Philip answered. "She is young, but she is not a child. In a good many ways, she is one of the most mature women I know. And that includes her mother."

"So you did come because of Katharine, is that it?" Connor asked him at the door.

Philip smiled, his sardonic smile. "That, and in the interest of justice. That is my major interest these days, you know," he joked.

"Thank you," Connor said, and the two men shook hands, Philip knowing by the other man's firm grip that what he had done was appreciated, and understood.

## ～ Chapter Twenty-Two

Kit wrote to us in Macao, a letter several weeks old by the time we received it but filled with bubbling good news. She said she had decided to stay on in San Francisco for a time. She was busy going to museums and the theater and had even accompanied Porter to some political rallies. The city was wonderfully exciting. She had had her hair cut in the new short bob, and had bought several dresses she described as "scandalous" at the City of Paris. They were, she said, in the new style, with shorter hems and longer waists. She was considering throwing out all of her corsets, in favor of some loose crepe de chine undergarments she had purchased. Near the end of the letter she mentioned that Sara had neglected to cancel a luncheon meeting with Connor McCord. "He came to pick you up," she wrote, "and since I hadn't anything to do at the moment, I was terribly forward and invited myself in your place. I pointed out that we were hardly strangers, since he had rescued Porter and me that time at the parade. Mr. McCord was singularly polite, though I think unimpressed with a young ranch woman up from the country."

I didn't like it. She was too flip. Sara said not to worry, that Connor could be trusted not to get involved. I hoped that she was correct. More than that, I hoped that Kit was not interested in seeing Connor again. I knew how willful she could be. She was like her mother in that respect. I had seen Kit when she was determined; I did not underestimate her resolve.

"What I am having difficulty understanding is the sea change," Kit told Connor, her hand on his arm lightly.

"Sea change?" he asked.

"In you; last week I was chasing you madly over the beaches and through the streets, this week you look at me, talk to me, agree even to take me to Chinatown. If I ask to go to an opium den, will you take me there, too?"

"What opium den?"

"The one Sara and my Aunt Lena went to in their wicked youth."

Connor smiled, rmembering. "I think all that is left of those wicked times are a few smoking rooms. The Chinatown squad lets them be—mostly it's just the old men who frequent them, more sad than wicked."

"Wasn't that always the case?" Kit asked.

"As long as you know that, I'll be glad to show you Chinatown."

"Let's walk," she said, pulling on a dark blue coat. "Can we see the back alleys too?"

Connor fell into step with her. "It's not romantic, Katharine, not at all. Poverty breeds all kinds of ills—and Chinatown is a slum. What goes on in the alleys isn't very pretty."

She nodded. "A ghetto, only a few short blocks from Nob Hill. If it weren't seen as exotic, I doubt it would be allowed to exist."

They made their way down the steep hill alongside the Fairmont, and continued until they reached St. Mary's Church, where Kit stopped to put on a kerchief, before beginning their stroll down Grant Avenue, through the heart of Chinatown.

When they stopped to look in the windows of apothecaries, she surprised him by knowing the Chinese names for the seahorses, snakes, birds and crabs that were arrayed in the windows. Inside, Chinese in black coats waited patiently in teakwood chairs while their prescriptions were filled.

The odor of camphor and strange herbs mingled with the smells of food cooking in hidden kitchens. They paused to stare at the live ducks and huge green frogs in window fronts of stores. "It's strange," she said, "when I visit in Cambridge, where my father's relations are, I get a sense that they think of us—Westerners, that is—as if we are somehow temporary, as if our cities and culture are young and inferior. But when I come here, to Chinatown, I feel a timelessness—the Oriental culture is so much more sophisticated..."

"Unfortunately," Connor told her, "other Westerners do not think of the Chinese in that way."

"Immigrants are perfect targets—you should hear my Boston relatives on the subject of the Irish," she said, raising her eyebrows. He touched her arm and murmured, "I can imagine!"

At a candy shop he bought her a sugared water lily and watched how delicately she held it between her fingers.

"On to the opium den," she said as she licked the sugar from her fingers.

"My friend Sergeant McGee tells me that if we walk down this alley," he pulled her into a narrow walkway that reeked of dampness and age, "we will come upon what is known as a smoking room." They made their way down the narrow passageway until they found an opening in the wall over which someone had hung a wet blanket, which served the purpose of screening out most, but by no means all, of the sweet, fetid fumes.

She breathed deeply, not letting herself cough or back away. "How do they get it, the opium?" she asked. "It's illegal, isn't it?"

"Oh, yes," Connor answered, "it's illegal. But you can buy almost anything, if you can pay the price."

Two old men entered the alleyway. They paused when they saw the two whites, then came on, chattering in the Cantonese dialect.

When they had passed, Kit chuckled. "They called us 'big noses.' They also had something to say about my virtue."

Back on the street, he asked where she had learned Chinese. She told him about Wing Soong, and how Porter had insisted they also learn the Cantonese dialect, since so many American Chinese came from the south.

He took her to dinner in a restaurant which had at least fifty tables, all covered in spotless white cloths, with only six of the tables occupied.

"It's early still," Connor explained. "It looks as if they have a large banquet scheduled for this evening. The Chinese are famous for their banquets, and this is a favorite place."

A young Chinese stopped and, in singsong English, told Connor how greatly honored he was to see him. When he left, Kit asked, "Who is that boy?"

"He's not exactly a boy. He's at least twenty, and he's a lottery runner. I'm one of his white customers."

Kit looked pleased.

Amused, he said, "You like it that I gamble?"

"I like it that you think twenty not young."

He looked at her and nodded. Then he picked up her chopsticks, deftly twirled a prawn in a mysterious sauce, and raised it to her mouth. She chewed cautiously, her expression at first wary, then delighted.

"What is it?" she asked.

"Do you really want to know?" he answered.

"No," she said, "I think not. I've never really felt I needed to know everything." And they both laughed.

"You said you wanted to know something about gambling in Chinatown," he said after a while. "Are you ready for a lecture?"

She looked at him steadily, trying to gauge if this could be the right moment to ask. She wasn't sure, but she felt she had to clear it up. She needed to know.

"Connor," she began carefully, "I know something and I want you to know I know it because . . . well, because I think it may have something to do with the sea change . . . why you wouldn't see me, at first. I know you've been in prison. I don't know why . . . I thought perhaps . . ." She watched the steel come into his eyes and it made her voice falter. "I don't need to know," she said softly. It wasn't the truth, but his eyes made her say it, "Really, I don't."

"I went to prison for smuggling," was his abrupt reply, "opium smuggling."

She chased a vegetable around her plate with her chopsticks, concentrating on the act. "Were you guilty?" she asked.

"I've done a great many things in my life that I regret," he told her.

She looked directly into his eyes then, and she said, "Please tell me about gambling now. The lecture."

He did as she proposed. "There are four games—or 'ac-

tions'—in Chinatown. Fan Tan, Mah-Jongg, Pai Gow and the
lottery. Fan Tan is a bean game—that is, each player takes a
handful of beans and puts them in a pile. The croupier removes
four and takes bets on if the remaining number is odd or even.
Pai Gow is like dominos—spectators tend to bet on the players,
not the game. Mah-Jongg you probably know. And the lottery
operates like all lotteries, with two drawings each day. I sometimes think everybody in Chinatown plays the lottery. The
drawings are in Oakland—the Chinatown squad ran it out of
San Francisco. So runners take the slips over each day on the
ferries. The police give them a merry chase."

He told her stories he had heard from men on the police
squad, and from Chinese who ran the numbers, about the adventures and misadventures of the Oakland run. By the time
he finished, the mood between them had been reestablished
and Kit decided she would not mention his past again, that it
was not important to her.

When they came out of the restaurant the sky was dark and
the lights of Chinatown glittered. "It's like being in a foreign
country," she said. They strolled silently, she listening to the
guttural snips of conversation around them, now and then translating. At the door to a soda parlor they paused and looked in.
Several young women sat at a Mah-Jongg table.

"Is it common for women to play in such a public place?"
she asked, and his hesitation made her look at him sharply.

"Are they prostitutes?" she whispered.

He nodded. At that precise moment a man sat down at one
of the tables. Connor would have moved on, but Kit pretended
to study a calligraphy brush in the store window, so she could
watch. She saw the man strike up a conversation, then the
woman rose and walked out of the store. In a minute, the man
followed.

"She's . . . she's not a woman," Kit said in a strained voice.
"Dear God, she's no more than a child . . ."

"I told you it wasn't pretty," he said roughly. Then, in a
softer voice, "Someone bought that girl for three or four thousand dollars in the old country. She is quite an investment, so
now she must work to make a return for her owner."

She is *owned*? But it can't be legal. My God, Connor, we
had a Civil War about slavery . . ."

"The law simply does not protect the Chinese in this country, that's about the long and short of it."

"No," she said, angry, "there has to be someone..."

"There is one person. Her name is Dina Cameron, she's a good Scotswoman at the Presbyterian Mission House. They call her 'Lo Mo' in Chinatown—the Mother. I suspect she's managed to get fifty or so of the girls out of their bondage. The Chinatown police cooperate with her, but she is the only one who is actively fighting the slave trade."

"Do you know her?" Kit asked.

He seemed surprised. "As a matter of fact, I do."

"Will you introduce me?"

"Why?" he asked, but before she could answer he saw something. Propelling her by the arm, he led her up a flight of stairs to a second-story balcony, and from there into a large room crowded with people.

It was a mixed group, including whites and a few women. The men made room for Connor at the table. She did as he had instructed, and stayed close by his elbow.

From a large jar of beans, he gathered a handful of beans. Fan Tan, she thought. Connor put a ten-dollar bill on the table in front of him. Everyone waited in silence as the men placed their bets.

At the last moment, one man put a tightly folded bill on the table in front of him. The chattering started up and stopped as quickly. Kit had not been able to understand the burst of talk.

Connor lost, as did the man who had put down the tightly folded bill. While Connor turned away, leaving his bet on the table, the other man insisted on replacing his bet with another bill from his pocket. The croupier began to shout. Kit felt Connor's hand on her back, moving her toward the door. When they were in the street again she asked, "Do you know what that was about?"

"If the man had won," Connor explained, "he would have opened that folded bet to show maybe a one-hundred-dollar bill inside."

"Would they have paid?"

"No, no more than they want to allow him to replace the bet on the table with a bill from his pocket. But winning or losing, in this case, isn't the point. What you saw was one tong harassing another's game. It is a way of creating trouble, maybe starting a tong war."

"How will it end?"

"In bloodshed, probably. A killing, not today but one day soon."

"Were we in danger?" she wanted to know.

"No," he said, "I wouldn't have taken you there if I thought there might be trouble. One thing the Chinese hired murderers—they call them highbinders—don't want is a white witness. They can get away with murder so long as they only kill each other."

"That's grotesque," she said.

"It is," he agreed.

They walked back up the hill in silence. At Sara's door he looked at her closely and asked, "Are you sorry you asked for a tour of Chinatown?"

She shook herself then. "No, not at all," she said, "in fact, I believe I've found what Porter has been after me about."

Kit sat in the ill-smelling foyer in the brick building on Stockton Street, waiting. The room was overheated, and she was sorry she had worn a wool dress. Finally, a young Chinese woman came in and motioned to her to follow. "Sit here," the girl said, nodding toward a straight-backed chair placed in front of a desk piled high with papers and assorted paraphernalia. After another long wait, when Kit was beginning to wonder if the girl had made a mistake, a tall, big-boned woman came thundering into the room, calling to someone who was out of sight. She saw Kit, but she made no motion that could be taken as greeting. She began to rummage through a stack of papers on the desk, obviously looking for something. After a while she gave up, sat down and said, "Connor says I should see you, and I always do what Connor tells me to do. What do you want?" she demanded.

"I want to learn about the slave trade in Chinatown—the girls who become prostitutes," she answered.

"Why?" Mrs. Cameron asked, voice booming.

"Because I'm appalled at what I saw the other night—a child prostitute—and I want to see if there is some way I might help."

"You want to volunteer, is that it?"

Kit was beginning to feel uncomfortable. She could feel herself flush. She hoped Mrs. Cameron would not notice the wave of red that would soon appear at her neckline.

"I want to do something if I can be effective, Mrs. Cameron. If I can't, obviously I would not wish to take up any more of your time."

Dina Cameron let out a large groan then, and leaned back in her chair. "I just remembered what Connor told me about you. I'm sorry I gave you my standard society lady reception."

"I'm sorry, too," Kit said, wanting but not daring to ask what Connor had said, "perhaps Connor told you that I speak the Cantonese dialect. I thought that I might be able to help by translating . . ."

Now Mrs. Cameron sat up straight, and she looked sharply at Kit. "He didn't tell me you could speak the language—Mandarin too?"

Kit nodded.

"Then you could be of help. But first I've got to tell you something—you hear me out, and then you decide if you want to have anything to do with the mission. The work that needs to be done is not amusing. What you will see is the underside of Chinatown, the dirt and the poverty and the degradation. It is sordid, repugnant, something a young woman like yourself perhaps shouldn't see. The smells are as bad as the morals. The girls—well, they are stupid, dirty creatures without the vaguest notion of what freedom means. A bar of soap, a bath, food twice a day, and a bed of their own where they can sleep and not have to open their legs to any man who asks, that's their idea of heaven. That's what I try to give them."

"I would like to be of help," Kit said.

"Come tomorrow and the next day, and the next, if you can stand it. Then tell me if you want to sign on—but promise me you will tell the truth. And don't be afraid to say if your stomach won't take it. Stronger men than you have been done in by Chinatown."

Kit smiled and offered her hand. The big woman shook it and smiled back, and Kit couldn't help but notice how it transformed her face.

Almost as an afterthought, Dina Cameron asked, "How do you happen to know Connor?"

"He's a friend of my godmother's," she told her.

"He's a rare good man," the older woman said, "a rare man."

\* \* \*

Kit sat soaking in the bathtub, her head back and her eyes closed, trying not to doze off. Porter was in the adjoining dressing room, sitting on a little stool and talking to her through the open door.

"You mean you actually went into the girl's room when she had a customer?"

"She was supposed to have given that up," Kit answered wearily, not opening her eyes, "I wasn't expecting her to have company."

"What were they doing?" he wanted to know.

"What do you think they were doing? Use your imagination, then turn that upside down."

"God!" Porter said, "So what did you do?"

"I used some of those wonderful new Cantonese words I told you about—the man didn't even bother to pull on his pants."

"And what about the girl? Was she contrite or what?"

"Lord no," Kit laughed, "she was amazed that I should be angry with her. After all, the man was a friend of her uncle's cousin, and therefore she could not refuse him...I should see how impolite it would have been. The Chinese are terribly polite, you know."

"And that's the sort of thing you do every day?" Porter asked.

"No, sometimes I get to fight with a girl's 'benefactor'— her owner. I do the talking, but Mrs. Cameron backs me up, towering and glowering. She is a wonder...bigger than life...literally and figuratively."

Porter coughed. "You never told me what Mother had to say about your decision to stay on and work at the mission. You must have heard from her by now."

"As a matter of fact, I received an eight-page letter from her just yesterday. I was certain I was in for a long, well-reasoned argument on why I should return. Instead, it was a complete resumé of her most recent court battles. Seems she is back in federal court this time. Her new lawyers assure her she has a strong case, that she should 'take it all the way to the Supreme Court.'"

"How many times does she have to hear that?" Porter said, mildly, considering how vehemently he disagreed with Willa.

"It was only at the end of the letter that she said she was disappointed, but would accept my decision to stay on in San

Francisco for the time being. She said my work at the mission sounded 'extremely interesting.'"

Porter chuckled. "I wonder if she would think so if she could see how dragged-out you're looking." He cleared his throat then, and although Kit couldn't see him she knew he would be leaning back, hands behind his head, staring at the ceiling. It was what he did when he had a prepared speech. "I've been thinking," he began, and she knew she was right, "you need some fun in your life—and a better class of people. I mean, all you do is associate with slavers and Chinese prostitutes and that monstrous big Scotswoman. I decided to organize a social outing. It's all arranged."

"A social outing? You, Porter Reade, have organized a *social outing*? I don't believe it."

"It's true," he called, "we're going to a dance."

"What do you mean 'we'? You don't even know how to dance," she said, incredulously.

"But you do, and Connor says it's fine with him."

"Connor? Oh, Porter, you can't mean it. You've actually asked him? And he said yes?"

He heard her climb out of the bath. In a moment she emerged, a towel wrapped around her, eyes wide. "Porter, what are you thinking?"

"I told McCord that since he was the one who sent you into the Chinatown brothels, the least he could do was take you dancing. He thought it a fine idea."

The look of anguish on her face made him laugh. "Don't worry. Actually, I only said that I thought you were working a bit too hard, and asked if he would like to join our group for some entertainment."

"What group?" she asked, suspiciously, stepping behind a door to pull on a robe.

"Some people I know from the Young Socialist League, and a girl from my political economics class—a fine student, you should like her."

Kit looked at him steadily, still not believing.

"Are you telling me you've arranged a...a *social evening*...a dancing evening with Connor McCord and some Young Socialists? You're mad!"

Porter grinned. "Probably, but don't worry. We're not going to a debutante ball, there's a place across the bay in Larkspur.

We'll have to take a ferryboat and a train to get there, but the dancing is outdoors—'under the stars' as they say, and a couple of thousand people turn out every week. There's this huge dance floor with trees growing up through it. It's supposed to be fun, at least that's what the Browns—the couple I told you about—say, and they grew up in a little town close by. They say people come from all over the bay, it's the big thing to do on Saturday night."

"The big thing to do," Kit repeated sarcastically. "Has it occurred to you that Connor is rich. A capitalist with a capital C. And your friends are not, and that might make them uncomfortable . . . not to mention Connor and, for that matter, me."

"I don't think so," Porter said, in a way that made her sure she would have a hard time convincing him otherwise. "Connor was very good about it."

She wrapped a towel around her head and lay back on the chaise. She would have to sort it all out, would have to put a stop to it, but first she had to get some sleep.

"When is this social outing supposed to take place?" she asked.

Porter ignored the question. "Better get your nap," he said, checking his pocket watch and making a mental note to waken her in a hour, so that she would have half an hour to dress.

The Browns interrupted each other, talking to show they were not intimidated by Sara's drawing room or Mrs. Weatherlee's superior attitude. Porter's date, a tall, handsome girl named Evelyn, said very little.

"Kit's never late," Porter explained, "it's just that she was so tired, I let her sleep until about twenty minutes ago. Then I had a hard time making her understand that she was supposed to get up and get dressed to go out."

Connor smiled to himself. He was mixing drinks at Sara's bar, politely asking each of them about their preferences, suggesting a mineral water when Evelyn seemed flustered.

"Does the lady who lives here have her own bootlegger, too?" one of the Browns wanted to know.

"Here's Kit," Porter broke in, turning to the stairs.

Kit's hair was still damp. She had brushed it back, away from her face, and put on a silk dress that fell straight from

the shoulder in the new, shorter length. She moved gracefully
down the stairs. It was not Kit's style to make entrances, but
this time it was unavoidable. For a long moment even the
Browns were silent, then both started talking at once.

"So pleased . . ."

"Porter's told us . . ."

Kit smiled timidly, almost, and shook hands all around.
She turned, then, to Connor.

"Connor," she said.

"Katharine," he replied, grinning.

*He knows,* she thought.

The Browns filled the uncomfortable silence with an en-
thusiastic description of the Rose Bowl, which was the name
of the dance in Larkspur. Only Porter seemed perfectly at ease.

While Porter gave Evelyn and the Browns a quick tour of
the lower floor of the mansion, pointing out Sara's collection
of paintings, Kit had a few minutes alone with Connor.

"I didn't know about this evening until . . ." she started.

"I guessed as much," he interrupted, his eyes crinkling with
laughter.

Kit lifted her shoulders in an elegant, humorous shrug, and
smiled back at him. "He's doing this for me, because he thinks
I should get out. It's not at all *his* idea of a good time."

Connor poured a small amount of scotch into a glass, filled
it with seltzer and handed it to her, saying, "I think we should
oblige your brother. To tell you the truth, I've never danced
under the stars before."

She let the bubbles from the seltzer spray her lips. Then
she said, "That really is good of you, Connor—to go along
with it. This just might be a very nice evening, after all."

They made their way to the bottom of Market Street, laughing and talking. Connor fit easily into the group, which surprised and pleased Kit. They boarded the ferry *Eureka* for the
trip to Sausalito, crowding around the marble counter to order
clam chowder and pie. Connor watched, amused, as Kit tipped
her soup cup to finish the last drops of chowder, then proceeded
to consume a large slab of apple pie. She smiled as she chewed,
enjoying being there, with him, more than she had enjoyed
anything in a very long time.

Leaving the others inside the cabin, they made their way to
the stern of the big boat, where people were throwing bread
to the gulls.

"Chinatown seems a million miles away," she said.

"That's good," he answered, "I was beginning to worry. Dina Cameron considers you a gift from God."

"And it bothers you, playing God?" she said. "You've been checking on me."

It was light still, and warm, though they could see the fog lying out beyond the Golden Gate. It would be clear in Larkspur. It was always warmer in Marin County than in the city. They would be able to see the stars, she thought. And when they returned, the city would be glittering across the water.

They took the train to Larkspur, as the Browns directed, and made their way to the Rose Bowl, hidden among towering redwood trees, its Chinese lanterns strung above the biggest dance floor she had ever seen, People of all ages converged on the place. In the crush, Kit and Connor got separated from the others. After Connor bought their tickets, they scanned the crowd for Porter and his party. After a full swing around the enormous floor—which, indeed, did have bay and ash and maple trees sprouting through the boards—they decided that Porter and his friends had not yet come into the dance.

"Then we're on our own," she smiled up at him.

"Looks that way," he answered and, with a slight pressure on the small of her back, guided her onto the dance floor.

She moved easily into his arms, her forehead against his chin. She closed her eyes and breathed in the fragrance of the bay trees and she felt light, she felt buoyant. The band was playing "Avalon." After a while, a tenor sang the lyrics, which came echoing out, clear and poignant and touching.

They danced without speaking, swaying to the music, her silk dress pressed against the rough tweed of his jacket. She lifted her face and let her lips graze his chin, which was clean shaven, smooth.

He shifted her in his arms as the music changed tempo, drawing her closer. Other couples swirled around them, a breeze played in the trees and the lights swept, amber and green and red, over them as the music drifted, bittersweet and perfect.

She saw Porter before he saw her, which was not difficult since he towered above most of the people on the dance floor.

"Shall we move that way?" Connor asked.

"Not yet," she whispered, "not quite yet."

\* \* \*

When the band swung into a lively rendition of "Ain't We Got Fun," he took her hand, and led her across the crowded floor toward Porter and his friends. Everyone was singing along.

When they reached Porter, she was still humming. "You are having fun, aren't you?" he asked.

"I am," she said.

"What did I tell you? Now aren't you sorry you yelled at me when I woke you up?"

"I am," she said again, looping her arm through his and giving him a quick hug.

He leaned down, as if to return her embrace, and instead whispered in her ear, "Then you won't mind if we ditch you, this time?"

"I won't," she said, and he laughed at her as he moved Evelyn onto the dance floor.

When they were alone again, Connor said, "I'm beginning to see how the two of you operate . . . it is fine to watch, I have to say."

She looked at him curiously for a moment, then she said, in a sultry voice of a moving picture vamp, "What about you, are you having a good time?" When he said yes, she added, "Stick with me, kid, and I'll show you what fun really is."

Connor and Kit took an early ferry back, leaving the others at the dance. The fog had swirled into the bay and the water was choppy. Kit wrapped her shawl around her. Though she was shivering, she didn't want to go into the brightly lit cabin.

"Let's stay out here," she said, balancing against the roll of the ferry. He started to take off his jacket for her, but she stopped him. "No, don't," she insisted, at the same time moving closer to him and tucking her arm in his. He must have felt her shivering, because he put his arm around her for warmth. She began to hum, softly, the tune to "Avalon."

They stood together that way, swaying as the boat swayed, alone on the afterdeck. She felt content, peaceful. She wished the trip would never end, that they would just go on floating around the bay. Angel Island rose, dark and ominous to port. They could see a few lights, and a sweep of light suddenly flashed into the sky. She looked up, then, into his eyes. A quiver ran along her spine. He kissed her softly at first, gently. She reached around him, under his jacket, her hands gripped his back. He kissed her eyes and her cheek and the hollow of her neck. He buried his face against her, and found her mouth again. She pressed into him, giving . . . taking . . .

Her hands felt the muscles of his back tighten. Her breathing slowed. *No, don't do that, don't move away,* went through her mind, but he *was* moving away from her.

"Please," she said out loud, "Connor, don't turn away from me again."

She thought she heard him moan, though it might have been something else. His arms were around her still, but when she tried to look into his face, he wouldn't allow it. He had turned away and when he turned back his face was set, the look gone from his eyes.

He said little to her for the rest of the trip. She searched her mind for the right words, the key words that would set everything right, but she could not find them. At the Ferry Building he hailed a taxicab and directed the driver to Sara's. Seated next to him, she held his hand tightly, but he said nothing, and she knew he wouldn't. He had locked himself away, and there was nothing she could do.

"Connor," she said, desperate, "we must talk. Somewhere, not at Sara's—Porter will be returning soon. But please, talk to me."

"Not now," he told her, his voice thick, "I need some time."

"Promise me you will see me again, promise me."

He nodded, and in the same hoarse voice told her he would call her within the week. She leaned to kiss him, and he allowed it, but it was worse than if she had not, he was so far removed.

She hurried inside. When Porter knocked lightly on her bedroom door she did not answer, but pretended sleep. For the first time in her life she did not want to talk to Porter.

She sat in the dark by the window, looking out as the rain swept across the hill in silver sheets, the wind riffling a coating of water that lay on the dark, rain-washed streets. She was alone in the mansion. She had sent the Weatherlees to a moving picture because she could not bear to have anyone there. It would be a half hour yet. She lit a cigarette but she did not remember to smoke it, and after a while she ground it out in the crystal tray on the end table.

She should turn on a light. He might wonder if she were there, inside the darkened house. No, he would know she was there, waiting. She should comb her hair, put on lip rouge, but she seemed unable to move from her place by the window, unable not to watch the rain fall in curtains of silver light. She shivered.

He moved across the street, facing into the wind. She knew it was Connor by the angle of his body, by the way he walked into the wind. A sharp, aching shock hit her. She swallowed and felt a terrible pleasure at knowing he would be here soon, in this room, alone with her... knowing, too, that it would be the last time, that he did not want to come...

The bell rang and startled her, though she was waiting for it.

He brushed the rain from his coat and hung it on the hall tree.

"I watched you cross the street," was all she could think to say.

He nodded, then moved into the small sitting room and switched on a standing lamp which threw out an amber light, enough to light only one small corner of the room. She had wanted to make every word count, but she knew it didn't matter. Nothing she would say would matter. He sat in a chair and motioned for her to sit across from him. He could have taken her hand in his, he was that close, but he did not. He would not touch her, she knew it.

"You weren't meant to look forlorn, Katharine," he said. "Since I seem to be the cause of your..." he groped for a word, "... your unhappiness, I want to tell you how it pains me. The other night at the dance, you were happy and it was..."

He stopped, dropped his hands between his legs as if he had lost the words, lost even the train of thought.

"Katharine," he started again, "I thought we might be friends, only that. I thought it possible, but now I don't believe it is. And it cannot be anything more, it can't. I'm sorry."

Tears fogged her vision. She tried to think what to say, but her throat closed. She felt helpless, impotent.

He sat across from her in the dim light, looking only at the floor, his hands limp from his wrists.

"I can't begin to tell you how sorry I am. You are so much... you have so much joy... it isn't right..."

"And you," she managed to say, "do you feel nothing, no pain, no sorrow?"

She could not see his eyes in the poor light. "I've lived with pain before, Katharine. It's not new to me." He tried to smile but couldn't. "I'll go to work in my garden in the country. Sometimes that helps, hard work . . ."

She pulled herself into a small knot in the corner of the chair, wrapping her arms around herself, making her body seem even smaller than it was, and more fragile.

Connor let himself out. For a time, outside, he stood so that the rain pelted him in the face and rivulets of water washed down his cheeks.

The man in the garage spread the map on the hood of the Stutz and traced the route for her with a black, thickened fingernail. She thanked him, slid back into the driver's seat and started the engine, but he was loath to let her go. Few enough people stopped in the small peninsula town, and rarely such a pretty woman. He stood, hands on the door, and shouted the directions again, to make himself heard over the noise of the engine, until, with no excuse to keep her any longer, he waved her off.

She found the turn-off easily enough, noting the grove of olive trees and then the house came into view: Wildwood, Connor's house, built of brick, solid and eloquent. Set deep in the green hills, it might have been an Irish country estate. As soon as she saw it she knew it had been built to satisfy some longing. At the same time she wondered if it had served its purpose.

A palsied old man answered the bell. With difficulty—his speech was stuttered—she was able to discover that Connor was working in the east gardens, trimming the yew trees.

"Is no one else about?" she asked, and the old man wheezed that only he and the cook were there, the cleaning girls and the gardeners would be out from town tomorrow.

She walked through a series of rooms, handsomely furnished in a traditional manner, until she discovered french doors that led into the gardens. A sound—she was not sure what sound—led her in one direction. The gardens were splendid. She skirted a maze and followed a narrow path until she rounded a corner and saw him. He was standing near the end of an avenue of yews, a vast stretch of perfect lawn between them. He was trimming the trees, reaching high with a pair of clippers, his shirt open to expose his chest.

She was halfway across the expanse of green before he saw her. By then she was unsteady, she seemed to be leaning, it was a peculiar sensation. She saw the earth, the grass coming to meet her.

He carried her into a tea house and put her on a cot covered with faded, flowered chintz, and for a moment she thought herself back in her old room in the townhouse in Los Angeles.

She saw him, and was confused. She wanted to know how he happened to be there, in her room, but she knew that was not right.

He was looking at her, his eyes filled with concern, and behind the concern something else, something much more confusing.

"I have to say..." she began, but he told her to be quiet, to lie still. He knelt in front of her and held her hand. She tried to smile, but she couldn't. And then the words came tumbling out, a torrent of words spilling from inside of her as if they had a will of their own, and would be said: "You went to prison and you smuggled opium and you were a cowboy on the Malibu, and it goes together, whatever it is that keeps you from me. It goes with my family, my family and the smuggling and whatever went wrong. But it doesn't matter to me, nothing that could have happened could matter to me. It was long ago, and I don't need to know. I don't want to know, unless you have to tell me, just don't send me away because of it."

She must have slept then, because the next thing she could remember was being held in his lap in a swing, rocking back and forth in a swing in the growing darkness, inside the tea house, and he was holding her so close she could smell his skin and with her tongue taste the perspiration on his chest.

She slept in his bed that night, curled in the curve of his body. He made love to her gently, tracing first his fingers down the slim line of her hips and into the inner curve of her legs, taking his time, looking at her. He told her the wonder he had discovered: that love was not fearsome, as he had thought, but perhaps even possible.

She stretched and pulled him into her then, and she shivered with exquisite pleasure. They slept, until she awakened him to make love again in the night.

"Don't ever push me away again," she said, "promise me, you'll never leave me again." He kissed her in answer. They would be together now, she knew, she was certain.

"I have never, never in all of the years of my life, all those years before you were born, felt what I feel now," he told her, "I want you to know that. It is important, Katharine, that you know."

When next she opened her eyes it was full light and she was alone in the big bed. She lay there for a while, remembering, and the pleasure threatened to overwhelm her. She jumped out of the bed and stood, perfectly naked, in the middle of the big room, wanting to throw open the windows and shout to the winds. Instead, she found the shower and let the water splash over her. She began to notice all the small things that were part of his life: the plain, unscented soap, the straight razor laid, with care, alongside an old kit, its leather cracked from years of use. She ran a finger over one of the cracks.

Wrapping a towel around her, she brushed her hair and began to examine the apartment, what Connor had called his "sleeping chambers."

She had been standing before the portrait, studying it, for several minutes when he returned with a breakfast tray.

She turned to him, glowing, her attention shifted.

"Woman," he said, "is there nothing you can't look ravishing in?"

She dropped the towel provocatively and said, "I'm ready for the ravishing..."

Being careful not to spill the coffee, he settled the tray onto a table with a show of efficiency, and picked up a robe which he brought to her, bending first to kiss the nipple of her right breast, laughing as he watched it grow hard and erect.

"Food now," he said, fixing the tie on the robe, "I don't want you fainting on me again."

Nibbling on a bun, she turned back to the portrait.

"Who is this beautiful child?" she asked.

A flicker of concern passed over Connor's face.

"What is it?" she asked, "Is something the matter?"

"Only... nothing, I think... only that I promised Sara... I hadn't expected ever to share this bedchamber, you see..."

"Sara painted this child?" Kit was surprised; she could see

now that it was Sara's style, and yet . . . she was perplexed. There was something about the child. "Do you know who posed for it?" she asked him.

"Sara never said—but I gather that her name was 'Rose'— see, it's written in the corner there."

"Of course!" Kit said. "That's why she seems so familiar. She looks just like all those old photos Auntie has, dozens of them—it has to be her——my sister Rose."

Connor stared at her. "Your sister? But I thought . . ."

"I know, that I had only brothers. But Rose died before I was born. There was an accident, she was only two when she died. It must have happened soon after this portrait was painted. Auntie speaks of her as a charming, magical child . . . and Sara has caught that quality, so much more than the photographs . . ."

She was very hungry, and for a few minutes she concentrated on spreading butter on the buns he had brought, and sipping the hot coffee. He watched as she ate, she felt his eyes following her every movement, as if to commit each to memory. When she had finished she smiled up at him, and he cupped her face in his hand and looked at her with such steady love that she closed her eyes and kissed his palm.

When she came downstairs, no more than twenty minutes later, he was gone.

# ~ *Chapter Twenty-Three*

*September 18, 1922:* The reliquary on my dresser began to jitter and jingle at 8:13 this morning, precisely. The house took a sudden jolt. Before my mind could register *earthquake*, it was over.

"Did you feel it?" Willa called from the hallway below. It was a small tremor, as they go, but it made us uneasy. The earth was shivering, deep down. A small quake could warn of some monstrous upheaval, the likes of which destroyed San Francisco not twenty years ago.

We spied Trinidad hurrying across the central courtyard, crossing herself and, we could tell by the way her lips moved, saying Hail Marys. Of all Trinidad's fears, the *temblor de tierra* is the greatest.

"It will take her an hour to settle down," Willa said with a trace of annoyance, "I was hoping she and Aleja could get into town early."

"When they do go, would you be sure to ask them to pick up my mail?" I said quickly, knowing that in another minute we would have to contend with Trinidad's hysteria. "I'm expecting a letter from Sara—with news of Kit."

When Sara and I returned to San Francisco from Macao, a letter had been waiting from Willa, asking if I could come to the ranch as soon as possible. She had noted some changes in Thad's behavior, and she wanted me to observe him before she went to the doctors. She asked that I say nothing of it, in case her mind was playing tricks on her and she was seeing what she wanted to see, rather than what was.

The tone of urgency in her letters was enough to send me on my way, with only one day's pause in San Francisco—scarcely enough time to begin to answer Porter's questions about Soong and the complicated political situation in China, which Porter assures me no one in this country is able to comprehend. Still, in all the confusion of homecoming, I could see that something was troubling Kit. She was wan, terribly quiet, and had lost weight she could ill afford. Porter says it is her work at the mission, the depressing conditions in Chinatown. He says that he has been after her about it, but I know Porter well enough to know he is not being forthright. Sara has promised to get to the bottom of it, and I am sure she will.

In my absence the Big House—which is not a house at all but a Moorish castle, of sorts—has nonetheless been renamed the Casa Blanca, since it's been painted a luminous white. The style is Mediterranean, with tile roofs and open courtyards and terraces everywhere. Tile makers brought over from Italy have set up a small factory near the old pier, where they are producing the most beautiful tiles of every imaginable shape and design. My favorite place is the tiled terrace that sweeps out to the west, offering a long view of the sea. Each tile requires examination: some have figures of mythical beasts, of antelopes, of spring-winged eagles, in shades of purple and blue and yellow. When it is finished, Willa's castle on the top of Peregrino Hill will be a crown for the Malibu. Work on the ballroom and upper floors continues. There is to be a widow's walk, and a children's playroom and a music room. Only the east wing is complete. Thad occupies one apartment with his companion (I made the mistake of calling him a caretaker, much to the young man's distress). Willa has another, Aleja and Trinidad share another and three are left for the rest of us. It seems to me that we rattle around in the expanse already, but Willa hasn't noticed. At times, I get the feeling that she expects the house, someday, to be filled.

Willa is, these days, consumed by blueprints and plans. She drives the workmen quite mad, checking everything—changing her mind at times, offering suggestions and opinions. I said to her yesterday that she reminds me of Owen. "He would have loved this house, think of the entertainments he would be planning!"

I sat on the terrace yesterday and realized how very quiet the world can be, so entirely different from the teeming, stinking streets of Macao. Here the earth smelled fresh; I breathed deeply the clean, country smell. I had had little time, since my return, to think of that other world. I smiled, remembering. Soong and I had been able to be seen together in public for the first time in our twenty-five years together. I was amazed that no one registered surprise that we should be together. It was thrilling to be seen in the company of such an impressive man. In that world, his world, Soong is revered.

I walked to the edge of the sprawling terrace and sat on a stone bench. I could hear the eucalyptus trees creaking as they stirred in the breeze. Rose's grave was but a few feet below, out of sight. I sighed, and tried to remember Soong's face our last day together in Macao: lined, weathered, yet stronger, somehow. And if not happy, determined.

*Happiness,* he had said to me, only partly in jest, *that is why I call on you now and then. You are my one source of happiness.* And I had said that he spoke of it as he would of petrol, a practical kind of necessity, and somewhat mundane. We did not, this time, speak of our future. Perhaps we have none. (I do not believe that. It is inconceivable that I should not see Soong again.)

Since my return to the Malibu, Willa has talked only of two things—the house and Thad. She has, on three separate occasions, noticed with what she describes as "some certainty" a change in him. Once, it had to do with the expression on his face. "There was nothing very noticeably different," she told me, "but something . . . as if some thought were occurring to him." Another time it had to do with a tone of voice, another with the way he walked. She was excited and wary at the same time.

"We can't know all that Thad has been through," she explained, "In the war and all . . . I wrote to Thad's battalion commander, and he answered that Thad was in the worst of it, that other of his men suffer as Thad suffers. I know that is so, but I can't help wonder if what happened here, before he disappeared—the bullfight—if that hadn't happened if he would be so . . . he's had such a dreadful time."

She pulled her arms around herself, thinking. "He is alive, and yet not alive . . . I feel that if we can bring him back, no matter how hard it might be, there is a chance the Malibu can heal him. He loved the ranch so, you remember that, Lena. It was important to him, and I have to believe that it can be again . . . that is what I am hoping."

Something sad shifted inside of me and settled more deeply into place. I could not offer comfort, I could only promise to watch closely now.

I decided to have one of the horses saddled to ride to the beach that afternoon, hoping to intercept Aleja and Trinidad upon their return. The sun was high and warm, but the afternoon breeze had risen so I sought a sheltered place behind some large rocks, with a view of the road to my rear.

It was a favorite spot, that section of beach. We came here often for picnics, besides which Thad fished here almost every afternoon, so I might have a chance to observe him.

I settled into my beach chair, removed my shoes and began to riffle through the notes I had made in Macao. The note-taking was a kind of self-protection. Porter, I knew, would expect me to remember my conversations with Soong verbatim; he grew impatient with me when my memory lapsed. Soong was working in the south of China, near Canton, with easy access to the Portuguese treaty port of Macao. We had spent the whole of the summer there, Sara and I, in heat that was at times unbearable . . . yet in spite of the heat and the hordes, it had been a precious time.

I scanned my notes. As usual, they began with great detail and, near the end of my stay, became quite abbreviated as I felt an urgent need to spend every possible minute with Soong.

Three days after our arrival in June, I wrote: "Soong has come here from the Chinese Communist party's Third Congress. He is quite disturbed. As a member of the party, he resisted the Russian Comintern's edict that the Chinese Communist party should work from within the Kuomintang—the Nationalist party that Soong has written so often to me about. The Third Congress has, he tells me, declared the Kuomintang to be 'the central force of the national revolution.' Soong does not agree. It is his fervent belief that the Communist party and the Kuomintang are opposing forces, with conflicting goals. Yet he must, once again, content himself with waiting—in the face of what he believes to be certain error. He has no choice, if he is to remain in the party, but to follow the Russian edict. He is sure, though, that the result will be a struggle for power from within—and once more the long-delayed reforms must wait, and the revolution stagnates. He is sick to death, he says, with petty, power-hungry men who talk revolution and spend their energies amassing private power and private fortunes. Even men of good will and ability are corrupted, he says.

"Soong understands the Western world's great horror of communism, and wants us to know why he has chosen this path. For a very long time, he said, he had hoped that China might find a way to achieve the kind of social democracy that exists in some Western nations—that it might evolve through a gradualist, reformist program. Now he is certain that can never be, not in a country so mired in feudalism. He believes that the only hope of bringing China into the twentieth century, of creating a better life for its long-suffering peasant class, is through Leninism.

"He has traveled twice to Moscow in the past several years. He does not believe that the Russian communists, who guide the Chinese party, have a grasp of the nature of peasant society, or the importance of the countryside in the coming struggle. Even so, he feels communism to be the most reliable answer left to a country so desperately in need of salvation."

I read these words over, trying to understand. Soong, a communist. I would not tell Willa, she would be appalled. I did, however, tell Porter, and was at once besieged with questions about Soong's rationale. His *rationale*. Dear God. Still, I would try. I would get some sense out of my notes, I promised myself.

All the while I was mildly distracted by a noise, worrisome in the way of bees buzzing close to one's ear, or a fly that won't quit circling. Now the noise grew loud enough to demand my full attention. Not far offshore—in fact, just beyond the breakers—thousands of sea birds were gathering to feed. With each new minute, scores more arrived. A school of herring was running, I guessed, and the birds were engaged in a frenzy of feeding. Gulls and snipes and pelicans gathered, converged, some riding the waves, others diving—beating the water and making it roil as they dived for fish. I watched, transfixed. In the midst of this scene, Thad came down the beach and stood staring at the orgy. It would mean good fishing. He must have thought the same thing, for more quickly than was normal for Thad, he began to pull on his high boots to wade into the surf.

I contemplated joining him, if only to get a closer look at the birds, but the breeze had picked up and it deterred me. Thad's tackle box was open. He had turned, his back to the sea, to rummage through it, when an errant wave swept in with force and spilled much of the fishing gear into the water. Thad's face contorted; for a time I could hear nothing above the raucous cacophony of the birds. And then a wail, one sustained, inhuman note that cut through the sound, shrill and chilling. Thad was standing, screaming at the wind and the birds and the sea.

I watched as he screamed at forces he could not control, and I understood, for one flashing moment, the frustration, the terrible frustration, pent up in this man. *Que laśtima,* the *rurales'* woman had said that day, *the gringo's manhood, gone.* I thought of the quake that morning, of the rumbling forces deep within the earth, and I wondered what it meant, what any of it meant?

The cacophonous cries of the birds seemed to swell; I put my hands over my ears. Perhaps the birds had made it seem more than it was; perhaps I was seeing more than was there. I watched the explosions on the water as the birds dived, watched one come up with a fish only to be robbed of it by a bigger bird. The noise was such that I didn't hear the motorcar until it was almost upon me, and I had to scramble to make myself seen.

"A bonanza, Miss Lena," Aleja called to me, "three letters—two from over the waters."

One from Soong, I knew that. And one, I hoped, from Sara. I was not disappointed. The third letter, however, was a mystery. I did not recognize the big, square hand.

Sara wrote: "Kit is working hard at the mission, yet I have satisfied myself that is not the cause of her malaise. As a matter of fact, it was Dina Cameron—who is enormously fond of Kit—who suggested what I suspect is the truth. Kit's trouble is a matter of the heart. The symptoms are classic, and severe. This is no ordinary affair, I think. Kit has not yet confided in me, but I feel that soon she will, and then we will know what we might do to help her. I admit to being somewhat relieved to learn the cause of her grief is something so universal. Still, it is hard for me to imagine the man who would turn Kit down. Perhaps he is married."

I shook my head, and smiled in spite of myself. *Perhaps he is married.* Dear Sara. I read on.

"After having spent the summer in the most sweltering climate in perhaps the whole world (in the name of love) I can only wonder if it is worthwhile. I tease, you know that. One has only to look at you after your weeks with Soong to be convinced of love's beneficial effects. I must say that I can hardly wait to transfer some of the Oriental images I sketched to canvas. I am planning a whole new Eastern series . . ."

I folded Sara's letter without finishing it. I would want to savor the details of her artistic plans later, when I could give them my full attention. At the moment, I was curious to open the letter with the unknown handwriting. It was to send me reeling with the third tremor of this shocking day.

"Dear Lena," it began, "you once wrote to thank me for being of assistance to you and the twins, on the occasion of the Preparedness Day Parade in San Francisco, in the year 1916. I hope now that you are willing to come to my aid. I have not wanted to trouble you, but I find no other way.

"I have only recently learned of the birth, and death, of the child Rose. I have been able to discover some of the facts of her life—the dates of her birth and her death, and the cause of death. The date of her birth told me much.

"I know that you reared the child, and were deeply affected by her death. I do not wish to cause you more distress than you have already suffered, yet I have some questions that I feel I must ask. I shall be deeply grateful if you will see me, for the purpose of sharing with me your memories and, perhaps, photographs or memorabilia of the child. I have no wish to speak to anyone else on this matter; what you tell me is for my own peace of mind, nothing more.

"I will leave Ireland within the week to return to California. Immediately upon landing in New York I will send you a wire, telling you the date of my arrival in Los Angeles. I pray you will grant me my request. Your grateful servant, Connor McCord."

I sat staring at the letter. The portrait, of course! He has put it together, as I knew he would. Sara . . . I told her, all he would need was the date of birth. He would have put detectives on it, his letter said as much. But what did he want from me? Was it memories only, could I trust him? I had once before, to my bitter regret. He had betrayed that trust. Was he going to make some kind of trouble now, after all these years? Still, he had helped us—the twins and me—that day. I felt sick and dizzy. I had to get out of the sun. I mounted my horse and managed, ever so slowly, to ride back up the hill, my mind and my heart in turmoil.

Thad was standing in the clearing by the gate, with the toe of his boot making small, circular motions in the carpet of tiny, dry oak leaves.

"Thad," I called to him.

He turned ever so slowly and looked at me with an empty, dutiful gaze. I searched his face for a long moment. He returned my gaze patiently, waiting for me to release him so he could return to the mechanical stirring of dead leaves.

I went to my room at once. I could telephone Sara now . . . God knows, I needed to share this burden of Connor with someone, and I couldn't talk to Willa. I told myself, *Calm down, there is time*. I took out pen and paper and began to write her instead, pouring it all out. Four days later, Sara telephoned me.

"Can you speak freely?" she asked.

"You know I can't," I snapped.

"Damnation!" Sara swore, and we could hear various clucking sounds echo over the party line.

"What am I to do?" I asked. "Tell me."

"Do? You don't need me to tell you. But listen now—I do need to know the time of arrival of your European visitor . . . when you expect to see this visitor at the townhouse. Do you understand?"

I understood. "All right," I said, "if you feel I must."

"I do. But remember, you will telephone me the time of arrival—or send me a wire if you can't manage the phone."

"I can manage the telephone quite nicely, thank you," I told her.

"I should hope so," Sara answered, not nearly so contrite as she should be, since she had caused this crisis in the first place by allowing Connor to take the portrait.

"Wait," I shouted into the mouthpiece. "Don't go before you tell me about Kit."

"I'm not deaf," Sara said. "Kit's going to be all right." I knew well enough that *is going to be* meant that Kit wasn't all right. I knew, too, that often enough Sara was less sanguine than she appeared to be. She would lie to calm my fears, and I could do nothing at all about it.

I observed Thad for another week, without incident. I was convinced he was not pretending, or hiding anything purposefully. I told Willa about the incident on the beach, trying not to make too much of it. She was as confused as I about what it could mean.

The telegram arrived, just as he had said it would, and I made my telephone call to Sara, as I had promised. Connor would come to my house on Saturday morning next. On the pretext of preparing the house for renters, I returned to Los Angeles with a mix of dread, apprehension and, strangely, excitement.

At ten o'clock precisely the car drew up to the house. I parted the curtains just enough to get a first glimpse of Connor McCord. I opened the door and blurted my first thought, "Time is so much kinder to men than it is to women. You seem hardly changed at all, Connor."

"Lena," he answered, with a smile that brought memories washing in, "thank you for seeing me. I was afraid you wouldn't."

I couldn't think what to answer to that, so I motioned him into the front parlor. "The house has been closed since the twins left—you know about the twins, of course, from Sara. Their pictures are there, on the piano."

He stood looking at them; he looked for quite a long time. I thought it peculiar that he touched the frame, briefly, awkwardly. For a moment neither of us could think what to say. Then something strange happened to me. I felt, quite unreasonably, a rush of warmth for the man—in spite of everything he had done those years ago. When I looked at him again, I knew why: his eyes, Rose's eyes. He was her father.

"You want to know about her?" I said, banishing the awkwardness. "Sit down and I will tell you. She was the most beautiful baby . . ." I took both of his hands in mind, then, and I said carefully, as carefully as I possibly could: "She was yours. You know, don't you?"

Again, he only nodded. I think he could not speak.

"You have the portrait, so you have seen . . . Sara captured the charm so perfectly. After Rose died, I couldn't look at that portrait. I'm not certain I could, even now. That is why Sara locked it away. When you saw it by accident, well . . . knowing what she knew, she couldn't deny you."

"She never told me," he said in a hoarse voice.

"She couldn't. She was sworn not to—but I know she wanted to, and I suppose her allowing you to take it meant it was only a matter of time . . ."

"She should have said something, she couldn't have known . . ."

I did not wait to hear what Sara couldn't have known. I needed to know something myself: "You said in your letter that you wanted me to tell you about Rose. Is that all you want?"

"That's all," he said. "She . . . Rose . . . was alive the same years I spent in prison. I tell myself there was no way I could have seen her, had I known about her existence. But . . . the portrait has had a strange effect on me. Lena, you may think me touched—but, well, it is almost as if she wanted me to know . . . the baby . . . So I've come to find out what she was like, the things she did . . . your memories, if you will share them."

Without a word I unlocked the cabinet, took out the dusty box that held all of my photographs of Rose, along with the memorabilia of her short life—her first shoes, a yellow hair ribbon, a picture she drew for me at Eastertime. We sat together on the divan, and I began to talk, touching each thing and giving it to him, letting the memories rise to the surface and float out . . . talking and talking, laughing sometimes.

It was joyous, speaking of her again. He hung onto my every word, he wanted to know it all . . . no detail was too small. I talked on and on, and it was as if I could smell her sweet baby's breath, could feel her arms around my neck.

"Her laugh," I told him, "if you could only have heard that laugh—spilling out of her like daisies. I told him then about her daisy bush, the chains she used to make us, the tea parties she held, how she looked when she ran full tilt across the lawn, her plump little legs churning, arms out for whoever would catch her and throw her into the air.

When it was time to tell him how she died, that awful day and night, I found myself speaking slowly, my words slurring.

I was not sure I could finish. Tears streamed down my face.
I looked at Connor and was amazed to see that he was weeping.
We looked at each other through our tears and laughed, gently.
"It happened so long ago," I said, blowing my nose, "and here
we sit, crying like babies."

I couldn't tell him how good it felt. I could not tell him
how *relieved*... at long, long last...I was.

Instead, I invited him to the kitchen for a cup of tea and a
bite of lunch. The servants were gone; we were quite alone.
He helped me search the cupboards for crackers and honey. I
had fresh cheese and fruit. We ate at the tall table, sitting on
high stools.

I felt that I could be utterly honest with Connor. "After she
died, I went a bit insane," I told him, "I drank too much...my
'medicine' was what the bootleggers would probably call white
lightning, though it had a good cure-all label." He grinned.
"Wing Soong and Sara took care of me. Soong cured me of
my habit...my *addiction*. I didn't want to live without something to dull the pain. Connor, you were her father and Willa
gave birth. But I was her mother."

He put his hand over mine. "I know you were, Lena. And
I have to tell you, even with all you went through, it is what
makes it bearable now, for me...knowing that she was not
needing for love, for care."

Those words seemed to bring all the elation of the morning
crashing in on me. I felt at once glad, and weary. "I'm glad
you know," I said, "I can see that Sara was right...you should
have known long ago."

"I've worn you out," he said. "I'll be going now. I want
you to know how much this has meant to me...and I want
you to know, too, that I won't be bothering you again." His
Irish accents seemed more noticeable. "I'll be going to San
Francisco now to make business arrangements—then I'll go
back to where I came from, back to Ireland for good."

"After all these years here?" I asked. "Is it because of Rose?"

He said it wasn't, and in a distracted way, said something
about it being better for everyone if he left. I shook my head,
not understanding. "Thank you again," he said, moving into
the front hallway.

The doorbell rang, startling us. Before I could get to it, Sara
pushed in and said in a loud, contentious voice: "I'm tired of

waiting. You've had enough time to talk of the past. Now, Connor, we must speak of the future."

"What in the world . . ." I began, but she raised her hand to silence me.

"You owe me quite a lot, Connor. Is that right?"

Connor looked grim. He didn't answer, but Sara didn't seem to require an answer. "I've talked to Kit," she said. "Or I should say, I've forced Kit to talk to me. I know."

"What is this?" I managed to put in. "What has Kit to do . . ." I looked at Connor then. *Kit* . . . that is how he found out, Kit would have recognized Rose. But Kit and Connor . . .

"Oh . . . no!" I gasped, looking at him.

He turned away.

"Oh, yes," Sara said. "He didn't tell you about Kit?"

"Don't do this, Sara," Connor warned her, "it isn't necessary. Lena's had enough for one day . . . and I've told her what you don't know—that I intend to return to Ireland permanently. I won't see Katharine again."

"Is that what you think?" Sara said enigmatically, and, turning to me, "I know you've been through a good deal these last days, Lena, but brace yourself. There is more, and I know you can be strong as an ox when you need to be.

"Connor, I'm constantly amazed at how such an intelligent man can be so stupid," Sara went on. "I can't imagine that you would think I could blame you for what happened. If any blame is to be laid it belongs on my doorstep . . . quite literally, since I seem to have negotiated your meeting with Kit. I'm not sure that my neglect to cancel that luncheon with you wasn't as conscious a decision as my allowing you to take the portrait. None of that matters now. You did take Kit to lunch, and the rest is history. Philip has told me his part in that business."

"What business?" I exploded, all patience lost.

"Lena, Kit has convinced me that she in unequivocally, absolutely, catastrophically in love with Connor. She pursued him relentlessly, she followed him, uninvited, to his country house, where she saw the portrait."

"In your bedroom?" I demanded of him.

He turned away, he stood with his back to us, his hands made into fists, and for a moment I thought he was going to pound the walls.

"I am old enough to be her father. That, in itself, should

be enough to prove the impossibility of it . . . I knew her mother, that compounds the issue. I do not have an explanation for what happened between Katharine and myself. I do not understand how I could have let it happen." He was struggling for words. We waited, sensing there was more. "Having fathered her sister, when I discovered that . . . I didn't think there could be anything more, but it was as if a sledgehammer was pounding it into me, the incestuous . . ."

Sara stopped him. "Kit knows," she said, in the gentle voice she had used with me on occasion. "She knows and she regrets it, but it doesn't change anything, she says. It doesn't change the way she feels. I believe you have underestimated the strength of her attachment. Rose was her half-sister, not her sister. You and Kit are not blood related, you know that. There is no question of incest. I believe . . ." she paused and started over, as if to stress those words, "I believe that Kit's happiness is at stake and I feel . . . you should know this, Lena . . . I feel that Connor is worthy of Kit. So, I intend to do something to set this whole crazy situation right. Kit and Philip have gone ahead to the Malibu. They are expecting us—the three of us—this afternoon. I have told them to explain to Willa that we will bring Connor, and to persuade her to hear us out. Connor?"

Before he could speak, I stood. Sara could, at times like this, carry me along on the strength of her will. I could not let that happen. I had to think, I had to explain something. "There is another issue here, an ethical—a moral—issue that you, Sara, seem determined to ignore." I pronounced every word, every syllable. "Connor committed a crime and he went to prison for it, but that wasn't the worst of it. Not from Willa's point of view, and not from mine. You betrayed us, Connor— our trust and our affection—and you did it for crass reasons. I almost was able to forget that this morning, when we talked of Rose. Perhaps you have changed, Connor. I know Sara thinks so. But what you did then, I don't think I can forgive you and I know Willa will never be able to. I'm quite certain that she will not tolerate the idea of you and Kit together. And Kit, well, Kit is the only one of her children she . . ." I couldn't finish.

"Kit knows the risk," Sara put in roughly. "If she is forced to choose, she will choose Connor."

I sat down, hard.

"Do you know what you are saying?" I asked Sara. "More than that, do you know what you are doing? My God, Sara. That would be a terrible blow, terrible."

Connor spoke up, "She's right, Sara. Listen to Lena. I think I know what you have in mind, but I tell you the risk is too great. I do not want to disturb Katharine's relations with her mother, or her memory of her father."

"She has no memory of her father," Sara said, rudely. "We haven't much time now, Lena. You will simply have to trust me. I feel certain that I am doing the right thing. Are you coming, Connor?"

"Please, Sara—please do not ask me to do this." He was pleading, which shocked me.

"I am asking," she said, "you owe it to me."

I could not believe Sara could be so unrelenting.

"I've sent your car away long ago, Connor," she said, "we'll go in mine."

On the drive down Sunset Boulevard, west toward the ocean, I asked: "You said Philip was with Kit. Why Philip?"

"Because he has been putting this puzzle together for a long time," Sara answered. "He knows a good deal, and I understand he shared what he knows with Connor. Philip is such a profound fellow, you know. He tends to linger over little pools of injustice, to worry them. He did not, however, know about Rose until I told him a few days ago. Then he felt something more than abashed, especially upon learning that the result had sent you bolting for Ireland, Connor. He figures little short of a thunderbolt could have sent you tearing for Mother and Country."

My head was swimming. "I think you should tell me what went on in San Francisco," I said to Connor. In short, clipped sentences he recited the events that led to Kit's appearance at Wildwood. He talked about the incident at the beach, about Philip's visit, and Chinatown, he spoke of evenings at the symphony and drives through Golden Gate Park, and the dance Porter arranged. He did not embellish, but it was not difficult to sense, from his voice, how much Kit had come to mean to him.

As we drove alongside the sea, a quiet fell over us. While I dozed off, Connor and Sara spoke in low, guarded tones.

The yelping of the dogs brought me full awake. They would

know we were coming now, there was no turning back. I remembered then that Joseph and Arcadia would be there this weekend.

"Good," Sara said, when I told her.

A fire had been lit in the great fireplace that filled one end of the dining hall.

Since the evening was cool, we gravitated there, drawn together for what Sara had spoken of as a "reckoning."

Joseph and Arcadia sat near where Willa stood. Kit joined me on an antique church pew Willa had discovered in her travels—it was hard, polished wood. I took a certain perverse pleasure in feeling it rub against the bones of my buttocks. Philip, Sara and Connor positioned themselves somewhat apart, the men standing and Sara perched on a fireplace stool. Her face was set, purposeful, strong. *Please Sara,* I prayed silently, *please know what you are doing.*

Connor had a fixed look on his face, while Willa seemed to be making an effort to control a rising anger. Kit, for her part, seemed dazed. She could not take her eyes off Connor, yet she had made no effort to speak to him. I took her hand in mine and squeezed it, but she didn't squeeze back.

Sara cleared her throat. "I need to say some things I have never said before, at least not so publicly. I shall try not to be maudlin." She smiled, a tight, dry smile. "Since the day in 1887 when I met Owen and Willa on the train that brought them West, I have been engaged—hopelessly, wonderfully, blessedly—with this family. I have made myself one of you, I suppose I could put it that way. This is my family, and I care deeply for each of you. I like to think not entirely for my own purposes.

"At times I have acted to preserve this family, and to protect my place in it. More often of late, I have thought that to be a major flaw in my character—that I have been so concerned with protecting my place that I have not always acted wisely, for the greater good. I have not wanted to risk upheaval...I suppose what I am saying is I have not wanted to risk an upheaval at the expense of my place. But that is what I am about to do now. I have been silent too long, and events have caught up with me. Now it is necessary to take that risk."

She took a deep breath. "It's time now for some plain talking. Willa . . ." She hesitated, shrugged and in the end did not say what she had been about to say.

Philip had been leaning against an Italian refectory table. Now he stood and, as if by prearrangement, began to speak. His years on the bench had given him dignity, a courtly bearing. "Joseph, Arcadia," he began, "I suppose you are the only ones in this room who have very little idea of what this is about. Perhaps we could all benefit if I attempted to explain it to you—to tell you the story in as much detail as I can. If I seem to wander, I can only ask that you bear with me. I have spent the past twenty-odd years putting together what I once called a 'puzzle.' Later, I came to think of it as a mystery. In its most recent chapter, I suppose it might be called a love story."

Philip looked at Willa, but she was staring at some point above the fireplace, her expression icy. "In the beginning," he went on, "my interest was purely professional. In time it became purely personal. For our purposes here tonight, however, let me tell you that the story begins on an afternoon in the year 1895. The month was August, late in August. Owen Reade had only the day before returned to Los Angeles from a protracted business trip East, during which he had fallen gravely ill. There was a reason why his family did not meet him at the train. Charles Emory had telegraphed to request an urgent, private meeting in Los Angeles, immediately upon Reade's arrival."

Philip paused and, for the first time, seemed to falter. Willa would not look at him, but maintained her gaze into the fire. "Emory met Reade's train, and he told him . . . he told him that his wife was engaged in an illicit liaison with the man he had hired as foreman—McCord."

Willa's neck whipped back, her eyes flashed with anger. She stood as if to leave, staring at Philip with something akin to hatred. "I am sorry, Willa. Terribly sorry to have to say this. But you must not leave until you hear what else I know, and you do not. What I should, I believe now, have told you long ago. Owen Reade was a sick man, he was extremely weak and he came home to confront the possibility that he could lose his wife. Charles played on that fear by suggesting a way to get rid of McCord. Reade agreed. Emory had already made the arrangements, and they were put into effect the very next night.

"Emory had a man in the Treasury Department—one Amos Proctor—who would arrange, for a price, for McCord to be arrested for smuggling."

Willa found her voice. "How dare you?" she gasped, "I do not believe this, I will not, and I will hear no more. What can you be thinking, Philip . . . dear God, Kit is here . . . what are you doing?"

"Willa," Philip said, softly, and again, "Willa . . ."

"I do not believe any of this. Owen was ill, yes, but he could never . . . he was not capable of . . . No."

Philip persevered, calling her name in an effort to get her attention. Finally she was quiet.

"I am sorry, but I have proof if you need it. Ignacio helped Reade. It was necessary to get McCord to a certain spot at a certain time. A great deal of opium smuggling was going on, and Point Dume was a favored spot—just as they are running whiskey there now. Ignacio's job was to make sure McCord was found with the gold on him, and to testify against McCord in court, perjuring himself."

Trinidad was standing outside the doorway listening. She lumbered in, carrying her heavy body like a great burden. "Is true, is true," she gasped. "*El Patrón*, he is so sick, is so sad to see, he say to Ignacio, 'You give gold to McCord, tell him is bonus for working so good. Then say McCord do one last job only, go to meet wranglers in cove with Ignacio late that night.' Ignacio say to McCord that our cousins from Mexico need work, they come by boat so *policía* not find them. Lies, all lies. Ignacio goes to court and swears to God in heaven that he say nothing to Mr. McCord, but always Ignacio is ashamed for what he do. He go to priest to confess once, twice, every week. God have mercy on his soul."

"That's enough, Trinidad," I said, not harshly, and I sent for Aleja to take her mother to their rooms.

For a time, the room was empty of sound. Connor stood staring out the window. He had said no more than two or three words since our arrival.

"I believed him," Willa said, "I believed Owen—your father." She was talking to Kit.

Kit answered, "Yes, Mother. You believed him that night, and in doing so you made your choice. But Connor was innocent."

Connor turned and addressed the two, the mother and the daughter. "No, Katharine. I was not innocent. Few of us there that night were. Your father was ill, and afraid, and he did what he thought he had to do. I don't know that I would act differently, under the same circumstances. Your mother..." Connor turned now to Willa, moving a few steps toward her, for the first time confronting her. "That night, as soon as I saw that you believed I was capable of smuggling, I understood something else. Whatever I might have thought was between us, whatever understanding, had no foundation, no firmness, as Katharine said, by believing Owen Reade you made your choice, and you did it without a single doubt. Now that I've said that, I would like also to say that enough people have suffered for the events we set in motion, you and I, that summer, and it seems to me now that this should end. Sara, what good can it do to go on with this?"

Sara answered, "Just what you've said—the innocent should not suffer, and Katharine is innocent. And so, I believe, is the love you feel for her."

Joseph cleared his throat in an embarrassed way. Arcadia gripped his hand. Philip returned to his narrative.

"I think Connor's point is well taken. Unless some good can come of this ... revelation ... Sara and I have made a terrible error in bringing you together like this. I think we must continue, let's have it all out now.

"The baby Rose ... that is, I think, the saddest part of the story. Joseph and Arcadia know about Rose, and unless I miss my guess they suspect that Connor was the father. If you are wondering how I came to know all of this, since I appeared on the scene somewhat later, I will tell you. I was one of T.R.'s boys charged with investigating corruption within the government. Amos Proctor had been under suspicion for quite some time. T.R. happened to be a friend of Owen's from their college days, so when we uncovered what we thought to be a connection, T.R. arranged for me to meet the Reades. I was here the night the century changed—along with some of you, and a couple hundred other partygoers ... including Amos Proctor. At about that time we were getting closer, and he was getting more desperate. He needed to leave the country, and for that he needed money. Fast.

"He didn't get it. I found him, two days later, in his rooming house in Long Beach, dead. He was murdered—quite professionally. No clues, no weapon, no murderer. What I was able to discover, however, about Proctor's various 'clients' I was able to put to use, some years later, in our campaign to rid the state of influence peddlers, men like Charles Emory, and the Southern Pacific.

"As for our gentle Sara here," he said, attempting a smile, "when she saw that I was about to confront Willa, she gave me more information than Willa could possibly provide—on the condition that I stay out of Willa's way. It was to my advantage to do so; soon enough it was no longer an issue.

"But to get on with the story. Sara had done enough detective work to discover that Amos Proctor was attempting to blackmail both Reade and Charles Emory for their part in the McCord episode. Proctor was in deep trouble already. Since he was planning to leave the country, he had nothing much to lose.

"Sara found out—I still do not know how—that Owen Reade turned Proctor down flat, that last night of the nineteenth century. He said he would risk exposure rather than compound a wrong. Emory was less willing to risk having his part in the plan exposed, so he had Proctor silenced permanently. I could never build a case that would see Emory stand trial, but there was enough circumstantial evidence to convince him that he should consider retiring from public service. That is how Sara kept him away from the Reades and the Malibu, and in part how Emory was convinced to relinquish control of the California legislature. So you see, Willa . . . McCord . . . what a tangled web of events were woven around what was—I have no doubt—a liaison swept along by emotion, by summer's heat."

Willa raised her hand to her hair, a hand we could all see was shaking. "This is all so . . . preposterous . . ." she said, "I don't think I can believe . . ." But she did believe, you could tell she did. She simply hadn't been able to sift through all the ramifications.

"The story has other twists, other turns," Philip went on, speaking directly to Willa now. "There was the matter of the man named Rodriguez, arrested with McCord here. Rodriguez was a well-known local lout who was hired to make the frame-up seem genuine. If you take a look at the record, you see that the judge—one Justice Peal—turned Rodriguez loose. Peal was another of Emory's men. At any rate, Rodriguez was found

one day in Calabasas with his throat slit. A sidelight, perhaps
pertinent, is that rumor had it Rodriguez was with the rustlers
the day Ignacio was killed. And three days after Ignacio's son,
Pablo, returned from Mexico, Rodriguez met his death. Frontier justice, perhaps."

Willa looked at him directly then, swallowed, and waited.
Perhaps she thought he was going to pursue Rodriguez' death,
but Philip had no such intention.

For the first time, Joseph started to speak, while searching
for a plate for his cigar ash. Those of us gathered, with the
exception of Connor, knew Joseph well enough to know the
search was as much a part of his delivery as the unlit cigar—
so no one made a move to help him. "What it seems to me
Philip is getting at is that nobody who was part of the events
of that summer—or who, like Philip himself, became involved
in the years to come—" he paused, looked briefly at Kit, and
continued "—can be free of the consequences. I do not exclude
myself. I knew something of what happened—though by no
means as much as Philip has told us this evening. My *inaction*
can be said to be a choice." Arcadia looked at him in amazement. Joseph only fumbled more erratically.

"The last time I talked to Porter," he went on, "he was quite
taken with the idea of time—of future time—as a multitude
of possibilities. That is to say, it was Porter's contention that,
if it were possible to tell the future, we would then be able to
change it. That future time was not a set, a given. If we had
known what was to happen at Sarajevo, for example, we might
have avoided the Great War—though of course, that is probably not the case. By which I mean, the assassination of the
archduke was only the *immediate* cause of the war." Joseph
was rambling. It occurred to me that he was being purposefully
obscure in order to calm us, to give us time to recover.

"What I am getting at," he went on in the same loquacious
way, "is that the false charges against McCord were the trigger,
only. In terms of future time—as Porter defines it—it was to
have the most complex reverberations. I'm sure the princi-
pals—Willa, Owen and Connor—would have liked nothing
so much as to put the whole episode behind them. But there
was the baby, and there were those who would find it useful
to know about the events of the summer. Charles, naturally.
And Philip here, too. It must have been difficult for you,

Philip—knowing all that you knew."

Philip's shrug was an eloquent gesture, at once sad and resigned.

"I thought as much," Joseph went on. "As McCord pointed out, we must share the guilt, some of us more than others."

I had something to say. My hands were shaking, as was my voice, but I had to speak. "Please," I coughed, and to my surprise everyone fell silent, waiting.

"I told Connor today, I told him about Rose—how beautiful she was, how touched with magic. I told him that when she died, I wanted to die too. For a time, I hated everyone...Connor, for what I thought then, and have all these years believed, was an act of supreme betrayal. Willa, I hated you for denying Rose's existence. And Wing Soong, because he wasn't here that day to keep her safe as he had promised he would. And Owen, oh, yes. I believe I hated Owen most of all...because he had gone off and left us here, alone, because he hadn't been able to look at Rose or touch her, and because he spread the poison. It seems to me now that the pain of her death almost overwhelmed the joy of her life. Almost, not quite. I knew that this morning, when I was able to talk about her as I never had. She was with us such a short time, but she was a source of such joy. And now that is what I am left with: the pleasure of her memory, only that. That is why I no longer blame anyone. It would be inconceivable. She was the innocent, Joseph. Rose was."

I looked at them now. Connor was standing by the window, staring out, but he heard me, I knew. Cadie's cheeks were tear-streaked; she sat close to Joseph and held his hand. I could feel the tension in Kit's body, next to me. She put her hand on mine.

Willa sat bolt upright, her expression frozen. It was all out, now. Everything that could be said, I believed, had been said. Now it was time for Willa to say what could be. I glanced at Sara, and saw my own concern mirrored in her face. Willa was not going to give way. Nothing that had been said could break through the fierce obstinacy born of habit. The eagle hunted, and fed, and each year returned to the same tree, the same nest, year after year until the tree fell, or the eagle died. When she spoke, it was forced.

"I suppose it is correct for me now to make an apology...to

remove the stigma, at least, that came with the false arrest, false imprisonment." She directed her words to Connor, but she did not look at him. "I believe that you did not betray us, and I apologize for my part in this sorry episode." The words were wooden, the sentiment hollow. Sara had miscalculated.

"It's long done," Connor answered. "Lena has been kind enough to help me. Now I intend to leave this country. I hope that we can consider this episode, as you say, closed, finished."

Sara cried out in anger: "You've finished nothing, McCord. Look at Kit . . . Look at her! You've damned near killed her."

*"Who killed Kit? Did I do it?"*

The words came from the doorway. We turned, all of us, to see Thad standing there, twisting his hands as if trying to keep them under control. His face contorted, he repeated the question: *"Did I do it? You've got to tell me!"*

His eyes were darting back and forth; they were wild, afraid. He walked the length of the room, his hands twisting faster and faster. "I think I must have done it," he said in a tormented cry, "I know I killed Rose. I poisoned her and I watched her die."

Willa rose, arms open to him, but he backed away from her like a child avoiding its mother.

"And Papa, I killed Papa, too. And Pablo. I suppose I killed Pablo. I went to find him and they told me he was dead, so I must have killed them all."

"Dear God in heaven!" Arcadia cried out, and immediately clasped her hand to her mouth. The men were standing, not certain what to do. I struggled to get to my feet. Kit was helping me, and she had turned toward me with her hands on my elbows when Thad screamed, "Sally!"

He grabbed Kit from behind, jerking her so violently away from me that I fell. Joseph and Philip rushed to my aid, and in the confusion Thad dragged Kit to the fireplace. His back was to the wall and he was holding her tightly, one arm around her throat so that she could not move her head. With the other hand, he waved everybody away.

"I've got her now," Thad said, in a voice of mad triumph, "I've got her and you can't take her away this time. She's going to stay with me. Tell them, Sally . . . tell them you're not going away."

"Thad," Willa said, straining to keep her voice calm. "Listen to me. It isn't Sally. You've got Kit and you're hurting her."

"You lie," Thad screeched, "Kit's dead, that's what you said. I'm keeping Sally. You can't send her away, not this time. I know your lies." His face changed, something sly came into his eyes, and when he spoke his voice was lowered, insinuating. "I'm going to keep Sally to show her that she was wrong. That you lied to her. I'm still a man, Mother. Nothing happened." He started dragging Kit toward the door, tightening his grip on her. He was breathing hard, his eyes were darting about. With his free hand he reached as if to caress Kit's body . . .

Then Connor was behind him and in one swift motion, he pinned Thad's arms and held him in an iron grip. Willa pulled Kit to her. Thad gave one long, piercing scream, as if to empty all of the sound from his body, before he slumped forward, unconscious.

They were waiting on the terrace: Connor, his white suit shining in the night, one foot resting on the low wall. He was looking out to the darkness that marked the Pacific. Kit was sitting on the wall, not far away, the red glow of her cigarette marking her presence. Sara, weary, sat very straight on a marble bench that was midway between the others. They did not speak, but only waited. There was, in the attitude of their bodies, the tension of the unknown. Philip and Joseph had gone with Thad, Arcadia and I had stayed with Willa. The four of us had done what we could do, and now I had to speak to Connor.

Kit quickly crossed the terrace to meet me. "He's quiet now," I told her. "They'll get some of the ranch hands to take turns sitting with him, and we'll take him to town tomorrow, to the doctor."

"Connor," I said, "we seem always to be asking each other for favors." He was looking out to the calm, moon-struck Pacific, which mocked the storm this house had witnessed. "But I have one more to ask. We would like for you to take Kit in to my house in Los Angeles and stay there with her. Sara and I will join you as soon as we can."

He leaned to kiss me. "Dear Lena," he said, touching my cheek with his fingers.

With his face close to mine, I told him, "Take care of her, Connor. Love her well."

* * *

Kit was a very good driver. She guided the big car down the twists and turns, racing along the straight run through the Palm Lane, saying nothing at all, but letting the soft night wind blow her hair about. She did not stop until they had traveled some distance down the beach road. Then she stepped quickly out of the car, and motioned him to follow her.

"This rock," she said, "this is where my parents sat to watch the new century come in. That was before I was born. I thought it had nothing to do with me. I was wrong. Their past, and yours—their *sins,* if you call them that, and yours, are inextricably mine."

She moved to him, wrapped her arms around him and they rocked gently, back and forth.

"What Auntie said about Rose... I will think of her now as some small angel, holding my happiness in her hands like a big, ripe peach—all those years ago."

He pulled her closer. She could feel the rise and fall of his breathing.

"She sent us away together, you know that, don't you?"

"She?" he asked, smoothing her hair with his hand.

"Mother."

"How do you know?"

"Auntie said 'we'—'we would like for you to take Kit away.' Mother told her to tell you that."

He looked at her thoughtfully, doubt in his face. "Katharine," he said softly, "it has been a wrenching night—for you, for your mother. I don't think anybody knows, yet, how they feel..."

"Wait," she put her finger on his mouth to stop him. "You don't know about Thad. You don't, or you would understand."

She told him, then, about the accident in the bullring, about Thad's impotence. She spoke of the long years when there had been no word at all from him, and of his startling reappearance, after the war. And she spoke of Willa's determined struggle to help him.

"The reason I believe she sent us away together has nothing to do with what was said tonight—what Sara and Philip told her about your innocence. I think it was because of Thad." She began to speak slowly, as if she were thinking it through as she spoke. "Until tonight, I don't think Mother had any idea—none of us had any idea—how much, in Thad's twisted mind, he blames her for all that happened to him. He believes she sent Sally away. She didn't, not at all. I suspect—and I'm sure Mother does too—that Thad blames her for his loss of manhood."

She shrugged, sighed. "It's all so mixed up."

He put his arm around her and they walked toward the ocean. The moonlight caught the edges of the waves as they broke, white against the darkened waters.

"You still haven't explained what that could have to do with us, why your mother would send us off together," he reminded her.

"Yes, well . . ." She leaned into him, close so he could hear above the sounds of the surf. "I think she is afraid now, afraid to try to stop my being with you. Afraid I'll blame her, or hate her. I know she doesn't want to hurt me. She loves me, Connor. I know that. And you protected me tonight, you were the one who got me away from Thad before he could . . ." She stopped, unable to say what Thad might have done to her. "Maybe that had something to do with it, I'm not sure."

He turned her to him, then. He smoothed the hair back from her face and looked at her for a long moment before he said, "I saved your father once. It was in the corral, at rodeo—a young bull got away and was charging him. I was there, I happened to throw the first rope. Could your mother have been thinking about that tonight?"

Kit's eyes widened. "Oh, Connor, yes. Yes, she would have remembered. I don't believe we have her blessing, but now I feel sure we have her permission."

"Is that important to you?" he asked.

"Yes," she answered, "but not nearly so important as it is to you."

They held hard together, then, on the moonlit beach—their bodies not distinctly two, but one in the translucent silver light, like survivors of some long-ago shipwreck by some miracle swept ashore, at long last, saved.

# Book VI

Sea Changes,
1922 - 1939

~ *Chapter Twenty-Four*

I have always thought it strange how time is measured in terms of decades, separate blocks of years, each ten of which would seem to have a temper of its own.

I am not at all sure that it is true. Yet, in retrospect, it is hard not to think of the third decade of the century as a time apart. More than that, the twenties were a bridge; the time between worlds. Machines had become a part of our everyday life, and they changed us irrevocably. The motorcar crowded horses off the streets in our cities. We talked to each other by telephone. Long journeys became jaunts, nothing was as it had been. In town, new buildings were rising in all directions. Business was booming. Hair was bobbed, dresses loose and short, all the old, tight Puritan rigidities were falling away. People danced and people sang, they drank and they laughed and only occasionally would the laughter stop and a sudden silence present an awful clarity.

Perhaps there were those among us who understood the twenties to be a last, long sigh. I was not one of them. For me, the decade was, for the most part, a sweet time, filled with satisfactions.

At five on the afternoon of December 21, 1922, Kit and Connor were married at Wildwood. Philip, in judicial robes, officiated. The ceremony took place before a bank of crimson poinsettias, in the drawing room. Porter and Sara and Dina Cameron were there. Arcadia, Joseph, Trinidad, Aleja and I came up from Los Angeles and Sally Fairleigh made the trip from Washington to see Kit wed.

Willa did not come, but her gift to Kit was eloquent: A Fortuny gown of sea-green Genoese velvet, printed in silver and gold designs—griffins and phoenixes. It fell in a straight line from shoulder to hem, a few inches from the floor in the fashion of the day, skimming over her small breasts and slim hips, accentuating the sweetness of her young body.

Sara and I helped Kit dress: the opulent gown gave her the look of a Renaissance princess. "Mariano Fortuny would be transported if he could see you," Sara told her, "when you return from your wedding trip I want you to sit for me. You must look exactly as you look now, glowing with happiness..." She backed away and began to study Kit with an artist's eye. "I believe I will put the portrait of Rose in the background, you will be standing... it can be my wedding gift to Connor."

"Sara," Kit said, twining her arms around her godmother's neck, "do you have any idea how much I love you?"

Caught by surprise, Sara's eyes brimmed. She waved at me for a handkerchief, so her tears would not stain the silk velvet.

Sara's were not the only tears of the day. I can think of no other time when our feelings, our affections, were so revealed. It would have been impossible to hear Kit and Connor repeat their vows—knowing what we knew—and not be touched by the breadth of their love.

The tears gave way to toasts, the toasts to laughter and the laughter was, at last, channeled into a convoy of limousines which delivered us to the gangplank of the Matson liner *Lurline*. We joined the newlyweds in their stateroom for champagne and more toasts. The send-off culminated in Porter's holding Kit high in the air, refusing to allow her to set foot on deck again until she had promised to take Connor on a "Kanaka" swim in Hawaii. Between gasps of laughter, Kit finally managed to explain that eight years before—when Sara and I had taken them to the islands—they had slipped out of our beach house one midnight to swim with the native children—the Kanakas—quite without the benefit of bathing suits. It was the first Sara and I knew of this breach of discipline, and I could not help expressing my chagrin, no matter how late.

"You might have drowned!" I wailed, at which everyone else burst into great peals of laughter.

Philip commented, drily: "I'm glad you weren't worried about them catching cold, Lena."

Sara added, "Do you know how much time Lena and I spent getting you those birds and bees books? And how worried we were that you wouldn't *understand*?"

Connor hugged me to him and said, "You've done everything exactly right, Lena. Don't let them fool you."

We were in high spirits as we left the *Lurline* and made our way to the train station in Oakland for the return trip to Los Angeles and on to the Malibu to spend Christmas with Willa and Thad.

Sally, Aleja, Porter and Philip waved us off. Sally and Aleja were to stay on at Sara's. Philip would return to Sacramento, and Porter had found a part-time job as a fledgling reporter for the *Oakland Tribune*. Although nothing had been said, it was understood that Sally would not go on to the Malibu, that she should not see Thad. If Willa had been protective of Thad before, she was doubly so now and she knew it would not be good for him to see Sally. To this end, she had gone so far as to suggest that Aleja stay behind after the wedding, to spend the holidays in San Francisco with her friend Sally. It was an agreeable solution all around.

For my part, I prayed there would never be an occasion when Sally would confront Thad. She, at thirty-two, was trim and almost pretty. Her hair was tamed, her carriage stately. She was vibrantly a woman now, her success in her work lending an air of dignity. By contrast, Thad seemed even more pathetic. His hair was thinning, his shoulders slumped, he walked with a slight shuffle, his eyes were often unfocused. It was difficult to remember the young man who had looked with adoring eyes at Sally ten years ago.

Not long after our return to the Malibu, I received the long letter Porter had promised. He wrote: "After we saw you off at the train station I took Aleja and Sally back to the city to my favorite restaurant in North Beach. Yes, Auntie, the one with the fifty-cent special. That particular night it was tagliarini with plenty of red wine. After all the champagne I could have fed them pickled pigs' feet and they would have thought it tasted fine. Sally said it was the perfect ending to an elegant day. She may even have meant it.

"I have seen them twice since, and I've had a chance to talk to Sally about the work she is doing in Washington. I had seen her in action, you remember, that year after I graduated from high school, so I am not surprised that much of what she was working on then has borne results. Child labor laws have been passed in many states, in no small part because Sally and her team made sure the lawmakers got accurate information on the abuse of children in the work place. She is now embroiled in the struggle to establish a minimum wage and that promises to pay off, too—if you will pardon a poor pun. She will be traveling to Sacramento to speak to some of the people who are working for a minimum wage in California. Philip is going to get an earful, you can be sure. You should have heard the speech she gave him at the wedding. It is exciting to me to see how intensely Sally feels about these issues, and how she translates that intensity into action. It makes me feel that people who are totally convinced, who know what is right and stick with it until they can make others see, are the ones who will change the world.

"I had a notion that newspaper reporting would be a good way for me to begin. After three months on the job, I am not so sure. So far, the only thing the job has taught me is that I can write. I know I don't want to be a newspaper writer—at least, not as a lifetime occupation. It's too slipshod. You have to do too many stories that are foolish or that mean nothing at all, and that takes time from the important stories.

"To give you one very good example—last week my editor sent me out to report on a fracas on the docks. I talked to the owners of the ship in question. I talked to the men who were complaining about a speed-up that they claimed was the cause of an accident that injured three men. Then I had to rush back to write the story without ever really sorting out the whole thing. It was superficial. In fact, it made me feel sick so I asked the editor to let me follow through, go back and dig and get the real story. He said that wasn't what I was hired to do. Then he sent me out to do a story on a bunch of fraternity boys whose idea of a good time is to see how many of them can jam into a Ford. Some fun.

"I decided to do the digging on my own time, hoping that if I came up with something the editors would reconsider and let me do a bigger story on the trouble on the docks. What I learned was that in 1919 the employers managed to destroy the union—the Longshoremen's Union, that is—by making people believe the Wobblies and other so-called radical elements were taking over. All anyone has to do is mention the Bolshies and totally rational men cannot seem to think straight. Anyway, since then the only union on the docks has been the 'Blue Book' and it's run by the employers. They have their own men in as hiring bosses and they hire the men who will do as they're told and never complain.

"Most jobs go to 'star gangs,' as they're called—about a thousand stevedores who follow the rules and hand back part of their pay, which isn't much in the first place. The other three thousand longshoremen—the 'casuals'—get what work is left. There's plenty of grumbling and a lot of discontent, but so far no rebellion. It is amazing to me, to see how far men can be pushed. And these are good men, not scared of anything much but losing their jobs. They put up with blacklists and speed-ups where they are pushed to work twice as fast so a boss can make a schedule. It's not only back-breaking work, but they don't get paid any more for it even though they do twice as much. They don't get paid for overtime, either. Most men work ten hours for eight hours' pay. But I believe there is a limit to how far they can be pushed, and one day there will be hell to pay. I want to be around when that happens. That's a story I will want to write.

"Unfortunately, my editors are not nearly so interested. They have nixed my doing another story about the docks."

Sara returned to San Francisco in time to spend the last week of Sally's visit with her. I had half a mind to go along, and I would have had not Willa seemed so blue. I knew why. She was missing Kit terribly; more than that, she knew that her time with her daughter would be limited now, and it made her sad. She and Kit had been so close, those years before Connor came back into our lives. Sara could see how Willa felt, so she didn't press me to return to San Francisco with her. Instead she said she would telephone me after Sally left, so we could have "a good, long chat."

Sara and her "good, long chats" on the telephone! She knew

I didn't like talking on that infernal machine, especially the long distance between San Francisco and the Malibu.

"I'm going to call you," she said, lecturing me as she did these days, "and I don't want you to keep trying to cut me off. I can afford to talk just as long as I like, and I much prefer it to writing those long letters."

"But I like writing long letters," I rejoined, weakly.

"Well I don't," she answered, "so if you don't feel like talking, just listen. It will save me a good deal of time."

She did as she said, and telephoned me the very day Sally returned to Washington.

"We have had the most sparkling good time," she bubbled over the long-distance wires. "I do believe Sally is good for Porter right now. She draws him out, though she is a good deal better informed on most issues. And Porter—Praise the Lord!—Porter understands. I believe he is finally past that phase when he felt he was expert on all subjects. Sally has been able to help him sort out what he wants for the future."

"And what is that?" I asked, standing on a wooden box so that I could speak into the transmitter.

"Well, yesterday the three of us were pedaling bicycles around Golden Gate Park. Sally is a physical culture devotee, and she will not hear of sitting and talking for more than half an hour at a stretch. You simply must be up and about with her . . ."

"You were telling me about Porter and the future," I reminded her.

"I'm getting to it," she said testily. "Anyway, we sat down to rest at the lake and before she got Porter out on the paddle boats where they scooted around like great water spiders, they continued a conversation about the labor situation on the docks in San Francisco. I think they've been talking about it between them . . ."

"I know, Porter's written me," I managed to say before Sara plunged on.

"Porter's plan is to go to work as a stevedore after graduation. That will give him the income he needs—and insists on providing for himself—at the same time it will allow him to study the problems of unionism firsthand, from the working man's point of view.

"He and Sally got to talking about how often it is necessary to sacrifice the work a person wants to do just to make a living wage, and how many people take menial jobs to support their private passions, be it writing or labor organizing or struggling to help women get legal rights.

"Sally said to me, 'It helps to have a benefactor,' I imagine to recognize the financial help I've given her. I decided right then that it was time I talked to Porter about my plan to make him and Kit my heirs, and maybe suggest that I set up a trust fund for him now, so that he would have a regular income."

"And did you?" I asked.

"I did," she answered, "and I can tell you I had no idea he would be so adamant. He jammed his hands in his pockets and began to pace. I told him he was driving me mad and to please sit down. Then he began to laugh. 'It's pretty damned funny, isn't it?' he said, 'I sit around complaining about having to earn a living and you offer me a way out. Just like that. I'm not even twenty-one yet, and twice in my life I've been offered a small fortune. Here's the money, sonny . . . now let's see what you do.'

"That's what he said, Lena," she told me, her voice rising.

"What did you say to him then?" I countered.

"I said, 'I'm not trying to call your bluff, Porter—nothing like that.' I told him I have been planning to make him my heir for a very long time—before he was born, if he only knew. I said that I thought he should look at it from my point of view. That is my way of taking part in something I believe in—what he wants to do. I explained how, by helping Sally, I felt that I had a hand in the reforms she was bringing about."

I knew what Porter would have said to that, but I asked anyway.

"He said that in one sense I was perfectly correct, that I handle my fortune more responsibly than most rich people, that it is a good thing for me to help Sally. But as for him—he said that it was an advantage he could not allow himself. He said it was better if he didn't have an inheritance, that if he planned to work on the docks and the men were to accept him, he should be as broke as they were. Otherwise, he said, he would be playing a part."

"He's right, Sara," I told her, raising my voice over some noises on the line.

"I know he's right," she called back. "It's just that I want him to be secure. I want to know that he is secure. I, I, I. Listen to me! But I couldn't budge him."

"I guess," I said haltingly, not certain she could hear me now, "I guess this is when we let go."

There was a long pause, and for a moment I thought she had not heard, that my words had not carried the long distance. But then she said, "I'm terribly proud of him, Lena."

And I called back, as loud as I could over the crackling noises, trying to keep the tears from welling into my voice: "So am I, Sara. So am I."

The years that followed Kit's marriage to Connor took on routine. I divided my time between San Francisco and the Malibu. When I was north, I was happy. When I was on the Malibu, I was not. My life was divided, but I had lived long enough to know to take satisfaction from the San Francisco days and to endure life on the ranch.

In San Francisco, I watched Kit and Porter move steadily, gaining power along the way, into maturity. On the ranch, Soong's letters helped sustain me, along with the gardening I had discovered could be a source of both comfort and joy. My flower gardens blazed with pansies and cyclamen, with Asian poppies and birds of paradise. Everything seemed to grow on the ranch, and my passion for gardening grew with it.

The one point of dread in my days at the ranch was the dinners we shared—Willa, Thad and I—in the small dining room. Thad was silent, his eyes lowered to his plate, while Willa and I attempted a conversation that did not exclude him. I would have preferred to take my evening meal alone, but I could not bring myself to suggest it. Willa was clinging to the hope that something would happen. She was as tenacious about Thad as she had been about everything else in her life; she could not let go.

A few months after Porter had graduated and was working on the docks as a "casual"—a stevedore not among the selected few who consistently were chosen to work—I went north for a visit. Porter was chosen to work only two or three days of each week, so he had time enough to visit with me.

Kit was working at the Mission House. She was also taking a class in accounting, and the remainder of the time she was looking over Connor's shoulder, learning all she could learn about his business.

"How do you put up with it," Philip teased Connor one night when we were all having dinner together, "having your wife know your business, I mean?"

Connor understood it was a joke, but he chose to answer as if it were not.

"She's quick, I have to give her that," he said, grinning at his wife. "I have to say, it seems to me that women are well suited to business," he went on in a serious tone, "Katharine grasps the central issue faster than most of the men I've worked with." Then, grinning again, "She's tough and she's hard. She drives a hell of a bargain." At that, Kit made as if to hit him, doubling her fist in mock battle, when he said, serious again, "The best thing is having someone you trust completely to talk over a question. But I suppose everybody needs that." Kit's fist opened, and she touched Connor lightly on the face.

"Hear! Hear!" Philip said, raising his glass, and we all echoed him.

Connor, grinning, raised his glass in answer and said, "I remember—it was the first thing you told me about her?"

"What, Philip?" Kit asked. "What did you tell him?"

"That you were a slow sort of a girl, but pretty," Philip quipped.

Sara was experiencing one of her most productive periods, often enough both Porter and I joined her in the studio as she worked and fussed at her to tell us exactly what she was trying to achieve.

I watched the portrait of Kit take shape; watched, entranced, as Sara captured Kit on canvas with much the same success as she had had with Rose. The wit was there, the intelligence, as well as the fragility. Sara painted the woman Kit was becoming, and it took our breath away.

Connor had been excluded from the sittings on Kit's orders. The portrait was to be a surprise. We were, each of us, exhilarated by the portrait and it was all we could do not to hurry Sara.

"It's hard work, posing," Kit said to us during one pause. She padded around the studio in the Fortuny gown, her feet bare, fixing tea and biscuits.

"Don't say that to Lena or she'll never agree to sit for me," Sara told her.

It was a sore point. I did not want Sara to paint my portrait, I'm not sure why. Perhaps I worried that she would reveal too much. Perhaps I feared I would not like the truth.

"I'm not vain," I said involuntarily. Both of them looked at me in surprise.

"Are you arguing with yourself again?" Sara chided.

I was embarrassed and made matters worse by snapping at her.

Silence.

"Why don't you move north?" Sara finally said. "You know you would rather live here just now." Her tone was worried.

"There's too much to do on the ranch," I said, annoyed. "We've talked about all this before."

Kit walked to the window and pretended to look down on the street. She would not encourage me to move, and I knew why. She was worried about her mother, alone now with Thad. Kit could do little about it, except for an occasional brief visit. It had been taken for granted that Connor would not go to the ranch—and Kit was loath to leave him for more than a few days at a time.

Defeated, Sara said, "Willa could at least pay us a visit now and then."

"She won't leave Thad."

"She won't leave the ranch," Sara corrected me.

"It's the same, isn't it?" Kit said, ending the argument.

I decided to stay until the portrait was finished, since I could not resist seeing Connor's face when he looked at it—Kit, standing, a hand reaching to touch a chair; the figure of Rose in the background as a portrait on the wall.

It was finished on a Wednesday. Sara agreed that we could hang it on Friday if we took great care, as the oil was still quite wet. It took us the better part of a sultry day to get it to Wildwood and find the proper place—over the marble fireplace in the green drawing room—and then to hang it.

Kit had stayed behind to bring Connor out. We were waiting for them, our task complete, under the Camperdown elm in the garden.

We heard the sound of the car on the gravel lane.

"They're early," Porter remarked as we hurried toward the

house. We stepped through the french doors at the very moment that Connor and Kit walked into the green room.

He stood, staring at the portrait. For a moment, he seemed stunned. Then he turned to Kit and took her face in his hands.

We turned away, embarrassed at witnessing something so intimate. But then Connor's arms were about us all. He did not appear to be weeping, yet his face was wet.

"If I had known you would go to pieces, I wouldn't have done it," Sara grumped.

"Yes you would have," Connor told her, "you have powers that do not belong to this world, Sara Hunt . . . and I'm blessed to have you touch my life."

"It's paint on canvas, that's all," she answered, but she held Connor's hand tightly for a moment before she said, "I hope you plan to feed us well after this."

We had dinner on the terrace. "I'm not at all sure what I had in mind when I built this big place," Connor began, and Porter finished for him: "You built it as a setting for Sara's portraits, obviously."

"Obviously," Connor answered, "but what I was getting at—Dina Cameron has suggested another use."

"Do you mean the charity ball?" Kit asked, explaining to us, "she says it's time some of the other rich San Franciscans help support the mission. She says Connor has done more than his share."

"That's probably a good idea," Sara put in, "my society friends—don't snicker, Porter—they tell me they are dying to see Wildwood, and of course Connor and Kit are the mystery couple in the city."

"Mystery couple?" I asked, intrigued.

"The current theory differs from the original theory—which had Kit a brazen young fortune hunter and McCord her unsuspecting victim, just a nice rich old man. When Kit turned out to be the 'heiress to the Reade fortune' and 'a daughter of the Boston Reades' we got the revised theory. Now Kit is the young innocent, duped by the old Irish satyr. It's all a matter of good and evil, don't you see? Your roles now seem firmly established in society."

Porter doubled over with laughter. "Now you see what you have to put up with when you are 'blessed' with your very own gnome," he told Connor, "Sara's not only going to draw pictures of your life, she's writing the book."

"Enough—Porter, Sara, both of you," I said, smiling in spite of myself.

Neither Kit nor Connor seemed to mind the banter, even if it was at their expense. "To get back to the charity ball," Kit said, "would we have to be here?"

"Of course," Sara answered for him, "you would be the main attraction."

"Perhaps you could make a recording, Kit... a few inanities... we could set the Victrola next to your portrait, and the guests could play it at will. You would be a real mystery woman then."

"That settles it, Porter," Kit answered. "If there's going to be a charity ball, you have to be here. I won't do it unless you are. We'll just see how you do with all the debutantes fawning over you."

I traveled between San Francisco and the Malibu with sporadic regularity, staying in the northern city until my conscience began to hurt or I got a cranky letter from Willa, inquiring when I thought I might be returning. Then I would try to convince myself—and Sara—that I did not really dread going back.

Thad had two "companions" now, strong young men who had worked as attendants in a veteran's hospital. It was their job to keep close watch on Thad, night and day. There had been other outbursts since the night of Sara's "reckoning." When they happened, he could not tolerate Willa's presence. Most of the time they occurred at night, brought on, perhaps, by nightmares. He would wake, drenched with sweat, crying and wild. Sometimes it took both men to restrain him; his bed had been fitted with straps for this purpose.

I could never sleep after one of these outbursts. I would lie awake and wish I were away, free of the constant dread that Thad would explode. I was ashamed of myself for feeling that way, for wanting to be rid of the burden. I looked at Willa and understood how much heavier hers was. Dark circles had appeared under her eyes and she was slimmer than she had been for many years. Her sixtieth birthday was behind her now; her long hair, pulled back in a knot, was gray, the lines at the corners of her mouth etched deeply. Yet she carried herself well, her back straight, her step firm, her health good.

*   *   *

That winter she made a detailed study of a pair of condors seen feeding on the northernmost border of the ranch. She was gone, at times, for two or three days, making camp at one of the cabins used by the herders. She returned refreshed and excited, with a wealth of stories about the giant birds and their amazing capacities. I looked forward to those times, I enjoyed being caught up in her enthusiasm, enjoyed seeing Willa with color in her face, the smell of the out-of-doors about her.

In the spring I went north for the first of three benefit balls scheduled for Wildwood. The rhododendrons were in full bloom, the trees were flowering and azaleas were blossoming everywhere. The spring at Wildwood was splendid. Dina Cameron was there, a flowered dress making her seem twice her usual size. Kit was in a pale yellow chiffon which floated to points at her ankles, a camellia in her hair. And, at Kit's insistence, Porter rented a dinner jacket and was standing in the reception line, next to Mrs. Cameron.

He was, I could see, a great attraction to the young women present. Working on the docks had done for Porter what none of his body-building programs ever had. He was tall and lanky, and the tendons in his neck looked like steel cords. With more enthusiasm than skill, he fox-trotted the young women around the dance floor. From their faces, I guessed they didn't mind his poor performance.

The benefit raised an unheard-of sum for the Mission House. It was such a success that two more balls were scheduled, each for a worthy cause. By the time the day for the third arrived, Kit had developed a positive dread of the evening ahead, having grown tired of the need to contend with young swells, fortified by liquor swigged from a flask. They would ask her to dance, holding her closer than she liked, breathing brandy into her face. They would suggest a walk in the garden, among other things. Most were dissuaded by a chilly look, a sharp word or two. One vacuous young man, convinced of his irresistibility, attempted to waltz her through the french doors and onto the terrace. That time, Porter saw what was happening and came to her rescue. After that, Connor and Porter agreed between themselves to keep her in view.

"You will not discuss politics with the mayor," Kit said to Porter as she straightened his tie before the last of the benefit balls, "and you will especially not discuss his shipping line."

Porter bristled. "The man's an ass."

"That may be," Connor put in, "but he's a decent sort of an ass."

"Those are the most dangerous—the 'Sunny Jims' who wear flowers in their lapels and sing and dance—the actors playing at politics."

Kit bared her teeth in a pseudo-smile. "No politics?"

"If you're threatening me," Porter told her, "I think you should know that I've been threatened by meaner-looking brutes."

She gave him a sidelong glance so he would know her patience was wearing thin. "Come along," she said, taking Connor and Porter by the arm, "let's dance."

"Tell the band to strike up Sunny Jim's theme song," Porter said in a loud voice as they descended the grand staircase.

Kit was fond of Mayor Rolph, whom she considered a genuinely good man. She enjoyed his ebullience. As he claimed her for the first dance she wrinkled her nose at Porter.

Later in the evening, Connor was at Kit's elbow when the band swung into "Avalon." "Did you ask them to play it?" she asked. "Remember that night at the Rose Bowl?" He kissed her ear in answer.

She was smiling at him still when the dance ended and, for a moment, she did not notice the stolid young man who claimed her next dance. She wanted to shrink from the heat of his hand on her back, pressing her into him. She could feel her own muscles constrict in an effort to hold back. The conversation was predictable: *He had graduated from Stanford two years ago; probably she had seen him play. Football. He had captained the team. She must have gone to the Big Game when her brother was at Berkeley.*

She made small, noncommittal answers. She did not want to be rude, she only wanted the dance to be over.

*He was in banking now, the family business. Probably she recognized the name. As a matter of fact, his father had known hers. Mr. Reade was a fine gentleman, his father said. Of course, his father was familiar with her husband, too.* He hesitated over the word "husband" as if it were distasteful.

When the music stopped she thanked him, her smile fixed, and walked purposefully off the dance floor so no one would stop her.

"You look like you've been sucking lemons," Porter gibed.

"I've managed to get a Stanford football headache," she told him. "If Connor wants me, tell him I've gone to our rooms to look for a remedy."

In their dressing room she rummaged through Connor's kit in search of a pill. She came upon a druggist's bottle marked *Digitalis*. She frowned and tried to think what it could be.

So preoccupied was she with the question that when she walked into the bedroom she did not, at first, see the football player. "I'm sorry..." she began, confused. Then she asked herself what she was sorry about and, angry, said, "These are private rooms. I believe you have made a mistake."

He was looking at her, his lips curved into a tight, brutal smile. He walked toward her and she backed away, until the wall stopped her.

"No mistake," he said, breathing into her face.

"Please leave," she told him, struggling to keep the fear from her voice, "leave now or..."

He grasped her arms and she winced with pain, but she did not cry out. She tried to raise her knee, to hold him off, but he was pressed too hard against her.

"What the devil!" Connor exploded, grabbing the man from behind. He released Kit, and shoved Connor with force enough to send him crashing against a chair before striding out.

Connor seemed to crumple on the floor, the color drained from his face. Perspiration appeared on his forehead.

"Darling," Kit cried.

"A minute," he gasped, "give me a minute..." He was speaking with difficulty. "Medicine..." he began, and she was off to get the kit before he could add anything.

In a few moments he was able to pull himself into a chair. She stared, worried, at his face.

"I'll be fine now," he said, trying to grin, "There was a time when I could have handled that young ox."

"That animal," Kit said, furious.

"Don't say anything, not yet," Connor told her. "Porter can be quick with his fists...don't..."

"I know," Kit reassured him, "just let me speak to Sara for a moment—she can finish downstairs for us. I'll be right back. Don't try to get up."

She was dismayed that he agreed so easily, knowing what it meant. When she returned no more than three minutes later, he was dozing. She helped him undress. Then she sat watching him sleep, a slight line between her eyes, a small dread in her stomach.

The next morning Connor seemed as hearty as ever, though he did cancel a business meeting in the city to stay on at Wildwood with us for a few days. Porter had nothing better to do, he said, since he hadn't worked for two weeks now and he was beginning to suspect that he had been blacklisted.

"Why would that be?" Connor wanted to know.

"The word is that I talk too much," Porter answered, "and I know my note-taking bothers them. The bosses don't like people who know how to write."

I sat under the Camperdown elm and watched Porter swim, stroking deliberately up and down the pool as if he were pacing himself. At the end of the avenue of yews, Connor and Kit walked together, heads close, his arm loosely around her shoulders. For an instant I felt a bubble of happiness rise in my throat.

On my third evening back on the ranch, I sat with my eyes on my plate, more to avoid looking at Thad than anything else. I concentrated on cutting the chorizo Trinidad had made.

We ate in silence, except for the sounds of Thad's chewing, until I felt Willa's hand on my arm. I followed her gaze, to Thad.

Using both knife and fork, he was cutting the sausages expertly, and eating them in the European fashion.

"Trinidad is a genius in the kitchen," he said in a voice so crisp it sent a chill through me, "has she ever written her recipes down?"

Stunned, we could not answer.

"Incidentally, Mother," he went on in the same intelligent tones, "at school one of the masters spoke of archeological digging sites. Isn't it true that the Malibu had several important Chumash Indian villages at one time? Perhaps we should form a Malibu Archeological Society. Do you think one of the universities might be interested?"

His voice was young, eager; his face was animated. Willa said something, I don't remember what. And then we watched as Thad faded before our eyes; in a matter of seconds his eyes were empty, his mouth drooped open.

"No," Willa cried pitifully, "oh, Thad, no . . ." It was as if he had held out something precious, something beautiful to her but before she could take it he jerked it back, pretended it was gone. I stared at him, angry and pained, as he sat chewing stoically, as if nothing at all had happened.

It had taken place in a matter of minutes, but the effect was shattering. Willa was excited beyond all reason; she was sure a full recovery was possible now, and she could talk of little else. As if to prove her right, Thad's periods of lucidity increased as the nightmares all but vanished. He would, quite suddenly, begin to speak and would carry on for two or three minutes at a time before sinking back into emptiness. The subjects he spoke on were banal—usually having to do with school—but the spirit and the liveliness were there. If the change took place when he was out of sight, in the hallway, or in another room, he sounded like Thad at thirteen or fourteen. His voice was higher, his laugh clear and spontaneous.

I know I should have rejoiced with Willa, but I could not. I came to dread being around Thad, watching the transformation—seeing the boy appear in the man's body. I was ashamed of myself for what I was thinking and feeling, but I could not but believe that Thad had made as much progress as he was going to make. He was locked in time, a boy forever . . . I did not believe that the Thad we had known before the accident would ever come back. I became convinced of this one rainy day when I came upon Thad in the parlor, poring over the stamp collection Owen had started for him the year he had sent Thad off to school. For Christmas one year when she was with us, Sally had given him several beautiful and quite rare stamps from her own father's collection.

"Do you remember who gave you this stamp?" I asked him, pointing to one of Sally's gifts.

Thad looked at me, his eyes clear and guileless.

"I don't, Auntie. Was it Papa?"

"No," I said. "It was Sally."

His eyes registered no recognition, none at all.

"Sally?" he said, "I don't remember any Sally."

I patted him on the arm and told him that my memory must be failing, that Sally must have been with us while he was away, at school. He accepted my explanation without question,

turning back to the study of his stamps without, it seemed to
me, any curiosity at all about Sally, who she was or why she
might have given him two extraordinarily beautiful and rare
stamps for his collection.

The incident had no effect on Thad so far as I could tell,
but it made me feel even more miserable, and the more miserable I felt, the less capable was I of leaving. I could not
abandon Willa, not while she was so besieged with problems.
Especially since she would not admit to so many of those
problems. Joseph had spoken to me twice since my return,
imploring me to help him make Willa understand how grave
the financial situation had become. The companies had done
well enough, but they were overextended. Willa had consistently drained off cash for legal fees and to build the Casa
Blanca.

Joseph was no alarmist. If he said that Willa was heading
for the most serious imaginable trouble, she was. Soon enough,
I understood Joseph's frustration. When Willa did not wish to
confront a problem, she distracted herself. She was going from
day to day, pushing away the problems, perhaps hoping that
a solution would present itself. It was easy enough to find
distractions. The house itself was a massive one.

The Casa Blanca. It was another reason that I no longer felt
entirely comfortable on the ranch. Sitting on its perch, looking
out and over everything, I felt we were above the ranch, not
of it. I couldn't step out of a door and onto the earth, but must
always tread across the smooth, hard surfaces of tile. The old
ranch house had been a place to live in. Dust gathered and was
ignored. The wooden floors were worn, walls spotted with rain
water were never corrected. The house had not been so important as the life within it, but the Casa Blanca was an art
object in itself. I grew bored and weary of examining bits of
cloth and talking about furniture and fittings and chandeliers.

One chandelier, in particular. The whole of one nervewracking week was spent—squandered is a better word—in
arranging for the purchase of a crystal chandelier that had hung
at Versailles during the signing of the peace treaty. It was not
an original, but rather a new, electrified copy thought necessary
to produce adequate light for the signing of the treaty that would
end the war to end all wars. One of Willa's agents had assured
her that it was a great stroke of luck, finding the piece at "quite

a good price." It was quite a price, to be sure. Nothing would do but that Willa have it for the ballroom, even though the ballroom was far from finished. She paid, and had the thing hung at once—a folly, it seemed to me, in more ways than I cared to list.

"I must speak to Joseph about arranging payment," she said.

And I answered, "You are impossible."

Willa's road war was, at this same time, winding down. She had spent the better part of two decades waging it, and though she had won several skirmishes and a few battles, the war itself was lost at a terrible cost. When it was too late by far, she offered to negotiate the site of the road. By then, the forces aligned against her, which included the county, state and federal governments, the people of the coastal cities and towns to the south, the settlers to the east, and the redoubtable Jacob Shurz, were in no mood to give quarter. The road would parallel the beach. It would slice through the most beautiful part of the ranch.

The rout had been total. The Supreme Court of the United States decreed that Willa must not only grant the right of way along the ocean, but laterally as well—with roads coming over the mountains. "Land may be condemned to build highways to places of pleasing natural beauty," the judges wrote.

The decision was read to Willa over the telephone, by one of the lawyers who had been so certain she could win. Before he signed off, he added a plea for quick payment of his already overdue charges.

"Yes," Willa had said in a voice drained of feeling.

Jacob Shurz appeared on the hilltop two days later. His face was weathered, his expression stoic. Willa walked out to meet him at the top of the road.

"I've come to say it's over now, done with," Shurz offered.

Willa looked at him. "I know what is over," she said. "Why did you think you had to come to tell me? Do you need to crow over it? Is that why you've come?"

"No, mum," Shurz said, "I never meant it personal. I just wanted what was right. Now it's done."

"I am really terribly pleased," she said in a voice filled with irony, "that you are so wonderfully infallible on the question of right and wrong. You and the judges who think you can build highways to 'places of pleasing natural beauty' and not

destroy the beauty in the process. You want to cover these hills
with houses and roads and clutter the beaches with shacks, so
that people can defile the beaches with their trash. They'll
invade these wild canyons, Shurz. They'll come like locusts
and cut the wood and drive the animals out, the birds and the
deer. One hundred years from now, no one will know what a
beautiful place this once was. The hawks will be gone, your
'people' will gouge out the hills and poison the waters. People
have a right to beautiful places, the judges say. You say people
have a right to plow and change the earth. You say they should
build roads through the wilderness, and start fires that rampage
and kill. Tell me, Shurz, who is to keep the land beautiful for
your children and your grandchildren? Have you thought of
that, Shurz?"

She was all but shouting now. She had not, since receiving
word of the Court's decision, had a chance to vent her anger,
and Shurz had provided the chance.

He listened, hat in his hand, and when she was finished he
nodded, mounted his horse and rode off. I watched from a side
terrace. Willa stood, watching him ride away, her face un-
changed—the anger and hurt and frustration there. I felt sorry
then, immensely sorry for them both. Each had felt so totally
right. It had never been possible for them to compromise. I
had never liked Jacob Shurz, but that day I admired him—for
coming to say what he had said and for giving Willa the chance
to say what she had to say.

Willa was not an easy woman to be around at that time.
There were days when I wanted to throw up my hands and tell
her that she was impossible, and that I had no intention of
standing by and putting up with her, that I had reached the end
of my tether. I never did; I hadn't the courage. Or maybe it
was just that so much of the world seemed lined up against
her. The local newspapers ran scathing editorials, calling her
"The High Priestess of the Holy Kingdom of the Malibu." They
said she believed herself above the law, that she was an im-
perious autocrat, feudal in her outlook. They scorned her for,
as they put it, "attempting to subvert the will of the people."

She deserved some of it. We tried to dissuade her from
getting a court injunction to prevent a picnic celebration that
would have marked the beginning of the road building. The
result was to delay the picnic for a month, and add hundreds
to her list of detractors.

Willa would spend the whole of a day answering an editorial that had been critical of her. She would pour out her frustrations, making long and complex arguments that, she was certain, would convince them of the righteousness of her position.

Thinking that Philip might be able to talk sense to her, I asked him to come to the ranch. It was a mistake. Philip had disqualified himself a number of times from proceedings involving the ranch. We all assumed that Willa understood his need to do this. Perhaps she did, but she used it now to attack Philip. She battered him, and the courts in general, until he lost all patience and told her that she was acting like a willful child. She glared at him, remaining silent until he could take it no more.

"Confound it, Willa, you're an intelligent woman. Why won't you listen? The Malibu is open now—there is no way in God's green world that you can keep it closed. If you try, you'll be carted off to the lock-up. Get your mind cleared out— once you talked persuasively about preserving the ranch, keeping it wild. Now all I hear is how you have been maligned— your rights, your money, your land, your reputation.

"And the fact of the matter is, most of it does belong to you and you can still have a great deal to do with how civilization infringes. The Malibu doesn't have to become an outpost of Iowa, as so much of southern California has been. As long as you can pay the taxes, this land is yours. So it's about time you looked ahead, there is so much that is still possible."

As he spoke, his anger dissipated, so that by the time he finished Philip was pleading for understanding.

"Is that all you have to say?" Willa asked, her voice chilly. "Perhaps you are right. You think like a judge, and I have to believe that you are all wonderfully wise, you judges. You say there is little I can do to keep people out of here, that they'll build anyway. I'm sorry you can't see the tragedy of it, Philip. I'm sorry you don't understand that the Malibu as we have known it is condemned."

She thought that Joseph had talked to Philip, that he knew about the taxes. A large payment was due and there was not enough to cover it and meet the company payrolls.

"You cannot delay any longer," Joseph had said, his voice taut with controlled anger. "We must make some decisions now, Willa. Now."

Willa hardly spoke for two days. She was not angry with

me, but preoccupied, and I knew she was turning the problem over in her mind. She needed to raise a quarter of a million dollars within the next three months. She was grappling with the problem with such concentrated energy that I felt she was regaining her sense of balance, her drive. I fully expected her to call me in to the office soon to see what I thought of this plan or that. In spite of our predicament, it was good to see Willa so occupied.

Had not Charlie Rich appeared at that precise moment, things might have gone differently. But he did show up—stouter, bald and older, like the rest of us, but with the same old evangelical claim to a first-rate, sure-fire, can't-fail solution to all of her problems. "Here's what we do," Charlie said with his big, know-it-all smile, and Willa listened.

She would sell off one section of the Malibu, Charlie explained. No plot would be less than two acres, none more than four. Building would be restricted, highly restricted. They would cut as few trees as necessary, so the homes would be hidden in the woods and hills. It would be a section close to the road, very tasteful, very discreet. No one would even know they were there.

But right now, speed was the good word, said Charlie in his rapid-fire speech. He must have power of attorney if he was going to get the money together for her as fast as she needed it. Otherwise it could take weeks, months, going through Joseph with all the paperwork. Willa hesitated for perhaps two minutes. Then she announced that Charlie Rich had helped get the Malibu for them, and now he would help her keep it. I wanted to remind her of what Owen had said, once, about Charlie—I didn't, because I knew she wouldn't believe me. I knew she needed to believe Charlie.

Within the week, newspapers in Los Angeles carried a remarkable advertisement. A limited number of homesites on the exclusive Malibu Ranch would be available for development. Charlie called in no time to say that people in limousines had been lining up at his office door, that the homesites were going like hotcakes.

Charlie had another idea that Willa liked even more—one that would bring in quick money without her losing control of the land. The pretty beach near the point would be offered for lease—that is, beachfront sites would be made available to anyone willing to put up a cottage. The lease could be renewed in ten years, but only if Willa wished.

"Who would want to put up a cottage for just ten years' time?"

"Lots of folks," Charlie had chortled, "Hollywood is full of crazy folks right now, all those people making moving pictures."

"I'm not sure I'd want them on the Malibu."

"They won't bother you, Mrs. R.," Charlie assured her, "count on me."

Count on me, Charlie kept saying. And Willa did.

As little as I liked the man, he did seem to be solving Willa's dilemma. As he had said, the moving picture people, as well as a shoe salesman from Baltimore and a dress manufacturer from Hoboken and any number of other wealthy, retired people, leased the beach property and started to put up little wooden cottages, each with a teahouse fronting on the ocean. (It was Willa's edict that these teahouses must be open on three sides and none must block the view of any other.)

I took over the ranch office for Aleja so that she could return, once more, to spend a month in Washington with Sally. This was her fourth visit in as many years. I was happy to take over the office duties, since there was little reason to go to San Francisco that summer. Connor and Kit were in Ireland. Sara was in Italy. I never knew where Porter might be.

Porter had written three long articles on the plight of the stevedores on the docks in San Francisco. The longest article had appeared in *The American Mercury* and had made Porter *persona non grata* on the docks. The owners labeled him a troublemaker. The men were afraid to be seen in his company.

"Will the articles make a difference?" I had asked him, and he had answered, "No. Not really."

And that was why, he explained very carefully, he had decided to give up writing for the time being, and take more direct action. He intended, he said, to become a labor organizer.

"Organizers get beat up," Kit had said, voicing my worry, "regularly. And they get killed."

"Somebody has to do it," Porter answered, "and I don't plan to get killed."

I sighed, and said nothing. He was his father's son. He would do what he had to do.

It was the beginning of what Porter called his "phantom life." We never knew where he was because he could never stay in any one place very long. When we had to reach him we called a number. A man with a rough accent would answer, listen. He would never acknowledge that he even knew Porter, but the message always got through. He traveled up and down the coast, between Seattle and Portland and San Pedro, sleeping who knows where—sometimes in flophouses that charged a quarter a bed, sometimes in the homes of longshoremen.

Once he came walking up the beach at the Malibu, a pack on his back like one of the transient workers who more often of late wandered into the ranch looking for work. He was grinning a big grin, which was not all that easy to see through a three-day growth of beard.

"I figured I'd be safe here for a while—that you would turn your *vaqueros* loose on anybody who came looking for me," he said to Willa. "If your own mother won't protect you, who will?"

"We read about you in the newspapers," Willa answered drily. "At least, we assumed the 'rabble-rousing labor organizer' they talked about might be you. Owen would turn in his grave if he knew a Reade was stirring up all that trouble."

"Beats working," Porter teased, and Willa threw up her hands in mock surrender. "I quit talking sense to you when you were thirteen," she laughed.

"Ah, yes, the disinheriting scene . . . smartest move you ever made, Mother." He was in good spirits, which made my own soar. Trinidad hovered over him making small clucking noises and sniffling at the same time so it was hard to tell if her joy at seeing him was overcoming her worry that he would be hurt.

"Have you been tarred and feathered yet?" Willa wanted to know.

"Chased out of town a few times—that's all."

Porter stayed only a few days, enough to hear me spill out my concerns about Willa and the ranch, about Thad, about everything. He listened carefully, nodding at times, asking a question now and then. He had no answers for me, but we explored possibilities together and I was aware, once more, of his capacity for reasoned thinking. It was comforting. When he left I felt relieved, somehow; I know I had a better understanding of what my own role might be. Certainly I knew how limited it was.

Aleja returned from her summer trip with startling news. At one of the embassy parties she and Sally attended she met the vice consul of the Argentinian embassy, Antonio Rodriguez de Cambon, a widower with two young children. He had, after a three-week courtship, proposed marriage. She had, she said, accepted. "Imagine," she added, "a bride at age forty."

Willa's response was to open her arms and hug Aleja. Trinidad's was to burst into tears. We were, all of us, happy for Aleja. Seeing her, beaming as she was, made it difficult not to be glad, even if it meant her moving across the continent and, one day surely, to the Southern hemisphere.

"My work here . . ." Aleja had said, "I will stay as long as . . ." Willa had interrupted to tell her that, as valuable as she was, it was more important to us to see her happily married and with a family of her own. We would, Willa said, find another young woman to take over the ranch office.

Aleja and Antonio were married at the old Franciscan mission in Santa Barbara on a bright afternoon in September 1929. We were all there for the wedding—Arcadia and Joseph, Willa and Porter and Kit and Connor, Philip and Sara and Sally, and Trinidad in blue lace. A friend of Porter's from college days took moving pictures of the group as we milled about the mission garden after the ceremony. I would view that film many times the following year. I can't say why, but it gave me a deep sense of calm to look at us as we were that day, happy to be together on a joyous occasion, a family event.

The film jumps in the beginning, a bit of grass and a stone step coming into view. And then Porter appears, raising his hand in salute to his friend who is behind the movie camera. Porter—tall, trim in his summer white suit. He smiles; his face is finished now. At twenty-five it is sharply chiseled, the gently shaped eyes, the high cheekbones seem so perfectly Eurasian to me. I cannot understand why others do not see it, but they don't. The camera follows Porter as he walks over to Willa, bends to kiss her on the cheek, says something that makes her smile. Then he turns to Trinidad, who throws her arms about him in one of her great hugs. Trinidad, her mountainous body covered in lace, an orchid corsage perched on her shoulder. Trinidad is laughing and crying and hugging everyone, in her happiness.

The bride and groom move into view. Antonio is a pleasant-looking man, gracious in the way of professional diplomats.

Aleja, wearing the ivory chiffon dress with its long, flowing sleeves that Sara and I helped her choose at the City of Paris, smiles modestly at her groom, and then they smile together for the camera, posing as if for a still photograph.

Sara says something that makes us all turn to her, laughing. She talks with her hands, waving them in the air as if directing a pageant. It seems to me that Sara, at sixty, is much handsomer than ever she was as a young woman. Celebrity has helped. It is as if her face has rearranged itself, has settled into softer, more interesting lines. Her eyes sparkle. She is dressed with her usual exotic élan, a paisley shawl with long silk fringe tossed over her thin shoulders, the flowered turban that has become her trademark framing her pixie face.

The camera moves to Arcadia and Joseph, who stand talking to Connor and Kit. Arcadia throws her head back and I can hear the laughter. That has not changed, even if Cadie has. The curves are gone now, her body has become thick with age. She colors her hair, and the blonde curls seem an echo of the sprightly girl of thirty years ago. Joseph has not been well for some time. He is much too heavy, his legs do not allow him to stand for long. Cadie flutters about him like a mother hen. She leans to whisper something in his ear, no doubt asking if he wants to sit down, if he is feeling well.

Kit comes into focus, Connor standing just behind her so that we look full in his face. Unaware of the camera, he is looking at her with such adoration that she bends toward him and, at that moment seeing the camera, stops and smiles, instead, into the lens. A dazzling, happy smile. At twenty-five, Kit is beautiful as a woman is beautiful. Connor, more than twice his wife's age, has managed to age flawlessly, if that is possible. His body is strong, trim in his perfectly tailored suit. Since his marriage, a look of contentedness has come into Connor's eyes. *Dear Connor,* I think when I see him on the film. I don't know why—just *dear Connor*.

At the end of the film, as it is beginning to run out, I glimpse myself walking across the garden with my awful, awkward side step. I raise my hands to my face, as if to hide. Then Porter rushes up, pulls me to him and makes me take my hands from my face. I do as he says, and his lips form the word "smile." I smile; we both smile into the camera together, our arms around each other. We laugh, and the film runs out.

I would look at that film in the years to come and remember that day in Santa Barbara with the bougainvillea spilling, blood-red, over the whitewashed garden walls, when Aleja became a bride. She stood erect, her olive skin lovely against the ivory chiffon gown, a triumph over the girl who had sobbed in my lap on the barn floor twenty-six long years ago.

No more than a week after Aleja left for Washington, I received a letter from Soong. It was not like him to complain, though he had much to complain about, I knew. But in this letter he recounted a long series of failures and frustrations. "The saying here is that the revolution is in a trough between two waves," he wrote. "The truth is, the revolution is becalmed. So, too, is the Chinese Communist party. The Kremlin insists that any revolution must arise from the proletariat because that is what happened in Russia, in spite of the fact that Chinese society bears no resemblance at all to pre-revolutionary Russia. It is like a religion with them, the scriptures according to Lenin. If the revolution fails, therefore, it is not the fault of those who give faulty orders, but of those who fail to carry them out.

"And the poor of China die . . . death is so much a daily part of life that one does not consider, after a time, the body of a child left in a frozen ditch alongside the road. One does not rummage through a pile of clothes left in a city alleyway, knowing that a frail body is collapsed inside.

"There is little that gives me hope. Mao Tse-tung, in a singular act of courage, has written a report on the peasant movement in Hunan. He is saying what nobody else is willing to say: that the peasants are capable of leading this revolution; that in China, any revolution must come from the countryside— not the proletariat. Mao is building a Red Army in Hunan near the Kiangsi border.

"I continue to be attached to the Central Committee in Shanghai. I cannot say how long we will be allowed to stay here. But now it is safe, perhaps more for Westerners than for Chinese. Shanghai is a comfortable city, there are many for-eigners here, many Americans. What I am suggesting—know-ing full well I have no right—is this: Should you be able to travel here, it may be the best opportunity left us to see each other again. I do not wish to put undue pressure upon you to come. I should definitely not want you to make the journey alone. If Porter could accompany you, that would be the most agreeable possible arrangement. I should feel you protected and, at the same time, I am selfish enough to want to see him now that he is grown and a man.

"I know that I ask too much. Forgive me. But if, by some miracle, it is possible, come quickly."

*If it is possible.* It had been seven years since the summer in Macao. Seven long and lonely years.

I would make it possible. I would go, nothing could stop me.

Not only did the prospect of seeing Soong lift some heaviness from my heart, but I also felt a need to come together, the three of us, one time. One last time.

*One last time.*

That was it, I knew it.

Willa frowned, but she did not discourage me. I had no compunction about leaving her now that it seemed Charlie Rich was going to prove me wrong and save the ranch.

My timing was perfect. I arrived in San Francisco three days later to find Porter tucked away in a back bedroom at Sara's, both eyes swollen shut and several ribs cracked.

She told me, "He turned up like this at two in the morning— and do you know what he said? He said, 'Would you pay the taxi, Sara?'"

I touched his swollen face and he grimaced.

"The police are looking for him," Sara said, as if Porter were not there. "Inciting to riot, I believe. Connor plans to move him to another hiding place after dark. It's not only the police who are looking for our brave boy here."

"I have to lie low a while, Auntie. Can you keep me company?" he asked.

"I can do better than that," I told him.

Three days later we were passing through the Golden Gate aboard the *Taiyo Maru,* en route to Kobe, Japan, and Shanghai.

The little missionary could scarcely stand still, He hopped up on his toes and down again and he opened and closed his mouth several times before anything came out. "There, with the spire— that's the Cathay Hotel and, to the right . . . there . . . is Jardine, Matheson, the great trading company, you know . . . and the British consulate, the guards are Sikhs, colorful with their turbans, quite fierce-looking, actually . . . and . . ." He shifted, jabbing a finger in a westerly direction, ". . . The Custom House and the *North China Daily News* . . ."

The great, gray buildings that lined the Bund, Shanghai's famous waterfront boulevard, might have loomed over almost any European city, only the thousands of junks and sampans that crowded the Whangpoo River reminded one that this was the Orient.

"Oh it's a wonderful city, wonderful," the missionary's wife, a birdlike woman, trilled. The two had attached themselves to us at Kobe. They were returning from home leave in the States, but clearly China was home to them.

As we waited for the launch that would take us ashore, I scanned the dock for some sign of Soong, knowing I could not possibly see him, knowing he could not meet us—but hoping nonetheless, now that we were so near. As we stepped ashore we were assaulted by utter confusion—noise and movement, and crowds that pressed in on us until I thought I might be lost in the crush. Porter put his arm around me protectively. I looked up at him and took confidence from the expression of excitement and anticipation on his face.

Before we knew what was happening, a giant of a man made himself heard over the din, addressing us by name and, booming directions all about, shepherded us into rickshaws, our baggage into a cart. His name was Sasha Malinovsky, and we were to put ourselves into his hands to be delivered to our mutual great, and very good, friend.

Soong's name was not to be mentioned, we had been forewarned. It would not do for it to be known that he was trafficking with white Westerners—or White Russians for that matter, not in his own camp, never mind the enemy.

In a short time we found ourselves entering the French Concession. "My home is humble," Sasha told us, "but it is yours, for as long as you will like." His accents were as lavish as his beard. We stopped at a small, walled house on the Avenue du Roi which was neither humble nor ostentatious but, it seemed to me, perfectly nondescript.

Malinovsky was a bohemian, an eccentric, a basso who sang in one of the city's many cabarets. He was larger than life, his gestures grand, his voice booming. And he could, we were to learn, be trusted totally.

Soong was waiting for us in the October light that golden afternoon. He grasped Porter by the shoulders and it was all I could do not to cry out. They stood equally tall. They looked so much alike in that moment that I thought—Porter will see!

"Wing Soong," Porter said, his voice befitting a solemn occasion, "there is no one I've seen less and know better."

Soong's eyes were locked on Porter's. He stared openly, appraising, his approval unmasked.

And then Sasha appeared from somewhere, silent for so large a man. He stoked the samovar and served us tea—a ritual too important to be delegated to the houseboy—and then he left again, as silently as he had come. The three of us talked that long afternoon, our news spilling out in a jumble—the beating Porter took for giving a rallying speech on the docks in San Francisco, Sara and Kit and Connor and the Malibu, the labor movement on the West Coast of the United States and the labor movement that was even then being crushed in Shanghai. There was so much to say. We interrupted each other in our haste, and laughed and said, "Sorry . . . you first." And we looked at each other, searchingly.

Sasha appeared once more to ask if Porter would, perhaps, wish to accompany him on a small errand on the Bund, so that he might give him a first preview of this city. Porter accepted and left us alone, to share the last light of the day.

For an awkward moment, we hesitated. I touched my hair, coughed slightly.

He took my hand.

"He is a fine man, Lena. A fine son. I am proud."

"He's as tall as you," I blurted, "my heart stopped when I saw you together—how can he not know?"

Soong smiled and took my other hand.

"He must not know, Lena."

"Why not?" I argued. "Soong, it's time to tell him. I want . . ."

He was shaking his head emphatically. "No, he cannot. Not now. There are many reasons, but the most important is that my position is far from secure. If he were known to be my son, it would put him in danger. Believe me, Lena."

I frowned, not understanding.

"I must be extremely careful, Lena. General Chiang Kai-shek will not tolerate the Communist party. He knows we are the enemy and he will obliterate us, if he can. I am not certain how much longer we will be able to stay here, in Shanghai.

But I am certain that I do not want Porter to be involved in this struggle. If he knew of his heritage, he might well decide that it was his as well. I don't want that."

"But..." I began.

"No," he said vehemently, "I've seen too many idealistic young men die senselessly. You cannot imagine the carnage, the venality...on both sides, Lena. And I don't want our son sacrificed. I am a communist because there is no choice left to me, no middle ground. Blood baths have already killed thousands, and it is not over. It is not over..."

I directed the talk to the Russian, an excuse to turn away from such painful decisions. Soong explained, "Sasha makes a business of being flamboyant. He is a favorite with the international set—the ladies particularly. He tells them his father was a count in Mother Russia. When he is feeling particularly devilish, he dresses up in white tie and wears a blue ribbon with an exotic decoration around his neck. Makes the ladies swoon, he tells me. But he is not so frivolous as he seems, though you must know him for quite a long while to discover that aspect of his character."

"It seems strange—you a communist and he a refugee from the Bolsheviks."

"Everything about Shanghai is strange—but I'm not so certain Sasha's background is as White as he pretends, and I think he may be a refugee from something else entirely." He looked at me then with candor and said, "Can I take you to the bed?"

A hot, wet sensation flashed in my groin. I felt as embarrassed as a girl.

"Are we alone?" I asked, my heart racing.

"Yes."

"I am not so..." I began, before he hushed me.

"You are beautiful, Lena. Age suits you. The gray in your hair suits you. I cannot say how perfectly beautiful you look to me."

We went together into a room lavishly furnished with Persian carpets and wall hangings, with couches covered with fur rugs and cushions, and we made love as we had long ago, when we were young and first discovering the pleasures of the body.

In the weeks to come, Soong appeared at odd hours, staying at times the whole of a day and at other times only an hour or two. He did not tell us what he did when he was away, and we did not ask. Occasionally Porter joined him away from the house, but only occasionally. They would go to another house, and there would be men there who would talk of world politics, asking Porter about conditions in America. It occurred to me that this was Soong's way of presenting his son to trusted friends, even if they could not know of the relationship.

On those days when I knew Soong could not come, I shopped along the Avenue Joffre, or went sightseeing with one of Sasha's many lady friends. Porter set out to explore the city on his own, and soon made friends among the young newsmen who worked for the foreign press. He drank pink gins at the Long Bar in the Shanghai Club, where the English referred to him as a "Yank." He went to the races and to the cabarets. He did, in short, whatever there was to do, moving from the faultlessly appointed dining room of the Cathay to the narrow, twisting streets of the Old City. One evening, after a concert, a group of us stopped at a popular American eating place operated by a retired sailor. It was called Joe's and its specialty was corned beef hash, served in gargantuan proportions, along with a bag. Leftovers, we were told, were to be given to the beggars who lined the sidewalks. They were everywhere, the beggars, some deformed and sitting on tiny platforms. It was Porter who pointed out that, in part at least, the excitement that so permeated this city had something to do with the thin edge of Western elegance, so close to the suffocating evidence of desperate poverty. "Sailor Joe's approach to the problem," Porter had said, "is typically American—peculiarly American."

"How so?" one of the Englishmen in our group asked.

"Do you think Sailor Joe is generous?" Porter asked.

"Indeed I do," the man answered, "he's a good chap, Joe."

"Then I was wrong," Porter answered, "it's not peculiarly American."

When the Englishman looked puzzled, Porter added, "We expect the starving peoples to be satisfied with leftovers from our table. They won't be, at least they won't be when they get enough in their bellies to satisfy the hunger pangs."

"Enough shop talk," another of the group said. One of the ladies—wearing a gardenia in her hair—tucked her arm in Porter's and said, "Hasn't anyone told you—it is eat, drink and be merry time."

"For tomorrow . . ." Porter began.

"No," she said, "there is no tomorrow."

Sasha introduced Porter to some of the city's more exotic plea-sures. He took him, Soong told me in confidence, to the Foo-chow Road to enjoy the company of the willowy sing song girls—young women who played a two-stringed lyre and were trained as courtesans. Now and then, when Sasha and Porter took short trips away from the city, Soong would stay the night with me. On one of these occasions I awakened at dawn to find him gone from our bed. He was in the garden, shadow-boxing. I watched, amazed at the elegance of movement, amazed at his physique, his strength.

"I must keep my body strong—I need to be strong physi-cally," he explained, "if I am to survive the revolution."

We drank our tea from glasses, the steam curling up and warming my face. At that moment I felt content. I must have smiled, for Soong asked what I was thinking.

"I was pretending that this was our house, that our son was away on holiday, but would return soon and we would live here together, the three of us."

Soong came around behind me and began to massage my shoulders and back, his hands gentle on me.

"Do you know what I once dreamed? Long ago, when I first came here from California, I used to tell myself that one day soon the revolution would end and that I would have served well enough to have earned a small house and a plot of land somewhere in the south, perhaps near Macao or Hong Kong, where the mixing of races is more acceptable. And you would come to be with me then. We would grow old together working in our garden. We'd grow flowers and vegetables. That is the dream that carried me through the worst times."

I could not see his face, so I put my hands on top of his and we remained so for a long time, that cool November morn-ing in 1929.

When finally Soong spoke his voice was not steady. "There is a word the people here, in this city, use. It is not Chinese, but Portuguese. The word is *maskee*! and it translates to some-thing like 'things are bad but they are sure to get better.'"

I looked at him then, wondering what he was trying to tell me. And then I knew, and wished I did not.

"When must we go?" I asked.

"Soon," he said. "The situation deteriorates. I need to be able to move quickly, and I do not want to have you here without me."

"Have we compromised you? Has our being here endangered you?" I asked, worried.

He took my hands in his, kissed them. "I have not been able to let you go. I am not sure now that I can."

I held his hands tightly in mine and told him we would leave as soon as we could book passage. And then I held close to him, as close as ever I could, pushing away the outside world for a few hours more, knowing it would be all that was left to us in this lifetime.

"I will not say goodbye," I told him, stubbornly.

"No," he answered.

"Instead, I'll think about the house and the vegetables."

"Peppers," he said, "sweet red peppers."

"And snow peas . . ."

"Yes, snow peas."

The last sight he had of us was of Porter with his arm around me, waving.

In Japan, a cablegram reached us. Porter read it, stumbling over the words. From Sara, it said: *Connor missing ocean swim stop presumed drowned stop Willa here*.

We boarded for the return voyage in a mist of sorrow. As our ship moved slowly across the winter Pacific, I think I should not have been able to persevere, had not Porter been with me. He was tender, attentive, denying his own hurt by ministering to mine. Occasionally he would blurt out "Damn," and add, "they had so little time together."

I could not let my mind dwell on Connor. *Dear Connor,* whose life had been inextricably tied to mine. And Kit, to suffer so. My mind returned, again and again, to Soong and the life we would never have.

Porter sat with me, making me play endless games of checkers—my mind unable to concentrate on anything more demanding. He made me read aloud, passages that he would select from books, or he read to me. It was as if by distracting me, he could distract himself.

A young woman passenger made several overt attempts to catch his attention, and for the first time I witnessed how rude he could be. Having managed to get herself seating next to him at our table, she proceeded to chatter constantly throughout the meal. The other diners, embarrassed, said little. I could see the anger growing in Porter, and I shot him a glance to show that I commiserated. Perhaps that is all that he was waiting for, for he said—looking down at the woman's hand on his arm—"I think you should know that shipboard romances are highly overrated. You'd do better to read a book or two, so you have something to talk about next time out." As if on cue, I rose and we departed.

"Sorry to have made a scene," Porter said.

"Sometimes it is necessary," I told him.

We talked then—about Soong and my long friendship with him, how Soong had been a substitute father in much the same way as I had been a substitute mother in their early years, his and Kit's. Porter believed, or so he told me often enough, that I had what he called "a positive genius" for friendships. I think it had not occurred to him that my feeling for Soong might be something more. I became convinced of this when he asked me, after considerable clearing of the throat, if Willa and Soong were ever "anything special" to each other.

I looked at him oddly. "What do you mean?"

"Well . . . Kit told me the whole story about Connor and Mother and the baby, Rose."

I nodded, having assumed that Kit would tell him.

"Well, I thought . . . if it were possible for Mother to have had a child by Connor perhaps it might be possible . . ."

"Oh, no, Porter. No. No." I was shaking my head to emphasize how wrong he was. "There was never anyone else with Willa. Only that one unhappy episode with Connor. Oh, no."

He nodded as if to say it was foolish for him to even think such a thing. "I know, Kit doesn't look anything at all like Soong. I just thought . . . well, maybe I hoped . . ."

Having regained my composure, I asked how he had happened onto that particular idea.

"Several times in Shanghai people who didn't know me would ask where I was from—and it turned out they expected me to say Hong Kong. They were convinced that I was Eurasian. You know how I've always been teased about my eyes looking Asian. I thought maybe that had something to do with why you've always maintained such a close friendship with Soong—that maybe he should be important to me in some . . ." He did not finish the sentence.

"Even as a little boy, you used to say that Soong and Joseph were your fathers. But remember, Owen Reade was a tall man with eyes not unlike yours." I was extremely careful with my wording. I wondered if Porter would notice that I had said "Owen Reade" rather than "your father." He did not.

"Is there something else, Porter," I suddenly asked, surprising myself a little, "something that is on your mind? Other than Kit and Soong?"

"Something, yes . . . well," he hesitated. "I suppose I would like to tell you about it," he said, as if he had just that moment decided. "Yes, I will."

What he told me explained the long hours he had spent away from Sasha's during the closing weeks of our Shanghai stay.

"I was out on Bubbling Well Road one day, it was crisp and cold and I had been moving about the city feeling—I don't know how to explain it, but I was feeling fine. Shanghai was exciting, being around Soong was exciting. Anyway, I noticed this girl . . . young woman. She was exceptionally pretty. Chinese, yes, and with that smooth face and high cheekbones and, well . . . she was just about the most exquisite woman I think I have ever seen." He looked at me, to see what I thought of what he was saying, and I was careful not to smile. I nodded for him to continue.

"She was standing with a dark little old lady, her amah, who was chattering away like some fierce little magpie, chastising the girl for lifting her eyes to look at me when I walked up. They spoke in Mandarin, and it didn't occur to them that I might understand, I was so obviously a 'white devil,' so I didn't let on. I gathered that the girl had wanted to visit a shop on the road, and the amah had insisted on going with her as a chaperone, which had embarrassed the girl somewhat, though she was remarkably kind to the old woman, I thought. I suppose I was having a hard time taking my eyes off the girl, because the amah began scolding her—because I was looking at her.

As I said, I was in high spirits that day. I guess I just felt like doing something crazy—so I walked over to them and asked if either of them happened to speak English. The girl lowered her eyes, as modesty demanded. The amah was almost apoplectic. She told me to get my Big Nose out of there and leave them alone. All in Mandarin, of course, but I didn't want them to know I understood so I tried to look puzzled, and maybe a little bit badly treated.

"I thought I detected a smile on the girl's lips, however, so—don't ask me why—I started speaking to her in English, above the amah's chatter. I told her she was the most beautiful woman I had ever seen, but I tried to make my voice sound as if I were talking about the weather or asking directions. I said something about her having a beautiful mouth, and eyes and . . ." He looked at me shyly, an embarrassed smile on his face. I smiled back, and motioned for him to continue.

"Well, the old lady just kept up this stream of invective, and then two rickshaws came along and they got in, the girl in the first one. And as she was pulling away, she looked back at me and said "Thank you for the compliments," in perfect English.

I had to laugh then. "What did you do?" I wanted to know.

"I chased the rickshaws—I followed them all the way into the International Settlement, to a very large estate. I don't know how the rickshaw drivers do it—I was almost dead by the time we finally got there."

"I believe it," I said, chuckling, "but did you get to meet her?"

"Not then," Porter continued, "but I knew where she lived, and I knew it was a good sign, her living in the Settlement. That would mean her father had Western connections, and might be more friendly to a Westerner. I asked around among the newspaper people I've met—and sure enough, the father is well-known. His background is interesting, as a matter of fact. He is wealthy, old Chinese wealth. He is a scholar who was educated in France. While he was there he became enamored with the idea of democracy. When he returned to Shanghai he started a magazine called "The New Youth"—*La Jeunesse*. It explored the idea of how Western ideas could be applied to ancient Chinese culture. He attacked Confucianism, and spoke out for human rights and social equality and individualism—unheard of, for China. He was, in effect, calling for an ethical revolution."

"And his daughter? Is she a revolutionary?"

Porter put his hands behind his head and tilted back in his chair. "No," he answered, "neither, really, is the father. As I said—he is enamored with the *idea* of democracy. The practice is something else. But the daughter—Liao Ch'ing-Ling..." He caressed the name.

"Yes, tell me about her," I put in.

"I managed to arrange an interview with her father, through a French journalist who had a friendly intellectual relationship with him. The father seemed to enjoy talking to me, probing for information about the United States, what is happening there. On the third visit I mentioned his daughter, that I had seen her. At first he looked shocked. Then he called her in and introduced us. You could tell he felt he was being extremely audacious, allowing me to speak to his daughter."

"What is she like?" I wanted to know.

"She was educated in Hawaii," he answered, "which is how she came to know English. Her English is so much better than her father's, in fact, that we were able to have rather private conversations, even when others were around."

"Yes," I prodded him to go on.

He smiled, remembering. "She is intelligent...extremely so. She is well-read, in English as well as Chinese and French. She is thoughtful, in the philosophical sense. In a classical sense...The family—her father, I mean—thinks himself to be progressive. I consider them to be traditional."

"Did you have time alone with her?" I asked.

"Alone? Oh, we would be in a room for a few minutes sometimes, that was all. When I suggested we meet somewhere, outside of the villa, she told me it would be impossible. She is not the kind of daughter who would defy her father. Traditional, as I said."

"But you care for her?"

He looked at me without smiling, and I knew he was answering the question for himself as much as for me.

"Yes," he said, "I do."

"Have you ever felt this way before—about another woman?" I asked.

He only shook his head. "Never," he said, biting his lower lip. "But I couldn't stay in China. I've work in San Francisco that needs to be finished. And it is work that Ch'ing-Ling can't understand, it simply does not fit into her life. Even if I stayed on, Soong's work is against their beliefs, too. Her father is not a communist, and that would be a problem for us. I talked to Soong about her . . . he told me not to say that I knew him, that it would do neither of us any good."

I shivered and Porter brought me a shawl. I did not tell him that my chill was not from the cold. I thought, once again, how wise Soong had been, not to want Porter to know about his heritage.

"Will you see her again?" I asked.

"If she will see me," he answered, with such a note of misery in his voice that I had to restrain myself from touching him.

"I see," I said. But I didn't.

# ᨆ Chapter Twenty-Five

*January 1, 1930, the Malibu:* I break habit the first day of the new decade. Today is Wednesday. Without fail, for the forty-five years I have been scribbling in these day books, I have made my entries on each Monday of the week.

So be it. Everything is subject to change, even old fools who try to compose a new coda . . . something to explain what has happened to bring us to this.

I am not alone in my confusion. The world outlook, at the beginning of this new decade, is precarious, at best. No other decade in memory has opened on such a disconsolate note. Porter, who has reason to know, says the working man is suffering, he says things are bad and that they are going to get worse. He does not believe that President Hoover's policies can do anything but plunge us more deeply into depression.

Perhaps my outlook is colored by Kit's grief, and my own, at Connor's death. Kit is here, on the ranch. She will stay, she says, until she feels she can tolerate the idea of a future without Connor.

She and Willa take long walks on the beach. They talk. They touch.

Willa was thirty-nine when Owen died. Kit is a widow at twenty-five. My heart aches for her.

"You are so young," people will tell her, as if that should be some comfort, "your whole life is before you."

Kit said to Willa, "I wish just once I could answer honestly. I would say, 'I don't know what is ahead, all I know is that one of the best parts of my life is gone.' . . . I miss him, I don't want to forget, not any of it." She went on to say, "Sometimes I feel as if he is standing behind me, that if I reach back, he will touch my hand . . . he is so close to me at times . . ."

Willa looked at her. The sun was an hour from setting, and they were perched on an old log that had been washed up by the tide. "After your father died," Willa began, deliberately, "there were problems . . . with Wen, and Lena was very ill and of course I was with child . . . with children, I should say . . . Sometimes it seemed as if it was all more than I could manage. My mind would get crowded and I would feel as if everything inside of me were in motion . . . I suppose I thought I was losing my mind. For a time I couldn't sleep, and then all I wanted to do was sleep. I could hardly force myself out of bed in the morning." She paused and glanced at Kit, who was listening and nodding agreement. "Well . . ." she went on, "twice when it was almost unbearable . . . Owen appeared. I mean, he would be standing at the foot of the bed, looking at me. He never said anything, he only . . . looked. It wasn't a dream, Kit. I've never told anyone about it, because I thought . . . well, what could they think? But I am certain that he was there."

Kit took her mother's hand. "I know. I do." After a time she went on, "The hard part is getting up in the morning. Sometimes the only way I can manage it is to think of what Connor would say to me . . . but at times, the emptiness of the bed . . ."

They spent long hours together, and it was good to see them so. I could not help thinking it ironic that Connor should have brought them together not as mother and daughter, but as wives, as widows . . . as women.

*February 17, 1930:* We went into town on Thursday last. I joined Cadie for a long chat—I had yet to tell her about my trip to Shanghai, so much has happened since our return. And Kit and Willa had to meet with Joseph on business matters.

About mid-afternoon Willa joined us, but without Kit, explaining that Joseph wanted a chance to talk to her.

Joseph moves more slowly now, having suffered a fall last

year that left one leg stiff. He walks with a cane, which is not entirely easy, given his bulk. Kit told me about the session later that same day. He eased himself into a chair, breathing noisily.

"Forgive me, Kitten," he said, calling her by the old, affectionate name, "I'm a nosy old man, you know that." He wheezed and shuffled some papers before he began, carefully. "I've heard some disturbing rumors . . . to the effect that Connor suffered heavy losses in the market crash and that . . ."

She interrupted to make it easier for him, "Joseph, yes—I know about the rumors and that is all that they are. I suppose the fact that Connor died—the circumstances—so soon after the market crash would make it inevitable that someone would say it was suicide. But it wasn't."

She opened her bag and took out a packet of cigarettes and a silver lighter. She had started to smoke again.

"Connor had a weakened heart . . . he had had two small attacks and several 'events,' as the doctors called them. He had been warned against continuing the morning swims, but he wouldn't stop. He decided he did not want to change the way he—we—lived. I've thought about it quite a lot, and I've decided that he may have wanted it this way. Just, to go off for his morning swim, having kissed me goodbye . . . I think if he had to leave, that was how he would have wanted it to be."

Joseph leaned forward and patted her hand. "I didn't mean to upset you, Kitten."

She smiled at him. "I know that, Joseph. As for business, well, Connor saw the stock market convulsion coming. We talked about it and I remember distinctly—it was a year ago last June—the day Giannini stock fell by one hundred twenty points on both the New York and the San Francisco exchanges. Connor said, 'If a strong outfit like Giannini can take that much of a drubbing, just think what's in store for the rest of the market.' So, very quietly, he got out. We have a good man in San Francisco who is marking a conservative course, as Connor directed. I know what's going on, I keep close touch. Connor taught me, and he left me a very rich lady."

"That's good, darling," Joseph said with obvious relief, "very good. I've always admired Connor, or maybe I should say, since I've come to know him—now more than ever. An uncommon man, your husband."

Kit bit her lip. It was too easy to cry, these days.

"I must say," Joseph went on, "it's very similar, isn't it, to the state of affairs when your father died? He left your mother one of the richest women in the country. She was not, at that time, as knowledgeable in business matters as you are now."

"But she learned quickly...Reade women are nothing if not quick," Kit quipped.

Joseph paused. "Of course, good business decisions are not always in concert with other considerations. Your mother has spent a million dollars a year on legal fees alone—that has been going on for a good many years, as you know. She is not in as good a position now as she was twenty-five years ago, even though the companies have, in themselves, done well."

"How bad is it?" Kit asked.

"The business outlook is not good for anyone these days ...let's hope that is a temporary state of affairs. Frankly, I don't believe for a moment that President Hoover is the man to handle it...but then, you know I was an Al Smith rooter all along and I'm sure you don't want me to rattle on about politics."

Kit smiled affectionately. "You haven't told me how bad it is, Joseph."

"Willa thinks Charlie Rich's schemes are going to make everything right again. I think they will bring in some fast cash, which will only prolong the problem. You have to realize— your mother has used all the cash we could generate to pay for her legal battles. And she got almost nothing from the government in recompense for the right of way, the land they condemned. The big winners have been the lawyers."

"But that's over now, isn't it?"

"I don't know," Joseph grinned, "she's still suing the local farm machinery dealer. And she has to defend herself against the suit Wen has pending to take control of the company out of her hands."

"Another suit?" Kit was surprised.

"This time he has a chance to succeed. Feelings against Willa, after all the road battles, run high in these parts. That should not have anything to do with it, but in reality—it may."

"Is there anything I can do?" Kit asked.

"I was hoping you would ask," Joseph answered. "The answer is yes, a very big yes. I wish I didn't have to ask it, but I believe there is no other way now. I would like to move to reorganize. Some new bankruptcy laws are coming out of Washington, designed to help faltering businesses, and I think they might be the means to survival for the Reade Land Company. But a reorganization would mean changes, and one change that I feel must be made is to replace Willa as president. I would like to see you take over that position."

For a moment, she only stared at him. Then she said, "Bankruptcy . . . is it that drastic?"

"Yes it is, and I haven't been able to make Willa understand. If we are going to save the ranch, it means taking harsh measures."

"But why must I . . . I can't see why Mother must be replaced."

Joseph looked grim. "To satisfy Wen. And to satisfy me, and the examiners."

"What are the alternatives?" Kit asked.

"There are none, Kitten. I'm sorry."

"What will you do if I say no?" she asked.

Joseph shook his head. "Willa will have to find someone to replace me, then."

"Joseph!" Kit gasped. "You can't mean it?"

"I have to mean it, dear," he said, "there's no time . . . and I don't know how many more years I've got left in me. I want to save the ranch, but I'll need your help."

*March 10, 1930:* The road graders are moving and the "Riviera," as we call it, is taking shape on a mesa overlooking the ocean. All electrical lines will be buried, so as not to mar the landscape. Building is scheduled to begin three months from now, as soon as all the "improvements" are in. There is a dredge in the cove, preparing a harbor. Willa had had to borrow to get this work done, but it will be repaid by the homeowners. Some lots are selling for as much as twenty thousand dollars. In this day and age! Don't tell me there isn't money around.

Kit says that the ranch has a potential sales value of one hundred million, if we can hold onto it long enough for land values to rise. For once, Wen and Willa are in agreement— the ranch should, under no circumstances, be sold.

Kit took over Willa's position on the Reade Land Company board with surprisingly little stir. Willa said only, "Wen wanted to relieve me of that burden once, but he was totally unprepared and—if the truth be known—unqualified. It's nice to be able to turn it over to someone better qualified than I am." I believe Joseph had something to do with making Willa feel she was being relieved to concentrate on the Riviera. Or at least, Joseph and Willa have agreed to play out that charade, for which I am thankful. I do not believe that Willa knows of Joseph's resolve to leave the company if she did not step down, and it is best that she does not.

Wen has been convinced that an effort is being made to put the companies on a firm footing, and recoup losses so as to protect his inheritance. He has dropped his suit, removing that annoyance. Wonder of wonders, he has even invited Kit to his home. It is the first invitation any of our family has received. We have seen Wen's girls a few times, always in strained circumstances. I have always regretted that and so has Willa. But each time we made some gesture, we were rebuffed.

"Should I go?" Kit asked at dinner last evening.

"Suit yourself," Willa answered flippantly, "it might be nice to know what else Wen is up to these days—besides suing his mother."

Thad looked up then and told us, to our embarrassment, a story about a time when he and Wen went into Boston together in search of a house of ill repute. Wen told Thad it would make a man of him.

Thad's memories are confined to the years before he finished school. He seems to be fixed in that time when a boy is becoming a man. His sense of humor is puerile at best, he laughs at inappropriate times, he is awkward and shy in the presence of strangers. At the same time he is anxious to please. He is both sweet and pathetic. We protect him as best we can—from strangers, from himself and from the elements. He has grown increasingly thin and has been sick several times this winter. I am always amazed to see him in heavy sweaters, even on the warmest of days.

*April 7, 1930:* Disaster. There is no other word. Charlie Rich is in the county jail. Criminal charges have been brought against him for mismanaging his clients' finances. He used the monies he collected for his own speculations, and lost it all. Willa reels under this latest blow. Troubles pile on troubles. She trusted him and I did not, not for a minute, but it would be cruel to say so. I cannot for the life of me understand how people can be so willing to believe charlatans. Willa is not his only victim. Can they have such a terrible need to believe what they want to believe, to hear what they want to hear? Now Willa must meet the heavy interest payments on the loan she took out for all those improvements at the same time that more and more of the people who turned money over to Charlie are demanding it back, claiming breach of contract. It is all so complicated. But Willa must make good, that much is clear. The money Charlie took is long gone. She is forced to sell more securities, and take a terrible loss.

Kit works night and day, trying to salvage something from this mess. Willa walks around and around, never sitting, at one moment looking as if she would like nothing so much as to take a whip to the county jail and apply it to the soft white hide of Charlie Rich, and the next instant she is so filled with self-loathing that she cannot bear to have anyone look at her.

In exasperation I told her, "I prefer Horsewhip Willa to Tail-Between-the-Legs Willa," and she sat down hard on a crate and cried straight out, not even bothering to cover her face. After that I rummaged around in her desk until I found the last of the notebooks she had done on the falcons. The covers were coated with dust, it has been that long since she worked in them. I told her it was time she got back to the peregrines, and to my surprise she agreed.

But I get ahead of myself. Before all this awful business with Charlie Rich, Kit paid a courtesy call at Wen's home and reported that while Abby is as sour as ever, the girls are quite delightful. They seemed happy that she had come, and asked about us. Caroline, who is sixteen, is the prettier of the two, Kit said, but it was clear that it was fourteen-year-old Lucy who caught her fancy.

Kit described Lucy as a pale child, small for her years, with straight hair and an even straighter back. She has a scar on her forehead near the hairline, memento of a fall from a horse, which she wears as a point of pride, pulling her hair back so that it can be admired. Her legs are so thin that her stockings sag, and Kit noticed they were of two slightly different shades of beige, the sort of calculated carelessness designed to ruffle a mother's feathers, which it did.

"I got the distinct impression," Kit laughed, "that Abby

would have liked to lock her in the nearest closet."

"Spunky girls run in the family," I noted. "I'll bet her grandmother would like her."

"I think so too." Kit told me, "and she would be good for Mother right now. Besides, Wen's children could be the only grandchildren she is going to have, so it would be a pity not to know them. I'd like to arrange a visit. I've already sounded Wen out . . ."

"What did he say?"

Kit mimicked Wen's stolid delivery: "I very much approve of the way you've taken over the reins of the family business, and I hear that you do admirably up in San Francisco, managing your late husband's holdings . . . I would, of course, be glad to put the good offices of my firm at your disposal . . ." She smiled, adding wryly, "I think Wen is counting on being the only Reade of our generation to produce heirs, and he would like his heirs to be ours . . ."

"In other words?"

"The girls may come at our convenience."

"Did you set a date?"

"If Mother agrees, next Sunday."

But as I said, the Charlie Rich debate exploded since then, and I haven't the slightest notion what lies in wait now.

*April 14, 1930:* This past week has been a bother. Willa and Kit are in town every day, all day long, trying to salvage what they can of the Charlie Rich mess. That, coupled with the generally dreary state of the economy, makes these dark days. Some say the worst is yet to come. In some perverse way, Willa seems to take heart from the nation's gathering woes. "I'm not the only one in trouble," she says, "a lot of us are in this together." I feel like hitting her when she says that. To think she has the gall to compare herself to those poor souls who are in far worse straits, and have had nothing at all to do with getting themselves there. They are the real victims. To be honest, however, I suppose I am most vexed because she wouldn't listen when I warned her about Charlie.

Like everything else, it is going to take time to sort out just how much damage has been done. According to Kit, Joseph feels the Charlie Rich business is a setback, but not a crippling blow. It has had one concrete effect, however. Finally, Willa is convinced she should stop work on the Casa Blanca.

When Wen's girls arrived on Sunday, their grandmother had regained enough of her composure to give them a tour of the house. Caroline was interested in the decorations, while Lucy wanted nothing more than to get out to the barns and the countryside, and would have been pleased to see the whole of the ranch in a day's time, had that been humanly possible. Willa has promised to cover it with her on horseback when school is out next month, if it is agreeable to her parents. From the look on Lucy's face, I sincerely doubt that either Wen or Abby would be able to stop her from coming. By the end of the day, she and Willa were chattering like old friends. I can always tell when Willa takes to someone. She gets quite excited. It has been a long time since she has allowed anyone new into her life, and I, for one, am glad. They will be good for each other, I suspect. Lucy is as plain as an old shoe, but there is something about her that is fetching. I am glad for yesterday. The girls offered us a small island of pleasure in dreary times.

*June 8, 1931: San Francisco.* The gloom gathers, the trouble deepens. Discontent lies like a gray fog over everything, though admittedly, one is hard put to see the real turbulence from the vantage point of the Malibu, or Nob Hill. Even so, the bright sun and the sea at Malibu seemed to mock everything, so I came to San Francisco to escape the heat, to hide in the summer fog. Kit is here too, tending to business. She has become a regular traveler on the overnight train. I think I prefer the night train these days. During the daylight, it is too easy to see—in those places where the railroad parallels the highway—the steady stream of refugees, that is all one can call them, pouring into California in search of work.

I am happy to report that Porter, at least, is feeling hopeful. The Wobblies are back in force, pricking the conscience of those who have called for reform, and this time the workers are listening. The International Longshoremen's Union is witnessing a revival, and Porter is in the midst of it all.

It does seem strange to me, and I told Porter this, that the men should choose this time to ask for what, admittedly, they are due: better pay, shorter working hours, a guaranteed number of hours each week. But to ask for it when company profits are down and the depression deepens, I don't know. It doesn't seem to make much sense. Porter says that it does. He insists that there would not be a depression had not wages for all workers been so low. It was, he says, a case of too many goods being produced and too few people able to buy them. The unemployment figures have been hovering at twenty percent... dreadfully high, and now they are up to twenty-five percent, one out of four workers.

In the meantime, Porter skitters up and down the coast between ports—Tacoma and Aberdeen, Stockton and San Diego—exhorting the men to stand together. "You are twelve thousand strong and you are the lifeblood of the docks," he shouts to them. "If we stand together, we can make the owners listen. The time for change is now."

And they cheer for him and shout and raise their fists.

Porter has heard from Ch'ing-Ling. She is living in Hawaii now, he told me, with her father's eldest brother and his family.

"Have you thought about seeing her again?" I asked. The look that flashed over his face said more than words ever could, and for the first time I glimpsed the depth of his longing for her.

"It would be more difficult to see her now," he said. "The elder uncle is much more traditional than her father. He would never permit me to call on her."

"And Ch'ing-Ling, does she want to see you?" I probed.

He nodded, clasping and unclasping his hands as he often did when struggling with strong emotions.

"Would she defy her uncle?" I asked.

"I don't know," he answered. "It would be difficult for her. I don't even know if I have the right to ask it of her."

"You'll find a way, Porter," I told him. It was all I could think to say.

*September 22, 1931:* Thad is in the hospital in Santa Monica. He weighs little more than one hundred pounds, and his lungs are weak as a result of the gassing during the war. Wen has been to the hospital several times, and I believe his concern is genuine.

It seemed a good time to tell him how much we enjoy Lucy's company at the ranch. "Lucy, well, yes," he said, as if the subject were not agreeable, "she seems to be fond of her grandmother. I think she is the only one who is. As Abby says, they deserve each other."

I was shocked and <u>dismayed</u> that he would speak so to me, not only about Willa but about his own daughter. Still, I held my tongue. I did not want to do anything that might hurt Lucy and Willa's friendship.

"Do you suppose Lucy might like to come north with me, the next time I go to San Francisco?" I asked. "Caroline is welcome too, of course."

"Oh, Caroline's busy all the time," he answered, "but Lucy can go. It would give us a bit of peace, to tell the truth."

I held my smile. Lucy had already let us know how she felt about her parents, her mother especially. I suppose I shouldn't be shocked at Wen, when the child is just as acid in discussing her parents. "I'm not much interested in Mother," she said one day, "because Mother is not very interesting. And don't tell me that is an arrogant and a rude thing to say about one's own mother, because I know it is."

I don't know why I like the little hoyden so much, but I do. And I believe she is blossoming under our wing. Speaking of which—the most wonderful thing has happened. Lucy, it turns out, has become fascinated with birds, not raptors so much as the shore birds that flock into the lagoon near the old pier. She is undertaking to catalog them, with Willa's expert guidance. In return, she goes hawking with Willa—always on horseback. Lucy loves to ride.

*December 7, 1931, San Francisco.* Lucy is on school vacation, so Kit and I brought her with us to the city. Willa had promised to come but, as usual, she found an excuse to stay on at the ranch. I thought that Lucy was going to stay with her, such was her disappointment. But in the end, she came.

Kit took her to the salon at the City of Paris and had her hair permed, then she bought her quite a beautiful, grownup dress and she is almost pretty. Porter calls her "Little Poker Face" but she seems to like it. Rather, she likes Porter. I do believe she is quite smitten, but we try not to let her know we notice.

Sara suffers from arthritis; it affects her hands and impedes her work. She spends several hours each day exercising, bathing and massaging her hands in an effort to keep them supple, but I fear it helps little.

I am worried about her. For the first time, she is succumbing to periods of depression. She has even said that perhaps it would be best if she gave up painting altogether. In desperation, I have offered to sit for a portrait. She accepted, but not until she had scolded me for fully an hour, saying such things as "now that my hands won't work properly, you agree. After all my years of pleading, now that I can't do you justice, isn't that just like you, Lena Kerr...to wait until my hands are crippled?"

Her ranting drove me to such distraction that finally I said, "Now that we're both cripples, maybe you will learn some patience."

I felt worse than awful when she answered, "I've always understood, Lena." We had a good cry together, after which Sara made a sensible schedule and I am to start sitting tomorrow. I had to agree to stay on as long as it would take. Anything to keep her at work.

Lucy must return to Los Angeles tomorrow, to her chagrin. She would like to live in San Francisco forever, she says melodramatically, looking at Porter.

Porter is oblivious. I have never seen him so distracted, and I thought I knew why. We were alone last evening for the first time. I approached the subject of his trip to Hawaii with care. "You were there three weeks," I reminded him, "can you tell me about it?"

He rose, clearly disturbed. He paced back and forth a few times, finally coming to rest by the window, looking down on California Street. For a while the only sound in the room was the continuously low singing hum of the cable on the street outside.

"Were you able to see her?" I probed.

"Twice," he answered. "I went to the university. She is escorted, even there, by an amah—the same old woman who was with her in Shanghai. But this time the amah was willing to help. She raised Ch'ing-Ling and she loves her enough to at least look the other way. And since she speaks no English, we could talk freely."

He fell silent again, staring down on the street, lost in thought.

"And?" I reminded him.

He sighed, and came to sit across from me. *"And,"* he said, "she says she feels love for me, she says that were it a matter of her personal happiness she would find no pleasure so perfect as to spend all of her life with me, in harmony and grace."

"Porter!" I could not help but exclaim, my feelings suddenly rose in my throat.

"No, wait," he cautioned, "that's not all. It seems that her personal happiness is pretty low on the list of priorities. We talked for no more than half an hour, most of the time just catching up on our feelings. God, Auntie..."

I swallowed. I could not let myself cry.

He went on, "The next day two very large Chinese men appeared at my door and told me I was to come with them. The next thing I knew I was standing before Ch'ing-Ling's uncle, who said nothing at all for a full five minutes, but just stared at me.

"Then they brought her in—she explained that she was to interpret for her uncle, but that I was not to speak directly to her or she to me. In this way, the uncle—speaking through Ch'ing-Ling—explained that a marriage had been arranged for her. She would return to China to become the wife of an officer in the army of General Chiang Kai-shek. It was explained that my friendship with the communist general Wing Soong was well known, that Soong was a mortal enemy of their family, and of Ch'ing-Ling's proposed husband. Therefore, it should be more than obvious that I should under no circumstances ever attempt to see her, or speak to her, again. As a postscript, he said that the amah had been sent back to China in disgrace, that she had lost her place in the family for allowing Ch'ing-Ling to speak to me the day before.

"What did you say?"

"I asked to be allowed to at least speak to Ch'ing-Ling. It was mad—talking to him through her and yet not being allowed to speak directly. He said no, not one word was to pass between us."

"And did she relay that message?"

"Oh, yes," he said in a voice so low I had to strain to hear, "there were tears in her eyes and her whole body was shaking but God! She did as she was told. I guess I got wild then. I started talking to her. I said I loved her and that this was crazy— that it was a medieval scene from some world that didn't exist anymore. And then. Jesus! Thinking about it makes me want to strangle him. That old man spoke up—in English. He hadn't needed a translator at all. He had done it to humiliate her. I swear, if his two goons hadn't thrown me out, I would have killed him."

He was sitting, running his hands through his hair, his head bowed. He looked so troubled, so terribly hurt and vulnerable, and I wanted nothing so much as to absorb the pain he was feeling.

He looked up at me, his eyes flashing with anger. "The bastard must have influence, because they put me on my ship and kept me there until it set sail. The reason they gave was that I was a 'known agitator.'" He stood once more and began pacing, pacing and thinking.

"And that, at least, is true, Auntie. I am an agitator, and it's something that doesn't fit at all with her life. Our worlds— they *are* too far apart . . . the chasm is just too great to bridge, if she hasn't the resolve, or the courage, to try."

*October 3, 1932, the Malibu:* I must return to San Francisco this week for the final sitting for my portrait. Dear Sara has struggled so, and at times she moved so painfully slowly that I think it may have been a mistake for me to have urged her to continue. I worry that she pushes herself beyond what is possible.

At the same time, she is impossible . . . she will not let any of us see the painting. If I get up to walk about to give my back a rest, she covers the canvas, as if I might try to peek behind her back. I tell her she is getting testier all the time and she is. But I also know that she does that rather than complain about the pain. Thad has been well all summer long. He even gained a bit of weight so we were hopeful that his health was improving, but he is ill again. I hope he won't have to go back into the hospital, he has been in and out so much of late. Willa says that I should not delay my trip to San Francisco on Thad's account. I didn't think that to be strange at first, but now it seems that not so long ago she would call me to observe the slightest change in his behavior or his health. I am not quite sure when it happened, or how, but some time during the last few years Willa stopped believing that Thad would make a full recovery, or that he would change very much. It had been so important to her for such a long time, and now it is not. The startling thing is, I don't know when the change occurred and neither, I think, does she. Perhaps hope does not rush out all at once but, rather, evaporates at such an infinitesimally slow rate that one day it is gone and we don't even notice.

*October 17, 1932, San Francisco:* Sara *would* have an un-veiling party last evening. (My objections never have deterred

ara when she has her mind set.) I agreed only because it was
st to be a few very close friends. Kit and Porter, Philip and
ina Cameron, and some of Sara's artist and museum friends
've known for years. It was dress up, champagne and all. Very
well, as Porter put it out of the side of his mouth, gangster
tyle.

I was a bit nervous, I must admit. But Sara, well. You
ould have thought she was about to give birth. When she did
nveil the painting and we got a look at it, I was at a loss to
ee what the fuss was all about. It doesn't look in the least like
ne as far as I can tell, so I can hardly be upset. I was pleased
o see that my back doesn't look grotesque, as I had imagined
t might.

The others are being quite silly about it. One of the museum
adies kept talking about "awesome power and force." I must
ay, it is a very strange experience to see yourself through the
yes of someone else. I don't believe I know the woman in
he portrait, but right away Kit said, "Oh, yes." And Porter
oo. He said, "Yes, you've got her." And Philip. Well, Philip
aid something that unnerved me, if the truth be told. Philip
aid, "I don't know, Sara—it's as if you are sharing our won-
lerful secret..." And Sara had answered, right off, "I know
hat, Philip. It's already been decided that the portrait will
emain in my estate, and that it will hang at Wildwood. The
ortrait is to be Porter's."

And Porter said, "If I never have a house to hang it in, I'll
carry it around on my back." We laughed at that, but it wasn't
entirely a joke, I could tell. I had to be careful, then, to make
ure my laughter didn't turn into tears.

Sara is basking in the praise, and for that it was worth every
minute. I've told her to find herself a proper subject, now that
she knows how she must work, but she says she is not in all
hat much of a hurry now.

*October 19, 1932:* Joseph called this morning to tell us that
Thad's condition is worsened, that we should return as soon
as we could.

*January 9, 1933:* I am too exhausted to write, so I shall
clip the obituary from last Thursday's *Santa Monica Evening
Outlook.*

*Thaddeus Reade, age 40, a native of California and lifelong
resident of the Rancho Malibu, died yesterday of injuries suf-*

*fered while serving with the U.S. Expeditionary Force in Franc*
*during the Great War. He was the son of Mrs. Willa Ker*
*Reade and the late Mr. Reade. He will be sorely missed by a*
*those friends and relatives he leaves behind.*

Sally sent white roses, which were placed on the casket
Kit sobbed throughout the service, until finally Porter had t
take her home. Willa is dazed. Lucy stays close by and I ar
thankful, having no reserves of energy myself.

*January 16, 1933, 3:00 P.M.:* How I envy the Catholics thei
confessional. I long to tell someone of my sin and be give
absolution. We poor Protestants are left with our conscience
and our notebooks. So I shall confess here: I have no feelin
at Thad's death, none at all. I do not miss him. More than that
I am glad. Glad? Perhaps only relieved. It is as if he lived s
on the periphery of our lives that when he slipped over th
edge into eternity, we scarcely noticed.

*11:30 P.M.:* I cannot sleep. Has something died within m
that I should be so unfeeling at Thad's death? Willa's pain i
real. I avoid her so I do not have to pretend. It is true, I an
glad. Sara stayed on after the funeral and, seeing the light i
my room so late, came to sit with me. I told her, I blurted i
all out and all she said was, "What is so terrible about that'
We've been mourning Thad for twenty years. We've watche
the life ebb out of him. Why aren't you angry, instead, at th
waste?"

Angry. She is right, it should be anger that I feel. At what'
At Thad? Or at the forces which came together to deny him a
good life? Dear Lord, I wish I knew.

I shall try my bed again; perhaps if I repeat the Lord's
Prayer, sleep will come.

*January 30, 1933:* I have a letter from Soong, written three
months ago. "Arrests and executions on orders of Generalis-
simo Chiang have decimated our ranks and made it impossible
for the Central Committee to remain in Shanghai. We leave
tomorrow for the Soviet Republic in Kiangsi, proclaimed by
Mao last year. The Central Committee is, now, firmly in the
hands of those 'students' who have been to Moscow for training
and who continue to insist that the urban proletariat must lead
the revolution in China. A few of us—Chou En-lai and myself
included—are tolerated by the party but only after we formally,
and publicly, confessed our 'cowardly rotten opportunism' for

having been involved in the debacle at Changsha."

*The debacle at Changsha.* I hadn't the slightest notion what it might be but I was sure of one thing. Soong had explained it in a letter that never arrived.

I was cheered, even so, by what seemed to me to be a stiffening of resolve on Soong's part. He wrote: "I am stubborn, but I have decided that I will see this revolution through. I cannot say why, but I have convinced myself that in my lifetime I will see a different China, one free of poverty and death and corruption and servitude. If that way is not democratic, it will at least be more humane. For the moment, however, Chiang Kai-shek is determined to exterminate as many of us as he can. Guerrilla units are fighting in the countryside, and soon I will be among them. I carry with me the picture I have in my mind's eye—of you and Porter as you stood together when last I saw you. It is a glorious picture."

*February 26, 1934, San Francisco:* The ILA—the Longshoremen's Union—is feeling its muscle and is determined to bring the Employers Association up short. It looks like trouble for certain, and Porter of course is in the middle of it. These are exciting times, he likes to tell me. I tell him they are nervewracking. On Saturday last, labor union delegates from every Pacific coast port gathered in San Francisco in common cause, and they have put forth these demands: one dollar an hour pay, a thirty-hour work week and a six-hour day. Not only that, but all hiring is to be done through the ILA halls.

Well, the employers rejected it out of hand.

I can only feel that the longshoremen are being unrealistic. There are four thousand of them and only thirteen hundred jobs, and there is an army of unemployed men who will work for any wage to feed their families. It is a ready-made pool of strikebreakers.

*March 12, 1934:* At President Roosevelt's request, the strike deadline has been postponed so a panel can study the demands. (Our President is a cousin of T.R.'s, and quite as flamboyant I do believe, in a different way. He is having a marvelous effect on the country, which is, of course, what I would expect from a cousin of T.R.'s.) At any rate, things seem cooled down now so that Kit and I could return to the Malibu, Kit to grapple with the continuing tangle of problems concerning the ranch and me—to be honest—to bury my head in the sand so I do not have constantly to be assaulted by the troubles of the Great Depression.

Our brothers in Illinois write that there is no market for their crops and they give away what they can. Porter Farm will hold, but many other smaller spreads have been taken over by the banks and it is a sorry sight, the boys say.

Traveling south through the Central Valley made me physically ill. Whole families with their possessions piled on top of broken-down cars can be seen along the highways. Dust seems everywhere—on the cars they come in, on the miserable camps they make for them on the outskirts of dingy little valley towns, even on their children. And yet they continue to make their way west, to California—the "land of milk and honey" and the old dream that will not die. They believe things will be better here. Or perhaps they simply must go as far as they can go, all the way to the Pacific.

Some, not many, find their way into the Malibu in search of work. We have none, we can scarcely afford to keep our own people. Even so, Willa has ordered a camp kitchen set up near the old pier, where anyone who wants can have a free meal. The ranch is still able to produce its own food. Who would have dreamed it could come to this?

A few days back, Kit and I were driving into town when we noticed a group of men waiting tentatively at the camp kitchen. We stopped to see what the matter was, and discovered that they were Danes—carpenters, actually, who live in a Danish settlement east of Santa Barbara. They had come in search of work.

We found the cook, and left them. Kit was uncommonly quiet. We drove for perhaps a mile and then suddenly she stopped the car and executed a turn so abrupt that I thought for a moment we would mire in the sand. She headed back, explaining, "Fate has just presented me with a decision."

She proceeded to hire the Danes to build her a house on the beach adjacent to the pier, with the ocean to its front and the lagoon to the back. She already had the architectural plans drawn up; she had, in fact, had them for some weeks.

"Whatever do you want a house for?" I asked as we continued on our way. "Isn't the Casa Blanca enough of a problem?"

"The Casa Blanca is Mother's house, not mine," was all

she would say. I supposed that there was more to it than that, but I would have to wait to find out, I could see.

As for the Casa Blanca—I wandered into the ballroom the other day. The lath and plaster is all exposed, and it seems terribly raw. The chandelier is missing several pieces, I can't imagine what could have become of them. Coated as it is with dust, it looks altogether forlorn. Like the whole of the country.

*July 9, 1934, San Francisco:* We rushed here, Kit and I, to be with Porter. He is in the hospital with second-degree burns on his hands and arms, suffered when he pulled a strikebreaker out of a blazing truck that had been overturned in the violence of Thursday last—"Bloody Thursday," as it is called.

Hundreds are hurt and two union men are dead in the ugliness that erupted last Thursday. I am thankful that Porter's injuries are not even more serious. I am grateful that they were suffered not in an act of destruction, but of courage.

I believe in Porter's work in support of the union. But I cannot condone violence or the wanton and reckless disregard for human life.

The strikebreaker Porter saved is a man of thirty-eight who has five young children. He hasn't worked in six months. How can anyone believe that man to be anything but a victim? Porter knows that, he believes it is wrong to set one poor man against another. And yet the police wade in with their tear gas and their nightsticks. Who is to blame? The governor talks of martial law and union men are calling a general strike. Ten thousand people marched up Market Street in memory of the dead. I saw it, and was moved to tears.

*July 29, 1934:* Porter is recovering, cheered by the knowledge that the general strike served its purpose. The union and the employers agreed to submit their differences to arbitration and, in the end, the union victory was all but total.

Kit is looking frazzled and worn, and Porter is mending. I suppose it seems irresponsible in a world so desperate, but I have suggested that we go to Hawaii to recuperate. Sara has started a new painting and does not want to leave right now. But to my great surprise, both Kit and Porter agreed.

Kit because she wants to get Porter away from the docks for a time, Porter because, in the midst of all the excitement on the docks, he has received extraordinary news. Ch'ing-Ling's arranged marriage did not take place. Her uncle died,

and her aunt is now head of the household, and amenable to
giving her niece the freedom to see a friend from California.

"I hope we get to meet her," Kit told me.

"That may not be possible," I answered, "it is rather a
complicated cultural problem."

She sighed. "I suppose I should have known we couldn't
expect a nice old-fashioned love affair from Porter."

"*Old-fashioned* it is," I laughed, "more than you know."

I think that neither Kit nor I expected the memories that would
wash over us when we returned to Honolulu. My last time on
the beach at Waikiki had been in 1914, when we went to meet
Soong. Kit was there last on her honeymoon, and she trembled
visibly when we walked into the elegant lobby of the Royal
Hawaiian.

Porter was too distracted to notice two women awash in
painfully sweet memories. I breathed in the scent of plumeria
from the leis that had been given us upon landing, and decided
to give myself over to the sun and the swaying palms.

For a time, Kit and I moved as in a trance. The Islands can
do that. We sipped cool drinks, rested in the shade the palms
threw on the raked enclosure that was the Royal Hawaiian's
private section of the beach, and listened to the ukelele music
played by supple young Hawaiians. We watched the clouds
billowing high offshore, watched the children stand, backs
straight, waiting for the next wave to wash over them, and we
let ourselves forget about the misery that was, even then, drawing closer.

We came in, that first day, in time to see Porter on his way
out, dressed in tropical whites and looking uncommonly handsome.

"Looks like a deluxe date," Kit teased, affectionately.

"Very deluxe," he answered, giving us both a quick kiss,
so that we felt his excitement.

"I think perhaps Porter is going to be well occupied," I said
to Kit, "why don't we make some plans of our own?"

We arranged to have dinner at the Officer's Club on the
naval base as guests of the commanding officer, a family friend
of some years. It was a large group. Kit's dinner partner was
a personable young lieutenant commander. His name was Michael Flannery and he made Kit laugh, which was nice to see.

The next evening, with my blessing, Kit agreed to see Flannery again, this time for dinner and dancing. Porter knocked on the door of the suite I shared with Kit just as she was preparing to leave. His eyes were red, he had neither shaved nor slept, it seemed.

"Where are you going?" he asked Kit.

"Out for the evening," she said flippantly, "on a date. Looks like you're just coming in."

When Kit left, he lay back on her bed and closed his eyes. I started to cover him, but he stopped me. "I'm going to go out again," he said. "I just wanted to rest for a few minutes."

"Porter . . ." I began, but he stopped me.

"I haven't been with Ch'ing-Ling all this time, Auntie. I've been on the beach, walking and thinking. I'm to see her again in an hour."

I sat, watching as he dozed, knowing some struggle was taking place and not knowing what I could do to help.

He pulled himself up. "You and Kit are invited to her aunt's home, for tea. You have been presented as friends of one of Ch'ing-Ling's teachers. I wanted you to meet her, and she thinks this is the best way—in the family home."

"We couldn't entertain her here, in the hotel?"

"She would rather you came there. She really is timid."

"That's fine," I said, not wanting him to suppose I minded, "did you find out why the arranged marriage didn't take place?"

He grimaced. "The man was killed. Chiang loses a good many of his officers, the ones who will go anywhere near a battlefield. Ch'ing-Ling's uncle died then, and he was the family patriarch. Her father was much more agreeable when she said she did not want to marry. She is in medical school, she plans to become a doctor."

"A doctor!" I exclaimed, surprise registering in my voice.

"I know. I was surprised too," he said, in such a way that I raised my eyebrows in question.

"I'm not sure how I feel about it. She is showing courage, and a willingness to strike out in new directions. China will need doctors when the war is finally over, she says. And she is right. It's just that . . ."

". . . she is planning a future, and not around you," I finished for him.

"Maybe," he said, "she hasn't said as much."

I wanted to know how it had been, seeing her again after so long a time, but I hadn't the courage to ask.

"You will know, when you meet her, how I could feel so strongly..."

"How do you feel about her?" I asked.

He rubbed his reddened eyes and grinned. "Like nothing I've ever felt before. Like I'm spinning. Like..."

"I see," I said, bending to kiss him on the top of his head. "Go shower, and take a fifteen-minute nap, at least. I'll call you."

On the afternoon of the fifth day of our visit we were received at the home of Ch'ing-Ling's aunt. With great courtesy, the aunt told us how honored she was to receive friends of her niece's professors at the university. Both Kit and I understood the subterfuge, and did not correct her.

We chatted, as best we could, with the aunt and her sister, neither of whom spoke English well. Kit had decided not to use her Mandarin, I suppose because she felt it would exclude me. The formality of taking tea made it all somewhat easier than it might have been. We smiled, and bowed, and I was impressed, as ever, with the Chinese ability to entertain graciously.

After a time, we were joined by a tall young woman in traditional dress. Porter was right; looking at her, I understood. She had a face of extraordinary clarity—beautiful, and more. There was in her eyes, in her expression, intelligence and warmth and a kind of wisdom that is not learned. Kit became aware of her presence after I did, I knew when I heard a tiny intake of breath, Kit's way of registering amazement.

Ch'ing-Ling made polite inquiries into the state of our health, our pleasure with our visit on Oahu. Only the politest of formalities passed between us, nothing that would suggest that we had a mutual acquaintance. And yet, when she called each of us by name—or so it seemed to me then—it was as if she were telling us how much she cared for him, for Porter. And I understood, then, how Porter could have fallen so completely in love with her.

As the taxi drove us through the streets of Honolulu on our way back to the Royal Hawaiian, we said nothing at all for a time. Finally Kit found the words. "I always thought the woman Porter would fall in love with would have to be extraordinary," she said, "I wasn't quite ready to find someone so...ethereal."

I do not know how much time they were able to spend together, or how they arranged to be alone. That they did, I am certain. I was happy for my son, and worried too.

For the rest of our vacation, Kit saw a good deal of Lieutenant Commander Flannery and his friends. I was pleased to see her having such a nice time, especially since Porter was so occupied.

On the voyage home, Porter kept to himself all the first day. On the second, we ran into heavy seas and I was obliged to stay in my bunk with a mild case of *mal de mer*. Porter and Kit fussed over me, as they tended to do whenever I could not disguise my discomfort.

Porter made, as he put it, a "run on the mess" to bring tea and toast, and as the three of us sat around the tiny table in my cabin, he said:

"I suppose you want to know about her."

"Are you going to tell us?" Kit asked.

Porter rested his chin on his clasped hands. "What do you want to know?" he fenced.

Kit was direct: "What she means to you."

"Lord," Porter said. "Everything. At least, that's the way it feels now. Maybe it won't be so bad after a while."

Kit took his hand. "Don't count on it," she said, and tears came stinging to my eyes.

Porter began to speak then, in a low and urgent voice he explained that Ch'ing-Ling had decided on a medical career in part to forestall another attempt by her family to arrange a marriage. While her father was by no means the autocrat her uncle had been, neither was he willing to entertain the idea of her marrying someone who, if not a communist himself, was connected to Wing Soong, a well-known comrade of Mao Tsetung, both of whom had prices on their heads. And Ch'ing-Ling could not bring herself to break with her family, or with her country. She "recognizes the wisdom of the old ways" she told him.

"So what is to happen?" Kit asked.

Porter shook his head. "We talked interminably. She is so totally intelligent, and yet I could not make her see some of the contradictions in her life. I could not get her to examine it . . ."

Kit turned to me. "The 'unexamined' life—was it Plato

who said the unexamined life was not worth living?"

"No," I answered, "not quite. What he said was, 'I tell you that to let no day pass without discussing goodness and all other subjects about which you hear me talking and examining both myself and others is really the very best thing a man can do, and that life without this sort of examination is not worth living.'"

"It isn't the same," Porter observed, "but it applies. Ch'ing-Ling will not discuss the questions that need to be asked at this moment in history."

"How old is she?" I asked.

"Twenty-five," he answered.

"It is quite young," I started, carefully. "Perhaps not so for Kit and you, but then you grew up in a world altogether different from Ch'ing-Ling's world. While she was being taught the importance of the old ways, you were being steeped in a commitment to change. Soong and Joseph and Philip were the men who guided you in your youngest years, and each of them was extraordinarily dedicated to a purpose, an ideal. You were brought up to believe that you should try to change the world, Porter. But you must learn to be patient with those who were taught other lessons."

Porter sat, locked in thought. We sipped our tea and maintained silence, balancing with the gentle roll of the boat, listening to the steady throb of the engines. Then Porter said what we were, each of us, thinking: "Ch'ing-Ling is everything I want . . . but I don't believe it is possible for our lives to work together."

*October 8, 1934:* Willa, Trinidad and I have moved into Los Angeles, into my townhouse. Let me explain.

The Casa Blanca has had to be sold, there was no way to keep it and meet ranch obligations. Miraculously, in the midst of the depression, a buyer was found. The Catholic church has agreed to purchase the Casa Blanca for use as a retreat. They are paying fifty thousand dollars. Willa had poured half a million dollars into the mansion, and had never finished it. The Catholics' money will pay back taxes.

Kit's house—the one built for her by the Danes—was finished in time to receive all of us. I should have realized that was what Kit had in mind when she built it. The old ranch house is in a dreadful state of repair, even if it weren't in use as a ranch office. Kit's beach house is altogether charming and beautifully situated, facing the sea with the lagoon filled with birds to the back, and hidden from the roadway. There are lovely tiled terraces, the Danes having put the leftover tiles from the Italians' kiln to good use. There are four large bedrooms upstairs, three of which have balconies that look up the coastline. It is much smaller than the Casa Blanca, of course, but in my opinion it is wonderfully elegant. It *feels* like the Malibu. The Danes' workmanship is extraordinary. They added artful touches, such as stenciled folk art on the open beams in the living rooms.

Kit was, I believe, greatly disappointed when Willa decided to move into town. Willa did not do it out of spite. If anything, it is a form of self-punishment, this self-exile.

Lucy, bless her, is a frequent visitor in our house. She is eighteen now and studying biology at the University of Southern California. Her serious interest, she tells us, is ornithology. At the present moment she is organizing Willa's notes—all of them—in hopes of publishing a scholarly book on raptors. The two of them spend long hours together in the library. Occasionally they drive out to the Malibu and do some hawking. Lucy has even persuaded Willa to take a group of fellow students on a birding study tour, concentrating on the shore birds at the lagoon.

*December 24, 1934, Los Angeles:* Today I received a letter, the third since Soong's arrival in Kiangsi two years ago. He writes: "Our very existence is threatened here. Chiang Kai-shek, with the help of the Germans, makes it imperative that we leave this redoubt and travel to the northern provinces, out of their reach. We will be cut off from everything and everyone. Perhaps that is not all bad, however, if it means—as it does—that the Kremlin will no longer be able to direct us, and as Chinese communists we will be free to wage our own brand of revolution. It will be a long journey. We must take a circuitous route and there will be fighting along the way. It will be months before we arrive, and it is unlikely that I shall have another chance to get a letter to you. So there are some things that I must say. First, that I am determined that I shall see the end of this quest, if it means I must live to be one hundred. I am fit, and I have faith. Second, when the time is right, and you will know, tell our son of his heritage, and tell him his father is filled with pride and love for him. Last, remember this. My love for you is eternal."

*February 1, 1937:* We had a belated birthday celebration over this past weekend, at Kit's beach house. It was the first time everyone has been able to get together, such is the temper of these times. Even Joseph, who has such trouble moving about, managed to be there.

Porter brought me a wonderful gift: a newspaper clipping from *The New York Times,* a Reuters report taken from the London *Observer.* A Reuters correspondent in China had managed to make his way into the communist stronghold in Yenan, and to come out again to write his story, part of which read: "The Long March is even now becoming the stuff of legend. Of the one hundred thousand Chinese communists who started from Kiangsi in October of 1934, only 20,000 eventually reached Shensi province, having traveled, in all, 6,000 miles, according to Wing Soong, a high-ranking official in the Chinese communist hierarchy and one of the survivors of the March."

I could not have received a more perfect gift, nor could it have arrived on a more perfect day. I read it over and over again, until Sara told me I was going to wear it out with my eyes. Soong was safe, he was alive and he was well. Knowing that gave me the strength to do what I had, all these thirty-three years since Porter's birth, longed to do. My gift to him on this birthday would be the truth. I felt a swelling within me, a wonderful sense of freedom. I began to prepare my speech, which I planned to deliver that evening, when we could be alone.

Dinner was a family affair, with Lucy holding forth on Spain, in a spirited defense of the Republic, while Joseph teased her by playing the devil's advocate, chiding the Spanish Republicans for repressing freedom of religion and thus inviting chaos. I only half listened. My mind was on that hour when I would tell Porter that he was my son, that Soong fathered him.

After dinner a small dance band began to play on the terrace, it being an unusually balmy night for February, and Kit and Porter's friends began to arrive. They drove out from Los Angeles and Santa Monica, and a few of the movie people came over from the beach colony. Trinidad and Lucy had strung Chinese lanterns at almost the last minute, which gave a festive glow to the setting, sheltered as it was from the open sea breezes, but with the moonlit beach in full view below.

It was a handsome group, swaying to the music, soft and sweet songs that were so popular—"June in January" and "Tea for Two" and "Stars Fell on Alabama." From a balcony, Sara and I watched, and felt glad. It was, I thought, a sweet respite— safe and sweet.

I heard Kit and Lucy come upstairs to bed after one. I waited until everything was still, then I put on my robe and made my way downstairs to the small guest room where Porter was sleeping.

He was not in the room. I found him in the living room, alone, standing by the big window that looked out to the sea.

"Porter?" I said, quietly.

He turned on a light.

"I was just wondering if it was too late to wake you," he said.

"What is it?" I asked quickly, "What's wrong?"

"I have something to tell you . . . I've been waiting for a good time to do it, and I guess there just is no good time."

I went cold inside. I felt weak and held onto a chair to keep my balance.

"Auntie," he said, "I'm going to Spain . . . I'm going to join the International Brigade."

*July 26, 1937:* We devour the news from Spain. There has been heavy fighting at a place called Brunete, just west of Madrid, these past three weeks, and the Fifteenth International Brigade was in the worst of it. The siege of Madrid has now been underway for nine months, and the Loyalists show no sign of giving in.

Porter is there, part of the Abraham Lincoln Battalion.

Abraham Lincoln, who slept in our farmhouse once, long ago.

I cannot make sense of it. I did not want Porter to go. I wanted to tell him that he was mine, my son, my only child— but I could not. He left without knowing, he does not know.

I could not tell him, not then. Not like that. It must be a gift, freely given.

He must live, he must. I could not bear to lose him.

Kit went with him, when he left. I could not. She told me about it, later—about that last hour in the train station. She had asked him, then, "Are you afraid?"

And Porter had answered her with a quotation: "You are mistaken, my friend, if you think that a man who is worth anything ought to spend his time weighing up the prospects of life and death. He has only one thing to consider in performing any action—that is, whether he is acting rightly or wrongly, like a good man or a bad one."

Plato, that old fool.

Kit had shook her head and whispered, "I hate it, Porter, all the death." He hugged her to him then and told her that he hated it, too, but that there was no other way, that Hitler and the fascists must be stopped in Spain, and now. He said if it could not be done, there would be a bloodbath beyond all we could imagine.

*April 3, 1939:* On March 28, the forces of fascism won in Spain. Democracy is in tatters everywhere. Madrid has fallen and the war is over. Porter and all of the men who fought for the Republic have learned what it is to lose. Plato is an old fool. Good does not triumph. But Porter is alive. He will be repatriated to England, we have learned. The message we received spoke of complications from a leg wound that has not properly healed.

*October 9, 1939:* Porter writes from England: "I apologize once more, Auntie, for the delay. I am also glad that I have convinced you to stay in Los Angeles. This is no time for you to be traveling in Europe. The British doctors hum and haw over my leg. They promise me they are doing everything humanly possible to save it, and I believe them. Next week, they say, a decision . . . I am confident that one day they will patch me up so that I can come home. Try not to worry."

I have not been able to sleep. I pace at night until I waken Trinidad and she comes out and cries. I can't seem to stop her from crying.

As for Willa, when I try to talk to her she only deflects me . . . usually to something that happened when we were girls. "I was thinking about Grandmother the other day," she will say. "What do you think she would have to say about airplanes and bombings?"

I confess, I haven't any idea.

When Kit told her that she was going to England to be with Porter, Willa set about getting a list of names of people that

Kit must look up—people Willa has neither seen nor heard from in thirty years.

I read the *Times* to Willa every morning. It has become a habit. I don't think she listens very much, but only pretends. She has not wanted to go out to the Malibu of late. Lucy told me of a conversation she had with Willa the other day.

Lucy said, "Don't you miss going out to the ranch, Grandmother? Don't you want to track the peregrines anymore?"

Willa didn't answer, but instead asked, "Did you know that an eagle builds a nest in one tree—it gets to be an enormous big thing. The pair returns to it every year until the tree dies or is cut down or simply topples under the weight of the nest."

"All birds are creatures of instinct," Lucy answered, "bound to the seasons, to the nest, to the ritual."

"Even so," Willa said, "to watch a falcon soar—to see it catch a thermal and sail so high in the sky that you can no longer see it, but only know it's there, until it flings itself into a stoop, diving at amazing speeds straight down . . . ah, my . . ."

"That is good, isn't it?" Lucy had asked.

And Willa had said, "Yes, it is. I do believe that it is."

## ~ *Epilogue*

I decided to commit this chronicle to paper on the day I learned that Porter was coming home from the Spanish Civil War. The truth was this: I knew I could not let him leave again without knowing the circumstances of his birth, and I was afraid to tell him.

Just that—afraid.

In Shanghai, with Soong, I had not been afraid, but Porter had been only twenty-five then, and young still. After Spain, he was thirty-five and no longer young. I became convinced that the truth had been hidden for so long that telling it could be devastating. Perhaps he would feel betrayed. Perhaps he would suddenly discover another truth—that I had been guilty of duplicity, that I was devious and deceitful and not worthy of his love. He would almost certainly think me a hypocrite, for having kept so large a truth hidden from him for so long. Porter's passion for justice was great. I became obsessively certain that in telling him, I would destroy whatever love he might feel for me.

And yet I knew I must tell him. I could not let him leave again without knowing. I would have to accept the consequences.

Kit brought him home from the long stay in the hospital in

589

England. He came limping up the walkway to the townhouse, Kit propping him on one arm. He was thin and weary and sad, you could see the sadness in the slope of his shoulders, but the sight of him filled me with thanksgiving.

It was a bittersweet homecoming. He was changed by Spain, you could see it in his eyes, in the way he entered a room or lifted a glass. He had learned a hard lesson in Spain.

He needed time to recover, spiritually and physically. Kit kept strict account of his exercises. She saw to it that he walked the prescribed number of miles each day on the beach, that he swam in the saltwater pool she added the beach house, that he slept.

Porter started writing again and, when his leg was completely healed, accepted a job with the International News Service—Hearst's wire service.

All the while I was working on my family "history," convincing myself that when it was finished I would give it to him to read, that any less of an explanation would not do. And each day the story got longer as more and more details were needed to explain all that has happened, to explain the deception.

Porter was to be in Los Angeles for two years. He was at the townhouse the morning that Willa did not appear in the library as usual, and he was there with us, at her bedside, two weeks later when she opened her eyes and said, "Lena, do you remember my telling you about waking in Cousin Minnie's house in Newton Center, and seeing the yellow rosebuds on the wallpaper and not knowing where I was?"

"Yes, darling," I murmured, taking her hand, "I remember."

She looked at me as if she meant to say something more, but before she could she lapsed into the sleep from which she would not awaken.

Willa knew, in the last months of her life, that Kit had put on the market two large blocks of land on the Malibu. She knew the earnings were enough to recoup losses and put the Reade Land Company on a firm footing. The family still owned vast tracts of land in the Malibu, land that was certain to increase in value so that, eventually, the family fortunes would be more than replenished.

Willa knew, but she chose not to acknowledge the sale. She did not leave the house in those last months, not until the day of her funeral.

I sold the townhouse then. It had served its purpose, and Kit wanted me to move back to the beach house with her, while Sara continued to prod me to come to San Francisco. I decided that as long as I was able, I would divide my time between the two.

Trinidad moved back to her old house on the ranch, to live with her daughter Marcella and her family. She was apologetic, telling me over and over again that she would worry about me, that she would be sure to come to see that I was eating properly. Porter and I drove her out to the old house in his big Buick. She cried all the way until finally I gave her a stiff poke in the ribs and said, sternly, "Trinidad, you are going to dry up and simply blow off into the hills if you don't stop leaking all those tears!" That made Porter laugh and Trinidad cry even harder, until I promised I would see her every week, and told her once more that if living with Marcella's family did not prove happy, she would always be welcome to come live with me.

Porter talked about Spain in the abstract; he spoke of campaigns and strategies and international politics. He did not talk of the people he knew, he did not speak of death or of disillusionment. When, once, Lucy blurted, "Did you ever have to shoot anyone?" his eyes had, for a flicker of an instant, a haunted look. He did not answer her question.

I believe he talked to Kit. They spent long hours together in the months following his return. Once they saddled horses and took enough supplies to camp deep in the canyons for five days. Kit was as responsible for his recovery as were the doctors.

She was another reason I delayed telling Porter. I could not know what it would do to them, to the way they thought about themselves, if they believed that being twins was the source of their almost mystical closeness.

December 7 was a particularly balmy winter Sunday in 1941. Kit and Porter had been invited to play roque, a game something like croquet, on the court at the beach colony. They insisted I go along, and took a folding chair for me to sit and watch the game. The roque court was laid out behind the row of beach cottages. I recognized one or two of the players from the moving pictures—a man with a neat little pencil mustache, a pretty girl in red slacks. It was a bright, sun-splashed afternoon, deceptively calm. The game was proceeding at a slow pace with a good many clever comments from the participants when a woman in a polka-dotted dress came running from one of the cottages, calling to us.

I can see her still, stumbling in her high heels—one arm raised ineffectually, as if to signal us—the attitude of her body telling us she had news of great moment.

"Pearl Harbor," she gasped, out of breath, "they've bombed Hawaii."

"The Japanese?" someone demanded, and the girl in the polka-dotted dress, out of breath, simply pumped her head up and down.

We followed her back to her cottage and gathered round a radio to listen to the news bulletins.

"This is it," the actor with the thin mustache said dramatically, "we're at war."

Someone giggled nervously at the voice of doom he affected, and the rest of us shifted uncomfortably, not knowing what to say.

"Could we be in danger here, on the coast?" a woman asked. "I mean, could we be invaded?" She glanced at her children playing in a teahouse on the beach, and I saw her check an impulse to gather them to her.

My own fear was mixed with dread. Porter would be leaving now. These two years with him had been the trough between the waves, as Soong would have said.

I sat up all that night, from Sunday and into Monday, sifting through the pages I had typed and stored in boxes. I put a towel under my door so that no one would knock to see why my light was on so late, and I went through it all, removing those few passages that seemed, in retrospect, too terribly private. In my resolve to be forthright, I had managed to become too graphic in certain delicate matters.

I finished before daylight, and thought to close my eyes for an hour or so. When I awakened at ten, Porter had left for the INS office and Kit was already on her way to San Francisco for a meeting planned weeks before.

After dinner that night I asked Porter if he would take me for a drive. I wanted to see the old house on Seaside Avenue in Santa Monica.

"I haven't been here in years," Porter said as he stopped the car in front of the house. "It looks a little run-down."

"Don't we all?" I tried to joke.

I took a deep breath. "I was seventeen years old when I first saw this house. Can you imagine that?" I asked him. "Fifty-odd years ago now. It changed my life forever."

"Are you glad?" he asked.

"Yes," I answered. "Oh, yes."

Then I said what I had to say. I told him I had something for him to read, that it was important to me—extremely important—that he read it as soon as possible. I could not trust myself to say more. We returned to the beach house and I handed him the box. He looked at it and nodded. He did not ask what it was, or why he should read it.

I could not sleep. I could see the reflection from the lamp in Porter's room from the balcony. It lit a small part of the coral tree that was outside of his window. He was reading.

I walked. I wrung my hands. I listened to the ocean and watched the steady glow of light on the coral tree until the sky turned a steel gray, and then so light a gray that I could no longer see the reflection of the lamp. I lay back on my bed then to wait for the day, and for Porter.

When I opened my eyes he was sitting beside my bed, his elbows propped on his knees, chin cupped in his hands, and he was watching me.

My heart lurched, sank.

He was looking at me and there were tears in his eyes.

"Porter . . ." I tried to say, but the words wouldn't come.

He took my hand, he kissed my gnarled fingers.

"I should have known," he said, in a voice that was husky. "I should always have known from the way I felt. You . . . are . . . my mother. Dear God, I've wanted it all my life!"

"Forgive me," I started again, but my voice stuck like a lump of porridge was in my throat.

"Forgive you?" he said, whimsically. "For what? For risking everything to give me life? For having the courage to love Soong? Soong . . ." he said, and his voice cracked, ". . . my father, after all."

He hugged me then, as he did when he was a little boy, and I put my arms around him and let myself cry.

I cried, and he rocked me and told me that he had been sitting there, watching me sleep, trying to decide if he felt differently about me . . . and finding that he did not, that he could not love me more, even if he had known ... but that knowing was a gift for which he thanked me.

Porter, my son, thanked me!

Porter, my son.

In the following days we talked. He had questions, more than I could have imagined. Many of them were about Soong. He was overwhelmed, and overjoyed, to learn that Soong was his father. It was unbelievable, he said. A child's dream come true. I tried to answer all of his questions. I told him there were no more secrets, none at all. My only concern was Kit.

"I've been thinking about Kit too," Porter admitted. "I have to tell her, and I've been trying to decide how. In some ways, Kit—the change from brother to cousin—is more difficult. She has always been my other half, in a way. I remember thinking once, in Spain, that if I didn't come back, Kit would still be here ..."

"Must that change?" I asked.

"I don't know," he answered, "I really don't."

We decided that Porter should meet Kit's train, that he should tell her before they returned. It was late when I heard the car on the gravel drive. I was waiting in the kitchen.

"Auntie," Kit said, smiling shyly and putting her arms around me, "at least, you are still *my* auntie."

Kit accepted the new order with amazing calm.

"It doesn't change anything," she said, "except that Porter now has a father to find."

That was when I learned of Porter's resolve to see Soong. "I have to," he told me, "I can't explain why, but it is important that we meet as father and son."

"I don't see how," I said. "Not now, not with the war."

"I've got to try," he insisted.

Porter left for Hawaii in the last week of December, just after Christmas, as an accredited war correspondent for the International News Service—INS. He had convinced his editors that with his command of the language he could best serve in the China theatre. His personal objective, we knew, was to get to the communist stronghold in Shensi province in the northwest of China. For the time being, he told no one of his personal connection to a high-ranking member of the Chinese communist regime. It would not, he reasoned, put him in good graces in

Chungking, where Chiang Kai-shek held forth.

His letters, during the months in Hawaii, were filled with details of life in the islands after the bombing of Pearl. He spoke of red tape and bureaucratic confusion, of a military in disarray, of the wangling he was doing to try to position himself in China. He asked that we pull any strings we could. Lucy got some help from the Nimitz family, with whom she had become acquainted when she was in graduate school at Berkeley. Kit suggested that Porter might look up Lieutenant Commander Flannery. She had seen him last six months before, when he was stationed in San Diego, but she knew that he was scheduled for another tour of duty in Hawaii.

Porter's return letter told her that he was sorry to have to report that Lieutenant Commander Flannery went down with the *Arizona* during the bombing of Pearl Harbor.

When Kit read of Michael Flannery's death, something seemed to harden inside her. He had made her laugh. They had danced together, had held close on the beach at Waikiki eight years before. They had seen each other, now and then, since. Now he was dead, and she knew it was only the beginning.

It was not until Porter wrote to tell us he had managed to get himself assigned to General Stilwell's staff and would be on his way to Chungking in a few weeks that he wrote us about Ch'ing-Ling.

"I had not thought to see her. I told myself it would be better not to, but the moment I set foot on the islands again, I knew I would. She is a doctor now, a pediatrician working in the children's hospital. She is more beautiful than I remembered, if that can be.

"The war has had a marked effect on Ch'ing-Ling. The day of the bombing—December 7—was a horror she will never forget. She was on duty, and saw the worst of it—the dead children.

"In a peculiar way, the practice of medicine and the war have accomplished what I could not. They have brought Ch'ing-Ling out of her traditional Chinese, protected life and into mine. And still, she is Chinese enough to tell me that it has all been ordained. That she has moved, inexorably, in planned patterns to this time, this place, to me.

"She has been waiting for me. I cannot believe it, but that

is what she says. She has been waiting, all this time. And I feel, when I am with her, that she is right. That everything is right. Even though we cannot be together for long, and perhaps will not be again."

Several weeks later we received another letter. In it was a photograph of Porter in his dress uniform, and Ch'ing-Ling in a Western dress of white crepe with a peplum, and a tiny hat with a veil. They were standing on a small bridge in what appeared to be a formal garden. She was holding a bouquet of flowers, ribbons trailing from it. Their smiles were fixed, for the camera. The letter that accompanied it was in Porter's hand, and it said: "We were married yesterday in a civil ceremony. I had not understood, until now, what a capacity for happiness I have. In two days I leave for Chungking, two more days of Paradise. Ch'ing-Ling sends her warmest regards. Someday, maybe she will become American enough to send hugs and kisses and a great deal of love, as I do now."

Three months later, Ch'ing-Ling was on her way to join us in San Francisco, where Kit and Lucy and I were staying with Sara. Pregnant with Porter's child, Ch'ing-Ling came to us. "I want our child to be born in the States, with you and Kit to help Ch'ing-Ling," Porter wrote. "In a manner of speaking, the future is in your hands."

So we wait, five women in a *petit palais* on Nob Hill, in the summer of 1942. Porter is attached to General Stilwell's staff in Chungking. We know he flies regularly over the Hump to Ramgarh in India, where Stilwell is training an army to retake the Burma Road.

Kit is mounting what seems to be a one-woman war effort of her own. She drives for the Red Cross and heads a civilian board assigned to find housing for those people who are pouring into the city to do war work. Her own house in Pacific Heights has been turned into a hostel for wives of servicemen. That is why she is living at Sara's with the rest of us.

Lucy is teaching biology at Balboa High School, there being a shortage of teachers now that the men are off to war. We have become accustomed to finding handsome young officers on our doorstep. Sara accuses Lucy of spending more time at the Top of the Mark than she does in class.

I wait with Ch'ing-Ling; I try to raise her spirits, knowing how difficult it must be, far away from all that she knows. She is a gentle creature, beautiful in her pregnancy. Still, the only time I glimpse excitement is when Porter's letters arrive. I only wish they did not have to be apart, not now with the baby coming.

We walk, she and I, in the park each afternoon. An old, elegantly dressed French woman takes her daily walk at the same time. Yesterday she told Ch'ing-Ling she was certain that the child would be a boy because, she explained, waving her hands, "you carry it so high."

After the woman continued on her way I asked Ch'ing-Ling, "Do you want a boy?"

Without hesitating she answered, "Naturally, a boy. For a Chinese it is important to have sons. But I think you know that," she added, touching my arm ever so gently.

I thought of Soong then, of the day I gave him his son. I cannot help but wonder what they will say to each other, Porter and Soong, when they meet as father and son.

In the midst of so much that is uncertain, I feel strangely at peace. I have come to welcome sleep, perhaps because so often of late I move, swiftly and softly, into dreams—lovely, summer dreams. Sometimes I am on the porch at Porter Farm, and a summer storm is gathering. The trees are blowing, bending in the wind, and the sky darkens and there is a sense of something tremendous about to happen. The Little Boys are tumbling down the grassy hillock in front of the farmhouse. They are wearing their Sunday best white blouses, and long green grass stains have begun to appear on them. Still they roll, laughing, over and over down the little hill.

Sometimes Thad is with them, sometimes Rose and Pablito and Wen and Kit and Porter . . . they all laugh and tumble together, and I smile to see it.

A strange, melodic tune is playing—the sort of music played by the sing song girls in Shanghai, a simple tune of great purity. I listen and watch and smile as the children play, even as the storm approaches.

Then the first big raindrops splash onto the porch and I call out to the children. They run, flinging themselves at me, gathering round, and we move back from the edge of the porch, where the rain is pounding . . . it drips off the chinaberry bush, it falls in great silver sheets, and we huddle together, close together, and watch, and wonder.